THE MASTER STORYTELLERS

WILBUR SMITH

THE MASTER STORYTELLERS

WILBUR SMITH

THREE NOVELS OF ANCIENT EGYPT

Reader's Digest – Sydney London New York

Published by Reader's Digest (Australia) Pty Ltd
26 Waterloo Street, Surry Hills, NSW 2010

ISBN 1 876689 80 3

Printed and bound by Dai Nippon Printing
Company (HK) Ltd, Hong Kong

River God *page 7*

The Seventh Scroll *page 215*

Warlock *page 401*

River God

River God

Astrologer, engineer, architect, scribe ... Taita is one of the most gifted men in all Egypt. Who better to be adviser to the omnipotent Lord Intef and tutor to his beautiful daughter, Lostris? But Taita is also Intef's slave and must submit to his cruel master's every command. How, then, can he help Lostris when she falls in love with the valiant Tanus, the son of her father's most hated enemy? How can he turn his back on the girl he has watched over and loved since childhood?

Taita must tread carefully—or risk his master's most dreaded retribution.

Wilbur Smith draws the reader irresistibly into the lives of his characters, setting his story during one of the most exciting periods in Ancient Egypt's dramatic history.

Book One

The river lay heavily upon the desert, bright as a spill of molten metal from a furnace. The sky smoked with heat haze and the sun beat down upon it all with the strokes of a coppersmith's hammer. In the mirage the gaunt hills flanking the Nile seemed to tremble.

Our boat sped close in beside the papyrus beds; near enough for the creaking of the water buckets of the shadoof, on their long counterbalanced arms, to carry from the fields across the water. The sound harmonised with the singing of the girl in the bows.

Lostris was fourteen years of age. The Nile had begun its latest flood on the very day that her red woman's moon had flowered for the first time; a happy coincidence, since her name meant "Daughter of the Waters". Her father was Lord Intef, second only in power and riches in this land to Pharaoh himself.

I remember her so vividly on that day. Every man aboard, every warrior at the rowing benches, was aware of her beauty. Neither I nor any one of them could keep our gaze off her. She filled me with a sense of my own inadequacy and a deep and poignant longing; for although I am a eunuch, I was gelded only after I had known the joy of a woman's body.

"Taita," she called to me, "sing with me!" And when I obeyed she smiled with pleasure. My tenor complemented her lovely soprano to perfection. We sang one of the old peasant love songs that I had taught her, and from the stern another voice joined with ours, a man's voice, deep and powerful.

Lostris turned her head and her smile shimmered like the sunbeams on the surface of the Nile. Although the man upon whom she smiled was my friend, still I felt the bitter gall of envy burn the back of my throat. Yet I forced myself to smile. I also loved Tanus. So why should I resent my mistress loving him? Poor neutered thing that I am, I knew that I could never have her for myself, not even if the gods had raised my state above that of slave. Yet such is the perversity of human nature that I hungered for what I could never have and dreamed of the impossible.

Tanus's father, Pianki, Lord Harrab, had been one of the grandees of the Egyptian nobility, but his mother had been the daughter of a freed Tehenu slave, a fair-headed, blue-eyed beauty. Tanus's mother had died while Tanus was still a child and so my memory of her was imperfect, but I had known and admired Tanus's father, before he had lost his vast fortune and great estates. He had been of dark complexion, a man with more physical strength than beauty, but he had had a generous and noble heart. It seemed that Tanus had inherited the best from both his parents, except only worldly wealth. In nature and in power he was as his father; in beauty as his mother.

Lostris sat on her cushion on the prow with her slave girls sprawled at her feet. She wore only a skirt of bleached linen, crisp and white as an egret's wing. She had set aside her formal wig and wore her natural hair in a thick dark rope. The green of her eyes was enhanced by the silver-green of powdered malachite cunningly touched to the upper lids. Between her breasts, suspended on a gold chain, she wore the figurine of Hapi, goddess of the Nile, fashioned in gold and precious lapis lazuli, which I had made for her.

Suddenly, Tanus lifted his right hand with the fist clenched. The rowers checked their stroke and held the blades of their paddles aloft. Then Tanus thrust the steering oar hard over, and the men on the port bank stabbed their backstroke deeply. The starboard side pulled strongly ahead. The boat spun sharply and then shot forwards as both banks of oars pulled together. The sharp prow brushed aside the dense stands of papyrus and she lanced her way out of the flow of the river and into the still waters of the lagoon beyond.

Lostris broke off the song and shaded her eyes to gaze ahead. "There they are!" she cried, and pointed at the other boats of Tanus's squadron, stationed across the southern reaches of the lagoon, cutting off any escape in that direction.

Tanus checked our rowers with a peremptory hand signal and the boat glided to a halt and lay rocking gently upon the waters. One of his staff officers ran up Tanus's personal standard to the masthead. It was the image of a blue crocodile, tail held erect and jaws open. Only an officer of the rank of "Best of Ten Thousand" was entitled to his own standard. Tanus had achieved such rank, together with the command of the Blue Crocodile Division of Pharaoh's own elite guard, before his twentieth birthday. But even so, if Lord Intef learned that I was responsible for allowing his daughter to be out for a fun day in the company of this young man, not even my privileged position would protect me from his wrath.

The standard at the masthead was the signal for the hunt to begin. Tanus lowered the gong—a long bronze tube—over the stern, allowing the end of it to sink below the surface. When it was struck with a hammer, the shrill ringing tones would be transmitted through the water, filling our quarry with murderous rage.

"Have a care for the safety of my mistress," I cried. "Do you hear me, boy? Do not encourage her to recklessness, for she is every bit as wild as you are." I could speak thus to an illustrious commander, for he was once my pupil. He grinned at me now as he had in those days.

"Come up here in the stern tower, Taita!" he ordered. "You can beat the gong for us. It will take your mind off your anxieties for a while."

I moved to do his bidding. Once in the tower, I watched him take up his bow and stand in the bows with my mistress at his side. They made a marvellous couple, but too obviously so for my peace of mind. I considered remonstrating with her, but my mistress was amenable to restraint only in certain of her moods, so instead I applied myself to beating the bronze gong.

The shrill reverberating tone carried across the waters of the lagoon, and instantly the air was filled with the susurration of wings as a vast cloud of waterfowl rose into the sky. At that moment, I saw far ahead a disturbance upon the glassy surface. Tanus gave tongue like a hunting hound, his men shouted with him and bent to their paddles, and the *Breath of Horus* shot forwards. We reached the spot where last we had seen movement, and the vessel glided to a standstill while every man upon her decks gazed around eagerly. I alone glanced directly over the stern. The water beneath our hull was shallow and clear. I shrieked and leaped back from the stern rail, for the monster was directly under us. The hippopotamus is the familiar of Hapi, the goddess of the Nile. It was only with her special dispensation that we could hunt it for the coming festival of Osiris. To that end Tanus had prayed and sacrificed at the goddess's temple that morning.

The beast that I saw beneath us was an enormous old bull. To my eye, he seemed as large as our galley; a gigantic shape that lumbered along the bottom of the lagoon, raising puffs of mud from beneath his hoofs. With the steering oar Tanus spun the boat about and we sped after the bull. But even at that slow and mannered gallop he drew away from us rapidly. Suddenly he broke through the surface and blew a great cloud of fetid steam from his lungs. For a moment his back formed a gleaming island in the lagoon, then he drew a whistling breath and with a swirl was gone again.

"After him!" Tanus bellowed.

"There he is," I cried as I pointed over the side, "doubling back."

"Well done, old friend," Tanus laughed at me, "we'll make a warrior of you yet." That notion was ridiculous, for I was, and still am, a scribe, a sage and an artist: my heroics are of the mind.

To the south of us the other galleys of the squadron were now weaving and pirouetting while other frenzied beasts fled before them. All was wild uproar and confusion and I found myself shouting and cheering along with the most bloodthirsty of them.

Tanus concentrated all his attention on the first and largest bull, drawing inexorably closer to him each time he surfaced. Suddenly the bull burst through the water not thirty paces from the bows. He came out gleaming in the sunshine, monstrous black and awful, clouds of steam spurting from his nostrils.

Tanus had an arrow nocked and now he threw up the great bow and loosed it in the same instant. And while the arrow still hissed in flight another followed it and then another. The bull bellowed as the arrows buried themselves in his back, and he dived again.

But Tanus was able to anticipate each of the bull's wild rushes and to send the *Breath of Horus* speeding to head him off. By now the waters were streaking and swirling red with blood.

Once again the bull came up dead ahead, but this time facing the *Breath of Horus* as she bore down upon him. His jaws gaped so wide that I could see far down his throat. It was a tunnel of bright red flesh that could easily have engulfed a man entirely. Tanus loosed yet another arrow which flew squarely down the gaping throat, yet the creature seemed not to notice this further injury. It charged headlong into the bows of our galley. The rowers were sent sprawling, while I was hurled forwards with such force against the rail of the stern tower that the air was driven from my lungs.

Yet even in my distress I saw my mistress, who had been in the very thick of the fray, flung forwards by the impact and teeter at the rail, her arms windmilling desperately. "Tanus!" she screamed and reached out one hand to him. He tried to catch it. For an instant their fingers touched, then she was plucked away and dashed over the side.

From my position I was able to follow her fall, down upon the vast back of the infuriated bull. For an instant she lay spread-eagled there like a human sacrifice upon the altar of some obscene religion.

The bull whirled about, his great jaws snapping at her. Somehow Lostris managed to cling to a pair of the arrow shafts that protruded from the bull's back as his curved fangs rang upon each other like the blades of duelling warriors. At each bite they seemed to miss her by only a finger's breadth.

In the prow Tanus recovered swiftly. He tossed aside his bow and jerked the blade of his sword free of its scabbard. He leaped up onto the gunwale and balanced there for an instant, watching the wounded bull in the water below, then he launched himself outwards and dropped like a falcon, the sword held in both his hands and pointing downwards. The full weight of his body was behind the sword as he struck. Half the length of the blade was driven into the hippopotamus's neck at the base of the skull. The immense carcass stiffened and the bull plunged below the waters of the lagoon, bearing Lostris and Tanus with him into the depths.

I choked back the wail of despair that rose in my throat, and bellowed an order to the deck below. "Back-water! Do not overrun them! Swimmers to the bows!" As I poised myself at the ship's rail, preparing to dive over the side in an attempt to rescue my mistress, the waters directly below me opened and two heads bobbed out making an unlikely sound. They were laughing. They were spluttering with laughter as they floundered towards the ship's side, locked so firmly in each other's arms that I was certain they were in real danger of drowning one another.

All my concern turned instantly to outrage at this levity, and I heard my own voice turn shrill and querulous as my mistress and

Tanus were dragged from the water onto the deck. "You reckless, unbridled little savage," I railed at her. "You thoughtless little hoyden. You promised me! You swore an oath."

She ran to me and threw both arms round my neck. "Oh, Taita!" she cried, still bubbling with laughter. "Did you see him? Did you see Tanus spring to my rescue? Just like the hero of one of your stories."

Realising that Lostris had lost her skirt, I shouted at her slave girls to find another for her. Then I rounded on Tanus. "As for you, you careless ruffian! I shall report you to my Lord Intef. He will have the skin flogged from your back."

Tanus laughed and threw one wet muscled arm round my shoulders. The *Breath of Horus* was separated from the other ships of the squadron, but by now the hunt was over. Tanus shook his head. "We did not make the most of our chances, did we?" he grunted, and ordered one of his officers to hoist the recall signal to the squadron.

Then he forced a smile. "Let us broach a jug of beer together—for now we have a while to wait and this has been thirsty work." He went to the bows where the slave girls were fussing over Lostris.

Although still angry, I joined their impromptu picnic on the deck. After all, the roast wild goose with figs that they were displaying was one of my favourite dishes. Even so I ate sparingly; I was, then, barely thirty years old but I had my figure to consider.

Tanus's squadron, scattered widely across the lagoon, now began to regroup. The galleys reassembled in line astern and their crews raised a cheer as they came level with the *Breath of Horus*. Tanus saluted them with a clenched fist. Every galley had killed at least one hippopotamus, while some had killed two and even three; I knew that Tanus was secretly lamenting the fact that our protracted encounter with the bull had limited our score to only that single animal. Anyway, he was not his usual ebullient self and he soon left us to supervise the repairs to the hull of the *Breath of Horus*.

The bull's charge had sprung the underwater planking and we were taking enough water to necessitate constant bailing of the bilges with leather buckets. Surely this inefficient procedure could be improved upon, I thought to myself, so I sent one of the slave girls to fetch my writing instruments. After a little further thought, I sketched out an idea for mechanically removing water from the bilges of a galley. It was based on the same principle as the shadoof water bucket: the clay pot at the end of a long arm was swung down into the river and then lifted to fill an irrigation ditch on the bank.

I was so engrossed that I did not hear Tanus come up behind me. He snatched the papyrus scroll from me and studied it avidly.

Of course, he understood instantly what I was about. When his father had lost his fortune, I had tried everything in my power to find a rich patron to sponsor him to enter one of the temples as a novice scribe, for I truly believed that he had every prospect of developing into one of the great minds of Egypt.

I had been unsuccessful, for the same enemy whose spite and guile had destroyed Tanus's father had set himself out to bar the way to Tanus himself. No man in the land could prevail against such a baleful influence. So I had instead helped Tanus to enter the army.

"How do you do it?" he now exclaimed as he studied my drawings. "You and your designing brush are worth ten squadrons to me!" And we were instantly immersed in a discussion of my design. Lostris could not be excluded for long, and she came to join us.

By now two of the huge corpses had been secured to our stern hawser and the rowers were straining at their paddles to move them through the water. As we approached the shore I shaded my eyes against the sun and peered ahead. It seemed that every man, woman and child in Upper Egypt was waiting upon the bank, dancing and singing and waving palm fronds to welcome the fleet.

As each galley drew up against the bank, teams of men waded out to fasten ropes to the carcasses. Oblivious to the ever-present threat of crocodiles lurking in the opaque green waters, they hauled the carcasses ashore, then swarmed like ants over the bodies, all wielding knives or axes in a delirium of greed.

From the stern tower of the *Breath of Horus* I watched the pantomime of human frailty that was being played out below me. Traditionally the populace was allowed to eat its fill of the meats of the hunt upon the foreshore. Living as we did then in a verdant land, fertilised and watered by the great river, our people were well fed. However, the staple diet of the poorer classes was grain, and months might pass between one mouthful of meat and the next. Many of the younger ones had probably never tasted the delicious flesh of the river cow before. Our people were starved of animal fat and the taste of it drove them wild.

I was content to keep aloof from this riotous mob, happy in the knowledge that my Lord Intef's bailiffs would secure the finest cuts and marrowbones for the palace kitchens, and the cooks would prepare my personal platter to perfection. My precedence in the vizier's household exceeded all other, even that of his major-domo or the commander of his bodyguard, both of whom were freeborn.

I watched the bailiffs at work now, claiming the share of my lord, the governor and grand vizier of all the twenty-two nomes of Upper Egypt. They swung their long staves with the expertise born of long practice, and shouted their demands.

The ivory teeth of the animals belonged to the vizier, and they were as valuable as the elephant tusks that were brought down in trade from the land of Cush, beyond the cataracts. Naturally, from the fruits of the hunt my lord was expected to tithe the priests of Hapi, titular shepherds of the goddess's flock of river cows. However, the amount of the tithe was in my lord's discretion, and I, who was in overall charge of the palace accounts, knew where the lion's share of the treasure would end up.

As for the hippopotamus hides, these belonged to the army and would be turned into war shields for the officers of the guards' regiments. Their battle armour, on the other hand, was made from the horny skin of the crocodile. Hence their honorific "the Blue Crocodile Guards", and their standard of the blue crocodile.

I went ashore. The army quartermasters were supervising the skinning and the handling of the hippopotamus hides. The meat that could not be consumed on the bank would be pickled in brine, or smoked or dried. Ostensibly it would be used to feed the army. However, in practice a large part of it would be discreetly sold and the proceeds would filter down into my lord's coffers.

Already those people who were stuffed with meat and gorged with beer were snoring where they had fallen. The younger and more shameless were dancing and embracing in the inadequate cover of the papyrus beds. This wanton behaviour was a symptom of the malaise that afflicted the entire land. It would not have been thus if only there had been a strong pharaoh and a moral and upright administration.

The sun sank and seemed to quench itself in the river, leaving a coppery sheen on the water and a smoky glow in the western sky.

Suddenly I realised that an hour had sped away since I had seen my mistress. I leaped to my feet in a panic. How could I have been so remiss? My mistress had been strictly raised—I had seen to that.

She was a good and moral child, fully aware of the duties and the obligations which law and custom placed on her. Of course I trusted her.

I trusted her as much as I would have trusted any other strong-willed young woman on a night such as this, alone in the darkness with the handsome young soldier with whom she was infatuated.

My lord's spies permeated every layer of society and every comer of our land. They were even more numerous than my own, for he had more money to pay his agents. If Lostris had disgraced her father, her family, and me, her tutor and guardian, then my Lord Intef would know of it in Karnak by morning, and so would I.

I ran from one end of the beach to the other, searching in desperation. I could see nothing of her or of Tanus, and my worst fears were encouraged. With an effort I controlled myself and considered how my mistress was likely to behave.

At that moment a soft yellow glow of torchlight further along the lagoon caught my attention. Immediately my intuition was aroused. I realised that, given my mistress's connections with the goddess Hapi, she would be drawn irresistibly to that deity's picturesque temple. I strode along the beach beside the dark waters to the stone jetty below the temple and hurried up the granite steps.

The goddess Hapi is one of my favourites. Strictly speaking, she is neither god nor goddess, but a strange, bearded, hermaphroditic creature with bounteous breasts. She is the deification of the Nile and the goddess of the harvest. The two kingdoms of Egypt and all the peoples in them depend utterly upon her and the periodic flooding of the great river.

I sped across the granite flags, my heart outrunning my frantic feet. At the entrance to the sanctum I paused. My instinct had been right. There they were, the two of them. I almost yelled aloud, then checked myself. My mistress was kneeling before the gigantic statue of Hapi, a blue woollen shawl spread over her head. The goddess beamed down upon her, bedecked in wreaths of water lilies.

Tanus knelt beside her. He had laid aside his weapons and his armour. They were piled at the door of the sanctuary. He was dressed only in a linen shift and short tunic, with sandals on his feet.

My base suspicions were refuted, and I was struck with shame. Quietly I began to withdraw. How could I have doubted her?

At that moment Lostris came to her feet and approached the statue. I lingered a moment longer to watch her, as from around her neck she unclasped the lapis-lazuli figurine which I had made for her. She stood on tiptoe to hang it on the idol's neck as a sacrifice, then she knelt and kissed the stone foot.

She rose and turned to go back to Tanus, but then she saw me in the doorway. I tried to melt into the shadows, for I was embarrassed at having spied upon so intimate a moment. However, her face lit with joy and she ran to me and seized my hands.

"Oh Taita, I am so glad that you are here—you of all people!" She led me forward into the sanctum and Tanus rose to his feet and came smiling to take my other hand.

"Thank you for coming. I know we can always count upon you."

I wished that my motives had been as pure as they believed them to be, so I hid my guilty heart from them with a loving smile.

"Kneel here!" Lostris ordered me. "Here, where you can hear every word we say to each other. You will bear witness for us before Hapi and all the gods of Egypt." She pressed me to my knees, and then they both resumed their places in front of the goddess and took each other's hands, looking full into each other's eyes.

Lostris spoke first. "You are my man," she whispered, "through this world and all the worlds to come."

"You are my woman, and I pledge you my love. I swear it to you on the breath and the blood of Horus," Tanus said clearly and openly.

"I take up your pledge," Lostris cried. "No one can ever come between us. Nothing can ever part us. We are one, for ever."

She offered her face to his and he kissed her, deeply and lingeringly. As they embraced a sudden chill wind off the lagoon swirled through the dimly lit halls of the temple and fluttered the torch flames. It passed as swiftly as it had come, but the whisper of it around the great stone pillars was like the distant sardonic laughter of the gods, and I shuddered with superstitious awe.

It is always dangerous to pique the gods with extravagant demands, and Lostris had just asked for the impossible. The pledge that she and Tanus had made to each other could never be. I felt my own heart tearing as, at last, they broke the kiss, rose to their feet and turned back to me. "Why so sad, Taita?" Lostris demanded, her own face flooded with joy. "Rejoice with me, for this is the happiest day of my life."

Now Tanus lifted me to my feet and embraced me. "You will speak to Lord Intef on my behalf, won't you?" he demanded.

What could I say to them? I could not be so cruel as to tell them the blunt truth. They were waiting for me to speak, to express my joy for them, and to promise them my help.

"Taita, what is it?" I watched the joy wither upon my mistress's beloved countenance. "Why do you not rejoice for us?"

"You know that I love you both, but—" For a moment I could not continue. "It is your father, my Lord Intef—"

"Exactly." Lostris was becoming angry. "My father! You will go to him and speak to him the way you always do, and it will be all right."

"Lostris," I began, and it was a sign of my distress that I used her name in this familiar fashion. "You know your father will never agree—"

She would not listen to me, she did not want to hear the truth, so she rushed in with words to drown out mine. "I know that Tanus has no fortune, yes. But he has a marvellous future ahead of him."

"Mistress, please hear me out. It is not only the lack of Tanus's fortune. It is more, much more."

"His bloodline, then? Is that what troubles you? You know full well that his family is as noble as ours. Pianki, Lord Harrab, was my own father's equal and his dearest friend—" She had closed her ears to me. She did not realise the depth of the tragedy on which we were embarking. Neither she nor Tanus did; but then I was probably the only person in the kingdom who understood it fully.

I had protected them from the truth all these years. How could I explain it to them now? How could I reveal the depths of the hatred that her father bore towards the young man she loved?

"Tanus is my equal in the lists of the nobility. How can my father deny it? You will go to him for us, won't you, dear Taita? Say you will, please say you will!"

I could only bow my head in acquiescence, and try to hide the hopeless expression in my eyes.

THE FLEET was heavily laden on the return to Karnak. The galleys were low in the water under their cargoes of raw hides and salted meat. Thus, our progress against the Nile's current was slower than on our outward journey, but still too swift for my heavy heart and mounting dread.

The lovers were gay and euphoric with their newly declared love and their trust in me to remove the obstacles from their path. I could not bring myself to deny them this day of happiness, for I knew that it would be one of the very last they would share. So instead I laughed and smiled as gaily as they did, and tried to hide my fears from them.

We sat together in the prow and discussed the re-enactment of the passion of Osiris that would be the highlight of the forthcoming festival. Lord Intef had madc me the impresario of the pageant, and I had written a new script for the occasion. I had cast both Lostris and Tanus in leading roles. She was to play Isis, sister and wife of Osiris, while Tanus would take the role of Horus, Isis's son.

Pharaoh would be the guest of honour when the pageant was performed in the temple of Osiris on the final night of the festival, so I was particularly anxious that it should be a success.

I was brought back from the passion of Osiris by a cry from the lookout. The fleet was sweeping round the last bend in the river, and there lay the twin cities of Luxor and Karnak, which between them made up Greater Thebes, strung out along the bank and sparkling like a necklace of pearls in the stark Egyptian sunlight.

Once we had docked at the palace wharf, I immediately made enquiry as to the whereabouts of my master and was relieved to learn that he had crossed the river to inspect Pharaoh's tomb and funerary temple on the west bank. The tomb had been under construction for the past twelve years; one of my lord's many titles was "Guardian of the Royal Tombs", and it was a serious responsibility.

His absence afforded me time in which to plan my strategy. As soon as I had seen my mistress safely ensconced in the harem, I hurried to my own quarters. Lord Intef had eight wives, all of whom brought him either a substantial dowry or influential political connections. However, as far as I was aware my lord had not visited the harem in the last fifteen years. The getting of Lostris had been the last occasion that he had performed his matrimonial duties. His sexual tastes lay in other directions.

I was the eldest of his select company of slave boys. I treated them, and tried my best to comfort them. That perhaps was why they called me Akh-Ker, a name which means elder brother.

I might no longer be my master's favourite plaything, but he valued me much higher than that now. I was many other things to him: physician and artist, musician and scribe, architect and book-keeper, adviser, confidant and engineer, and also nursemaid to his daughter.

I am not so naive as to believe that he loved me or that he trusted me, but I think that at times he came as close to it as he was capable. That was why Lostris had prevailed upon me to plead on her behalf.

That evening I retired early to my private quarters, where my first concern was to feed my animals. The wild birds flocked to my terrace and perched on my shoulder or on my hand. While this was going on my tame gazelle brushed against my legs and my two falcons squawked at me from their perches. Only after I had taken care of this menagerie did I call for my evening meal.

On the terrace overlooking the wide green expanse of the Nile I savoured the dish of wild quail that the head chef had prepared especially to welcome me home. From there I was able to watch for the return of my lord's barge from the far bank. It came with the sunset glowing on the square sail, and I felt my spirits sink. He might send for me this evening, and I was not ready to face him.

Then I heard Rasfer, the commander of the palace guard, shouting for my lord's favourite of the moment, a sloe-eyed Bedouin lad. It was not I who would be called this evening and I was relieved.

I woke before dawn with the feeling of dread still strong upon me. Even my ritual swim in the cool waters of the Nile did nothing to relieve it. I hurried back to my chamber where two of the slave boys were waiting to oil my body and comb out my hair. I wanted to look my best in order to please my lord especially today.

I was the first member of my lord's entourage awaiting his arrival in the water garden where he held his assize every morning. Gradually I was joined by the rest of the court. Many of them were yawning from sleep, for my lord kept early hours and liked to complete the bulk of the business of state before the main heat of the day. We waited respectfully in the first rays of the sun for my lord's arrival.

"He's in a good mood this morning," the chamberlain whispered as he took his place beside me, and I felt a tiny prickle of hope. I might yet be able to escape the serious consequences of my foolhardy promise to Lostris.

There was a stirring among us and my Lord Intef came out. His walk was stately, for he was mighty with the weight of his honours and his power.

He singled me out without seeming to have done so. The yellow gaze, as implacable as that of a wild leopard, touched mine and he inclined his head slightly. I stepped in behind him as he passed. He was an outrageously handsome man with long, clean limbs and a flat, hard belly. His head was leonine and his hair dense and lustrous. At this time he was forty years of age and I had been his slave for almost twenty of those.

Lord Intef led us to the barrazza in the centre of the garden, a thatched building without enclosing walls, open to the cool breeze off the river. He seated himself cross-legged on the paved floor at the low table on which lay the state scrolls. The day's business began.

At noon my lord dismissed the officials and called for his meal. For the first time that day we were alone together, except for Rasfer. He took his post at the gate, in sight but out of earshot.

With a gesture my lord invited me to move up to his elbow and to taste the delicious meats and fruits that had been laid out before him. While we waited for the effects of any poisoning to manifest themselves upon me, we discussed the morning's business in detail.

Then he questioned me about the expedition to the lagoon of Hapi. I described it to him and gave him the figures of the profits that he might expect from the meat and hides and teeth of the river cows. I inflated the estimate of profits a little and he smiled. His smile was frank and charming. I screwed up my courage and began my plea.

"My lord should know that I allowed your daughter to accompany me on the expedition." I could see that he already knew.

"You did not think to obtain my permission?" he asked mildly.

"My lord was in council at the time. I would not have dared disturb him. Besides, there was no harm in it that I could fathom."

"You are so glib today, aren't you, my darling?" he chuckled. "Yet whatever it is you are up to, you are still very attractive, Taita. After all these years you can still make me smile. But tell me, you took good care of the Lady Lostris, did you not? Is there something that you wish to report to me? Speak out like a man, even though you are not."

It was a cruel little gibe, but it steeled me. "There is indeed something I wish humbly to bring to my lord's attention," I said. "And it does indeed concern the Lady Lostris. She is now of marriageable age. She is a woman of an ardent and loving nature. I believe it would be wise to find a husband for her, as soon as we can."

"No doubt you have one to suggest?" he asked drily.

I nodded. "There is indeed a suitor, my lord."

"Not one, Taita. You mean another one, don't you? I know of at least six who have already made offers."

"I did mean another, but one that the Lady Lostris approves."

"The child's approval or disapproval is of no interest to me whatsoever." He smiled and stroked my cheek to encourage me. "But go on, Taita, tell me the name of this lovelorn swain who will do me the honour of becoming my son-in-law." I steeled myself to reply, but he stopped me. "No, wait? Let me guess . . ."

His smile turned into that sly foxy grin that I knew so well, and I realised that he had been toying with me.

"For Lostris to welcome him he must be young and handsome." He pretended to muse on it. "And for you to speak out for him he must be a friend or a protégé of yours. There must have been an opportunity for this paragon to declare his suit. What would be the time and the place for that to have happened, I wonder? Could it have been at midnight in the temple of Hapi, perhaps? Am I right?"

I felt myself pale. How did he know so much? He slid his hand around behind my head and caressed the nape of my neck.

"I can see that my guesses are close to the target." He took a handful of my hair and twisted it hard enough to bring tears to my eyes. "Now it remains only to divine the name of this bold lover. Could it be Dakka? No, no, Dakka is not so stupid as to incur my wrath." He twisted harder and a clump of hair came away in his hand. "Tanus, then? Answer me, my darling, was it Tanus?"

I choked back the whimper in my throat. "No, my lord."

"Are you sure?" He pretended to be puzzled. "If it was not he, then I am at a loss to guess who else might be so stupid as to approach the virgin daughter of the grand vizier of Upper Egypt."

Abruptly he raised his voice. "Rasfer!" he cried.

My head was twisted so that through streaming eyes I could watch Rasfer approach. In his great hairy fist he held a whip of hippo hide.

Rasfer was an artist with this awful tool. He could flick out and leave only a crimson weal that never broke the skin but stung as viciously as a scorpion; or with a dozen strokes he could strip the flesh from a man's back. He grinned as he flexed the long lash in his hands. Rasfer loved his work.

My Lord Intef stroked my naked back and sighed. "You should know better than to press the suit of that young jackanapes upon me. Also, you have endangered the market value of the goods that I placed in your care." He twisted my head up so that I could answer him. "For that you must be punished. Do you understand?"

"Yes, my lord," I whispered.

Once again Lord Intef spoke to Rasfer above my head. "With all your cunning, Rasfer. Do not break the skin—I do not want this delightfully smooth back marred permanently. Ten will do as a start."

I had watched a hundred or more unfortunates undergo this punishment. Not one was able to remain silent under the lash.

"One!" grunted Rasfer and the lash fluted. I screamed.

"You are fortunate, dear Taita," Lord Intef murmured. "I had the priests examine the goods last night. They are still intact."

"Two!" Rasfer cried, and I shrieked again.

ONE OF Lostris's slave girls was waiting for me on the terrace of my quarters when I limped painfully up the steps from the garden.

"My mistress bids you attend her immediately," she greeted me.

Shouting for one of the slave boys to dress my injuries, I hurried through into my chamber. "Go and tell your mistress that I am injured, and I cannot come to her," I snapped over my shoulder.

"She told me that you would try to wriggle out of it, but she told me also that I was to stay with you and see that you did not."

"You are insolent for a slave," I reprimanded her as the boy anointed my back with a healing salve of my own concoction. Then I capitulated. "Go and tell your mistress that I will come to her."

"She said I must wait and make sure you did."

So I had an escort as I passed the guards at the gate of the harem. The guards were eunuchs like myself, but powerful and fierce. The harem was not nearly as grand or as comfortable as the quarters of the slave boys. It was a compound of mud-brick hutments surrounded by a high wall. The only gardens or decorations were those that Lostris and her maids had undertaken, with my assistance, round her quarters; a pretty garden with a lily pond and songbirds twittering in cages woven of split bamboo.

I pushed my way past the slave girls huddled at the doorway and heard my mistress's sobs from the inner chamber. She was lying face down on the low bed, her entire body shaking with the force of her grief, but she heard me enter, whirled off the bed and rushed to me.

"Oh, Taita! They are sending Tanus away. Pharaoh arrives

tomorrow, and my father will prevail upon him to order Tanus to take his squadron upriver. Oh, Taita! I shall never see him again. I wish I were dead . . ." All this in one rising wail of despair.

"Softly, my child." I rocked her in my arms. "How do you know these terrible things? They may never happen."

"Oh, they will. Tanus has sent me a message. My father has found out about Tanus and me. He knows that we were in the temple of Hapi alone. Oh Taita, my father sent the priests to examine me . . ."

I hugged her gently. "I shall never see Tanus again," she cried. "My father will destroy him."

"Even your father cannot touch Tanus," I tried to reassure her. "Tanus is a commander of a regiment of Pharaoh's own elite guard. He is the king's man." I did not add that this was probably the only reason that her father had not already destroyed him, but went on gently, "While as for never seeing Tanus again, you will be playing opposite him in the pageant."

"My father will never let the pageant go on now."

"He has no alternative, unless he is prepared to risk Pharaoh's displeasure—and you can be certain that he will never do that."

"He will send Tanus away, and have another actor play Horus."

"There is no time to rehearse another actor. Tanus will play the god Horus. We will find a way for the two of you to talk."

She gulped back her tears. "Oh, Taita. I know that you will find a way. You always do—" She broke off suddenly and her expression changed. Her hands moved over my back, then she stepped behind me and lifted the light linen tunic I had donned to hide my injuries, and she gasped. "This is Rasfer's work. Oh, my poor dear Taita . . ."

At least her own misery was forgotten for the moment in her concern for my injuries. She ordered me to sit on her bed and remove my tunic while she ministered to me. Soon she was chattering in her usual fashion, making plans to reunite herself with Tanus.

"I shall play such a fine role of Isis in the pageant," she declared, "and I shall make myself so agreeable to Pharaoh that he will grant me any boon that I ask of him. Then I shall beg him for Tanus as my husband. It could happen, could it not, dear Taita?"

"No natural man could resist you, mistress." I smiled at her nonsense. "Not even great Pharaoh himself."

If I had known then how my words would turn out to be true, I think I should have placed a live coal on my tongue before speaking.

On the fifth day of the festival of Osiris, Pharaoh came downriver to Karnak from his palace at Elephantine. He came in full state with all his retinue to officiate at the festival.

Tanus's squadron had left Karnak three days previously to meet the great flotilla and escort it on the last stage of the voyage, so neither Lostris nor I had seen him since the great river-cow hunt.

It was a special joy for both of us then to see his galley come flying round the bend in the river, leading the fleet up from the south.

Lostris was in the grand vizier's train, standing behind her two brothers, Menset and Sobek. The two boys were well favoured, but there was too much of their father in them for my taste.

Tanus stared sternly ahead with his unsheathed sword held in salute before his face, and the rest of his squadron followed, their standards streaming out in a fluttering blaze of rainbow colours, a noble show that set the crowds cheering. Almost a quarter of a million souls had turned out to welcome their pharaoh.

It was some time before the first vessel of the main convoy came trundling round the bend behind them, laden with ladies and nobles of the king's entourage. It was followed by another and then by a great untidy horde of vessels great and small, transports filled with palace servants, barges laden with oxen, goats and chickens for the kitchens, gilded vessels bearing cargoes of palace furniture and treasure, until at last Pharaoh's state barge lumbered round the bend and the cheering of the crowd rose to a crescendo.

The state barge was as long as five of the fighting galleys laid end-to-end, its massive hull painted in the riotous colours that were the fashion of the age, and its figurehead of Osiris gilded with real gold leaf.

Amidships stood a tall deckhouse, Pharaoh's private quarters, so stuffed with heavy furniture that the sailing characteristics of the barge were sadly affected. Atop this edifice, behind a railing woven of fresh lilies, sat Pharaoh Mamose in majestic isolation. On his feet were sandals of gold filigree and his robe was of pure linen. On his head he wore the tall double crown: the white crown of Upper Egypt, combined with the red crown of the Delta.

Despite the crown, the truth was that this sovereign of ours had lost the Delta almost ten years previously. Another pharaoh ruled in Lower Egypt, a pretender who was our sovereign's deadly adversary, and whose constant wars against us drained both kingdoms of gold and the blood of young men.

In order to bring the unwieldy vessel to her moorings at the palace wharf, the captain should have steered close in to the far bank, giving himself the full breadth of the Nile in which to complete his turn. However, he had misjudged the strength of wind and current and he began his turn from midstream.

At first the barge swung ponderously across the current, listing heavily, as under the goading of the lash the rowers plied their paddles in a frenzy. Then the rate of the barge's turn bled away until she was no longer swinging but was heading straight for where we stood on the bank.

As everyone realised what was about to happen, an awful hush fell upon both banks of the Nile. Then suddenly all eyes were drawn downstream, as the *Breath of Horus* broke from her station and came tearing upriver. She cut in so sharply under the bows of the barge that the crowd gasped. Collision seemed inevitable, but at the last moment Tanus signalled, both banks of rowers backed water and the helmsman steered hard over. The *Breath of Horus* checked and paid away before the advance of the great barge. The two vessels touched lightly, and in that instant Tanus poised himself on the bulwark, a light flax line trailing behind him, and leaped out across the gap between the two vessels.

"Tanus!" I am sure that it was my mistress, Lostris, who first called out his name, but I was next.

"Tanus!" I yelled, and then all those around me took up the cry.

The moment he landed on the deck of the barge, Tanus whirled and raced into the bows, hauling in the thin line as he ran. The crew of his galley had spliced a heavy hawser, as thick as a man's arm, to its end, and now they sent this across as Tanus lay back against the weight of it, the muscles of his arms and back shining as he dragged it in.

The moment it was secured Tanus signalled his galley away, and the *Breath of Horus* leaped into the current, gathering speed swiftly. Then abruptly she came up short against the hawser, and the weight of the heavy vessel threw her back on her haunches.

The barge's captain, Admiral Nembet, was the commander of all Pharaoh's fleet with the rank of Great Lion of Egypt. Years ago he had been one of the mighty men, but now he was old and feeble. Tanus took over from him effortlessly, and the crew responded.

Pull!" He gestured to the port bank of oarsmen.

"Back-water!" He stabbed his fist at the starboard side.

Now Tanus signalled to the helmsman of the *Breath of Horus*, masterfully coordinating the efforts of both crews.

At last the gaudily painted bows began to swing up into the current as the galley dragged them round. Once again the cheering died away and that fateful hush fell upon us all as we waited for the enormous ship to crash into the wharf.

I stood helplessly and trembled for my dear friend, and then a miracle occurred. The barge was so close to running aground and Tanus so near to where I stood that his voice carried clearly to me.

"Great Horus, help me now!" he cried.

There is no doubt at all in my mind that the gods often take a hand in the affairs of men. Tanus is a Horus man, and Horus is the god of the wind. At that moment, the desert wind that had blown for three days out of the west dropped. It did not taper off, it simply ceased to blow. Released from the claws of the wind, the barge yielded to the pull of the *Breath of Horus*. Her bows turned up into the current, and she came parallel with the wharf at the exact moment that her side touched the dressed stone and the rush of the Nile stalled her motionless in the water. One last command from Tanus and the mooring ropes were cast onto the wharf and swiftly gathered up. The great barge lay safe at her berth.

We, the onlookers, burst out in a roar of praise for the feat. Modestly and very prudently, Tanus made no attempt to acknowledge our applause. Instead he dropped overside onto the galley's deck. To draw any further attention to himself that might detract from the welcome that awaited the king would have been folly indeed. Pharaoh was always jealous of his royal dignity.

However, I saw the fury on the face of Nembet, the ancient admiral, the Great Lion of Egypt, as he came ashore behind Pharaoh, and I knew that Tanus had made himself another powerful enemy.

It wasn't until the afternoon of the sixth day of the festival that Pharaoh moved in solemn procession to the temple of Osiris on the bank of the Nile. The great sledge on which he rode was drawn by twenty white bullocks with wreaths of flowers on their heads.

One hundred musicians led the procession, strumming the lyre and the harp, beating the cymbal and the drum, and blowing on the long straight horn of the oryx and on the curling horn of the wild ram.

A choir of a hundred of the finest voices in Egypt followed them, singing hymns of praise. Naturally I led the choir. Behind us followed a guard of honour from the Blue Crocodile regiment led by Tanus himself. The crowds raised a special cheer for him as he strode past.

Behind the guard of honour came the vizier and his high office bearers, then the nobles and their wives and children, then a detachment of the Falcon regiment, and finally Pharaoh's sledge.

As we approached the temple of Osiris, the abbot and all his priests were drawn up on the staircase between the tall entrance pylons to welcome Pharaoh Mamose.

At the base of the staircase Pharaoh descended from his carriage and in solemn majesty began to climb the 100 steps.

The choir lined both sides of the staircase. I was on the fiftieth step and so I was able to study the king minutely during the few seconds that it took for him to pass close to me. His hairless arms were folded across his chest in the ritual posture and he carried the crook and the flail of his royal office and his godhead. He wore rings on all his fingers and on his toes, amulets on his upper arms and bracelets on his wrists. The massive pectoral plate of red gold on his chest was inlaid with many colours of faience depicting the god Thoth.

Under the double crown, his face was powdered dead white. His eyes were outlined in black and his lips were rouged crimson. Under the heavy make-up his expression was petulant. His eyes were shifty and nervous, as well they might be, I reflected.

The foundations of the great House of Egypt were riven. Even a god has his worries. Once his domain had stretched from the sea, across the seven mouths of the Delta, southwards to Assoun and the first cataract—the greatest empire on earth. Now his enemies swarmed at his shrunken borders, clamouring like jackals to feast on the carcass of his Egypt. I was certain that this pharaoh was not capable of leading the nation back to its former glories. He was incapable even of breeding a male heir. He had taken twenty wives so far. They had given him a virtual tribe of daughters, but no son. He had consulted every doctor of renown in the Upper Kingdom and visited every oracle and every important shrine.

I knew all this because I was one of the learned doctors he had sent for. I admit that I had felt some trepidation in prescribing to a god, but nevertheless I had recommended a special diet and counselled him to find the most beautiful virgin in Egypt and take her to his marriage bed within a year of the first flowering of her woman's moon.

I had no great faith in my own remedy, but I consoled myself that, if not actually efficacious, my recommendations would do no harm. That was what I believed. How wrong the fates would prove me.

Now the king was swiftly past me and gone into the temple. The grand vizier, my Lord Intef, and all his train followed closely and then there was an undignified rush of lesser citizens to find places from which to watch the passion play.

Before the pageant could begin we were obliged to endure a succession of flowery speeches. This interlude gave me the opportunity to make certain that all the arrangements for the pageant were perfect. I went from tent to tent checking costumes and make-up, and soothing attacks of stage fright.

When I came to Rasfer's tent he was drinking wine with two of his cronies from the palace guard. I had created his make-up to render him even more repulsive, which was not an easy feat given the high plateau of ugliness from which we started. He was a natural for the evil god Seth, and my Lord Intef had been insistent that I cast him in the part.

Tanus too was already in costume. Relaxed and smiling he clasped my shoulder. "Well, old friend, this is your opportunity. After this evening your fame as a playwright will spread throughout all Egypt."

"As yours has already. Your name is on every lip," I told him, but he laughed it away with careless modesty as I went on. "Do you have your closing declamation prepared, Tanus?"

Traditionally the actor who played Horus would close the pageant with a message to Pharaoh, ostensibly from the gods but in reality from his own subjects. In olden times this had been an occasion when the populace could bring to the king's notice matters of concern they were not able at any other time to address to him. Recently the tradition had fallen away, and the speech had become another eulogy to the divine Pharaoh.

For days past I had been asking Tanus to rehearse his speech for me, but every time he had put me off with excuses. I was now thoroughly suspicious of his intentions, but he laughed at me.

"I have decided to let my speech be as much a surprise to you as

I hope it will be to Pharaoh. That way you should both enjoy it more." There was nothing I could do to persuade him. I left him in not a little dudgeon, and went to find more convivial company.

As I stooped in through the entrance of Lostris's dressing tent I gasped aloud at the ethereal vision that stood before me.

"Isn't this fun?" she said. "I cannot wait to see Tanus in full costume. I am sure he must look like the god himself."

"No more godlike than you, my lady," I whispered.

"When will the play begin?" she demanded impatiently.

I cocked my ear to the panel of the tent and listened for the drone of the speeches in the great hall. Realising that this was the final oration, I took Lostris's hand and squeezed it.

"At any moment your father will call for the play to begin. Remember the long pause and the haughty look before your opening speech," I cautioned her.

She slapped my shoulder playfully. "It will all go perfectly, you'll see." And at that moment I heard my Lord Intef's voice raised.

"The divine God Pharaoh Mamose, the Just, the Great, the All-Seeing, the All-Merciful . . ." The titles and honorifics continued while I made my way to my opening position behind the central pillar. The inner courtyard of the temple was packed, Pharaoh and his senior wives sitting in the front rank on low benches.

The main body of the stage was still hidden from the audience by linen curtains. My masons had built a stone cistern at the back of the temple from which a stream could be diverted across the stage to represent the River Nile, and at the rear of the stage, hanging from floor to ceiling, were tightly stretched sheets on which artists had painted marvellous landscapes.

". . . Mamose, Son of Ra, may you be granted eternal life. We your loyal subjects, the citizens of Thebes, beg you to give your divine attention to this poor play that we dedicate to Your Majesty."

Lord Intef concluded his address of welcome and resumed his seat, and to a fanfare of hidden rams' horns I stepped out from behind the pillar and faced the audience. A raucous cheer greeted my entrance and even Pharaoh smiled in anticipation. I held up both hands for silence, and only when it was total did I begin to speak.

"While I walked in the sunlight, filled with the vigour of youth, I heard the fatal music in the reeds by the bank of the Nile. The music was of surprising beauty. Joyously I went to find the musician, and could not know that he was Death and that he played his harp to summon me alone." We Egyptians are fascinated by death, and I had at once touched a deep chord within my audience. They sighed and shuddered and I knew that I had them.

"Death seized me and bore me up towards Ammon-Ra, the sun god, and I was become one with the white light of his being. Then Death set me down in a high place from which I could see the world. There were no men upon the earth and only the gods existed. I watched the passion of the gods played out before me."

My audience all sat silent and enthralled as I went on.

"Out of chaos and darkness rose the sun, Ammon-Ra, and beneath him Geb and Nut, the earth and the heaven. Geb and Nut coupled, and from their dreadful union were born the gods Osiris and Seth and the goddesses Isis and Nephthys."

I made a wide gesture and the linen curtains were drawn slowly aside to reveal the fantasy world that I had created. The audience gasped with amazement.

With measured words I continued. "And the god Osiris, with his crook and his flail made mystical gestures, declaiming in sonorous tones, 'Behold Atur, the river!' "

Once more the audience rustled and murmured as they recognised the Nile. The Nile was Egypt and the centre of the world.

Secretly I signalled for the cistern to be opened, and the waters began to flow across our stage. A shout of approval went up from a thousand throats.

"Now, behold the insects and birds upon the earth!"

Cages at the rear of the stage were opened and a chattering cloud of wild birds and gorgeously coloured butterflies filled the temple.

The watchers were like children, reaching up to snatch at the butterflies. Then one of the wild birds, a long-billed hoopoe marvellously patterned in colours of white, cinnamon and black, by chance flew down unafraid and settled on Pharaoh's crown.

The crowd was delighted. "An omen!" they cried. "A blessing on the king. May he live for ever!" and Pharaoh smiled as I continued.

"But Seth was jealous of his brother's great works, the world Osiris had created, and the two gods fought. And Seth the evil one triumphed, the bronze blade of his sword hissing as it swung, striking off an arm and then a leg, full thirteen fragments, until finally the head was struck from Osiris's body. And these fourteen blood-soaked pieces Seth scattered to the far corners of the earth . . ."

The audience woke from their trance. "Spare him! Spare the great god Osiris!" They sighed, knowing that the struggles and passions of the gods were beyond the influence of mortal men.

Slowly the linen curtains behind me closed. I stepped forward to face my audience. Every one of them, from Pharaoh to the meanest vassal, was captive to my voice as I described the mourning of Isis and her sister Nephthys at the death of their brother.

When I stepped down and the curtain was drawn aside to reveal the grieving figure of Isis, the audience gasped aloud at her loveliness. She began to sing the lament for the dead, and her voice thrilled through the gloomy halls of the temple. I watched Pharaoh attentively as she sang. His eyes never left her face.

Nephthys entered and sang a duet with her sister, then hand in hand they went in search of the scattered fragments of Osiris's corpse.

To represent the body of the god I had ordered the funeral artists from the necropolis to build for me a magnificent mummy cartonnage depicting Osiris in his full regalia. This container I had cut into sections that fitted together like a child's building blocks.

As the sisters retrieved each of these sections they sang a hymn of praise to the god's parts, to his hands and feet, to his limbs and trunk, and finally to his divine head. When at last the two sisters had reassembled the body of Osiris, they pondered aloud how they could return it to life once more. This was my opportunity to add to the pageant that essential element that makes any theatrical production appeal to the popular taste.

"There is but one certain way to bring our dear lord and brother back to life." I placed the words in the mouth of the goddess Nephthys. "One of us must perform the act of generation with his shattered body to make it whole again and to fan the spark of life within it."

I had agonised over how I would represent upon the stage this episode in the myth of the resurrection of Osiris. My mistress's reputation was too valuable to trifle with, so I had hired a wench whose body resembled hers. And now, at my signal, the linen curtains were drawn once more and my Lady Lostris quickly left the stage.

As soon as the substitute goddess was in position the torches at the rear of the stage were lit so as to cast her shadow upon the curtain. She began to disrobe and the audience cheered on her shadowy gyrations, convinced they were watching my Lady Lostris. The girl responded to this encouragement with an increasingly lewd display, the audience egging her on with whistling and hooting.

At the climax of this exhibition the torches were extinguished and the temple plunged into darkness.

In the darkness the substitution was made once more and when the torches were relit and the curtains drawn back my Lady Lostris stood in mid-stage with a newborn infant in her arms. One of the kitchen slaves had been considerate enough to give birth a few days previously, and I had borrowed her child for the occasion.

"I give you the newborn son of Osiris, god of the underworld; and of Isis, goddess of the moon and of the stars."

My Lady Lostris lifted the infant high and he, astonished by the sea of strangers before him, screwed up his tiny face and howled.

Isis raised her voice above his and cried, "Greet the young Lord Horus, god of the wind and the sky!" Half the audience were Horus men and their enthusiasm for their patron was unbounded. They came to their feet in a roaring tumult, and the act ended in triumph.

I opened the second and final act with another of my recitations describing the childhood and the coming to manhood of Horus. I spoke of the sacred charge laid upon him by Isis, and as I did so the curtains were drawn aside to reveal the goddess bathing in the Nile, attended by her handmaidens.

Tanus as Horus entered in his polished armour, and immediately dominated the stage. For at this moment he was the darling of the crowd. The long list of his battle honours in the river wars, together with his most recent exploit in saving the royal barge, had focused the attention of the populace full upon him.

While the cheering swirled around Tanus, I picked out certain faces in the audience and watched their reactions.

Nembet, the aged admiral and Great Lion of Egypt, scowled and muttered fiercely into his beard. Pharaoh smiled graciously and nodded slightly so that those seated behind him were made aware of his approbation, and my Lord Intef, never one to fly against the prevailing winds, smiled his most silky smile. His eyes, however, were deadly.

At last the applause abated and Tanus could speak his lines—not without difficulty, however, for every time he paused to draw breath another outburst of cheering broke out. It was only when

Isis began to sing that complete silence fell upon them once more. In verse she warned her noble son, and held out her arms to him in supplication and in command.

"The curse of Seth is upon us all,
And only you can break it.
Seek out your monstrous uncle,
And when you find him, strike him down.
Bind him to your will,
That the gods and all men
Will be freed for ever from his sway."

The goddess withdrew and left her son to his quest. Like children following a well-loved nursery rhyme, the audience knew full well what to expect and they leaned forward in eager anticipation.

They greeted Seth with a chorus of hatred. In defiance Rasfer leered and gibbered at them, strutting about the stage, driving them wild with fury. Their reaction to him was in no way moderated by the fact that they knew this was no Seth, but Rasfer.

"Kill the murderer of the great god Osiris!" they roared.

At last Seth pretended to see his nephew for the first time, and swaggered up to him. "Who is this child?" he demanded.

"I am Horus, son of Osiris."

Seth let out a mocking peal of laughter. "And what is it you seek, boy-child of a dead god?"

"I seek vengeance for the murder of my noble father. I seek the assassin of Osiris."

"Then search no further," Seth shouted. "For I am Seth the vanquisher of lesser gods and the destroyer of worlds."

The two gods drew their swords and rushed at each other, to meet mid-stage with a clash of bronze as blade struck blade. Simultaneously the two swordsmen pushed each other backwards and then rushed in again, thrusting and cutting, feinting and parrying.

What seemed to the observer the chaos of real battle was in fact a meticulously choreographed ballet, carefully rehearsed. Each man knew exactly how each blow must be launched and each parry timed. The crowd was mesmerised and so was I. Therefore it must have been some deep instinct that made me tear my eyes away from the spectacle and glance at my Lord Intef where he sat in the front row.

Again, was it instinct or my own deep knowledge of him, or the intervention of the god who protects Tanus, that placed the thought in my mind? A little of all three of these perhaps, but I knew with utter certainty the reason for my Lord Intef's wolfish smile.

I knew why he had chosen Rasfer to play Seth. And I knew why he was smiling now. Before this final act was played out Rasfer would ply his special talents.

"Tanus," I screamed as I started forwards. "Beware! It's a trap. He intends—" My cries were drowned out by the crowd and I was seized by each arm from behind. I tried to struggle free, but two of Rasfer's ruffians held me fast and started to drag me away.

Instead of resisting them I hurled myself back in the same direction as they were pulling me. For an instant they were thrown off-balance, and I broke half free of their grasp. I managed to reach the edge of the stage before they could control me again, and screamed with all my breath, "Tanus! Beware! He means to kill you!"

This time my voice carried above that of the mob, and Tanus heard me. I saw his head flick and his eyes narrow slightly. Rasfer responded instantly, breaking the rehearsed routine, and with an upward sweep of his own blade he forced Tanus's sword arm high.

Now he launched a thrust behind which was the full weight of his massive shoulders. The point of his blade was aimed an inch below the rim of Tanus's helmet and directly at his right eye.

But my shouted warning had given Tanus that fleeting moment in which to react. With the pommel of his sword he managed a glancing blow to Rasfer's wrist. It had just sufficient force to deflect the sword point a finger's width, and at the same moment Tanus tucked in his chin and rolled his head. It was too late to avoid the blow entirely. However, the stroke that might have split his skull merely laid open his eyebrow to the bone and then flew on over his shoulder.

Instantly blood gushed from the wound and flowed over Tanus's face, blinding his right eye. He was forced to fall back before the savage onslaught that Rasfer now launched at him.

Tanus was able to survive that first attack, weaving, parrying and ducking. Rasfer kept coming at him, never letting him recover his balance or his full vision, grunting like a giant forest hog.

Though no great swordsman myself, I am a student of the art. So often had I watched Rasfer at practice in the weapons' yard that I knew his style intimately. I knew he was an exponent of the attack Khamsin, the attack "like the desert wind", and I divined by his footwork that he was gathering himself for it.

I screamed at Tanus again, struggling in the grip of my captors. "Khamsin! Be ready!" I thought that my warning had been drowned by the uproar that filled the temple, for Tanus showed no reaction. Later he told me he had indeed heard me, and that with his impaired vision my second warning had saved him once again.

Rasfer dropped back a pace, then his weight shifted and his left foot swung forwards into the lead, launching his entire body into the attack. At that precise instant, Tanus launched himself with equal power and flew straight at Rasfer. As they met in midair Tanus gathered up Rasfer's blade with his own and let it run down onto the pommel, where it came up hard and short, stopping it dead.

The mass and speed of the two big men was thrown onto the bronze blade in Rasfer's fist, and it could not withstand the shock. It snapped cleanly, and left him clutching only the sheared-off hilt.

Then they were locked chest to chest once more. Although Tanus's sword was undamaged, Rasfer had got in under his guard and he could not wield it. Both Tanus's hands, the sword still held in his right fist, were locked behind Rasfer's back. They spun about the stage, each attempting to unbalance the other, equally matched in strength.

The audience had long since sensed that this was a fight to the death. They were insatiable, howling for blood. Women screamed and men roared their fury. But not one of them mounted the stage to try to prevent the tragedy from being played out.

At last Rasfer tore his arm free of Tanus's encircling grip. He still clutched the hilt of the broken sword in his fist, and with the jagged edge he struck at Tanus's face, deliberately aiming at his eyes. Tanus twisted his head to avoid the blows and used the moment to adjust his crushing hold round Rasfer's chest. The strain that he was exerting was such that Rasfer's features began to engorge with blood. The air was being forced out of him, and he struggled against suffocation.

Tanus felt him falter, and changed the angle of his effort, dropping his shoulders slightly and forcing his opponent backwards and upwards onto his heels. Rasfer was off balance, and Tanus heaved again and forced him backwards across the stage, steering him at one of the gigantic stone pillars. Then we saw him drop the point of his sword to the horizontal and press the hilt hard against Rasfer's spine.

At a full run the point of Tanus's sword hit the unyielding column.

The metal screeched against the granite, and the shock was transmitted up the blade. It stopped the two men in their tracks, and the force of it drove the hilt into Rasfer's spine. It would have killed a lesser man, and even Rasfer was temporarily paralysed by it. He let out a cry of pain and his knees buckled. Tanus hurled him over backwards. He landed heavily and the back of his skull struck the stone flags. He groaned in agony. He had barely the strength to lift his arms in capitulation. Tanus stood over Rasfer and lifted his sword high, gripping the hilt with both hands.

"Kill him!" roared the congregation. "Kill the evil one!"

The point of Tanus's sword was aimed at Rasfer's chest, and I steeled myself for the downstroke that would impale that gross body. I willed Tanus to do it, for I hated Rasfer more than any of them.

It was in vain. I should have known my Tanus better. He shook his head slightly, as if to regain control of himself. Then, instead of stabbing down, he lowered his sword point slowly until it just pricked Rasfer's chest. The keen point raised a drop of blood, bright as a garnet. Then Tanus picked up the lines of his script.

"Thus I bind you to my will, and I expel you from the light. May you wander through all eternity in the dark places. From henceforth you are the god of all evil. Get you gone, and carry away with you the curse of Horus and of his resurrected father, Osiris."

Tanus lifted the point of his sword from Rasfer's chest and tossed the weapon aside. Then he strode to the waters of our stage Nile and went down on one knee to scoop a handful and dash it into his own face, washing away the blood.

Rasfer's two apes released me and rushed on stage to succour their fallen commander. They lifted him to his feet and he staggered between them, heaving and grievously injured. They dragged him from the stage and the crowd howled their derision.

I watched my Lord Intef and his expression was for the moment unguarded. I saw my suspicions confirmed there. This was how he had planned to wreak his vengeance on Tanus—to have him slain before the eyes of the entire populace, and of his own daughter.

Tanus was still gasping from the exertions of the duel, but now, as he moved to the front of the stage, he drew breaths to steady himself for the declamation that would bring the pageant to an end.

As he faced them the congregation fell silent.

He was an awe-inspiring sight. He lifted up both his hands to the temple roof and cried out in a loud voice, "Ammon-Ra, give me voice! Osiris, give me eloquence!" The traditional entreaty of the orator.

Pharaoh made a gesture of invitation to him to speak, inclining his head gracefully.

"It is I, Horus, that speaks," Tanus began. "I speak to you of this ancient land given to us in the time when all the gods were young. I speak to you of the two kingdoms that in nature are indivisible."

Pharaoh nodded. This was the standard dogma, approved by both temporal and religious authorities, neither of whom recognised the impostor in the Lower Kingdom.

"I speak to you also of this land divided, torn by civil war, bleeding and drained of treasure."

My own shock was mirrored on the faces of all those that listened to him. Tanus had just given voice to the unspeakable.

"I speak to you," he continued, "of old and feeble generals and of admirals too indecisive to wrest back the stolen kingdom from the usurper. I speak to you of ancient men in their dotage who waste your treasure and the blood of your finest young men."

In the second row of the audience I saw Nembet, the Great Lion of Egypt, flush with anger. The other elderly military men around him frowned and moved restlessly on their benches.

"I speak to you of the robber who waits in ambush on every hilltop and in every thicket. The farmer is forced to plough with his shield at his side, and the traveller must go with his sword bared."

The common people at the rear of the great hall stamped their feet in agreement with what Tanus had said. The depredations of the robber bands were a terrible scourge upon them all.

Tanus had struck exactly the right note with the people, and suddenly I was moved by the notion that revolutions had been forged by just such appeals to the masses.

"While the poor cry out under the lash of the tax collector, the nobles anoint their fancy boys with the most precious oils—"

A roar went up from the rear of the hall, and my fears were replaced by a tremulous excitement. Had this been carefully planned? The land is ripe for revolution, I cried in my heart. And who better to lead it than Tanus? But why, oh why had he not consulted me before embarking on this perilous venture?

With his next breath he made the reason plain. This was no plot. This was simply Tanus speaking his mind. The commoners were now given the sharp edge of his tongue as he rounded upon them.

"Hear me, oh Egypt! What is to become of a land where the mean-spirited try to suppress the mighty among them; where the patriot is reviled; where no man is revered for his wisdom; and where the envious seek to tear down all men of worth to their own base level?"

There was no cheering now as those at the back of the hall recognised themselves in this description. Effortlessly my Tanus had succeeded in alienating every man among them, rich and poor.

Tanus went on relentlessly. "Pharaoh, you are the father of the people. We cry out to you for protection. Give the affairs of state and war into the hands of honest and clever men. Call off the faithless priests and the usurious servants of the state, those parasites upon the body of our nation."

I was as good a priest hater as the best of them, but only a fool or a very brave man would call down the wrath of every god-botherer in Egypt upon his own head, for their power was infinite. While as for the civil servants, their lines of influence had been set up over the centuries and my Lord Intef was the chief of them all.

Tanus fell to his knees in the centre of the stage and spread his arms wide. "Oh Pharaoh, you are our father. We protest our love to you. In return, show us a father's love. Hear our entreaties, we beg of you."

Up to that moment I had been stupefied by the depths of my friend's folly, but now I regained my wits and signalled frantically for my stagehands to drop the curtain. As the gleaming cloth floated down and hid him from their view the audience sat in stunned silence.

It was Pharaoh himself who broke the spell. He rose to his feet, and as he swept from the temple the congregation prostrated itself before him. Before my Lord Intef too went down in obeisance I saw his expression. It was triumphant.

I ESCORTED TANUS back from the temple to his quarters close to the dock at which his squadron was moored. He was quite unrepentant. Indeed he seemed inordinately pleased with himself.

"It was time somebody stood up and said what needed to be said, don't you agree, old friend?" His voice rang clear and loud down the darkened alley. "You did not expect it of me, did you now? Be honest with me, Taita. It took you quite by surprise, did it not?"

"It surprised us all. Even Pharaoh was taken aback."

"He listened, Taita. He took it all in, I could tell."

When I raised the subject of Rasfer's treacherous attack upon him and suggested that it might have been inspired by my Lord Intef, Tanus would have none of it.

"That is impossible, Taita. Lord Intef was my father's dearest friend." Besides, I am to be his son-in-law." Despite his injuries he let out a happy shout of laughter. "No, it was simply Rasfer working out his spite. Well, he'll know better next time." He laughed again.

How could I stifle his joy? This was not the time to point out the danger in which he had placed himself. So I took him home, stitched the gash in his forehead and washed his wounds. Then I left him.

When I reached my own quarters well after midnight, there were two summonses awaiting me. One from my Lady Lostris and the other from the vanquished Rasfer. There was no doubt as to which of them I would have responded if I had been given the choice, but I was not. Rasfer's two thugs almost dragged me away to where he lay on a sweat-soaked mattress, cursing and moaning.

It is a strange thing about those of us who are healers that we cannot find it in our hearts to deny our skills to even the most abominable creatures that require them. I sighed with resignation and unpacked the leather bag containing my medical equipment.

As well as numerous contusions and shallow wounds, at least three of Rasfer's ribs were broken and there was a lump on the back of his head almost the size of my fist. One of the broken ribs was out of alignment and there was a danger that it might pierce the lung. While his two thugs held him down I manipulated the rib back into place and strapped up his chest. Then I dressed the lump on the back of his skull. Rasfer would survive, but I wondered if I had truly done mankind a great service by helping to preserve him.

When I left Rasfer I found that I was completely exhausted. However, there was to be no rest for me yet, for my Lady Lostris's messenger still hovered on the terrace of my quarters and pounced on me as I set foot on the first step. Yet, as I tottered into her chamber, I felt the tiredness fall from my shoulders like a heavy load. Her mere presence had the power to revitalise me.

"My lady, what a wondrous role you played this night. It seemed to me that it was indeed the goddess that walked among us—"

"Don't you dare try your tricks with me." She stamped her foot, but without conviction. "How dare you keep me waiting so long? I was ready to have you flogged, I truly was . . . But come and sit beside me on the bed and tell me how the play has been received. I am still so excited that I am sure I will not sleep for a week."

She took my hand and led me to the bed, babbling on happily about Tanus, and how he must have won every heart as well as Pharaoh's with his wonderful performance and fearless speech.

At last I had to stop her. "My lady, it is almost dawn and we must be ready to leave with all the court to accompany the king when he crosses the river to inspect his funerary temple and his tomb. You must get some sleep if you are to look your best."

"I'm not sleepy, Taita," she protested and went chattering on, only to fall asleep in mid-sentence a few minutes later.

Gently I slipped her head down onto the carved wooden head-rest and covered her with a rug of colobus-monkey furs.

I COULD SCARCELY drag myself from my couch at dawn, and I was among the last to join the throng upon the grand vizier's private dock where the great state barge lay moored. My Lady Lostris was already on the deck of the barge. I watched her for a while.

She had been invited to join the royal women. It was difficult to believe that, like me, Lostris had not slept more than an hour or two, for she seemed fresh as one of the desert roses in my garden. I looked for Tanus, but his squadron was already lying well upstream, ready to escort Pharaoh's crossing. At that moment there was the boom of a drum, and the populace craned to watch Pharaoh's stately progress from the palace to the royal barge.

This morning he wore the light nemes crown of starched and folded linen, secured round his forehead with a gold band. The erect golden cobra, with its hood flared and its garnet eyes glittering, rose up from his brow. The cobra was the symbol of the powers of life and death that Pharaoh held over his subjects.

Despite all the ceremonial he wore no make-up. Under the direct rays of the early sun, Mamose was unremarkable. Just a soft little godling of middle age, with a small paunch bulging over the waistband of his kilt and features carved with lines of worry.

As he passed where I stood it seemed he recognised me, for he nodded slightly. I immediately prostrated myself on the paving, and he paused and made a sign for me to approach.

I crawled forwards on hands and knees.

"Are you not Taita, the poet?" he asked.

"I am Taita the slave, Your Majesty," I replied. There are times when a little humility is called for. "But I am also a poor scribbler."

"Well, Taita the slave, you scribbled to good effect last night. I have never been so well entertained by a pageant."

He announced this loud enough for all the court to hear. However, he was not finished with me yet.

"Tell me, Taita the slave, are you not also the same surgeon who recently prescribed to me?"

"Majesty, I am that same humble slave who has the temerity to practise a little medicine."

He dropped his voice. "Then when shall your cure take effect?"

"Majesty, the event will take place nine months after you have fulfilled all those conditions that I listed for you." I felt emboldened to ask, "Has Pharaoh found the companion I suggested?"

"Alas, doctor, it is not as simple as it would seem. The prettiest flowers are soonest visited by the bee. You did stipulate that she must be completely untouched, did you not?"

"Virgin and untouched and within a season of her first red moon," I added quickly, making it as difficult as possible to put my recipe to the test. "Have you found one who meets that description, Majesty?"

He smiled thoughtfully. "We shall see," he murmured and turned and mounted the boarding ladder of the barge.

As my Lord Intef drew level with me he made a small gesture, ordering me to follow him onto the deck of the royal barge.

He drew me aside as soon as we reached the deck. "You still have the power to surprise me sometimes," he whispered. "Just when I was seriously beginning to doubt your loyalty."

I was taken aback by this sudden flush of goodwill. However, I bowed my head to shield my expression and waited.

"I could not myself have written a more appropriate declamation for Tanus to recite before Pharaoh. Where that imbecile Rasfer failed so dismally, you retrieved the day for me."

He believed that I was the author of Tanus's monumental folly, and that I had composed it for his downfall.

"I am pleased that you are pleased," I whispered back to him.

I felt an enormous sense of relief. My position of influence had not been compromised. Tanus and Lostris would need every bit of help that I could give them during the stormy days that lay ahead.

Soon we were across the river and pulling into the mouth of the canal that led across the plain to Pharaoh Mamose's great funerary temple at the foot of the gaunt Saharan foothills.

As the barge nosed into the canal, 200 sturdy slaves seized the tow ropes in the bows and began to draw her smoothly across the plain. They sang one of their sad melodious work chants as they marched in ranks along the towpath.

When at last we slid into the stone dock below the outer walls of the half-finished temple, the slaves made the tow ropes fast to the mooring rings. As the huge vessel came to rest, the trumpeter seated in the bows blew a fanfare and the portcullis was raised slowly, to reveal the royal hearse waiting in the gateway attended by the company of embalmers and fifty priests of Osiris.

The priests began to chant as they eased the hearse forwards on its wooden rollers, onto the deck of the barge. Pharaoh hurried forwards to examine this grotesque vehicle.

I had taken no part in this celebration of bad taste. It was entirely the work of the priests. In the naked sunlight, the gold work shone so brightly as to offend the eye almost as painfully as did the actual design. Such weight of gold forced the priests to sweat as they manhandled the ark on deck, and it listed the ship alarmingly.

At my Lord Intef's suggestion, the king mounted the vehicle and took his seat on the platform designed to carry his sarcophagus. From there he beamed all about him. On what was clearly an impulse, he beckoned my lord to join him, then looked around the crowded deck as if seeking someone else in the throng. He stooped slightly and said something to the grand vizier.

My Lord Intef smiled and, following his direction, singled out my Lady Lostris. With a gesture he ordered her to join them. She was clearly flustered, but mounted the carriage with long-legged grace.

She knelt before the king and, in front of all the priests and the entire court, he did an extraordinary thing. He reached down and took Lostris's hand and lifted her to her feet, and seated her beside him on the platform. It was beyond all protocol, and I saw his ministers exchange looks of amazement.

The shock of it was like the blow of a fist in my stomach.

Had I been blind, I berated myself, or merely stupid? My ill-considered advice to the king had directed his attention towards my Lady Lostris. The most beautiful virgin in the land, to be taken within the first season after her moon had flowered—it was her exactly.

Before I could recover my wits, the sweating priests had shoved the hearse off the deck and through the gateway, and I was borne along with the crowd into the forecourt of the funerary temple. I began to push my way forwards to reach the hearse before it came to the main entrance of the royal mortuary.

As one team of priests pushed the vehicle forwards, a second team picked up the wooden rollers that were left behind it and ran forwards to place them ahead of the ponderous golden vehicle.

When I reached the near side of the ark I found myself directly below Lostris. She had completely recovered her poise, and was now setting herself out to be as agreeable as possible. Miserably I recalled how she had planned to do exactly this, and to use Pharaoh's favour to secure his agreement to her marriage to Tanus.

If, earlier in this chronicle, I have given the impression that my Lady Lostris was a flighty child with not a thought in her pretty head, then I have fallen short in my efforts as historian of these extraordinary events. Although still so young, she was at times mature far beyond her years. She was a diligent scholar, with a bright and enquiring mind. She was an accomplished conversationalist, with an enchanting voice and a merry laugh. Truly, no man or god could resist her. I had to warn her, and yet how could a slave intrude upon persons so infinitely high above his own station?

The funeral ark passed into the inner court of the temple and rolled down the long colonnaded atrium, past the guarded doors to the six treasuries in which were manufactured and stored the funerary offerings. At the end of the atrium the acacia-wood doors, on which were carved the images of all the gods of the pantheon, were swung open, and we entered the mortuary.

Here in this solemn chapel the king dismounted and went forward to inspect the massive table on which he would lie for the ritual of mummification. The grand master of the guild of embalmers was standing beside the table, ready to explain the entire process to the king, and Pharaoh seemed fascinated by every gruesome detail.

He examined the embalmer's instruments and the four Canopic jars, carved from gleaming translucent alabaster, which would receive Pharaoh's viscera. The stoppers of each were fashioned in the shapes of the animal-headed gods: Anubis the jackal, Sobeth the crocodile, Thoth the ibis, Sekhmet the lioness. These would be the guardians of his divine parts, until his awakening in eternal life.

Once the king had satisfied his curiosity at the mortuary table my Lady Lostris directed his attention to the painted bas-relief engravings that covered the temple walls from floor to ceiling.

I had drawn most of the original cartoons with my own hand, and had closely supervised the others drawn by the palace artists. These had been traced onto the walls with charcoal sticks, and now a company of master sculptors was engraving them into the sandstone blocks, while behind them a second company of artists was painting in the completed bas-relief.

Naturally, the theme that I had chosen for the mortuary was the *Book of the Dead*, that detailed description of the route to the underworld that Pharaoh's shade must follow, and the depictions of all the trials and dangers that he would confront along the way.

It was almost noon before Pharaoh had completed his inspection of the mortuary temple and led the way out into the forecourt where the palace chefs had laid out a sumptuous alfresco banquet. And once again the king ignored precedent to place my Lady Lostris close to him at the banquet table. During the meal he directed most of his conversation towards my mistress. She was now completely at her ease and kept the king and all around her enthralled with her wit.

Of course, as a slave I did not have a seat at the table, nor could I even inveigle myself within range of my mistress to warn her to moderate her demeanour in the king's presence. Instead I found myself a place on the pedestal of one of the granite horns that lined the carriageway, from where I could watch everything that took place. I was not the only observer, for my Lord Intef sat close to the king and yet withdrawn, watching with glittering implacable eyes.

After the midday meal it was customary for the court to rest for an hour or so, especially at this the hottest season of the year. However, Pharaoh was so wrought up that today he would have none of it. "Now we will inspect the treasuries," he announced.

The guards at the doors of the first treasury stood aside and presented arms as the royal party approached, and the doors were swung open from within. The hall that we entered was the armoury that housed the weapons and accoutrements of the battlefield and the chase, which the king would take with him into the afterworld.

As the king passed slowly down the row of benches, his questions were so astute and technical that those nobles and priests to whom he addressed himself could provide no answers. I was summoned hastily and pushed forward to face the king's interrogation.

"Ah, yes." Pharaoh grimaced bleakly as he recognised me. "It is none other than the humble slave who writes pageants and cures the sick. No one here seems to know the composition of the wire that binds the stock of this war bow."

"Gracious Pharaoh, the metal is a mixture of one part of copper to five parts of silver and four of gold. The gold is the red variety found only in the mines of Lot in the western desert. We extrude the hot metal by swinging it in a special pendulum. Later we can watch the process in the gold foundry, if Your Majesty so wishes."

Thus, during the rest of the tour I was able to remain at the king's side and to deflect some of his attention away from Lostris, but I still could not find the opportunity to speak to her alone.

From the armoury we crossed the atrium to the furniture store, where a hundred cabinet-makers laboured to build the funeral furnishings for the king's long journey. Then we passed on to the hall of the sculptors. In marble and sandstone and granite of a hundred differing hues the sculptors whittled and chipped with chisel and file so that a fine, pale dust hung in the air. The granite sarcophagus, only partially completed, lay in the centre of the masons' hall. Originally it had been a single block of pink granite quarried from the mines at Assoun, and ferried downriver by barge.

The masons had begun by sawing a thick slab from the top of it. Upon this granite lid a master mason was fashioning the likeness of the mummiform Pharaoh, with his arms crossed. Another team of masons was now engaged in hollowing out the interior of the main granite block to provide a nest into which the seven inner coffins would fit perfectly. Seven was, of course, one of the magical numbers. The innermost coffin would be of pure gold, and later we watched it being beaten out in the hall of the goldsmith.

Here, on a dais in the centre of the hall, the most skilful smiths were at work. They had perfectly captured Pharaoh's living face in the shimmering metal. The mask would fit exactly over his bandaged head. It was a divine image with eyes of obsidian and rock crystal, and with the cobra-headed crown encircling the brow.

Even after Pharaoh had admired the golden mask from every angle, he seemed unable to tear himself too far from it. He spent the remainder of the day on the dais beside it, seated on a low stool, while box after cedarwood box of exquisite jewels were laid at his feet and the contents catalogued for him. There were 6,455 pieces already in the cedarwood boxes, and each day more were added to the collection. All of this the king intended taking with him to the tomb.

Who am I, a humble slave, to question the price that a king was willing to pay for eternal life? Suffice it only to state that in assembling this treasure, while conducting the war against the Lower Kingdom, Pharaoh had plunged Egypt into beggary.

LAVISH QUARTERS had been prepared in the necropolis in which the king would spend that night upon the west bank of the Nile. The necropolis, the city of the dead, was home to all those associated with the building and the care of the funerary temple and the royal tomb.

There was also a full regiment of the elite guard to protect the holy places, for the usurper in the north was avaricious, while the robber barons in the desert became more daring each day. It was with relief that we moved into the king's quarters to spend the night, for it had been a wearying day. But once again there was little rest for me.

I tried to reach my Lady Lostris, but, as I waited in the antechamber of her quarters, a summons reached me from her father.

As soon as I entered his bedchamber he dismissed all the others in the room. I was disturbed by his excited manner.

"How often the gateway to power and fortune is found in the most unexpected place," he laughed. "This time it lies between the thighs of a woman. No, old darling, don't play the innocent. I know just what a cunning hand you have taken in all of this. Pharaoh has told me how you have cajoled him by promising him a male heir to his line. By Seth, but you are the cunning one.

"I have just come from the king's presence. Tomorrow at the culmination of the festival he will announce his betrothal to my daughter. The wedding will take place the same day, immediately after the closing ceremony of the festival."

I felt a sudden chilly dew upon my skin but my lord did not notice my distress, being too concerned with his own immediate interests.

"Before I gave my formal consent to the union, I prevailed on the king to concede that if she bore him a son then he would elevate my daughter to the rank of principal wife and queen consort."

He clapped his hands in unrestrained triumph. "Of course, you realise what that means. If Pharaoh should die before my grandson is of age to rule, then I would become regent—"

He broke off suddenly. I understood exactly what was running through his mind. Nobody should ever have heard that thought expressed. It was purest treason. My Lord Intef had given voice to his intended regicide, and he was now considering removing the only one who had heard the indiscretion spoken.

"My lord, I am only grateful that it has turned out the way I planned it. But there remains a great deal for us to do, before we can count ourselves secure—" and I began to extemporise a list of all that might go awry before he could gain control of the crown of Egypt. Tactfully I made it clear how much he still needed me if he were to achieve this. I saw him relax as he followed my arguments, and I knew that at least for the immediate future I was safe.

It was some time before I could escape from his presence. There was only one person that I could turn to now. I left the necropolis and set off along the towpath of the canal, back towards the river bank where I knew that Tanus's squadrons were camped.

The moon was only three days from full and it lit the jagged hills of the western horizon with a cold yellow radiance and threw black shadows on the plain below. The squadron's sentries challenged me and then, when they recognised me, led me to Tanus's tent.

Tanus was at late supper with Kratas, his second-in-command, and four of his subordinate officers. He rose to greet me with a smile. "This is such an unexpected pleasure, old friend. Sit down beside me. You look hot and out of sorts—"

I cut short these pleasantries, all my fear and anxiety tumbling out in a flood of invective. "To Seth with you, you senseless oaf. Do you not understand what jeopardy you have placed us in?"

His expression changed and he held up one hand as though to shield himself. "Whoa! You take me unawares. I am unarmed and unable to defend myself—" His smile was thin as he seized my arm, steered me out of the tent and half dragged me beyond the regimental fines into the open moonlit fields beyond.

"Now puke it up!" he ordered me grimly. "Are you talking about my declamation at the pageant? How can you say it was folly? All my officers are delighted with what I had to say—"

"You fool, don't you see that you have played directly into the hands of my Lord Intef?"

"Lord Intef?" He stared at me hard. "You speak of him as though he were my enemy. The grand vizier was my father's dearest friend."

"Oh. Tanus!" I curbed my anger. "I have been unfair to you. There is so much that I should have told you, and never did. I was a coward, and I could not tell you that Intef was your father's enemy. One day I will explain it all to you. I will give you all the proof you need. But there is no time now. You must trust me. Both you and my Lady Lostris are in danger of losing each other for ever."

"But how is that possible, Taita?" He was confused and shaken. "Have you not spoken to my Lord Intef about our union, then?"

"Yes, I have spoken to him." I seized Tanus's hand and thrust it up under the back of my tunic. "That was his reply. Feel the welts left by the lash. He had me flogged for even suggesting the marriage of you and my Lady Lostris. That is how he hates you."

He stared at me speechlessly, but I saw that he believed me at last. "Hear me now, dear friend, and brace yourself. My Lord Intef has this very night pledged his daughter's hand to Pharaoh Mamose. The king will make the announcement himself tomorrow, at the end of the festival. The marriage will take place that very same evening."

Tanus swayed on his feet and turned away from me, finding an outcrop of black rock and seating himself upon it with a weary air.

"Has Lostris consented to this marriage?"

"Of course not. As yet she probably knows nothing about it. But do you think for one moment that her objections would count against the will of her father and the king? She will have no say in the matter."

"What are we to do, old friend?"

Even in my distress I was grateful to him that he used the plural, including me, reassuring me of our friendship.

I drew a deep breath, and then blurted it out. "Pharaoh is a weak man who has divided the two kingdoms and brought our country to her knees. He does not deserve your allegiance. Your men would follow you to the gates of the underworld—" I faltered, for his expression gave me no encouragement.

He was silent for twenty beats of my racing heart and then he ordered me softly, "Go on! Say what you have to say."

"Tanus, you would make the noblest pharaoh that this land has known. You with my Lady Lostris on the throne beside you could lead us back to greatness. Call out your squadrons and lead your men to where that unworthy Pharaoh lies. By dawn tomorrow you could be the ruler of the Upper Kingdom. By this time next year you could have defeated the usurper and have reunited the two kingdoms." I faced him. "Tanus, your destiny and that of the woman you love await you. Seize them in both your strong warrior's hands."

"Warrior's hands, yes." He held them up. "Hands that have fought for my motherland and have protected her rightful king. You do me a disservice, old friend. They are not the hands of a traitor, of a blasphemer, who would seek to cast down a god and take his place."

I groaned aloud in my frustration. "Do it, I beseech you, for the sake of Egypt and of the woman we both love."

"You cannot convince me. Lostris is a woman of virtue and of honour. As a traitor and a thief, I would forfeit all right to her respect. I would never respect myself again if I did what you urge. Speak of it no more. I have no claim to the crown, nor will I ever make such claim."

The matter was closed. I knew him so well. "Then what will you do? Nothing that I say has any weight with you."

"Come, Taita, help us. Lostris and I need you now as never before. Don't desert us. Help us find the honourable way."

"There is no such thing," I sighed. "But if you will not seize the crown, then you must sweep Lostris up and bear her away from here."

He stared at me. "Leave Egypt? You cannot be serious. This is my world. This is Lostris's world. The world of the true pharaoh!"

"That true pharaoh is the same one who will marry your love, and will order the strangling rope to be twisted round your neck," I pointed out grimly.

He sprang to his feet and began to prowl about, muttering to himself. At last he stopped in front of me.

"I am not prepared to play the traitor, but with a heavy heart I will force myself to play the coward. If Lostris agrees to accompany me, and only if she agrees, then I am prepared to take flight. I will take her away."

"Where will you go?" I asked.

"I know that Lostris can never leave the river. It is her life and her god. We must stay with Hapi, the river. That leaves only one direction open to us. We will follow the Nile southwards into the depths of Africa, into the land of Cush and beyond. There, perhaps, we will carve out another homeland for ourselves."

"Who will be your companions?"

"Kratas, of course, and those of my officers and men who are game for the adventure. I'll address them tonight and give them the choice. We must be ready to leave by dawn. You go and fetch Lostris."

"And me?" I asked quietly. "You'll take me with you?"

"You?" He laughed at me. "Would you truly give up your garden and your books, your pageants and your building of temples?"

"I could not let you go alone. What follies would you lead my mistress into, if I were not there to guide you?"

"Come!" He clapped me on the back. "I know that Lostris would not leave without you, anyway. Enough chatter! We have work to do."

I was as excited as he was as we hurried back to the regiment's encampment below the temple. Indeed, I was so elated that my sense of danger was dulled. It was Tanus who picked out the sinister movement in the moonlight ahead of us and seized my arm.

"An armed party," he whispered, and I saw the glint of bronze spearheads. There was a band of men, thirty or forty, I estimated.

At that instant a voice hailed us from out of the darkness.

"We are Pharaoh's men on the king's business. Who are you?"

Tanus drew his sword and called back, "Which pharaoh do you serve, the red usurper or the true pharaoh?"

"We serve the true king, the divine Mamose, ruler of the Upper and the Lower Kingdoms. I am the king's messenger."

"Come forward, king's messenger, and state your business!"

The leader of the band stepped forward. "My name is Neter. I am commander of Pharaoh's bodyguard. I bear the hawk seal for the arrest and detention of Tanus, Lord Harrab."

Tanus raised his voice again. "Show us the seal, Captain Neter."

Neter held it aloft. A small statuette in glistening blue faience, in the shape of the royal hawk, the king's personal empowerment. The bearer acted with all the force and validity of Pharaoh himself.

"I am Tanus, Lord Harrab," Tanus conceded. "And I acknowledge the hawk seal."

He drew me a little to one side. "Old friend, the gods frown on our enterprise. I must trust myself to the king's good sense. If he is truly a god then he will be able to look into my heart and see for himself that it contains no evil." He touched my arm, and that light gesture was to me more significant than the warmest embrace. "Go to Lostris, tell her what has happened. Tell her I love her, and I will do so through this life and the next. Tell her I will wait for her."

Then Tanus ran his sword back into his scabbard and with empty hands stepped forward to meet the bearer of the hawk seal.

"I stand ready to do the king's bidding," he said.

The king's guard closed in round him, and then they moved away along the towpath of the canal, back towards the necropolis.

WHEN I MYSELF reached the necropolis, I went directly to my Lady Lostris's quarters. I was distressed to find that they had already taken her to Pharaoh's own harem. I had no influence there, and as I feared, the guards had orders that not even the closest members of her retinue were to be allowed to go to Lostris. I was not to see either her or Tanus again until the evening of the last day of the festival of Osiris. It ended as it had begun in the temple of the god. It seemed once more that all the populace of Greater Thebes was packed into the courtyards.

I was feeling wretched, for I had slept little for two nights in succession. Apart from the uncertain fate of Tanus, I had been burdened by my Lord Intef with the onerous duty of arranging the wedding ceremony of the king to his daughter.

Twice during Pharaoh's interminable speech from the throne, I was on the point of fainting. However, I forced myself to hold on, and after he had spoken for a while it became plain to me that he was referring to every one of the points that Tanus had raised and attempting to offer remedies for each. It was clear that Pharaoh had taken serious notice of every issue that Tanus had brought forward. Could he now go on to condemn him for sedition?

"It has been brought to my notice," Pharaoh continued, "that certain officials of the state, concerned with the collection of taxes, have abused the trust that I placed in them. These officials will be called upon to account for the moneys placed in their care, and those found guilty of embezzlement or corruption will be sentenced to death." The populace stirred and sighed. Would the king truly seek to restrain his tax collectors? Then a single voice cried out, "Long live Pharaoh!"

The cry was taken up until the temple rang with the cheering. It must have been an unusual sound for the king to hear, that spontaneous applause. Even at the distance that I was from the throne I could tell that he enjoyed it.

When the cheering eventually subsided, the king went on: "My trusted grand vizier, the noble Lord Intef, will be placed in sole and absolute charge of this investigation of the civil service, with the full powers of search and arrest, of life and of death vested in him."

There was just the softest echo of applause to greet this appointment. Pharaoh was sending a hungry leopard to count the birds in his chicken-coop. What sport my Lord Intef would have, milking the tax collectors of their secret hordes of savings.

"I must speak now," Pharaoh continued, "of Tanus, Lord Harrab. He has been arrested for the crime of sedition. My councillors are divided on the subject of this person's guilt. There are those among them who wish him to pay the supreme penalty, and there are those who feel that his declamation at the festival was inspired by divine forces. If this latter be the case, then clearly there can be no culpability to the mortal through whom the gods chose to speak."

The king gave a command to the captain of his bodyguard, who stood below the throne.

I recognised him as Neter, the officer who had been sent to arrest Tanus. Neter marched away smartly and returned a moment later leading Tanus from the sanctuary at the rear of the hall.

My heart leaped to see my friend, and then with joy I realised that he was unbound and I felt my optimism revived.

Tanus made his obeisance before the throne, but when he rose to his feet again, Pharaoh spoke in a voice without pity.

"Tanus, Lord Harrab, I find you guilty of treason and sedition, for which the traditional punishment is death by strangulation."

A groan went up from the people. A woman wailed, and soon the temple was filled with cries of lamentation. Nothing could demonstrate more clearly the love which the populace bore Tanus.

Only when Pharaoh raised his voice again were the people at last silent, so that everyone heard his next pronouncement.

"The condemned man has complained of the lawless state of the kingdom. He has called upon the throne to stamp out the bands of robbers who ravage the land. The condemned man has been called a mighty warrior. If this be true, then he himself would be better suited than any other to carry out those measures he demands. Therefore, the sentence of death is deferred for two years. If the condemned man was truly inspired by the god Horus when he made his seditious speech, then the god will assist him in the task I now place upon him."

The silence was profound as, at a signal from the king, one of his ministers stepped forward and offered Pharaoh a tray on which lay a tiny blue statuette. Pharaoh held it aloft.

"I issue to Lord Harrab the hawk seal of the pharaohs. Under the auspice of the seal he may recruit all the men and materials of war that he deems necessary to his task. For two full years he is the king's man, and he answers only to the king. At the end of that time, on the last day of the festival of Osiris, he will come before the throne once again, wearing the noose of death. If he has failed in his task he will be strangled on the spot where he now stands. If he has completed his task then I will lift the noose from round his neck and replace it with the gold chain of valour."

A roar went up from the crowd, but though they cheered, I lamented. The task that Pharaoh had set was too great for any mortal man to achieve.

The cloud of death had not been lifted from over Tanus. I knew that in two years from today he would die on the very same spot where he now stood, so young and proud and tall.

FORLORN AS a lost waif she stood alone in the midst of the multitude, with the river that was her patron god at her back. Her long linen shift was dyed to the colour of the finest wine, a colour that proclaimed her a virgin bride. Her hair was loose. It flowed down onto her shoulders in a soft dark tide that shone in the sunlight as though with an inner fire. On those shining locks she wore a bridal wreath woven from the long stems of the water lily.

The priests had built a wedding canopy of river rushes on the bank above the Nile, and my Lady Lostris waited beneath it for her bridegroom to come to claim her, her father at her side.

The royal bridegroom came at last, to the solemn beat of the drum and the bleat of gazelle-horn trumpets, and to me this wedding march was the saddest sound in all the earth.

Pharaoh wore the nemes crown and carried the sceptre, but behind all the pomp he was still a little old man with a pot-belly. His ministers and high officials attended him so closely that my view of my mistress was obscured.

Despite the fact that it was I who had been forced to arrange it, I was excluded from the wedding. It was only when the crowd beneath the canopy opened and Pharaoh led his newest bride to the front of the platform that I knew it was done and that Lostris was forever beyond the reach of Tanus's arms. The people showed their love for Lostris in a chorus of adulation that went on until my ears rang and my head swam.

At last my Lord Intef came forward to take his farewell of his daughter. As the crowd subsided into silence he embraced her, then offered the ritual gift to his daughter.

It was the usual practice for the gift to be agreed in private before the ceremony. In this case, however, my Lord Intef had told his daughter unequivocally what she was entitled to ask for. Now, however, he continued the ancient formula, as though the sentiments were his own.

"Ask any boon of me, my beloved child. I will refuse you nothing on this joyous day."

It remained only for her to give voice to the prearranged request before her groom and all the wedding guests. But she stood pale and silent, seeming withdrawn.

"Speak up, my child. What is it that you desire from me?" My Lord Intef's tones of paternal love were becoming strained. "Come, tell your father what he can do to make this happy day complete."

My Lady Lostris stirred, and this time she opened her mouth and her request rang out over our heads, clear as the music of the lyre. "For my gift give me the slave, Taita!"

My Lord Intef reeled back a pace and stared at her aghast. Only he and I knew the value of the gift that Lostris had demanded. He recovered swiftly, his expression calm and benign.

"You are too restrained, my darling daughter. A single slave is no fitting gift for Pharaoh's bride."

"Father, you have always been too generous with me, but I want only Taita."

My Lord Intef smiled a white smile; white teeth, white lips and white rage. I could see that his mind was racing.

I was the most valuable of all his possessions. It was not simply my wide range of talents that made up my worth to him. Even more, it was that I knew every convoluted thread of the intricate tapestry of his affairs. He could not let me go. Yet before Pharaoh and the population of Thebes he could not deny Lostris her request.

"Let the slave Taita stand forward," he called. I pushed my way to the foot of the wedding platform.

"I am here, my lord," I cried.

He stared down at me with those deadly eyes. At last he said in soft, almost affectionate tones, "Taita, you have heard my daughter's request. You have been with me since you were a child. I have come to regard you as a brother more than as a slave. I know that it is unusual for a slave to be given a say in his own disposal, but then your circumstances are unusual. Choose, Taita. If you wish to stay in your home, then I cannot find the heart to send you away. Not even at the request of my own daughter."

He never took his eyes off me. I am not a coward but I am careful of my safety. I tore my gaze from his and looked towards my Lady Lostris. There was such appeal there, such loneliness and terror, that my own safety counted for nothing. I could not desert her.

"How can a poor slave deny the wish of Pharaoh's wife?" I cried. "I am ready to do the bidding of my new mistress."

"Come, slave!" my mistress ordered me. "Take your place behind me."

As I mounted the platform, I was forced to pass close to my Lord Intef. His lips barely moved as he spoke for my ears alone. "Farewell, my old darling. You are a dead man."

I STAYED CLOSE to Lostris during the rest of the ceremony and I waited on her personally at the wedding feast. She was so wan that I was certain she had eaten nothing in the two days since her betrothal.

In the end I succeeded in getting her to take a little watered wine, but that was all. Pharaoh saw her drink and lifted his own gold chalice, smiling at her as he returned the toast, and the wedding guests cheered the couple delightedly.

"Taita," she whispered to me as soon as the king's attention was diverted. "I fear that I am going to vomit. I cannot stay here another moment. Please take me back to my chamber."

It was a scandal, and had I not been able to adopt the role of surgeon I could never have achieved it, but I was able to whisper to the king without causing an undue comment among the guests.

As I grew to know him better I found that Pharaoh was a kindly man, and this was the first proof he gave me of it. He listened to my explanations and then clapped his hands and addressed the guests.

"My bride will go to her chamber now to prepare for the night ahead."

In her bedchamber my mistress collapsed upon the bed. "I don't want to live without Tanus," she moaned.

"Tanus is alive," I tried to console her. "He loves you and he promises to wait for you. The king is old, he cannot live for ever—"

She sat up on the fur bedcover and her voice became stern. "I am Tanus's woman and no other man shall have me. I would rather die. I order you to prepare a draught of poison for me to drink."

"Please, my little one, let us talk of this in the morning. Everything will be different in the sunlight."

"It will be the same," she contradicted me. "I will be parted from Tanus, and that wrinkled old man will want me in his bed. Mix me the poison draught now, this instant. I order you to do it."

I dared not argue longer.

"Very well, my lady. I will do it. I must fetch my chest of medicine from my rooms."

When I returned with the chest under my arm, she was up from the bed and pacing her chamber. With glittering eyes she watched as I prepared the draught from the scarlet glass bottle. She knew that colour warned of the lethal contents.

When I handed the bowl to her she showed no fear, and paused only to kiss my cheek. "You have been both father and loving brother to me. I thank you for this last kindness. I love you, Taita."

She lifted the bowl in both hands. "Tanus, my darling," she toasted him with it, "they shall never take me from you. We shall meet again!" and she drained the bowl at a swallow, then dropped it to shatter on the floor.

At last with a sigh she fell back upon the bed.

Taken on her empty stomach the effect of the draught was very rapid. She had only time to whisper, "Tell Tanus again how much I loved him." Then her eyes closed and she was gone.

She lay so still and pale that for a moment I was truly alarmed, afraid I had misjudged the strength of the narcotic Red Shepenn that I had substituted for the essence of the deadly Datura Pod. It was only when I held a bronze hand mirror to her mouth that the clouded surface reassured me she still breathed.

I covered her gently and left the bedchamber in search of Aton, the royal chamberlain. "There has been a small mishap," I told him, and led him through to see Lostris for himself.

He puffed out his cheeks in consternation when he saw her. "What can I tell Pharaoh?" he cried. "He will have me beaten. I will not do it. The woman is your responsibility. You must answer to the king."

Reluctantly I agreed to accompany him to the royal bedchamber, my medical chest under my arm. Pharaoh had removed his crown and his wig. His head was shaved as bare and white as an ostrich egg. He seemed as startled to see me as I was to see him. We stared at each other for a moment before I fell to my knees and made my obeisance.

"What is this, Taita the slave?"

"Merciful Pharaoh, on behalf of the Lady Lostris I come to beg your understanding and indulgence." I launched into a harrowing description of my Lady Lostris's indisposition. Aton stood beside me, nodding in anxious corroboration.

"Your Majesty," Aton interrupted my explanations, "with your permission I will fetch you another female companion for the night."

"No, no," the king dismissed him. "There will be plenty of time when the child is recovered. Leave us now, chamberlain. There is some other matter that I wish to discuss with this slave."

As soon as we were alone the king said, "These are troubled times, Taita. I must have an heir. The dynasty is in jeopardy. Will your treatment provide me with a son? I am no longer a young man, Taita. You are a doctor and I can tell you this. Of late I have failed when I most had need to succeed."

"Pharaoh, I am pleased that you have discussed this with me. Sometimes the gods work in mysterious ways—" We both made the sign to avert evil before I went on, "Your first congress with my virgin mistress must be perfectly executed. There will be only one opportunity; the first union must be successful."

"What must we do?" he demanded anxiously, and I was silent for a long while, relieved that I had been offered a perfect excuse for keeping her maidenhead intact for at least a little longer.

"I can help you, but it will take some time." My mind was racing. I had to wring every drop out of this sponge. "We will have to go onto a very strict diet—and of course I will prepare special potions for you."

He looked relieved. "You are certain this will work?"

"It has never failed before, but one other measure is essential."

"What is that?" He sat up and peered at me anxiously.

"Complete abstinence. You must forsake your harem and all its pleasures for a while."

The king's reaction surprised me. He simply lay back on his headrest and smiled. "For how long?" he asked quite cheerfully.

Clearly Pharaoh was content to be relieved of a once pleasurable duty that by reason of being so often performed had become onerous.

"Ninety days," I said. "Nine Egyptian weeks of ten days each."

"Ninety days? Very well." He nodded without rancour and changed the subject easily. "My chamberlain tells me, doctor, that apart from your medical skills, you are also an eminent astrologer."

I inclined my head modestly. "He flatters me, Your Majesty. But perhaps I do have some little knowledge of the heavenly bodies."

"Cast a horoscope for me!" he ordered, sitting up eagerly.

"Now?" I asked with surprise.

"Why not?"

I fetched my scrolls from the palace library and he watched avidly while I made the first cast of the royal horoscope. Before I had half finished it I saw the great red wandering star that dominated his destiny: the star of conflict, of confusion and war, of sadness, and in the end of violent death.

How could I tell him all these things? I put together a scantily veiled resume of the well-documented facts of his life, and laced these with a few less well-known details that I had gathered from my spies. Then I followed these with assurances of good health and long life.

The king was impressed. "You have all the skills that your reputation made me expect. So tell me what I really want to know. Will I have a son and will my dynasty survive?"

"Alas, Pharaoh, those matters cannot be predicted by the stars."

"Ah, yes," he interrupted me, "but there are other means of seeing into the future, are there not? I have made enquiry about you, Taita. You are an adept." I was distressed. How had he found this out? Very few knew of this esoteric gift of mine, and I wanted it to remain thus. However, I could not blatantly deny it, so I remained silent.

"Tell me if I am to have an heir and whether or not my dynasty will survive," he ordered.

A divination requires an expenditure of the life forces, a burning up of something deep inside the seer that leaves him exhausted.

However, a slave cannot deny a king, so with a sigh I prepared a mixture of the herbs that were necessary to open the eyes of the soul, to enable them to look into the future. I drank the potion, and then waited.

I felt dreamy and far from reality as Pharaoh repeated his questions. "Will I have a son? Will my dynasty survive?"

I closed my eyes and from the darkness shapes began to emerge and strange sounds filled my ears.

"I hear a newborn infant cry." My voice was distorted.

"Is it a boy?" Pharaoh's question throbbed in my head, so that I felt rather than heard it.

I looked down a long tunnel through the darkness to a light at the far end, where I saw a child, lying in its own birth waters.

"I see a boy," I confirmed, and the image faded.

"The dynasty? What will become of my line? Will it endure?" The king's voice reached me, and then was lost in a cacophony of other sounds that filled my head—battle trumpets, the shouts of men in mortal conflict, and the ring of bronze on bronze. I saw the sky above me, and the air was dark with flights of arrows arcing overhead.

"War! I see a mighty battle that will change the shape of the world."

"Will my line survive?" The king's voice was frantic, but I paid it no heed, for now there was silence in my head and I saw a great acacia tree standing upon a river bank. On the topmost branch perched the royal hawk, and before my eyes the waters of the river rose and fell, and rose and fell again. Five times in all the waters flooded.

While I still stared with burning eyes, the sky above the tree darkened, and a dense cloud of locusts descended upon it. When they rose again the tree was devastated and fell to earth. The shattered trunk turned to dust.

"What is it that you see?" Pharaoh demanded, but it all faded and I found myself seated on the floor of the king's bedchamber.

I gasped for breath. Pharaoh was staring at me and I realised what a haggard and dreadful sight I presented to him.

He whispered, "Will my line survive?"

I could not tell him the truth of my vision, so I invented another.

"I saw a forest of great trees that reached to the horizon of my dream. There was no end to their number and on top of each tree there was a crown, the red and the white crown of the two kingdoms."

Pharaoh sighed and covered his eyes with his hands for a while.

At last I lied softly. "The forest that I saw was the line of your descendants," I whispered. "They reach to the boundaries of time, and each of them wears the crown of Egypt."

He uncovered his eyes and his gratitude was pathetic. "Thank you, Taita. You may go now and rest. The day after tomorrow the court will sail for my palace on Elephantine Island. I will have a galley set aside for the safe passage of you and your mistress."

I was so weak that I had to use the frame of the bed to lift myself to my feet. Slowly I made my way back through the palace to my own rooms in the quarters of the slave boys. Soon the royal flotilla would sail for the south. I had to pack my possessions quickly if my mistress and I were to be ready for the departure.

My animals seemed to sense that something untoward was happening. They fretted, each trying in his own way to attract my attention. I noticed the jug of goat's milk beside my bed. It was one of my favourite drinks, and the slave boys made certain that the jug was always refilled. My animals also enjoyed the milk, so to distract them I carried the jug out onto the terrace and filled their bowls. They crowded round the bowls and I went back to my task.

I stood for a while in the centre of my room, suddenly aware of the silence. I went to the rush awning and drew it aside. The sunlight burst into the room and for a moment blinded me. Then my sight returned and I cried out with horror. They were scattered upon the terrace and down into the garden; every bird and animal in the abandoned attitudes of death. I rushed out to them, kneeling by each of them as I searched for signs of life. There was no flicker of it in any.

I knelt on the terrace with my family dead around me and I wept.

It was some time before I could bring myself to think about the cause of this tragedy. Then I stood up and went to one of the empty bowls. I sniffed at it to try to fathom the nature of the poison that had been intended for me. The odour of milk disguised any other smell; all that I knew was that it had been swift and deadly.

It did not matter who had placed the jug beside my bed. I knew with utter certainty who had given the order for it.

"Farewell, my old darling. You are a dead man," Lord Intef had told me, and he had not waited long.

Anger seized me. I checked it, forced myself to gather up the pathetic bodies of my pets. I had planned to plant a row of trees along the border of my garden. The holes to take them had already been dug. They would never be planted now that I was leaving Karnak, and the pits would now serve as graves for my beloved creatures.

When I had filled the last grave, I returned to my mistress's chamber.

Lady Lostris was still asleep. I settled at the foot of her bed, intending to wait for her to wake on her own. However, the exertions of the past night and morning had been too much for me. I slumped down and fell asleep on the tiles.

I WOKE under attack. Something struck the side of my head such a painful blow that I was on my feet before I was properly awake.

"You cheated me," Lady Lostris screamed at me. "You did not let me die." She swung the bamboo fan again. Fortunately she was still groggy from the drug. Her aim was erratic and I ducked the blow.

She burst into tears. "Why did you not let me die?"

It was some time before I could approach her and put one arm round her to comfort her.

"Did I hurt you, Taita?" she asked. "I have never beaten you before."

It was time to change the subject. "Mistress, I have important news for you. Last night I went to Pharaoh's bedchamber and I spoke to him for half the night. I worked a divination for him."

Instantly I had her complete attention. She said, "Tell me! What did you see?"

"First you must swear secrecy."

"I swear. I swear."

"Very well, listen to my vision. I saw a great tree upon the bank of the Nile. Upon the summit of the tree was the crown of Egypt—"

"Pharaoh! The tree was the king." She saw it at once and I nodded. "Go on, Taita. Tell me the rest of it."

"I saw the Nile rise and fall five times."

"Five years, the passing of five years!" She loved to unravel the riddles of my dreams.

"Then the tree was devoured by locusts and turned to dust."

She stared at me, unable to utter the words, so I spoke for her.

"In five years Pharaoh will be dead and you will be a free woman. Free to go to Tanus, with no man to stop you."

"If you are lying to me, it will be too cruel to bear."

"It is true, my lady, but there is more. In the vision, I saw a new-born child, a son, and I knew that you were his mother."

"And the father? Who was the father of my baby?"

"In the dream I knew with absolute certainty that the father was Tanus." This was a deviation from the truth, but I had the consolation of believing that it was for her benefit.

She was silent for a long time. Then at last she whispered, "I can wait for five years. It will be hard, but I can wait five years for Tanus. You were right not to let me die, Taita."

My relief buoyed me up, and I now felt confident that I would be able to steer her safely through all that lay ahead.

AT DAWN the following day the royal flotilla sailed south from Karnak. My Lady Lostris and her entourage were on board one of the small, fast galleys of the southern squadron. I sat with my mistress on the poop, looking back at the buildings of the city shining in the rising sun.

"I cannot think where he has gone." She was fretting over Tanus. "Did you look everywhere for him?"

"Everywhere," I confirmed. "He has disappeared. But I left your message with Kratas. You can be sure he will deliver it."

"Five years without him—will they ever pass?"

Book Two

THE VOYAGE upriver passed pleasantly enough in long leisurely days spent in conversation with my mistress. Although I was torn between these two dear children of mine, Tanus and my mistress, my first duty was to my mistress. I knew that I could not launch her alone into court society without a friend or a mentor.

The flotilla sailed only during the day, so every evening we moored and a forest of tents sprang up on the river bank. The entire court was still in festive mood. Every camp was treated as a picnic. There was dancing and feasting in the light of the bonfires, while in the shadows the courtiers intrigued and flirted. I myself used every moment to the best advantage of my mistress. Of course she was now one of the royal ladies, but there were already several hundred of those, and she was still a very junior wife. Her future status might change, but only if she bore Pharaoh a son. In the meantime it was up to me.

Almost every evening after we had gone ashore, Pharaoh sent for me, ostensibly to cure a minor attack of ringworm, but in reality to review the preparations for begetting a male heir. While he watched, I prepared my tonic for potency and virility, then went on to deal with the ringworm. To the king's gratification my ointment cured his ringworm within three days, and my reputation as a physician was enhanced.

The king boasted of my accomplishment to his council of ministers, and within days I was in huge demand throughout the court. Then it became known that I was an astrologer, whom even the king consulted, and thereafter, every evening, a succession of messengers came to our tents bearing expensive gifts for my mistress from this lady or that lord, and begging that she allow me to visit them for a consultation.

Pharaoh Mamose, beneath his glum exterior, was a kind and decent man. My Lady Lostris soon realised this and, like me, she began to grow quite fond of him. Before we reached his palace on Elephantine Island she was treating him like a favourite uncle, and Aton confided to me that he had never seen the king so gay.

All this was noted by the court, who swiftly recognised her as the king's favourite. Soon there were other visitors to our tents, those who had petitions that they wished her to bring to Pharaoh's notice. The gifts they proffered were even more valuable than those offered for my services, and before the voyage was done my mistress had accumulated a comfortable fortune.

Our success brought with it some drawbacks. There was jealousy from those who felt themselves displaced in Pharaoh's favour, and there was also the matter of Pharaoh's mounting carnal interest in my mistress. This was aggravated by the period of abstinence that I had enforced upon him. Soon its ninety days would be up. I began to condition my mistress for that night, pointing out to her that it was inevitable and she would have to submit to the king's will.

"Will he hurt me?" she asked, and I hastened to reassure her.

"The king is a kind man, I am sure he will be gentle."

I went on to outline the fundamentals and to make it seem so commonplace as not to alarm her unduly.

As we sailed deeper into the south, so the belts of green land on each side of the river narrowed. Now the desert began to squeeze in upon us, and soon we could hear the distant thunder of the first great cataract as we approached Elephantine Island.

Elephantine was the largest of an assembly of islands that were strung through the throat of the Nile, where the harsh hills constricted its flow and forced it through the narrows.

Elephantine Island took its name from the smooth grey granite elephant-like boulders that clustered along its bank. The wide stretch of water that surrounded the island secured it from enemy attack, but much of the city had now overflowed onto both main banks. After great Thebes, west and east Elephantine together made up the largest and most populous city in the Upper Kingdom.

As at no other place in the whole of Egypt, Elephantine Island was clad with trees. Their seeds had been brought down by the river on a thousand annual floods, and they had taken root in the fertile loams that had themselves been transported by the restless waters.

The royal palace was a very modest affair, and its sprawling jumble of red clay walls and roofs offended both the instincts of the mathematician and the architect in me. Yet I suppose it did have a sort of bucolic charm.

Naturally we were lodged in the walled harem on the northern tip of the island, but the size and the furnishings of our lodgings confirmed our favoured position with the king. A side gate led directly down to the riverside and a stone jetty. That very first day I purchased a skiff which we could use for fishing and waterfowling.

The rest of our new home, my mistress and I immediately set about improving and beautifying. With the cooperation of the head gardener, we laid out and planted our own private garden in the courtyard, with a thatched barrazza under which we could sit in the heat of the day.

By this time my mistress was completely resigned to her future role as the king's favourite, while my promise that there would be a term to her captivity made it easier for her to bear.

In all fairness, though, our sojourn on the island could not truly be described as captivity. A wife of the king is not confined to the harem, but, if escorted by her entourage, may walk abroad in city street or countryside.

Thus my mistress and I were free to explore the cities on each bank of the Nile and the surrounding countryside. On other days we fished together from our little skiff in the lagoons that the inundation of the Nile had created.

We took possession of a deserted fisherman's shack, which we had discovered on the fringe of the swamp below Karnak, and made this our secret hunting lodge.

From the earliest age I had allowed Lostris to accompany Tanus and myself on our hunting and fishing forays. Thus Lostris had picked up the lore and the wisdom of the outdoors, until she could wield a harpoon or a hunting bow with equal skill.

From Tanus and myself she learned to respect the quarry, but not to burden herself with guilt when she exercised her god-given rights over the other creatures of the earth. We may have dominance over the beasts, but in the same way, all men and women are Pharaoh's cattle, and none may gainsay him.

ON THE NINETIETH night the king sent Aton to fetch my mistress.

Next morning we went out hawking as though nothing untoward had happened, and she only mentioned the subject once during the day. As we picnicked on the bank of the river, quite unexpectedly she smiled at me.

"I don't know what all the fuss was about," she murmured. Then she asked thoughtfully, "Will it be the same with Tanus, do you think, Taita?"

"No, mistress. You and Tanus love each other. It will be different. It will be the most wonderful moment in your life."

"Yes. I know deep in my heart that is how it should be," she whispered, and both of us looked northwards towards Karnak, reminding me where my duty towards Tanus lay.

Yet life on the island was so idyllic, and I so much enjoyed the exclusive company of my mistress, that I delayed my departure, procrastinating until one evening, after a full day out in the field with the king, we returned late to the palace. I saw to it that my mistress's evening meal was laid out for her, then I went to my own rooms.

As I entered, the delicious odour of ripe pomegranates filled the air, while in the centre of the floor stood a large closed basket. I carried the basket to the doorway to have the benefit of the last light of the dying day. As I lifted the woven lid and reached for the reddest and ripest of the pomegranates, the fruit spilled and rolled across the floor.

There was a sharp hissing sound and a great black ball of writhing coils and gleaming scales flopped out of the basket and lashed out at my legs.

I leaped backwards, and threw myself against the wall in the far comer of the room. The cobra and I confronted each other across the width of the floor. Half its body was coiled upon itself, the front portion of it raised half as high as my shoulder. It watched me with glittering eyes, and I realised that it stood between me and the only door to the chamber.

I sidled along the wall trying to outflank it. It launched itself at me, the gape of its jaw a pale sickly yellow, with tendrils of venom that drooled from the tips of its fangs. Involuntarily I yelled with terror as I sprang away from it and cowered in my corner again. The serpent recovered swiftly from the strike and reared upright.

As I watched, its lower body uncoiled slowly and it began to glide across the floor towards me, its flaring head held high. Then suddenly I saw a movement beyond the swaying cobra. Lady Lostris appeared in the doorway, summoned by my terrified cry.

My mistress had been at her dinner when she heard my cry for help. She stood now with a half-peeled melon in one hand and a silver knife in the other, and she reacted with the swift instinct of a true huntress, hurling the melon with the force and aim of a trained javelineer.

It struck the cobra upon the back of its extended hood, and for a fleeting instant the blow knocked it flat upon the tiled floor. She leaped forwards and landed with both her neat little sandalled feet upon the back of its head, pinning it to the tiles with her full weight.

Perhaps she had expected to crush its spine, but the snake was as thick as her wrist. Although its head was pinned, the rest of its long body whipped up and over and coiled round her legs.

She screamed out, "Help me, Taita!"

I dived and thrust my hands into the coils of the serpent's body that coiled round her legs. I groped along its sinuous length, down to where it narrowed into the neck, and I seized it and locked both my hands round the cobra's throat, with my fingers entwined.

"I have him!" I yelled. "I have him! Get away from us! Stand clear!"

My mistress leaped back obediently, and I came to my feet trying to keep the creature's gaping jaws away from my face.

The tail whipped back and wound round my neck, threatening to strangle me as I clung to the head. I held it at arm's length, but with its terrifying strength it was pulling itself towards my face, drawing closer to my eyes every moment. Waves of power pulsed through its body, contracting and tightening the coils round my throat.

"On the table!" My mistress spoke close beside me. "Hold its head on the table!" I saw that she still brandished the table knife.

Carrying the cobra with me, I staggered across the floor. With a supreme effort I managed to force the snake's head down across one edge of the table, and to hold it there. It gave my mistress a chopping-block against which to wield the knife. She hacked at the base of the cobra's neck, behind the hideous head.

The snake felt the first cut and redoubled its struggles. Coil after coil lashed and contorted round my head. But the little blade was sharp, and the scaly flesh parted under it as it bit down to the bone of the spine, found the joint between the vertebrae and slipped through.

Now my fingers were lubricated by the cobra's blood. I felt the head slither out between them and the serpent was free. Dangling by a thread of skin, the head was thrown about loosely by the cobra's death throes. Although almost severed from the body, its fangs still oozed poison. The lightest touch would be enough to drive them into my flesh.

I tore at the body and at last managed to unwind it from around my throat and hurl it to the floor. As the two of us backed away to the door, it continued its contortions.

"Are you harmed, my lady?" I asked.

"I am all right," she whispered. "And you, Taita?"

The tone of her voice alarmed me enough to make me forget my own distress. The reaction from danger had already seized her, and she was beginning to shake. I had to find some way to release her from the icy grip of shock.

"Well," I said briskly. "He came in a basket. I wonder who sent him. It must have been somebody who does not like my singing!"

She was not put off so easily. "Don't play the clown with me, Taita. I think you know who it was, and I think I do as well."

I stared at her, not sure how to deal with what was coming.

"It was my father," she said with such finality that there was no denial I could give her. "Tell me about him, Taita. Tell me all the things you have never dared tell me before."

It came hard at first. A lifetime of reticence cannot be overcome in a moment. But she had charged me to tell her everything, so I obeyed her, and the full moon was halfway up the sky before I was done.

We sat in silence for a long time afterwards. I had left out nothing, nor had I tried to deny or to excuse my own part in any of it.

"No wonder he wants you dead," she whispered at last.

"Do you not despise me also for what I have done?"

She reached across and touched my hand.

"You forget that I have known you all my life, since the day that my mother died giving birth to me. Anything you did, you were forced to do.

"Tanus is in terrible danger from my father. I never realised just how much until this evening. He must be warned so that he will be able to protect himself. You must go to him, Taita, without delay."

"Mistress—" I began, but she cut me off brusquely.

"No. Taita, I will not listen to any more of your excuses. You will leave for Karnak tomorrow."

So, BEFORE sunrise the next morning, I set out fishing, alone in the skiff. I made certain that at least a dozen slaves and sentries saw me leave the island. Then, in a backwater of the lagoon, I opened the leather bag in which I had concealed a tomcat that had befriended me. He was a sad old animal, with agonising canker in both ears. For some time I had been steeling myself to give him release from his misery. Now I fed him a lump of raw meat laced with Datura essence. I held him on my lap and stroked him as he slipped into oblivion.

I sprinkled his blood over the skiff, and dropped his carcass overboard where I knew that the crocodiles would dispose of it. Then, leaving my harpoons and lines on board, I pushed the skiff out into the current and waded through the papyrus beds to hard ground.

It would be noon tomorrow before they found the blood-smeared skiff and concluded that I had been taken by a crocodile or been murdered by bandits.

Once I was ashore, I changed swiftly into the costume I had brought with me. I had chosen to impersonate one of the priests of Osiris. The priests are always on the move along the river, travelling between one temple and another, so I would excite little interest.

At the docks I approached one of the barge captains who was loading a cargo of corn, and demanded free passage to Karnak in the name of the god. He shrugged but allowed me to come aboard.

Five days later, we rounded the bend of the river and saw the city of Karnak lying before us.

My stomach was queasy as I went ashore, for this was my town and if I were recognised Lord Intef would hear about it before I could reach the city gates. However, my disguise held up, and I kept to the back alleys as I hurried to Tanus's house near the squadron base. His door was unbarred and I closed it securely behind me. The rooms were deserted. Tanus had obviously been gone for a long time.

I wished to avoid moving around the city in daylight, so I remained in Tanus's rooms until nightfall, when I slipped out and went down to the riverside. The *Breath of Horus* was at her moorings. She had obviously been in action since last I had seen her, and had suffered battle damage. However, neither Tanus nor Kratas were on her deck, so I set out to tour the sailors' haunts around the docks.

I found Kratas in one of the more respectable taverns. He was drinking and playing at dice with a group of his brother officers. I made no move to approach him, but I watched him across the crowded room until at last he gave his companions a hearty good night and made his way out into the alley. Then I followed him.

"What is it you want from me now, beloved of the gods?" he growled when I hurried up beside him. "Is it my gold you crave?"

"No, friend Kratas," I told him.

He stopped dead in his tracks and stared at me suspiciously. "How do you know my name?" He seized me by the shoulder, dragged me into a lighted doorway and studied my face. At last he snatched the wig from off my head. "It's you, Taita!" he roared.

"I'd be obliged if you could refrain from shouting out my name to all the world," I told him, and he turned serious at once.

"Come! We'll go to my rooms."

Once we were alone he poured two mugs of beer. "Haven't you had enough of that?" I asked, and he grinned at me.

"How now, Taita! Don't be stingy with me. We have been down-river raiding the red usurper's fleet for the past three weeks. Don't grudge me a mouthful of beer now. Drink with me!"

He raised his mug, and I was also thirsty. I saluted him in return but as I put the mug down again I asked, "Where is Tanus?"

He sobered instantly. "Tanus has disappeared, gone. I have had my men scour every house in Thebes. There is no sign of him."

"When did you last see him?"

"The day that you sailed with the royal flotilla for Elephantine. I tried to talk some sense into his thick head, but he would not listen."

"What did he say?"

"Using the authority of Pharaoh's hawk seal, he handed over the command of the entire squadron to me, and then he disappeared. But first he cursed the gods and Pharaoh. He even cursed Lady Lostris and called her a royal whore."

I winced to hear it. Yet I knew that this was not Tanus speaking. It was the voice of despairing and hopeless love.

"That was all? He gave you no hint as to what he intended?" Kratas shook his head and refilled his beer mug.

"What happened to the hawk seal?" I asked.

"He left it with me. He said he had no further use for it. I have it safe aboard the *Breath of Horus*."

"I will find Tanus and bring him back. But you must be ready to help. You must take a hundred picked men of the Blue Crocodile Guard and wait with them at the first oasis on the caravan road to the Red Sea. I will find him and join you there."

He slammed down his mug. "I am a soldier. I cannot leave my duties and take half the squadron to go off on some mad adventure. It was one thing when Tanus had the hawk seal—"

"You have the hawk seal now," I told him softly.

He stared at me. "I cannot use it without Tanus—"

"You are his lieutenant. Tanus gave you the hawk seal to use. You know what to do with it. There is desperate and bloody work ahead, and Tanus needs you. Don't let him down."

I was uncertain as to how I would make good my promise to find Tanus, but I left Kratas and went out into the town again to try.

Once more I made the rounds of every one of his old haunts, but as dawn broke I stood tired and disconsolate on the bank of the Nile. High above me a straggling skein of geese was outlined against the eastern sky. Immediately they brought to my mind those happy days that the three of us, Tanus, Lady Lostris and myself, had spent wildfowling in the swamps.

"Fool!" I reviled myself. "Of course, that's it!"

THE INUNDATION was at its height and the lands along the river were in the fecund embrace of the Nile. The river was laying down another rich layer of silt. When she receded again those glistening expanses would once more bloom, raising three crops to harvest before the Nile poured over her banks once more to deliver her bounty. The borders of the flooded fields were hemmed with the raised dykes that controlled the flood and also served as roadways. I followed one of these footpaths eastwards until I reached the rocky ground along the foothills, then I turned southwards.

I kept a wary eye on the rough and broken ground to my right, for that was just the terrain that would afford a fine ambush for bandits. At the shoulder of the next hill I paused and saw movement on the track ahead of me. I stopped short and, shading my eyes against the dazzle of the noonday sun, was relieved to make out a small and innocent-seeming party coming in my direction. I moved forwards cautiously to meet it, and as we drew together my heart leaped as I thought that I recognised Tanus. He was leading a donkey, heavily burdened with a woman and a child. I saw that the woman was herself heavily burdened, her belly swelling out with her pregnancy. The child balanced behind her was a girl on the verge of puberty.

I was about to hail Tanus when I realised that I was mistaken. The man was a stranger—it was his tall, broad-shouldered figure and the shining shock of gold-blond hair that had deceived me. He was watching me suspiciously and had drawn his sword.

"The blessings of the gods upon you, good fellow." I played out my role as priest.

He grunted and kept the point of the sword aimed at my belly. No man trusted a stranger in this Egypt of ours.

"You risk the life of your family on this road, my friend. You should have sought out the protection of a caravan. There are brigands in the hills." I was truly worried for them.

"Pass on, priest!" the man ordered. "Keep your advice for those who value it. We want no truck with strangers."

He urged the donkey past where I stood, and with a helpless shrug I went on my way.

It was late afternoon before I looked down on the spur of rock in the green swampland on which stood the shanty. I ran down the path until I reached the edge of the water.

I found our old boat tied up at the landing, and poled out cautiously through the papyrus. At the Nile's low ebb the shanty stood on dry land, but now there was deep water under the stilts that supported it. A second boat was tied to one of the hut stilts. I moored mine beside it, climbed the rickety ladder and peered into our old hunting lodge. It had never before been in such disorder.

I crossed the floor gingerly to an unwashed mattress in the far comer, and looked at Tanus as he slept. I hardly recognised him. His face was mottled with drink and it was clear that he had not shaved since last I had seen him.

I sat beside his mattress for a while, letting my sympathy for him run its full course. He had tried to destroy himself, and although I was angry with him for abusing himself in such a fashion, I did not despise him for it. His love for my mistress was such that without her he did not wish to continue living. After all, she had tried to take poison for the very same reason. I had understood and forgiven her. Could I do less for Tanus?

I took Tanus by the heels and dragged him across the floor of the hut and tumbled him through the doorway. Cursing weakly, he plunged into the swamp head first and raised a mighty splash as he went under. I waited for him to come up.

Coughing and choking he floundered to the ladder and hung upon it with his hair streaming into his eyes. He peered about and focused on me at last. "Taita! Damn you! You tried to drown me!"

"What a sorry, disgusting sight you are," I told him.

I went back into the hut and left him in the water, shaking his head and mumbling to himself. I set about tidying up the mess.

It was some time before Tanus followed me up the ladder. I ignored him and went on with my work, until at last he was forced to break the silence. "How are you, old friend? I have missed you."

"Others have missed you also; Kratas for one. The squadron has been fighting downriver. Lady Lostris for another. She speaks of you every day. She is still your woman and always will be."

He groaned and held his head.

"By Horus, she puts me to shame," he muttered.

"No," I disagreed. "Your shame is of your own making."

"Enough, Taita. You have had your say. Mock me no more." He looked up at me pitifully. "Tell me about her, Taita. How is she? Does she still think of me?"

"More is the pity," I grunted. "She thinks of little else. She would have you take up Pharaoh's challenge, so that you will still be a man of honour in five years' time, when she is free to come to you."

I had his full attention now. "Five years? What is this about, Taita? Will there truly be a term to our suffering?"

"I worked a divination for Pharaoh. He will be dead in five years from now," I told him simply. "Can you wait that long for your love? My mistress swears that she can wait for you through all eternity. Can you wait a few short years for her?"

"She has promised to wait for me?" he demanded.

"Through all eternity," I repeated, and I went on to tell him about the vision I had had. We talked until night fell, and then on. I told him the things that I had told Lady Lostris, all the details that I had kept from them both over the years. When I came to the details of how his father, Pianki, Lord Harrab, had been destroyed by his secret enemy, his anger was so fierce that it burned away the last effects of the debauchery from his mind. He sprang to his feet and girded on his sword scabbard.

"Let us get on with this enterprise of yours!" he cried. "Back to Karnak at once! Kratas is waiting and the lust to avenge my father's memory burns like a fire in my blood."

As soon as the sun came up above the horizon we left the swamp at a run. Although Tanus panted wildly he never paused to rest or even moderated his pace. It was I who pulled him up with a shout. We stood and stared ahead. The birds had caught my attention.

"Vultures," Tanus grunted. "They have found something dead among the rocks." We went forwards cautiously.

We found the man first. I recognised him from his blond hair as the husband I had met on the road the previous day. A dozen stab wounds were thrust through his ribs. I walked on and found the dead body of his wife, huddled against a boulder, and then on deeper into the broken ground, to where the bandits had dragged the little girl and cut her throat. I began to weep.

"Did you know them?" Tanus asked.

I nodded. "I met them on the road, yesterday. I tried to warn—" I broke off, for it was not easy to continue. I took a deep breath. "They had a donkey. The Shrikes will have taken it."

Tanus nodded. The bandits who terrorised the Upper Kingdom called themselves the Shrikes, after these fierce birds. His expression was bleak as he turned away.

"This way!" he called and broke into a run.

"Tanus, I feel for that family even more than you do," I protested. "But this is folly. Kratas waits for us. We do not have time—"

He cut me off without even glancing in my direction. "I always have time to see justice done." He headed out into the rocky desert.

I joined him and we picked up the trail of the donkey.

It was almost noon when at last we spotted our quarry far ahead. There were five of them, and the donkey. Tanus pulled me down behind the shelter of a rock while we caught our breath, and he growled at me, "We'll circle out ahead of them. I want to set up an ambush." We overtook the band of Shrikes well beyond their line of sight. Then we cut in again to meet the track ahead of them.

Tanus laid a hand on my arm, "Don't move until I do, do you hear me? I want no heroics from you now, mind."

I nodded vigorously.

The Shrikes came on directly to where we waited among the rocks. They were all heavily armed. A tall bearded Bedouin, who was obviously their leader, walked ahead. Two others followed him, leading the donkey, and the last two sauntered along behind.

Tanus let them all pass, and then he stood up quietly and moved in behind the last two men. He swung his sword at the neck of the man on the right, and the legs buckled under the decapitated trunk. As the blow reached the limit of its arc, Tanus smoothly reversed the stroke. With the same movement he struck back-handed at the next brigand, severing the second neck just as cleanly.

The other three Shrikes spun round in alarm, and with a wild shout they drew their swords and rushed at Tanus. Tanus charged them ferociously, splitting them apart. He swung to face the man he had isolated, and his thrust ripped a bloody flesh wound down his chest. The man reeled backwards as the other two fell upon Tanus from behind. Tanus spun round to face them, and bronze clashed on bronze as he stopped their charge.

He held them off at sword's length, engaging first one and then the other. His swordsmanship was breathtaking to watch, but Tanus was tiring and his features were contorted with the effort. He retreated before the Bedouin's next rush until his back was pressed against one of the boulders. With the rock to cover his rear, both of them were forced to come at him from the front. But this was no real respite. Their attack was relentless, and Tanus's right arm tired.

The spear carried by the first man whom Tanus had beheaded had fallen in the middle of the track. With a huge effort I gathered up my courage and crept from my hiding place.

I reached the spot where the spear lay and snatched it up. The Bedouin was standing closest to me with his back towards me. I levelled the spear and rushed at him. The spear point skewered his right-hand kidney with a surgeon's precision.

The Bedouin froze, instantly paralysed by my thrust. Then the sword fell from his fist and he collapsed with such a dreadful cry that his comrade was distracted enough to give Tanus his chance.

Tanus's next thrust took the last one in the centre of his chest, with sufficient power to fly cleanly through and protrude a handspan from between his shoulder blades. Tanus cleared his blade, took a few paces back, then gasped, "I'm all done in."

He pulled the water-skin from the back of the donkey and drank, his eyes tightly closed with the pleasure of it. "By the sweet breath of Isis, I am soft as an old woman. Even that little piece of swordplay nearly finished me."

As I led the way back to where we had left the bodies of the murdered family, I began to regret my callous murder of the brigand. "After all he was a human being, as we are," I told Tanus.

He snorted. "He was a rabid jackal and you did a fine job. Forget him. Tell me, instead, why we must make this detour back to look at dead men, instead of heading straight for Kratas's camp."

"I need the husband's body." I would say no more until we stood over it. "Look at that hair," I told Tanus. "Who else do you know with a mane like that?"

For a moment he looked puzzled and then he grinned and ran his fingers through his own dense ringlets.

"Help me load him on the donkey," I ordered. "Kratas can take him into Karnak to the morticians for embalming. We'll buy him a fine tomb with your name on the walls. Then, by sunset tomorrow, all of Thebes will know that Tanus, Lord Harrab, perished in the desert."

"If Lostris hears of it—" Tanus looked worried.

"I'll send a warning letter to her. The advantage we will win by letting the world believe you dead will far outweigh any risk of alarming my mistress."

KRATAS WAS camped at the first oasis on the caravan road to the Red Sea, less than a day's march from Karnak. He had with him a hundred men of the Blue Crocodile Guards, as I had commanded.

Tanus and I reached the encampment in the middle of the night. We had travelled hard and were close to exhaustion, yet instantly Tanus was mingling with his men. Their delight at having him back was transparent. The officers embraced him and the men cheered him and grinned with pride as he greeted each of them by name.

At breakfast Tanus gave Kratas instructions to take the corpse back to Karnak for burial and to make certain that the news of his death was the gossip of all Thebes. I gave Kratas a letter for my Lady Lostris, and instructions on how to have it delivered to her.

Kratas selected an escort of ten men, and they prepared to set off with the donkey and its odorous burden back to Thebes.

"You'll find us camped at the oasis of Gebel Nagara. We will wait for you there," Tanus shouted after him as the detachment trotted out of the encampment. "And bring my bow when you return!"

No sooner was Kratas out of sight beyond the first rise on the westerly road than Tanus led the rest of the regiment in the opposite direction along the caravan road towards the sea.

The caravan road from the banks of the Nile to the shores of the Red Sea was long and hard. A caravan usually took twenty days to make the journey. We covered the distance in four days, for Tanus pushed us in a series of forced marches. Once we had reached Gebel Nagara, Tanus kept his men exercising at arms and at competitions of archery, wrestling and running, while we waited for Kratas.

Kratas arrived only two days later. He handed over both the bow and the hawk seal with a grin, delighted to be back with Tanus.

In the morning we left Kratas in command of the guards and

Tanus and I set out alone for the coast. It was only half a day's travel to the small fishing village that was our goal, and at noon we topped the last rise and looked down onto the glittering sea.

As soon as we entered the village Tanus called for the headman, and when he showed the old man the hawk seal he fell to the earth in obeisance. When I lifted him to his feet he led us to the finest lodgings in the village, his own filthy hovel, where we ate a bowl of dubious fish stew. Then Tanus and I went down to the beach, and after bathing away the dust of the desert, I embarked on one of the tiny fishing vessels that had just unloaded a huge catch.

I waved back to Tanus on the beach as I put out through the pass in the reef. He was to remain there until I returned with the equipment that we needed for the next part of my plan. His job now was to prevent any of the fishermen sneaking away to report to the Shrikes the presence of a golden-headed lord, who bore the hawk seal, in their village.

I had but a short way to go, and before nightfall the helmsman pointed over the bows at the clustered stone buildings of the port of Safaga on the distant shoreline.

For a thousand years Safaga had been the entrepôt for all trade coming into the Upper Kingdom from the east, and I had visited the port regularly on Lord Intef's nefarious business. It was dark by the time I stepped ashore on the beach, and the streets were almost deserted. I made my way swiftly to the home of Tiamat, the merchant. An armed slave barred the door to me.

"Tell your master that the surgeon from Karnak who saved his leg for him is here," I ordered, and Tiamat limped out himself to greet me. Some years previously he had been carried in to me on a litter, after his caravan had been pillaged by the Shrikes. I had stitched him together, and managed to save the leg that had already mortified.

Tiamat was taken aback when he saw my priestly disguise, but did not remark on it in front of his slave. He drew me into his walled garden, and as soon as we were alone he chuckled and exclaimed, "Is it really you, Taita? I heard that you had been taken by the crocodiles at Elephantine. I am delighted to see that the reports are premature."

After a decent interval of polite conversation, I drew out the hawk seal from under my tunic. His expression became grave, and he listened to all I had to say without another word. When I had finished he sent for his bailiff and gave him his orders in front of me.

After the bailiff had left, we sat on talking for half the night. Tiamat heard every rumour and whisper from the farthest reaches of the empire, and from beyond the sea. I learned as much in those few hours in his garden as I would in a month at the palace.

It was long past midnight before Tiamat called a slave to light me to the chamber he had set aside for me.

"You will be gone before I rise tomorrow." Tiamat embraced me. "Farewell, my good friend. My debt to you is not yet paid in full. Call upon me again whenever you have need."

The same slave woke me before dawn, and led me down to the sea front in the darkness. Tiamat's vessel was moored inside the reef. The captain weighed anchor as soon as I came aboard.

In the middle of the morning we dropped anchor in front of the little fishing village, where Tanus had managed to gather together six decrepit donkeys. The sailors from Tiamat's ship waded ashore carrying the bales that we had brought with us from Safaga, and loaded them onto these miserable creatures.

Tanus and I left the captain of the trading vessel with orders to await our return. Then, leading the donkeys, we headed back towards Gebel Nagara, where Tanus ordered Kratas to parade his men. The warriors watched as I unpacked the first of the bales that we had brought in on the donkeys, and laid out the costume of an Assyrian slave girl. The bales yielded up a further seventy-nine female costumes.

Two officers helped me place one of these on the sand in front of each guardsman, and then Tanus gave the order: "Disrobe! Put on the dress in front of you!"

There was a roar of protest, and it was only when Kratas and his officers sternly reinforced the order that they began to obey it. But once they had weathered the first shock of seeing each other in such outlandish apparel, the men entered into the spirit of the moment.

Unlike our women who dress but lightly, the women of Assyria wear skirts that sweep the ground and even veil their faces when they walk abroad. Thus there were soon eighty veiled slave girls prancing on the sand. I congratulated myself that they would be able to carry through my plan, with a little schooling in feminine deportment.

THE FOLLOWING morning our strange caravan wound its way down onto the beach, where the trading vessel waited. Kratas and eight of his officers dressed in the motley garb of mercenaries made up the escort, since a complete lack of armed escort for such a valuable consignment would have aroused suspicion. Nine armed men would be sufficient to allay this, but would not deter the Shrikes.

At the head of the caravan marched Tanus, dressed in the rich robes and beaded headdress of a wealthy merchant from beyond the Euphrates River. I followed close behind him, wearing the long skirts and veil, together with the gaudy jewellery, of an Assyrian wife.

On the beach at Safaga, Tiamat had forty donkeys waiting for us, as he had promised. Twenty of them were laden with filled waterskins and the remainder with pack saddles to carry the bales and bundles that we brought ashore from the trading ship.

Kratas and his escort hurried our slave girls through the narrow streets, making certain that the soldiers kept their veils in place. We camped that first night still within sight of the town.

I was certain that we were already being watched by the spies of the Shrikes, so while it was still light I made sure that our slave girls conducted themselves as women. It was only after darkness fell that Tanus ordered the bundles carried by the donkeys to be opened and the weapons they contained to be issued. Each of the soldiers slept with his bow and his sword concealed under his sleeping mat.

It was still cool the following morning when the column started out. Tanus was at the head of the caravan, with myself in all my womanly grace and beauty following him closely.

Behind us the donkeys were harnessed in single file, moving down the middle of the well-beaten track. The slave girls were in columns on the outer flanks of the file of donkeys. Their weapons were concealed in the packs upon the backs of the animals. Each of the men needed only to reach out to lay a hand upon the hilt of his sword.

Kratas had split his escort into three squads of three men each, commanded by Astes, Remrem—warriors of renown—and himself.

The escorts now slouched along beside the column, making every attempt to forsake their military bearing. It would seem to the spies, who were certainly watching us from the hills, that they were there solely to prevent any of the slaves from escaping.

From the crest of the first pass we looked back at the cool blue of the sea for the last time and then dropped down into that sweltering wilderness of rock and sand that stood between us and the Nile. It was impossible to continue the march during the hottest hours of the day. We lay in the flimsy shade of the linen tents that Tiamat had provided, and panted like hunting dogs after the chase.

When the sun sank towards the jagged horizon we went on, our long slow column following the ancient road along which countless other travellers had passed before us. We marched on for half the night before Tanus gave the order to fall out. Then he had us up before dawn and we marched on again.

When we rested in the middle of the day the whirlwinds pirouetted across the plains, and the cupful of water that was our ration seemed to turn to steam in my mouth.

"Where are the Shrikes?" Kratas growled angrily.

"They are cunning," I told him. "They will let us tire ourselves with the journey before they strike."

On the fifth day, we reached the oasis of Gallala. Centuries ago the oasis had supported a thriving city, but then an earthquake had damaged the wells and the water in them had dwindled to a few seeping drops. Now roofless walls stood forlorn in the silence.

Our very first concern was to refill the water-skins. While the men were busy drawing water at the well, Tanus and I made a swift tour of the ruined city. It was a melancholy place. In its centre was a dilapidated temple, its roof fallen in and the walls collapsing.

"This will do admirably," Tanus muttered.

When I questioned him on his intentions, he shook his head. "Leave the fighting to me."

That evening when we sat round small, smoky fires of dried donkey dung in the ancient temple, we heard baboons barking in the hills that surrounded the ruined city.

I nodded at Tanus across the fire. "Our friends have arrived at last. Their scouts are in the hills up there watching us now. It is they who have alarmed the baboons."

Swiftly a new mood infected the camp as they realised that the enemy was near. The long hours drew out and the fires died down but none of us slept. Through the open roof I watched the constellations of the stars wheel overhead, and still the attack never came.

Just before dawn Tanus made his round of the sentries for the last time. On his way back to his place he stopped by my mat and whispered, "You and your friends the baboons, you deserve each other. All of you bark at shadows."

"The Shrikes are here," I protested. "I can smell them."

"All you can smell is the promise of breakfast."

I smiled complacently to myself. There were few pleasures in my life compared with those of making Tanus eat his words.

Above us the stars began to fade, and the dawn crept upon us stealthily. Then abruptly I heard a sentry on the west wall of the temple whistle and instantly a stir ran through the camp.

Without rising, and with my shawl masking my face, I looked up at the crests of the cliffs that stood higher than the temple walls. Their silhouette had begun to alter. Slowly I turned my head in a full circle, and it was the same in whatever direction I looked. The skyline all about us was picketed with the menacing shapes of armed men.

I knew then why their leader had so long delayed his retaliation. It would have taken him all this time to gather together such an army—there must be a thousand or more of them. We were outnumbered at least ten to one.

As the light strengthened so the silence drew out until I thought that my nerves might tear. Then suddenly a voice rang out, shattering the dawn silence and echoing along the cliffs.

"Merchant! Are you awake?" the Shrike called. He was standing in the centre of the west wall of the cliff, where the road cut through it.

"Merchant!" he called again. "I want everything you have!"

Tanus rose from his mat. "Then you will have to come down and take it from me!" he shouted back, and drew his sword.

The Shrike raised his right arm, then brought it down abruptly.

At his signal a shout went up from his men and they streamed down the cliffs into the narrow valley of Gallala.

Tanus's officers ran to join him, while the slave girls and I crouched on our mats and covered our heads, wailing with terror.

Tanus leaped up onto the altar with his great bow, and faced the main gateway through which the horde of Shrikes must enter.

Below the altar Kratas had drawn up his men, a pitifully small cluster, and they, too, faced the entrance to the square.

Only five men abreast could pass through the opening, and the distance to where Tanus stood on the altar was less than forty paces. As the mob of bandits burst through into the square, the small band round the altar met them with volley after volley of arrows, shooting them down so that their corpses almost blocked the opening, until at last a mass of fighting men poured into the square and surrounded the altar. It was too close quarters for the bows now, and Tanus and his men cast them aside and drew their swords.

"Horus, arm me!" Tanus shouted his battle cry, and the men around him took it up as they went to work. Bronze rang on bronze as the Shrikes tried to come at them, but no matter from which side they came the Shrikes were met by the deadly swordplay of the guards. Soon there were more than a thousand men crowded into the confined space. Choking in the dust, I was kicked and pummelled by the battling horde, until I managed to crawl away into a comer of the wall. The other women still cowered on their sleeping mats, their heads covered.

I looked about me quickly. The plight of the small group of guards round the altar had worsened. Two men were down and another was wounded. Tanus was still untouched. But he had left it too late to spring the trap, I thought. The entire band of Shrikes were crowded into the square and baying around him. Even as I watched, Tanus killed another of them with a straight thrust through the throat, then threw back his head and let loose a bellow that rang from the crumbling walls around us.

On the instant cringing slave girls leaped up and flung aside their trailing robes. Their swords were already bared and they fell upon the rear of the robber horde. The surprise was complete and overwhelming. I saw them kill a hundred or more before their victims even realised what they were about. But when they did turn to face this fresh attack, they exposed their backs to Tanus and his little band. Suddenly it was no longer a battle but a massacre.

I danced on the fringes of the fighting, screaming at Tanus, trying to make myself heard in the uproar.

"Stop them! We need prisoners!"

Eventually he heard me. I saw the madness fade, and he was once more in control of himself. "Give quarter to those who plead for it!" he roared, and the guards obeyed him. But even so, out of the original thousand, in the end fewer than 200 Shrikes remained alive.

Tanus strode across to me now, stepping over the dead and wounded. He clapped me on the back.

"There is plenty of work for you, Taita. There are at least a dozen wounded—"

"What about their camp?" I asked.

He stared at me. "What camp?"

"A thousand Shrikes did not spring up from the sands like desert flowers. They must have pack animals and slaves with them. You must let nobody escape to tell the tale of today's battle."

"Sweet Isis, you are right." He hailed Kratas across the length of the temple. "Take fifty men. Go to their base camp. Destroy it. A thousand pairs of feet will have trodden a road for you to follow."

ONE OF THE smaller ruined buildings near the wells was turned into a field hospital. There I worked through the day, sewing together the wounded guardsmen. As always I was impressed by their stoicism, for many of their wounds were grave and painful.

I slept well that night, and Tanus sent for me as soon as it was light. When I entered the temple Tanus called me to where he stood with a group of his officers. The prisoners were being held in the temple. Their wrists were bound behind their backs, and they squatted in long lines along the north wall, the guards standing over them.

"There are thirteen clans of Shrikes, isn't that what you told me, Taita?" Tanus asked and I nodded. "Each clan with its own baron. And above them all the man they call Akh-Seth, the brother of Seth. Let's see if you recognise any of the leaders among this gathering of the fair and gentle."

He indicated the prisoners with a chuckle, and took my arm to lead me down the rank of squatting men.

I kept my face veiled so that none of the prisoners could recognise me. I glanced at each face as I passed, and recognised three of them. Shufti, who was obviously their leader, was the most notorious of Shrike barons; Akheku was head of the southern clan that preyed on the lands around Assoun; while Setek was from further north, the baron of Kom Ombo.

When we reached the end of the line Tanus asked, "Are you sure that you missed none of them?"

"How can I be sure? I never met all of the barons."

Tanus shrugged. "We could not hope to catch every little bird with one throw of the net. But let us look at the heads. We might be lucky enough to find a few more."

This was a gruesome business that might have affected a more delicate stomach than mine. While we sat at our ease on the steps of the temple enjoying our breakfast, the severed heads were displayed to us, held up one at a time by the blood-caked hair.

I recognised a score or so of common thieves but only one more of the barons, Nefer-Temu of Qena.

"That makes four of them." Tanus grunted with satisfaction and ordered Nefer-Temu's head to be placed on the pinnacle of the pyramid of skulls that he was erecting in front of the well of Gallala.

"Now let us begin putting the questions to our prisoners."

Tanus sprang up onto the stone altar, and with the hawk seal in one hand looked down on the ranks of squatting prisoners. "I am the bearer of the hawk seal of Pharaoh Mamose, and I speak with his voice. I am your judge and your executioner."

He paused and let his gaze pass slowly over their upturned faces. "You are guilty of pillage and murder. In the name of Pharaoh I sentence you to death by beheading."

Tanus nodded and the first prisoner was dragged forward and forced to his knees before the altar.

"If you answer three questions truthfully," Tanus told the prisoner, "your life will be spared. You will be enlisted as a trooper in my regiment of the guards, with all the pay and privileges. If, however, you refuse to answer the questions, your sentence will be carried out immediately. This is the first question. What clan do you belong to?"

The condemned man made no reply. The blood oath of the Shrikes was too strong for him to break.

"This is the second question. Who is the baron that commands you?" Tanus asked and still the man was silent.

"This is the third and the last question. Will you lead me to the secret places where your clan hides?" Tanus asked, and the man looked up at him, hawked in his throat and spat. Tanus nodded to the guardsman who stood over the prisoner with the sword. The stroke was clean and his head toppled onto the steps at the foot of the altar.

Tanus lopped twenty-three heads before the first of the condemned men broke down. He was not much more than a boy and he gabbled out the replies before Tanus could pose the questions.

"My name is Hui," he said. "I am a blood brother of the clan of

Basti the Cruel. I know his secret places, and I will lead you to them." Tanus smiled with grim satisfaction and gestured for the lad to be led away.

"Care for him well. He is now your companion-in-arms."

After that it went more readily, until we had informers to lead us to the strongholds of all the remaining robber barons.

That night Tanus sent for Hui from the clan of Basti the Cruel, the youngster who had been the first to capitulate to the threat of execution, and turned all the irresistible force of his personality upon him. Soon Hui was pouring out every detail that he could remember of the clan to which he had once sworn a blood oath. I listened quietly, and recorded all he had to tell us.

The stronghold of Basti was in the desert of Gebel-Umm-Bahari, on the summit of a flat-topped mountain that was protected by sheer cliffs on every side, but less than two days' march from the east bank of the Nile and the busy caravan routes.

"There is one path to the top, cut like a stairway from the rock. It is wide enough for only one man to climb at a time," Hui told us.

"There is no other way to the summit?" Tanus asked.

Hui grinned. "There is another route. It is a dangerous climb. but a dozen men could make it and hold the top of the cliff while the main force came up the pathway to them. I will lead you up it, Akh-Horus."

It was the first time that I heard the name: Akh-Horus, the brother of the great god Horus. Naturally, Hui could not know Tanus's real identity. But this was a good name for him, in his struggle against evil, against Akh-Seth, the brother of Seth and lord of the Shrikes.

Tanus was eager to lead his men into the Gebel-Umm-Bahari to hunt Basti down. It was not only that he was the most rapacious and pitiless of all the barons. There was more to it than that. From me Tanus had learned that Basti had been instrumental in destroying the fortune of Pianki, Lord Harrab, Tanus's father.

"I can lead you up the cliffs of Gebel-Umm-Bahari," Hui promised. "I can deliver Basti into your hands."

Tanus was silent in the darkness as he savoured that promise. After a while he sighed and dismissed Hui. Then he leaned across and clasped my shoulder. "You have done enough here, old friend. I could never have accomplished so much without you. I owe you more than I can ever repay, but I must send you away now. Basti is my meat, and I don't need you to share the feast with me. I am sending you back to where you belong—at the side of Lady Lostris."

I protested, of course, and swore that all I wanted was another chance at those villains, but the truth was I had enjoyed my fill of wild heroics. I was not by nature a soldier, so at last I allowed him to convince me.

Tanus had ordered Kratas back to Karnak, to assemble and bring up reinforcements for the expedition into the desert of Gebel-Umm-Bahari, and I travelled that far under his protection. We made the journey in less than a week.

Fearful of discovery by Lord Intef, I spent as little time in my beloved city as it took me to find passage on one of the barges heading southwards.

We had the north wind in our sails all the way, and tied up at the royal Island of Elephantine twelve days after leaving Karnak. I was still dressed in the wig and garb of the priesthood, and nobody recognised me as I came ashore by the steps that led up to our garden in the harem.

My heart pounded against my ribs as I bounded up the stairs. I had been away from her far too long. A Cushite maiden met me at the gate and tried to prevent me entering. "My mistress is unwell, priest."

"She will see me," I told her and stripped off my wig.

"Taita!" She fell to her knees, making the sign to ward off evil. "You are dead. This is some evil apparition from beyond the grave."

I brushed her aside and hurried to my mistress's private quarters.

The odour of sickness filled the chamber, and a wild grief seized me as I looked down at her sleeping figure. She seemed to have shrunk and her skin was pale as ashes.

Tenderly I placed my hand in her armpit to feel for the heat of fever, but her skin was cool. What kind of disease was this? I had not encountered any like it before. I ran to my own rooms. Thankfully, my medicine chest was still in the alcove where I had left it. With it in my arms I hurried back to my mistress.

My hands were shaking as I lit a twig of the scorpion bush from the flame of the oil lamp beside her bed and held the glowing end under her nose. Almost immediately she gasped and sneezed.

"Mistress, it is me, Taita. Speak to me."

She opened her eyes, held out her thin pale arms to me, and I took her to my breast.

"Taita," she sobbed. "Tanus is dead. I cannot live without him."

I stared down at her in bewilderment. Clearly the messenger, whom Kratas had dispatched with my message of comfort, had never reached Elephantine.

I fell on my knees beside my mistress's bed.

"No! No! He is alive. I come from him with messages of love."

"You are cruel to mock me so. I know he is dead. I have not eaten a mouthful since that day. His tomb is sealed—"

"It was a subterfuge to mislead his enemies," I cried. "Tanus lives. I swear it. He loves you. He waits for you."

"Can it be?" I saw the strength of hope flow back into her, and a faint colour bloom in her cheeks. "Oh, Taita, can it truly be?"

"Would I look so joyful if it were not? You know I love him. Could I smile thus if Tanus were truly dead?"

While she stared into my eyes I launched into a recitation of all that had occurred since I had left her side so many weeks ago. She said not a word, but her pale face glowed like a pearl as she listened to my account of our adventures at Gallala.

When I ended she said, "If he is alive, then bring him to me."

I reached for the mirror and held it before her. "First you must eat. Do you want him to see you as you are now?"

She stared at her reflection. I watched her struggle with her emotions. "I am ugly," she whispered. "I look like an old woman."

"Your beauty is still there. But you must eat."

"You promise," she wavered, "you promise that he is still alive, and that you will bring him to me as soon as I am well again?"

"I promise," I said.

Then I hurried to the kitchen where I mixed a bowl of warm milk and honey. We would have to begin slowly for she had driven herself to the very edge of starvation.

The news of my miraculous return from the grave swept through the island and before nightfall Pharaoh sent for me.

He greeted me with a mixture of respect and nervousness. "Where have you been, Taita?" he asked suspiciously.

I prostrated myself at his feet, my answer ready. "Divine Pharaoh, as you yourself are part of the godhead, you clearly ask that question just to test me. You know that it would be sacrilege for me to speak of these mysteries. Please convey to the other deities who are your peers that I have kept the oath of silence imposed upon me beyond the grave. Tell them that I have passed the test that you set me."

I could see him forming question after question, and then discarding each of them in turn. I had left him no opening to exploit.

In the end he blurted out lamely, "Indeed, Taita, you have passed the test I set you. Welcome back. You have been missed."

I crawled closer to him and dropped my voice to a whisper. "Great Egypt, you know the reason I have been sent back."

He nodded uncertainly, and I continued. "Lady Lostris. Her illness was caused by the direct influence of—" I did not say the name, but made the horn sign with two fingers, the sign of the dark god, Seth.

His expression changed from confusion to dread, and he shivered involuntarily and drew closer to me, as if for protection, as I went on. "Never fear, Great Egypt, I have been sent back by forces greater than those of the dark one, so that the destiny that I foresaw may run its allotted course. There will be a son."

He was distraught.

"You must not leave the side of Lady Lostris until she is well again." His voice shook with emotion. "If you save her and she bears me a son, you may ask from me whatever you wish."

"With your permission, Your Majesty, I shall go to her this instant."

"This instant," he agreed. "Go! Go!"

MY MISTRESS'S recovery was swift. Her flesh filled out and firmed almost as I watched. Fresh young blood suffused the chalk of her skin until it glowed once more. Very soon it was impossible to keep her to her bed. Within three weeks of my return to Elephantine she was playing games with her handmaidens and dancing about the garden.

Each morning Lady Lostris would reach for her mirror and study her reflection to determine if it was ready yet to be looked upon by Lord Tanus. And each evening she would make me repeat my promise to her. "Swear you will bring Tanus to me, just as soon as I am ready to receive him."

I tried to ignore the dangers that this promise would bring. "I swear it to you," I repeated and she went to sleep with a smile upon her face.

MY RETURN from the underworld was not the most popular fare of the palace gossips for long. Soon they had something else to keep them busy, the advent of Akh-Horus into the consciousness of every person living in the land along the great river.

The first time I heard the name Akh-Horus whispered in the palace corridors I did not immediately place it, for I had forgotten the name that Hui had bestowed upon Tanus. When, however, I heard the accounts of the extraordinary deeds ascribed to this demigod, I realised who they were speaking about.

In a fever of excitement I ran all the way back to the harem and found my mistress in the garden. I seized both her hands. "Come," I whispered. "Let's go where nobody can hear us." "

I led her down to the jetty and handed her into our little skiff.

"There is a fresh clean wind blowing through the land," I told her when we were safe from flapping ears. "They call this wind Akh-Horus."

"The brother of Horus . . ." She breathed it with reverence. "Is this what they call Tanus now?"

"None of them knows it is Tanus. They think he is a god. They say that every bandit in the land now runs in terror of his life, that the clans of the Shrikes are being shattered one by one."

"Tell me more!" she cried.

"They say that at every crossroads and beside every caravan route he has built tall monuments to his passing, high pyramids of skulls, the heads of the bandits he has slain, as a warning to others."

My mistress shuddered. "Has he killed so many?"

"Some say he has slain five thousand, some say fifty thousand."

"Is all of this possible?"

"For a god anything is possible."

"He is my god. Oh, Taita, when may I see him?"

"Soon," I promised. "Your beauty burns brighter every day. Soon it will be fully restored."

"In the meantime you must go to the shipping wharf every day and gather every story and rumour of Akh-Horus and bring them to me."

PHARAOH, of course, had full reports of my mistress's recovery and came in person to visit her. He brought her a new ornament of gold and lapis in the form of an eagle and sat until evening playing word games and setting riddles with her.

When he was ready to leave he called me to walk with him as far as his chambers.

"The change in her is extraordinary, Taita. When can I take her to bed? Already she seems well enough to bear my son and heir."

"Not yet, Great Egypt," I assured him vehemently. "Her slightest exertion might trigger a relapse."

And fortunately he no longer questioned my word, for now I spoke with all the authority of the once dead.

IN THE afternoons my Lady Lostris and I resumed our old practice of strolling through the streets and the marketplaces. As before her illness, my mistress was welcomed by an adoring populace, and she stopped to speak with all of them no matter what their station.

Always she was able to turn the conversation to Akh-Horus, who had been promoted in the popular imagination from demigod to a full member of the pantheon.

There was a new spirit of confidence abroad. As the caravan routes were made secure, so the volume of trade between the Upper Kingdom and the rest of the world blossomed. Because it was now safe to work the fields furthest from the protection of the city walls, crops were planted where for decades only weeds had grown, and the farmers, who had been reduced to beggars, began to prosper again. The markets were filled with fresh produce and the volume of traffic on the Nile swelled dramatically. More craft were needed and the shipyard workers spent their new wealth in the taverns and markets.

Egypt was coming to life again, after being strangled for all these years by the depredations of Akh-Seth and the Shrikes.

Then one day there was a fresh rumour in the marketplace. A caravan coming down the northern road had encountered a pyramid of heads at the roadside not two miles beyond the city walls.

"This means only one thing," the gossips told each other. "This means that Akh-Horus is in the nome of Assoun, probably within sight of the walls of Elephantine."

This was the best news I had heard in weeks and I was in a fever to take it to my mistress. I pushed my way through the fishermen on the wharf to find a boatman to take me back to the island.

A beggar tugged at my arm. "I have a message for you," he whined. "A message from one of the gods."

I gaped at him. "Hui!"

My heart soared as I recognised the erstwhile robber. "What are you doing here?" I did not wait for a reply to my fatuous question but went on swiftly, "Follow me at a distance."

I led him to a narrow alley beyond the harbour. "What news of your master?" I demanded, the moment we were alone.

Hui chuckled. Already he had adopted all the swagger of a trooper. "The god Akh-Horus sends greetings, to you and to another whose name cannot be mentioned. He bids me tell you that the task is completed and that all the birds are in the cage. He reminds you that it lacks only a few months to the next festival of Osiris."

"Where is he? How long will it take for you to return to him?"

"I can be there before the sun plunges beyond the western hills."

I glanced up; the sun was halfway down the sky. Tanus was lying up very close by. I rejoiced anew and turned back to the city.

It was almost dark when I stepped ashore on our little jetty and hurried up the steps to my mistress's quarters.

"He is here." I announced at the doorway, and then dropped my voice. "Tanus is here," I whispered, so that the slave girls could not hear.

She leaped up and threw her arms round my neck in joy. "The day after tomorrow I will make good my promise to you," I vowed.

AS PART OF his annual tribute from his kingdom across the Red Sea, the vassal king of the Amorites had sent Pharaoh a pair of trained hunting cheetahs. The king was eager to run these magnificent creatures against the herds of gazelle that abounded in the desert dunes of the west bank. The entire court, including my mistress, had been commanded to attend the course.

We sailed across to the west bank in a fleet of small river craft. There was laughter and music, and my mistress, knowing my plan, was in a gayer mood than any.

It seemed that I alone was not carefree. I kept glancing anxiously at the western sky. The wind had a harsh, abrasive edge to it, and was blowing from the wrong quarter. I put aside my misgivings and tried to enter into the spirit of the outing. But I had more than the weather to worry about, for if my plan went awry, my life would be in danger and other lives more valuable.

When we landed on the west bank, there was an army of slaves waiting for us. Grooms held splendid white riding donkeys from the royal stables, all caparisoned with silk. The cheetahs' cage was loaded on a sledge drawn by a team of white oxen, and the court gathered round to admire these rare and beautiful beasts.

Pharaoh was dressed in light hunting garb and for once seemed relaxed and happy. He stopped beside my mistress and enquired graciously about her health. I was filled with dread that he might decide to keep her by his side throughout the day, but the hunting cheetahs caught his attention and he passed on by.

We made our way to where a donkey was being held for Lady Lostris. While I helped her to mount, I spoke quietly to the groom. When he told me what I wanted to hear, I slipped silver into his hand.

With one slave leading her and another holding a sunshade over her, my mistress and I followed the king out into the desert.

It took us half the morning to reach the Valley of the Gazelles. On the way we passed at a distance the ancient cemetery of Tras, which dated from the time of the very first pharaohs. Without making it obvious, I studied the entrances of the tombs keenly as we passed.

The nobles dismounted on the crest of a hill overlooking the broad brown valley. I made certain that my mistress and I secured a good vantage point from which to watch the hunt, but one from which we could withdraw discreetly without attracting attention.

In the distance I could make out the herds of gazelle through the wavering watery mirage on the floor of the valley. The hunt was beginning. Two of the royal huntsmen opened the cage and the hunting cheetahs leaped down to earth, while along the far side of the brown, scorched valley bottom a line of beaters moved slowly in our direction the herds of antelope beginning to drift ahead of them.

While the king and his huntsmen, with the cheetahs on leashes, moved down the slope towards the valley bottom, we and the rest of the court remained on the crest.

"When can we go?" my mistress whispered.

"Once the hunt begins all their eyes will be upon it. That will be our opportunity." Even as I spoke, the wind that had blown us across the river suddenly dropped. The air became almost too hot to breathe, and once again I looked to the western horizon. The sky above it had turned a sulphurous yellow. It made me uneasy.

Now that the hunting party was at the bottom of the hill we

began to edge away towards a clump of rocks that would screen our retreat from the rest of the company. The bribe of silver to the groom had procured for us a donkey that was now tethered out of sight among the rocks. As soon as we reached it, I checked that it carried what I had ordered, a water-skin and a leather bag of provisions.

I boosted my mistress into the saddle and led the donkey down into the dead ground where we were out of sight of the company behind us, and on towards the cemetery of Tras. Soon I felt sweat break out upon my skin, for the day was close and heavy. "The air is dry as old bones," I told my mistress. "You should drink a little water—"

"Keep on! There will be plenty of time to drink our fill later. Every moment we waste will give me that much less with Tanus."

As we drew closer to the cliffs so her eagerness increased until she could no longer abide the pace of her mount. She leaped off its back and ran ahead to the next rise. "There it is! That is where he will be waiting for me," she cried and pointed ahead.

As she danced on the skyline the wind came at us like a ravening wolf, howling among the hills and canyons. I turned and looked back and saw the storm coming out of the Sahara. It towered into the sullen yellow heavens, billowing upon itself like storm surf.

I broke into a run, dragging the donkey behind me. "We must be quick!" I shouted. "We must reach the shelter of the tombs."

Dragging my mistress with one hand and our donkey with the other, I staggered into the dark mouth of one of the tombs. The entrance shaft led us deep into the hillside.

My mistress sank down against the rock wall. I unsaddled our donkey, drew a cup of water from the skin and made her drink.

"What will happen to the others, the king and all our friends?" she asked between gulps from the cup.

"They have the huntsmen to care for them," I told her. "They are good men and know the desert."

"And Tanus?" she asked. "What will become of him?"

"Tanus will know what to do. He is like one of the Bedouin."

By now it was almost completely dark in the tomb, and I fumbled for the lamp from the pack and blew upon the smouldering wick. It flared and lit the tomb with a cheery yellow light.

While I was still busy with the lamp and my back was turned to the entrance, my mistress screamed.

I spun round and reached for my dagger, but when I saw the monster whose bulk filled the doorway, I froze. In the feeble light of the lamp the form was indistinct and distorted. I saw that it had a human shape but it was too large to be a man, its grotesque head gleamed with reptilian scales, and the beak was that of an eagle.

Then suddenly, while we were still frozen by this horrible presence, it raised both hands and lifted off its gilded war helmet, the visor fashioned like the head of an eagle. Then it shook its head and a mass of red-gold curls tumbled down onto the broad shoulders.

My mistress screamed again, this time with joy. "Tanus!"

She flew to him, and he gathered her up and lifted her so high that her head brushed the rock roof. Then he brought her down and folded her to his chest. From the cradle of his arms she reached up with her mouth for his, and it seemed that they might devour each other with the strength of their need.

I stood forgotten in the shadows. Although I had risked so much to bring them together I felt bitterness as I witnessed their rapture. I began to slink from the tomb, but Tanus saw me leaving and broke that kiss which was threatening to destroy my soul.

"Taita, don't leave me alone with the wife of the king. Stay with us. Our honour is in jeopardy."

"Go!" cried Lady Lostris from his arms. "Leave us, gentle Taita. I'll listen to no talk of honour. Our love has been too long denied."

I stumbled from the chamber. Finding a corner of the shaft where the wind would not harry me, I sank to the stone floor. I pulled my shawl over my head as the storm outside roared along the cliff.

At length the wind abated. The light strengthened and I roused myself and called to them. For a while there was no reply, and then my mistress spoke in a husky voice that echoed down the shaft.

"Taita, is that you? I thought that I had died in the storm and been carried to the fields of paradise."

Once the storm had dropped we had little time remaining. The royal huntsmen would already be searching for us.

On the other hand, Tanus and I had barely spoken, and there was much to discuss. Hastily we made our plans, then I embraced Tanus in farewell and urged the donkey out into the late evening sunlight.

My mistress lingered, and I waited for her in the valley below.

Looking back I saw them emerge from the cave at last. They stood gazing at each other for a long moment without touching, and then Tanus turned and strode away. My mistress watched until he was gone from her sight, then she came down to where I waited. She walked like a woman in a dream.

I helped her to mount, and while I adjusted the saddle girth, she reached down and took my hand.

"Thank you," she said simply.

"I do not deserve your gratitude."

"I am the happiest creature in the world. Everything that you told me of love is true."

I think I loved her more in that moment than I had ever done before. I took up the reins, and led her back towards the Nile.

ONE OF THE royal huntsmen spied us from a far hilltop and hailed us. "We have been searching for you at the king's command," he told us as he hurried down to join us. "He has commanded that Lady Lostris be brought to him directly she is found."

Pharaoh was truly moved to have my mistress returned to him. I am sure he had come to love her and not merely for the promise of immortality that he saw in her. A tear tangled in his eyelash and smeared the paint on his cheek as she knelt before him.

"I thought you were lost," he told her. "Instead I find you prettier and livelier than ever." Love had gilded her with its special magic.

"Taita saved me. He guided me to a shelter and protected me."

Pharaoh smiled at me. "You have rendered us many services, Taita. But this is the most valuable of them all."

Once back on Elephantine Island he commanded a banquet in my mistress's honour, and bade me make the arrangements. I hired and rehearsed the best musicians and acrobats in the city. I set out leather cushions and garlands of flowers for each guest, and jars of perfumed oil to cool them in the sultry night and drive away the mosquitoes.

At nightfall the royal ladies and other guests began to arrive.

The wine was robust and the music rousing. It was in this convivial mood that Pharaoh rose to his feet and called for the attention of his guests. Then he commanded me to kneel before him.

Warily I obeyed, and as I did so there was a murmur of comment, for Aton stood beside him, holding a small cedarwood box.

He lifted the lid and proffered it to the king, who lifted out a gold chain.

The king held the chain over my head and intoned, "For your services to us we bestow upon you the Gold of Praise."

He lowered it onto my shoulders, and the oppressive weight was a delight to me. This decoration was the highest mark of royal favour, usually reserved for high officials. I doubted that ever in the history of Egypt had the gold chain been placed round the neck of a lowly slave.

At Pharaoh's other side my mistress lifted a wine cup to her lips, but before she drank she smiled at me over the rim.

THE MORNING after the banquet we woke to find that during the night the river had swollen with the commencement of the annual flood. Still heavy with wine I left my bed and ran down to the river. Both banks were already lined with the populace of the city. They greeted the waters with prayers and songs.

I hurried back to find my mistress and to prepare for the ceremony of the waters. We dressed in our finest and I placed my new gold chain round my neck. Then, with the rest of our household and the ladies of the harem, we trooped out to the temple of Hapi.

Pharaoh and all the great lords of Egypt led us. The priests were waiting for us on the temple steps. Before the king the statue of the god was carried from the sanctuary. We sang psalms of praise and thanks to the god for sending down the flood, and the king made sacrifice of corn and wine and silver and gold. Then, by torchlight, I followed the high priest into the mouth of the Nilometer, a dark opening in the rear of the sanctuary. We descended the incline shaft, the stone steps slippery with the effusions from the river, and made the first and most crucial reading. After five days of observation, we could calculate how high the waters would rise that year. On those levels hung prosperity or famine for the whole land.

Finally, to close the ceremony Pharaoh announced the date of the annual pilgrimage to Thebes to participate in the festival of Osiris. In eight days' time the royal flotilla would sail northwards to Thebes on the rising flood of the Nile.

ON THE TENTH night after leaving Elephantine the royal entourage camped on a pleasant promontory above a bend in the river. The entertainment that evening was to include one of the most famous storytellers in the land. To my surprise Lady Lostris declared herself too fatigued to attend the storyteller. Although she urged me to go, I could not leave her alone when she was unwell. I gave her a hot draught and I slept on the floor at the end of her bed.

I was truly worried in the morning when I tried to wake her. She pulled the covers back over her head and mumbled, "Leave me to sleep a little longer. I feel heavy and dull as an old woman."

The king had decreed an early start, so I dared not let her sleep. I poured boiling water over a bowl of herbs, then prodded her awake and made her drink the tonic.

Without warning, she vomited.

"What is wrong with me, Taita?" she whispered. "Nothing like this has ever happened to me before."

Only then the meaning of it dawned on me.

"The cemetery of Tras!" I cried. "Tanus!"

She stared at me blankly for a moment, and then her smile lit the gloom of the tent like a lamp.

"I am making a baby," she cried.

"Not so loud, mistress," I pleaded.

"Tanus's baby! I am carrying Tanus's son!"

It could not be the king's infant, for I had successfully kept him from her bed since her starvation sickness.

"I must speak to Aton immediately," I told her firmly. "You will share the king's couch this very night."

She stared at me in bewilderment.

"Even Pharaoh, who believes most things I tell him, would not believe that you were impregnated by the seeds blown in on the wind. We must have a foster-father for this little prince of ours." Already I considered the infant ours, and not hers alone. Though I tried to conceal it behind my levity, I was every bit as delighted with her fecundity as she was.

Aton came to fetch her to the king's tent that night, soon after the king had eaten his dinner. She went with a calm expression and a firm step, dreaming perhaps of her little prince's true father, who waited for us in Thebes.

BELOVED THEBES, how we rejoiced as we saw it appear ahead of us. My mistress sang out with excitement as each of the familiar landmarks revealed itself to us. Then, as the royal barge put in to the wharf below the palace of the grand vizier, the joy of homecoming went out of us both and we fell silent, for we had seen my Lord Intef.

Lord Intef stood with his two sons, Menset and Sobek, at the head of the great concourse of nobles and city fathers that waited upon the quay to greet the king. And not far behind the grand vizier stood Rasfer. I felt my spirits quail.

"You must be vigilant now," Lady Lostris whispered. "They will seek to have you out of their way. Remember the cobra."

At that moment Rasfer recognised me and grinned at me across the narrow strip of water.

"I promise you, my lady, that my hand will be upon my dagger and I will eat nothing but fruit that I have peeled with my own hands while Rasfer and I are in Thebes together," I murmured.

Over the following days I kept my promise. Naturally, we were often in the company of the grand vizier, for it was his duty to escort the king through all the ceremonies of the festival, but Lord Intef played the role of loving father to Lady Lostris, and treated me with the consideration due to my position in Pharaoh's favour. Yet I remembered his patience and his persistence when dealing with an enemy and was uneasy.

Meanwhile the festival rolled on with all the usual ceremony and tradition. However, this season it was not Tanus's regiment but another that hunted the river cows in the lagoon of Hapi, while a company of actors played out the passion in the temple of Osiris.

THE FESTIVAL ended with the assembly of the people in the temple of Osiris to hear the proclamation from the throne.

Pharaoh was seated on his tall throne on the raised stone dais so that all the congregation could have a clear view of him. He wore the double crown and carried the crook and the flail.

My mistress and myself were seated on a stand directly opposite the throne and a little above the height of the king's head, so we had a fine view of the whole of the inner courtyard.

All around us were assembled the noblest in the land, lords and ladies, guild masters and rich merchants, priests and ambassadors from all the vassal states of the empire. In front of the king extended the courts of the temple, packed with the common people, the overflow spilling out into the gardens beyond the temple walls.

Finally, around the throne was gathered a small group of the highest dignitaries, their heads at the level of Pharaoh's feet. One of these was the high priest of Osiris who had collaborated with me in certain unusual arrangements for today's ceremony. However, the most impressive figure in the group, rivalling Pharaoh himself, was Lord Intef.

Lord Intef opened the ceremony in the traditional manner with a lengthy address of welcome to the king. When at last he finished, the high priest stepped into his place, reporting to the king on the ecclesiastical affairs of Thebes.

Eventually the high priest ended his address. The crowd craned forward eagerly to hear Pharaoh speak. Pharaoh rose to his feet and spread his arms in benediction.

But at that moment the great doors to the sanctuary, situated behind the throne, swung open, and a gasp passed like a wind through the temple courts. I was one of the few in the crowd who was not surprised by what followed, for I had done more than my share to arrange it.

Suddenly a woman screamed and immediately a groan of superstitious horror shook them all, as a godlike figure strode out through the burnished copper doors. His helmet was crowned with a plume of egret feathers and his features were half-eagle and half-man, with a hooked beak and dark slits for eyes.

"Akh-Horus!" screamed a woman.

"Akh-Horus!" The cry was taken up. "It is the god."

Row after row they fell upon their knees, until in all the temple only two persons remained on their feet: Pharaoh posed on the steps of his throne like a painted statue; and the grand vizier stood tall and arrogant.

Akh-Horus stopped in front of the king. Pharaoh never flinched. "Who are you?" he challenged. "Why do you disturb our proceedings?" Pharaoh's voice was strong and clear. I could detect no tremor in it.

"Great Pharaoh, I come before you in response to the command you laid upon me in this place on this day of Osiris two years ago."

He lifted the helmet from his head and the fiery curls tumbled down. The congregation recognised him instantly. A shout went up that seemed to rock the foundations of the temple.

"Lord Tanus! Tanus! Akh-Horus!"

Suddenly Tanus drew the sword from his scabbard and held it aloft in an unmistakable command for silence. The crowd obeyed.

"Great Egypt, do I have your permission to speak?"

The king made a gesture and then dropped back on his throne.

Tanus addressed him in the same ringing tones. "Two years ago you charged me with the destruction of those murderers and robbers who were threatening the life of the state. In order better to carry out your orders, I pretended my own death. Then I led a thousand brave men into the wild places and sought out the Shrikes. There we slew them in their hundreds and broke the power of the barons. Only their leader remains at liberty. He hides behind the name of Akh-Seth, and his deeds of infamy rank with those of his brother, the dark god."

"Give me his true name," Pharaoh commanded, rising to his feet.

Tanus drew out the moment. He looked round the temple slowly and deliberately.

"I will name this Akh-Seth for you, Divine Pharaoh." Tanus pointed with his sword. "There he is, wearing the Gold of Praise about his traitor's throat. That is Akh-Seth, governor of the nome of Thebes, grand vizier of the Upper Kingdom."

An awful hush fell upon the temple. There must have been 10,000 or more in the congregation who had every reason to hate Lord Intef, but not a voice spoke out against him. All knew how terrible was his wrath, and how certain his retribution.

In that hush Lord Intef laughed, a sound full of disdain. He turned his back upon Tanus and spoke directly to the king. "The desert sun has burned his brain. I am saddened that a warrior of his reputation has fallen so low." He held out both hands to Pharaoh, a dignified and loyal gesture. "All my life I have served Pharaoh and my people. I see no need to defend myself against these wild rantings. Without fear I place my trust in the wisdom and justice of the divine king."

I saw confusion on the king's painted face, but before he could utter any judgment Tanus lifted his sword yet again, and through the open copper doors came Kratas, leading two bound captives.

I was watching Lord Intef's face, and I saw shock assail him as he recognised the men. Then he looked back at the throne and lifted his chin in a confident and defiant gesture.

The two prisoners dropped to their knees before the throne.

"Who are these creatures?" Pharaoh demanded. The first of them hauled himself to his feet. His skin was studded with the old healed scars of the smallpox and his blind eye reflected the light like a silver coin.

"Great Egypt, I am Shufti," he said. "I was once a baron of the Shrikes before Akh-Horus scattered and slew my clan."

Tanus stood over him. "Tell the king who was your overlord."

"Akh-Seth was my overlord," Shufti replied. "I swore a blood oath of allegiance to Akh-Seth, and I paid a bounty of one-quarter of all my plunder to him."

"Point out to the king the man you know as Akh-Seth," Tanus ordered.

Shufti shuffled forward until he faced Lord Intef. "This is Akh-Seth," he cried.

Lord Intef showed no emotion at the accusation. Kratas dragged Shufti to one side and Tanus lifted the next captive to his feet.

"Tell the king who you are," he ordered.

"My name is Basti." He spoke more clearly than the other. "Men call me Basti the Cruel, though I know not why." He grinned with a hangman's humour. "I was a baron of the Shrikes until Akh-Horus destroyed my clan. Lord Intef was my overlord."

Tanus spoke to him again. "Tell the king. Did you know Pianki, Lord Harrab, who in former times was a nobleman of Thebes?"

"I knew him well. I had dealings with him."

"What were these dealings?"

"I plundered his caravans. I burned his crops. I raided his mines at Sestra, and I slew the miners. I burned his villas. I helped to destroy him so that in the end he drank poison from his own cup."

"Who was it who ordered these things?"

"Lord Intef commanded them and rewarded me with gold."

"What did Lord Intef hope to gain from this persecution?"

Basti shrugged. "Lord Intef is grand vizier, while Pianki, Lord Harrab, is dead. It seems to me Lord Intef achieved his purpose."

"You acknowledge that I have offered you no clemency in return for this confession?" Pharaoh said. "Do you understand that death awaits you?"

"Death?" Basti laughed. "I have never been afraid of that. It is the flour of the loaf I bake. I have fed it to countless others, so now why should I be afraid to feast on it myself?"

"Take him away, to await the king's pleasure," Tanus rasped.

He composed himself with an effort, then went down on one knee before the king. "I have done all that you asked of me, Divine Mamose. I wait for you to command me further."

The silence in the temple persisted. Beside me I felt my mistress squeeze my hand with a strength that threatened to crack my bones.

At last Pharaoh spoke. There was doubt in his voice. He had trusted Lord Intef for so long that it shook the foundations of his faith. "Lord Intef, you have heard the accusations against you. How say you?"

"Divine Pharaoh, are these accusations? I thought them merely a young man's fantasies. He is the son of a traitor, yet in some perverse fashion he holds me responsible for his father's downfall."

The king wavered. His doubts were growing stronger. "What of the accusations of the barons? What reply do you make to them?"

"Barons? Must we flatter them with such a title? They are criminals of the basest kind. Divine Majesty, would you take the word of one of these against a man who has served you faithfully all his life?"

I saw the small nod of the king's head as he accepted this reasoning and Lord Intef sensed his advantage.

"So far I have had only words thrown at me. Surely there must be some evidence? If there is no one who has evidence, then I have nothing to answer to."

His words troubled Pharaoh deeply. "Lord Tanus, what proof do you have of these things, apart from the word of murderers?"

"The evil one covers his tracks well," Tanus admitted. "I have no further evidence against Lord Intef, but there may be some other who does. I beg you, Royal Egypt, ask your people if there is not one of them who can bring forth anything to help us."

The king then addressed the congregation. "My people! Citizens of Thebes! You have heard the accusations made against my trusted grand vizier. Is there one of you who can bring forward evidence against the Lord Intef? If so, I charge you to speak."

I was standing before I realised it, and my voice was loud. "I am Taita, who was once the slave of Lord Intef. I have evidence."

Pharaoh looked across at me. "You are known to us, Taita the physician. You may approach."

As I left my seat and went down to stand before the king, Lord Intef's hatred was tangible.

"Divine Egypt, this thing is a slave," he cried. "The word of a slave against a high officer of the state—what mockery is this?"

Pharaoh silenced him with a gesture. "You presume on our good opinion of you, Lord Intef. The codes of law are mine to interpret."

Lord Intef bowed in submission, but his face was haggard.

Now the king looked at me. "Taita, let me remind you that Lord Intef has demanded not words but proof. I, too, demand proof."

I drew breath. "For half my lifetime I was the scribe and the treasurer of the grand vizier. I kept the record of his fortune. I gathered in the bounty that the barons of the Shrikes paid to Lord Intef, and I disposed of all this wealth."

"Can you show me your scrolls, Taita?"

"No, Majesty, I cannot do so. The scrolls are in the possession of Lord Intef. But I can lead you to the treasure that the grand vizier has stolen from you. It was I who built his secret treasuries for him, and hid within them the bounty that I gathered from the barons."

Although every eye in the temple was fastened upon me, I myself was watching Lord Intef's reflection in the burnished copper doors of the sanctuary. I had taken a risk in trusting that his treasure had not been removed from the secret places where I had stored it for him. Now I saw from the panic in his expression that the arrow I had fired at him had struck the mark. I had won.

"I do not want to believe this." Pharaoh's expression was sorrowful as he looked at his grand vizier. "I have trusted you all my life."

Lord Intef fell to his knees. "Great Egypt, hear me!"

"I have listened to you long enough." Then the king nodded to Tanus. "Have your men guard him well, but show him courtesy, for his guilt is not yet fully proven."

Finally Pharaoh addressed the congregation. "I adjourn these proceedings to consider the evidence that Taita the slave will present to me. The population of Thebes will assemble to hear my judgment in this same place at noon tomorrow. I have spoken."

WE ENTERED through the main doorway to the audience hall of the grand vizier's palace. At the far end of it stood his throne, carved from a solid block of alabaster.

I led Pharaoh and his royal train down the hall to the throne wall and we stopped below a huge mural depicting the sun god, Ammon-Ra. Tanus marched only a pace behind the king. He and his soldiers had taken over the duties of the royal bodyguard.

The king turned to Tanus now. "Have your men bring forward the Lord Intef!"

Treating him with elaborate courtesy Kratas led Lord Intef to face the wall, then stood between the prisoner and the king with his blade at the ready.

"Taita, you may proceed," the king told me.

I measured the wall, stepping out paces from the furthest comer and marking the distance.

"Let the masons approach!" I called out, and a small band of these sturdy rogues in their leather aprons came down the aisle.

"Behind this wall lies a secret compartment," I told the king. "I had it constructed on Lord Intef's orders."

I borrowed a wooden set square from the master mason, and with it marked out an oblong shape on the clay-plastered wall. Then I stepped back, and with their wooden mallets and their chisels of flint, his men fell upon the wall and attacked the sealed doorway. Soon a dark opening was revealed and Pharaoh called excitedly for torches to be lit.

When the torches were brought, the king stepped through the gaping door. I was the next to enter after him and Tanus.

The chests and casks of acacia wood and cedar were stacked exactly as I had left them. I pointed out to the king those cases to which he should first devote his attention, and he had them carried out into the audience hall. It took three men to lift each case.

"I have never seen these boxes before," Lord Intef protested. "I had no knowledge of a secret chamber behind the wall. It must have been built by my predecessor."

"Your Majesty, observe the seal on this lid," I said.

"Whose seal is this?" he demanded.

"Observe the ring on the left forefinger of the grand vizier, Majesty," I murmured. "May I respectfully suggest that Pharaoh match it to the seal on this chest?"

"Lord Intef, hand me your ring," demanded the king.

The grand vizier slid the ring from his finger, and Pharaoh bent studiously over the chest to make the comparison of ring to seal.

"It is a perfect match. This seal was struck from your ring, Lord Intef." The grand vizier made no reply.

"Break the seal! Open the chest!" Pharaoh ordered, and Tanus cut away the clay tablet and prised up the lid with his sword.

The king cried out involuntarily as the lid fell away and the contents were revealed. "Gold!" He scooped both hands full with the glittering rings, and then let them cascade back between his fingers. "How many cases are there in the secret storeroom?"

"If my memory serves me well, there should be fifty-three cases of gold and twenty-three of silver in this store."

"Is there no one I can trust? You, Lord Intef, I treated as my brother, and this is how you have repaid me. Your guilt is as high as the heaven. I will have to devise a suitable punishment."

THE FOLLOWING morning, the congregation in the temple of Osiris was, if anything, even larger than it had been on the day before. There was not a soul in Thebes who had not heard of the downfall of the grand vizier, or who was not eager to witness his humiliation.

The two barons of the Shrikes, and Rasfer, were led before the throne in bonds, but Lord Intef wore fine linen and silver sandals and the chains of the Gold of Praise hung round his neck.

Pharaoh rose and stood before us in all his grandeur and his rage. He seemed a true king and I was overcome with a sense of awe.

"Lord Intef, you are accused of treason and murder. I have heard the testimony and I have seen the contents of your secret treasury. I, Mamose the eighth of that name, Pharaoh and ruler of Egypt, hereby find you guilty of the crimes of which you are accused."

"Long live Pharaoh!" shouted Tanus, and the salute was taken up and repeated ten times by the people of Thebes.

When silence fell, Pharaoh spoke again. "Lord Intef, you wear the Gold of Praise. The sight of that decoration on the breast of a traitor offends me." He looked across at Tanus. "Captain, remove the gold from the prisoner."

Tanus lifted the chains from Lord Intef's neck and carried them to the king. Pharaoh took the gold in his two hands, but when Tanus started to withdraw he stayed him.

"Your father was hounded to a traitor's death. You have proven your father's innocence. I rescind all sentences passed against Pianki, Lord Harrab, and posthumously restore to him all his honours and titles that were stripped from him. Those honours and titles descend to you, his son."

"May Pharaoh live for ever!" shouted the congregation. "Hail, Lord Harrab!"

"In addition to those titles which now come to you as your inheritance, I bestow upon you new distinction. You have carried out my charge to you. You have destroyed the Shrikes and have delivered their overlord to justice. In recognition of this, I bestow upon you the Gold of Praise. Kneel, Lord Harrab."

"Hail, Lord Harrab!" they cried as Pharaoh placed the gold chains, which had so recently belonged to Lord Intef, about Tanus's neck. As Tanus withdrew, Pharaoh turned his attention back to the prisoners.

"Lord Intef, your estates and all your possessions, including your illicit treasure, are forfeited to the crown. Except those that once belonged to Pianki, Lord Harrab. These are now returned in their entirety to his heir, Tanus, Lord Harrab."

The people cheered wildly, and beside me my mistress was weeping unashamedly, but then so were half the royal women.

At last the king was ready to pass sentence on the four prisoners, though he looked only at Intef as he spoke.

"At dawn on the day after the end of the festival of Osiris, you will be marched through the streets of Thebes, bound and naked. While you still live you will be nailed by your feet to the main gate of the city, with your heads hanging downwards. You will be left there until your bones are picked clean by the crows. Then your bones will be taken down and ground to powder and cast into Mother Nile."

Even Intef paled and swayed on his feet as he listened to the sentence. By dispersing their earthly bodies so that they could never be embalmed and preserved, Pharaoh was condemning the prisoners to oblivion. For an Egyptian there could be no harsher punishment.

AT DAWN on the day of the execution the gardens of the palace were still shrouded in darkness when I left the harem. As I approached the wing of the palace where Lord Intef was being held in his own quarters, I heard frantic invective from within.

I broke into a run. Tanus was in the antechamber, roaring like a lion in a trap.

I went straight up to him and shouted in his face. "Tanus! Control yourself! In the name of all the gods, are you mad?"

I saw him wrestle with his emotions and at last take control of them. "See what you can do for my men." He pointed at the bodies that were scattered about the antechamber.

With horror I recognised that one of them was a captain of the regiment and a man I respected. I touched his cheek and the skin was cold and dead. "He is past all help that I can give him." I lifted his eyelid with my thumb and gazed into his dead eye, then I leaned forward and smelt his mouth.

"Poison." I stood up. "The others will be the same." There were five of them dead on the tiles. I took a deep breath to calm myself before I asked. "No doubt your prisoner has escaped?"

Tanus did not reply but led me through into the grand vizier's bedchamber. Immediately I saw that a painted panel had been removed from the far wall of the empty room, leaving an opening.

"Did you know that there was a secret passage?" Tanus demanded.

I shook my head. "I thought I knew all his secrets, but I was wrong." My voice was resigned. In my heart I had known that we would never bring Intef to justice. "Has Rasfer escaped with him?" I asked.

"I have him locked in the arsenal with the barons," Tanus told me. "But Intef's two sons, Menset and Sobek, have disappeared. Almost certainly they arranged their father's escape. You know Intef so well, Taita. Where will he go now? How can I catch him?"

"One thing I know, he will have made plans against such a day as this. I know he has treasure stored for him in the Lower Kingdom. He has even had commerce with the false pharaoh. He would receive a friendly welcome in the north."

"I have already sent five fast galleys to the north, with orders to search all vessels they overtake," Tanus said.

"He has friends across the Red Sea," I said. "And he has had dealings with the Bedouin. They would help him to cross the desert."

"By Horus, he is like a rat with a dozen escape routes to his hole. How can I cover all of them?"

"You cannot," I said. "And now Pharaoh is waiting to witness the executions. You will have to report this to him."

"The king will be angry, and with good reason. By allowing Intef to escape, I have failed in my duty."

But Tanus was wrong. Pharaoh accepted the news of Intef's escape with remarkable equanimity. When Tanus admitted his responsibility for the prisoner's escape, Pharaoh brushed it aside.

"The fault lies with the captain of the guard, and he has already been sufficiently punished from the poison bowl that Intef's sons provided for him. You have sent galleys and troops in pursuit of the fugitives. You have done all that can be expected. It remains only for you to carry out my sentence on these other criminals."

Great was the public interest in the executions. Few had not suffered from the ravages of the Shrikes. The condemned men had been led through the streets, suffering hurled dung and filth, screamed insults and shaken fists. Now they were at last led out through the open gates.

Rasfer was the first prisoner to be lifted onto the wooden gate. When the thick copper nails were driven through the flesh and bones of his spread hands and his huge calloused feet, he roared and swore and twisted in the grip of the men who held him, while the crowd cheered and laughed and urged on the sweating armourer.

Then the two other condemned men, Shufti and Basti the Cruel, were lifted onto the gate and nailed there, and the crowd applauded. Basti, as brave as ever, made no sound and gave them poor sport.

As the day wore on the sun beat down and the heat grew steadily stronger. The spectators began to lose interest and drifted away. Shufti and Basti died quickly but Rasfer went on breathing all that day. Only as the sun was setting did he take one last shuddering breath and finally hang inert.

Book Three

At Pharaoh's command the return of the court to Elephantine was initially delayed for a month. The king had his new treasure to dispose of and was in buoyant mood. I was pleased for him. By this time I held the old man in real and warm affection.

Nevertheless the king found time to send for Tanus to ask his advice on military matters. He had now recognised Tanus as one of the foremost generals in his army. The threat from the false pharaoh in the Lower Kingdom was ever present and such was Tanus's influence that the king was persuaded to divert a part of Intef's treasure to the building of five new squadrons of war galleys, and to re-equipping all the guards regiments with new weapons.

Apart from his military duties, Tanus these days was much occupied with the reorganisation of his father's estates that he had at last inherited. On these matters he consulted me almost daily. Not surprisingly, the estates had never been preyed upon by the Shrikes while they belonged to Lord Intef, and accordingly they were all prosperous and in good repair. Thus Tanus had become overnight one of the most wealthy men in the Upper Kingdom.

So the days passed swiftly, until one morning I consulted my calendar and discovered that over two months had passed since Lady Lostris had resumed her marital duties. It was time to apprise the king of his approaching paternity.

When I told my mistress what I intended, only one matter engaged her consideration. She made me promise that before I discussed it with the king I must first tell Tanus that he was the true father of the child she was carrying. I set out to fulfil my promise that very afternoon. I found Tanus at the shipyards on the west bank of the river, where he was swearing at the shipwrights. He forgot his anger when he saw me, and led me to the far end of the yard where none of the sailors could overhear us. "How goes it with your mistress? Tell me, is she well? What a loving heart she has, what beauty!"

"There will soon be two of her for you to love," I told him and he stared at me with his mouth agape like a man suddenly bereft of his senses. "Lady Lostris is carrying your child. She sent me to tell you so that you should be the first to know it, even before the king."

He seized me in a hug so powerful that I could not breathe. "My child! My son!" he cried. It was amazing how both of them had made that immediate assumption of the poor mite's gender. "This is a miracle. This is a direct gift from Horus." He was grinning like an idiot. "My woman and my son! I must go to them this very moment."

I had to run to catch him. It took all my powers of persuasion to prevent him storming the palace.

In the end I led him to the nearest tavern to wet the baby's head. Fortunately there was already a gang of off-duty Crocodile Blues drinking there. I ordered and paid for a butt of the tavern's best wine and left them to it, then went directly to the palace.

"Pharaoh!" I cried. "Great and Divine Egypt! I have wonderful tidings. The goddess Isis has kept her promise. Your dynasty will be eternal. The prophecy will be fulfilled. Lady Lostris is bearing your child!"

Like Tanus, Pharaoh's first instinct was to go to her. My mistress was waiting for him in the garden of the harem. She was seated on a low bench with flowerbeds around her and the broad river behind her. The king showered her with congratulations and compliments and earnest enquiries after her health.

Finally he asked her, "My dear child, is there anything you lack for your happiness? Is there anything I can do to make you more comfortable?"

I knew she had been dreading the court's return to Elephantine Island. Even so, her reply surprised me. "Your Majesty, Thebes is the city of my birth. I cannot be truly happy anywhere else in Egypt. I beg you to allow your son to be born here in Thebes."

I held my breath. The siting of the court was an affair of state.

Pharaoh looked amazed. "You want to live in Thebes? Very well, then, the court will move to Thebes!" He turned to me. "Taita, design me a new palace." He looked back at my mistress. "Shall we site it there on the west bank, my dear?" He pointed across the river.

"It is cool and pretty on the west bank," my mistress agreed. "I shall be very happy there."

"On the west bank, Taita. Do not stint yourself in the design. It must be fit for the son of Pharaoh. His name will be Memnon, the ruler of the dawn. We will call it the Palace of Memnon."

With such simple ease my mistress saddled me with a mountain of labour, and accustomed the king to the first of many such demands in the name of the child in her womb. From this moment on, Pharaoh was not disposed to deny her aught that she asked for, whether it was titles of honour for those she loved or hated, or rare and exotic dishes that were fetched for her from the ends of the empire.

Once she was present when Tanus delivered a report to the king on the Egyptian fleet. My mistress sat quietly until Tanus had finished and taken his leave, then she remarked quietly, "I have heard it said that Lord Tanus is the finest general we have. Don't you think it may be wise, divine husband, to promote him to Great Lion of Egypt and place him in command of the northern corps?"

I gasped at her effrontery, but Pharaoh nodded thoughtfully. "That same thought had already occurred to me, my dear, even though he is still so young for high command."

The following day, Tanus was summoned to a royal audience from which he emerged as Great Lion of Egypt and the commander of the northern wing of the army. The ancient general who had preceded him was palmed off with a substantial pension. Tanus now had 300 galleys and almost 30,000 men under his command.

On the same day that the work began on the construction of the Palace of Memnon, a blockade runner docked in Thebes with a cargo of cedarwood from the Lebanon. The captain was an old friend of mine and he had interesting news for me.

First he told me that Lord Intef had been seen in the city of Gaza. It was said that he was travelling in state with a large bodyguard towards the east.

The captain had other news that at the time seemed insignificant, but which was to change the destiny of Egypt and all of us who lived along the river. It seemed that a new and warlike tribe had come out of an unknown land to the east of Syria, carrying all before them. They called themselves the Shepherd Kings, the Hyksos. Nobody knew much about them except that they seemed to have developed a form of warfare that had never been seen before. They could cross vast distances very swiftly, and no army could stand against them.

When I mentioned this story to Tanus, he smiled. "No one can stand against this mysterious foe? I would like to see them come against my lads. I'll show them what the word invincible truly means."

He was much more interested in my news of Intef. "If only we could be certain of his true whereabouts, I could send a detachment of men to bring him back to face justice."

"Would that it were so easy." I shook my head. "Intef is as cunning as a desert fox. I don't think we will ever see him in Egypt again."

As I said it the dark gods must have chuckled to themselves.

As the day of my mistress's confinement approached I lay awake at night worrying. The king was not expecting his heir to arrive so expeditiously. Even a god can count the weeks from the first day of the festival of Osiris.

Pharaoh had now conceived an interest in the subject of pregnancy and parturition, so I was able to inform him of the interesting but little-known fact that many of the great athletes, warriors and sages of history had been prematurely exposed to the light of day.

"It would not surprise me," I told him, "to learn that you yourself experienced a premature birth." I knew that he had not, but naturally he could not now contradict me. "It would be a most propitious circumstance if this prince of yours should imitate his sire and start early from his mother's womb."

In the end the child cooperated by overstaying its allotted term by almost two weeks. The time span was now so close to the normal that no tongues could wag, but Pharaoh was blessed with the premature birth that he had come to believe was so desirable.

It was no surprise to me that my mistress began her labour at a most inconvenient hour, the third watch of the night. But once she had begun, Lady Lostris carried it off with dispatch. I barely had time to shake myself fully awake, scrub my hands in hot wine and bless my instruments in the flame of the lamp, before the child came out like a stone from a slingshot.

Before I had a good hold on it, my mistress struggled up on her elbows. "Is it a boy? Tell me! Tell me!"

The roomful of royal ladies crowding round the bed were witnesses and a dozen voices answered her together.

"A boy! Hail, Memnon, royal Prince of Egypt!"

I could not speak yet, for my eyes burned with tears of joy as his birth cry rang out. As my vision cleared I was able to make out his strong, lean body and his proud head, not with the shock of red-gold curls I had dreaded, but rather with a pelt of thick dark hair.

I left my mistress to the joy of her son and went to report to the king. I was in no hurry. I knew that the news would have been carried to him long since, and so I dawdled a while in the water garden. Dawn was breaking and the sun god showed the tip of his fiery disc above the eastern hills.

As I stood with my eyes uplifted, a flock of the palace pigeons circled above the gardens. Then I saw a falcon high above the circling flock. It folded back its wings and began its stoop. It had chosen the leading bird in the flock and it struck the pigeon in a burst of feathers. The falcon then opened its talons and released the pigeon. The shattered carcass fell at my feet, and with a harsh scream the falcon circled over my head. Three times it circled and three times it uttered that thrilling call.

I realised that this was no natural occurrence. The falcon was a messenger, or even the god Horus himself, and the pigeon was a token from the god, a sign of his protection and patronage for the infant prince. I understood also that it was a charge to me. The god was commending him to my care.

I took the dead pigeon in my hands and lifted it to the sky. "Joyfully I accept this trust that you have placed upon me, O Horus. Through all the days of my life I will be true to it."

The falcon called again and then it flew out across the wide Nile waters, back towards the western fields of paradise.

I plucked a single wing-feather from the pigeon. Later I placed it under the mattress of the prince's cot for good luck.

PHARAOH DECLARED a nativity feast. For one entire night the citizens of Upper Egypt sang and danced in the streets, gorged on the meat and wine that Pharaoh provided, and blessed Prince Memnon.

So young and resilient was my mistress that within days she was well enough to appear before the full court of Egypt, bearing her infant. Seated on the lesser throne below that of the king, she made a picture of lovely young motherhood.

Pharaoh rose to address us.

"I acknowledge this child to be my issue and the direct line of my blood and succession. He is my first-born son, and shall be Pharaoh after me. To you, noble lords and ladies, to all my subjects, I commend the Prince Memnon."

The cheers went on and on, while during all of this I was standing with the other slaves in one of the upper galleries which overlooked the hall.

When at last the king ordered silence and he had their attention once more, he continued, "I commend to you also the mother of the prince, the Lady Lostris. Know all men that from this day forward she is elevated to the rank of the senior wife of Pharaoh. From henceforth in name she will become Queen Lostris, while in precedence she ranks after the king and his prince alone. Furthermore, until the prince has reached the age of his majority, Queen Lostris shall act as my regent."

To end the ceremony of the naming of Pharaoh's heir, the royal family left the hall and were drawn in the sledge of state to the temple of Osiris to make sacrifice to the god.

That night as I waited on Queen Lostris and the child, she whispered to me, "Oh, Taita, did you see Tanus in the crowd? What a day of mixed joy and sorrow this has been. I could have wept for my love. Is there no way that we can let him enjoy our baby as we do?"

I thought about it for a while and then made a suggestion which, on the very next day when Pharaoh came to visit his son, the queen put into effect. "Dear husband, have you given thought to selecting official tutors for Prince Memnon?"

Pharaoh laughed indulgently. "He is still only an infant. Should he not first learn to walk and talk, before he is instructed in other skills?"

"I think his tutors should be appointed now, so they can grow to know him, and he them."

"Very well." The king smiled and lifted the child onto his knee. "Who do you suggest?"

"For his schooling we need one of our great scholars. Some person who understands all the sciences and mysteries."

The king's eyes twinkled. "I cannot think of one who answers that description," and he grinned at me. Since Memnon's birth he had become almost jovial.

The queen continued, "Then we need a soldier to train him as a warrior. He should, I think, be young and of good breeding. Trustworthy, of course, and loyal to the crown."

"Who do you suggest for that position, my dear? Very few of my soldiers answer to all those virtues."

My mistress inclined her head gracefully. "The king is wise, and knows who from all his generals best suits that role."

At the very next assizes the king announced the prince's tutors. The slave, Taita, was to be responsible for Memnon's schooling and deportment. This surprised very few, but there was a buzz of comment when the king went on, "For his training in arms, the Great Lion of Egypt, Lord Harrab, shall henceforth be responsible."

Accordingly it became the duty of Lord Harrab, when he was not on campaign, to wait upon the prince at the beginning of each week. Very often there were a score of other officials or courtiers present at this audience, and occasionally Pharaoh himself arrived. However, once in a while there were just the four of us present.

On the first occasion that we had such privacy, Queen Lostris placed the prince in his father's arms for the first time and I was witness to the incoherent joy with which Tanus looked down into the face of his son.

The prince was blessed with his father's abundant health and strength. He crawled when others had only begun to sit up. He took his first tottering step when others would only begin to crawl.

Tanus was present on that remarkable day. He had been on campaign for the past two months, for the forces of the red usurper had captured Asyut. Pharaoh had ordered Tanus downriver with all his fleet to retake the city.

Much later I heard from Kratas just how terrible had been the fighting, but in the end Tanus breached the walls and was at the head of his beloved Blues when they broke in. They drove the pretender back beyond his own borders with bloody losses.

Tanus sailed back to Thebes and the gratitude of the kingdom. Pharaoh laid another chain upon his shoulders, the Gold of Valour.

Tanus came almost directly from the king to the water garden where we were waiting for him. While I stood guard at the gateway, Tanus and my mistress embraced with all the fire that had burned up so brightly while they had been apart.

At last I had to separate them. "Lord Tanus," I called sharply, "Prince Memnon grows impatient." Reluctantly they drew apart, and Tanus went to where the infant sprawled on a robe I had spread for him in the shade.

"Greetings, Your Royal Highness. I bring you tidings of the triumph of our arms—" Tanus mocked him lovingly, and Memnon gave a happy shout as he recognised his father. Then the sparkling gold chain caught his eye. He hoisted himself to his feet, took four lurching steps, seized the chain and clung to it with both hands.

All of us applauded this feat, and supporting himself by the chain Memnon beamed about him, accepting this praise as his due.

THE INUNDATION of that summer was as benevolent as any that we had forecast at the ceremony of the waters in Elephantine. When the flood had receded, the mud on the fields was soon obliterated by dense green stands of corn and fruits.

By the time the prince took his first upright step the granaries of Egypt were brimming, and the larders of even the poorest of her subjects were filled.

On the west bank the Palace of Memnon was taking shape, and the war in the north was running in our favour. The gods smiled on Pharaoh and all his realm.

The only discontent in all this was that the two lovers, though close enough to touch, were cleaved apart by a gulf wider than the valley in which we lived.

Thus the old year died, and the river began to rise once more, completing the endless cycle. This was the fourth flood that my vision had foretold.

Then another year passed without any change in our circumstances, and yet another. I began to lose faith in my prophecy. I came to believe that what I had seen was my own wishful fantasy. In the end Prince Memnon was almost five years old and his mother twenty-one when the messenger came flying wild-eyed from the north, in one of our scouting galleys.

"The Delta has fallen. The red pretender is dead. The Lower Kingdom is in flames. The temples are burnt to the ground and the images of the gods thrown down," he shouted to the king.

Pharaoh replied, "It is not possible. I long to believe this dispatch, but I cannot. For twenty years we have been unable to overthrow the usurper. How has this been accomplished, and by whom?"

The messenger was shaking with exhaustion, for his journey had been onerous. "The red pretender was destroyed with his sword still in the scabbard. His forces were scattered before the war trumpets could sound the alarm."

"How was this accomplished?"

"Divine Egypt, I know not. They say that a new and terrible enemy has come out of the east, swift as the wind. Though they have never seen him, our army is in full retreat from the northern borders."

"Who is this enemy?" Pharaoh demanded.

"They call him the Shepherd King. The Hyksos."

Pharaoh called his war council into secret conclave. It was only long afterwards that I learned all that transpired in those deliberations. The council was divided between the ancients, headed by Nembet, and the new blood of which Tanus was the leader. Unfortunately the final authority lay with the old men.

Tanus wanted to draw our main forces back from the frontier and to set up a series of deep defences along the river. At the same time, he intended sending forwards scouting parties to assess the nature of the enemy.

"Until we know what we are facing we cannot devise the correct strategy to meet it," he told the council.

Nembet and his faction countered all of Tanus's suggestions.

"We will not yield a cubit of our sacred soil. To suggest it is cowardice. We will meet the enemy and destroy him wherever we find him."

"My lord!" roared Tanus. "Only a fool will make a decision before he knows the facts. We have no scrap of intelligence to act upon—"

It was in vain. The seniority of the generals above Tanus prevailed. Tanus was ordered north immediately, to steady and rally the retreating army.

He was to hold the frontiers before Asyut and to make his stand on the boundary stones.

In the meantime, Nembet would bring up the rest of the army, so that within a month there would be an invincible strength of 60,000 men and 400 galleys lying before Asyut. Until then, Tanus must hold the frontier at all costs.

Pharaoh himself announced his intention of taking his place at the head of his army. Naturally the king would not travel northwards to the battlefront alone. His entire court would attend him, including his senior wife and his son. Prince Memnon must, of course, be attended by his tutors, and so I, too, would be going north to Asyut and the battlefront.

THE FURTHER north we sailed, the more troublesome were the reports coming down from the front. Soon we encountered the first elements of the retreating army, straggling groups of deserters who were looting the villages as they fled southwards. Tanus beheaded several hundred of them and had their heads spiked on spears and planted along the bank as a warning. Then he gathered up the others and regrouped them under reliable officers.

There were no further desertions and the troops stood to the colours with a new spirit.

Our flotilla came to the walled city of Asyut. Here Tanus left a small strategic reserve of 5,000 men under the command of the loyal warrior Remrem.

Then we sailed on northwards to take up our positions on the border, there to await the approach of the Hyksos. The fleet lay at anchor across the river in its battle formations, its fighting men disembarked with the main body of infantry and deployed upon the east bank of the river.

I remained with my mistress and the prince on board the royal barge. It was cooler and healthier out on the water, and their escape would be swifter if our army met with any reverse of arms.

The king went ashore with the army, and set up his camp on high ground above the fields. There was a deserted village here; the peasants had years ago fled from this disputed border with the false pharaoh. The name of the derelict village was Abnub.

The regiments encamped in their order of battle. Astes commanded the fleet on the river, Tanus himself had the centre with his western flank anchored on the Nile, while Kratas had the right wing.

The desert stretched to the eastern horizon, dun and forbidding. It was our right flank, secure and impregnable.

All that we knew of the Hyksos was that he had come overland, and that he possessed no fleet of his own. Tanus expected to meet him on land, and to fight an infantry engagement.

I went with Tanus to inspect the troops under his command and I could not imagine an enemy powerful enough to overwhelm us. There were 12,000 archers, 8,000 heavy spearmen, and 10,000 swordsmen who were also armed with slingshots.

I felt more confident with each day that passed, as I watched Tanus exercising these huge masses of armed men. Yet it worried me that we still knew so little about the Hyksos.

When I pointed this out to Tanus he ordered Hui to take a single squadron of fast galleys northwards as far as Minieh, or until he encountered the enemy. This was the same Hui who had been one of Basti's Shrikes. Under Tanus's favour, that young rogue had advanced swiftly, and now commanded a squadron of galleys.

Hui had strict orders to avoid action and to report back within four days. Dutifully, he returned on the fourth day. He had reached Minieh without seeing another ship or encountering any resistance. The villages along the river were all deserted, and the town of Minieh itself had been sacked and was in flames.

Hui had, however, captured a handful of actual eyewitnesses of the Hyksos invasion, but their reports were so far-fetched as to be incredible. How could we believe in the existence of an army that sailed across the open desert on ships that were as swift as the wind?

"These are not men," the prisoners reported, "they are fiends, and they ride on the devil winds out of the desert."

On the tenth day of waiting at Abnub, we received word that Nembet was at last on his way with reinforcements, and that he expected to reach Asyut within the next two weeks. Tanus issued an extra ration of beer and meat to celebrate the news, and the cooking fires were a field of stars upon the plain before Abnub.

I had left my mistress on the barge with her son, and had come ashore to attend the final war council with Tanus's commanders.

Our deliberations went on until after midnight. It was too late to return to the ship that night, so Tanus gave me a straw mattress in the corner of his tent. When I woke before dawn, Tanus was gone from his bed and the camp was already astir. I hastened out to watch the dawn breaking over the desert.

I climbed the hill behind the camp. From there I looked first towards the river. The blue smoke from the cooking-fires was smeared out across the surface, mingling with the streamers of river mist.

I turned then towards the east and saw the light bloom over the desert with the glow of pearly oyster shells. In the limpid air a cloud seemed to be suspended beneath the unblemished aquamarine sheen of the sky. It was no larger than the end of my thumb, and my gaze wandered past it, then drifted back. I had stared at it for a while before I realised that it was moving.

Even as I pondered it, the cloud grew taller. It must be dust, and yet I still could not believe it. Swiftly it grew, and drew ever closer.

Suddenly I saw reflected light twinkle at the base of the towering cloud. Instantly I knew that those beams of light were from war armour and from blades of polished bronze. I started to my feet, and alone upon the hilltop I shouted a warning that nobody heard.

Then I heard the war trumpets sounding in the camp below me. The pickets on the heights had also seen the approaching dust cloud and sounded the alarm. Now the camp below me was a tumult of men running to arms.

I saw Pharaoh carried from his tent in the centre of a knot of armed men. They hustled him up the slope of the hill where he sat like a marble statue on his throne, overlooking the plain.

I ran down the hill to be near the king. Tanus had disposed his force in the classical formations. His heavy spearmen formed the front ranks, their shields interlocked and their spear butts grounded. Drawn up behind them were the archers.

The swordsmen were in reserve; they were light troops that could rush in to stop a breach or to exploit a weak point in the enemy formations.

Reviewing Tanus's dispositions, I could find no fault in them. My confidence soared. How could an enemy prevail against this mighty host of hardened veterans?

Then I looked once more beyond our ranks at that ominous rolling yellow cloud, and my confidence wavered. It was now so close that I could make out dark shapes and my skin crawled with a kind of religious horror as I recognised the shiplike shapes that our prisoners had warned us of. Behind them, the dust cloud extended back to the horizon from which they had come.

It was then I realised that the dust cloud was no longer advancing upon us. It had begun to settle and clear so that I was able dimly to make out the vehicles in the vanguard. A stillness had fallen on us.

Suddenly there was movement again. From the Hyksos's front ranks some of these strange vehicles started towards us. A murmur went up from our lines as we saw how fast they moved. The range closed and another cry went up as we realised that these vehicles were each being drawn by a pair of extraordinary beasts.

They stood as tall as a wild oryx, with the same stiff mane along the crest of their arched necks, but they were not horned and their heads were more gracefully formed. Striding out with a peculiar daintiness, they seemed merely to brush the surface of the desert.

Even now, after all these years, I can recapture the thrill of gazing at a horse for the first time. In my mind the beauty of the hunting cheetah paled beside these marvellous beasts.

The leading vehicle swung away and sped parallel to our front rank. It moved on spinning discs, and I stared at it in wonder.

If anything, my first sight of a chariot was as moving as the sight of the horses that drew it.

There was a long yoke-pole between the galloping pair, connected to the centre of the axle. The high dashboard was gilded with gold leaf and the side panels were cut low to allow the archer to shoot his arrows to either side.

All this I took in at a glance and then my attention focused on the spinning discs on which the chariot sailed so swiftly over the ground. I stared at the first wheel I had ever seen and the simplicity and the beauty of it burst in upon me like lightning flaring in my head.

As the golden chariot drew opposite us I looked at the two men riding inside it. One was clearly the driver. He leaned out over the dashboard and he seemed to control the galloping team by means of long plaited cords of leather attached to their heads. The taller man who stood on the footplate behind him was a king. There was no doubting his imperial bearing.

I saw instantly that he was an Asian, with amber skin and a hooked, aquiline nose. His beard was black and thick, curled and intricately plaited with coloured ribbons. His body armour was a glittering skin of bronze fish scales, while his crown was tall and square and set with precious stones. His weapons hung on the side panel of the chariot, close to his hands. His bow was of a shape I had never seen before, its upper and lower limbs recurved at the tips.

As the chariot flew down our line the king leaned out and planted a lance tipped with a crimson pennant in the earth. The men around me growled in perturbation. "What is he doing? Is it a challenge?"

The chariot sped on, still just out of bowshot, and the Asian planted another lance, then wheeled and came back. He had seen Pharaoh on his throne and he halted below him. The Hyksos greeted Pharaoh Mamose with an ironic wave of his mailed hand, and he laughed.

The challenge was as clear as if it had been spoken in perfect Egyptian. The ranks of our army growled with anger.

A small movement below me caught my attention and I looked down just as Tanus let loose an arrow. It rose high against the milky blue sky, reached its zenith and then dropped, full at the centre of the Asian king's chest. Our watching multitude gasped with the power and aim of that shot. At the very last moment the Hyksos threw up his bronze shield and the arrow buried its head in the centre of the target. It was done with contemptuous ease.

Then the Hyksos seized his own strangely shaped bow from the rack beside him. With one movement he nocked an arrow and drew and let it fly. It rose higher than Tanus's had reached, and it sailed over his head. It struck the base of Pharaoh's throne behind me. It quivered in the cedar like an insult. The Hyksos king laughed again and sped away in his chariot, back across the plain to rejoin his host.

I knew then that we were doomed. How could we stand against these speeding chariots and the recurved bows that so easily outranged the finest archer in our ranks?

The flying chariots merged into columns four abreast and came directly at us. Only then my mind cleared and I ran to Tanus's side and shouted at him. "The pennant lances mark the weak points in our line. Their main strike will come through us there and there."

Somehow the Hyksos had known our battle order, and had recognised the gaps in our formation. Their king had planted his pennants exactly between our divisions.

Tanus responded to my warning instantly, and shouted an order for our pickets to race forwards and seize the pennants, but, before they could reach them, the spearhead of flying chariots bore down upon them. Some of our men were shot down with arrows from the bouncing, swerving chariots.

The survivors turned and raced back, trying to regain the illusory safety of our lines. The chariots overhauled them effortlessly. The drivers did not run down their victims directly, but swerved to pass close by them, and it was only then that I noticed the knives that curved outwards from the spinning hubs of the wheels.

The chariots crashed into our defensive wall of shields and spears, and tore through it as though it were a drift of river mist. In one instant our formation was shattered.

The horses spurned our strongest and heaviest men under their hoofs. The whirling wheel-knives hacked through their armour and lopped off heads and limbs, while the charioteers showered arrows into our tightly packed ranks, then tore on through the breach they had forced, driving full tilt along our rear files.

The first assault split our army in two, dividing Tanus from Kratas on the right wing. Then those that followed swiftly cut up the two halves into smaller isolated groups.

Across the plain on wings of swirling dust, the Hyksos came on endlessly.

Behind the light two-wheeled chariots followed the heavy four-wheeled war carts, each carrying ten men. The sides of the carts were screened with sheep fleeces. Our arrows slapped ineffectually into the thick soft wool, our swords could not reach the men in the high bodies of the carts. They shot down into us and broke up our fighting men into scattered knots of terrified survivors.

Only the Blues stood firm around Tanus. They were a little island in the torrent of defeated, retreating men. Even the chariots could not break them up, for, with the instinct of a great general, Tanus had gathered them and pulled them back into the one patch of rocks and gullies where the Hyksos could not come at them. The Blues were a wall, a bulwark round the throne of Pharaoh.

I saw Kratas fight his way through from the shattered right wing to join us. His plumed helmet attracted the Hyksos arrows, but he came through unscathed.

Tanus tapped the side of his helmet with the flat of his sword in greeting, but his expression was grim. "Our work here is finished for today," he told Kratas. "Let us see if these Hyksos monsters can swim as well as they run. Back to the river!"

Then, shoulder to shoulder, the two of them shoved their way through the ranks towards the throne where I still stood. I saw the golden chariot of the Hyksos king wheel out of formation and cleave its way towards us. The driver brought the horses to a rearing halt before he reached the barrier of rocks which protected us. Balancing easily on the footplate, the Hyksos drew his recurved bow and aimed at me, or so it seemed. Even as I ducked I realised the arrow was not meant for me. It shrieked over my head, struck Pharaoh high in the chest and buried half its length in his flesh.

Pharaoh gave a hoarse cry and slid from his high throne. The king collapsed forward towards me and I opened my arms to receive him. His weight bore me to my knees.

Tanus stooped over me. "How badly is he struck?"

The angle of entry and the depth of the wound could mean only one outcome was possible, but I knew that our men would lose heart if Pharaoh were slain. I said, "He is hard hit. But if we carry him back aboard the state barge, he may recover."

"Bring me a shield here!" Tanus roared, and when it came we gently lifted Pharaoh onto it. Quickly, I felt for the head of the arrow, but it had not emerged from his back. I snapped off the protruding shaft.

"Taita," he whispered. "Will I see my son again?"

"Yes, Mighty Egypt, I swear it to you."

"And my dynasty will survive?"

"Even as my vision has foretold."

"Ten strong men here!" Tanus bellowed. They crowded round the litter and lifted the king. "All together now. Back to the ships!"

The moment we left the shelter of our little rocky redoubt, the chariots came at us.

"Leave the men!" Tanus had found the key. "Kill their beasts!" As the first chariot bore down upon us, his bowmen drew with him, and they all fired on his example. Half our arrows flew wide, for we were running over uneven ground and the archers were winded. But others struck home and each horse went down like an avalanche, tangling the traces and dragging its team-mate down in a cloud of dust and kicking hoofs.

The charioteers were hurled from the cockpits and the other chariots veered away to avoid the wreckage. A jubilant shout went up from our ranks, and our pace picked up as we raced for the river.

The chariots circled us with the first wariness they had demonstrated all that day. They had seen the fate of their comrades. Then three of them swung across our front and charged at us head-on.

"Shoot at the heads of the beasts!" Tanus shouted, and led them with an arrow that brought another horse crashing to its knees.

We were rapidly approaching the morass of muddy fields and flooded irrigation ditches that marked the river bank, where the wheeled enemy could not follow us. Yet ours was the only surviving detachment that still showed any cohesion. The rest of the Egyptian army was a terrified rabble streaming across the plain. Most had thrown aside their weapons, and when the chariots drove at them they dropped to their knees and held up their hands in supplication. The Hyksos showed them no quarter. I had never seen such butchery. For 1,000 years our armies had been invincible. Here on the field of Abnub an age had come to an end.

The first irrigation ditch was just ahead when another chariot formation came driving hard at us. I could hear the squeal of the chariot wheels bearing down on us. I attempted to hurdle the ditch but it was too wide for me to cross in a single leap, and I landed knee-deep in the black mud. The chariot that was following me struck the bank of the ditch and one of its wheels shattered.

Swiftly the Blues stabbed and hacked at the horses and men as they lay helplessly in the mud, but I took the moment to wade back to the chariot. The upended wheel was still spinning. I placed my hand upon it and let it rotate beneath my fingers. I stood there only as long as it took me to draw three deep breaths, but at the end of that time I had learned as much about wheel construction as any Hyksos.

Then I seized one of the recurved bows from the chariot and an arrow from the quiver, and waded across the ditch with them in my hand. I caught up with the litter bearers by the time we reached the main bank of the Nile, where Tanus called me to him. "I place Pharaoh in your hands now, Taita. Take him on board the royal barge and do all you can to save his life."

"When will you come aboard?" I asked him.

"My duty is here, with my men. I must save all of them that I can and get them embarked." He strode away, shouting his orders.

I went to the king and knelt beside the litter. He was still alive. His skin was clammy and his breathing shallow. There was only a thin rim of blood around the arrow shaft but when I laid my ear to his chest I heard the blood bubbling in his lungs with each breath he drew. I shouted for a boat to take him out to the barge.

The litter bearers lifted him into the skiff and I sat in the bilges beside him as we sculled out to the great state barge.

THE KING'S SUITE crowded the ship's side to watch us approach. I recognised my mistress standing among the royal women. Her face was pale and she held her son in her arms.

Of all the women, my mistress stood closest at hand as the king was lifted up the ship's side and his litter laid on the deck. He recognised her and asked for his son. She held out the prince to him and he smiled softly and tried to raise his hand to touch the boy, but he did not have the strength and the hand dropped to his side.

Then Pharaoh reached out to my mistress. "Take my hand, and listen to my words," he ordered, and she sank down beside him.

"If I should die, you will stand as regent for my son. Instruct my son in all the virtues of kingship that you and I have discussed. You know my mind in all these matters." The king fell silent for a while, then he grasped the hand of my mistress more firmly. "There is one last charge I have for you. My tomb and my temple are incomplete. Now they are threatened, as is all my realm. I charge you most strictly that you will see me embalmed and interred with all my treasure in accordance with the strictest protocols of the *Book of the Dead*."

My mistress was silent. I think that she realised even then just what an onerous charge this was that Pharaoh had laid upon her.

"I swear on Hapi, and on all the gods, that this shall be done," Queen Lostris said, softly but clearly, and I knew that she would honour her word at all and any cost to herself.

The king sighed with satisfaction. "Then I am ready for you, Taita, and for whatever the gods have decreed."

I ordered the crew to carry him to his quarters, and my mistress came to me quickly. "What of Tanus? Is he safe?"

"He is safe. Nothing can harm him. All this was foreseen. But now I must go to the king, and I will need your help. Leave Memnon with his nursemaids and come with me."

Queen Lostris and two of the other royal women stripped and bathed Pharaoh and laid him on fresh white linen sheets while I prepared a draught of the Red Shepenn, the sleeping flower, for him. When he had drunk it all I waited for the pupils of his eyes to contract and for the lids to droop over them, then I blessed my instruments in the lamp flame and washed my hands in hot wine.

On leaving Thebes I had expected to have to deal with arrow wounds, so I had brought my spoons with me. I had designed this instrument myself, and my method allowed me to enclose the arrowhead snugly within the spoons, masking the wicked barbs with the metal as they were drawn out.

"If I leave the arrow, it will certainly mortify," I told my mistress, and for a moment we looked into each other's eyes. If the king should die, Queen Lostris would be free to go to her love. She would become regent of this very Egypt. Tanus would be able to lift Memnon in his arms and kiss him and call him son. If the king lived none of these things would be possible.

"He is my husband. He is Pharaoh." My mistress took my hand to emphasise her words. "Save him, Taita, if you can."

"You know that I will," I answered.

By this time the drug had worked its full magic, and Pharaoh lay unconscious. I laid my ear on his chest once more and heard his breath sigh and gurgle in his lungs.

Satisfied that he still lived, I greased the spoons that I had selected with mutton fat, to lubricate their entry into the wound. I laid the spoons close at hand and took up one of my keenest scalpels.

I worked swiftly, opening a slit on each side of the shaft. The human skin is tough and would inhibit the entry of the spoons, so I had to get through it.

I dropped the knife and took up the pair of lubricated spoons. Using the arrow shaft as a guide I eased them deeper and deeper into the wound until only the long handles still protruded.

By this time the drug had ceased to be effective and Pharaoh was writhing and twisting in the grip of the four strong guards holding his wrists and ankles. I slid the spoons deeper until I felt them touch the arrowhead. This was the delicate part of the operation. I levered the spoons apart and worked them over the arrowhead. When I felt them close of their own accord, I hoped that I had entirely enclosed the barbs.

I took a careful grasp of the handles of the spoons and of the reed shaft of the arrow, and pulled back on them until the arrow came free in my hands and blood spurted from the wound.

I stemmed the blood, smeared the wound with precious myrrh and crystallised honey, then bound it up tightly with clean linen bandages.

Pharaoh seemed much easier after the binding up, and I could leave him sleeping in the care of his women and go back on deck. I needed the cool river airs to revive me, for the operation had drained me almost as much as it had Pharaoh.

By this time it was evening, and the sun was setting. There had been no assault by the Hyksos infantry, and Tanus was bringing off the remains of his vanquished army to the galleys anchored in the stream. Then I saw that the dust cloud of the Hyksos chariots had already begun to move southwards towards Thebes.

IT WAS DARK by the time that Tanus himself came aboard the state barge. In the light of the torches he looked like one of the corpses from the battlefield, pale with fatigue and dust.

When he saw me his first concern was to ask after Pharaoh.

"I have removed the arrow," I told him. "He is very weak, but if he survives three days then I will be able to save him."

"What of your mistress and her son?"

"Queen Lostris is tired but she is with the king now. The prince is bonny as ever and sleeps now with his nurses."

I saw Tanus reel on his feet, and knew that he was close to the end of even his great strength.

"You must rest now—" I began but he shook off my hand.

"Taita, fetch your writing brushes and ink and scrolls. I must send a warning to Nembet, lest he walk into the Hyksos trap as I did."

So he and I sat half that night on the open deck, and I wrote out four copies of the message he dictated to me; and as I completed each, Tanus called for messengers to carry them by separate means to the Lord Nembet.

"Surely one of your scrolls will win through to Nembet." I reassured him. "You must sleep now, for if you destroy yourself, then all of Egypt is destroyed with you."

Even then he would not go to a cabin, but curled up on the deck like a dog, so that he could be instantly ready for any new emergency. But I went to the cabin to give comfort to my mistress.

I WAS ON DECK again before the first glimmer of dawn. I arrived to hear Tanus giving orders to burn half our fleet.

When the messengers had been sent away he told me brusquely, "I have just received the roll call from my regimental commanders. Only seven thousand of my men remain, many of whom will still die. I am left with only sufficient men to work half our ships. I must abandon the rest of our ships, but I cannot let them fall into the hands of the Hyksos."

The men used bundles of reeds to start the fires, and once they were set they burned fiercely. It was a sad and terrible sight to watch.

At last Tanus gave the order to his remaining galleys to weigh anchor, and our little fleet turned back into the south. I was absorbed with my duties as physician to the king, who rallied strongly, and on the second day he asked to see the prince again, and Memnon was brought to him.

Already Memnon was a beautiful boy with clean strong limbs and his mother's skin and great dark eyes. Pharaoh's delight in him was poignant. The child was his hope of immortality. Against my wishes he kept the child with him until after sunset. I knew that Memnon's boundless energy was tiring the king, but I could not intervene until it was time for the prince's supper and he was led away by his nurses.

The next day was the third since the wounding, and the most dangerous. If he could survive this day, then I knew I could save him. But when I woke in the dawn the cabin was thick with the musky stench of corruption, and when I touched Pharaoh's skin it burned my fingers. I called for my mistress and she came stumbling through from her alcove behind the curtain where she slept.

She stood beside me as I unbound the wound. When I peeled away the linen bandages, the crusted scab that corked the mouth of the wound burst open, and pus poured out.

"Mortification!" I whispered. "He will be dead before nightfall."

We waited beside his bed for the inevitable. As the word spread through the ship that Pharaoh was dying, the cabin filled with priests and women and courtiers. We waited in silence.

Tanus was the last to arrive, and he stood at the back of the throng. His gaze rested not on the deathbed, but upon Queen Lostris. She kept her face averted from his, but I knew that she was aware of him in every fibre of her body.

Pharaoh tossed about restlessly and cried out in delirium, haunted by all the terrors and monsters of the other world, who waited to receive him. Gradually his voice and his movements became weaker, and a little after noon he gave one last shuddering sigh and was still.

"Pharaoh is dead," I said softly, and closed the lids over his staring eyes. "May he live for ever!"

The mourning cry went up from all who were assembled there. It was a sound that chilled me so I left the cabin as soon as I was able.

Tanus followed me out. "You did all in your power to save him?" he demanded roughly. "This was not another of your devices?"

I knew that this unkind treatment of me was an expression of his own guilt and fear, so I was gentle in my reply.

"He was slain by the Hyksos arrow. I did all that was in my power to save him. It was his destiny and there is no fault in any of us."

He sighed. "I should rejoice that the queen is free, but I cannot. Too much is lost and destroyed."

"There will be a time of happiness for all of us hereafter," I reassured him. "But there is still a sacred duty on my mistress."

And I told him of the oath that Queen Lostris had sworn to the king, that she would preserve his earthly body and give it proper burial.

He said, "The Hyksos is sweeping through the kingdom ahead of us; I cannot guarantee that Pharaoh's tomb will not be violated."

"Then we must find another tomb for him. Our first concern must be to preserve his body. I am not skilled in the embalmer's art, but I do know about one way in which we can keep our trust."

Tanus sent his sailors down into the barge's hold and they swung up one of the huge clay jars of pickled olives from our stores, which he emptied and refilled with boiling water. While the water was still hot he mixed into it three sacks of salt. Then he filled four wine jars with the same brine and set them all out on the deck to cool.

In the meantime I was working alone in the cabin, removing the liver, lungs, stomach and entrails from Pharaoh's corpse. I then packed the cavity with salt and sutured it closed with catgut.

At last I ordered the sailors to bring in the cool jars of brine. Tanus helped me to fold Pharaoh's body into the foetal position and we placed him in the olive vat. His viscera we packed into the smaller wine jars. We sealed all the jars with pitch and wax and lashed them securely below deck.

I had done my best to help my mistress make good her vow.

WHEN WE reached the walled city of Asyut, it was apparent that the Hyksos had not invested it, but had continued southwards with their army. Thus Remrem and his 5,000 who had been within the city were waiting for us, and before nightfall he and all his men were safely embarked.

Immediately, Tanus signalled the flotilla to weigh anchor and we continued upstream under oars.

Remrem told us that he had captured two Egyptian traitors who had gone over to the enemy, and under torture they had given him much information about the Hyksos.

The Hyksos king, whom we had so disastrously encountered on the plain of Abnub, was named Salitis. His tribe was of Semitic blood and originally a nomadic and pastoral people who had lived in the Zagros Mountains. Although they had evolved such an extraordinary vehicle as a wheeled chariot, in other areas it seemed that they were a backward people. They were unable to read or write, and their government was a harsh tyranny by their single king and ruler.

The chief god of the Hyksos was named Sutekh, the god of storms. It needed no deep religious instruction to recognise in him our own dreaded Seth.

It seemed that Remrem's captives were not the only Egyptian traitors; some great Egyptian lord from the Upper Kingdom actually sat upon King Salitis's war council. If any of this was true, then we must expect that the enemy knew all our strengths and weaknesses. They must also know of the rich treasure that Pharaoh had accumulated in his funerary temple.

That afternoon the state council of Upper Egypt convened before the throne on the royal barge. The high priest of Osiris represented the spiritual body; Lord Merseket, the chancellor, stood for the temporal body; Tanus, Lord Harrab, stood for the military.

Between them the three lords lifted Queen Lostris to the throne of Egypt, placed her son upon her lap, and every man and woman on board the barge raised their voices in a loyal salute.

It seemed to me that this marked a new beginning for all of us. Up until that moment we had been overwhelmed by the shock of defeat and the loss of Pharaoh. But now, as the great lords of Egypt went forward one at a time to kneel before the throne and swear their allegiance, a fresh spirit sprang up in us. Our will to fight returned.

WE CAME UPON the first of the Egyptian dead before noon. He came floating down the river with his bloated belly buoying him up.

"He wears the kilt of the Lion Guards," Tanus said quietly. "The Lions are the spearhead of Nembet's army. I pray there will be no others following this one down the river."

But there were. Ten more, then more and still more until the surface of the river was carpeted by floating corpses. At last we found one who still lived, a captain of the Lion Guards whom we fished from the water. I attended to his wounds and when he had recovered sufficiently to speak, Tanus asked, "What of Lord Nembet?"

"Lord Nembet is slain, and all his staff with him."

"Did Nembet not receive my warning?"

"He received it on the eve of the battle, and he laughed as he read it. He said that the puppy was destroyed—forgive me, Lord Tanus, but that was what he called you."

"The arrogant old fool," Tanus lamented. "But tell me the rest of it."

"Lord Nembet deployed upon the east bank with the river at his back. The enemy fell upon us like the wind and drove us into the water. The slaughter was beyond my power to describe."

"All our most famous regiments decimated," Tanus mourned. "What happened to Nembet's fleet? Was it anchored in midstream?"

"Lord Nembet anchored the greater part of the fleet, but he

beached fifty galleys in our rear, to re-embark our troops expeditiously, should your warning prove justified."

"What then is the fate of our fleet?"

"Of the ships that were anchored in midstream, most are scuttled."

"And the fifty ships that lay upon the beach?"

"They have fallen into the hands of the Hyksos." The captain trembled as he answered, for he dreaded Tanus's anger.

Tanus stood up and strode to the bows. I went to stand at his side.

"So the old fool has sacrificed his life, and the lives of all his men, simply to spite me. Also he has given the Hyksos the means to cross the river. And once they are across the Nile we are finished."

At that moment, I felt the wind that had blown so long into our faces veer. Tanus felt it also. He roared an order to his officers.

"The wind turns fair. Make a general signal to the fleet. Set all sail. Relieve the men at the oars every hour. Make all haste southwards."

The wind settled strongly into the north. Our sails filled and the whole battle fleet raced southwards.

"All thanks to the goddess for this wind," Tanus shouted. "Divine Isis, let us be in time to catch them on the water."

The state barge was slow and ungainly. She began falling astern of the fleet. It seemed that the fates intervened once more, for Tanus's old galley that he had loved so well, the *Breath of Horus*, was sailing close to us in the formation. Tanus hailed her alongside the state barge and transferred his standard into her, taking over the command from her captain. My place was with my mistress and the prince. I am not certain, therefore, how I found myself on board *Breath of Horus*, standing on the poop beside Tanus as we tore along upstream.

From the deck of the *Breath of Horus*, Tanus issued his orders. The wounded were transferred to the slower vessels, which fell back to keep pace with the state barge. The faster galleys in the van were cleared for action.

At last we saw the dust of the chariots mingling with the smoke from the cooking-fires of the Hyksos camp in the sky ahead of us.

"It is as I had hoped," Tanus exulted. "They have halted their advance on Thebes now that Nembet has presented them with the means of crossing the river. But they are not sailors, and they will have difficulty embarking their men and chariots. If Horus is kind, we will arrive in time to help them on their way."

In extended battle order we swept round the last wide bend of the river to find the fifty captured galleys straggling across the river, sails and sheets in a tangle and every oarsman keeping his own stroke. The Hyksos manning the decks in full bronze armour stared at us in consternation as we bore down upon them.

I shouted to Tanus above the bloodthirsty cheers of our soldiers, "They have taken their horses across already. Look over there!"

Almost unprotected, except for a few armed guards, there was a huge herd of these terrible animals gathered on the west bank. They were a disturbing sight, and I turned my attention back to the galleys in the stream ahead of us, their decks piled high with chariots and equipment.

As they realised their predicament, some of the Hyksos tried to turn back. They collided with the ships that followed them, and locked together they drifted helplessly on the current.

Tanus laughed to see their confusion and shouted, "Light the fire arrows."

Suddenly I stiffened. "Tanus!" I seized his arm. "Look! Look at the galley dead ahead! On the poop—there is our traitor."

For a moment Tanus did not recognise the stately figure at the rail of the galley, for he wore armour and a tall Hyksos war helmet. Then he roared with anger.

"Intef! Why did we not guess it was him?"

"I see it so clearly now. He has guided Salitis to Egypt. He went east and deliberately tempted the Hyksos with accounts of our treasures."

Tanus threw up his bow and loosed an arrow, but the range was long and the point glanced off Lord Intef's armour. His head jerked round and he looked across the water. He singled us out, Tanus and myself, then ducked out of sight below the gunwale of the galley.

Our leading squadron flew into the Hyksos pack. With a tearing crunch our bronze ramming-horn struck Intef's galley amidships, then disengaged from the stricken ship. At the same time our archers were pouring fire arrows into her sails.

The waters flooded in through the gaping hole in her belly, and she listed over sharply. The sails caught fire with startling rapidity. She was almost gone when Lord Intef reappeared. He had thrown off his helmet and armour, and wore only a breech clout as he dived overboard.

He was a son of the Nile, at home in her waters. He knifed through the surface, and came up a minute later and fifty paces from where he had struck, reaching out for the east bank.

Tanus gave the order and we shot in pursuit, but by now Lord Intef was close in to the bank where Hyksos archers waited, ready to give him covering fire.

Tanus was forced to put the tiller over, and to signal urgently for his oarsmen to back-water. All down the line the Hyksos galleys were ablaze and sinking. A burning galley drifted by, hiding Lord Intef from my view, and when I saw him again, three brawny Hyksos charioteers were dragging him from the water.

We wheeled away and Tanus turned his attention to the west bank and to the small party of the enemy guarding the horses. Like hounds after a jackal our men isolated and surrounded them, and left their bleeding corpses scattered across the fields of corn.

I had jumped ashore behind the first wave of our troops. I had serious business in mind. Even so, it required an enormous act of courage to start me towards that herd of terrible creatures.

I was certain that at any moment they would rush at me like wounded lions, and at a distance of a hundred paces my courage evaporated and I could go no closer.

This was my first opportunity to study these animals. They were mostly of a dun colour but one or two of them were black. They stood as tall as a man, and their hides glowed in the sunlight.

One of them nearest to me threw back its head and rolled its upper lip, and I recoiled as I saw the great square white teeth that lined its jaw. It kicked its hind legs and emitted such a terrifying neighing sound that I turned and started back towards the ship.

Then a hoarse yell from one of our soldiers near me arrested my retreat. "Kill the Hyksos monsters!"

"No!" I cried. "No! Save the horses. We need them."

My voice was lost in the angry shouting of our troops as they rushed at the herd of horses, and a glossy black stallion reared and screamed with an arrow standing out of his chest.

"No! Please no!" I screamed again as one of the sailors ran in with a light war axe and hacked at a young mare. "Leave them!" I pleaded, but the arrows and swords brought down a dozen of the lovely animals before the herd bolted towards the desert.

When they had disappeared I ran to protect those animals that were left maimed among the papyrus beds. Behind an isolated clump of reeds stood the black stallion that I had first seen hit by an arrow. He was sorely struck and staggering as he limped forwards, the arrow deep in his chest. I ran towards him.

His eyes were swimming with pain: gentle eyes, eyes that made my heart swell with pity. I held out my hand and touched his muzzle and it felt like warm Arabian silk. He came directly to me, and pressed his forehead to my chest in a gesture of trust that was almost human.

Instinctively I flung my arms round his neck and embraced him, knowing that he was hit through the lungs and far beyond any help that I could give him. The stallion's legs collapsed under him and he fell heavily on his side. Bright red bubbles frothed from the wound in his chest. I crouched beside him, lifted his noble head into my lap and waited with him until he died. Then I went back to the *Breath of Horus*.

"Damn you, Taita! Where have you been?" Tanus railed at me as I scrambled aboard. "There is a battle raging. The whole army cannot wait around while you have another of your famous daydreams."

He would not hear me out, but cut brusquely across my request for leave to follow the herd of runaway horses out into the desert.

"I want no truck with those unholy creatures. My only regret is that my men let them escape and did not slaughter the lot."

"Were you there on the plain of Abnub?" I do not usually indulge in loud argument, but his intransigence infuriated me.

"Did you not see the future charge at you? Do you not understand that without chariot and horse, you and this Egypt we know are finished?"

His officers were stiff with shock to hear a slave so address the Great Lion of Egypt, but I was past all restraint. "The gods have given you this wonderful gift. Three hundred horses. I will build you the chariots to go with them. Are you so blind that you cannot see it?"

"I have my ships!" Tanus roared. "These beasts are an abomination. I want no part of them. That is final." He stamped away.

"Final, is it?" I muttered. "We will see about that."

There have been very few occasions when I have not been able to have my own way with my mistress, and hers was now the highest authority in all Egypt.

First, therefore, I crafted a tiny working model of a chariot with miniature horses in the traces. Then I went to her that very evening.

Queen Lostris was enchanted by the model.

"You must go immediately and rescue these marvellous animals," she cried. "When you have them, build a squadron of chariots for my armies."

If Tanus had spoken to her before I had the chance to persuade her, I doubt that she would have given that order, and the history of our world would have been very different. As it was, Tanus was furious with my deception. It was fortunate that I had been ordered ashore by Queen Lostris, and was able to escape the full force of his wrath. I had only a few hours in which to gather a few helpers, and the chief of these was the most unlikely of them all.

I had never taken to Hui, the Shrike captured at Gallala. He had commanded one of the galleys that Tanus had scuttled at Abnub and was now without a ship. As soon as rumour of my mission spread through the fleet he sought me out.

"What do you know about horses?" I challenged him.

"I was once a groom, one who cares for horses," he replied. "As an infant my parents were killed, and I was captured by a tribe who were people of the horse. As a child I lived each day with those animals, and when I escaped it was upon the back of my favourite stallion. He died long before we reached the Euphrates."

Thus Hui was with me when a galley set us down upon the west bank. At Hui's suggestion we were equipped with light linen ropes and bags of crushed durra corn. By this time the tracks of the horses were two days old, but they had stayed together in a single herd and so had beaten a road that was easy to follow. Hui assured me that the herd instinct was strong among them, and that with such lush grazing along the river bank they would not have wandered far. We found the herd grazing peacefully before noon the second day.

Even after my experience with the wounded stallion, I was still rather nervous of these mysterious creatures. "It will surely be a difficult matter to capture them," I confided in Hui.

"I had heard that you have the reputation of being very clever." He grinned. "Clearly, it is a reputation that is ill-founded."

He showed me how to braid a halter from the ropes. We made a dozen of these, then each of us armed himself with a halter and a sack of crushed corn and started towards the herd. Following Hui's example, I strolled obliquely past the fringe of the group.

"Slowly now," Hui cautioned me when they flung up their heads and studied us with that peculiarly frank gaze. "Sit down."

We sank into the standing corn and remained motionless until the horses started feeding again. Then we moved forwards until they became restless once more.

"Down," Hui ordered, and when we were crouched in the corn one of the mares closest to us took a few steps towards me. She had a foal at her heels, a lovely little creature with pricked-up ears.

I gently scooped a handful of crushed cornmeal and held it out to the mare, who took another few paces towards me.

Even now I can remember the thrill that almost stopped the beating of my heart when she took the last pace up to me and delicately lowered her muzzle into my hand to taste the white meal.

"The halter," Hui reminded me softly, and I slipped it over her head as he had shown me. "She is yours," Hui said.

"And I am hers," I replied without thinking, but it was true.

As soon as the halter was on the mare the rest of the herd settled down and trustingly allowed Hui and me to walk freely among them.

Hui had selected and haltered one of the other mares. "Very well," he said at last. "We will mount up now." And to my utter astonishment he placed both hands on his mare's back, drew himself up and flung one leg over her, to sit astride her back.

I expected the mare to react violently, but instead she stood quietly until Hui dug his heels into her ribs, and then she started forwards obediently, first at a trot, then at a gallop. Hui guided her in patterns across the field and then circled back to where I stood.

"Come up, Taita. Try a gallop!"

I could see that he was expecting me to refuse, and it was that which made me overcome my reluctance.

My first attempt at mounting up was unsuccessful, but the mare stood stoically, and Hui laughed. "She has a great deal to teach you. You should call the poor animal 'Patience'."

I did not see the humour of it then, but the name stuck and the mare was Patience from then onwards.

"Pull yourself higher before you swing your leg over," Hui counselled. "And sit up straight!"

Thus Hui began my instruction, and Patience assisted me with her sweet and forgiving nature. I rode ahead on the mare, her foal at heel. The herd trailed after us compliantly, all 316 of them. Hui brought up the rear to sweep up stragglers.

With each league we covered, I became more confident and proficient upon Patience's back, and the rapport between us became firmer. And so I led my herd up the west bank of the river towards Thebes.

By the time we reached the city, Thebes was already lost and the whole east bank of the river as far as Dendera. King Salitis with his chariots had swept on, surrounded the city walls and stormed them. From the west bank, where Tanus now had his headquarters in the half-built Palace of Memnon, we could see the burnt and blackened roofs of the city across the river. Each day we watched the dust clouds of the Hyksos chariots as they prepared for the coming battle.

With his sadly depleted fleet, Tanus had thus far managed to hold the river line, and during my absence had beaten back another attempt by the Hyksos to get across the Nile in strength. However, our defences were thinly spread, and the crews of our galleys stood to arms every watch of the day and night. Tanus slept only when he could, which was not often.

Every night saw the arrival on the west bank of hundreds of refugees. They crossed the Nile in an odd assortment of rafts and small craft, all of them desperate to escape the Hyksos terror. Their numbers strained our resources, but fortunately the date palms were in full bearing, and the supply of fish from the river was inexhaustible.

My mistress had appointed me Master of the Royal Horses. I made Hui my deputy, and he managed to recruit 100 grooms, whom we later trained as our first chariot drivers.

It was no hardship for me to make time every day to visit our makeshift stables in the necropolis. Patience always came running to greet me. Often I was able to sneak Prince Memnon away from his mother and his nurses and I carried him into the stables on my shoulders. He squealed with excitement as soon as he saw the horses.

I also spent a great deal of my time in the armoury workshop of Pharaoh's funerary temple, where I had the assistance of some of the finest craftsmen in the world to help me build my first chariot.

It was here, while working on the design of these vehicles, that I conceived the long wooden staves sharpened at both ends, which were to become our first line of defence against the Hyksos chariots. Each of our infantrymen would carry ten of these in a bundle upon his back. The staves were planted in the earth at an angle, with the points at the level of the horses' chests. Our men would take up their positions behind this barrier and fire their arrows over them.

When I first demonstrated these to Tanus, he threw his arm round my shoulders for the first time since our quarrel over the horses, and said. "Well, at least you have not turned senile on me yet," and I knew that I had been at least partially forgiven.

My workmen and I at last completed the first chariot. It was so light that two charioteers could lift it between them and carry it over broken ground where the horses could not pull it.

By the time the embalmers in the funerary chapel had completed the ritual seventy days of royal mummification, we had built our first squadron of fifty chariots and had trained drivers for them.

SINCE WE HAD returned to the Palace of Memnon from our defeat at Abnub, my mistress had been occupied with the business of state. Long hours were spent with her ministers and advisers.

Now, on the seventieth day after his death, the mummification of Pharaoh was completed. My early efforts in preserving the king's body had been successful, and the grand master of the guild of embalmers had found no evidence of decay when he removed the king's corpse from the olive jar.

Laid out upon the diorite slab in the mortuary, he was wiped and dried, and his empty stomach was filled with linen pads soaked in resins and wax, and then sutured closed. Meanwhile, his internal organs had been desiccated and sealed in their alabaster jars.

For the remaining forty days, the body of the king was allowed to dry out, until it was dry as a stick of firewood. Then the first layer of pure white linen bandages was wound into place around his body, leaving his head and neck exposed. Under the bindings were laid amulets of gold and precious stones. The bandages were then soaked with resins that dried to a stony hardness.

My mistress and I went to the chapel together in the gloom of dawn, and we were witnesses as the linen sheet that covered the king was drawn aside. Pharaoh's head was miraculously preserved.

The eyes were closed and his expression was serene. The embalmers had painted his face, and he looked better in death than he had in life.

We waited while the embalmers bound up Pharaoh's head in the neat swathes of bandages, painted them with resin and moulded the bandages to the shape of his face beneath them.

Finally they placed over his blind bandaged face the first of the four funeral masks.

Then the wrapped mummy was placed in the golden inner coffin which was sealed, and this went into the second golden coffin with another death mask embossed upon the lid. There were seven coffins in all, including the massive stone sarcophagus standing upon the golden sledge, which waited ready to carry Pharaoh along the causeway to his tomb in the gaunt hills. But my mistress refused to give her sanction for this to happen.

"I have given my sacred vow. I cannot place my husband in a tomb that may be plundered by the Hyksos barbarians. Pharaoh will lie here until I am able to find a secure tomb in which he may lie through all eternity."

THE WISDOM of Queen Lostris's decision to delay the entombment was proved three nights later. The Hyksos made a determined effort to cross the river, and succeeded in making a beachhead near Esna on the west bank before Tanus could rush his galleys to the spot. He arrived before they could unload their chariots and destroyed their boats with the chariots still on board, and he then had almost 3,000 Hyksos stranded on our side of the river. Their horses, which had swum across in a mass, bolted away into the night when Tanus's troops made their first charge.

Without their chariots the Hyksos were on even terms with our troops, but they had no means of escape and fought with grim determination.

It was only by the wildest coincidence that Hui and I had brought a squadron of fifty chariots and fledgling charioteers to Esna the previous day on a training exercise.

I was exhausted after a long day of manoeuvring at high speed, and I was dead asleep when Hui shook me awake.

"There are fires burning on the bank of the river downstream," he told me. "And you can hear the sounds of battle. I think there is a fight going on down there."

I told him to rouse the camp and harness the horses. In the chilly drift of the river mist we trotted along the road two chariots abreast. I was driving the lead chariot, while Hui had command of the rear guard. Our fifty chariots had been reduced to thirty by the previous day's exercises, for I had not yet succeeded in perfecting my wheels. They had a tendency to fly to pieces when driven at speed. The track we were following took a turn to the left, and the field lay open before us. The sun was just above the horizon, and the ships of Tanus's squadron lay just offshore, crowding in close in an attempt to bring the archers on the decks in range of the Hyksos.

The stranded enemy regiment was making a stand in the centre of a field of knee-high green corn. They had formed a circle, facing outwards, shoulder to shoulder, with their shields locked together. As we came into view they had just repulsed another attempt by Tanus's troops to break their circle.

I am no soldier. I had intended simply to perfect my chariot, train the first squadron of charioteers and then hand it over to Hui. Yet now I heard my voice giving the order to deploy in arrowhead formation, as we had practised the previous day.

"Squadron will advance."

I had only to lift my left hand that held the traces and the horses bounded forwards and we went straight at the Hyksos circle.

Beneath me the chariot leaped and jolted over the lumpy ploughed earth, and ahead I saw the wall of Hyksos shields glittering in the early sunlight, drawing closer with every stride we took.

On either side of me, men were howling and cheering to hide their terror and I howled with them. We tore through the lines of retiring Egyptian infantry and they scattered out of our path.

On my right I saw Tanus's battle standard waving, and recognised his crested helmet. "What do you think of my cursed brutes now?" I yelled at him as we tore past.

The first rank of the enemy was now so close that I could see their eyes staring at me over their shields. Their arrows hissed round my ears—and then we were into them.

My horses leaped together into the barrier of shields and it shattered before our charge. On the footplate behind me my javelineer was making deadly practice.

The chariots behind us tore into the gap we had opened, and we hardly checked as we raced along, breaking out through the far side of the Hyksos circle, then wheeling round and coming back at them.

Tanus seized the moment and threw his infantry into the breach that we had torn open. The Hyksos formation disintegrated and the men panicked and ran for the river, where they came within range of the archers on the decks of our galleys.

Ahead of me there was an isolated pocket of Hyksos warriors still fighting. I swerved the chariot and drove at them at full gallop.

Before I reached them, my right wheel burst asunder, the chariot flipped over, I soared free and with a gut-tearing lurch fell back to earth. My head struck first, and my eyes filled with darkness.

I woke again under the awning on the deck of Tanus's flagship, lying on a sheepskin mattress with Tanus leaning over me. I tried to sit up, but my head ached abominably and I groaned, then clutched at his arm as it all came back to me. "Tanus, the enemy horses that swam across last night. I must have them."

"Don't worry—I have already sent Hui to gather them up," he assured me. "If I am to have five hundred of those contraptions of yours for my new chariot division, I will need a thousand of those cursed brutes to pull them. However, those newfangled wheels of yours are more dangerous than a regiment of Hyksos. I will not ride with you until you do something about them."

Tanus had quashed his pride and given in to me. My chariot squadron was at last to be part of the standing army. He would even ride with me, if I could fix my wheels. But what truly filled me with joy was that he had forgiven me and we were friends once more.

THE SUCCESS of my chariots at Esna, and the feeling of confidence that it instilled in us all, was short lived.

When Salitis swept through the Lower Kingdom, he had captured most of the fleet of the red pretender in the docks of Memphis. Soon he would recruit enough mercenaries in the ports along the eastern coast of the great sea to man several hundred of these galleys.

When our spies on the east side of the river opposite Asyut warned us of the approach of a fleet from the Delta, Tanus rushed his own ships northwards to meet them. The battle they fought lasted for almost a week before Tanus drove them back into the Nile Delta. However, Salitis had brought his transports up behind the screen of fighting galleys, had embarked two full regiments of horse and chariot, and had ferried them intact to our side of the river.

These regiments comprised nearly 300 of his fast war chariots, his elite divisions which he led himself. At last he had turned our flank. There was nothing to stop him now as his chariots came bowling southwards along our side of the river.

Queen Lostris called her war council when the news of the Hyksos crossing reached us in the Palace of Memnon. She addressed Tanus.

"Now that he is across the river, can you check the barbarian?"

"I can slow him down, perhaps," he replied. "But his chariots are so fast that he can swing round our positions. No, I cannot stop him."

Queen Lostris looked at me. "Taita, what about your chariots? Can they not give battle to the Hyksos?"

"Your Majesty, I have forty chariots that I can send in to meet Salitis. He has three hundred. My chariots are swifter than those of Salitis, but my men cannot match his in skill. And we dare not risk the horses. They are our only hope for eventual victory."

While we thus debated, another messenger arrived, this time from the south. While our fleet was busy at Asyut the barbarian had made another crossing at Esna. Two Hyksos regiments were across and they would be here in three days.

None of us spoke until Tanus sent the man away with orders that he be fed and cared for. When we were alone, Tanus said softly, "Salitis has four regiments across the river. Six hundred chariots. It is over."

"No!" My mistress's voice shook with the force of her denial. "The gods cannot desert this Egypt now. Our civilisation cannot perish." She turned to me. "Taita, I have not asked you before because I know how dearly it costs you. But I must ask you now to work the divination for me. I must know what the gods require of us."

I bowed my head in acquiescence.

THE SITE that I chose for the divination was the inner sanctuary of the shrine to Horus in the half-completed Palace of Memnon.

My mistress sat before me with Tanus at her side and they watched in fascination as I drank the potion to open the eyes of my soul.

I felt the drug in my blood grow stronger and the beat of my heart slow as the little death crept over me and I let it carry me away.

I heard my mistress's voice as though from a great distance. "What will become of the double crown? How can we resist the barbarian?"

The visions began to form before my eyes, and I was carried up into the days that were still to come.

When at last I returned from this far journey, I was trembling with the memories of the sights that I had seen.

My mistress and Tanus had stayed with me. My mistress was anxious. "Taita, are you all right? Speak to us. Tell us what you saw."

"There was a serpent." My voice still echoed strangely in my own ears. "A great green serpent that crawled through the desert. It shimmered green in the sunlight, though I couldn't see its head. It crawled through a strange land, in which lived tall naked men and strange beasts."

"Where were you? Where did you stand?"

"I was riding upon the back of the serpent," I answered. "But I was not alone. You were at my side, and Memnon with you. Tanus was on my other hand, and the serpent carried us all."

"The Nile! The serpent was the river!" she cried triumphantly. "You foresaw a voyage that we were making upon the river."

"At last I saw the heads of the serpent ahead of us. The body of the serpent was bifurcated, and on each branch was a head."

"Does the Nile have two branches?" my mistress wondered aloud.

"Let us hear the rest of what Taita has to tell us." Tanus stopped her speculation. "Continue, old friend."

"Then I saw the goddess," I went on. "She sat upon a high mountain. Both the heads of the serpent worshipped her."

"It was the goddess Hapi. The river god," my mistress whispered.

"What else did the vision show you?" Tanus demanded.

"The goddess said to us, 'Let my child come to me. I will make her strong so that she will prevail against the barbarian.' "

"I am the child of the river goddess," said my mistress simply. "At birth I was dedicated to her. Now she summons me, and I must go to the place where she dwells at the end of the Nile. But we will come back. This is my land, this is my city. I cannot leave them for ever. I will return to Thebes. This I swear. We shall return."

THERE WAS little time for us to make our preparations. Tanus placed Kratas in charge of half his available force and sent him to meet King Salitis, who was driving hard from the north, ordering him to delay the barbarian army as long as possible.

Tanus took the other half of our army south to fight another delaying battle against the Hyksos coming at us from Esna.

While they were thus engaged, my mistress was to embark our people and all their possessions aboard the remaining ships. The planning and execution of this evacuation fell squarely on my shoulders, but before I could turn my mind to this I had to take care of my horses, for they were the key to our survival.

With those animals that we had captured at Esna, we now had several thousand. I sent Hui and my charioteers south with the horses towards Elephantine.

Once the horses were dispatched I could turn my attention to the humans. The ships would be gunwale-deep under a great weight of humanity, but I had no choice. Still, I had some satisfaction in first embarking all the most useful and creative citizens. I chose men from every trade and profession, masons and weavers, coppersmiths and carpenters, tanners and sailmakers, scribes and artists, shipbuilders and carpenters, all leaders in their particular discipline. These I saw safely on board the waiting transports.

I had to be careful in choosing what cargo we would load. I gathered up the weapons and tools and raw materials that we would need to build up another civilisation in unknown lands, the seeds of every desirable plant in clay jars sealed with wax.

There was barely room for the living, but there still remained my mistress's promise to Pharaoh.

We opened the massive granite sarcophagus and lifted out the six inner coffins. The two innermost coffins we covered with a thick linen canvas shroud. The size and weight was thus reduced to acceptable proportions, and we stowed these two coffins in the hold of the *Breath of Horus*.

The bulk of Pharaoh's treasure was packed into cedarwood boxes, which were carried down to the wharf, and I distributed these so that every ship carried at least one chest. In this way, the risk that the entire treasure could be lost at a single stroke was reduced.

Before the last ship was loaded, the lookouts on the roof of the palace shouted that the dust clouds of the Hyksos chariots were in sight. Within the hour our exhausted troops began to pull back into the necropolis and to embark on the waiting galleys.

I met Tanus as he came up onto the causeway. "Queen Lostris and the prince?" he asked. "Have they gone aboard?"

"My mistress will not leave until all her people are on board the ships. She is waiting in the palace."

He looked at me aghast. "The enemy are pressing us hard. If she will not come on her own, we shall have to go and fetch her."

We pushed our way through the long lines of passengers that were streaming down to the dock to go aboard the ships.

At last we broke out of the crowd and ran to the palace gates. The halls and corridors were empty and deserted except for a few looters who were picking through the empty rooms.

The private quarters of the queen were unguarded and the door standing wide. We rushed through it. My mistress sat alone on the terrace with Prince Memnon on her lap. She was pointing out to Memnon the fleet of ships on the Nile below the terrace.

Queen Lostris stood up smiling when she saw us, and Memnon slid off her lap and ran to Tanus, who swung him onto his shoulder.

"Where are your slaves?" Tanus demanded.

"I sent them to the ships."

I seized her arm. "King Salitis will be here soon enough. Can we please go to the ships?"

We raced across the palace gardens to the stone staircase that led up onto the causeway. That was the shortest way to the temple dock. Ahead of us the last of the refugees had gone on board the ships, and beyond the stone battlements I could see their masts moving slowly down the canal towards the open river. We were the last persons left ashore, and we had still half a mile to cover before we reached the empty dock.

All of us stopped together, and watched the last galleys sail away. "What can we do now?" my mistress breathed.

"If we can reach the river bank, surely Remrem or Kratas will see us and send in a skiff to pick us up," I suggested.

Tanus agreed immediately. "This way! Follow me!"

I took my mistress's arm to help her along the causeway, but she was agile as a shepherd boy and ran at my side. Then suddenly I heard horses, and the squeal of chariot wheels, terrifyingly near.

"The Hyksos!" I said softly and we stopped in a tight little group. "It must be one of their advance scouting parties."

"It sounds like only two or three of their chariots," Tanus agreed. "But that is enough. We are cut off."

Suddenly the sounds of turning wheels stopped and we heard the horses blowing and stamping below us. Tanus made an urgent signal for silence.

Prince Memnon was not accustomed to restraint; he had also heard and recognised the sounds. "Horses!" he shouted. "I want to see the horses!"

There was an instant outcry below. Weapons rattled in their scabbards, then heavy footfalls pounded upon the stone staircase as a party of the enemy came dashing up onto the causeway. There were five of them and they rushed up at us with drawn swords.

One of them was taller than the rest. I did not recognise him at first, for he had grown a beard and decorated it in the Hyksos fashion, but then he shouted in that voice that I would never forget: "So it's you, young Harrab! I killed the old dog, and now I will kill his puppy!"

Despite his boast, Lord Intef did not advance to meet Tanus, but waved the Hyksos charioteers forward to do the job for him.

Tanus swept Prince Memnon from his shoulders and tossed him to me. "Run!" he ordered us. "I will buy you a little time here." He rushed the Hyksos while they were still bunched on the staircase and had no room to wield their swords.

With the child clutched to my chest I knew how futile was his command. Burdened as I was I would never reach the river bank. Instead I stepped to the parapet of the causeway and looked over. There were two Hyksos chariots parked directly below me, the horses blowing and stamping in the traces. Only one man had been left to hold them and he had not seen me on the causeway above his head.

Still clutching Memnon, I threw my legs over the parapet and pushed myself outwards. The prince shrieked with alarm as we dropped.

I might easily have broken a leg in the fall except that I landed neatly on the unsuspecting Hyksos's head. The impact broke his neck and he crumpled under us.

I scrambled to my feet with Memnon howling at this rough treatment. I dropped him into the cockpit of the nearest chariot and looked up at my mistress.

"Jump!" I shouted. "I will catch you!"

She flung herself over the edge, hit me squarely and knocked the wind out of my lungs. We went down in a heap together.

I scrambled up wheezing for breath, and dragged her to her feet. I shoved her roughly over the footplate of the chariot and shouted, "See to Memnon!" for the boy was still howling with anger and fright.

I had to scramble over them to reach the reins. "Hang on tight!"

The pair of horses responded instantly, and I wheeled the rig smartly under the wall. "Tanus!" I screamed. "This way!"

High above us he jumped up onto the parapet and balanced there easily, exchanging parry and thrust with the charioteers.

"Jump, Tanus, jump!" I yelled and he stepped out over the edge of the stone wall and let himself drop. With his cloak billowing around him he landed astride the back of the outside horse. His sword jerked out of his hand and clattered onto the hard earth.

"Hi-up!" I called to the pair and whipped the end of the reins round their hindquarters. They surged forwards into a full gallop across the open fields that led down to the river. We had half a mile to go to reach the bank, and I glanced over my shoulder.

Lord Intef and his men had rushed down the staircase and were climbing up into the other chariot. I cursed myself that I had not disabled it. Now Lord Intef was coming after us. His chariot was faster than the one I was driving, for Tanus's weight on the back of the offside horse was hampering its gallop.

I heard the shouts of the Hyksos charioteer closing with us, and the pounding of hoofs. I glanced back to see them not three lengths behind. Lord Intef was leaning out eagerly over the dashboard. "Taita, my old darling, do you still love me?" he shouted.

There was an irrigation ditch ahead of us, and I swerved to run alongside it for the sides were deep and sheer. The Hyksos chariot followed us, gaining on us with every stride, until Lord Intef no longer needed to shout to make himself heard.

"Lord Harrab, this is a pleasure. What shall we do with you, I wonder? First we will watch the soldiers entertain my daughter—" I tried to stop my ears to his filth, but his voice was insidious.

As the heads of the Hyksos pair drew level with our vehicle the archer on the footplate behind Intef nocked an arrow to his short recurved bow. At that range he could not miss hitting one of us.

It was only then that I realised the mistake the Hyksos driver had made. He had pushed his horses into the gap between us and the irrigation ditch. He had left himself no room to manoeuvre.

The archer lifted his bow and aimed at me. I was looking into his dark, implacable eyes over the barbed flint of the arrowhead.

The Hyksos horses were running level with the hub of my near-side wheel, and I swerved towards them. The flashing bronze knives that stood out of my wheel-rims spun towards the legs of the horses.

The Hyksos driver realised his error. His horses were trapped between the ditch and those cruel knives. At the same instant the Hyksos archer loosed his arrow, but my sudden swerve had beaten him. The arrow flashed like a beam of sunlight over my shoulder.

The other driver had tried to counter my swerve by turning away from me, but now his far wheel was running along the lip of the irrigation ditch, and the chariot lurched and teetered on the edge.

I gathered my horses and swung them again, turning into the other chariot. My wheel-blades hacked into the legs of the nearest horse, and the Hyksos chariot went over the edge of the ditch. The two passengers were thrown clear, but the driver was carried over and crushed beneath the capsized vehicle and the spinning wheels.

"Whoa!" I slowed my horses, and turned to look back. The Hyksos archer who had fired his arrow at me lay in a broken heap where he had been thrown, Lord Intef lay a little further from the edge of the ditch. At that moment he sat up and then pushed himself unsteadily to his feet. Suddenly all my hatred of him came back to me. A savage cry burst from my throat and I wheeled the horses in a tight circle until we were headed back towards the causeway.

Lord Intef stood directly in my path. I whipped the horses up into a gallop once more and the heavy wheels rumbled forwards. I aimed the chariot directly at him. His eyes were dull and bemused, but as I drove the horses down on him, suddenly they cleared.

"No!" he shouted and began to back away. But his dark gods had finally abandoned him. One of the spinning blades tore through his coat of mail and hooked into his belly. His screams were a sound that I wish never to hear again as long as I live.

I pulled up the horses and Tanus slid down off the back of his mount and came back to the chariot. He lifted my mistress and the prince down and held them close to his chest.

My mistress was weeping. "It's all right now." Tanus hugged her. "It's over now."

Prince Memnon was peering back over his mother's shoulder at the figure of his grandfather with all the fascination that children have for the macabre. Suddenly he piped up, "Is the nasty man dead now?"

"Yes, Mem," I told him softly. "He is dead."

I had to drive the horses hard along the river bank to catch up with our departing flotilla, but at last I drew level with Kratas's galley and he recognised us. Even across that wide stretch of water, his astonishment was apparent. Later he told me that he had believed we were safely aboard one of the leading ships of the flotilla.

I turned the horses loose before I left the chariot. Then we waded out to reach the small boat which Kratas sent in to pick us up.

THE HYKSOS would not let us go that easily. Day after day their chariots pursued our flotilla down both banks of the Nile as we fled southwards.

"Their horses cannot keep up this chase much longer," I told Tanus on the morning of the twelfth day.

"Don't be too smug about it. Salitis has the lure of the treasure of Pharaoh Mamose and the legitimate heir to the crown," Tanus replied simply. "We have not seen the last of the barbarian yet."

Confined as we were to the deck of the galley, Prince Memnon and I spent much time together sitting under the awning on the poop deck. There he listened avidly to my stories, or watched me design and whittle the first model of a new bow for our army, based on the Hyksos recurved type. He had by now learned the old trick of asking questions to keep my attention focused upon him.

"What are you doing now, Tata?"

"I am making a new bow."

"Yes, but why?"

"All right, I will tell you. Our own single-curve bows, apart from lacking the power, are too long to be used from the chariot." He listened gravely. From the very first he had been an exceptionally intelligent child, and under my influence he developed his gifts more swiftly than any other I had instructed, even my mistress.

For such a small boy he missed very little that was happening around him. It was no surprise to me when he was the first of any of the crew of the *Breath of Horus* to spot the figures far ahead of us on the right bank of the river.

"Horses!" he shrieked, and then moments later, "Look! It is Hui!"

I rushed up to where he stood in the bows and my heart soared as I realised that he was right. Hui had got the horses through to Elephantine. He had saved my horses.

WE WERE GIVEN a respite once we reached Elephantine. There had been no sign of the pursuing chariots for so many days that a new optimism spread through the fleet and the city.

Men started speaking of abandoning the flight south, and of remaining here below the cataracts to build up a new army with which to oppose the invader. I never allowed my mistress to be seduced by this confidence. I think by this time it was the adventure itself that had cast its spell over me, even more than the necessity of running from the Hyksos. I wanted to see where this great river that was our life began.

At the very first opportunity, Tanus and I went upriver to scout the cataracts, which extended for many miles. The water was low. All the islands were exposed, and the channels between them were so shallow that in places it was possible for a man to wade through. Even I was daunted by the task that lay ahead of us.

When we returned to the palace on Elephantine Island, Tanus and I went directly to report to Queen Lostris.

She listened to everything that we told her, and then shook her head. "I do not believe that the goddess has deserted us so soon."

She led us and all her court to the temple of Hapi on the south tip of the island. There she made a generous sacrifice to the goddess and we prayed all that night and asked for guidance.

As soon as the rays of the sun struck through the doors of the sanctuary, my mistress sent me down the shaft of the Nilometer. I had not reached the bottom step before I found myself ankle-deep in water. Although it was weeks early, the Nile had begun to rise. Hapi had listened to our prayers.

The very next day after this, one of our fast scouting galleys came speeding upriver on the wings of the north wind. The Hyksos were on the march again. They would be in Elephantine within the week.

Lord Tanus left immediately with his main force to prepare for the defence of the cataracts, leaving me to see to the embarkation of our people. This time we were able to avoid the chaos that had overtaken us at Thebes, and the fleet prepared to sail for the tail of the cataracts in good order. Fifty thousand Egyptians lined both banks of the river, weeping and singing psalms to Hapi and waving palm fronds in farewell as we sailed away.

Queen Lostris stood in the bows of the *Breath of Horus* with the little prince at her side, and both of them waved to the crowds on the bank as they passed slowly upriver. At twenty-one years of age my mistress was at the zenith of her beauty. Those who gazed upon her were struck with an almost religious awe. That beauty was echoed in the face of the child at her side, who held the crook and flail of Egypt in his small determined hands.

"We will return," my mistress called to them, and the prince echoed her. "We will return. Wait for us. We will return."

The legend that would sustain our oppressed land through all the long, bitter years of the Hyksos tyranny was born that day on the banks of the river.

Book Four

WHEN WE reached the tail of the cataracts the following noon, the rock-studded gorge had been transformed into a smooth green chute of rushing waters, which were now high enough to allow our ships through without grounding.

Tanus himself managed the ships, while Hui and I managed the shore party. The heaviest linen lines were laid out upon the bank, and our horses were harnessed into ten teams of ten, 100 horses. In addition to the horses, we had almost 2,000 men upon the secondary ropes and the guide lines. At every dangerous turn of the river we stationed other men, all armed with long poles to fend the hulls off the rocks as they were dragged through. Tanus and I arranged a system of signals between the ships and the shore party that functioned more smoothly even than I had hoped.

The *Breath of Horus* was the first to make the attempt. We hauled her forwards and she thrust her bows into the first chute of smoothly racing waters. The green flood piled up against her bows, but its thrust was unable to overcome our determination and the strength of 2,000 men and 100 straining horses. We dragged the

Breath of Horus up the first rapid and we cheered when she glided into the deep green pool at the head. But there were six miles still to go. We changed the men and horses and dragged her bows into the next stretch of broken water, with death and disaster swirling around every rock. But the ropes held and the men and horses plodded on.

My mistress walked along the bank beside the sweating teams, and her laughter and banter gave them fresh purpose. She sang the working songs with them. I joined with her in the choruses, and the men laughed and hauled on the ropes with renewed strength. When at last we broke out into the deep, unruffled flow of the main river above the rapids, the working chant of the boatmen turned to a hymn of praise to Hapi.

It had taken us a full day to bring the *Breath of Horus* up the rapids. But we became more expert, and within the following week we were making the transit in half that time, and we had five or six vessels in the gorge simultaneously.

There were over a hundred galleys moored along the bank in the quiet, deep green reach of the Nile above the rapids when the Hyksos fell upon us once more. King Salitis had been delayed by his sack of the city of Elephantine, whose citizens had long held out against the Hyksos in order to give our flotilla a chance to complete the transit.

Of course, it could not last indefinitely, and when at last some poor soul revealed under torture that we had continued upriver with Pharaoh's treasure, Salitis harnessed up his horses yet again and came storming after us into the gorge of the cataracts. However, Tanus was well prepared to meet him, and the terrain was our greatest ally. At every turn of the river rose high cliffs, each of them a natural fortress for us to exploit.

In the confines of the gorge the chariots were unable to manoeuvre, but there was no alternative; they were forced to come at us in single file along the narrow river bank.

As the Hyksos vanguard came up the gorge, they were met with a downpour of arrows from stone-walled redoubts on the high ground above them. Then, when they dismounted from their chariots and went forwards to clear the stone barriers that had been placed across the track, Kratas yelled the order and wedges were knocked from under rock slides balanced on the lip of the precipice. The avalanches came rolling down upon the Hyksos, sweeping men and horses and chariots off the bank into the river.

Their losses in men and horses were frightful, while we were almost unscathed. Before he had fought halfway up the gorge, King Salitis was forced to abandon the pursuit, leaving the path strewn with the wreckage of their chariots and abandoned equipment.

We watched Salitis out of sight. In my heart I knew that he would not come after us again. Hapi had fulfilled her promise, and offered us her protection once more.

Then we turned and followed the pathway back to where the flotilla was moored.

THE MASONS had finished work on the obelisk. I had marked out the proportions and the shape of it upon the mother rock before the masons had made their first cut. Now it was set above the last wild stretch of the cataract on the summit of the bluff overlooking the scene of our triumph, and all our people had gathered below it as Queen Lostris dedicated the stone to the goddess of the river.

She read aloud the inscription that the masons had engraved upon the polished stone. "I, Queen Lostris, regent of Egypt and widow of Pharaoh Mamose, mother of the crown prince Memnon, who shall rule the two kingdoms after me, have ordained the raising of this monument.

"This is the mark of my vow to the people of this Egypt, that I shall return to them from the wilderness whence I have been driven by the barbarian. Let this stone stand immovable as the pyramid until I make good my promise to return."

Then, in sight of all the people, she placed the Gold of Valour upon the shoulders of Tanus and Kratas and Remrem and Astes, all those heroes who had made possible the transit of the cataract.

The following morning we went back on board the *Breath of Horus* and turned our bows once more towards the south.

WE FOUND that the river had changed its character. It was no longer the broad, serene presence that had sustained us all our lives. This was a sterner, wilder being. It was narrower and deeper, and the land on each side was steeper and more rugged.

As the weeks wore on, we saw little sign of any human presence. We were anxious to make our first contact with the tribes of Cush, for we needed slaves. Our civilisation was based on the work of slaves, and we had been able to bring very few of them with us from Egypt. All wealth can be counted in four commodities, land and gold, slaves and ivory. If we were to grow strong enough to return and drive the Hyksos from Egypt, then we must discover this wealth.

Queen Lostris sent out her gold-finders into the hills along the river as we passed. They climbed up through the gorges, scratching and digging in every likely spot, and the royal huntsmen went with them to search for game with which to feed our multitudes. They searched also for the first sign of those great grey elephants who carried the precious teeth of ivory in their monstrous heads.

The months passed, and below our keels the river began to dwindle as the inundation abated.

At night Memnon and I sat up on deck as late as his mother would allow, and together we studied the stars that illuminated the firmament of the sky with a milky radiance. By watching the heavenly bodies I was able to determine that the river had begun to veer towards the west.

The second cataract was a series of rapids more extensive and formidable than those we had already negotiated. Over a vast area, the stream of the Nile was split by several massive islands and hundreds of smaller ones. It was low water now and at most places the bed of the river was exposed. A maze of rock-strewn canals and branches extended for miles ahead of us.

We could not attempt a transit of these rapids until the next inundation in many months' time, so our farmers went ashore and cleared land to plant the seeds that we had brought with us. Within days the seeds had sprouted, and in the hot sunlight the plants seemed to grow taller under our eyes.

Within a few short months the durra corn was ready to be harvested, and we were gorging on the fruits and vegetables that we had missed so much since leaving Egypt.

I for my part had at my disposal the timber from those trees we had felled on the islands. I was able to experiment with these. There was an acacia whose wood was resilient and strong. It made the finest chariot wheels of any material which I had so far tested, and so I put my carpenters to work on building new chariots.

At the same time I was able to complete the first successful recurved bow upon which I had been working since we left Elephantine. Tanus finally agreed to shoot the bow at a series of targets that I had erected. After he had shot twenty arrows he said little, but I could see that he was astonished by its range and its accuracy. I knew him so well. He was a conservative to the marrow of his bones. I did not pester him for an opinion but let him come to it in his own time.

ONE DAY, when I returned to the fleet from a hunting expedition with the prince, Queen Lostris was waiting for me. "When did you and I last go fishing together?" she asked. "Fetch your fishing spears, Taita. We will take one of the skiffs. Just the two of us on the river the way we used to in the old days."

I knew that we would do little fishing. She wanted me alone on the water where we could not be overheard.

I paddled downstream until the bend of the river and the high rocky bluff hid us from the fleet. At last she looked up at me, and her eyes were filled with a strange mixture of joy and worry.

"Taita, I think I am going to have another baby."

I can think of no reason why this statement should have surprised me. After all, every night since we had left Elephantine she and the commander of her army had been locked in secret conclave, while I kept guard at the door of her cabin. Nevertheless, I was so alarmed that it was some moments before I could regain my voice.

"My lady, did you use the effusion of herbs that I prepared for you?"

"At times I did, but at others I forgot." She smiled. "It is rather serious, isn't it, Taita?"

"Rather serious? Oh, I think that is the wrong word. If you give birth to a bastard, then you will be obliged to relinquish the regency. That is the law. Lord Merkeset would be the next in line as regent, but there will be covert warfare among all the nobility for the position. The prince would be in great danger—" I broke off, and shuddered at the prospect.

"There must be something that you can do?" She looked at me with that blind trust that angered me.

"There is something, but you will not agree to it."

"If you care anything for me you will not even suggest it." She had understood me immediately, and recoiled as though I had struck her. "I would rather die myself than kill this miracle of love."

"Then, Your Majesty, there is nothing more that I can suggest."

She smiled at me with such sublime trust and confidence that it took my breath away. "I know you will think of something, my dear Taita. You always do."

And so I had a dream.

I RELATED my dream before a full session of the council of state called by the regent of Egypt.

Queen Lostris and Prince Memnon were seated upon the throne, the members of the council below her. Lord Merkeset and the nobility represented the secular arm of the state. The priests represented the sacred arm. Lord Harrab and his officers stood for the military.

I stood below the throne and faced this distinguished gathering.

"Your Majesties." I made the low salutation to the throne. "Your Majesties, last night I dreamed a strange and wonderful dream which I feel it is my duty to relate. I beg your leave to speak."

Queen Lostris replied graciously, "Every person in this company is aware of the sacred gift that you have. The prince and I know that you are able to see into the future, and to divine the wishes of the gods. I command you now to speak of these mysteries."

I bowed again and turned to face the council.

"Last night I slept at the door to the royal cabin as is my duty. Queen Lostris lay alone upon her couch, and the prince slept in his alcove beyond her bed. In the third watch of the night I awoke, and there was a strange light glowing throughout the ship."

My audience stirred with interest. They all loved a good story.

"Then I heard footsteps echoing through the hull, slow footsteps such as never were made by mortal man." I paused dramatically. "These sounds came from the hold of the galley where the gold coffin of Pharaoh Mamose lies awaiting burial. These footsteps drew closer to where I lay at the queen's door. The heavenly glow of light grew stronger, and while I trembled a figure appeared before me. It was the shape of a man, but it was not human, for it glowed like the full moon and its face was a divine reincarnation of the king."

They were rapt and silent, not a man stirred. I searched their faces for any sign of incredulity, but I found none.

Then suddenly the prince cried out high and clear, "It was my father. It was Pharaoh!"

They took up the cry. "It was Pharaoh. May he live for ever."

"Pharaoh came towards me and I could neither move nor utter a sound. He passed me and entered the cabin of Her Gracious Majesty, Queen Lostris, while the queen still slept."

There was still no sign of disbelief. "When Pharaoh returned from the sleeping queen, he looked upon me and he spoke thus."

I spoke now in the voice of Pharaoh Mamose. "I have endowed the queen with my godhead. She has become one with me and the gods. I have impregnated her with my divine seed. She, who has known no man but me, will bear a child of my royal blood. This will be a sign that she enjoys my protection and that I watch over her still.

"Then the king passed back through the ship and entered once more his golden coffin where he now rests. That was all my vision."

"May Pharaoh live for ever," shouted Lord Tanus, just as I had coached him, and the cry was taken up.

That night when I prepared to retire, my mistress called me to her. "Your vision was so vivid and you told it so well that I shall not be able to sleep lest Pharaoh come again. Guard the door well."

"I dare say there may be one bold enough to disturb your slumber, but I doubt that it will be Pharaoh. If some rascal does come to take advantage of your loving nature, what should I do?"

"Sleep soundly, dear Taita, and stop your ears." Her cheeks glowed pink in the lamplight as she blushed.

The Nile flooded once again, reminding us that another year had passed. We gathered in our herds. We packed the chariots on the open decks of the galleys. We rolled up the tents and stowed them in the holds. Finally, we laid out the ropes upon the bank and put every able-bodied man and horse into the traces.

It took us almost a month of heartbreaking labour to make the transit of this fearsome cataract. We lost sixteen men drowned, and five galleys broken. But at last we were through, and we set sail upon the smooth flow of the river above the rapids.

As the weeks turned to months, the Nile described a slow and majestic bend beneath our keels, until at last we found that we had made a vast loop out into the west and were now heading back full circle into the east.

Since leaving Elephantine I had charted the course of the river, and when it seemed that we were headed back towards Elephantine and the first great cataract, I showed my findings to Tanus and the queen. Many nights we sat late in the royal cabin discussing the course of the river and how it would affect our plans to return to Egypt.

"There might be a way to cut across the bight of the river, and to halve the distance of our return journey," I pointed out to her.

"Keep your charts well, Taita. I trust you to find the easy way home for us, when the time comes."

So our river caravan journeyed onwards. We observed the festivals and prayed to our gods. We feasted and fasted in the correct season, and danced and sang and studied the sciences. I held lessons for the older children and Memnon was my prize student.

Before the year was out we came upon the third cataract. Once again we went ashore and cleared the land and planted our crops, while we waited for the Nile to rise and help us through. And it was here at the third cataract that another joy came to fill my life.

In a linen tent upon the bank of the river, I attended my mistress in her labour and brought forth into this world the Princess Tehuti, the acknowledged daughter of the long-dead Pharaoh Mamose.

The river rose at last and we made the transit of the third cataract. We sailed on, and before the year was out it was necessary for me to dream another of my dreams. For my mistress had once more suffered a pregnancy that could only be explained by supernatural means. The ghost of Pharaoh had been on the prowl again.

While we waited for the waters of the Nile to rise, we planted our crops on the cleared islands and the river banks. However, the lie of the land was steeper than at the other sites lower downriver. It was more difficult to raise the water with our traditional shadoofs to irrigate the crops, and I foresaw a time of famine, unless we were able to bring more water to the fields.

I do not know what made me think of the wheel for this purpose, except that the science of the wheel had by this time become an obsession in my life. I was still plagued by the occasional bursting of our chariot wheels, and I had heard from one of the priests of Hapi that some varieties of timber could be made more resilient by soaking them in water, so I was driven to experiment with this idea.

As we were lowering one of the chariot wheels into the river for this purpose, the current playing in the rim began to turn the wheel on its hub. I watched this idly, but would have thought no more about it had not Memnon been with me.

"It would go faster, Tata, if it had paddles fixed around the rim," he said, using his pet name for me, and I stared at him in wonder.

He was but ten years old, yet he had a fresh and enquiring eye.

By the time the full moon came round again we had built a wheel that was driven by the river and which lifted the water in a series of clay jars and spilled it into a canal at the top of the high Nile bank.

Thus the fields of durra soon grew dense and green in the loamy soil on the high banks, and the ears of golden corn drooped heavily in the bright Nile sunlight.

This was not the only harvest that we gathered in at the fourth cataract. Queen Lostris gave birth to another little royal princess. It was strange that Princess Bekatha was born with a cap of golden red curls. Her ghostly father, Pharaoh Mamose, had been swarthy and her mother's hair was dark. No one could think of any reason for this aberrant coloration, but all agreed how pretty it was.

Princess Bekatha was two months old when the Nile began to rise once more, and we made our preparation for the transit of the fourth cataract. By now we were experienced in what had become an annual labour to beat the rapacious river.

WE HAD NOT travelled more than a month before we realised how our fortunes had changed. We had come through the worst, the desert was behind us, and the broad smooth flow of the river turned south once more, carrying us into a land such as none of us had ever seen.

It was here that for the first time many of our company witnessed the miracle of rain. Although of course I had seen it in the Lower Kingdom, they had never seen water fall from the sky. The rain beat down into our upturned faces, while thunder rolled across the heavens and lightning blinded us.

These copious rains engendered a new and exciting landscape. On either bank of the Nile, as far as we could see, stretched a broad savannah grassland, rich with grazing for our horses. For antelope too, gazelle, giraffe, rhinoceros and buffalo.

This was not the only blessing that the goddess had bestowed. Wood was to us Egyptians a rare and treasured commodity. Each stick of it had to be carried in by ship or on beasts of burden, from far lands. Now, wherever we looked we saw great trees, growing in lofty groves with broad grassy spaces between the majestic trunks.

This was not the only treasure we found in this legendary land of Cush that we had reached at last. I saw them first in the distance and thought that they were monuments of grey granite on the yellow grass plain.

Then, as I watched, these great rocks began to move.

"Elephants!" I had never seen one before, but they could be nothing else. The cry was taken up by those on the deck around me. "Elephants! Ivory!" Wherever we looked the vast herds stood.

"Unload the chariots from the holds!" Tanus roared. "Put the horses into the traces! The hunt is on!"

Tanus was bristling with impatience to go out against this new quarry. As soon as the first division of fifty chariots was ready, he gave the order to mount up. If I had known the danger that we were riding into, I would never have allowed Prince Memnon to mount the footplate behind me as we drove out on our first elephant hunt. To us they appeared such docile brutes, slow and clumsy.

We shouted challenges to the other drivers, and made our wagers on the outcome of the hunt as the long columns of chariots rolled out through the groves along the river bank. Ahead of us was a small herd of elephants. I studied them as we approached. They fanned out enormous ears and turned to face us. They lifted their trunks, and I guessed that they were taking up our scent. There were small calves with them, and the mothers gathered them into the centre of the herd and stood guard over them.

"These are all females," I called over my shoulder to Tanus on the footplate. "Their ivory is small and of little value."

"You are right." Tanus pointed over my shoulder. "But look beyond them. Those two must surely be bulls. Look at their tusks."

I gave the signal to the chariots that followed us and we veered away from the cows and calves, towards the two great bulls.

"That one on the right is the biggest," cried Memnon as we approached. "We should take him first."

"You heard the royal command," Tanus laughed. "We will take the one on the right. Let Kratas have the other."

So I raised my fist and gave the hand command that split the column into two files.

Kratas wheeled away on our left, while we ran on straight at the huge grey beast that confronted us.

"Hi-up!" I called, and the horses opened up into a gallop. We both expected the huge animal to run from us. No other game we had ever hunted had stood to receive our charge.

"His head is so big, it will make a fine target," Tanus exulted as he nocked an arrow. "I will kill him with a single shaft."

We were right on the bull now, but still he stood his ground. He threw up his trunk and loosed a blast of sound that deafened us. The horses shied wildly, so that I was thrown against the dashboard. For a moment I lost control of the team, and we swerved away.

Then the bull squealed again, and he ran directly at us in a furious charge. He was swifter than any horse, and was on us before I could get the horses under control again.

Tanus got off a single arrow. It struck the bull in the centre of his forehead but he did not even check or swerve.

Hui in the second chariot of our line saved us, for we were defenceless against the old bull's fury. Hui came in from the side and his archer fired an arrow into the bull's cheek a hand's-breadth below the eye, and that pulled his attention from us.

The elephant wheeled to chase after Hui, but his horses were at full gallop and raced clean away. The next chariot in line was not so fortunate. The driver lacked Hui's skill, and his turn away was inept. The bull lifted his trunk high and struck the nearside horse across the back. The horse went down and dragged its team-mate with it.

As the elephant placed one forefoot on the fallen charioteer, the next chariot in line tore in, distracting the bull from his victim.

I pulled up my horses, and we stared back aghast at our shattered squadron.

There were broken chariots scattered across the field, for Kratas out on the left had fared no better than we had. The two great bull elephants bristled with arrow shafts, yet the wounds had not weakened them but seemed only to have aggravated their fury.

Kratas raced up alongside us and shouted across at us. "This is hot work! We have lost eight chariots in the first charge."

"Better sport than you expected, Captain Kratas," Prince Memnon yelled back at him.

He would have done better to keep his opinion to himself, for up until that moment we had forgotten about the boy in the confusion. Now, however, Tanus rounded on him.

"As for you, my lad, you have had enough sport for one day," he said firmly, and at that moment an empty chariot cantered by, its crew having been thrown from the cockpit.

"Catch those horses!" Tanus ordered, and when the empty chariot was brought back to us he told the prince, "Take that chariot back to the beach and wait there for our return."

"My Lord Tanus," Prince Memnon drew himself to his full height, reaching as high as his father's shoulder, "I protest."

"None of your royal airs with me, young man. Go back and protest to your mother, if you must." And with that he lifted the prince and dropped him into the vacant cockpit of the other vehicle. Then Tanus turned his back on him. We put the boy out of our minds.

"Gathering ivory is not quite as easy as picking up mushrooms," I remarked. "We will have to think up a better plan."

"We will go in again and try an arrow through the ribs," Tanus growled. "If they have no brain in their skulls, then surely they have lungs and a heart."

I gathered up the reins and lifted the heads of the team. "I'll go at him head-on," I told Tanus, "and then turn out to give you a broadside shot into his ribs."

I put the horses into a trot, and then gradually pushed up their speed. Dead ahead of us our bull saw us coming and let out another of those terrible squeals that chilled my blood, and the horses flicked their ears and shied.

The bull charged to meet us, a terrible sight in his rage, but I held my team steady, not yet pushing them to the top of their speed. Then, as we came together, I swung out hard left, and at a range of less than twenty paces Tanus fired three arrows in quick succession. All went in behind the shoulder, finding the gaps between the ribs. The bull squealed again, but this time in mortal agony. I looked back and saw him standing in our dust, blood spurting from the end of his trunk.

"Good work, Tanus!" I shouted. "You have hit his lungs."

"We have found the trick of it now," Tanus exulted. "Take us back. I will give him one through the heart."

Though he was mortally struck, the tenacious old bull was still far from death. The magnificent beast charged to meet us once again with a courage that filled me with reverence.

Just then the offside wheel of the chariot burst. There was a giddy moment as I somersaulted through the air, but the earth was soft and I rode the shock.

I came up on my feet unhurt and with my wits still all about me.

Tanus had not come through as well as I had. He was sprawled flat out and unmoving.

I made sure that the bull was turned away from me, then I ran to where Tanus lay. "Up! Get up!" I croaked in a hoarse whisper.

I tried to lift him to his feet, but he was a heavy man and only half conscious.

Desperately I looked back at the bull. He was moving away from us now.

I draped Tanus's arm round my neck and with all my strength I managed to lever him to his feet. He hung against me unsteadily and took only one pace before he gave a groan and fell back upon me. "My leg," he grunted. "Can't move. Knee twisted."

The elephant lifted his head and shook it. He had heard Tanus's voice and he swung round, ears flaring. He stared full at us, and we were less than fifty paces from him.

I dragged Tanus with me, forcing him to hop on his good leg beside me. The bull saw the movement and charged straight for us.

As tall as a cliff and black as death he came. I could see every crease in the folded skin round his eyes which glared with such rage that my heart turned to a stone in my chest. I stood and watched death bear down upon us, and could make no move to avoid it.

"Tata!" A child's voice rang in my head. "Tata, I am coming."

Across the open ground a chariot was tearing towards us at full gallop, the driver's head barely showing above the dashboard.

"Mem!" I cried. "Go back! Turn back!"

The wind blew his hair out in a cloud behind his head, and he came on without a pause or check.

"I'll thrash the little ruffian for disobeying me," growled Tanus as he teetered on one leg. We had both of us forgotten our own danger.

"Whoa!" Memnon cried and brought the team down from a full gallop, cutting in front of us, shielding us for an instant from the charging bull, and as the chariot spun about there was a moment when it was standing still. It was beautifully done.

I heaved my shoulder up under Tanus's armpit and threw him sprawling on the footplate. The very next instant I hurled myself headlong on top of him.

"Go, Mem!" I shouted. "Go for all you're worth!"

"Hi-up!" Memnon screamed. "Yah hah!"

The chariot careered away with the horses driven to full flight by the enraged squeals of the charging bull close behind.

And then suddenly it was all over. One of the arrows buried in his chest had worked in deeper and sliced open the heart. The elephant died in his tracks, coming down with a crash that jarred the earth.

Memnon pulled in the horses, and Tanus and I stumbled out of the carriage and stood staring at the mountainous carcass. Tanus clung to the side of the chariot to favour his damaged leg, and slowly turned back to look at the boy. "By Horus, I have known some brave men in my time, but none of them better than you, lad," he said, then he lifted Memnon in his arms and hugged him to his chest.

WE GATHERED on the deck of the galley, those closest to the queen and the commanders of all the divisions of her army. The standard-bearers stood to attention behind the throne, and the trumpeters blew a fanfare as the prince knelt before the queen.

"My beloved subjects!" The queen spoke out clearly. "Noble officers of my council, generals and officers of my army, I commend to you the crown prince, Memnon, who has found favour in my sight." She smiled down on the eleven-year-old boy.

"For his courageous conduct in the field I command that he be received into the regiment of the Blue Crocodile Guards with the rank of subaltern, and I bestow upon him the Gold of Valour."

I felt tears coming on as the people cheered my beautiful prince, but I fought them back with an effort. In the same manner as his parents, the boy had a way with the affections and loyalties of men. Every officer of the Blues came forward at the end to salute the prince and embrace him as a comrade-in-arms.

That evening as we drove together along the bank of the Nile in the sunset, Memnon suddenly reined in the horses and turned to me. "I have been called to my regiment. I am a soldier at last, so you must make me my own bow now, Tata."

"I will make you the finest bow that any archer has ever drawn," I promised him.

THERE WAS another cataract across the river, the fifth and what would prove to be the penultimate that we would encounter upon our voyage. While we waited for the Nile to rise again, we planted our crops as usual. We also sent our chariots southwards across the savannah, to pursue the elephant herds.

These sage creatures learned their lessons swiftly, and very often now the hunting expeditions returned after being out for many weeks without having gathered a single tusk. However, those chariots ranging southwards did not return entirely empty-handed. They found something even more valuable to us than ivory. They found men.

We had expected to come across people as soon as we passed the first cataract. For centuries the land of Cush had produced slaves, captured by their own people and carried down with other commodities of trade to the outposts of our empire. I still cannot explain, therefore, why we had not found people before this.

However, now that we had finally caught up with them, Tanus ordered a full-scale expeditionary force to be sent out immediately.

The first villages we came across were on the river bank, three days' travel above the cataract. Tanus sent scouts forward to reconnoitre and then in the dawn we surrounded them with a single swift rush.

The people that stumbled out of the huts were too dazed and shocked to offer any resistance.

"A fine catch!" Tanus was delighted as we looked them over. The men were tall, dark-skinned and lean, and towered over most of the men in our ranks. Their women were strong and healthy. Yet they were the most primitive people I had ever encountered. They had forged no metal artefacts. Their weapons were wooden clubs and sharpened sticks. They planted no crops, but lived on fish they caught and on the herds of stunted, long-horned cattle which were their most prized possessions.

The first raid gave us no warning of the true warlike nature of the Shilluk, which was what these people were called. It had all gone too easily, and we were unprepared for what followed when we swept down on the next straggle of villages.

By this time the Shilluk had been alerted, and they were ready to meet us. Armed only with wooden clubs, they came in their hordes against our chariots, with a courage that surpassed belief.

In the end we ran them to exhaustion with the chariots, and only when they fell to their knees could the slave masters put the ropes on them.

Tanus selected the best of them for new infantry regiments. He armed them with shields and bronze-tipped spears, and his sergeants drilled them in all the classic evolutions of war. We learned swiftly to integrate these tactics with those of the chariots.

ONCE WE HAD brought the fleet up through the fifth cataract, the entire land of Cush lay open to us.

Soon we reached a wide river, which we named the Atbara, that joined the main flow of the Nile from the east. Queen Lostris dispatched an expedition of gold seekers, with Shilluk guides, to follow the Atbara as far as they were able. The fleet sailed on southwards, hunting and slave raiding along the way.

I worried to see how often these days Prince Memnon's chariot was at the head of one of these flying columns. I felt he should spend more time with me studying his scrolls, but when I protested to Tanus, he merely laughed. "If he is to wear the double crown one day he must learn to spurn danger and lead men." My mistress agreed with him.

At least I had my two little princesses. Tehuti and Bekatha grew more enchanting each day, and I was their slave in more than name alone. I think that this was the most happy period in my life. I felt that I was at the centre of my family, and solid in their affections.

We encountered one last cataract on our voyage southwards, but this transit proved easier than all the others. And so at last we reached the mystical confluence of the two mighty rivers that between them became the Nile.

"This is the place that Taita saw in his vision. This is the sacred site of the goddess," Queen Lostris declared. "We have completed our voyage. I name this place Qebui, the Place of the North Wind, for it is that wind which blew us here. It remains only for us to find a site for the tomb of my husband, Pharaoh Mamose. Once the tomb is built and Pharaoh sealed in it, then my vow will have been fulfilled and it will be time to return in triumph to Egypt."

My mistress chose me as the one to seek out the site of the royal tomb, and ordered Prince Memnon to escort me on this expedition with his squadron of chariots.

At fourteen years of age the prince was placed in command of the expedition. This was not exceptional. There have been pharaohs in our history who commanded great armies in battle when they were no older.

The prince took his responsibilities seriously, and we deliberated at great length as to which direction we should follow in our search for the ideal site for the king's tomb.

Where we stood now was the meeting point of two rivers. The western branch was slow and yellow, but greater in volume than the other. The eastern branch was a murky grey-blue, an overbearing flood.

"Which river must we follow, Tata?" Memnon demanded, and I sent for the Shilluk guides.

"The yellow river comes out of a vast and pestilent swamp," the Shilluk told us. "No man can enter there. It is a place of fever where a man might lose his way and wander for ever."

"What of the other river?" we asked.

"The dark river comes out of the sky, down cliffs of stone that rise up into the clouds. No man can climb the dreadful gorges."

"We will follow the dark left-hand fork," the prince decided. "In those rocky places we will find a resting place for my father."

So we journeyed into the east until we saw the mountains rise on the horizon, a blue rampart so formidable as to surpass anything that we had ever seen. We ventured no further than the foothills, for there we found a hidden valley with vertical sides, and for twenty days the prince and I explored this wild place until at last we stood before a black cliff face and Memnon spoke quietly.

"This is where my father's earthly body will rest for all eternity." He stared up at the sheer stone. "It is as though I can hear his voice speaking in my head. He will be happy here."

So I surveyed this place and marked out the cliff, driving bronze pegs into the cracks in the rock, setting out the direction of the entrance passage for the masons who would come to begin this work.

MY MAJOR duty now, laid upon me by my mistress, was the construction of Pharaoh's tomb. Although I had 8,000 slaves to carry out the task, and the unstinted assistance of all our finest craftsmen and artists, I knew it would take many years to complete the elaborate mausoleum which my mistress insisted we build.

When I was not up in the mountains working at the tomb, I spent my time by the river, where a myriad different tasks and pleasures awaited me. These ranged from the education of my two little princesses to devising new military tactics with Tanus and the prince.

Of all these pleasures, none for me could compare with the hours that I was able to spend with my mistress. In this her thirty-third year she was in the high summer of her beauty, enhanced by her poise. She had become a queen indeed, a woman without peer.

All her people loved her but none of them as much as I did. It was my pride that she still needed me and relied upon my advice.

I should have been contented, but a new wanderlust had come to plague me. Whenever I paused from my labours at Pharaoh's tomb, and looked up, the mountains beckoned me. I began to make short excursions into their lonely gorges, often alone but sometimes with Hui or some other companion.

Hui was with me when I first saw the herds of wild ibex. They were of a species we had never seen before, twice as tall as the wild goats that we knew from the Nile valley, and within the month Lord Tanus arrived at the valley of the king's tomb with his bow over his shoulder and Prince Memnon at his side.

As for myself, I welcomed the chance to explore those fascinating highlands in such company. We had meant to venture only as far as the first line of peaks, but when we climbed to their crest we were presented with a breathtaking vista and were lured on deeper.

We saw other mountains against the sky that were shaped like flat-topped anvils and were the tawny colour of lions. The Nile climbed with us up through precipitous valleys and dark gorges that churned its waters to gleaming white. And we were camped in one of these gorges when the mountains loosed their full fury upon us.

It began to rain, then a cold wind raced down the valley and chilled our bodies and our spirits. We huddled together in dismay. The rain came down upon us as though we stood under one of the cataracts of the Nile when the river was in full flood.

Then, above the sound of the falling rain, I heard a new sound, as down the narrow valley where we lay swept a wall of grey water. It stretched from cliff to cliff and carried everything before it.

I was caught up in it and tumbled end over end. I felt life being beaten out of me as I was thrown against the rocks. Darkness overwhelmed me.

I have a vague recollection of hands dragging me from the floods. I smelt woodsmoke, and felt the warmth of the flames.

"Tata, wake up, speak to me." The voice was insistent and I

opened my eyes. Memnon smiled down at me. Then he called over his shoulder. "He is awake, Lord Tanus."

I found that we were in a rock cave and that outside the night had fallen.

Tanus came across from the smoky fire of damp wood and squatted beside the prince. "How are you, old friend?" he asked.

I struggled into a sitting position, and gingerly tested every part of my body before I replied, "My head is cracked through, and every limb aches. Apart from that I am cold and hungry."

"You will live then," Tanus chuckled, "but we have to get out of these cursed mountains. It was madness ever to venture into a place where the rivers come out of the sky."

"What about the horses?" I asked.

Tanus shook his head. "They are all drowned."

"Food?"

"Nothing," Tanus replied. "Even my bow is lost in the river. I have only the sword at my side and the clothes on my body."

AT DAWN we started back down the valley. At the foot of the gorge we found the bodies of our horses strewn upon the rocks.

We scavenged among the rocks and scree, and managed to recover some of our equipment. To my great joy I found my medical chest still intact. I laid out the contents on a rock, and while they dried I fashioned a sling to carry the chest upon my back. In the meantime, Memnon had cut strips of meat from the carcass of one of the horses and grilled this over another fire of driftwood. When we had eaten our fill we set out on the return journey.

There seemed to be no end to this terrible wilderness, and by the second day our bruised feet in open sandals protested against every step. I was certain that we were doomed to die in these mountains.

Then we topped the next saddle between peaks and found the infant Nile winding through the depths of the gorge below us. And on the banks of the river we saw a collection of coloured tents, and among them men moved.

"Civilised men," I said immediately, "for those tents must be of woven cloth. We must find out who these people are."

"We will get our throats cut," Tanus growled. "What makes you believe they are not as savage as the land in which they live?"

In the end curiosity got the better of us and we crept down to spy upon these strangers. They were tall, well-built people, their hair thick and dark, and they wore full-length brightly coloured robes. Their women were unveiled and cheerful. They sang and called to each other in a language I had never heard before.

Suddenly I felt Tanus grip my arm, and he whispered in my ear, "Look at that!"

One man was clearly the chief of the party. He wore the richest apparel of any of them. His robe was striped in scarlet and blue and his earrings were stones that glowed like the full moon. But I could not see what had excited Tanus.

"His sword," Tanus hissed. "Look at his sword."

It was longer than one of our weapons and the pommel was gold filigree-work. The blade was made of a metal that was not yellow bronze or red copper, but of a strange silvery glittering blue.

"What is it?" Tanus breathed. "What metal is that?"

"I do not know."

The chief had laid the sword across his lap, and with a piece of volcanic rock was lovingly stroking the edge of the blade.

"I want it," Tanus whispered. "I will never rest until I have it."

I gave him a startled glance. He meant what he said.

"We cannot remain here longer," I told him softly. "We will be discovered. Let us go to look at their horses."

He allowed me to draw him away. I led Memnon by the other hand, and at a safe distance we circled the camp, towards the horses. They were taller, more elegantly proportioned than ours.

"They are beautiful," whispered Memnon at my side. "Look at the way they hold their heads and arch their necks."

Tanus longed for the sword; the prince and I coveted the horses.

We found a secure hiding place further downriver among a heap of boulders. As we debated what to do next, we were suddenly aware of voices approaching along the river bank. A party of women came into view and they stopped below us at the water's edge.

There were three older women, and a girl. The women wore robes of a drab hue and cloths of black round their hair. I thought that they were servants or nursemaids, for they treated the girl with deference. She was tall and slim, and wore a short robe of rich wool.

The women stood together below our hiding place, and one of them began to disrobe the girl. The other two filled the clay jars that they had carried down on their heads with water from the river, which was still swollen with floodwater. No one could safely enter that icy torrent, and it was clear that they intended bathing the girl from the water jars.

One of the women lifted the girl's robe over her head and she stood naked at the water's edge, her brown skin glowing in the sunlight. Her features were delicate, her nose narrow and chiselled. Her eyes were large and dark, slanted above high cheekbones. She was beautiful. I have only known one other woman who was more so.

Suddenly she said something to the women with her. They stood aside and she left them and climbed towards us. But before she reached our hiding place, she stepped behind a boulder that shielded her from her companions but left her full in our view.

She glanced round quickly, and would have squatted, had not Memnon been standing a little to one side of Tanus and me. While we were concealed, he was full in her view.

The two of them stared at each other. The girl was trembling and I expected her to scream. Instead, she looked back over her shoulder as if to make certain that the women had not followed her. Then she turned back to Memnon and in a soft voice she asked a question, at the same time holding out her hand to him in a gesture of appeal.

"I do not understand," Memnon whispered.

The girl stepped up to him and repeated the question impatiently, and when Memnon shook his head she seized his hand in agitation.

"Masara?" One of her attendants was calling her. "Masara?" The girl made a gesture of caution and silence to Memnon and turned to go back.

However, the three women had started up the slope after her. They came round the side of the boulder in a pack and screamed when they saw Memnon.

The naked girl seemed poised to run to his side, but the women seized her and screamed as the girl struggled to be free. From the direction of the camp came shouts also.

"Time to go home." Tanus jerked my arm, and I was after him in a bound. But Memnon had not followed us, so we turned back and grabbed him and hauled him away. He came reluctantly.

"I'll come back for you," Memnon shouted at her, as we ran with him between us. "Be brave. I will come back for you."

When somebody tells me that there is no such thing as love

at first sight, I smile and think of the day that Memnon first saw Masara.

We had lost time in the struggle to get Memnon away, and when I paused to look back I saw men coming over the ridge in a body.

We were in single file along the narrow path. Memnon led us and Tanus followed him. I was last in the file and burdened by the heavy medical chest on my back; I began to fall further behind.

An arrow passed over our heads and a second struck the pack on my back with a force that made me stagger. The next arrow hit me in the thigh, and I went tumbling across the path.

I rolled into a sitting position and looked with horror at the reed shaft of the arrow that protruded from my leg, then I looked back at our pursuers. The chieftain in the striped robe led them, and he had outdistanced his own men by a hundred paces.

"Taita!" Tanus called back at me. "Are you all right?"

He had paused on the brow of the slope and was looking back anxiously. Memnon had crossed over and was out of sight.

"I am arrowed!" I yelled back. "Go on and leave me."

Without a moment's hesitation he came leaping down towards where I lay. The chieftain saw him coming and bellowed a challenge, drawing his glittering blue sword.

Tanus reached the spot where I sat, but the chieftain was almost upon us. Tanus drew his own sword, and the two of them came together in a murderous rush.

The chieftain swung first with a full-blooded overhand cut at Tanus's head. Tanus responded with a parry. The two blades met, but there was no ringing clash. The blue blade hacked clean through Tanus's yellow bronze as though it were a wand of green willow. Tanus was left with the hilt in his hand.

"Run, Tanus!" I screamed. "Or he will kill us both."

Tanus leaped backwards. The chieftain went for him again, but I was lying in the middle of the path. I seized him round the knees with both arms and brought him down on top of me. Both of us rolled off the path and began to slide away down the steep slope of loose scree.

As we rolled more swiftly, gathering momentum, I had one last glimpse of Tanus peering down over the edge of the path.

"Run!" I cried. "Take care of Memnon!"

The shale and loose scree were treacherous and gave no purchase. The chieftain and I were flung apart but both of us were carried to the brink of the river. I was battered to the edge of consciousness, and lay there groaning until rough hands dragged me to my feet, and blows rained upon my head.

The chieftain stopped his men from killing me and they began to drag me away towards their encampment. I looked around desperately and saw my medical chest among the rocks.

"Bring that," I ordered my captors, pointing. They laughed at my insolence, but the chieftain sent one of his men to retrieve the chest.

Two men were obliged to support me, for, with the shaft in my thigh, every pace back to the camp was agony. When they reached it they threw me to the ground while they discussed what to do with me.

There was a distraction when the party that had pursued Tanus and Prince Memnon returned empty-handed. There was much shouting and arm-waving as bitter recriminations were exchanged. I was cheered that they had got away. After that most of them lost interest in me and wandered away.

The chieftain resumed his seat in front of the largest tent, and while he stropped the edge of his sword he regarded me. It seemed that my immediate danger was past.

I judged my moment carefully, and then addressed him directly. I pointed to my medical chest which had been thrown against one of the tents.

"I need my chest. I must tend this wound."

Although he did not understand the words, the chieftain understood my gestures. He ordered one of his men to bring the chest across to him. He made them set it down in front of him and opened the lid. He examined each separate item and seemed satisfied that, apart from my scalpels, the chest contained no dangerous weapon. With signs I showed him what I needed to do, making a pantomime of pulling the arrow from my leg.

He stood over me with the sword in his hand but he allowed me to use my instruments.

The pain that I inflicted on myself, as I used the spoons to trap and mask the barbs buried deep in my flesh, brought me more than once to the point of fainting away. I was panting and drenched in sweat when at last I was ready to draw the arrowhead. By this time I had an audience for my surgery of half the men in the camp.

At last I took a firm hold on the handles of the spoons, placed a wooden wedge between my teeth and bit down on it hard, and drew the clamped arrowhead out of the wound. There were shouts of amazement from my audience.

In any nation and in any culture, the healer has a special place. I had demonstrated my credentials in the most convincing manner; at the orders of the chief, I was carried to one of the tents and laid on a straw mattress. My medical chest was placed at the head of my bed, and one of the women brought me a meal of corn bread and chicken.

In the morning, when the tents were struck, I was placed in a pole litter behind one of the horses and pulled along the rough tracks. To my dismay I saw that we were headed back into the mountains, and I knew that I was lost to my own people, probably for all time.

DESPITE THE jolting of the litter, my leg began to heal cleanly. This further impressed my captors, and soon they were bringing to me any member of the band who was sick or injured.

When my leg had healed sufficiently for me to walk again, I was given the run of the camp. However, I was not allowed out of sight, and I was kept away from Masara and only saw her from afar. She was always accompanied by her female jailers, and usually surrounded by armed guards. It was obvious that she was a prisoner of rank and importance.

Without a knowledge of the language I could not hope to understand these people, so I set out to learn their tongue. Very early on I was able to deduce that they called their country Ethiopia, and that the chieftain's name was Arkoun.

While I learned their language and treated their ailments I studied their mores. I discovered that I had underrated Arkoun. He was not a chieftain but a king. His full name was Arkoun Gannouchi Maryam, ruler of the Ethiopic state of Aksum.

Arkoun's nearest neighbour was one Prester Beni-Jon, also claiming to be ruler of the Ethiopic state of Aksum. There appeared to be ill feeling and rivalry between these two monarchs. They had already fought a number of battles.

Masara was the favourite daughter of Prester Beni-Jon. She had been kidnapped by robbers and sold to Arkoun for a horseload of silver bars. Arkoun intended using her to gain political ground from her doting father. Not trusting any of his own men with such a valuable commodity, Arkoun had gone himself to take possession of Princess Masara. Our caravan was carrying her back to Arkoun's stronghold.

By the time we reached Amba Kamara, the mountain fortress of King Arkoun, I was aware of an increasing excitement running through our caravan. These "ambas" were the flat-topped mountains that made up the mountain range of central Ethiopia, and each was a natural and impregnable fortress.

Arkoun rode up beside me and pointed to the mountains on the southern skyline. "That is the hiding place of the scoundrel Prester Beni-Jon. He is a man of unsurpassed treachery." He hawked in his throat and spat over the edge of the cliff.

At the far end of the amba the path led us to a most extraordinary natural stronghold. From the main table of the mountain, a buttress had eroded, until it stood alone, a pinnacle of rock with precipitous sides, separated from the table by an awe-inspiring abyss which was bridged by a narrow, natural arch of stone.

Perched on top of this pinnacle of rock was an ungainly castle of stone blocks and reed thatch. As soon as our caravan had crossed the causeway and pulled into the central courtyard, Masara was whisked away by her female jailers and I was allotted a single stone cell, dark and draughty. Though I wore the woollen robes of the land, I was never warm in Adbar-Seged. How I longed for the sunlight on the Nile and the bright oasis of my very own Egypt!

I sat on those windswept battlements and pined for my family, for Memnon and Tanus, for my little princesses, and for my mistress.

Often I pleaded with Arkoun to release me.

"But why do you want to leave me, Taita?"

"I want to go back to my family."

"I am your family now," he laughed. "I am your father."

THEY CAME for me in the night and led me shivering through the passages to Masara's cell. The room was lit by a dim oil lamp and smelt of vomit. The girl lay curled on a straw mattress. She was in terrible pain, groaning and weeping and holding her stomach.

I set to work immediately. There was no fever in her blood and though she groaned and screamed with agony when I touched her, I could not find any cause for her condition. I was puzzled and I sat back to think about it.

Then I realised that although her face was contorted with agony, she was watching me with a candid gaze.

"This is worse than I feared."

I turned to her two female attendants. "If I am to save her, I must have my chest. Fetch it immediately."

They scrambled for the door, and I lowered my head to hers and whispered, "You are a clever girl and a good actress."

She smiled up at me and whispered back, "I could think of no other way to meet you. I have been so lonely. Perhaps between us we will find a way to escape from this dreadful place."

At that moment we heard the women returning. Masara seized my hand. "Quickly, tell me—what was his name? The one who was with you on that first day beside the river."

"His name is Memnon."

"Memnon . . ."

The women burst into the room, and Masara clutched her belly and groaned as though she were at the point of death.

I mixed a herbal tonic and told them that I would return in the morning.

In the morning there was only one of the women present and she soon became bored and wandered away to the far side of the room. Masara and I exchanged a few quiet words.

"Memnon said something to me that day. What was it he said?"

"He said, 'Be brave. I will come back for you.'"

"He could not mean that. He does not know me." Tears filled her eyes. "Do you think he meant it, Taita?"

"He is Crown Prince of Egypt, and a man of honour. Memnon would not have said it unless he meant it."

That was all we could say then, but afterwards I told Arkoun that although Masara was improving in health, I must be allowed to see her each day. "Otherwise I cannot answer for her health."

Since she was a valuable asset he gave his permission, and thus Masara and I were able to spend most mornings together strolling around the walls of Adbar Seged.

She wanted to know everything about Memnon, and I racked my memory for anecdotes to entertain her. She particularly enjoyed the account of how he rescued Tanus and me from the wounded bull elephant.

"Tell me about his mother, the queen," she demanded, and then, "Tell me about Egypt. Tell me about your gods. Teach me your language." I was glad to satisfy her demands, for I longed for my family and my country. Speaking about them made them seem closer to me. When I was not teaching her Egyptian or telling her about Memnon, we were discussing our plans of escape.

"Even if you escape from this fortress, you will never pass through the mountains without help," she warned me. "You must go directly to my father. He will protect you."

"But if I go to your father he will think I am one of Arkoun's spies. He will have my head."

"I will tell you what to say to him. Things that only he and I know. That will prove to him that you come from me. Then he will guide you back to your own people and Memnon will come to rescue me."

She said this with such confidence that I dared not shatter her hopes. "How will I find my way to your father's fortress?"

"I will explain the way to you."

For two long years we languished on the height of Adbar Seged, devising plans of escape.

In the end I left Adbar Seged riding on a fine horse. Arkoun was going out on a raid against King Prester Beni-Jon, and I was commanded to accompany him, as his physician.

As I walked my horse across the causeway, I looked back and saw Masara standing on her terrace looking down at me. She was a lovely, lonely figure. She called to me in Egyptian.

I could just make out her words above the sough of the wind. "Tell him I am waiting for him. Tell him I love him."

The wind turned the tears upon my cheeks as cold as ice, as I rode away across Amba Kamara.

THE NIGHT before the battle, Arkoun kept me sitting late in his tent. He asked my opinion of his battle plan for the next day. He had learned that I was a student of military tactics. Naturally I told him his plan was brilliant.

In fact, the terrain would not allow full use of the horses, and they had no chariots, so Arkoun's strategy would be to split his forces into four raiding parties that would hide among the rocks, rush out, seize a few hostages, slit a few throats, and then run for it.

It seemed that King Prester Beni-Jon was a commander of equal panache. We met his forces the following day and to begin with he came forward to shout insults at Arkoun from a safe distance.

Once Prester Beni-Jon had had his say, Arkoun went forward and replied at length. When he subsided at last, there were several other warriors who wished to speak. I fell asleep against a rock in the sun.

It was afternoon when I woke and started up at the clash of arms. Arkoun had loosed his first assault. One of his detachments raced forwards against Prester Beni-Jon's positions, beating their swords against their copper shields. Within a short space of time they returned to their starting point without having inflicted or suffered casualties.

Further insults were exchanged, and then it was Prester Beni-Jon's turn to attack. He charged and retired with equal verve and similar results.

So the day passed, and at nightfall both armies retired. We camped at the foot of the valley and Arkoun sent for me.

"What a battle," he greeted me triumphantly. "It will be many months before Prester Beni-Jon will dare take the field again."

Seven of our men had been wounded in this ferocious encounter. I drew the barbs and dressed and bandaged the wounds. The following day I saw the wounded loaded onto litters and walked beside them as we started back to Adbar Seged.

Late that afternoon we came to a ford in the river. There had been rain over the preceding days and the level of the water was high. I began the crossing, wading beside the litter of a patient with a stomach wound. Halfway across the ford the flood caught the side of the litter and swung it sideways, dragging the horse into deeper water.

I was hanging onto the harness, and the next moment the horse and I were both swimming. We were washed away downstream, the wounded man was tumbled out of the litter, and when I tried to reach him I lost my hold on the horse's harness. I was swimming for my life.

For a while some of Arkoun's men ran on the bank beside me, but soon the river swept me through a bend and they could not find a way round the base of the cliff. The horse and I were alone in the river.

Below the bend, the speed of the current slackened. I was able to swim back to the horse and throw one arm over its neck. For the first time I realised that the gods had made an opportunity for my escape. Two days later, following Masara's directions, I reached one of the fortified hilltop villages in the domain of King Prester Beni-Jon.

The guides who were escorting me to Prester Beni-Jon spoke of him in warm and affectionate terms. The villages that we passed along the way were cleaner and more prosperous than those of Arkoun. The horses I saw were magnificent and when at last we came in sight of his castle high on another amba, it was in a better state of repair than that of Arkoun.

King Prester Beni-Jon was an extremely handsome man. His silver hair and beard endowed him with a singular air of dignity. His complexion was fair and his eyes dark and intelligent.

At first he was sceptical of my story, but his manner changed towards me as I recited the intimate knowledge with which Masara had armed me. He was deeply affected by the messages of love and duty that I brought, and he questioned me eagerly as to her health.

"Your Majesty, Masara has been a prisoner of Arkoun these past two years," I pointed out. "She pines for you in his stinking dungeons." I embroidered the facts a trifle, to bring home to him the urgency of her plight.

"I have tried to assemble the ransom that Arkoun demands for my daughter," Prester Beni-Jon excused himself. "But I would have to melt down every plate and bowl in Aksum to put together such a hoard of silver as would satisfy his greed."

"I could lead your army to his stronghold of Adbar Seged. You could lay siege to the castle and force him to hand over Masara."

Prester Beni-Jon looked startled by this proposal. "Adbar Seged is impregnable. My men are lions, but we have never been able to defeat Arkoun's mighty army."

I rejoined with another proposal. "Great Emperor, as you well know I am of the Egyptian nation. Queen Lostris, the regent of Egypt, lies with her armies at the confluence of the two rivers."

He nodded. "This I know. These Egyptians have entered my territory without my leave. They are digging mines in my valleys. Soon I will fall upon them and annihilate them."

It was my turn to be startled. Prester Beni-Jon was aware of the work on Pharaoh's tomb. I modified the suggestion I was about to put to him.

"My people are skilled in the art of siege and war," I explained. "I have influence with Queen Lostris. If you send me back safely to her side, I will prevail on her to extend you her friendship. Her troops will storm Adbar Seged and free your daughter."

Although Prester Beni-Jon tried to disguise the fact, I could see that my suggestion appealed to him. "What would your queen require in return for her friendship?" he asked carefully.

We haggled for five days, and in the end a bargain was struck.

"You will allow Queen Lostris to continue building the tomb in your valley, and your own people will be forbidden to enter there on pain of death."

"I agree," said Prester Beni-Jon.

"Once she is free, the Princess Masara shall be allowed to marry any man she chooses."

"It is against our custom," he sighed. "But I agree."

"When we capture them, Arkoun and the stronghold of Adbar Seged will be handed over to you, but we shall be allowed to keep all the spoils of war that we capture from Arkoun, including his sword." That was for Tanus.

"I agree," said Prester Beni-Jon, and I could see that he thought he had made a bargain.

I set out the following day on the return to my people, riding a fine stallion that was the king's parting gift to me.

Book Five

I WAS STILL five days' ride from Qebui when I saw a swift dust cloud racing towards me across the plain. As the chariots approached, their dressing was perfect, the spacing between each vehicle so exact that they looked like a string of beads. I guessed who commanded them. Even so, I did not recognise the leading charioteer.

It was almost three years since I had laid eyes on Memnon. The difference in age between sixteen and nineteen is the difference between the boy and the man.

I had taken to riding with saddlecloth and stirrups in the Ethiopian manner, and so now I stood high in the stirrups and waved. When he recognised me he pulled up his horses, sprang from the footplate and dragged me from my horse. First he hugged me, and then he held me at arm's length and we studied each other avidly.

"You are pale and thin, Tata. The bones are sticking out of you. Are those grey hairs I see here?" He tugged at my temples.

He was now taller than I, broad in the shoulder, and even more handsome than when I had last seen him.

He set me on the footplate of the chariot. "Take up the traces," he ordered. "I want to see if you have lost any of your old skill."

"Which way?" I asked.

"West, to Qebui, of course. My mother will be angry if I do not bring you directly to her."

That night we sat at a campfire together, away from the other officers, so that we could talk in private. We sat in silence for a while, looking up at the silver blaze of stars, and then Memnon said, "When I thought I had lost you, it was as though I had lost a part of myself. You are woven into my very first memory of life."

I, who deal in words, could find no words to answer him.

We were silent again, and then at last he laid a hand on my shoulder. "Did you ever see the girl again?" he asked.

"Which girl?" I asked, to tease him.

"The girl at the river. They called her Masara."

"I spent two years imprisoned with her," I told him, "in the fortress of Adbar Seged. There I learned to love her, for her nature is even sweeter than her face."

"Tell me about her, Tata! Tell me everything."

So we sat the rest of that night beside the fire and we talked about the girl. I told him how she had learned to speak Egyptian for his sake. I told him how his promise to her had sustained her through the dark lonely days, and in the end I told him the message that she had called out to me as I rode away and left her.

"Tell him I am waiting for him. Tell him I love him."

He was silent for a long while, staring into the flames, then he said softly, "Will you help me make good my promise to her, Tata?"

I HAVE NEVER in my life known such joy as was mine when I went aboard the *Breath of Horus*. Memnon had sent a messenger ahead to warn them of my return, and they were all waiting for me.

"I thought we had got rid of you at last, you old rogue," Kratas said, and crushed me to his chest.

Tanus stared into my eyes and grinned. "But for you, that hairy Ethiop would have had me. Thank you, old friend." I saw Tanus had aged. Like me there was grey in his hair.

My little princesses were no longer little, but they were still adorable. They were shy towards me, for their memory of me had faded, but at last they recognised me.

My mistress smiled at me as I walked towards her along the deck. She had thickened round the waist, and the heavy affairs of state had furrowed her brow. To me, however, she was still the most lovely woman in the world.

She stood up from the throne as I knelt before her. This was the highest mark of her favour. She laid her hand on my bowed head, and it was a caress. "You have been away too long, Taita," she said.

I took her to see the stallion that Prester Beni-Jon had given me, and pointed out to my mistress his finer points of breed.

Then I reminded her of her promise to dead Pharaoh, and told her, "Prester Beni-Jon will cede the valley of the tomb to you, and his warriors will guard against grave-robbers. He will place a taboo upon the valley, and his Ethiops are superstitious people. They will respect the prohibition."

I had already warned Memnon not to mention to Queen Lostris his amorous interest in an expedition against Arkoun. No mother takes pleasure in seeing her son led away by another woman.

Memnon and I had planned our tactics meticulously. Tanus had been easy to convince. His defeat by Arkoun still rankled, and by the time I had finished with him, he was hot for the venture. No woman could have resisted the combined charm and cunning of Tanus and Memnon and myself. Queen Lostris gave her consent to our expeditionary force marching on Adbar Seged.

WE LEFT the wagons and the chariots at the valley of Pharaoh's tomb, and struck out into the mountains. Prester Beni-Jon had sent a company of guides to meet us, a hundred of his most reliable men.

Tanus had selected a full division of his bloodthirsty Shilluk, and Memnon a small band of his finest swordsmen and rough fighters, including Remrem and Astes.

For support we had three companies of Egyptian archers, led by Lord Kratas. That old ruffian had been elevated to the peerage during my sojourn in Adbar Seged.

I impressed on both Tanus and the prince how vital it was to move swiftly. Not only for reasons of surprise, but also because the rains must soon break, and if they caught us in the valleys they would prove a more dangerous enemy than any Ethiop army.

Twenty-five days after setting out we stood in the valley below the massif of Amba Kamara and looked up the winding track to the heights looming over us.

Tanus sent his Shilluk warriors bounding up the path in small parties. They were held up only by Arkoun's archers, hidden behind stone redoubts. When this happened, Kratas led his archers up the mountain. With their superior bow-range, the Egyptians were able to shoot massed volleys high into the air, to drop down onto the redoubt so steeply that the wall afforded the men behind it no protection. We heard their screams and then saw them break and scurry away up the slope, the Shilluk already after them.

I had difficulty keeping up with Memnon and the rest of our small group. We were wearing heavy woollen Ethiopic robes and carrying the traditional round shields of our enemies, and the years were beginning to take their toll. I was no longer a young man.

When at last I came out on the flat tableland of the amba, I called to Memnon and his band. "The wigs!" Each of them pulled a wig of black horsehair over his scalp. Clad in the long striped robes and with the wigs on our heads we could pass as a mob of Arkoun's clansmen.

"This way! Follow me!" I cried. We skirted a village and ran in a disorderly bunch through the cornfields. As we neared the head of the causeway I shouted to the guards there, "We are under King Arkoun's direct orders. Stand aside!"

"The password?" The captain of the guard poked his sword at me.

During my imprisonment I had heard the password a thousand times, for my cell had been above the main gate. It might have been changed since then, but I tried yelling it at him.

"Go across!" He stood aside and we ran out onto the bridge. So urgent was the need to reach Masara that I barely noticed the drop on either hand, and without a qualm I led the way across the void.

"Where is King Arkoun?" I shouted at the guards who blocked the gateway. "I have urgent dispatches for him! Let us pass!"

We barged through the open gate before they could decide to oppose us, and with twelve men at my back I raced for the outer staircase that led to the upper terrace. There were two armed guards at the door to Masara's chamber.

"Who are you?" one of them shouted and drew his sword. "By what authority—" He did not finish the challenge. I stepped aside and allowed Memnon and Remrem to brush past me. They flew at the guards and cut them down before they could defend themselves.

The room beyond the door was in deep gloom. I could barely make out the huddle of women in the far comer.

"Masara!" I called her name as I plucked the wig from my head, and let my own hair fall round my shoulders.

She recognised me by it. "Taita!" She bit the wrist of the woman who tried to hold her, and ran to me. She flung both arms round my neck, and then she looked over my shoulder. Behind me Memnon, too, had pulled off his wig. The two of them stared at each other.

"You came," Masara said softly in Egyptian. "You kept your promise. I knew that you would."

Memnon could only nod his head. He stood there blushing.

Behind me one of the women darted away down the inner staircase. Her screams reverberated up the stairwell. "Guards! The enemy has broken into the east wing!"

Almost immediately there was a rush of booted feet on the staircase, and in an instant Memnon was transformed. "Take care of her, Tata. Let no harm come to her," he told me grimly, and stepped past me to the head of the stairs.

He killed the first man coming up, then kicked him backwards down the stairwell. The falling corpse tumbled into the other men coming up from below, and swept the stairs clean.

"Remrem, lead us. Tata and the princess in the centre. I will bring up the rear guard," he said crisply, and stabbed the next man coming up the stairs in the chest.

"Follow Remrem!" he shouted at me. "Don't stand there. After him!" I grabbed Masara's arm and the sunlight dazzled us as we ran onto the terrace. I blinked to clear my vision, then looked across the causeway. Tanus's Shilluks were there, on the far side of the gulf.

Two or three hundred of Arkoun's soldiers were there also. They had the abyss at their backs, and necessity made heroes of every one of them. Although a score of them were driven back over the edge, the survivors hurled back the first charge of the Shilluk.

I saw Tanus then, exactly where I expected him to be, holding the centre. They hacked their way through the defenders, and Tanus was the first man onto the bridge.

Halfway across he stopped.

From the gateway of Adbar Seged, below where I stood, another man had stepped out onto the bridge to confront Tanus. I could not see his face, but there was no mistaking the weapon in his hand. The blue sword flashed like a sheet of summer lightning.

"Arkoun!" Tanus bellowed. "I have been looking for you."

Arkoun could not understand the words, but the sense of them was unmistakable. He laughed into the wind.

"I know you!" He swung the blade. "This time I will kill you." He started forwards, out along the narrow arch of stone.

Tanus altered his grip on the handle of his bronze shield and tucked his head in behind it.

As they came together Arkoun gathered himself to thrust straight at Tanus's head. Tanus lifted the shield and caught the blue blade in the centre of the heavy bronze target. The blue sword sheared through it. Half its silver length was buried in the yellow bronze.

Now Tanus twisted the shield at an angle so that the blade was trapped. Arkoun struggled to withdraw his weapon, wrestling and heaving, but Tanus had the blue sword in a vice of bronze.

Arkoun gathered all his strength and pulled back again. This time Tanus did not resist him, but stepped forwards in the direction that Arkoun was heaving. This unexpected move threw Arkoun off balance and he staggered away, tripped, and teetered on the brink of the chasm. In order to keep his balance he was forced to relinquish his grip on the blue sword, leaving it still embedded in the shield.

Arkoun swayed out over the drop, then Tanus put his shoulder behind his shield and barged forwards. Arkoun was thrown backwards into empty space. He turned a slow somersault in the air and then went straight down with his robe ballooning round him, until he struck the rocks a thousand feet below. He screamed all the way down, on a high receding note that cut off abruptly at the end.

Slowly the fighting died away. The Ethiopians had seen their king vanquished and the heart went out of them. They threw down their weapons and were dragged away to the waiting slave masters.

I had no eyes for any of this for I was watching Tanus. He began to walk towards the gateway of the fortress, and the men cheered him and raised their weapons in salute. But he walked with a slow and hampered gait, and as he came down the bridge he lowered the shield. Only then did I see the stain spreading on his breastplate.

I thrust Masara into Memnon's arms and ran down the outer

staircase out onto the causeway. Tanus saw me and smiled. The smile was lopsided. He stopped walking and his legs buckled beneath him. He sat down heavily in the middle of the bridge.

I dropped on my knees beside him and saw the rent in the crocodile skin of his breastplate. Blood oozed from it. Arkoun had driven the point through the bronze shield and into Tanus's chest.

Carefully I untied the straps that held his armour and lifted away the breastplate. Tanus and I both looked down. Every breath he drew frothed through the wound in a rash of pink bubbles.

"You are wounded." I could not look him in the face as I said it.

"No, old friend, I am not wounded," he replied softly. "I am killed."

His Shilluk made a litter with their spears and carried him into the fortress of Adbar Seged, where we laid him on the king's bed. When they were gone I placed the blue sword upon the bed beside him. He smiled and laid his hand on the hilt.

"I have paid a high price for this treasure," he murmured. "I would have liked to wield it just once upon the battlefield."

I could offer him no hope or comfort. He had seen too many lung wounds: I could not hope to deceive him as to the final outcome. I mixed a draught of the sleeping flower, but he would not drink it.

"I will live every minute of my life," he told me.

"What else is there that I can do for you?"

"You have done so much already," he said. "But these last things I ask of you. Firstly, you will never tell Memnon that I am his sire. He must always believe that the blood of the pharaohs runs in his veins. He will need every strength to meet the destiny that awaits him."

"He would be proud to share your blood."

"Swear to me you will not tell him."

"I swear it," I replied.

He lay a while, gathering his strength. "There is one other boon," he said. "Take care of my woman who was never my wife. Shield and succour her as you have done all these past years. Take care of Lostris and of our children. I give them all into your hands."

He closed his eyes, then said, "I wish to see the prince."

"He waits for you on the terrace," I answered, and went to the doorway.

Memnon stood at the far end of the terrace. Masara was with him, and the two of them stood close together but not touching.

Memnon came immediately, leaving the girl standing alone. He went directly to Tanus's bed. Tanus smiled unsteadily up at him.

"Your Highness, I have taught you all I know of war, but I cannot teach you about life. Each man must learn that for himself. There is nothing else I have to say to you before I start out on this new journey, except to thank you for the gift of knowing and serving you."

"You were ever more than a tutor to me," Memnon answered softly. "You were the father I never knew."

Tanus closed his eyes and his expression twisted.

"I have a gift for you." He groped for the handle of the blue sword but he did not have the strength to lift it.

He took Memnon's hand and placed it upon the jewelled hilt. "This is yours now," he whispered.

"I will think of you whenever I draw it from its scabbard. I will call your name whenever I wield it on the battlefield."

Memnon stood up and touched the blade to his lips, saluting the man lying on the bed.

Tanus nodded. "There is nothing more that I can teach you. It is not too soon for me to go."

"I will wait with you," Memnon said.

"No." Tanus made a weary gesture. "Your destiny waits for you beyond these walls. Taita will stay with me. Take the girl with you. Go to Queen Lostris and prepare her for the news of my death."

"Go in peace, Lord Tanus." Memnon did not degrade the solemn moment with argument. He crossed to the bed and kissed his father. Then he turned and strode from the room.

"Go on to glory, my son," Tanus whispered and turned to face the stone wall. I sat beside him that night, and mourned for him.

In the dawn I sent for the embalmers.

EVEN THOUGH there was no more for me to do, I waited with Tanus through the forty long days of the mummification. Then we carried him down from the mountains. I walked beside his bier all that weary way. His Shilluk easily bore the weight of his body. They fought each other for the honour.

At last we descended through the final pass and the great plains lay before us. As we approached Qebui, my mistress came to meet us. She rode on the footplate of the chariot behind Prince Memnon.

As they came towards us through the grassland, I ordered the Shilluk bearers to lay Tanus's coffin under the spreading branches of a giant giraffe acacia. My mistress dismounted from the chariot and went to the coffin. I was shocked to see what ravages sorrow had wrought upon her. She placed one hand upon it and bowed her head.

I went to her side to warn her. "Mistress, you must not make your grief clear for all to see. For the sake of his memory and the honour that he held so dear, hold back your tears."

"I have no tears left," she answered me quietly. "My grief is all cried out. Only you and I will ever know the truth."

We placed Tanus's humble coffin in the hold of the *Breath of Horus*, beside the magnificent gold coffin of Pharaoh.

I stayed at the side of my mistress until the worst agonies of her mourning had subsided. Then, at her orders, I returned to the valley of the tomb to supervise the completion of Pharaoh's sepulchre.

Obedient to my mistress, I also selected a site further down the valley for the tomb of Tanus. I did my very best with the material and craftsmen available to me, but he had accumulated no treasure in his lifetime of service to the state and the crown. His tomb was a peasant's hut compared with the funerary palace of Pharaoh Mamose.

When at last it was completed, I stood alone in Tanus's modest tomb, where he would spend all eternity, and I was consumed by anger. In my eyes he was more a man than any pharaoh—the crown could have been his, it should have been his, but he had spurned it.

To me he was more a king than ever Pharaoh had been.

AFTER THE RAINS had passed, my mistress ordered the funeral procession to set out for the valley of the tomb.

Prince Memnon led the first division of chariots. Behind him followed fifty carts loaded with the treasure of Pharaoh Mamose.

Queen Lostris rode on the wagon that carried the golden coffin. I saw her glance back more than once towards the end of the long caravan where the wagon that carried the lighter wooden coffin was followed by a regiment of Shilluk.

There were to be two separate funerals. The first was the lesser, that of the Great Lion of Egypt. The second would be the more elaborate royal funeral.

So it was that three days after our arrival at the valley the wooden coffin was placed in the tomb that I had prepared for Tanus, and the tomb was consecrated by the priests of Horus.

During this ritual my mistress was able to restrain her grief and to show nothing more than the sorrow of a queen towards a faithful servant, although I knew that inside her something was dying.

Early the following morning I returned secretly to the burial chamber. I carried with me a long bundle wrapped in a linen sheet. When I stood for the last time beside the sarcophagus, I opened the bundle I carried. From it I took a long bow I had made especially for him. I placed it upon the sealed stone lid of his coffin.

As I left the tomb I paused at the entrance and looked back for the last time. "Farewell, old friend," I said. "I am richer for having known you. Wait for me on the other side."

TEN DAYS after the first funeral the golden coffin was placed on its wooden sledge and dragged into the vast royal tomb.

It required the efforts of 300 slaves to manoeuvre the coffin through the narrow passageways. To thwart all future grave-robbers and any others who would desecrate the royal tomb, I had designed a maze of false passages and dummy burial vaults beneath the mountains.

In all there were four burial chambers, but three of these would remain forever empty. There were three hidden doors and two vertical shafts. The coffin had to be lifted up one of these, and lowered down the other.

It took fifteen days for the coffin to be inched through this maze, and installed at last in its final resting place. Five storerooms led off from the chamber, and into these were packed the treasure that Pharaoh Mamose had accumulated over his lifetime, which had come close to beggaring Egypt.

Finally the golden coffin was placed within the stone sarcophagus that had been hewn out of the native rock. With a system of ropes and levers the heavy lid was lifted over it and lowered into place.

The royal family and the priests and the nobles entered the tomb to perform the last rites.

My mistress and the prince stood at the head of the sarcophagus, and the priests droned on with their incantations and their readings from the *Book of the Dead.*

In the dim yellow fight I saw my mistress's face turning pale and the perspiration beaded on her forehead. I worked my way through the tightly packed ranks of people, and I reached her side just as she swayed and collapsed.

I was able to catch her before she struck her head on the granite edge of the sarcophagus.

IT TOOK US many months to complete the work on the royal tomb. As we retreated through the labyrinth, I personally inspected every sealed doorway and every secret device we left behind us.

I was alone, for my mistress and the prince had gone up into the mountains to the fortress of Prester Beni-Jon. They had gone with all the court to prepare for the wedding of Memnon and Masara.

When at last my work in the tomb was completed and my workmen had sealed the outer entrance in the cliff face, I also set off into the mountains. I was anxious not to miss the wedding feast, and I travelled as hard as the horses could stand.

We reached Prester Beni-Jon's palace five days before the wedding, and I went directly to that part of the fortress where my mistress and her suite were lodged.

"I have not smiled since last I saw you, Taita," she greeted me. "Sing for me. Tell me your stories. Make me laugh."

It was not an easy task she set me, for the melancholy had entered deeply into her soul. Soon we abandoned our attempts at merriment, and fell to discussing affairs of state.

It might have been a love match as far as the two lovers were concerned, but for the rest of us the joining of Memnon and Masara was a royal wedding and a contract between nations. There were treaties to negotiate, dowries to be decided, trade agreements to draw up between the ruler of Aksum and the regent of Egypt. Additionally, my mistress had been at first less than enchanted by the prospect of her only son marrying a woman of a different race.

"In all things they are different, Taita. The gods they worship, the language—oh! I wish he had chosen a girl of our own people."

"He will." I reassured her. "He will marry perhaps a hundred Egyptians. All the races and nations he conquers in the years to come will provide him with wives. Cushites, Hittites, Assyrians—"

"Stop your teasing, Taita." She stamped her foot. "You know full well what I mean. Those others will all be marriages of state. This, his first, is a marriage of two hearts."

What she said was true. The promise of love that Memnon and Masara had exchanged, in those fleeting moments beside the river, was now blossoming.

I did not share my mistress's misgivings. Though they were different in every way that she had listed, their hearts were turned from the same mould. I knew that Masara would not distract Memnon from his destiny, but rather that she would encourage and incite him to greater endeavour.

One bright mountain day, watched by 20,000 men and women of Ethiopia and of Egypt, Memnon and Masara stood together and broke the jar of water that the high priest of Osiris had brought there from the Nile.

Then the bride and groom led our caravan down from the mountains, laden with the dowry of a princess and the treaties of kinship sealed between our two nations.

WHEN THE FLOODS came, the priests sacrificed on the banks of the river, each to his own god, and they consulted the auguries for the year ahead. Some consulted the entrails of the sacrificial sheep, others watched the flight of the wild birds, still others stared into vessels filled with water from the Nile. They divined in their separate ways.

It is not usual for the gods to agree with each other. However, this year was different from any other that I had known. All the great gods, Ammon-Ra and Osiris and Horus and Hapi and Isis, gave the same counsel: "The time has come for the return to Egypt."

Queen Lostris summoned the high council of state, and when she made the proclamation that endorsed the dictates of the gods, the nobles and the priests stood and cheered her. I cheered as loud and as long as any, and that night my dreams were filled with visions of Thebes, and images of those far-off days when Tanus and Lostris and I had been young and happy.

Since the death of Tanus there had been no supreme commander of our armies. Now, therefore, the war council met, and after long argument the command was offered to Kratas.

He stood before them, grizzled and scarred, and he laughed that great laugh of his and said, "I am a soldier. I follow. I do not lead.

Give me the command of the Shilluk, and I will follow one man to the borders of death and beyond." He drew his sword then and pointed with it at the prince. "That is the man I will follow. Hail, Memnon! May he live for ever."

Thus, at the age of twenty-two years, Prince Memnon was elevated to the rank of Great Lion of Egypt and commander of all her armies. Immediately he began to plan the Return.

Though my rank was only that of Master of the Royal Horse, I was on Prince Memnon's staff. Often he appealed to me to solve the logistical problems that we encountered. During the day I drove his chariot as he reviewed the regiments and led them in exercises of war.

Many nights the three of us, the prince and Kratas and I, sat up late over a jar of wine as we discussed our plans for the Return. Our main concern was to avoid the hazardous transit of the cataracts on the way downriver. These could only be navigated in flood season, and would thus limit when we could travel.

It was proposed that we transport our army by barge down to the departure point below the fifth cataract for a desert crossing of the great bight of the river. Then, when our army regained the river above the first cataract, we would rebuild a squadron of fast fighting galleys to carry us down to Elephantine.

If we timed this correctly, and if we could shoot the rapids and surprise the Hyksos fleet, we would deal the enemy a painful blow and be able to capture the vessels we needed to augment our fighting ships.

Once we had secured a foothold, we would then be able to bring down our infantry and our chariots through the gorge of the first cataract, and engage the Hyksos on the flood plains of Egypt.

We began the first stage of the Return the following flood season, when the main fleet sailed back downriver to the head of the fourth cataract. Before us lay the desert road across the great bight of the river, and for the whole of the following year caravans of wagons set out from here laden with clay jars that were filled to the brim with Nile water, and sealed with wooden plugs and hot pitch.

Every ten miles along the road we set up watering stations. At each of these, thousands of water jars were buried to prevent them cracking in the rays of the sun. The water carts set out from the river each evening. Their task was unending, for we would be nearly 50.000 souls, and as many animals.

Thus we were obliged to wait on the river bank for a further full year.

Two days before we were due to begin the crossing, my mistress said to me, "Taita, how long has Tanus been gone from us?"

My voice choked as I answered, "He set out on his journey to the fields of paradise over three years ago, mistress."

"I have dreamed of him almost every night since then," she mused. "Is it possible that he might have returned to leave his seed in my womb while I still slept?"

"All things are possible," I replied carefully. "We told the people that was how Tehuti and Bekatha were conceived. However, in all truth, I have never heard of it happening before."

We were both silent for a while.

Then she spoke again. "I think I am to have another child," she whispered. "My red moon has waned and I feel the infant growing within me."

I stared at her, feeling the wings of tragedy brush lightly past me.

"You do not have to ask me if I have known another man," she said. "You know that I have not."

"This I know full well. Yet I cannot believe you have been impregnated by a ghost, no matter how beloved that ghost might be."

"Feel my womb, Taita," she commanded. "This is a living thing within me. Each day it grows."

My mistress lay naked upon the linen sheets, and I studied first her face and then her body. She was still lovely to me, but I could see how the hardships of this life in the wilderness had wrought their cruel change. The cares of the regency had chiselled their grim message on her brow.

And she was thin. I should have noticed that before. It was an unnatural thinness, almost an emaciation. Yet her belly protruded out of proportion to her slim arms and legs.

I laid my hands lightly upon it. I felt the thing within her and knew at once that this was not life beneath my fingers. This was death.

I could not find words. I turned and went out onto the deck, for I knew this thing that was growing within my mistress. I had felt it in the bodies of other women. When they died, I had opened the womb and seen the ball of red flesh that had killed them.

It was a long time before I could return to the cabin.

My mistress had covered herself with a robe. She was sitting in the centre of the bed, looking like the little girl I once had known.

"Mistress, why did you not tell me about the pain?" I asked gently.

"How do you know about the pain?" she whispered back. "I tried to hide it from you."

OUR CARAVAN set out into the desert, travelling by moonlight. Sometimes my mistress walked at my side and the two little princesses frolicked along with us, excited by the adventure. At other times, when the pain was bad, my mistress rode in her wagon. Then I sat beside her and held her hand until the powder of the sleeping flower worked its magic.

Every night we travelled just as far as the next watering station. During the long days we lay beneath the awning of the wagon and drowsed in the sweltering heat.

After thirty days and nights upon the road we saw a remarkable sight in the dawn—sails moving gently over the sands. It was not until we had journeyed many more miles that we saw how we had been deceived. The hull of the galley had been hidden from us by the bank of the Nile. We had crossed the loop.

Prince Memnon and all his staff were there to greet us. Already the squadron of new galleys had almost completed their fitting out. All the chariots were assembled. Hui had herded the horses across the desert, and the wagons had carried their fodder with them. The main body of our nation had been brought across. It had been an undertaking that almost defied belief.

Now only the first cataract still stood between us and the sacred earth of Egypt.

A new barge had been built for my mistress and the princesses. There was a large and airy cabin for her, equipped with every luxury. The hangings were of embroidered Ethiopian wool, and the furniture was of dark acacia wood inlaid with ivory and gold. I decorated the bulkheads with paintings of flowers and birds.

As always, I slept at the foot of my mistress's bed. Three nights after we sailed, I woke in the night. She was weeping.

The pain had come again, and I mixed her a draught of the sleeping flower, stronger than I had ever given to her before.

She drank it and lay quietly for a while. Then she said, "Can you not cut this thing out of my body, Taita?"

"No, mistress, I cannot."

"Then hold me, Taita. Hold me the way you used to do when I was a little girl."

I took her in my arms. I cradled her, and she was thin and as light as a child. I rocked her tenderly and after a while she slept.

THE FLEET reached the head of the first cataract above Elephantine, and we moored in the quiet flow of the river, waiting for the Nile to rise and open the cataract for us to pass down into Egypt.

While we waited we sent spies down through the gorge, dressed as peasants and priests and merchants with goods to trade, and when they returned they brought us the very first news of our motherland that we had heard in all the years of exile.

King Salitis still reigned, but he was old now and his two sons were the mighty men of the Hyksos legions. Prince Beon commanded the infantry and Prince Apachan commanded the chariots.

The might of the Hyksos exceeded all our estimates. Our spies reported that Apachan disposed of 12,000 chariots. We had brought down only 4,000 from Cush. Beon had 40,000 archers and infantry. Even with Kratas's Shilluk, we could muster only 15,000. We were heavily outnumbered.

There was cheering news also. The great bulk of the Hyksos force was held at the city of Memphis in the north, where Salitis had made his capital. It would take months for him to move his forces south to Elephantine and Thebes. For the moment there was only a single squadron of chariots guarding the city of Elephantine.

Prince Memnon's battle plan was simple. We would pass through the cataract on the flood, and seize Elephantine. Then, while Salitis moved southwards to oppose us, we would march on Thebes, raising the populace in insurrection as we went.

We learned from our spies that although all Salitis's senior officers were Hyksos, many of his captains and sergeants had been recruited from among the Egyptians, and half the common soldiers were of our own nation. Most of these would have been infants or not yet born at the time of our exodus. We wondered where their loyalties would lie when Prince Memnon led our army down into Egypt.

All was in readiness now. The scouts had marked a road through the desert on the west bank, and our galleys were rigged for battle. When the Nile flooded we would sail, but in the meantime there was one last ritual to complete.

We climbed the bluff above the river to where the obelisk that my mistress had raised almost two decades before still stood, pointing into the cloudless African sky.

My mistress walked painfully slowly to the foot of the pillar on the arm of Prince Memnon, and gazed up at the inscription.

Our whole nation watched her, all those souls who had found their way back to this point from which we had set out so long ago, as my mistress read aloud the inscription. Her voice was soft but carried clearly to where I stood behind the great lords and the generals.

"I have done that which was required of me. I have led you back to the border of your land. My task is completed and I relinquish the regency." She paused and for a moment her eyes met mine. I nodded slightly to encourage her, and she went on.

"Citizens of Egypt, it is fitting that you have a true pharaoh to lead you the last step of the way home. I give to you the divine Pharaoh Tamose, once the Crown Prince Memnon. May he live for ever!"

"May he live for ever!" the nation roared in one voice.

Pharaoh Tamose stepped forward to face his people. He drew the blue sword from its jewelled scabbard and saluted them with it.

His voice rang and echoed from the gaunt red crags of the hills. "I take up this sacred trust. I swear on my hope of eternal life to serve my people and my land all my days. I shall not flinch from this duty, and I call upon all the gods to witness my oath."

THE FLOOD came. The waters rose and the cataract began to growl like a beast in its lair.

I sailed aboard the leading galley with Lord Kratas and Pharaoh. We dropped our mooring and the rowers on the benches turned to watch Kratas, gripping the steering oar in the stern.

I stood beside Kratas, with a map of the rapids spread on the deck in front of me. I did not really need the map for I had memorised every line drawn upon it. In addition to which I had stationed reliable men onshore with signal flags to show us the way through.

The current quickened beneath our keel and the rowers touched the surface lightly with the blades of the oars, just to keep our bows pointed downstream.

We floated so smoothly that we seemed to be drifting, and it was only when I looked at the banks, and saw them streaming past us, that I realised how fast we were running. The rock portals of the gorge flew to meet us.

"Come on, you rogues!" Kratas shouted at his crew. "This day I'll make your mothers proud of you, or else I'll find work for the embalmers."

The river was split by three islands, and the channel narrowed. "Bear to port!" I cried.

The deck tipped beneath my feet and we flew down a chute of grey water. I thought that we were out of control and waited for the crunch of rock. Then I saw the bows steady, and I picked out the man on the centre island flagging us into the turn.

"Hard to starboard as we come up to the flag!"

Kratas put the rudder over and the deck canted sharply. A wall of rock flashed past us at the speed of a galloping horse.

One more turn and the first rapids lay ahead. My stomach clenched as we leaped over the edge and dropped down the slope. At the bottom we wallowed and spun like a stalk of dry grass in a whirlwind.

"Pull left!" Kratas bellowed, and we steadied and aimed for the next gap in the black rock. The white water dashed over the deck and into my eyes. It hissed alongside, and the waves stood taller than our poop deck. We touched once, and rocks rasped along our belly, then Memnon's team poled us free and we raced on down.

Behind us I heard the shattering crash as one of the galleys behind us struck hard. I dared not look round as I judged our next turn, but soon there was wreckage and the heads of drowning men bobbing in the torrent on both sides of us.

At last we were hurled from the bottom of the cataract into the main body of the river. Of the twenty-three galleys that had entered the gorge, only eighteen followed us out.

There was not time for us to celebrate our deliverance, or to grieve for the dead. Ahead lay the Island of Elephantine, and on both banks of the river stood the well-remembered walls and buildings of the city.

"Archers, string your bows!" Tamose called from the bows. "Hoist the blue pennant!"

Our tiny squadron flew into the mass of shipping that clogged the roads of Elephantine. Most of it was made up of trade barges and transports. We passed these by and went for the Hyksos galleys.

The Hyksos had manned their fighting ships with Egyptian

sailors. Only their officers were Hyksos, most of whom were ashore, carousing in the pleasure palaces of the docks.

Our spies had told us which was the flag of the southern admiral, a swallowtail of scarlet and gold. We steered for the ship that flew it, and Memnon boarded her with twenty men at his back.

"Freedom from the Hyksos tyrant!" they roared. "Stand up for this Egypt! Cast out the tyrant!"

The crew gaped at them. They had been taken completely by surprise and most of them were unarmed. Their weapons were locked away below decks, for the Hyksos officers trusted them not at all.

The other enemy galleys were boarded as swiftly. On all of them the reaction of the crew was the same. After the first surprise they embraced our men, roaring out a welcome. "For Egypt! For Tamose! For Egypt and Tamose!"

The cheering jumped from ship to ship. Men danced upon the rails and swarmed up the masts to tear down the Hyksos banners. They broke open the arms stores and passed out bows and swords.

Then they poured ashore. They dragged the Hyksos from the taverns and hacked them to bloody shreds. They ran through the streets to the barracks of the garrison, and fell upon the guard.

"For Egypt and Tamose!" they chanted.

Some of the Hyksos officers rallied their men, and held out for a while in pockets. Then Kratas and Memnon came ashore with their veterans, and within two hours the city was ours.

The populace went wild with the joy of liberation. They were dancing through the streets, waving any piece of blue cloth that came to hand. Blue was the colour of Pharaoh Tamose.

As soon as Memnon and Kratas had stamped out the last pockets of Hyksos resistance, they set about restoring order to the city. Squads of disciplined troops trotted through the streets, using the shafts of their war spears as clubs to beat sense into the drunken, delirious mob. By nightfall the city was quiet, and decent men and women were once more safe to walk the streets.

MEMNON set up his headquarters in Pharaoh Mamose's palace where the Hyksos garrison commander had lived. The palace had escaped the looters and within days I restored the rooms and water garden to a state in which they were fit to receive my mistress. Then I went to Memnon to ask permission to bring her home.

"Leave at once, Tata," he commanded, "and bring Queen Masara with you."

One hundred slaves carried the litters of the two queens along the banks of the Nile to the Palace of Elephantine. Queen Lostris was exhausted by the journey. Each day the thing in her womb grew larger as it fed upon her wasting body.

I laid her on a couch in the water garden and she closed her eyes and rested for a while. Then she opened them once more and smiled at me softly. "We were happy here once, but will I ever see Thebes again before I die?"

I could not answer her. It would have been idle to make promises that were not mine to keep.

"If I die before that, will you promise to take me back and build me a tomb in the hills from where I can see my beautiful city?"

"That I promise you with all my heart," I replied.

IN THE DAYS that followed, Aton, the old king's chamberlain, and I resuscitated our web of spies and informers across the Upper Kingdom. Through them we learned which Hyksos regiments were billeted in each town, and which of them were on the march south. We learned their strength, and had an exact count of the numbers of their ships and their chariots.

I smuggled secret messages in the name of Pharaoh Tamose to those Egyptians in the regiments of the enemy, urging them to revolt. They started to trickle in through our lines, bringing more valuable intelligence with them. Soon the trickle became a flood. The crews of a hundred galleys mutinied and slew their Hyksos officers, and two full regiments of archers deserted to us.

Each day we were growing stronger, and the whole of Egypt was in a ferment of excitement and anticipation. The heady aroma of freedom perfumed each breath we drew.

Aton and I, poring over our secret dispatches, saw a different picture emerging. We saw the Hyksos giant shaking itself awake and stretching out a mailed fist towards us. From Memphis and every city and town in the Delta, King Salitis's regiments were on the march, moving south upon Thebes.

I waited until I knew that Lord Apachan, the commander of the Hyksos chariots, had reached Thebes and was encamped outside the city walls with all his vehicles and all his horses. Then I went before the war council of Pharaoh Tamose.

"Your Majesty, I have come to report that the enemy now have twenty thousand horses and six thousand chariots massed at Thebes. Within two months the Nile will have subsided to the level that will enable Apachan to begin his final advance upon this island."

Pharaoh Tamose gripped my shoulders and stared into my eyes. "Are you ready to ride to glory with me?"

"I am ready, Pharaoh."

"Then put the horses into their traces and fly the blue pennant over my chariot. We are going home to Thebes."

So we stood at last before the city of Thebes with four divisions of chariots and 30,000 foot. King Salitis's host lay before us, but beyond his multitudes the walls of Thebes beckoned to us in the dawn light.

The Hyksos army deployed ponderously in front of us, column after column, rank upon rank. Their spearheads glittered and the golden helmets of the officers blazed in the early sunlight.

Apachan had five chariot divisions in the centre, and my spies told me he was holding six more in reserve, hidden beyond the city wall.

The king touched my shoulder. "The dice are in the cup, Tata. It is too late to change them now. Drive out in review."

I took up the reins and wheeled the chariot out in front of our army. The king was showing himself to his troops. His presence would give them heart, and stiffen their spines. The carriage of the royal chariot was dressed in a thin skin of gold leaf, and it made a dazzling display. This was the only concession I had made in my quest for lightness, yet no one who looked upon it could doubt that this was Pharaoh's chariot. On its long bamboo rod the blue pennant streamed in the breeze high above our heads, and the men cheered us as we drove down their ranks.

We passed in front of the massed regiments of the Shilluk spearmen in the centre. Apart from their long spears, each of them carried a bundle of javelins, and they had set sharpened wooden staves into the earth to form a palisade in front of their line. The Hyksos chariots must break through that spiny barrier to reach them.

The Egyptian archers were drawn up behind them, ready to move forwards through their ranks or retreat again as the battle required. They raised their recurved bows and cheered Pharaoh.

"Tamose! Egypt and Tamose!"

Pharaoh wore the blue war crown, with the golden circlet round his brow, the heads of the vulture and the cobra of the two kingdoms entwined, their jewelled eyes glittering.

He returned their salute with the bare blade of the blue sword held high.

We wheeled round our own left flank and started back to where our chariots were holding in the rear. Remrem headed the first division; Astes had the second; and Lord Aqer, Lord Merkeset's noble son, the third. Newly promoted to the rank of Best of Ten Thousand, Captain Hui commanded the fourth division.

We heard the horns sounding in the centre.

"It begins now." Memnon pointed to the front, and we saw the Hyksos chariots looming through the dust clouds. "Yes, Apachan has turned loose his chariots."

He looked back at our divisions and signalled to Lord Aqer.

The third division came forwards in a column of fours behind us, and Pharaoh led them out.

The Hyksos chariots lumbered forwards and aimed at the centre of our line. Memnon cut across in front of them, interposing our thin column between their hordes and the infantry. Then at his signal we wheeled into line abreast and flew straight at them.

It seemed suicidal. As we came together our archers fired head-on into them, aiming for the horses. Gaps opened in their line as the horses were brought down by our arrows, then at the last possible moment our drivers used their superior speed and manoeuvrability, swerving into the gaps and racing through them. Not all our chariots escaped, but Lord Aqer led four out of every five of them through.

We emerged in the rear of the Hyksos charge and spun round in a full-locked turn, reforming the line at the gallop to overhaul the Hyksos, coming into them from behind and firing our arrows.

The Hyksos chariots were designed to give protection to the crew from the front, and their archers were stationed on the footplate to fire their arrows forwards. Confusion spread down their fine as they tried to meet our attack from the rear.

Hard-pressed, some of the drivers attempted to turn back to confront us and collided with the chariots alongside. Those fearsome wheel scythes cut into the legs of the neighbouring horses and brought them down, confusion spreading as the first volley of arrows from the Egyptian archers dropped among them.

Now Memnon gave the order and we wheeled away and let them run down on that palisade of sharpened staves. Half their horses were maimed or killed. Those who broke through were met by the Shilluk and a hail of javelins.

Those chariots that were still under control hurled themselves into the Shilluk phalanx. But they met no resistance. The black ranks opened before them, allowing the horses to run through, but then they closed behind them. Every one of those tall black devils was an athlete, and they leaped up onto the footplates of the chariots from behind, stabbing and hacking at the crews with dagger and spear.

The Hyksos spearmen had been moving forwards to follow up and exploit the chariot charge, but now they were stranded in the middle of the field, and Memnon seized the opportunity. As we wheeled back into line, Pharaoh signalled to Astes. The second division moved forwards behind us and formed up at the trot.

The Hyksos infantry was still tangled in the middle of the field. Their line was crumpled and, with a general's eye, Memnon picked out its weakest point, a salient in their left flank.

"The second division will advance," he cried. "Trot-march! Forward! Charge!"

We tore into the salient in the line, eight chariots abreast, and ripped them open. We had them canted across the field, their centre was shearing and Memnon reformed the third division at the gallop, and set them up to tear open the enemy centre.

At the moment before we were committed to the charge, I glanced across at the city. Dust had almost obscured the range, and I glimpsed movement beyond the eastern fort.

"Sire!" I cried, and pointed back. The king followed my arm, and saw the first reserve squadron of Hyksos chariots trot out from concealment behind the curve of the wall. The others followed, like a column of black warrior ants on the march.

"Apachan is throwing in his reserves to save his infantry!" Memnon shouted above the din of battle. "A moment more and he would have had us in enfilade! Well done, Tata!"

We had to let the infantry escape, as we wheeled into line to face Apachan's chariots. We charged at each other across a field littered with overturned chariots and dead and wounded men and horses.

As we came together, we opened before their charge, peeling away on either side of them, drawing them back to where Hui's fourth division was drawn up alongside Remrem's first.

I turned my chariot in alongside that of Hui. A team of grooms slipped our sweat-soaked horses from the traces and led in a fresh pair. While Lord Aqer's exhausted division streamed back past us, we faced the oncoming Hyksos.

"Are you ready, Captain Hui?" Memnon called to him.

Hui raised his bow in salute. "For Egypt and Tamose!"

"Then forward march. Charge!" Memnon laughed, and our horses jumped against the traces and we shot forwards.

There were six full divisions of Apachan's chariots scattered across the field in front of us. We went out to meet them, face to face. In the centre of their charge rode a man so tall that he towered above his driver. He wore the high golden helmet of Hyksos royalty, and his dark beard was plaited with coloured ribbon.

"Apachan!" Memnon challenged him. "You are a dead man."

Apachan heard him, and he picked out our golden chariot. He swerved to meet us, and Memnon tapped my shoulder.

"Lay me alongside the bearded hog. It's time for the sword, at last."

Apachan loosed two arrows at us as we closed. Memnon caught one on his shield. I ducked under the other, but I was watching those terrible spinning scythes on the hubs of Apachan's wheels. They could hack my horses' legs out from under them.

Behind me I heard the rasp as Memnon drew the blue sword from its scabbard on the side panel. I swung my horses' heads over, feinting to the right to confuse the Hyksos driver, but the instant he started to turn away I changed direction again. I avoided his scythes and passed him close, then I turned in sharply behind him. With my free hand I snatched up the grappling hook and tossed it over the side panel of the other chariot. Now we were locked together, but I had achieved the advantage, for we lay across his stern.

Apachan swivelled round and aimed a sword-cut at me but I fell to my knees under it; Memnon gathered up the blow on his shield and then swung the blue sword. A shard of bronze curled from the edge of Apachan's weapon, sliced away by the steel, and he shouted in angry disbelief and flung up his copper shield at the next blow.

Apachan was a superb swordsman, but no match for my king and the blue sword. Memnon mangled his shield to strips, and then swung hard at his bronze blade as Apachan tried to defend his head. The silver blade sheared it cleanly, and drove on into Apachan's open mouth. His angry bellow was drowned out by a torrent of blood.

I cut the rope of the grappling hook and let the Hyksos chariot run free. The horses were out of control, and they slewed away and ran down the line of locked and battling chariots. Apachan clutched at the dashboard, holding himself erect even though he was dying, and the blood flowed from his mouth and down his breastplate.

It was a sight that struck dismay into the hearts of his charioteers. They tried to disengage their staggering horses, but we ran hub to hub with them all the way back until we were forced to break off.

"It's not over yet," I warned Memnon as we walked our tired horses back. "You still have to deal with Beon's infantry."

"Take me to Kratas," Pharaoh ordered.

I stopped our chariot in front of the massed regiments of Shilluk, and Memnon called across to Kratas, "What heart, my lord?"

"I fear, sire, that my fellows will fall asleep if you cannot find a little work for us to do."

"Then let us hear a tune from them as you take them forwards to seek employment."

The Shilluk began their advance. They moved with a curious shuffling gait, and every third pace they stamped in unison with a force that made the ground jump. They sang in deep African voices, and they drummed their spears upon their shields.

The Hyksos were disciplined and brave; they could not have conquered half the world if they had not been so. We had smashed their chariots, but they stood to meet Kratas's advance behind a wall of bronze shields.

The two armies came together like fighting temple bulls, battling it out breast to breast and spear to spear.

While the two armies of foot soldiers mauled each other, Pharaoh held back his chariots, using them with skill and daring only when there was an opening in the enemy positions. The Hyksos rallied every one of their remaining chariots, and every one of their horses that could still stand, and threw them against our right.

Memnon sent Hui and Astes out to break up their attack.

Pharaoh and I circled the fighting in the golden chariot, watching each shift in the conflict. He pushed in his reserves in exactly those places they were most needed, and with the timing that can never be taught or learned. It was as though he sensed the pulse of the battle beating in his heart.

Always I looked for Kratas in the thick of it. Many times I lost him and I dreaded that he was down, but then his helmet showed again and it was there in the centre where Kratas fought that the Hyksos ranks began to give. Their line bulged and stretched. Their rear ranks began to fall in upon themselves under the relentless pressure.

"By Horus, Tata, this is the moment of our victory."

We galloped across to where Remrem still waited, and Pharaoh hailed him. "Are you ready, my Lord Remrem?"

"I have been ready since dawn, sire, but I am no lord."

"Would you argue with your king, sir? You are a lord now. The enemy centre is breaking. Chase them back to Memphis!"

"May you live for ever, Pharaoh!" Lord Remrem sprang to the footplate. He led out the first division. Their horses were fresh and their fighting spirit was chafed raw with long restraint. They crashed into the Hyksos right flank, cut through them with barely a check and swung round. They went into the enemy centre from the rear. Within the time it takes to draw a breath the Hyksos were in rout.

They streamed back towards the city gates, and even Kratas's Shilluk were too far gone to follow them.

This was when the genius of Memnon was made apparent. He had kept the first division in hand for this moment.

The first of the fleeing enemy reached the city gates, but they found them slammed in their faces. My agents had done their work well. The populace of Thebes was in revolt and the city was ours. They barred the gates to the broken Hyksos legions.

Remrem drove the Hyksos back thirty miles, and every yard of the north road was littered with the bodies of the slain.

I DROVE the Pharaoh's golden chariot up to the main gate of the city, and he stood on the footplate and shouted, "I am Tamose, ruler of the two kingdoms. Open the gates! Let me pass through!"

"Hail, Pharaoh! May you live for ever!"

The gates swung open, and Memnon touched my shoulder. "Drive through, Tata."

I turned to face him. "Forgive me, Majesty. I have taken oath that I will not enter the city, except at the side of my mistress, Queen Lostris. I must pass the reins to you."

"Dismount," he ordered me gently. "Go! Fetch your mistress and make good your oath."

FASTER THAN any ship could sail, I carried the news to Elephantine. I was one man in this chariot, and the horses ran lightly.

I changed the teams at every relay station along the south road, and galloped on without a check. I never slept nor even rested. Horus guided my weary hands upon the traces, for though I ached in every limb and reeled on the footplate with fatigue, I met with no mishap.

At each relay station and in each village along the way, I shouted the joyous news. "A victory! A mighty victory! Pharaoh has triumphed at Thebes! The Hyksos is cast down!"

"Praise to all the gods!" they cheered me. "Egypt and Tamose!"

I drove from Thebes to Elephantine in two days and two nights, and when I reached the palace I barely had the strength left to stagger into the water garden where my mistress lay, and throw myself down beside the couch.

"Mistress," I croaked through cracked lips and a throat that was parched with dust. "Pharaoh has won a mighty victory. I have come to take you home."

WE SAILED downriver to Thebes.

The princesses were with me to keep their mother company and to cheer her. They sat with her on the open deck and sang to her. They rhymed and riddled and laughed, but there was sadness in their laughter as they watched over her.

Queen Lostris was as frail as a wounded bird. There was no weight to her bones and her flesh was as translucent as mother-of-pearl. The power of the sleeping flower was no longer able to still the pain that gnawed her belly. I carried her to the bows when at last the walls of Thebes opened to our view round the last bend in the river. With her arm round my shoulders I supported her as we lived again a thousand joyous memories of our youth.

But the effort tired her. When we docked below the Palace of

Memnon, half the populace of Thebes was waiting to welcome her. Pharaoh Tamose stood at the head of this vast throng.

When the litter bearers carried her ashore they cheered her. Although most of them had never laid eyes upon her, her legend had persisted during her long exile.

Mothers lifted up their infants for her blessing and reached out to touch her hand. "Pray to Hapi for us," they pleaded. "Pray for us, Mother of Egypt."

Pharaoh Tamose walked beside her litter like the son of a commoner, and Tehuti and Bekatha followed close behind. Both the princesses smiled brightly, though tears jewelled their eyelids.

Aton had prepared quarters for the queen. I sent them all away, even the king, and laid her on the couch beneath the vine arbour on the terrace. From there she could look across the river to the shining walls of her beloved Thebes.

When darkness fell I carried her to her bedchamber. As she lay upon the linen sheets she looked up at me.

"Taita," she murmured. "Will you work a divination for me?"

"Mistress, I can refuse you nothing." I bowed my head and went to fetch my medicine chest.

I sat beside her bed, cross-legged upon the stone slabs, and she watched me prepare the herbs.

"Thank you," she whispered as I drained the steaming cup. I closed my eyes and waited for the familiar slide into the world of visions.

When I returned, the lamps were guttering and smoking in their brackets and the palace was silent. The only sound was the light breath of my mistress as she lay upon her pillow.

I thought she was sleeping. But the moment I lifted my trembling hand to wipe the cold sweat from my face, she opened her eyes.

"Poor Taita, was it so bad?"

It was worse than ever before. My head ached and my vision swam. I knew that I would never work a divination again. This was the last time and I had done it for her alone.

"I saw the vulture and the cobra stand on either side of the river, divided by the waters. I saw the waters rise and fall two hundred seasons. I saw the dust of battle and the flash of swords. I saw the smoke of burning cities mingle with the dust.

"At last I saw the cobra and the vulture come together. I saw them entwined on a sheet of pure blue silk. There were blue banners on the city walls and banners of blue flew on the temple pylons.

"I saw the blue pennants on the chariots that drove out across the world. I saw monuments so tall and mighty that they would stand for ten thousand years. I saw the peoples of fifty different nations bow down before them."

I sighed and pressed my fingers into my temples to still the throbbing in my skull.

Then I said, "That was all my vision."

Neither of us spoke or moved for a long while thereafter.

Then my mistress said quietly, "Two hundred seasons must pass before the two kingdoms are united, two hundred years of war and striving before the Hyksos are at last driven from the sacred soil of Egypt. It will be hard and bitter for my people to bear."

I interpreted the rest of my vision for her. "But they will be united upon the blue banner, and the kings of your line will conquer the world. All the nations of the world will pay homage to them."

"With this I am content." She sighed and fell asleep.

I did not sleep, for I knew that she still needed me near her.

She woke again in that hour before dawn which is the darkest of the night. She cried out, "The pain! Sweet Isis, the pain!"

I mixed the Red Shepenn for her. After a while she said, "The pain has passed, but I am cold. Hold me, Taita, warm me with your body."

I took her in my arms and held her while she slept.

She woke once more as the first rays of dawn crept in through the doorway from the terrace. "I have loved only two men in my life," she murmured, "and you were one of those. Perhaps in the next life the gods will treat our love more kindly."

She closed her eyes for the last time. She stole away quietly and left me. Her last breath was no louder than the one before, but I felt the chill in her lips when I kissed them.

"Goodbye, my mistress," I whispered. "Farewell, my heart."

I HAVE WRITTEN these scrolls during the seventy days and nights of the royal embalming. They are my last tribute to my mistress.

Before the undertakers took Lostris away from me, I opened her womb and I took from it that terrible incubus that had killed her. When I cast it into the fire I cursed it and I cursed the foul god Seth who had placed it in her.

I have prepared ten alabaster jars to hold these scrolls. I will leave them with her. I am painting all the murals of her tomb with my own hand. Each stroke of my brush is an expression of my love.

I wish that I could rest with her in this tomb, for I am sick and weary with grief. But I still have my two princesses and my king to care for. They need me.

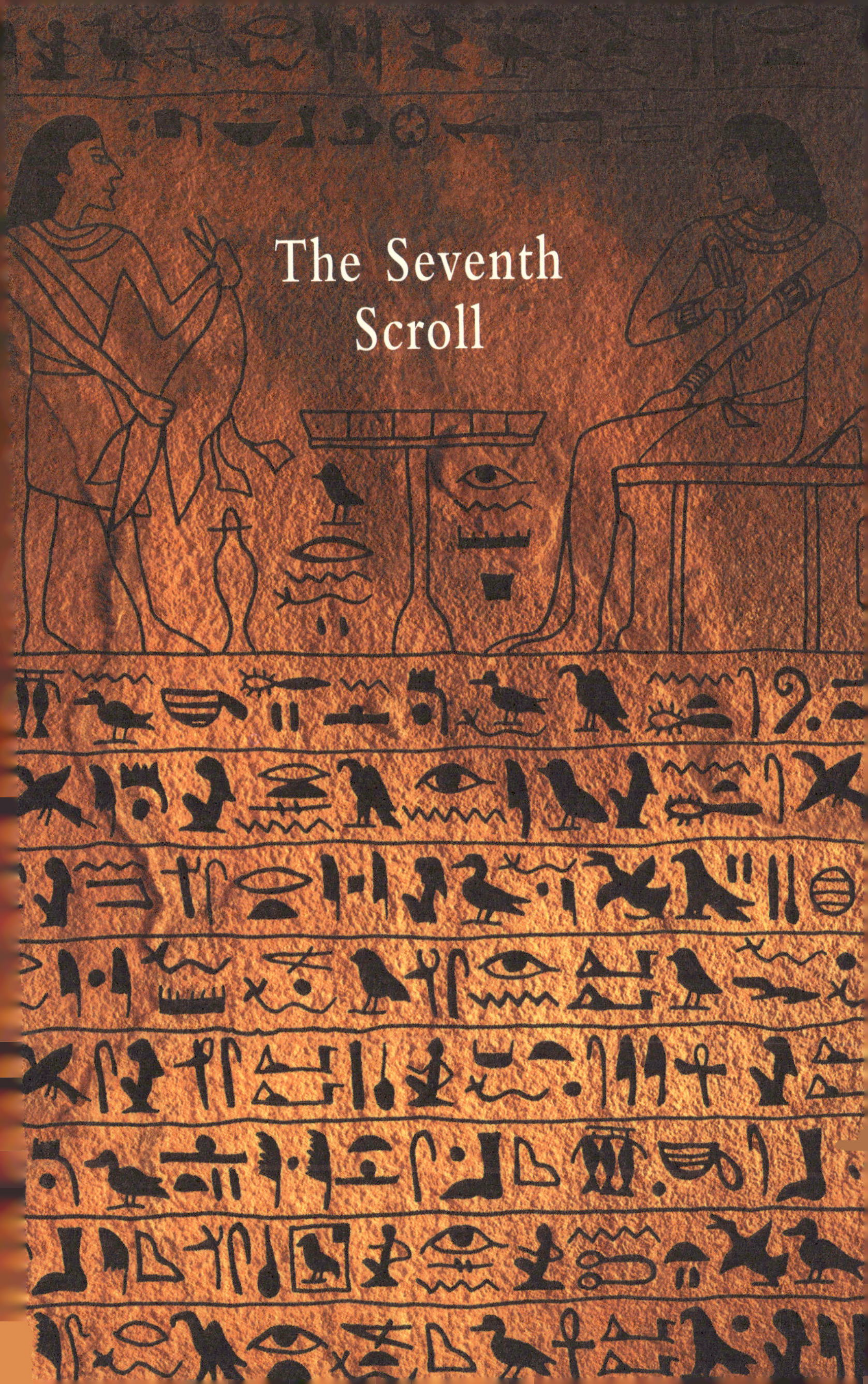
The Seventh
Scroll

The Seventh Scroll

For nearly four thousand years the scroll has lain buried, and with it the secret of Pharaoh Mamose's final resting place. Now, the research of two archaeologists, Duraid and Royan Al Simma, has brought the ancient manuscript to light. For Royan it promises the fulfilment of a dream—the chance to restore to Egypt part of its ancient heritage. For others, less scrupulous, it is the key to riches beyond compare. But for all of them, there will be a price to pay for disturbing the dead ...

THE DUSK crept in from the desert and shaded the dunes with purple. Like a thick velvet cloak it muted all sounds, so that the evening was tranquil and hushed. From where they stood on the crest of the dune they looked out over the oasis. The buildings were white with flat roofs, except for the Islamic mosque and the Coptic Christian church. These bastions of faith opposed each other across the lake.

The man and the woman made a disparate couple. He was tall, slightly bowed, with silvering hair. She was young, in her early thirties, slim, alert and vibrant. Her hair was thick and curling, restrained now by a thong at the nape of her neck.

"Time to go down now." He smiled at her fondly. She was his second wife. When his first wife died he had not expected this last period of happiness in his life. Now he had her and his work. He was a happy man.

They set off towards the village, skirting the reedbeds of the oasis, crossing the rickety bridges over the irrigation canals. As they passed, the peasants returning from the fields greeted him with deep respect.

"*Salaam aleikum, Doktari!* Peace be with you, Doctor." They honoured all men of learning, but him especially for his kindness to them and their families over the years. It mattered little that most of them were Muslim, while he and his wife were Coptic Christians.

When they reached the villa, the old housekeeper greeted them with mumbles and scowls. "You are late. You are always late. Why do you not keep regular hours, like decent folk?"

He sent her away gently, and they ate the simple meal on the terrace together, dates and olives and unleavened bread and goat's-milk cheese. It was dark when they finished.

"Royan, my flower." He reached across the table and touched her hand. "It is time to begin work." He stood up from the table and led the way to the old books and scrolls in the study.

Royan Al Simma went directly to the tall steel safe against the far wall and tumbled the combination. When the heavy steel door swung open, she stood back for a moment. She always felt this prickle of awe whenever she saw this relic of the ages.

"The seventh scroll," she whispered, and steeled herself to touch it. It was nearly four thousand years old, written by a genius whose words spoke to her clearly from beyond the grave. She carried the scroll to the long table at which Duraid was already at work. He always wanted the scroll there on the table, even though he had the photographs and the microfilm to work with.

"Your eyes are better than mine," he said. "What do you make of this character?"

She leaned over his shoulder and studied the hieroglyph on the photograph of the scroll that he pointed out to her.

The two of them laboured on into the cool of the night. This was when they did their best work. Sometimes they spoke Arabic and sometimes English. They had both received their education at universities in England and the United States, so far from this very Egypt of theirs. Royan loved the expression "This very Egypt" that Taita, the ancient author of the scrolls, used so often in them.

Royan's mother was an Englishwoman who had worked at the British Embassy in Cairo. She had met and married Royan's father, a young Egyptian officer on the staff of Colonel Nasser. It was an unlikely union and had not persisted into Royan's adolescence.

Her mother had insisted upon returning to England for Royan's birth. She wanted her child to have British citizenship. After her parents had separated, Royan had been sent back to England for her schooling, but all her holidays had been spent with her father in Cairo. Her father's career had prospered exceedingly, and in the end he had attained ministerial rank in the Mubarak government.

It was her father who had arranged her marriage to Duraid. It was the last thing that he had done for her before his death. All her modern training had made her want to resist the old-fashioned Coptic tradition of the arranged marriage, but her breeding and her family were against her. She had acquiesced and over time had grown to respect and like Duraid. She had known him ever since she had returned from England with her doctorate in archaeology and won her job with the Department of Antiquities, of which he was the director.

She had been Duraid's assistant when he had opened the tomb in the Valley of the Nobles, the tomb of Queen Lostris, the tomb that dated from about 1780 BC.

She had shared his disappointment when they had discovered that the tomb had been robbed in ancient times and all its treasures plundered. And it had been she who had been working at the wall behind the plinth on which the sarcophagus had once stood when a section of the plaster had fallen away to reveal in their niche the seven alabaster jars. Each of the jars had contained a papyrus scroll. Every one of them had been written and placed there by a man, a eunuch, whose seal identified him as Taita, the slave of the queen.

Since then their lives, Duraid's and her own, had revolved around those scraps of papyrus. What a story they contained: of the people of the Nile attacked by a superior enemy, armed with horse and chariot that were still alien to the Egyptians at that time. Crushed by the Hyksos hordes, the people of the Nile were forced to flee. Led by their queen, Lostris of the tomb, they had followed the great river southwards almost to its source among the brutal mountains of the Ethiopian highlands. Here Lostris had entombed the mummified body of her husband, the Pharaoh Mamose, who had been slain in battle against the Hyksos invaders.

It was a story that had fascinated Royan as they unravelled each hieroglyph that the old slave had penned on the papyrus.

It had taken them many years, working at night here in the villa on the oasis after their days at the museum in Cairo were done, but at last the scrolls had been deciphered—all except the seventh. This was the one that was the enigma, the one which contained symbols that had never figured before in all the thousands of texts they had ever studied. It was obvious to them both that Taita had not intended that the scrolls should be read by ordinary eyes. It had taken all their combined skills, all their imagination and ingenuity, but at last they were approaching the conclusion of the task.

Duraid picked up the top photograph from the pile in front of him. It was an extract from the central section of the scroll.

"It is the worst luck that the damaged piece of papyrus falls where it does." He placed his reading glasses on his nose and read aloud: "'There are many steps to ascend on the staircase to the abode of Hapi. With much hardship we reached the second step and proceeded no further, for it was here that the prince received a divine revelation.'" Duraid looked across at Royan. "'The second step.' It is a precise description for once. Taita is not being his usual devious self."

"Let's go back to the satellite photographs," Royan suggested, and drew the glossy sheet towards her. "To me it seems most logical that the natural feature that would obstruct them in the gorge would be something like a set of rapids or a waterfall. If it were the second waterfall, that would put them here—" Royan placed her finger on a spot on the photograph. At that moment the lights went out.

The soft thudding of the decrepit diesel generator in its shed at the back of the palm grove had ceased. Duraid crossed the room and took the oil lamp down from the shelf beside the door where it waited for just such a contingency. He lit it. "I will have to go down. I am sure it is nothing to be alarmed about."

He went to the door, and for no good reason she called after him, "Duraid, be careful!" He shrugged and stepped out onto the terrace.

She thought for an instant that it was the shadow of the vine over the trellis moving in the night breeze off the desert. Then she realised that it was a human figure crossing the flagstones silently and swiftly.

"Duraid!" She screamed a warning and he spun around.

"Who are you?" he shouted. "What do you want here?"

The intruder closed with him silently.

Royan did not see the knife in his right hand, but she could not mistake the upward stabbing motion aimed at Duraid's stomach. Duraid doubled up at the blow, and his attacker stabbed again. This time Duraid dropped the lamp and seized the knife arm.

The flame of the fallen oil lamp was guttering and flaring. The two men struggled in the gloom, but Royan saw a dark stain spreading over her husband's white shirt front.

"Run!" he bellowed at her. "Go! Fetch help! I cannot hold him!" The Duraid she knew was a gentle person, a soft man of books and learning. She could see that he was outmatched by his assailant.

"Go! Please! Save yourself, my flower!" She could hear by his tone that he was weakening, but he still clung desperately to his attacker's knife arm.

Royan had been paralysed with shock these few fatal seconds, but now she broke free of the spell and ran to the door. Spurred by her terror and her need to bring help to Duraid she crossed the terrace, swift as a cat, and vaulted over the low stone wall into the grove. At first she ran without purpose or direction. Then gradually she brought her panic under control. She glanced back, but saw nobody following her. As she reached the edge of the lake she slowed her run to conserve her strength, making for the housekeeper's shack across the nearest irrigation canal. She had covered less than a hundred paces when a voice called from the grove behind her, speaking in Arabic: "Yusuf, has the woman come your way?"

Immediately an electric torch flashed from the darkness ahead of her and another voice called back, "No, I have not seen her."

Another few seconds and Royan would have run full into him. She crouched down and looked around her desperately. There was another torch coming through the grove behind her.

She was blocked on two sides, so she turned back along the edge of the lake. Behind her the two men with torches were sweeping the grove and she could not keep her lead ahead of them. They were gaining on her—she could hear them calling to each other.

She turned and plunged down the bank to the lake. She knew that there were thick clumps of reeds ahead of her, that might give her shelter, and so she waded out until the bottom sloped away steeply under her feet and then broke into an awkward breaststroke, hampered by her skirts. However, her stealthy movements created almost no disturbance on the surface, and before the men had arrived at the point where she had descended the bank, she reached a dense stand of reeds. She eased her way into the thick of them and let herself sink. She could make out the voices of the men.

"Go in there, Yusuf, and bring the whore out."

She heard Yusuf slipping and sliding down the bank and the splash as he hit the water. "It is too deep. You know well I cannot swim. It will be over my head." Yusuf splashed around heavily, moving back to the bank, and not any of the other man's threats could persuade him to continue the hunt.

"The woman is not as important as the scroll," he protested, as he climbed back onto the roadway. "Without the scroll there will be no money. We always know where to find her later."

Royan saw the torches move away towards the villa. She was too shaken and terrified to make any attempt to leave her hiding place. She feared that they had left one of their number to wait for her to show herself. It was only a few minutes later, when she saw the glow of the flames flickering through the trunks of the palm trees, that she forgot her own safety and dragged herself back to the bank.

"The villa!" she whispered. "Duraid! Oh please God, no! No!"

She pushed herself to her feet and began to stagger towards her burning home. When she reached the steps at the far end of the terrace, she stopped and stared in horror into the burning room. The heat was like a solid wall. At that moment the roof collapsed, sending a roaring column of sparks and flames high into the night sky. She backed away from it, shielding her face with a raised arm.

Then she saw Duraid on the terrace and fell on her knees to take him in her arms. His hair was gone, frizzled away, and his face was a black crusted mask. All she could do was hold him and try to comfort him. She realised that he was dying—he had lost much blood and no man could survive such fearsome injuries.

"They will come soon to help us," she whispered to him. "Someone must see the flames. Be brave. Help will come very soon."

He was twitching in her arms, tortured by his mortal wounds.

"The scroll?" His words were barely intelligible. "All our work—"

Royan shook her head. "It's gone," she said. "Burnt or stolen."

"Don't give it up." His voice was faint but fierce. "Promise," he demanded. "Promise me!"

"I am alone. I cannot do it alone."

"Harper!" he said. Royan leaned closer so that her ear touched his lips. "Harper," he repeated. "Strong—hard—clever man—" and she understood then. Harper, of course. Nicholas Quenton-Harper. He had spoken often of this man with respect and warmth, and when the government had refused to fund their work he had even considered approaching the Englishman for sponsorship.

"But what do I tell him? How will I convince him? The seventh scroll is gone."

"Trust him," he whispered. "Trust him—"

Then she remembered the notebook in their Cairo flat, and the material stored in her PC. Not everything was gone.

"Yes," she agreed. "I promise you, my husband, I promise you."

There was a faint echo of satisfaction in his voice as he whispered, "My flower!" Then his head dropped forward, and he died in her arms.

The peasants from the village found Royan still kneeling beside him, holding him. By that time the flames were abating, and the faint light of dawn was stronger than their fading glow.

ROYAN LEFT the oasis as soon as she was able to escape from the condolences of the peasants, many of whom had worked for Duraid's family most of their lives. She felt numbed and isolated, so that their pious exhortations were meaningless and without comfort.

The tarmac road back through the desert to Cairo was busy, but she was able to make reasonably good time. Nevertheless, it was afternoon when she made out the green line against the tawny desolation of the desert that marked the start of the narrow strip of irrigated and cultivated land along the Nile.

She left the old green Renault in the underground garage of the apartment building and rode up in the lift to the top floor. She let herself into the flat and then froze in the doorway. The sitting room had been ransacked—even the paintings ripped from the walls. In a daze she picked her way through the litter of broken furniture and smashed ornaments. She glanced into the bedroom as she went down the passage, and saw that it had not escaped, but she could not bring herself to go in. Instead she continued down the passage to the large room that they had used as a study.

In the chaos she moved like a sleepwalker to her desk. Her PC was wrecked. They had shattered the screen and hacked the mainframe with what must have been an axe. She could tell at a glance that there was no information left on the hard drive; it was beyond repair. She glanced down at the drawer in which she kept her floppy disks. That and all the other drawers were empty, of course; along with the disks, all her notebooks and photographs were missing. Her last connections with the seventh scroll were lost. After three years of work, gone was the proof that it had ever existed.

She slumped down on the floor, feeling beaten and exhausted. She was alone and vulnerable as she had never been before. She sat in the wreckage of her life and wept until there was nothing left within her.

THE MINISTER kept her waiting only a few minutes before his male secretary ushered her into his presence. Atalan Abou Sin wore a dark, shiny silk suit, although Royan knew that he preferred a more comfortable robe. He noticed her glance and smiled deprecatingly. "I have a meeting with some Americans this afternoon."

She liked the Minister of Culture and Tourism. He had always been kind to her, and she owed him her job at the museum.

He asked after her health and they chatted for a while in a polite manner. Only Westerners would have the gaucherie to come directly to the main business to be discussed. However, to save him embarrassment Royan took the first opportunity he gave to tell him: "I feel that I need some time to myself. I need to decide what I am to do with the rest of my life, now that I am a widow. I would be grateful if you would consider my request for at least six months' unpaid leave of absence. I want to go to stay with my mother in England."

Atalan showed real concern. "Please do not leave us for too long. The work you have done has been invaluable. We need you to help carry on from where Duraid left off." But he could not entirely conceal his relief. She knew that he had expected her to put before him her application for the directorship. Things in Egypt were changing, women were emerging from their traditional roles, but not that much or that swiftly. They both knew that the directorship must go to Nahoot Guddabi, the minister's nephew, whose relationship to the minister fully made up for his lack of experience and qualifications in archaeology. He walked with her to the door of his office and shook her hand in parting, and as she rode down in the lift she felt a sense of freedom.

She had left the Renault standing in the sun in the ministry car-park. When she opened the door the interior was hot enough to bake bread. She opened all the windows and doors, but still the surface of the driver's seat burned the backs of her thighs when she slid in behind the wheel.

As soon as she drove through the gates she was engulfed in the swarm of Cairo traffic. She crawled along behind an overloaded bus that braked and forced her to a halt. She glanced in the rearview mirror. There was a taxi stopped only inches from her bumper, and behind that the traffic was backed up solidly. As she watched in the mirror, a battered red 200cc Honda came weaving through the congestion with suicidal abandon. There was a passenger perched on the pillion as, passing on the wrong side, the Honda skimmed through the narrow gap between the taxi and the cars parked at the kerb with nothing to spare on either side. It slowed slightly as it drew level with Royan's Renault, and the pillion passenger leaned out and dropped something through the open window onto the passenger seat beside her. Immediately the driver accelerated away down an alleyway.

As the Honda disappeared Royan looked down at the object on the seat beside her. It was egg-shaped and the segmented metallic surface was painted military green. She had seen the same thing so often on old TV war movies that she recognised it instantly as a hand grenade.

Without thinking, she grabbed the door handle beside her and flung all her weight against the door. It burst open and she tumbled out in the road. Her foot slipped off the clutch and the Renault bounded forward and crashed into the back of the stationary bus.

As Royan sprawled in the road under the wheels of the following taxi, the grenade exploded. The car's back window burst outwards and sprayed her with diamond chips of glass, and the detonation drove painfully into her eardrums.

A stunned silence followed the shock of the explosion, broken only by the tinkle of falling glass shards, and then immediately there was a hubbub of groans and screams. Royan sat up. The Renault was wrecked, but she saw that her leather sling bag had been blown out of the door and lay in the street close at hand. She pushed herself to her feet and hobbled over to pick it up.

All around her was confusion. Nobody was taking any notice of her, but she knew the police would arrive within minutes and then she would be tied up in days of interrogation. She slung the bag over her shoulder and walked as swiftly as her bruised leg would allow her to the alleyway down which the Honda had disappeared. In the horror of Duraid's murder she had not considered her own safety. Now she remembered the words of one of the assassins spoken beside the oasis: "We always know where to find her later!"

The attempt on her life had failed only narrowly. She had to believe that there would be another. I can't go back to the flat, she realised. They would look for me there. She walked a few blocks, doubling back on her tracks and watching behind her to make sure she was not being followed, before she hailed a taxi in the street.

She made the driver drop her in the street behind her bank, and walked the rest of the way. She withdrew what money was in her account, which amounted to less than five thousand Egyptian pounds. It was not a great sum, but she had a little more in her account in England, and she had her Mastercard.

"You should have given us notice to withdraw an article from safe deposit," the bank official told her severely.

She apologised so meekly that he relented, and was soon handing over to her the package that contained her British passport and her British banking papers.

Duraid had numerous relatives and friends who would have been pleased to have her to stay with them, but she chose instead one of the two-star tourist hotels away from the river where she hoped she could remain out of sight and anonymous.

As soon as she was alone in her room she phoned British Airways reservations. There was a flight to Heathrow the following morning at ten o'clock. She booked a one-way economy seat and gave them the number of her Mastercard.

It was after six o'clock by then, but the time difference between Egypt and the UK meant that it would still be office hours there. She looked up Leeds University in her notebook. Her call was answered on the third ring.

"Archaeology Department. Professor Dixon's office."

"Is the Prof in? It's Royan Al Simma speaking."

Professor Dixon came on the line. He was over seventy and should have retired years ago.

"Royan, is it really you? My favourite student." She smiled. Even at his age the pretty ones were still his favourites.

"This is an international call, Prof. I just want to know if the offer is still open."

Two months ago Prof Dixon had invited her to lecture on the discovery and excavation of the tomb of Queen Lostris, and the discovery of the scrolls.

"My goodness, I thought you said that you couldn't fit us in?"

"Change of circumstances. I'll tell you about it when I see you."

"Of course, we'd love to have you come and talk to us. When can you manage to get away?"

"I'll be in England tomorrow. I'm staying with my mother near York. I'll call you in a few days' time."

She hung up and turned her thoughts to other problems. If she was to lecture she would need her slides, and these were still at her office at the museum. The best way to get hold of them without fetching them in person was for her to phone the administration office and have them sent out to the airport in a taxi with one of the secretaries.

When the secretary handed them over to her at the check-in desk the following morning, he told her, "The police were at the museum when we opened this morning. They wanted to speak to you, Doctor."

Obviously they had traced the registration of the Renault. She was pleased that she had her British passport. If she had tried to leave the country with her Egyptian papers she might have run into delays. As it was, she passed through the checkpoint with no difficulty.

During the flight she passed the time by writing down in her notebook everything she could remember from what Duraid had told her of the man that she was going to find. She headed the page: *Sir Nicholas Quenton-Harper.*

According to Duraid, Sir Nicholas had served in Africa and the Gulf States with the British Army. He was a fluent Arabic and Swahili speaker and a noted amateur archaeologist and zoologist. He had written a number of articles for various scientific journals and had lectured at the Royal Geographical Society.

When Sir Nicholas had inherited the title and the family estate at

Quenton Park, he had resigned from the army to run the estate, but more especially to supervise the family museum that had been started in 1885 by his great-grandfather. It housed one of the largest private collections of ancient Egyptian and Middle Eastern artefacts.

However, from Duraid's accounts she concluded that there must be a wild, even lawless, streak in Sir Nicholas's nature. Duraid had first met him a number of years previously, when Sir Nicholas had recruited him to act as an intelligence officer for an illicit expedition to "liberate" a number of Punic bronze castings from Gaddafi's Libya. Sir Nicholas had sold some of these to defray the expenses of the expedition, but had kept the best of them for his private collection.

More recently there had been other expeditions, including one involving an illegal crossing of the Iraqi border to bring out a pair of stone basrelief friezes from under Saddam Hussein's nose. "He is a bit of a devil," Duraid had told her, "but the man to have with you when things are tough."

She smiled. The venture that she hoped to lead Sir Nicholas into was not exactly without its risks, and she supposed that lawyers might debate the legality of it endlessly. At Heathrow Royan phoned her mother. "Hello, Mummy. It's me. I'm at the airport and I'm coming up to stay with you for a while. Is that all right?"

"I'll go and make your bed." Her mother sounded as unflappable as ever. "What train will you be coming up on?"

"I had a look at the timetable. There's one from King's Cross that will get me into York at seven this evening."

"I'll meet you at the station. What happened? Did you and Duraid have a tiff? Old enough to be your father. I said it wouldn't work."

Royan was silent for a moment. This was hardly the time for explanation. "I'll tell you all about it when I see you this evening."

GEORGINA LUMLEY, her mother, was waiting on the platform in the gloom and cold of the November evening, with Magic, her cocker spaniel, sitting obediently at her feet. For Royan they painted a comforting and familiar picture of the English side of her lineage.

Georgina kissed Royan's cheek in a perfunctory manner. "Never was one for all that sentimental fiddle-faddle," she often said, and she led the way to the old mud-splattered Land-Rover in the carpark.

They drove in silence for a while and Georgina lit a cigarette. "So what happened to Duraid then?"

For a minute Royan could not reply, and then the floodgates within her burst and she let it all come pouring out. It was a twenty-minute drive north of York to the little village of Brandsbury and Royan talked all the way. Her mother made only small sounds of encouragement and comfort, and when Royan wept as she related the details of Duraid's death, Georgina reached across and patted her daughter's hand.

It was all over by the time they reached her mother's cottage. Royan had cried it out and was dry-eyed and rational again as they ate the dinner her mother had prepared.

Over the next few days Royan arranged her slides and notes for the lectures, and each afternoon she accompanied Georgina on long walks over the surrounding countryside.

"Do you know Quenton Park?" she asked her mother during one of these rambles.

"Rather," Georgina replied enthusiastically. "Magic and I help out at the shoots there four or five times during the season. Some of the best pheasant and woodcock in Yorkshire."

"Do you know the owner, Sir Nicholas Quenton-Harper?" Royan asked.

"Seen him at the shoots. Don't know him. Good shot, though," Georgina replied.

"I hear there is a private museum on the estate. They have a world-renowned Egyptian collection. I wanted to get a look at it."

"Not open to the public any more. Invitation only. Sir Nicholas is an odd chap, secretive and all that."

"Couldn't you get an invitation for me?" Royan asked, but Georgina shook her head.

"Why don't you ask Prof Dixon? He is often one of the guns at Quenton Park. Great chum of Quenton-Harper."

IT WAS THE end of the week before Prof Dixon was ready for her. She borrowed her mother's Land-Rover and drove to Leeds. The Prof folded her in a bear hug and then took her through to his office.

Being back in the cluttered room filled with ancient artefacts made her nostalgic for her days as a student. Royan told him about Duraid's murder, and Dixon was shocked and distressed, but she quickly changed the subject to the slides that she had prepared for the lecture. He was fascinated by everything she had to show him.

It was almost time for her to leave before she had an opportunity to broach the subject of Sir Nicholas and the Quenton Park museum.

"I'm amazed that you never visited it while you were a student," he said. "It's an impressive collection. As a matter of fact, I'm shooting on the estate next Thursday. I'll have a word with Nicholas. I'm afraid he isn't up to much at the moment. Last year he suffered a terrible tragedy. Lost his wife and two little girls in a motorway accident." He shook his head. "Awful business. Nicholas was driving. He blames himself." He walked her out to the Land-Rover.

"So we'll see you on the twenty-third," he told Royan as they parted, and he gave her a cheery wave as she pulled away in a cloud of exhaust smoke.

ROYAN'S LECTURE went off extremely well. She was a good speaker and she knew her subject intimately. She held them fascinated with her account of the opening of the tomb of Queen Lostris and of the subsequent discovery of the scrolls.

Afterwards Prof Dixon took Royan to dinner. He was delighted with her success, and ordered the most expensive bottle of claret on the wine list to celebrate.

Under the benign influence of the wine the Prof became expansive, and entertained her with accounts of the archaeological digs he had been on. It was only over the coffee that he turned to her and said, "Goodness me, I almost forgot to tell you. I have arranged for you to visit the museum at Quenton Park any afternoon this week. Just ring Mrs Street the day before, and she will be waiting to let you in. She is Nicholas's PA."

ROYAN DROVE through the massive cast-iron gates to the Quenton Park estate and followed the road signs pointing the way to the museum. Through the misty landscape she caught glimpses of the big house, designed in 1693 by Sir Christopher Wren. The museum was set in a grove of copper beech trees half a mile beyond it. Mrs Street was waiting for her at the side door. "There are no other visitors today. You will have the place to yourself. If I can help you in any way my office is at the end of the passage."

From the first moment that Royan walked into the African room she was enthralled. The primate room housed a complete collection of every single species of ape and monkey from that continent. It was obvious that the museum must employ a staff of skilled artists and taxidermists. She came up short as her eyes fell upon a fifteen-foot-high figure of Rameses II, depicted as the god Osiris in polished red granite. The god-emperor strode out on muscular legs, wearing only sandals on his feet and a short kilt. In his left hand he carried a war bow, and in his right a seal embossed with his royal cartouche. Upon his majestic head he wore the tall double crown of the Upper and Lower Kingdoms. His expression was calm and enigmatic.

Royan recognised the statue instantly, for its twin stood in the grand hall of the Cairo museum. She passed it every day on her way to her office. She felt anger rising in her. This was one of the major treasures of Egypt. It had been plundered and stolen from one of her country's sacred sites. It did not belong here.

The royal cartouche stood out in the centre, with the arrogant warning: "I am the divine Rameses, master of ten thousand chariots. Fear me, O ye enemies of Egypt."

Royan had not read the translation aloud; it was a soft, deep voice close behind her that spoke, startling her. She had not heard anyone approaching. She spun around to find a man standing close, his hands thrust into the pockets of a shapeless blue cardigan.

"Sorry. Didn't mean to startle you." He smiled a lazy smile of apology. "Nick Quenton-Harper," he introduced himself. "You must be Percival Dixon's old student."

She was surprised at how young he was. She had expected him to be a man of Duraid's age. She saw now that he was no older than forty for there were only the first strands of silver in the wings of his thick, rumpled hair. His features were tanned and weather-beaten, those of an outdoors man, and his eyes were green and penetrating under dark, beetling brows.

He was friendly and forthright, so she felt her hackles subsiding as she responded, "Yes, I am Royan Al Simma. I think you knew my husband, Duraid Al Simma."

"Duraid! Of course I know him. Grand fellow. We spent a lot of time in the desert together. How is he?"

"He's dead." She had not meant it to sound so bald, but then there was no other reply she could think of. "He was murdered."

"I am so terribly sorry. I didn't know." She saw the sympathy in his eyes, and she remembered that he also had suffered. "I telephoned him in Cairo not more than four months ago. He was his old charming self. Have they found the person who did it?"

She shook her head and looked around the hall to avoid having to face him and let him see that her eyes were wet. "You have an extraordinary collection here."

He accepted the change of subject at once. "Thanks mostly to my great-grandfather. We are very proud of our collection. Please let me show it to you." She followed him to a huge display case that occupied one complete wall of the hall. It was lined with shelf after shelf of royal *ushabti*, the doll-like figures which had been placed in the tombs to act as servants and slaves for the dead kings in the shadow world.

With his own key Nicholas opened the glazed doors of the case and reached up to bring down the most interesting of the exhibits. "This is the *ushabti* of Maya who served under three pharaohs, Tutankhamun, Ay and Horemheb."

He handed the doll to her and she read aloud the three-thousand-year-old hieroglyphics as easily as though they had been the headlines of that morning's newspapers. She spoke in Arabic to test him, and his reply in the same language was fluent and colloquial.

"It seems that Percival Dixon told me the truth. You must have been an exceptional student."

Engrossed now in their common interest, they moved slowly around the hall, lingering before each display case to handle and examine minutely each object that it contained.

It was as though they were transported back over the millennia. Hours and days seemed of no consequence in the face of such antiquity, until eventually Nicholas glanced at the Rolex Submariner on his wrist. "Five forty already, what on earth happened to the day?" He turned back to Royan. "Can't let you go without showing you something that Duraid was in on with me. Can you stay for a few minutes longer?" She nodded and he led her out of the exhibition halls through a door marked "Private. Staff Only," and down a corridor to the room at the end.

"The inner sanctum." He ushered her in. "Excuse the mess. I must really get around to tidying up in here one of these years. My wife used to—" He broke off abruptly. Royan glanced sideways at him and saw the devastating sorrow in his eyes. So as not to embarrass him she looked around the rest of the room, which was obviously his study and workshop. It illustrated the contradictions of his character—the bookish scholar set against the man of action. Among the muddle of books and museum specimens lay fishing reels and a canvas shotgun slip.

Nicholas went to the fireplace and threw a log on the fading coals. He kicked it until it flared up brightly and then beckoned her to a tall armoire against the opposite wall. He opened the double doors and said, "This is what Duraid and I brought back from Libya, without the consent of Colonel Gaddafi." He took down one of the exquisite little bronzes and handed it to her. It was the figure of a mother nursing her infant, and it had a green patina of age.

"Hannibal, son of Hamilcar Barca," he said, "about 203 BC. These were found at one of his old camps on the Bagradas River in North Africa. Hannibal must have cached them there before his defeat by the Roman general, Scipio. There were over two hundred bronzes in the hoard, and I still have fifty of the best of them. Had to cover expenses by selling the rest of the booty."

He went to his desk and brought out a bottle of whisky from the bottom drawer. "Can I tempt you?" he asked, but she shook her head. "Then may I offer you something a little more ladylike?"

"Do you have a Coke?" she suggested.

She took the glass he brought to her and returned his toast with it.

"To life!" she agreed, and then she went on, "Duraid told me about your visit to Libya." She replaced the Punic bronze in the armoire, then came to face him at the desk. "It was also Duraid who sent me to see you. It was his dying instruction to me."

"Aha? So none of this is coincidence then. It seems I am the unwitting pawn in some deep and nefarious plot." He pointed to the chair facing his desk. "Sit!" he ordered. "Tell!"

He perched above her on the corner of the desk, one denim-clad leg swinging as lazily as the tail of a resting leopard. Though he was smiling, he watched her face with a penetrating gaze.

First she told him about Duraid's murder. She left out nothing. He listened intently as she told him of the second attempt on her life in the streets of Cairo.

"Any suspicions?" he asked, when she had finished. "Anybody you can think of who might be responsible?" But she shook her head.

"There was no warning of any kind," she said.

They finished their drinks in silence, each of them thinking their own thoughts. Then Royan took a deep breath and asked, "Have you heard of an ancient Egyptian queen called Lostris, coexistent with the first Hyksos invasions?"

He laughed a little derisively. "Of course I have. And about the supposedly unviolated tomb of Pharaoh Mamose, somewhere near the source of the Blue Nile. I spoke to Duraid about it and he assured me the rumours were all a load of bunkum."

"It's not bunkum," she contradicted him, and then corrected herself quickly, "well, at least not all of it."

"I see. Duraid was lying to me, was he?"

"Not lying. Just delaying the truth a little. He wasn't ready to tell you the whole story then. He didn't have the answers to all the questions that he knew you would ask. He was going to come to you when he was ready. Your name was at the top of the list of potential sponsors that he had drawn up."

"Duraid didn't have the answers, but I suppose you do?" He was smiling sceptically.

Royan took a deep breath and said, "Several scrolls from that period are in existence. Six of them are still in the vaults at the Cairo museum. I was the one who discovered them in the tomb of Queen Lostris. But the scroll that most concerns us is the seventh, the one that was stolen by the men who murdered my husband."

Nicholas went to the fireplace and threw on another log. "What's the significance of that particular scroll?"

"It's the one that contains the account of Pharaoh Mamose's burial and, we believe, directions that might enable us to find the tomb."

"You believe, but you aren't certain?" Nicholas swung around to face her.

"Large parts of the seventh scroll are written in some sort of code. Duraid and I were in the process of deciphering these when"—she broke off and drew a long breath—"when he was murdered."

"You must have a copy of something so valuable?" He glared at her, so that she felt intimidated. She shook her head.

"All the microfilm, all our notes, were stolen along with the original scroll. Then whoever killed Duraid went to our flat in Cairo and destroyed my PC onto which I had transposed all our research."

"So you have no evidence? Nothing to prove that this is true?"

"Nothing," she agreed, "except what I have here." With a long slim forefinger she tapped her forehead. "I have a good memory."

He frowned and ran his fingers through his thick curling hair. "And so why did you come to me?"

"I have come to give you a shot at the tomb of Pharaoh Mamose," she told him simply. "Do you want it?"

Suddenly his mood changed. He grinned like a naughty schoolboy. "At this moment I cannot think of anything I want more. Tell me all the details."

"You know most of the story. Queen Lostris and her people are driven out of Egypt by the Hyksos. They journey south up the Nile until they reach the confluence of the White and Blue Niles. In other words, present-day Khartoum. In the holds of their river galleys they are carrying the mummified body of Queen Lostris's husband, Pharaoh Mamose the Eighth. Twelve years previously she had sworn to him as he lay dying that she would find a secure burial site for him, and that she would lay him in it with all his vast treasure. When they reach Khartoum she determines that the time has at last come for her to make good her promise to him. She sends out her son, Prince Memnon, with a squadron of chariots to find a burial site. Memnon is accompanied by his mentor, the narrator of the history, Taita."

Before she could continue, Nicholas interjected. "I know the area. When I was younger and even more stupid than I am now, I conceived the grandiose plan of boating down the Abay gorge from Lake Tana. The Abay is the Ethiopian name for the Blue Nile."

"Why did you want to do that?"

"Because it had never been done before. I thought I could write a book about the voyage and earn myself a fortune. I talked my father into financing the expedition. It was the kind of mad escapade that appealed to him. It was a fiasco. The gorge is the most hellish corner on this earth. It smashed up our kayaks before we had covered twenty miles out of the five hundred."

He looked serious for a moment. "I lost two members of our party. We were not even able to recover their bodies. They are still down there somewhere. I had to tell their parents—" He broke off as he remembered the agony of it.

"Has anybody ever succeeded in navigating the Blue Nile gorge?" she asked, to distract him.

"Yes. I went back a few years later. This time not as leader, but as a very junior member of the official British Armed Forces Expedition. It took the army, the navy and the air force to beat that river."

She stared at him. He had actually rafted the Abay. It was as though she had been led to him by some strange fate. Duraid was right. There was probably no man in the world better qualified for the work in hand.

"So you know as much as anybody about the real nature of the gorge," she said. "I will try to give you a general indication of what Taita actually set down in the seventh scroll. You will have to tell me how this agrees with your own knowledge of the terrain."

"Go ahead," he invited her.

"Taita described the escarpment as a sheer wall from which the river emerged. They were forced to leave their chariots and go forward on foot, leading the packhorses. Soon the gorge grew so steep and dangerous that some of these animals fell from the tracks they were following and plunged into the river far below. This did not deter them and they pressed on at the orders of Prince Memnon."

"I can see it exactly as he describes it. It's fearsome countryside."

"Taita then describes coming to a series of obstacles, which he describes as 'steps.' Duraid and I could not decide with certainty what these were. But our best guess was that they were waterfalls."

"No shortage of those in the Abay gorge," Nicholas nodded.

"This is the important part of his testimony. Taita tells us that after twenty days' travel up the gorge they came upon the 'second step'. It was here that the prince received a message from his dead father, in the form of a dream, in which he chose this as the site of his tomb. If we are able to determine what it was that stopped them, that would tell us just how far into the gorge they penetrated."

Nicholas stood up and stretched. "Before we can go any further we'll need maps and satellite photographs of the mountains, and I'll have to go over my expedition notes and diary," he said. "Let's start again tomorrow."

He walked with her to the old green Land-Rover in the carpark, and as she started the engine he told her through the open window, "We have a lot of work to do before we can even think of leaving for Africa. What time will I see you?"

"I have to stop off at my bank in York first thing. I won't be here before eleven," she said as she let out the clutch.

AFTER BREAKFAST Georgina and Royan climbed into the Land-Rover for their trip into York, Georgina driving.

As they turned into the village street, Royan noticed a large truck parked near the post office, but she thought no more about it.

Once they were out in the countryside they found there were patches of fog that in places reduced visibility to thirty yards. Royan glanced over her shoulder to check the road behind them, and saw that the truck was following them. Even as she watched it, the fog swallowed it up. She turned back to listen to her mother.

"This government is a troop of incompetent nincompoops."

Georgina squinted her eyes against the smoke from the cigarette that dangled from her lips. "And when they start fiddling around with my pension I get really mad." Her mother's pension from the Foreign Service was her sole income and it wasn't much.

"You don't want a Labour government, now tell the truth, Mummy," Royan teased. Her mother had always been the arch-Conservative.

Georgina wavered. "All I say is bring back Maggie." Royan turned and glanced through the dirty rear window again. The truck was still behind them, looming out of the trail of blue exhaust smoke that Georgina was laying behind her. Up until now it had hung back, but suddenly it accelerated up behind them.

"I think he wants to pass you," Royan told Georgina mildly.

"Everybody wants to pass me," lamented Georgina. "Story of my life." She held the centre of the narrow road doggedly. "Anyway, can't let him through here. There's a narrow stone bridge ahead of us."

At that moment the truck driver sounded his klaxon so close that it was deafening.

"Stupid bastard," Georgina swore. "What does he think he's playing at? Write down his number plate. I'll report him to the police."

"His plate's covered with mud. Can't make it out, but it looks like a continental registration. German, I think."

As if the driver had heard her protest he slowed slightly and fell back until a gap of twenty yards opened between the two vehicles. Royan had swivelled right around in the seat to watch him.

"That's better," Georgina said smugly. She peered ahead. "There's the bridge—"

For the first time Royan was able to see up into the driver's cab of the truck. The driver wore a balaclava helmet that covered all but his eyes and nose with dark blue wool. It gave him a sinister aspect.

"Look out!" Royan screamed suddenly. "He's coming straight at us!"

The engine beat of the great truck rose to a bellow as the truck smashed into them from behind and carried the Land-Rover forward on the steel bars that protected the shining chromed radiator.

Georgina wrestled with the wheel, trying to maintain control. "Can't hold her. The bridge! Try and get clear—"

Royan hit the quick-release buckle on her seat belt and reached for the door handle. The stone walls of the bridge were racing towards them at a terrifying pace. The Land-Rover was slewing across the road, completely out of control.

The door burst open in Royan's grip, but she could not push it all the way before the Land-Rover was flung into the solid stonework columns that guarded the approaches to the bridge.

The two women screamed as the vehicle crumpled and then flipped over the wall. It went down the embankment and began to roll.

Royan was flung clear. The slope of the bank broke her fall, but it knocked the wind out of her. She rolled down the incline and dropped into the icy waters of the stream below the bridge.

Just before her head went under, she found herself looking up at the sky and the bridge above her. She caught a glimpse of the truck as it roared away, but before she could register the large red trademark and company name painted on its side she was plunged below the surface of the stream. Impeded by her sodden clothing, she floundered to the bank and hauled herself out.

She knelt in the mud, coughing up the water she had swallowed. Then her own plight was forgotten as she heard the terrible sounds of her mother's agony coming from the wreck of the Land-Rover.

In frantic haste she clawed herself to her feet and stumbled through the wet and frosted grass to where the Land-Rover lay on its back. The bodywork was crumpled, the front wheels still spinning.

"Mummy! Where are you?" she cried, using the body of the vehicle to steady herself as she dragged herself towards the sound.

Georgina sat on the wet earth with her back against the side of the car, her legs thrust out straight in front of her. The left one was twisted so that the toe of the booted foot was pointed down into the mud at an unnatural angle. The leg was obviously broken.

Royan sank down beside her mother, placed one arm around her shoulders and hugged her. Then, fearing that the driver of the truck might return to finish the job, she crawled up the bank and tottered onto the road to stop the next car that arrived on the scene.

NOT UNTIL Royan was two hours late for their meeting did Nicholas become sufficiently worried to phone the police in York. Fortunately he had noticed the licence plate of Royan's Land-Rover.

There was a delay while the woman constable checked her computer, and then she came back. "I am sorry to have to tell you, sir, that Land-Rover was involved in an accident this morning."

"What happened to the driver?" Nicholas demanded brusquely.

"The driver and one passenger have been taken to the York Minster Hospital. I have no further information, sir."

It took Nicholas forty minutes to reach the hospital and almost as long again to trace Royan. She was in the women's surgical ward, sitting beside her mother's bed. Her mother had not yet come around from the anaesthetic.

She looked up when Nicholas stood over her. "Are you all right? What the hell happened?"

"My mother—her leg is badly smashed up. She's going to be here for ten days at the very least."

"How are you?"

"A few bruises and scrapes. Nothing serious."

"How did it happen?"

"A truck—it pushed us off the road. The driver crashed into us from behind. It must have been deliberate."

"Did you tell the police?"

She nodded. "Apparently the truck was reported stolen early this morning, while the driver was stopped at one of those Little Chef cafés. He is German. Speaks no English."

"That is the third time they've tried to kill you," Nicholas told her grimly. "So I am taking over now."

He went out into the hospital waiting room and used the telephone there. The chief constable of the county was a personal friend, as was the hospital administrator.

By the time he returned, Georgina had come around from the anaesthetic. Although still woozy, she was comfortable as they wheeled her off to the private ward that Nicholas had just arranged.

"Right you are," Nicholas told Royan as they left Georgina sleeping. "My housekeeper has made up a room for you at the hall. I'm not letting you wander around on your own any more. Otherwise, next time they try to cull you they may have a little more luck."

She was still too shaken and upset to argue, and she climbed meekly into the front seat of the Range Rover and let him drive her back to Quenton Park. Her trip to the bank could wait. As soon as they arrived, he sent her up to her bedroom.

"The cook will send dinner up to you. Somebody will fetch your gear from Brandsbury if you give the key to your mother's cottage to Mrs Street. In the meantime my housekeeper has set out some nightclothes and a toothbrush in your room for you. I don't want to hear from you again before tomorrow morning."

It was good to have him take control of her life. For the first time since that terrible night at the oasis she felt secure and safe.

In the morning a young housemaid woke her with a copy of *The Times* and a pot of tea. "Sir Nicholas would like you to take breakfast with him in the dining room at eight thirty."

While she showered Royan inspected her body in the bathroom mirror. There was a dark bruise on her thigh and her shin was scraped raw, legacies of the car crash. Gingerly she pulled a pair of slacks over the injury, then, limping a little, she went down the main staircase to find the dining room.

"Please help yourself." Nicholas looked up from his newspaper and waved at the display of breakfast dishes on the sideboard.

"Did you sleep well?" He didn't wait for an answer, but went on: "I've heard from the police. They found the truck abandoned in Harrogate. They're going over it now but they don't expect to find much. We're dealing with someone who knows what he's doing."

"I must phone the hospital," she said, spooning scrambled eggs onto her plate.

"I already have. Your mother had an easy night. I left a message that you would visit her this afternoon."

"This afternoon?" She looked around sharply. "Why so late?"

"I intend to keep you busy until then." He stood as she came to the table, and drew back her chair for her.

"The first attack on you and Duraid at your villa in the oasis—we can draw no conclusions from that, apart from the fact that the assassins knew exactly what they were after, and where to look for it." She found the abrupt change of subject disconcerting. "However, let's give some thought to this latest attempt. Who knew you were leaving Cairo? Who knew you were staying at your mother's cottage?"

"One of the secretaries from my office brought my slides out to the airport."

"Did you tell anyone what flight you were leaving on?"

"I told the minister about my plans when I asked for leave of absence. Not him—surely not?" Her expression reflected her horror at the thought.

Nicholas shrugged. "Some funny things happen. Of course, the minister knew all about the work that you and Duraid were doing on the seventh scroll?"

"Not all the details, but—yes—he knew what we were up to."

"All right. Next question, tea or coffee?" He poured coffee into her cup, and then went on, "You said that Duraid had a list of possible sponsors for an expedition. Might that give us some ideas as to a short list of suspects?"

"The Getty Museum," she said, and he smiled.

"Cross that one from the list. They don't go around murdering people. Who else was on the list?"

"Gotthold Ernst von Schiller."

"Hamburg. Heavy industry. Metal and alloy refineries." Nicholas nodded. "What was the third name on the list?"

"Peter Walsh," she said. "The Texan."

He nodded again. "Lives in Fort Worth. Fast-food franchising. Mail-order retail." There were very few collectors with the substance to compete with the major institutions when it came to making significant acquisitions of antiquities or to financing archaeological exploration. Nicholas knew them all, for it was a circle of no more than a couple of dozen men.

"Those are two beady-eyed bandits. We must believe that they both knew that Duraid had something going on. What would they do if they thought you stood in their way to the tomb of Mamose? We will put their names on our list of suspects." Then he inspected her plate. "Enough? Another spoonful of egg? No? Very well, let's go down to the museum and see what Mrs Street has found for us to work on."

When they walked into his study, she was impressed by the amount of organisation that he had accomplished in such a short time. In the centre of the room stood a large easel and blackboard on which were pinned a set of overlapping satellite photographs of southwestern Ethiopia along with a large-scale map covering the same area.

Royan crossed to one of the two chairs he had set up at a table facing the board. He stood at the board and picked up a silver-topped swagger stick from the table, brandishing it like a schoolmaster's pointer. "Class will come to order." He rapped on the board. "The first thing you have to do is convince me that we will be able to pick up the spoor of Taita again. Let us first consider the geographical features of the Abay gorge."

Nicholas described the course of the river on the satellite photograph with his pointer. "Along this section the river has cut its way through the flood basalt plateaus. Where there are intrusive strata of harder igneous schists the river has not been able to erode them, forming a series of gigantic waterfalls. I think your assumption that Taita's 'steps' are actually waterfalls is correct."

He came to the table and picked out a photograph from among the bundles of papers that covered it. "I took this in the gorge during the Armed Forces Expedition in 1976."

He passed her a riverscape of towering cliffs and a cascade of water that seemed to dwarf the men and boats in the foreground.

"I had no idea it was like that!" She stared at it in awe.

"You can see how that waterfall would halt a party of Egyptians coming upriver. There is usually some sort of wild-game path alongside cataracts, but there is simply no way to bypass this waterfall and get around those cliffs."

She nodded, and he went on, "However, there are a number of factors to consider, not least the fact that the river may have altered its course since our friend Taita visited it."

"Surely it could not have escaped from such a deep canyon," she protested. "Even the Nile must be held captive by that?"

"Yes, but it would certainly have altered the existing bed. In the flood season the river rises twenty metres up the side walls and bores through at speeds of ten knots or more."

They both stared at the photograph in silence for a minute, imagining the terrors of that mighty stretch of water in its full fury.

Then Nicholas picked up the swagger stick and on the satellite photograph traced the course of the river. "The gorge proper begins on the Ethiopian side of the border. No roads or towns in there. Nothing for five hundred miles except racing Nile waters and savage black basalt rock." He paused to let that sink in.

"Here, where one of the tributary rivers enters the main flow of the Abay, there is a Coptic Christian monastery, built into the rockface about four hundred feet above the surface of the river."

"Down there in the depths of the gorge?" She sounded incredulous. "Why would they build a monastery there?"

"Ethiopia is one of the oldest Christian countries on earth. It has over nine thousand churches and monasteries, a great many of them in similarly remote places. This one is the reputed burial site of St Frumentius, the saint who introduced Christianity to Ethiopia in the early third century."

"Could you find your way down?"

"No, but I have a few ideas on the subject. We will come to that later. Firstly, we must decide what we expect to find down there after four thousand years." He looked at her expectantly. "Your turn now. Convince me." He handed her the silver-headed pointer, dropped into the chair beside her and folded his arms.

She exchanged the pointer for her bag and brought out another photograph.

"Let me start with one of the inscriptions in the tomb of Queen Lostris. This photograph is an enlargement of a section of the murals from the burial chamber, that part of the wall that later fell away and was lost when the alabaster jars were revealed. Duraid and I believe that the fact that Taita placed this inscription over the hiding place of the scrolls was significant." She passed him the photograph.

"'The father of the prince who is not the father,'" he translated haltingly, "'guards eternally hand in hand with Hapi the stone testament of the pathway to the father of the prince who is not the father, the giver of blood and ashes.'"

He shook his head. "No, it doesn't make sense," he protested, "I must have made an error in the translation."

"Don't despair. You are making your first acquaintance with Taita, the champion riddler. Duraid and I puzzled over it for weeks," she assured him. "To work it out, let's go back to the history books. Do you remember Tanus, the Great Lion of Egypt?"

"Of course. He was the commander of the Egyptian armies who led the exodus from Egypt when they were driven out by the Hyksos."

"He was also the Queen's secret lover and, if we are to believe Taita, the father of Prince Memnon," she agreed. "And so 'the father of the prince who is not the father' is Tanus. Similarly, Pharaoh Mamose was Memnon's father in name only, but not his biological father. Again the father who was not the father. Mamose passed down to the prince the double crown of Egypt, the red and white crowns of the Upper and Lower Kingdoms—the blood and the ashes."

"What about the rest of the inscription?" Nicholas was clearly intrigued.

"The expression 'hand in hand' is ambiguous in ancient Egyptian. It could just as well mean very close to, or within sight of, something. Hapi is the god or goddess of the Nile. Throughout the scrolls Taita uses Hapi as an alternative name for the river."

"So if we put the seventh scroll and the inscription from the queen's tomb together, what then is your full interpretation?" he insisted.

"Simply this: Tanus is buried within sight of, or very close to, the river at the second waterfall. There is a stone monument or inscription in his tomb that points the way to the tomb of Pharaoh."

Nicholas exhaled through his teeth. "I am exhausted from all this jumping to conclusions. So what if Taita was indeed pointing us towards the second waterfall at the Dandera River? Just what do we look for when we get there? If there is a rock inscription, will it still be intact or will it be eroded away?"

"Howard Carter had an equally slender lead to the tomb of Tutankhamun," she pointed out mildly. "A single piece of papyrus, of dubious authenticity."

He grinned at her. His grin was irresistible and it was settled. They were going to Ethiopia.

LATER, HE drove her in his Range Rover to visit her mother in hospital, dropping her off at the hospital entrance. "I'll pick you up at three o'clock," he told her and drove on into the centre of York.

From his university days Nicholas had kept a small flat in one of the narrow alleys behind York Minster. The entire building was registered in the name of a Cayman Island company, and the flat's telephone number was unlisted. He used the flat for confidential and clandestine business.

He hadn't used the flat for months, and it was cold and musty-smelling and uninviting. He put a match to the gas fire in the grate and filled the kettle. With a mug of steaming tea in front of him he checked his watch. It was still early morning in Florida, but Alison picked up the phone on the second ring. She was the blonde feminine dynamo who ran Global Safaris, a company that arranged hunting and fishing expeditions to remote areas around the world.

"Hello, Nick. We haven't heard from you in over a year. We thought you didn't love us any more."

"I've been out of it for a while," he admitted. How do you tell people that your wife and two little girls had died?

"Ethiopia?" She did not sound at all disconcerted by the request. "When did you want to go?"

"How about next week?"

"You have to be joking. We only work with one hunter there and he is booked two years in advance."

"Is there nobody else?" he insisted. "I have to be in and out again before the big rains."

She hedged a little, then told him reluctantly, "This is without our recommendation, you understand. There is only one hunter who may take you on at such short notice, but I don't even know if he has a camp on the Blue Nile. He is a Russian, and we have had mixed reports about him. Some people say he is ex-KGB."

"I'm desperate," he told her. "I promise I won't come back to you with any complaints."

"Okay, then, no comebacks—" and she gave him a name and a telephone number in Addis Ababa.

"I love you, Alison darling," Nicholas told her.

"I wish," she said, and hung up on him.

When at last he got through to Addis a woman answered and switched to fluent English when he asked for Boris Brusilov.

"He is out on safari at present," she told him. "But I am Woizero Tessay, his wife, and if it is in connection with safari business I can help you." In Ethiopia a wife did not take on her husband's name. Nicholas remembered enough of the language to know the name meant Lady Sun, a pretty name.

NICHOLAS PICKED Royan up outside the hospital entrance.

"How is your mother?"

"She is doing well."

He paused and then asked delicately, "Will you be able to leave her? I mean, if we're going out to Africa?"

"I spoke to her about that. There is a woman from her church who will stay with her until she's well enough to fend for herself."

Royan turned to examine his face. "You have been up to something since I last saw you," she accused him. "I can see it in your face."

He made the Arabic sign against the evil eye. "Allah save me from witches!"

"Come on!" He could make her laugh so readily. "Tell me what you have up your sleeve."

"Wait until we get back to the museum."

As soon as they entered the building he led her to the hall of African mammals, and stopped in front of a diorama of mounted antelope. "*Madoqua harperii.*" He pointed to a tiny creature in the corner. "Harper's dik-dik, also known as the striped dik-dik."

It was a nondescript little animal, not much bigger than a hare. The brown pelt was striped in chocolate over the shoulders and back.

"A bit tatty." She gave her opinion carefully, unwilling to offend him. "Is there anything special about it?"

"Special?" he asked with wonder in his voice. "It is only one of the rarest creatures on earth. So rare that it is probably extinct by now. Which is why we are going to Africa to hunt for another specimen."

"I don't understand."

"Come with me and all will be explained." He led her back to his study and sat her down. "As you know, to cater for our own expedition would require months of planning and would mean having to obtain approval and permission from the Ethiopian government. That could take months, if not years. On the other hand, there are a number of legitimate safari companies operating throughout the country that have all the necessary permits, governmental contacts, vehicles and camping equipment. The authorities are quite accustomed to foreign hunters arriving and leaving with these companies, whereas a couple of feringhee nosing around on their own would have the local military down on them like a herd of angry buffalo."

"So we are going to travel as a pair of dik-dik hunters?"

"I have already made the booking with a safari operator in Addis Ababa, the capital. My plan is to look upon the whole of our project in two distinct stages. The first stage will be this reconnaissance. If we find the lead we are hoping for, then we will go back again with our own men and equipment. That will be stage two."

"When do we leave?"

"Before I tell you when, let me ask you one more question. Your interpretation of the Taita riddle—did you explain that in the notes that were stolen from you at the oasis?"

"Yes, everything was either in those notes or on the microfilm."

"So the uglies will have it all neatly laid out for them, just the way you laid it out for me."

"I am afraid they will, yes."

"Then to reply to your question as to when, the answer is I have booked two seats on a flight to Nairobi this Saturday—that is, in two days' time. We must get into the Abay gorge before the competition beats us to it. For all we know they are on their way already. We will drive down to London this evening and stay over at my house there. Are your yellow fever and hepatitis shots up to date?"

"Yes, but I have no equipment and hardly any clothing with me."

"We'll see to that in London. We both need visas for Ethiopia, but I have a contact who can arrange that in twenty-four hours. And we'll both start malarial prophylactics immediately." He worked swiftly through his list and then sent her up to her room to pack the few personal items she had brought with her from Cairo.

By the time they were ready to leave Quenton Hall it was dark outside, but still he stopped at the York Minster Hospital to allow her to say goodbye to her mother. He waited in the pub across the road, and he smelt of real ale when she climbed into the Range Rover beside him. It was a pleasant, yeasty aroma, and she felt so much at ease in his company that she lay back in the seat and fell asleep.

ON SATURDAY morning, when a taxi deposited them at the departures level of Heathrow Terminal 4, Nicholas surveyed their combined luggage with approval. She had only a single soft canvas bag, no larger than his, and her sling bag over her shoulder. His hunting rifle was cased in travel-worn leather, with his initials embossed on the lid. A hundred rounds of ammunition was packed in a separate brassbound magazine and he carried a leather briefcase that looked like a Victorian antique.

She had to step out to keep up with him as he strode through the crowded departures hall. Miraculously the throng opened before him. He tilted the brim of his panama hat over one eye and grinned at the girl at the check-in counter, so that she came over all girlish and flustered.

Once they were aboard the aircraft he set up a tiny chessboard on the arm of the seat between them, and when they landed at Jomo Kenyatta Airport in Kenya they were still locked in combat.

At the Norfolk Hotel in Nairobi he had booked a pair of garden bungalows, one for each of them. Within ten minutes of her flopping down on the bed, he called her on the house phone.

"We're going to dinner with the British High Commissioner. He's an old chum. Dress informal. Can you be ready at eight?"

One did not have to rough it too onerously when travelling around the world in this man's company, she thought.

IT WAS A relatively short haul from Nairobi up to Addis Ababa, and the landscape below them unfolded in fascinating sequences that kept her glued to the cabin window until the bleak brown deserts of the northern frontier district finally gave way to the highlands of the great central plateau of the ancient land of Ethiopia.

"In Africa only the Egyptians go back further than this civilisation," Nicholas remarked as they watched it together. "They were Christians when Europeans were still worshipping pagan gods."

From the air Addis was like so many other African cities, a mixture of the old and the new, of traditional and exotic architectural styles, thatched roofs alongside blocks of flats and the villas of the affluent, the government buildings and the grandiose, flag-bedecked headquarters of the Organization of African Unity.

After Nairobi the high-altitude air was cool and sweet when Royan and Nicholas left the aircraft and walked across the tarmac to the terminal building. As they entered, before they had even approached the row of waiting immigration officers, someone called his name.

"Sir Nicholas!" They both turned to the tall young woman who glided towards them with all the grace of a dancer, her dark and delicate features lit by a welcoming smile. She wore full-length traditional skirts which enhanced her movements.

"Welcome to Ethiopia. I am Woizero Tessay." She looked at Royan with interest. "And you must be Woizero Royan." She held out her hand to her. "If you will let me have your passports, I will see to the formalities while you relax in the VIP lounge. There is a man from your British Embassy waiting there to greet you, Sir Nicholas. I don't know how he knew that you were arriving."

The man waiting in the VIP lounge was dressed in a well-cut tropical suit and wore a Sandhurst tie.

"Nicky, how are you? It's good to see you again. Must be all of twelve years, isn't it?"

"Hello, Geoffrey. I had no idea they had stuck you out here."

"Military attaché. His Excellency sent me down to meet you."

Geoffrey looked at Royan with marked interest, and Nicholas introduced them. "Geoffrey Tennant. Be careful. No girl is safe within half a mile of him."

"I say, steady on," Geoffrey protested.

He quickly gave them a résumé of conditions in the country. "*He* doesn't like the idea of you swanning around on your own in the Gojam. I told him that you knew how to look after yourself."

In a remarkably short time Woizero Tessay was back. "I have cleared all your luggage, including the firearm and ammunition. This is your temporary permit. Here are your passports—the visas are stamped and in order. Our flight to Lake Tana leaves in an hour, so we have plenty of time to check in."

Geoffrey Tennant walked with them as far as the departures gate, where he shook hands. "Anything I can do, it goes without saying. *Serve to lead*, Nicky."

"*Serve to lead*?" Royan asked, as they walked to the plane.

"Sandhurst's motto," he explained.

IN THE HIGH, thin air the Twin Otter aircraft pitched and yawed in the updraughts from the mountains below. The land had an impoverished look, and bones of rock showed through the red earth.

Abruptly ahead of them the plateau over which they were flying was rent through by a monstrous chasm. Tessay leaned forward in her seat to tap Royan's shoulder. "The Abay River!"

The rim of the gorge was clear-cut, and the bare plains of the plateau gave way immediately to the heavily forested walls of the gorge. Down and down it plunged, a mile and more, on to the glittering snake of the river in the depths. In places the gorge was forty miles across, in others it narrowed to under ten. Deep down there between its terrible cliffs the river gouged dark pools and long slithering runs through the red sandstone. Man had made no impression upon it.

The aircraft banked into its descent and Tessay pointed over the starboard wing tip. "Lake Tana," she told them. It was a wide and lovely body of water, over fifty miles long, studded with islands. The Otter touched down on the dirt strip beside the lake, swung in, and stopped engines beside the run-down terminal building.

Only one vehicle was parked out there, a sand-coloured Toyota Land Cruiser. A white man lounged behind the wheel.

As Nicholas came down the ladder behind the two women, the driver slipped out of the truck and strode out onto the strip to meet them. He was dressed in a faded khaki bush suit, and he was tall and lean and walked with a spring in his step. His ginger hair was cropped short, his eyes were pale killer-blue. There was a puckered white scar that ran across one cheek.

Tessay introduced Royan to him first, and he made a short, choppy bow as he shook her hand. "*Enchanté*," he told her in an execrable French accent and then looked at Nicholas.

"This is my husband, Alto Boris," Tessay introduced him. "Boris, this is Alto Nicholas."

"My English is bad," Boris said. "My French is better."

Not much to choose between them, Nicholas thought, but he smiled easily and said, "So we will speak French then. *Bonjour*, Monsieur Brusilov. I am delighted to make your acquaintance." He offered the Russian his hand.

Boris's grip was hard—too hard. He was making a contest out of the greeting, but Nicholas had expected it. He knew this type of old.

"So you have come for a dik-dik?" he asked, just short of a sneer. "Most of my clients come for big elephant or at least mountain nyala."

"Bit rich for my nerves," Nicholas grinned, "all that big stuff. Dik-dik will suit me fine."

Boris grunted and turned to his wife. "Have you got all the stores I ordered?"

"Yes, Boris," she answered meekly. "They are on the aircraft." She is afraid of him, Nicholas decided, probably with good reason.

"Let's get loaded up then. We have a long journey ahead of us."

The two men rode in the front seats of the Toyota, and the women sat behind them with many of the packages of stores packed in around them. Good African protocol, Nicholas smiled to himself: men first, women fend for themselves.

The road swung away into the west, below the high mountains. This was the Gojam, a well-populated country; both men and women wore woollen shawls and baggy white jodhpurs, their feet in open sandals. Most of the men were heavily armed. They carried two-handed swords in chased-silver scabbards, and AK 47 assault rifles.

"Makes them feel like big men," Boris chuckled. "Very macho."

The condition of the road surface was appalling; in places it had been torn up by the tyres and tracks of heavy traffic.

"Military traffic?" Nicholas asked, and Boris grunted.

"Some of it. There is a lot of activity along the gorge—bandits and dissident warlords. Once Ethiopia was known as the breadbasket of

Africa, but when Mengistu seized power he used starvation as a political weapon. The people are still suffering terribly. However, most of this traffic is mineral-prospecting. One of the big mining companies has got concessions in the Gojam and they are moving in to begin drilling."

The sun was lowering as the road dropped into a rocky valley, down the length of which ran a river with steep, eroded banks. Above the river nestled a circular, white-walled church with a wooden Coptic cross set high on its reed-thatched roof. The village of thatched *tukuls*, circular huts, huddled around the church.

"Debre Maryam," Boris announced with satisfaction, "the hill of the Virgin Mary, and the river is the Dandera. I sent my men on ahead. They will have the camp ready for us. We will sleep here tonight, and tomorrow we will follow the river until we reach the gorge."

Boris's camp staff had set up the tents in a eucalyptus grove just beyond the village. "The second tent is yours." Boris pointed it out.

"That will do fine for Royan," Nicholas agreed. "I will need a tent on my own."

"Dik-dik and separate tents." Boris looked at him with a flat, pale stare. "A hell of a man. You impress me." He shouted for his men to erect Nicholas's tent alongside the other. "You may get up your courage during the night," he leered.

The shower under which they bathed was an oil drum hung in the lower branches of one of the bluegum trees, with a canvas screen set up around it. Royan used it first and came back looking cheerful and refreshed, and with a damp towel wrapped around her hair.

It was dark by the time the evening meal was ready. By the end of dinner the vodka bottle at Boris's elbow was empty and his face was flushed and swollen.

"Let me tell you something, a little secret." He grinned at Nicholas. "There is no such animal as a striped dik-dik these days, even if there ever was one. You are wasting your time and your money."

"Fine," Nicholas agreed mildly. "It's my time and my money."

Boris laughed scornfully, got up from the table and disappeared into the darkness in the direction of his tent, swaying on his feet.

"I apologise," Tessay told them quietly. "It is only in the evenings. In the day he is fine. It is a Russian tradition, the vodka." She smiled brightly; only her eyes stayed sad.

"It is a lovely night, and too early yet for bed. Would you like to walk up to the church? It is very old and famous. I will have one of the servants bring a lantern, so that you may admire the murals."

The servant walked ahead of them, lighting their way, and ushered them into the interior. The walls were covered with a magnificent display of paintings. In the lantern light they blazed like gemstones. There was a strong Byzantine flavour to the style: the saints' eyes were huge and slanted, with great golden halos over their heads. Nicholas wandered around the church, moved by the beauty of the moment, while Tessay and Royan knelt before the altar side by side.

I wish I had that kind of faith, he thought, as he had so often before. It must be a comfort. I wish I were able to pray like that for Rosalind and the girls. He could not stay longer, and went out and sat on the church portico where he watched the night sky. After a while his sadness abated. It was good to be back in Africa.

"NICKY!" Royan shook him awake. When he sat up and switched on his torch, he saw that she had thrown a woollen shawl over striped pyjamas before she had come into his tent.

"What is it?" he asked, but before she could answer he heard the sound of a hoarse and angry voice shouting invective in the night, and then the unmistakable thud of a clenched fist striking flesh and bone.

"He's beating her." Royan's voice was tight with outrage. "You have to make him stop."

There was a cry of pain after the blow, and then sobs.

Nicholas hesitated. Only a fool interferes between a man and his wife. Reluctantly he swung his legs out of the camp bed and stood up. He slept in boxer shorts, and he did not bother to find his shoes. She followed him, also on bare feet, to Boris's tent.

There was a lantern burning within, and it threw magnified shadows on the canvas walls. He saw that Boris had his wife by the hair and was dragging her across the floor.

"Boris!" Nicholas had to shout his name three times. Then they saw the shadow play on the canvas as he dropped Tessay and flung open the tent flap.

"What the hell is going on here?" Nicholas demanded.

"I am giving this black whore a lesson in good manners," Boris gloated. "Go away, English bastard! Mind your own business. Go away, before I give you a little lesson in good manners also."

He staggered forward and thrust his open hand against Nicholas's chest. Nicholas moved as smoothly as a matador avoiding the first wild charge of the bull. He swayed to one side and used Boris's own momentum to send him on in the direction in which he was already committed. Completely off-balance, the Russian reeled across the open ground in front of the tent until he collided with one of the camp chairs and went down in a sprawling heap.

"Royan, take Tessay to your tent!" he ordered softly. Royan ran into the tent and lifted Tessay to her feet.

"Please, don't do this," Tessay sobbed. "You don't know him when he gets like this. He will hurt somebody."

Royan dragged her, still protesting and weeping, out of the tent, but by now Boris was on his feet again. He bellowed with rage and picked up the camp chair that had tripped him. With a single jerk he tore off one of the legs and hefted it in his bunched fist.

"You want to play games, English? All right, we play!" He rushed at Nicholas, swinging the chair leg. As Nicholas ducked under it Boris reversed the swing, going for the side of his chest. Nicholas twisted away. Then he straightened, with all his weight rolling into the punch, and his fist slogged into the pit of Boris's belly just under the sternum. The Russian's breath was driven out of him in a great gusty belch.

The chair leg flew from his grip and he doubled over and collapsed. Clasping his middle, and heaving and wheezing for breath, Boris lay curled in the dust.

Nicholas straightened up and spoke to Royan. "Get her to your tent and keep her there." He combed his hair back from his face with his fingers. "And now, if you have no serious objections, may we get a little sleep?"

NEXT MORNING, Boris greeted Nicholas heartily. "Good morning, English. We had some fun last night. I still laugh to remember it."

Tessay was withdrawn as she supervised the servants handing around breakfast. One eye was swollen, and her lip was cut.

"We will go on ahead," Boris explained jovially as they drank coffee. "My servants will break camp and follow us in my big truck. With luck, we will be able to camp tonight on the rim above the gorge, and tomorrow we will begin the descent." As they were climbing into the Toyota, Tessay was able to speak to Nicholas softly for a moment, without danger of Boris overhearing her. "Thank you, Alto Nicholas. But it was not wise. You must be careful now. He does not forget, nor does he forgive."

Twice during the morning the Toyota became stuck in the foul ground. Each time this happened, Nicholas stripped to the waist and worked in the mud to free it. When they stopped beside the river for an alfresco lunch, therefore, he went down to the pool beside the road to wash off the filth of the morning's labours. Royan followed him down the slope and perched on a rock above the pool while he knelt at the verge to splash himself with the cold mountain water.

"I don't think Boris believes your story about the striped dik-dik," she warned him. "Tessay tells me that he is suspicious of what we are up to." She watched as he sluiced his chest and upper arms. She decided that his body was good to look at.

"He's the type that would go through our luggage if he got a chance," Nicholas agreed. "You didn't bring anything with you that has any clues for him? No papers or notes?"

"Only the satellite photograph, and my notebooks are all in my own shorthand. He won't be able to make anything of them."

"Be very careful what you discuss with Tessay. Her first allegiance is to Boris."

There was no improvement in the surface of the track as they drew nearer to the rim of the gorge. As they approached the end of the day's bone-jarring journey at last, they passed a signpost beside the track. Across the top of the board an arrow indicated a newly bulldozed road that headed off to the right, and the directions read:

PEGASUS EXPLORATION
BASE CAMP – ONE KILOMETRE
NO ENTRY TO UNAUTHORISED TRAFFIC

A scarlet horse reared in the centre of the board with its wings spread wide, on the point of flight.

A strong feeling of *déjà vu* overcame Royan as she stared at the image. Then she gasped aloud as the memory came upon her with stunning clarity. In an instant she was transported back into the icy waters of an English salmon river, the huge truck roaring over the bridge above her, and the prancing red horse upon its side.

It cannot be a coincidence, she assured herself silently, and I am not mistaken. It is the same company. Pegasus Exploration.

She was withdrawn for the last few miles of the journey, until the track they were following ended abruptly on the brink of the sheer cliffs of the escarpment. Boris pulled over onto the grassy verge. "This is as far as we ride. We camp here tonight. My big truck is not far behind. They will make camp as soon as they arrive. Tomorrow we will go down into the gorge on foot."

As they dismounted, Royan tugged at Nicholas's arm. "I must speak to you," she whispered urgently, and she followed him as he led her along the bank of the river.

He found a place for them to sit side by side, with their legs dangling over the drop. The cliff below them was a sheer wall of rock almost a thousand feet deep. It was so high that in the evening light the abyss far below was a dark, mysterious place, its bottom hidden from them by shadow and spray from the falls.

It was with a conscious effort that Royan pulled her mind away from the awe-inspiring scene and back to the troubled present.

"Nicky, do you remember I told you about the truck that forced my mother and me over the bridge in the Land-Rover?"

"Of course." He studied her face. "You are upset. What is it, Royan?"

"The truck had signwriting down the side. It was the same as the sign we passed this afternoon. The red Pegasus, the flying horse."

Nicholas stared out over the magnificent panorama of the gorge spread below them.

"A coincidence?" he wondered at last.

"Pegasus in both Yorkshire and Gojam? A strange coincidence."

"It doesn't make sense. The truck that hit you was stolen—"

"Was it?" she demanded. "If you were planning an assassination, would you rely on stealing a truck? Why not arrange for your own truck to be placed there for you, and for your driver to report it stolen only after you had a good head start on the police?"

"It's possible," he agreed.

"Whoever murdered Duraid, and made two further attempts to kill me, obviously has considerable resources at his disposal. On top of that, he has the seventh scroll in his possession. He has our notes, which point him clearly to this spot on the Abay River. Just suppose that he has control of a company like Pegasus—is there any reason why he can't be here in Ethiopia, just as we are?"

Nicholas was silent for a while. He picked up a stone and tossed it out over the cliff. They watched it drop away, dwindling until it vanished in the veils of spray far below where they sat.

Abruptly Nicholas stood up and reached for her hand to pull her to her feet beside him. "Come on," he said. "We're going to Pegasus base camp. Let's have a chat with the site foreman."

Boris protested angrily when Nicholas climbed into the Toyota. "Where the hell do you think you're going?"

"Sightseeing." Nicholas let in the clutch. "Back in an hour."

They reached the signposted turnoff and followed the side track over the ridge. The Pegasus camp lay on the far side. Nicholas braked to a halt on the crest of the rise and they studied it in silence.

An area of about ten acres had been enclosed by a security fence, with a single closed gate. Three massive diesel trucks in green and red livery were parked inside the fence. There were also smaller vehicles, several Quonset buildings and a tall mobile drilling rig.

"A big, well-organised outfit," Nicholas commented. "Let's go down and see who is in charge."

There were two armed guards on the gate, dressed in the camouflage uniform of the Ethiopian Army. One of them came forward suspiciously with his AK 47 rifle at the ready.

"I want to speak to the manager here," Nicholas told him in Arabic.

The soldier grunted, lifted the handset of the two-way radio and spoke into the mouthpiece. After five minutes the door of the nearest building opened and a white man came out. He was dressed in khaki overalls and a soft bush cap, and his eyes were covered by mirrored sunglasses. "What's going on down here?" he demanded in a Texan drawl, speaking around the stub of an unlit cigar.

"The name is Quenton-Harper." Nicholas dismounted from the truck to greet him and held out his hand. "Nicholas Quenton-Harper. How do you do?"

The American hesitated, and then took the hand. "Helm," he said. "Jake Helm, from Abilene, Texas. I'm the foreman here."

"Terribly sorry to worry you, but I will be hunting in this area over the next few weeks. I wouldn't like to endanger any of your employees with a stray shot. Can you give me some idea of where you will be working?"

He shook his head. "I'm running a prospecting outfit here, mister. I don't give out newsflashes on my movements."

"Your company—Pegasus. Can you tell me where your head office is situated? Who is your managing director?"

"I'm a busy man. You're wasting my time. Beat it!" Helm walked to the gate and gave brusque orders to the guards before marching back to his office building.

"Satellite dish on the roof," Nicholas remarked. "I wonder who our lad Jake is speaking to at this very moment."

"Somebody in Texas?" Royan hazarded.

"Doesn't follow, necessarily," Nicholas demurred. "Pegasus is probably a multinational. Just because Jake is Texan doesn't mean his boss is." He started the engine and U-turned the Toyota. "But if someone at Pegasus is the ugly mixed up in this, he will recognise my name. We have given them notice of our arrival. Let's see what we flush out of the bushes." When they arrived back at the river, they found that Boris's truck had arrived and the tents had been erected. Boris was less than welcoming, and maintained a sullen silence while Nicholas tried to placate him for commandeering his Toyota. It was only after his first vodka of the evening that he mellowed sufficiently to speak again.

"The mules were supposed to be waiting for us here. Time means nothing to these people. We cannot start until they arrive."

"Well, at least while we're waiting for them I'll have a chance to sight in my rifle," Nicholas remarked with resignation. "In Africa it never pays to be in a hurry. Too wearing on the nerves."

After a leisurely breakfast the next morning, when there was still no sign of the mules, Nicholas fetched his rifle case. Using the open hillside as a safe backstop, he stepped out two hundred yards and set up a cardboard carton on which he had taped a Bisley-type target. He came back to where Royan waited and then settled down behind the rock on which the weapon lay.

Royan was unprepared for the report of the rifle's first shot, which struck three inches right and two inches low. She jumped involuntarily and her ears sang.

"What a horrible, vicious thing!" she exclaimed. "I don't understand why you would want to kill any of God's creatures deliberately."

"That I can't explain," he said as he adjusted the telescopic sight. "It's something to do with an atavistic urge that few men, no matter how cultured they deem themselves, can deny completely." He fired a second time, then worked on the sight again. "Some of them work it out in the boardroom, others on the golf course, and some of us on a salmon river." He fired a third shot, merely to confirm the previous two, and went forward to retrieve the target.

He found that his shots had punched a tiny symmetrical rosette with all three bullet holes just touching.

He slid the rifle back into its case and they walked back together. As they came in sight of the camp, Nicholas pulled up short.

"Visitors," he said. "Aha! We have flushed something out of the undergrowth. Let's go and find out what is going on."

As they drew closer to camp, they realised that there were a dozen or more heavily armed, uniformed soldiers clustered around a green truck, and that an Ethiopian army officer was seated under the awning of the dining tent in conversation with Boris.

As soon as Nicholas entered the tent, Boris introduced him to the Ethiopian officer: "This is Colonel Tuma Nogo, the military commander of the southern Gojam region."

"How d'you do?" Nicholas greeted him, but the colonel chose to ignore the courtesy. "I want to see your passport, and your firearms licence," he ordered.

"Yes, of course." Nicholas went to his own tent to fetch his briefcase. He opened it on the dining table. "I'm sure you will also want to see my letter of introduction from the British Foreign Secretary in London. Here is another from the Ethiopian Ambassador to the Court of St James, and this firman is from your own Minister of Defence, General Siye Abraha."

The colonel stared in consternation at this fruit salad of official letterheads and scarlet beribboned seals.

"Sir!" He jumped to his feet and saluted. "You are a friend of General Abraha? I beg your pardon for this intrusion."

He saluted again. "I came to warn you only that the Pegasus Company is conducting drilling and blasting operations. There may be some danger. Please be alert. Also there are many bandits and outlaws operating in this area. I have been ordered to provide an escort for the employees of the Pegasus Company. If you yourself experience any trouble while you are here, or if you need assistance for any reason, you have only to call on me, sir."

"That is extremely civil of you, Colonel."

"I will detain you no longer, sir." He saluted a third time and backed off towards the truck, giving Nicholas his fourth and final salute through the cab window as the truck pulled away.

Nicholas acknowledged the salute with a nonchalant wave. "Now at least we know that Mr Pegasus definitely does not want us in his hair. I think we can expect his next move fairly promptly."

THE MULES arrived early the next morning, six big sturdy animals, each accompanied by a driver dressed in the ubiquitous jodhpurs and shawl. By midmorning they were loaded and ready to begin the descent into the gorge.

The pathway clung to the cliff and at places entered the body of the mountain, passing behind butts and needles of rock that time and erosion had prised away from the cliff face.

All that day they clung to the precipitous track as they eased their way down that terrible wall. It was late afternoon, and they were only halfway down, when they heard the rumble of the falls ahead. The sound became a thunderous roar as they moved around the corner of another buttress and came in full sight of the falls.

The wind created by the torrent tugged at them and forced them to clutch for handholds. The spray blew around them and wetted their upturned faces, but the Ethiopian guide led them straight on until, miraculously, the waters parted and they stepped behind the great translucent curtain into a deep recess of wet, moss-covered rock. The only light in this place was filtered through the waterfall, green and mysterious like some undersea cavern.

"This is where we sleep tonight." Boris pointed to bundles of firewood piled at the rear of the cave, and the smoke-blackened wall above the stone hearth. "The muleteers carrying supplies down to the priests in the monastery have used this place for centuries."

As they moved deeper into the cavern, the sound of falling water became muted to a dull background rumble. Once the servants had lit the fire, it became a warm and comfortable lodging.

"Just think!" Royan whispered to Nicholas. "Tomorrow we will be retracing the footsteps of old Taita himself."

NEXT DAY the party was on the pathway again as soon as the light was strong enough to reveal their footing. When the early sun struck the upper walls of the cliff face, they were still high enough above the valley floor to have an aerial view of the terrain. Nicholas drew Royan aside and they let the rest of the caravan go on ahead.

He found a place to sit and unrolled the satellite photograph.

"We can't see the Abay River from here," Nicholas pointed out. "It looks as though the Dandera has changed its course many times over the centuries. I can see at least two gullies that look like ancient riverbeds." He pointed down. "There, and there. They are all choked with jungle now." He squinted up at the sun and said, "We must get on. It looks close, but it will take us two more days to reach the Abay."

As they approached the bottom of the cliff, the gradient of the trail smoothed out and followed the Dandera River for a while. Sometimes they were several hundred feet above it, and shortly afterwards they splashed waist-deep through a ford, hanging on to the panniers of the mules to keep themselves from being swept away on the flood.

All day they followed the winding trail, and in the late afternoon they camped in a clearing above the river where it was evident that other caravans had camped many times before them on the way to the monastery.

As they sat at the campfire after the evening meal, Nicholas looked up suddenly. "Am I hearing things?" he wondered aloud.

"No," Tessay laughed. "That is singing you hear. The priests from the monastery are coming to welcome us."

They saw the torches then, winding up the hillside, flickering through the trees as they approached the camp. The muleteers crowded forward to greet the deputation from the monastery.

Young acolytes, bareheaded and barefooted, were followed by monks wearing long robes and tall turbans, an honour guard for the canopied palanquin as it was carried forward and placed in the centre of the camp. The crimson and yellow silk curtains shimmered in the light of the camp lanterns and the torches of the procession.

"We must go forward to welcome the abbot," Boris told Nicholas in a whisper. "His name is Jali Hora."

As they stepped up to the litter, the curtains were drawn aside and a tall figure stepped down. Tessay and Royan sank to their knees respectfully and clasped their hands at the breast. However, Nicholas and Boris remained on their feet, and Nicholas inspected the abbot with interest.

Jali Hora was skeletally thin. His robe was green and gold, worked with gold thread that glittered in the firelight. On his head he wore a tall hat with a flat top embroidered with a pattern of crosses and stars. The abbot's face was dead sooty black, the skin wrinkled and riven with the deep etchings of age. His beard was a startling silver white, breaking like storm surf on the old bones of his jaw. One eye was opaque and blinded, but the other eye glistened like that of a hunting leopard. He began to speak in a high, quavering voice.

"A blessing," Boris warned Nicholas, and they both bowed their heads. After the blessing two white-robed servants brought forward a stool of African ebony, took Jali Hora's elbows and gently seated him on it. Then the rest of the company sank to the earth around him, their faces lifted towards him attentively. The abbot smiled, exposing the yellow stumps of his teeth, and spoke briefly.

Tessay translated for him. "He says, 'Welcome to the monastery of St Frumentius and the season of Timkat.' He wishes you good hunting on the banks of the Abay River."

Immediately the solemn mood of the company changed. They broke out in smiles, and the abbot looked expectantly at Boris.

"The abbot says it has been a thirsty journey," Tessay translated.

"The old devil loves his brandy," Boris explained, and shouted to the camp butler.

With some ceremony a bottle of brandy was brought and placed on the camp table in front of the abbot, who tossed back a dram that made his good eye weep with tears, and his voice was husky as he directed a question at Royan.

"He asks you, Woizero Royan, where do you come from that you follow the true path of Christ the Saviour of Man?"

"I am an Egyptian, of the old religion," Royan replied. The abbot nodded with approval.

"We are all brothers and sisters in Christ, the Egyptians and the Ethiopians," he told her. "You are welcome, my daughter."

His servant poured another dram and the old man swallowed it at a gulp. Then Jali Hora turned to Nicholas. "He wants to know what animals you have come to hunt here," Tessay told him. Nicholas steeled himself and replied carefully. There was a moment of disbelief, then the abbot cackled happily.

"A dik-dik! You have come to hunt a dik-dik! But there is no meat on an animal that size."

Nicholas let them get over the first shock, and then produced a photograph of the mounted specimen of *Madoqua harperii* from the museum. He placed it on the table in front of Jali Hora.

"This is no ordinary dik-dik. It is a rare and holy dik-dik," he told them in portentous tones, nodding at Tessay for the translation. "Have any of your men ever seen one of these animals?"

One after the other they shook their heads. The photograph completed the circle and was passed to the rank of squatting acolytes.

Suddenly a young boy leapt to his feet, brandishing the photograph. "I have seen this holy creature! With my very own eyes!"

There were cries of disbelief from the others. One of them snatched the print from the boy's grasp and waved it out of his reach. His eyes were wild as he tried desperately to recapture the photograph but they teased him and jeered at his antics.

"The child is soft in the head, and often possessed by demons," Jali Hora explained sorrowfully. "Take no notice of him, poor Tamre!"

At that moment something tripped in the boy's mind and he fell to the ground. His back arched, his limbs twitched and white froth creamed on his lips.

Before Nicholas could go to him, four of his peers picked him up bodily and carried him away. The others acted as though this was nothing out of the ordinary. Their laughter dwindled into the night.

It was late when at last Jali Hora took his leave and was helped into the palanquin by his deacons. He took the remains of the brandy with him, clutching the half-empty bottle in one clawed hand and tossing out benedictions with the other.

"You made a good impression, English," Boris told him.

WHEN THEY set out the next morning, the path followed the river for a while. But within a mile the waters quickened, and then raced through a narrow opening between high red cliffs and plunged over another waterfall.

Nicholas and Royan left the well-trodden trail and went down to the brink of the falls. They were unprepared for the stunning vista that opened up before them.

They stood high on a ledge above the subgorge of the Nile. Below them was a mighty cauldron of red rock five hundred feet deep. The main flow of the river plunged in a green torrent into the shadowy abyss. It was so deep that the sunlight did not reach down into it. Beside them the sparser waters of the Dandera River took the same leap, the waters mingling and churning together in a welter of foam until at last they found the exit gorge and tore away down it.

"You sailed through that in a boat?" Royan asked.

"We were young and foolish, then," Nicholas said.

They were silent for a long while, both of them considering the magnitude and uncertainty of their task. Then Royan said softly, "One can see how this would have stopped Taita and his prince as they came upstream." She pointed down the gorge towards the west. "They must have followed the line of the top of the cliffs, right along here where we are standing." Her voice took on an edge of excitement at the thought.

"Unless they came up the other side of the river," Nicholas suggested to tease her, and her face fell.

"I hadn't thought of that. Let's consider that only when it's forced upon us."

Her face was upturned to his, and it seemed to glow under a light dew of perspiration and the strength of her commitment. He was seized by an almost overwhelming urge to take her in his arms and kiss her moistly parted lips, but instead he turned away and started down the trail, and said, "Let's catch up with Boris and find out what he intends to do."

They followed the trail along the edge of the cauldron to a spot where the track forked. One branch turned away from the river into a wooded depression, while the other still hugged the rim of rock.

Boris was waiting for them, and he indicated the track that led away from the river. "There is a good campsite up there in the trees where I stayed last time I hunted down here."

There were several tall wild fig trees throwing shade across this glade, and a spring of fresh water at the head. To minimise the loads, Boris had not carried tents down into the gorge. So as soon as the mules were unloaded he set his men to building three small thatched huts for their accommodation.

While this work was going on, Nicholas beckoned to Royan and Tessay, and the three of them set off to explore the monastery. Where the trail forked, Tessay led them along the path that skirted the cliff top, and soon they came to a broad rock staircase that descended the cliff face.

They came out onto a wide terrace that had been hewn by man from the living rock. The red rock overhung it, forming a roof to the cloister with arches of stone left in place by the ancient builders to support it. Over the ages the interior wall of the long covered terrace had been mined and burrowed to form the halls and cells and shrines of the monastic community.

There were groups of monks seated along the length of the terrace. Some of them were listening to one of the deacons reading aloud from an illuminated copy of the Scriptures, while from the interior of the cells and caves there came the hum of voices raised in prayer or supplication. The air was thick with the smell of incense.

They came at last to the entrance to the cavern cathedral of St Frumentius, the surrounds of the portal painted with a border of stars and crosses, and of saintly portraits. The eyes of the saints were huge and outlined in charcoal, their expressions tranquil and benign.

A deacon guarded the entrance, but when Tessay spoke to him he smiled and nodded and gestured for them to enter. The lintel was low and Nicholas had to duck his head to pass under it, but on the far side he raised it again to look about him in amazement.

The roof of the cavern was so high that it was lost in the gloom. The rock walls were covered with murals, a celestial host of angels and archangels who flickered and wavered in the light of candles and oil lamps. This was the outer nave of the church. In the far wall the doorway to the middle chamber was guarded by a massive pair of wooden doors that stood open. The visitors crossed the stone floor to the inner doors, but their way was blocked by two robed deacons, one of whom addressed Tessay sternly.

"They will not let us enter the middle chamber," Tessay told them regretfully. "Beyond that lies the *maqdas*, the holy of holies. Only ordained priests are allowed to enter the *maqdas*, for it contains the entrance to the tomb of the saint."

Disappointed and frustrated, they made their way out of the cavern and back along the terrace.

THEY ATE their dinner under the stars. The air was still stiflingly hot, and clouds of mosquitoes hovered just out of range of the repellents with which they had all smeared their exposed skin.

"And so, English, I have got you where you wanted to be. Now, how are you going to find this animal that you have come so far to hunt?" The vodka was making Boris belligerent again.

"At first light Royan and I will work the riverine bush along the banks of the Dandera River. It looked very promising habitat for dik-dik. Warn your people to keep clear of the river. I don't want the game disturbed."

They left camp the next morning in the glimmer of dawn. They moved slowly, stopping every dozen paces to look and listen. The thickets were alive with the sounds and movements of small mammals and birds. "Do you really expect to find your great-grandfather's dik-dik?" she asked.

"Of course not," he grinned. "Still, it gives us a wonderful excuse to fossick about in the bushes." He glanced back to make certain that they were well clear of the camp, and then gestured for her to sit beside him on a fallen tree trunk. "So, let's get it clear in our minds what we are looking for. You tell me."

"We are looking for the remains of a funerary temple, or the ruins of the necropolis where the workers lived while they were excavating Pharaoh Mamose's tomb."

"Any sort of masonry or stonework," he agreed, "especially some sort of column or monument."

"Taita's stone testament," she nodded. "Probably badly weathered, fallen over, covered with vegetation—I don't know. Anything at all."

"Well, why are we sitting here?" Nicholas stood up. "Let's get on."

A little after noon they reached the spot where the river issued from between the cliffs of the chasm. They explored as far as they were able before their way was blocked by the rocks that fell straight into the flood and would not allow them to penetrate further.

They retreated downstream, and crossed to the far bank over a primitive rope suspension bridge that Nicholas guessed had been built by the monks from the monastery. Once again they tried to push on into the chasm, but were forced to abandon the attempt.

"If we can't get through there, then it's highly unlikely that Taita and his workmen would have done so," Nicholas told Royan.

They went back as far as the hanging bridge and found a shady place close to the water to eat their lunch. The heat in the middle of the day was stupefying. Royan wetted her cotton neckerchief in the river and dabbed at her face as she lay on the ground. Nicholas lay beside her and studied the cliffs through his binoculars.

It was late afternoon when they arrived back at the camp, and Tessay hurried out to greet them.

"I have been waiting for you to return. Jali Hora has invited us to a banquet to celebrate Katera, the eve of Timkat. There is just time for you to change and shower before we go down to the monastery."

THE ABBOT sent a party of young acolytes to escort them to the banqueting hall. Royan recognised one of these as Tamre, the epileptic boy. Once more they descended the stone stairway down the cliff and came out onto the torchlit terrace. They stooped through the low entrance to the outer nave of the cathedral, where the monks were seated crosslegged on a carpet of rushes.

The visitors were led forward to a spot that had been left clear for them directly in front of the wooden doors to the middle chamber. As soon as they were settled, another party of acolytes came in from the terrace bearing flasks of *tej*, the local honey mead, and knelt to place a separate pottery flask in front of each of them.

The monks were concentrating their hospitality on Royan. The fact that she was a Coptic Christian, a true believer, had impressed them. It was obvious also that her beauty had not gone entirely unremarked by this company of celibate men.

Suddenly there was the sound of music and drums, and at last Jali Hora, the ancient abbot, appeared at the head of the steps. He wore a full-length robe of crimson satin, with a gold-thread-embroidered stole around his shoulders. On his head was a massive crown of gilt brass. A weighty silence fell upon the company.

"Now he will say the grace," Tessay told them, and bowed her head.

Jali Hora's grace was fervent and lengthy. When at last he came to the end, two servants helped him down the stairs and seated him on his carved stool at the head of the circle of priests.

A procession of acolytes entered from the terrace, each of them bearing upon his head a flat woven reed basket filled with unleavened *injera* bread, and two more acolytes staggered in carrying a steaming brass pot filled with gallons of spicy mutton stew.

The assembly fell on the food voraciously. They tore off wads of *injera* and scooped up the stew with it, and then stuffed the parcel into their mouths. They washed it down with long swallows from the *tej* flasks before wrapping another parcel. Soon every one of them was greasy to the elbow as they chewed and drank and laughed.

Only a churned-up mess of bread and grease remained when the acolytes came tottering in under the weight of another set of pots, this time filled to overflowing with curried chicken.

"I don't think I can take much more of this," Royan told Nicholas queasily.

"Close your eyes and think of England," he advised her. "You are the star of the evening. They aren't going to let you escape."

Jali Hora, by now warmed with *tej*, lurched to his feet and walked unsteadily across the chamber. He came to a halt in front of Royan, sank stiffly to his knees and embraced her, almost losing his shiny crown in the process. Then, without relinquishing his embrace, he made himself a place beside her.

"It looks as though you have made another conquest," Nicholas told her drily.

Suddenly Royan started violently as she stared at Jali Hora's crown, which had slipped forward over his eyes.

"What is it?" Nicholas demanded quietly.

She reached down and grasped his wrist. "Look at his crown! The jewel! The blue jewel!" she gasped.

He saw it then, among the semiprecious garnets and rock crystal. The size of a silver dollar, it was a seal of blue ceramic, perfectly round, and in its centre was an etching of an Egyptian war chariot. Around the circumference was a legend engraved in hieroglyphics. It took him only a few moments to read it to himself:

I COMMAND TEN THOUSAND CHARIOTS.
I AM TAITA, MASTER OF THE ROYAL HORSE.

Royan desperately wanted to escape from the oppressive atmosphere of the cavern. She knew it was unwise to draw attention to the scrap of ceramic, but when she glanced across the circle she saw that Boris was far past noticing anything. In the end it was Boris who gave her the excuse for which she had been seeking. He tried to get to his feet, but his legs collapsed under him. He sagged forward quite gracefully, and lay there snoring noisily.

Nicholas considered the unlovely spectacle. "I rather suspect Prince Charming has had enough for one night," he murmured. Then he stood up, stooped over Boris and with a sudden jerk heaved him over his shoulder in a fireman's lift.

"Good night, all!" he told the assembled monks, few of whom were in any condition to respond. Then he carried Boris away, followed by the two women, who had to hurry to keep up with Nicholas as he strode down the terrace and up the stairway without a pause.

Back at camp, Nicholas threw his burden down on Boris's own bed and stood back panting heavily. Boris groaned, rolled over and vomited copiously.

"On that pleasant note I will bid you good night," Nicholas told Tessay, stepping out of the hut into the warm African night.

He breathed in the smell of the forest and the river with relief, and then turned to Royan as she gripped his arm and led him excitedly to her own tent.

"Did you see it?" she demanded. "Could you read it?"

" 'I command ten thousand chariots,' " he recited.

" 'I am Taita, master of the royal horse.' " She completed it for him. "He was here. Oh, Nicky! He was here. Taita was here. That's the proof we wanted. Now we know that we're not wasting our time."

She flopped down on her camp bed and hugged herself ecstatically. "Where do you suppose the seal came from? Who found it?"

He sat down beside her. "Steady on, dear girl. Maybe the seal was manufactured in Hong Kong. There is a little factory there that turns them out by the thousands."

She punched his arm. "Be serious."

"Okay. Maybe Taita dropped the seal in the gorge while he was working on the construction of Pharaoh's tomb. Three thousand years later an old monk, one of the very first to live here at the monastery, picked it up. Of course, he could not read the hieroglyphics. He took it to the abbot, who declared it to be a relic of Frumentius, and had it set in the crown."

"And they all lived happily ever after," Royan agreed. "Then this proves that Taita really was here, and our theories are correct."

" 'Proves' is too strong a word. Let's just say that it points in that direction," he demurred.

She wriggled around on the bed to face him squarely. Her eyes were bright, and her cheeks flushed a warm rosy brown. He leaned very slowly towards her, treating her gently, giving her every opportunity to pull away. She did not move, but stared into his eyes, as if seeking something, some reassurance. When their lips were an inch apart, Nicholas stopped, and it was she who made the last movement. She brought their mouths together.

At first it was soft, just a light mingling of their breath, and then it became harsher, more urgent. Then suddenly she whimpered and with a huge effort of will tore herself out of his arms.

"No," she whispered. "Please, Nicky, not yet. I'm not ready yet."

He picked up her hand and turned it between his palms. Then lightly he kissed the tips of her fingers. "I'll see you in the morning." He dropped her hand and stood up. "Early. Be ready!" he said, and stooped out through the doorway of the hut.

"BORIS IS not awake yet," Tessay told them as she served their breakfast early next morning.

"Now that is a great surprise to me," Nicholas said, without looking up from his plate. He and Royan were still slightly awkward in each other's presence, remembering the circumstances in which they had parted the previous evening. However, as Nicholas slung the rifle and the pack over his shoulder and they set off up the valley, their mood changed to one of anticipation.

They had been going for an hour when Nicholas glanced over his shoulder and frowned.

"We are being followed."

Taking her wrist, he drew her behind a slab of sandstone. He poised himself, and suddenly leapt forward to seize the lanky figure in a dirty white *shamma* who was sneaking up the valley behind them. With a howl Tamre fell to his knees.

Nicholas hauled him to his feet. "Tamre! What are you doing following us? Who sent you?" he demanded in Arabic.

The boy rolled his eyes towards Royan.

"Leave the child, Nicky. You will precipitate another fit." Tamre scurried behind Royan and clung to her hand for protection.

"Peace, Tamre," Nicholas soothed him. "I will not hurt you, unless you lie to me. Who sent you to follow us?"

"I came alone. Nobody sent me," blubbered the boy. "I came to show you where I saw the holy animal."

Nicholas stared at him for a moment. "I'll be damned if the boy doesn't actually believe he saw Great-grandfather's dik-dik." Then he laughed softly. "All right, Tamre. I will give you a chance. Take us to where you saw the holy animal."

Tamre would not relinquish his grip on Royan's hand. He clung to it as he danced beside her, leading her along.

For an hour he led them up over the high ground above the valley, until they were back to the Dandera River, at a point where it still ran in the bed of the deep ravine.

"I saw the holy thing over there." Tamre pointed to the far side of the chasm where a small feeder spring meandered out of the thorny bush and trickled down into the river two hundred feet below.

Nicholas shrugged. "Well, seeing that we're here, we might as well sit a while and see if Great-grandpa's dik-dik puts in an appearance."

He picked a spot in the shade of one of the stunted thorn trees that hung on the lip of the chasm, sat with his back against its trunk and laid the rifle across his lap.

By this time it was past noon and the heat was stifling. He passed the water bottle to Royan and, while she drank, glanced at Tamre and suggested to her in English, "This might be a good time to find out what, if anything, the lad knows about the tomb of Frumentius. He is besotted with you. He will tell you anything you want to know."

She began gently, chatting softly to the boy. Occasionally she stroked his head. She spoke to him of the previous night's banquet, the beauty of the underground church and the murals, and then at last asked if he had seen the tomb of Frumentius.

Tamre looked around him guiltily. "Only the ordained priests are allowed into the holy of holies."

"You have seen it, Tamre," she accused him gently, intrigued by the boy's guilt. "You can tell me. I will not tell the priests."

"Only once," he admitted. "The other boys sent me to touch the *tabot* stone. All the new acolytes are made to do this. I was very afraid. It was after midnight when the priests were asleep."

"Did you see the tomb of the saint?" Royan asked, and the boy nodded vigorously.

"I saw the coffin of the saint through the bars across the entrance. It is wood and there is painting on it, the face of the saint."

"Is he a black man?"

"No—a white man with a red beard. The painting is very old."

"Is there anything else you remember about the tomb of the saint?" Royan tried to prod his memory, but Tamre shook his head.

"It was very dark," he apologised.

"It does not matter. Tell me about the *tabot*," she suggested, but Nicholas forestalled her.

"No, you tell me about the *tabot*," he demanded of her. "Is it similar to the Jewish Tabernacle?"

She turned to him. "Yes. It is usually wrapped in an embroidered cloth. The only difference is that the Jewish Tabernacle is carved with the Ten Commandments, but in our Church it is carved with the words of dedication of the particular church that houses it."

Nicholas frowned with concentration. "Tell us about the *tabot* stone, Tamre," he asked.

"It is so high, and so square." He indicated a height of a little above his own shoulder and the width of his spread hands. "The *tabot* stands on top of it."

"What does the stone look like? Are there paintings on it also?"

"I don't know. I don't know. The stone is wrapped with cloth."

Nicholas and Royan exchanged startled glances, and then Royan turned back to the boy.

"Covered?" Royan leaned closer to him. "The stone is covered?"

"They say that it is only uncovered by the abbot on the birthday of St Frumentius."

Nicholas smiled thoughtfully. "I would rather like to have a look at the *tabot* stone—in its uncovered state."

Royan whispered softly, "The covered stone? Taita's testament?"

"Don't say it aloud," he pleaded. "The Devil is listening."

They were silent again, both of them thinking furiously. Then Royan started: "Nicky, what if—?" She broke off. "No, that won't work." She relapsed into frowning silence again.

Tamre broke the quiet with a sudden squeak of excitement. "There it is. Look!" He seized her arm and shook it. He was trembling with emotion. With his other hand he was pointing out across the river. "There at the edge of the thorn bushes. The holy creature."

Nicholas scrabbled in his pack and brought out his binoculars. He lifted and focused them, and then he began to chuckle.

"Hallelujah! Great-grandpa's reputation is safe at last." It was three hundred yards away, but through the ten-power lens he could make it out in detail. It was almost half as large again as the common dik-dik and instead of drab grey its coat was a rich red brown. Its most striking feature, however, was the distinct dark bars of chocolate colour across its shoulders and back.

"It's *Madoqua harperii*, no less," Nicholas whispered. "I'm sorry, Great-grandfather, for doubting you." He passed Royan the glasses.

The dik-dik stood half in shadow, wriggling its nose as it snuffled the air. Royan heard the snick of the rifle action as Nicholas worked the bolt and chambered a round. Hurriedly she lowered the glasses and glanced at him. "You aren't going to shoot it?"

"No, not at that range. Over three hundred yards, and a small target. I'll wait for it to get closer."

"But it's so beautiful."

"I take it, then, that it would be perfectly all right if it were ugly?"

She said nothing, but raised the binoculars again. The dik-dik had lowered its head to nibble at a tuft of coarse grass. Then it lifted its head again and came on down the clearing in the thorn scrub.

"Go back!" She tried to will it into safety, but it kept on coming.

Nicholas settled himself behind the root of the tree. He screwed up his hat into a soft pad on which to rest the rifle.

Abruptly the dik-dik came to a halt, quivering with tension, then bolted back into the thorn scrub.

"Go, dik-dik, go!" said Royan.

Nicholas sat up and grunted with disgust. "I can't make out what frightened him." Then he cocked his head. There was an alien sound on the air, growing each second—a clatter and a shrill whistle.

"Chopper!" Nicholas recognised the sound. He took the binoculars from Royan and turned them to the sky. "There it is," he said grimly. "A Bell Jet Ranger. Green and red fuselage, and the red horse emblem. Your old friends from Pegasus Exploration."

The sound of the rotors crescendoed, and Royan could make out the flying horse on the fuselage of the helicopter. Tamre crouched behind her trying to hide, his teeth chattering with terror.

"It looks as if our friend Jake Helm has got himself some fancy transport. If Pegasus is in any way connected with Duraid's murder and the attempts on your life, we can expect them to be breathing down our necks from now on. Unless he's just on a joy ride, he's probably looking for our camp, and he'll have no trouble finding it."

"When your enemy is up in the air, it gives you a helpless feeling. Still, they haven't spotted us—" But even as Royan said it, Jake Helm looked directly at them across the open void. Although his expression did not change, he tapped the pilot's shoulder and pointed.

Nicholas put on his hat and tipped the brim forward over one eye, then he gave Jake Helm a laconic wave.

The foreman made no response to the greeting. Still without change of expression, he said something to the pilot out of the corner of his mouth, and immediately the helicopter banked away to the north, heading back directly towards the base camp.

"Mission accomplished. He found what he was looking for." Royan sat up. "Us!"

"And he must have spotted the camp. He knows where to find us again," Nicholas agreed. He stood up. "I don't think we're going to see Great-grandfather's dik-dik again today. He's been thoroughly shaken up by the chopper. I'll come back for another try tomorrow."

Tamre was still shivering and weeping, but he calmed down quickly when Royan soothed him, and followed them back towards the camp. However, when they neared the grove he slipped away in the direction of the monastery.

THAT EVENING at dinner Boris showed no ill effects from the previous night's debauch. During the day he had taken out his shotgun and shot a bunch of pigeons. Tessay had marinated these and barbecued them over the coals.

During the meal Tessay replied only in low monosyllables when Royan tried to draw her into the conversation. She looked tragic and defeated. When the meal ended, they left her sitting with Boris at the fire, a fresh bottle of vodka on the table beside him.

"The way he's pumping the liquor, it looks as if I might be called out on another midnight rescue mission," Nicholas remarked as they made their way to their own huts.

"Tessay has been in camp all day with him. There has been more trouble. She told me that as soon as they get back to Addis Ababa she is going to leave him. She can't take any more of this, and she has asked me if she can come with us tomorrow. She cannot stand another day in camp with Boris on her own."

"Tell her to come along," Nicholas said resignedly. "The more of us the merrier. Perhaps we will be able to frighten the dik-dik to death by sheer weight of numbers. Save me wasting ammunition."

It was still dark when the three of them left camp the next morning. There was no sign of Boris and when Nicholas asked about him Tessay said simply, "After you went to bed last night he finished the bottle. He won't be out of his hut before noon. He won't miss me."

The sun was well up by the time they again reached the spot under the thorn tree on the lip of the chasm and settled down to wait.

"How will you retrieve the carcass, if you do manage to shoot the poor little creature?" Royan asked.

"I made certain of that before we left camp," he explained. "I spoke to the head tracker. If he hears a shot he will bring up the ropes and help me to get across to the other side. They teach you some useful things in the army." By noon there was still no sign of the dik-dik. The valley sweltered in the midday sun and the women lay somnolent in the heat. The whole world was silent and heat-struck. Nicholas found his own eyelids becoming leaden. On the very edge of sleep he heard a sound, close by in the thorn scrub behind him.

It was a tiny sound, but one that he knew well. It was the metallic sound of the safety catch on an AK 47 assault rifle being slipped forward into the "Fire" position.

In one fluid movement he lifted the rifle out of his lap, picked up his target immediately and swung onto it.

There was a man crouched twenty paces away, the assault rifle he carried aimed into Nicholas's face. He was black, and dressed in tattered camouflage fatigues. His webbing held a bushknife and grenades, water bottle and all the other accoutrements of a guerrilla fighter.

Shufta! thought Nicholas. A real pro. He realised that if the intention had been to kill him, then he would be dead already.

The man gave an order in Arabic. "Salim, cover the women. Shoot them if he moves."

Another guerrilla stepped out of the scrub, a Soviet RPD light machine gun on his hip. There were other stealthy rustling sounds in the bush all around them. These two were not the only ones, Nicholas realised. Very slowly and deliberately he lowered the muzzle of the rifle, laid the weapon down and raised his hands.

The guerrilla leader acknowledged his surrender by coming to his full height and speaking rapidly to his men, still in Arabic. "Get the rifle and his pack."

"We are British subjects," Nicholas told him loudly. "We are simple tourists. We are not military. We are not government people."

"Be quiet. Shut your face!" he ordered, as the rest of the patrol emerged from cover. They were very professional as they searched their prisoners for weapons, then hustled them onto the path.

"Where are you taking us?" Nicholas demanded in Arabic.

"No questions!"

They were forced to keep marching through the heat of the afternoon, heading westwards towards the Sudanese border. It was late afternoon before they came upon the guerrilla camp, which consisted of a few crude lean-to shelters and a ring of weapons emplacements. They were led to the guerrilla commander who was seated at a table in one of the shelters. He straightened up from the table and came out into the sunlight.

"My men tell me that you speak Arabic," he said to Nicholas.

"Better than you do, Mek Nimmur," Nicholas told him. "So now you are the leader of a bunch of kidnappers? I always told you that you would never get to heaven, you old reprobate."

Mek Nimmur stared at him in astonishment. "Nicholas! I did not recognise you. You are older." He opened his arms wide, folded Nicholas into a bear hug and kissed him on each cheek. Then he held him at arm's length and looked at the two women.

"He saved my life," he explained to them. "How long ago was it, Nicholas?"

"It doesn't bear thinking about."

"Fifteen years ago at least," Mek said. "Are you still in the British Army? What is your rank? You must be a general by now!"

Nicholas shook his head. "I'm back in Civvy Street now."

Mek Nimmur turned to the women. His eyes flicked from Royan to Tessay, and then stayed on the Ethiopian girl's dark and lovely face. "I know you," he said. "I saw you in Addis, years ago. You were a young girl then. Your father was Alto Zemen, a great and good man. He was murdered by the tyrant Mengistu."

"I know you also, Alto Mek. My father held you in high esteem. There are many of us who believe that you should be the president of this Ethiopia of ours, in place of that other one."

"I am flattered by your opinion of me," he said. Then he turned back to Nicholas. "I'm sorry for the rough welcome. Some of my men are over-enthusiastic. I knew that there were feringhee asking questions at the monastery. But enough, you are with friends here. I bid you welcome."

Mek Nimmur led them to his shelter, where one of his men brought viscous black coffee in mugs for them.

He and Nicholas plunged into reminiscences of the days when they had fought side by side, Nicholas as a covert military adviser and Mek as a young freedom fighter opposing the tyranny of Mengistu.

"But the war is over now, Mek," Nicholas remonstrated at last. "Why are you still out in the bush with your men?"

"Alto Mek is a crusader for Christ and the rights of the common man," Tessay told Nicholas in awed tones.

"And he dearly loves a good fight," Nicholas laughed. The two men embarked into a spirited discussion of African politics, so complicated that Royan knew very few of the personalities whom they were discussing. She was, however, impressed by Nicholas's knowledge and understanding of the situation.

In the end Mek punched Nicholas's shoulder affectionately. "What are you doing here yourself, Nicholas, if you are no longer a soldier? There was a time when you also loved a good fight."

"I am completely reformed. No more fighting. I have come to the Abay gorge to hunt dik-dik."

"Dik-dik?" Mek Nimmur roared with laughter. "I don't believe it. Not you. Not dik-dik. You are up to something."

"It is the truth."

"You are lying, Nicholas. I know you too well. You are up to something. You will tell me about it when you need my help."

"And you will still give me your help?"

"Of course."

While they talked, the sun slanted down the sky.

"You are my guests for tonight," Mek Nimmur told them. "In the morning I will escort you back to your camp at the monastery. That is also my destination. My men and I are going to celebrate the festival of Timkat."

THE GUERRILLA column moved out before dawn the next morning. They marched in full battle order, with scouts moving ahead and flankers covering each side of the path.

Tessay was watching Mek Nimmur as they marched; indeed, she had seldom taken her eyes off him. Now she murmured to Royan, "He is a truly great man, a man who could unite our land, perhaps for the first time in a thousand years. I feel humble in his presence."

The march back to the monastery took the entire morning. When they came in sight of the Dandera River, Mek Nimmur drew his men back off the path and sent one scout forward. After an hour's wait, a party of acolytes came up from the monastery, carrying large bundles which they handed over to Mek's men.

The bundles contained priestly *shammas*, headcloths and sandals. Mek's men changed out of their camouflage fatigues into these garments, wearing only their side arms under the robes. All their other equipment they cached in one of the caves in the cliffs.

Now as a party of monks they covered the last few miles to the monastery, to be welcomed joyously by the community there. Here Nicholas and the women left Mek, and climbed the steep path up into the camp. Boris was waiting for them, angry and frustrated.

"Where the hell have you been, woman?" he snarled at Tessay.

"We lost our way yesterday evening." Nicholas fed him the cover story that they had agreed with Mek Nimmur. Boris was hardly the man to trust. "And we were picked up by a party of monks from the monastery this morning. They brought us back."

"You are the big hunter and tracker, are you?" Boris sneered at him. "I see now why you want only to shoot dik-dik." He guffawed without humour and looked at Tessay with pale dead eyes. "I will talk to you later, woman. Go and see to the food."

While they ate lunch Royan sat close to Nicholas, and throwing a cautionary glance in the direction of where Boris sat at the other end of the table, she dropped her voice and said in Arabic, "Tessay and I were talking on the march this morning. We were discussing the festival of Timkat. Apparently on the fourth day the abbot takes the *tabot* down to the river. Everybody joins the procession: the abbot, all the priests, the acolytes, every true believer, they all go down to the river and they stay there overnight. For one whole day and night the monastery is deserted. Empty. Nobody there at all."

He stared at her over the rim of his glass. "Now that is very interesting indeed," he agreed. "But before we start planning this thing, have you considered the possible consequences?"

"You mean, if the monks catch us at it?"

"At the very least we can expect them to run us out of the valley. It could go as far as a knife between the ribs. After all, this is one of their most sacred sites. There is a great deal of danger involved."

"I have thought about it," she admitted. "And all I know is that, no matter what, I have to go in there. Even if I give offence to Tessay and Mek and all the priesthood, I have to do it."

"All right. That is settled, then." He glanced at his wristwatch and stood up. "Now," he said, "I am going back after that damned little Bambi. It has made a fool of me once too often."

"I am coming with you," she said firmly.

THE TINY antelope stepped out from the deep shadow of the thorn thicket, and the afternoon sunlight gleamed on the silky pelt. It kept walking steadily across the narrow clearing.

Nicholas's breathing quickened as he followed it with the telescopic sight. It was ridiculous that he should feel so wrought up with the hunting of such a humble little animal, but his previous failure had sharpened his anticipation and now, suddenly, procuring this specimen had become a matter of supreme importance to him.

The dik-dik made for the thick scrub on the far side of the clearing, then stopped abruptly and thrust its tiny head into one of the low bushes. Standing broadside to Nicholas, and angled slightly away from him, it was in the perfect position for the heart shot which would inflict the least possible damage to the skin.

He settled the reticule of the scope on the precise spot, and squeezed the trigger. The tiny antelope bounded high, coming down to touch the earth at a full run. It was dead already, running only on the last dregs of oxygen in its bloodstream—straight towards the cliff. Blindly it leapt out into empty space and fell, dropping from their sight, down into the chasm of the Dandera River.

"That was a filthy bit of luck." Nicholas ran to the rim of the chasm. Royan followed him and the two of them stood peering two hundred feet down into the giddy void.

"There it is!" She pointed, and he nodded. "Yes, I can see it."

The carcass lay directly below them, caught on an islet of rock in the middle of the stream.

"What are you going to do?" she asked.

"I'll have to go down and get it." He straightened up and stepped back from the brink. "Fortunately I've brought a length of rope."

He anchored the rope end to the bole of one of the wiry thorn trees and lowered the other end down the cliff until it touched the surface of the water to check the rope was long enough. Then he tested its strength meticulously.

"That should do it." He stripped to his shirt and khaki shorts and pulled off his chukka boots. On the lip of the cliff he leaned out backwards with the rope now draped over his shoulder and the tail brought back between his legs in the classical abseil style.

"Coming in on a wing and a prayer!" he said, and jumped out backwards into the chasm. He controlled his fall by allowing the rope to pay out over his shoulder, swinging like a pendulum and kicking himself off the rock wall with both feet. He went down swiftly until his feet dangled into the rush of water, a few yards short of the spur of rock on which the dead dik-dik lay. He let himself drop into the river. With the end of the rope held between his teeth he swam the last short distance with a furious overarm crawl, just beating the current's attempt to sweep him away downstream.

He dragged himself up onto the island and took a few moments to catch his breath before he could admire the beautiful little creature he had killed. He felt the familiar melancholy and guilt as he stroked the glossy hide but there was no time for regrets. He trussed up the dik-dik, tying all its legs together securely, then he stepped back and looked up. He could see Royan's face peering down at him.

"Haul it up!" he shouted, and the dik-dik lifted clear of the island and rose jerkily up the wall of the chasm. Nicholas watched it anxiously. There was a moment when the rope seemed to snag when the carcass was two-thirds of the way to the top, but then it freed itself and snaked on up the cliff.

Eventually the dik-dik disappeared from his sight, and there was a long delay until the rope end dropped back over the lip. Royan had been sensible enough to weight it with a stone and was hanging over the top of the cliff, watching its progress and controlling the descent.

When the end of the weighted line touched the surface of the water she pendulumed it close enough for Nicholas to grab it. Then he started to climb. He began to ascend in a series of spiralling jerks and heaves. As he rose, the belled wall of the chasm arched in to meet him, until he could fend off from the rock with his bare feet. He was thirty feet from the top of the cliff when suddenly one of the strands of the nylon rope sheared against the cutting edge of the rock and began to uncurl like a long green worm.

He looked down. The surface of the water seemed far below. He looked up again as the second strand of the rope parted and unravelled. There was only a single strand holding him now.

It was going to go at any moment, he realised. Then, with a pop like a champagne cork, the third and final strand of the rope parted. He plunged downwards, with the loose end of the severed rope fluttering above his head. Flinging both arms upwards over his head to stabilise his flight, he straightened his legs, arrowing his body to hit the surface of the water feet first.

The impact drove the air out of his lungs and then the river swallowed him under. Kicking off the bottom, desperate for air, he broke out through the surface, wheezing and coughing. He trod water on the racing stream, shook the water from his eyes and looked around him. The walls of the chasm were streaming past him, and he estimated his speed at around ten knots—fast enough to break bone if he hit a rock. He rolled onto his back and thrust both feet out ahead of him, ready to fend off.

You're in for the whole ride, he told himself grimly. There was only one way out, and that was to ride it to the bottom.

He looked up. The walls canted in from each side, so that at places they almost met directly over his head. There was only a narrow strip of blue sky showing, and the depths were gloomy and dank.

Gradually he became aware of a new sound in the canyon. It was a dull roar, growing stronger as he sped onwards. The walls of the chasm converged upon each other, the gut of rock narrowed and the flood seemed to accelerate as it was confined. The sound of water built up rapidly into a thunder.

Abruptly the air opened under him and he was launched out into space. All around him white spuming water filled the air, and he was tossed like a leaf in the torrent. The drop seemed to last for ever and his stomach swooped against his ribs. Then once more he struck with all his weight and was driven far below the surface.

He fought his way up and burst out through the surface. The waters revolved and eddied, and as he turned he saw first the high sheet of white water of the falls down which he had tumbled, and then, still turning, the narrow exit from the basin through which the river resumed its mad career downstream. But for the moment he was safe here in the back eddy below the falls. He reached out and found a handhold on a clump of mossy fern growing out of the wall.

His only way out of the chasm was to follow the course of the river and to take his chances with whatever lay downstream. If only there were some way up the wall! He looked up, but quailed as he considered the overhang high above him.

While he still stared upwards, something caught his eye. A double row of dark marks ran vertically up the wall of rock, beginning at the surface of the water and climbing to the rim almost two hundred feet overhead. He relinquished his hold on the clump of fern and dog-paddled slowly down to where these marks reached the water. They were niches, cut about four inches square into the wall, deep enough to accommodate his arm to the elbow. The two rows were twice the spread of his arms apart, and the niche in one row lined up in the horizontal plane exactly with its neighbour in the second row.

The nearest opening, being below the flood level of the waters, was smoothed and worn, but those higher up the wall, above the watermark, had retained their shape. The edges were sharp and square.

How old are they to have been worn like that? he marvelled. And how the hell did anybody get down here to cut them? And why?

Then suddenly something else caught his eye. It was a circular indentation in the rock, precisely between the two rows of niches and above the high-water mark. He paddled further around, trying to gain a clearer view of it. It seemed to be some sort of rock engraving, but the light was too poor for him to be able to recognise any script or lettering that might have been incorporated in the design.

Using the stone niches as foot- and handholds, he managed to lift himself out of the water, but the distances between the holds were too great and he fell back with a splash. Only then did he realise how close he was to total exhaustion.

Reluctantly he pushed himself away from the wall of rock and felt the current pick him up and bear him forward. He stopped swimming and let it take him.

The Devil's rollercoaster! he told himself. Down and down she goes, and where she stops nobody knows.

The first set of rapids battered him. They seemed endless, but at last he was spewed out into the run of slower water below them. He floated on his back, taking full advantage of this respite, and then went cascading down the next steep slide.

After a while he lost track of how far he had been carried and how many cataracts he had survived. It was a constant battle against the pain of sodden lungs and strained muscle. The river mauled him.

Suddenly he felt the force and ferocity of the river abating. He squinted up into bright sunlight and saw that he had passed into that familiar part of the river which he had explored with Royan. Coming up ahead of him was the rope suspension bridge, and he had just sufficient strength remaining to paddle feebly towards the small beach of white sand below it. He tried to crawl fully ashore, but collapsed with his face in the sand and vomited out the water he had swallowed. His lower body still hung into the river, but he fell into a state halfway between sleep and unconsciousness.

"EFFENDI, wake up! The beautiful Woizero seeks you."

With a huge effort Nicholas roused himself and sat up slowly. Tamre knelt over him. "Please, effendi, come with me. The Woizero is searching the river bank. She is weeping and calling your name."

Nicholas looked beyond him and saw that it must be late afternoon, for the sun sat fat and red on the lip of the escarpment. "Help me up!" he ordered Tamre.

The boy put his shoulder under Nicholas's armpit and hoisted him to his feet. He ached in every muscle, but he could detect no broken bones. The two of them had hardly reached the bank when there was a joyous shout from close at hand.

"Nicky! Oh, dear God! You are safe." Royan threw her arms around him. "I have been frantic. I thought that—" She broke off and held him at arm's length to look at him. "Are you all right?"

"You know me." He grinned at her. "You don't get rid of me that easily. I only did it just to get a hug from you."

"Don't read anything into that," she said. "I'm kind to all dumb animals." But her smile belied the words. "Nevertheless, it's good to have you back in one piece."

"What have you done with my dik-dik?"

"There is certainly nothing much the matter with you if you can worry about that. The skinners have taken it down to the camp."

"Damn it to hell! I must supervise the skinning and preparation of the trophy myself. They will ruin it!" He put his arm around Tamre's shoulder. "Come on, my lad! Let's see if I can break into a trot."

BY THE white glare of a butane-gas lantern Nicholas had only just completed the initial skin incisions down the inside of the dik-dik's legs when Boris pushed open the door of the hut.

"Did you have a good swim, English?"

"Bracing, thank you." Nicholas smiled. "I don't expect you want to eat your words about my striped dik-dik, do you?" he asked mildly. "No such bloody animal, I think you said."

"It is like a rat. A true hunter would not bother himself with such rubbish," Boris replied haughtily. "Now that you have your rat, perhaps we can go back to Addis, English?"

"I paid you for three weeks. It is my safari. We go when I say so," Nicholas told him. Boris grunted and backed out of the hut.

Nicholas worked swiftly, but before he had completed his task Mek Nimmur stooped into the hut, dressed in a priest's *shamma* and headcloth.

"I hear that you have been looking for trouble again, Nicholas. I came to make sure that you were still alive." He squatted opposite Nicholas. "Give me a knife. It will go quicker if I help you."

Without comment Nicholas passed him one of the knives. The sooner the skin was off, the less chance there would be of deterioration. They worked in companionable silence for a while until Mek asked, "How well do you know Boris Brusilov?"

"I met him for the first time when I stepped off the plane. He was recommended by a friend."

"Not a very good friend." Mek looked up at him and his expression was grim. "I came to warn you about him, Nicholas. Brusilov used to be a KGB interrogator. He retired when Mengistu fled. I don't know how he persuaded Woizero Tessay to marry him, but knowing what I do of the man, I expect she did not have much choice in the matter. I came to tell you that I may have to kill him."

He stood up. "These days life is uncertain, Nicholas. If I have to leave here in a hurry, there is somebody in Addis who will pass a message to me if you ever need me. His name is Colonel Maryam Kidane in the Ministry of Defence. He is a friend." They embraced briefly. "Go with God!" said Mek, and left the hut quietly.

It was late by the time Nicholas finished his work. He carried the lantern to the dining hut. The others had eaten and gone to bed hours earlier, but Tessay had left his dinner in the charge of the Ethiopian chef. He had not realised how hungry he was until he smelt it.

NEXT MORNING he was so stiff that he hobbled to the dining hut like an old man. Royan was already there. He sat down at the table beside her. "I'm glad you're here. I want to tell you about what I found in the river yesterday."

He described the niches carved into the canyon wall. "They reach from the lip right down to the water's edge, and they are very old."

"What do you think was their purpose?" she asked. "Could they be the anchor points for some sort of scaffolding?"

"Good thinking. They could be," he agreed.

"Why would anybody want to erect scaffolding in a place like that?" She picked up a piece of bread which she nibbled reflectively.

He shrugged. "To gain access to the bottom of the chasm?"

"If that is the motive, then they were fairly committed to the project. It must have been designed to support the weight of a lot of men or heavy material. Was that all you saw down there?"

"High up the wall, aligned between the lines of stone niches, there was something that looked like a basrelief carving."

She sat up with a jerk and stared at him avidly. "Could you see it clearly? Was it script? What was the style of the carving?"

"No such luck. It was too high, and the light was very poor."

Her disappointment was palpable, but after a pause she asked, "What are we going to do about this putative basrelief of yours?"

"I don't like the idea in the least, but I will have to go back in there and have another look."

"When?"

"Timkat tomorrow is our one chance to get into the *maqdas* of the cathedral. After that we will make a plan to explore the gorge."

TWO SERVANTS who had been detailed by the abbot to escort them tried to force a way for them through the crowds. However, they had not reached the foot of the staircase before the escort itself was swallowed up and lost. Nicholas and Royan then contrived to lose Boris and Tessay in the crush also, and it all worked nicely to plan.

At last they reached a position where Nicholas could set his back firmly against one of the stone columns of the terrace, to prevent the crowd jostling him. He also had a good view of the entrance to the cavern cathedral.

The worshippers kept up a low monotonous chant, while musicians tapped their drums and rattled their sistrums. Suddenly, from within the precincts of the cathedral there came the chiming of brass bells, and immediately a hundred horns and trumpets answered. The men's faces were alight with religious fervour. The women held their infants aloft, and tears streaked their dark cheeks.

From the gateway of the underground church emerged a procession of priests and monks. First came the acolytes who were to be baptised at the riverside. Royan recognised Tamre. She waved over the crowd and he saw her and grinned shyly before he followed the others onto the pathway to the river.

Following the baptism candidates through the stone gateway came the ordained priests bearing processional crosses of silver and glittering brass, and behind them, borne by two priests in the most sumptuous robes, came the *tabot*, the Ark of the Tabernacle, covered with a crimson cloth that hung to the ground.

Last in the procession came Jali Hora. Two servants held his elbows and guided his uncertain footsteps onto the stairway that led down to the Nile. As the procession descended, there was a general movement along the terrace to join the flow, and as it began to empty Nicholas took Royan by the hand. With his other hand hanging on to the strap of his camera bag, he allowed them to be carried forward, but all the time he was edging across the stream of humanity towards the entrance to the church.

As they reached the gateway to the outer chamber of the church, he eased them out of the throng into the dim, deserted interior. With a quick glance he made certain that they were alone, then he moved quickly along the side wall, to where tapestries hung from the ceiling to the floor. He lifted the folds of heavy woven wool and drew Royan behind them, letting them fall back into place, concealing them both.

They were only just in time, for hardly had they let the tapestry settle when they heard footsteps approaching. There was a weighty thud from outside as the locking beam of the main doors was dropped into place, and then a profound silence pervaded the cavern.

"I didn't reckon on that," Nicholas whispered. "We're locked in."

"At least it means that we won't be disturbed," Royan replied briskly. "We can get to work right away."

Stealthily they emerged from their hiding place and moved across to the doorway of the middle chamber.

It was smaller and lower than the room they had left. The wall hangings were richer and in a better state of repair. As they crossed the floor towards the *maqdas*, Nicholas took two electric torches from his camera bag and handed one to Royan. "New batteries," he told her, "but don't waste them. We may be here all night."

They stopped in front of the doors to the holy of holies. Quickly Nicholas put his shoulder to one leaf of the door and pushed it open only just wide enough for them to squeeze through.

They stood side by side on the threshold of the *maqdas* and gazed about them in silent awe.

The holy of holies was a small chamber, much smaller than either of them had expected. From the floor upwards the walls were lined with shelves upon which stood the gifts and offerings of the faithful, icons of the Trinity and the Virgin rendered in Byzantine style, framed in ornate silver. In the centre of the floor stood an altar of cedarwood, the panels carved with scenes of revelation and creation, of the temptation and the fall from Eden, and of the Last Judgment. The altar cloth was raw silk, and the cross and the chalice were in worked silver. The abbot's crown gleamed in the candlelight, with the blue ceramic seal of Taita in the centre of its brow.

Royan crossed the floor and bowed her head in prayer. Nicholas waited respectfully until she rose again, and then he went to join her. "The *tabot* stone!" He pointed beyond the altar, and they went forward. At the back of the *maqdas* stood an object as tall as a man, covered with a heavy damask cloth. Fearful that their expectations might prove unwarranted, Nicholas broke the tension that gripped them by turning away from the covered stone to the barred gate in the back wall of the sanctuary.

"The tomb of St Frumentius!" he said, and together they peered through the bars. The interior was in darkness. Nicholas prodded his torch through and pressed the switch.

The tomb lit up in a rainbow of colour so bright that their eyes took a few moments to adjust, and then Royan gasped aloud.

The coffin was set into a stone shelf in the rear wall of the tomb. On the exterior was painted the likeness of the man within. Although it was badly faded, the pale face and reddish beard of the dead man were still discernible.

This was not the only reason for Royan's amazement. She was staring at the walls above and on either side of the shelf on which the coffin lay. Every inch of them was covered with intricate paintings that had miraculously weathered the passage of the millennia.

Nicholas played his torch beam over them in awestruck silence. There were scenes of great battles, fighting galleys locked in terrible combat upon the blue waters of the river. There were scenes of the hunt, and of regiments plumed and armoured, raging in their fury.

The foreground of each mural was dominated by the same tall heroic figure. In one scene he drew the bow to full stretch, in another he swung high a blade of bronze. His enemies quaked before him.

Nicholas played the beam over all this splendid array of art, and brought it to a stop upon the central panel. Here the same godlike figure rode the footplate of his chariot, and his hair flowed out behind him, a thick golden braid like the tail of a lion.

Below him was a legend in classical Egyptian hieroglyphics. In a whisper Royan translated them:

"Great Lion of Egypt.
Best of One Hundred Thousand
Holder of the Gold of Valour
Pharaoh's Sole Companion
Warrior of all the Gods
May you live for ever!"

Her hand shook upon his arm. "I know this artist," she said softly. "I have spent five years studying his work. I would know it anywhere." She drew a breath. "Nearly four thousand years ago Taita the slave decorated these walls and designed this tomb." She pointed to the coffin. "This is not the tomb of a Christian saint. Centuries ago some old priest must have stumbled upon it and, in his ignorance, usurped it for his own religion." She drew a shaky breath. "Look there! That is the seal of Tanus, the commander of all the armies of Egypt, lover of Queen Lostris and the natural father of Prince Memnon, who became the Pharaoh Tamose."

They were both silent then, lost in the wonder of their discovery.

Nicholas broke the silence at last. "It's true, then. The secrets of the seventh scroll are here for us, if we can find the key to them."

"Yes," she said softly. "The key. Taita's stone testament."

They turned back towards the *tabot* stone and approached it slowly. Nicholas jerked away the damask cloth that covered it and they stared at the tapered pillar of mottled pink granite.

Royan stepped forward. "Taita's letter to us," she whispered. "Written almost four thousand years ago."

Slowly she circled the granite pillar, studying each of the four sides in turn. She picked out a line of hieroglyphics and followed them with her finger as she read aloud, "'The vulture rises on mighty pinions to greet the sun. The jackal howls and turns upon his tail. The river flows towards the earth. Beware, you violators of the sacred places, lest the wrath of all the gods descend upon you!'"

"It's nonsense. It doesn't make sense," he protested.

"Oh, yes, Taita always makes sense, once you follow the way his mind is working." She turned to face him squarely. "Don't look so glum, Nicky. Taita has set us a riddle that may take weeks of work to unravel."

"Well, one thing is certain. We can't stay here in the *maqdas* for weeks while we puzzle it out. Let's get to work."

He set down the camera bag and opened the flap. "I will shoot two rolls of colour first, and then use the Polaroid. That will give us something to work on until we can have the colour developed."

She stood out of his way as he took shots of each of the four sides of the pillar, using different shutter speeds and exposures, and of the blue ceramic seal in the centre of the abbot's crown. Then he went to the grille gates and photographed the walls of the tomb.

"That's the lot," he told her at last. "Now for the Polaroids." He changed cameras and repeated the entire process, but this time Royan held a small tape measure against the pillar to give the scale.

After almost two hours' work they had a complete set of Polaroids, and Nicholas packed his cameras away, stepped back and massaged his aching back.

"That does it, then. All finished."

"What time is it?" she asked, and he checked his wristwatch. "Nearly midnight. We had better tidy up in here. Make certain we leave no sign of our visit."

He spread the cloth over the pillar and they adjusted the folds to hang as they had found them. From the threshold of the door they surveyed the *maqdas* for the last time, then he followed her out into the church.

"How will we get out through the main doors?" she asked.

"I don't think that will be necessary. The priests probably have another entrance from their quarters." He looked around carefully. "It must be on this side if it leads directly into the monks' living quarters—" He broke off with a grunt of satisfaction. "Aha! You can see where all their feet have actually worn a pathway over the centuries." He pointed out a smooth area of worn stone near the side wall, crossed quickly to the hanging and drew a fold aside. "I thought as much." There was a narrow doorway concealed behind the hanging. "Follow me."

They found themselves in a dark passageway through the rock. Nicholas flashed his torch into the doorless entrance to a monk's rock cell. A wooden cross hung on the wall with a truckle bed below it. They went on past a dozen others which were almost identical.

At the next turning of the passage Nicholas paused. He felt a tiny draught on his cheek.

"This way," he whispered.

They hurried on, slipped down the passageway and out onto the deserted terrace. They stopped briefly at the foot of the staircase and breathed the sweet cool night air.

Dawn was flushing the serrated crests of the escarpment by the time they reached the sleeping camp. They separated at the door to Royan's hut. "I'm bushed," she told Nicholas. "The excitement has been too much for me. You won't see me again before noon."

It was early next morning, however, when Nicholas was woken from a deep sleep by Boris. "English, wake up! I must talk to you. Have you seen my wife?"

Nicholas rolled over and thrust one arm out from under the mosquito net as he groped for his wristwatch. "Damn you, Boris! What has your wife got to do with me?"

"She has gone! I have not seen her since last night."

"The way you treat her, that comes as no surprise. Now go away and leave me to sleep."

"The whore has run off with that bastard, Mek Nimmur. I know all about them. Don't try and protect her, English. I know everything that goes on around here. You are trying to cover for her—admit it."

"Get out of here, Boris. Don't try and involve me in your sordid private life."

"You think I will let the whore get away with this? You are wrong. I am going to follow them and kill them both. I will shoot him in the belly and let that whore Tessay watch him die."

"If you are going after Mek Nimmur, then my bet is that you won't be coming back."

"You don't know me, English. You beat me up one night when I had a bottle of vodka in my belly, so you think I am easy, *da*? Well, Mek Nimmur will see now how easy I am."

Boris flung out of the hut. Nicholas pulled on a shirt over his shorts and followed him.

Back in his own hut, Boris had flung a few essential items into a light pack. Now he was stuffing cartridges into the magazine of his hunting rifle. "The safari is over, English." He flung a pair of keys on a leather tag on the floor at Nicholas's feet. "There are the keys of the Land Cruiser. You can make your own way back to Addis. I will leave four of my best men to look after you. Leave the big truck for me to use. When you get to Addis, leave the keys of the Land Cruiser with my head tracker, Aly. I will send you the money I owe you for cancellation. Don't worry—I am a man of principles."

"How could I ever doubt it?" Nicholas smiled. "I wish you luck. You'll need plenty of that if you're going up against Mek Nimmur."

Boris was several hours behind his quarry, and as soon as he had left the camp he broke into a jog trot that carried him with an easy swinging gait down the pathway towards the Sudanese border.

Looks as though he is still in good shape, even with the vodka, thought Nicholas. Despite himself he was impressed as he watched him go. He turned back to his own quarters, but as he passed her hut Royan popped her head out. "What was all the shouting about?"

"Tessay has done a bunk. Boris has guessed that she's gone off with Mek, and he's chasing after them."

"Oh, Nicky! Can't we warn them?"

"No chance of that, but unless Mek has gone soft he'll be expecting Boris to come after him. No, Mek doesn't need any help from us. Go back to sleep!"

"I can't possibly sleep. I've been looking at the Polaroids we took last night. Come and have a look at this."

In her hut she had the Polaroids spread out on the camp table, and she beckoned him to take the seat beside her.

"While you were snoring your head off, I made some progress." She laid four Polaroids side by side. "Taita has headed each of the sides of the stele with the name of one of the seasons of the year. I think he is telling us in which order to read the panels. This one is spring. The Egyptians considered spring as the beginning of all life.

"It starts with four standard quotations from the *Book of the Dead*. As far as I can see, they do not differ substantially from the original. My instinct is to set these aside for the time being."

"Let's go with your instinct," he said. "Read the next section."

She peered at the Polaroid. "Taita can be as earthy as Rabelais when he's in the mood. Anyway, here goes. 'The daughter of the goddess pines for her dam. She roars like a lioness as she hurries to meet her. She leaps from the mountain, and her fangs are white. She is the harlot of all the world. Her sex eateth up the masons and the workers of stone. She has swallowed up a god.'"

"Whoa there!" Nicholas chuckled. "Pretty fruity stuff!" Then he became serious. "Hapi is the goddess of the Nile. Is the Dandera River not then her daughter, pining to meet her, leaping from the mountain top, roaring like a lioness, her fangs white with spume?"

They stared in silence at the Polaroid.

"The workmen swallowed up in there!" Her voice became even more excited. "Pharaoh Mamose was a god. The river has swallowed up a god with her—with her stone cleft. I must admit that I wouldn't have made the association if you hadn't explored the interior of the chasm and found those niches in the wall." She shook his arm. "Nicky, we have to get in there again. We have to get a clearer look at that bas-relief you found on the cavern wall."

"It will take some preparation," he said dubiously. "I will have to splice ropes and make some sort of pulley system. We won't be ready to make the attempt until tomorrow morning at the very earliest."

"You get on with it. I will have plenty to keep me occupied with the translation." Then she stopped and looked up. "Listen!" she whispered.

He cocked his head and heard the whining flutter of rotors in the air. "Damn it!" he snapped. "I thought we had lost the Pegasus presence." They sat quietly and listened to the helicopter approaching swiftly. Suddenly the engine beat changed as the pitch altered and the pilot pulled up the collective.

"Sounds as if he's going for a landing in the hills," Nicholas said. "I would feel a lot easier without them snooping around."

"I don't think we have too much to worry about," Royan disagreed. "Even if they are in some way connected with Duraid's killers, we're still way out ahead of them."

"I hope you're right."

WHILE ROYAN pored over her photographs, Nicholas spliced nylon rope to make a single length five hundred feet long. Then he cannibalised the canvas fly of the cooking hut, cutting it up to make a sling seat. He fashioned the ends of the rope into a harness which he spliced into the four corners of the canvas seat. He had no block and tackle, so he put together a crude gantry of poles which would be extended out over the cliff to keep the rope clear of the rock.

It was the middle of the afternoon by the time he had completed his preparations. Then, leaving Royan in camp, he led Boris's men, burdened with the coils of rope and the pole sections of the gantry, back up the pathway to the spot where he had abseiled down into the ravine to retrieve the carcass of the dik-dik. From there they worked their way downstream, following the rim of the cliff, until the rock seemed to quiver under their feet with the roar of falling waters. Finally, by leaning out over the edge and peering downwards, Nicholas could make out the flash of spray in the depths below, and the double row of niches in the rockface.

"This is the spot." He grunted with satisfaction and explained to Aly in Arabic what he wanted done.

They set up their gantry and extended the long pole out over the drop. Then they rigged and secured it with a crude cantilever system of ropes and lighter poles.

When they were finished, Nicholas crawled out to the end to run the rope through the slot he had prepared for it. The whole structure seemed firm. Nevertheless, it was with relief that he crawled back to solid ground.

He stood up and looked over the tops of the thorn scrub to where the lowering sun was fuming red and angry on the horizon.

Enough for one day, he decided. The rest can wait for tomorrow.

NEXT MORNING Nicholas and Royan were both up and drinking coffee at the campfire while it was still dark. Aly and his men were squatting at their own fire nearby, talking quietly. The project seemed to have caught their imagination. They had no inkling of the reason for this descent into the chasm, but the enthusiasm of the two feringhee was infectious.

As soon as it was light enough to see the path, Nicholas led them back up into the hills, and they came out on the rim of rock just as the sun broke out over the eastern escarpment of the valley. Nicholas had drilled the men the previous day, so each of them knew their part and they lost little time in setting themselves up for the descent.

Nicholas stripped to shorts and tennis shoes and an old rugby jersey. Then he took his seat in the sling and swung out over the cliff. Dangling from the end of the gantry he gave Aly the sign, and the men lowered him down into the gorge.

When he reached the surface of the water he slipped out of the sling and dropped in. The water was very cold. He trod water, gasping, and gave Aly three tugs on the signal rope. While the canvas seat was hauled up he swam to the side of the pool and held on to one of the carved stone niches for support. He had forgotten how gloomy it was here in the bottom of the chasm.

After a long delay Royan came into sight, dangling in the sling seat and revolving slowly at the end of the nylon rope. She looked down and waved at him cheerfully. He wanted to shout encouragement, but he knew it was futile because of the thunder of the falls, so he contented himself with returning her wave.

Halfway down he saw her tugging on the signal rope. Aly had been warned to expect this, and her descent was halted. Then she groped for the binoculars which hung around her neck and held the glasses to her eyes. She was obviously having difficulty picking up the round mark on the wall and keeping it in the field of the lens, for the sling was still revolving slowly. But eventually she dropped the binoculars onto her chest and Aly began paying out the rope once more.

When her feet were almost touching the water she signalled on the rope to stop her descent and hung there, fifty feet away from him.

"What did you find?" he shouted across.

"You were right, you wonderful man! It's an inscription. Taita's ego got the better of him once again." She laughed. "He couldn't resist signing his work."

"Marvellous! Plain bloody marvellous!" he exulted.

"Proof that Taita was here, Nicky. To carve that cartouche he must have been standing on a scaffolding. That niche you're holding on to is part of his ladder to the bottom of the gorge."

"Yes, but why, Royan?" he yelled back at her. "Why was Taita down here? There is no evidence of any excavation or building work."

They both looked around the gloomy chasm. Apart from the tiny rows of niches, the walls were unbroken. She was silent. Then she called again, "Nicky, how far do those niches go down? Do they go below the surface?"

Still clinging to his handhold, he groped down as far as he could reach with his toes.

"By Jove!" he shouted. "There's another niche down there!"

"How far do the niches go down?" she called. "Will you dive down and see?"

He hung in the water, pumping air in and out of his lungs, flushing his bloodstream with oxygen to increase his underwater endurance to its limits. Finally, he duck-dived headfirst down the submerged wall, groping for the next niche below the surface. He found it, and used it to accelerate his dive, pulling himself on downwards.

Swimming deeper, he found another niche, another, then another, all about six feet apart. Four rows of niches, twenty-four feet below the surface. His ears were popping. Just one more niche, he promised himself, and then back up to the surface. He saw the vague shape of a fifth niche appear out of the murk below him.

They go right to the bottom, he realised with amazement. How on earth did Taita do it? They had no diving equipment. He grasped the niche and hovered there for a moment, undecided if he should risk going further. He knew he was almost at his physical limit.

He was bracing himself to push off when something grabbed his legs and dragged him hard against the rock wall. He tried to kick out, but his legs were bound as if by the arms of a sea monster.

Taita's goddess! He meant it literally. She's got me, he thought.

He was pinned against the wall. Terror seized him, and flushed away the hallucinations of his oxygen-impoverished brain. He realised what had happened to him. No goddess. This was water pressure. He was being sucked into a narrow opening in the rock, the mouth of an underwater tunnel.

Spreading his arms, he resisted with all his strength, but his fingers slid over the polished surface of the rock. He hooked his fingers and felt his nails tear and break, then suddenly they locked into the last niche in the wall above the sinkhole.

Now at least he had an anchor point. With both hands he clung to the niche and fought the pull of the water. He fought it with all his remaining strength. Then suddenly he was free and shooting towards the surface. When he came out he didn't know that he had done so. He wallowed there like a waterlogged carcass, face down and dying. Then Royan's fingers locked into the hair on the back of his head, and he felt the cold air on his face as she lifted it clear. "Nicky!" she screamed at him. "Breathe, Nicky, breathe!"

He opened his mouth and let out a spray of water, realising that she must have dropped out of the sling seat and come to his aid.

"You're still alive! Oh, thank God. You were down for so long. I thought you had drowned."

The air tasted good and he felt his strength returning.

"We have to get you up," she told him. "A few minutes more to get yourself together, and then I'll help you into the sling."

She swam with him across to the dangling sling and signalled to the men at the top of the cliff to lower it into the water. Then she held the folds of canvas open so that he could slip his legs into them.

Once they had both been hauled safely up out of the ravine, Nicholas ordered Aly to dismantle the gantry and hide the sections in the thorn scrub. From the helicopter it would be highly visible and he did not wish to stir Jake Helm's curiosity. He was in no shape to give the men a hand, but lay in the shade of one of the thorn trees with Royan tending to him. When he felt sufficiently well, he told her everything that he had discovered and how he had been caught in the inflow of the underwater sinkhole. She listened without interrupting, and even when he had finished speaking she said nothing for a while, but frowned with concentrated thought.

At last she looked up at him. "You mean that Taita was able to take those stone niches right down to the very bottom of the pool?" and when he nodded, she said, "How on earth did he do that?"

"Four thousand years ago the water level might have been lower. There might even have been a drought year when the river dried up."

"Then why go to all the trouble of building a scaffold? Why not just use the dry riverbed as an access?"

"Beats me. I have no idea," he admitted.

"All right. Let's leave that for the moment. Now let's go over your description of the sinkhole that almost sucked you in. Was the entrance directly between the two rows of niches?"

"No, not directly," he said thoughtfully. "It was at the bottom of the pool, and slightly downstream from the scaffolding."

She stood up. "We're going back to the camp. I need my notes, and the photos from the stele that the monks call their *tabot* stone."

When she helped him to his feet and they started back towards camp, he moved like an old man, lame and stiff. Every muscle in his body ached.

Once they reached camp Royan led him to his hut and fussed over him as she settled him under the mosquito net. It was pleasant to have a woman caring for him again. She brought him a couple of aspirin tablets and a steaming mug of tea, stiff with sugar. Then she spread her papers around her.

"Yesterday, while you were busy building the gantry, I was able to decipher most of the rest of the 'spring' face of the stele." She moved her notebook so that he was able to look at the pages she had opened. "These sections that I have highlighted with green are quotations from the standard version of the *Book of the Dead*. On the other hand, these parts of the text that I have highlighted in yellow are original Taita writings."

She traced a section with her forefinger as she read it aloud: " 'The daughter of the goddess has conceived. She has been impregnated by the one who is without seed. She has begotten her own twin sister. Her twin shall never see the light of Ra. She will live for ever in the darkness. The unborn twin becomes the bride of the god who was a man. Their destinies are intertwined. They shall live for ever.' "

She looked up from the notebook. "The daughter of the goddess must be the Dandera River. I'm also pretty sure that the god that was once a man must be Pharaoh. Mamose was only deified on his ascension to the throne of Egypt. Before that he was a man."

Nicholas nodded. "The seedless one is obviously Taita himself. He makes repeated references to the fact that he was a eunuch. But now," he suggested, "if you have some ideas about the mysterious twin sister, let's hear them."

Mediterranean Sea
Cairo
Memphis
LOWER KINGDOM
Abnub
Asyut
Safaga
EGYPT
Thebes
(Luxor, Karnak)
Assoun
UPPER KINGDOM
First cataract
Elephantine Island
Red Sea
Second cataract
Third Cataract
River Nile
Fourth cataract
Fifth cataract
Atbara
Sixth cataract
Qebui (Khartoum)
Atbara River
CUSH
Pharaoh's Tomb
Adbar Seged
ETHIOPIA
N

"The twin of the river would most likely be a branch or a fork of the stream. I'm suggesting that the sinkhole is the twin. Down there in the gorge it will never see the light of Ra. Taita, the seedless one, claims paternity, so he is telling us that he made it, marrying it to Pharaoh Mamose for all eternity. Putting that all together, I have come to the conclusion that we will never find the location of Pharaoh Mamose's tomb until we explore that sinkhole."

"How do you suggest we do that?" he asked, and she shrugged.

"I'm not the engineer. I leave that to you to arrange. All I know is that if Taita devised some way of doing it, then you can do it also."

SINCE BORIS and Tessay had left the camp there was no longer any reason for Nicholas and Royan to skulk in Royan's hut when they discussed their search for the tomb. Nicholas transferred their headquarters into the dining hut, and had the camp staff build another table on which they could spread the satellite photographs and all the other maps and material that they had accumulated.

"We will never be certain if that shaft was made by Taita until we can get back in there, but I think we can safely say that we have found enough evidence both in Tanus's tomb and Taita's pool to make it imperative that we return with scuba-diving equipment."

She nodded. "But you're not going to be able to pose as a tourist sportsman next time around. What possible excuse are we going to find for returning that won't set off all the alarm bells in the minds of Ethiopian bureaucracy?"

"You are speaking to the man who once paid an uninvited visit to Gaddafi. This should be a Sunday-school picnic in comparison."

"When do the big rains start up in the mountains?" she asked.

"Yes!" His expression became serious. "That is the jackpot question. You only have to look at the high-water mark on the walls of Taita's pool to have some idea what it must be like in there when the river's in full flood." He flipped over the pages of his pocket diary. "Luckily, I think we can spare just a few more days to work out some ideas that I have about Taita's pool and the sinkhole, to try to arrive at some sort of informed guess about what we'll need when we return."

"What are these ideas that you have?"

"What goes in must come out," he said. "The water going into the sinkhole must be going somewhere. One thing is certain. Nobody is going to get into the sinkhole from the pool. The pressure is lethal. But if we can find the outlet, we may be able to explore it from the other end."

"That's a fascinating possibility." She looked impressed, and turned to the satellite photograph. Nicholas had identified the monastery and ringed it on the photograph, and had marked in the approximate course of the river through the chasm. "Here is where the river enters the chasm." She pointed it out to him. "And here is the side valley down which the trail detours. Okay?"

"Okay," he nodded. "What are you driving at?"

"On our approach march we remarked that this valley might at one time have been the original course of the Dandera River, and that it seemed to have cut a new bed for itself through the chasm. Well, do you recall we crossed another smaller, but still pretty substantial, stream on our way down the dry valley? That stream seemed to emerge from somewhere on the eastern side of the valley."

"All right, I'm with you now. You're suggesting that this may be the overflow from the sinkhole. Clever little devil, aren't you?" He stood up. "Why don't we go and take a look?"

Nicholas went to fetch his camera bag and the light day pack from his hut, and when he returned he found Royan ready to go. But she was not alone. Tamre stood at her side.

"I see that you are bringing your chaperone with you," he remarked.

"Unless you are tough enough to send him away." Royan smiled encouragement at the boy who stood grinning at her side.

"Oh, very well." Nicholas gave in without a struggle. "Let the little devil come along."

Tamre lolloped away up the path ahead of them, his grubby *shamma* flapping around his long skinny legs, as they made their way up the side of the valley. The stream tumbled down a series of cascades, each with a pool at its foot. The bush crowded the banks, lush and green where the roots had been able to reach the water. Clouds of black and yellow butterflies danced over the pools, and a wagtail patrolled the moss-green rocks along the edge.

At the top of the slope they came to the source. There was a low cliff of red sandstone, from a grotto at whose foot the stream gushed. The entrance was screened by a heavy growth of ferns, and Nicholas went down on his knees to peer into the low opening, which narrowed down into a shaft of some sort.

"Do you think it is the work of humans?" she asked.

"Impossible to tell. The water is coming out of it like the spout of a bath tap. A solid jet."

"Could a man get into the opening, if it wasn't for the water pressure?"

"If he was a pygmy. Or a child?"

"Or a child," she agreed. "The ancients often used child-slaves. Taita might have done the same."

Nicholas sat down on the bank and ferreted in his pack. She looked at him quizzically when he brought out a small instrument.

"Aneroid barometer," he explained. "Every good navigator should have one." He studied it and then made a note of the reading. "I want to know if this spring is below the level of the sinkhole in Taita's pool. If it is not, then we can cross it off our list of possibilities."

He stood up. "If you're ready, we can move on to Taita's pool. We need a reading there to establish the difference in altitude between the two points."

Once Tamre knew where they were headed he showed them a short cut, so it took them just under two hours from the fountainhead to the top of the cliff face above Taita's pool.

While they rested, Royan remarked, "Tamre seems to know every path and game trail. He is an excellent guide."

"Better than Boris, at least, wherever he may be." Nicholas fished out his barometer and took another reading.

"You look particularly pleased with yourself." Royan watched his face as he studied the instrument.

"Every reason to be," he told her. "The entrance to the sinkhole is over a hundred feet higher than the fern grotto on the other side of the ridge. Which means that there's a distinct possibility that the inflow is here in Taita's pool and the outflow is from the grotto."

"How on earth did Taita do it?" she puzzled. "How did he get to the bottom of the pool?"

Nicholas shrugged. "The accepted technique is to build a dam," he said casually, and then broke off and stared at her. "A dam! What if that old ruffian Taita dammed the whole flipping river!"

"Would that have been possible?"

"I'm beginning to believe that with Taita anything is possible. He certainly had unlimited manpower at his disposal."

"Where would he have built the dam?" she asked excitedly.

"There is one natural place for it," he answered. "The spot where the trail leaves the river and detours down the valley, and the river falls into the chasm." They both turned their heads and looked upstream.

"What are we waiting for?" she asked, and sprang to her feet. "Let's go look-see!"

Their excitement was infectious, and Tamre giggled and danced ahead of them along the trail through the thorns and then up the valley to the point where it rejoined the river.

"If Taita had thrown a dam across here"—Nicholas made a sweep of his arms across the mouth of the gorge—"he could have diverted the river down the side valley here."

"It's a big river," Royan said. "What method would he have used? An earthen dam? Surely not?"

"The Egyptians used earthen canals and dams for a great many of their irrigation works," Nicholas mused. "On the other hand, when they had rock available to work with they used it extensively. They were expert masons. You have stood in the quarries at Aswan."

"Not much topsoil here in the gorge," she pointed out. "But on the other hand, there is plenty of rock. It's like a geological museum."

"I agree," he said. "Rather than an earthen wall, Taita would most probably have used a masonry and rock fill. So where did he get it?"

When she looked puzzled, he went on: "Don't you see! We should be looking for the quarry, not the remnants of the dam."

"So where do we start?"

"I hoped you were going to tell me." He laughed, and immediately Tamre bubbled with uncomprehending sympathetic laughter. They both looked at the boy.

"I think we should start with Tamre, our faithful guide," she said, and took his hand. "Listen to me, Tamre. Listen very carefully!" Obediently he cocked his head and stared into her face.

"We are looking for a place where the square stones come from." He looked mystified, so she tried again. "Long ago there were men who cut the rock from the mountains. Somewhere near here they left a big hole. Perhaps there are still square blocks of stone lying in the hole?"

Suddenly the boy's face cleared. "The Jesus stone!" he cried happily.

He sprang to his feet without relinquishing his grip on her hand. "I show you my Jesus stone." He dragged her after him as he bounded away down the valley.

"Wait, Tamre!" she pleaded. "Not so fast." But in vain. Tamre kept up the pace and burst into an Amharic hymn as he ran. Nicholas followed at a more sedate pace and caught up with them a quarter of a mile down the valley. Tamre led Royan to the rock wall and in front of Nicholas's eyes the two of them seemed to vanish. He looked about him in mild alarm.

"Royan!" he called. "Where are you? What's going on?"

"This way, Nicky. Come this way!"

He went to the wall. "My oath! We would never have found this in a year of searching."

The cliff face was folded back upon itself, forming a concealed entrance. He walked through the opening, gazing up the vertical sides, and within thirty paces came out into an open amphitheatre that was at least a hundred yards across. The walls had been quarried out of the rock, leaving tiers rising up to the top. The recesses from which blocks had been hacked were still plain to see and had left deep steps with a stockpile of finished granite blocks scattered about the bottom of the excavation.

Tamre led Royan to the centre of the quarry where one large slab, finished and dressed into a perfect rectangle, lay on its own.

"The Jesus stone!" Tamre chanted, kneeling before the slab and pulling Royan down beside him. "Jesus led me here. The first time I came here I saw Him standing on the stone. He had a long white beard and eyes that were kind and sad." He crossed himself and began to recite one of the psalms, swaying to the rhythm.

As Nicholas moved up quietly behind them he saw evidence that Tamre had visited this sacred place of his regularly. The Jesus stone was his own private altar, and his pathetic little offerings were lying where he had laid them, bunches of wild flowers that had long ago dried out, tortoiseshells and porcupine quills, and models of animals and birds moulded from blue river clay.

Nicholas stood and watched the two of them praying in front of the primitive altar. He felt deeply moved by this evidence of the boy's faith, and by his childlike trust in bringing them to this place.

At last Royan stood up and came to join him. Together she and Nicholas began to make a slow circuit of the quarry floor. It was a perfect illustration of the quarrying methods used by the ancients. Work could be seen in progress in all the various stages, from the marking out of the blocks by the master craftsman, the drilling of the tap holes, the wedging of the cleavage lines, right up to the finished product lifted out of the wall and ready for transport to the dam site.

The sun had set and it was almost dark by the time they came around to the entrance of the quarry again. They sat together on one of the finished blocks, with Tamre sitting at their feet like a puppy.

"If he had a tail he would wag it," Nicholas smiled.

"We can never betray his trust," Royan murmured. "He has made this his own temple. Will you promise me that we will always respect it, no matter what?"

"That is the very least I can do," he agreed.

Then, looking up at the last rays of the sunset above them, Royan suggested that they should start back to camp.

"I don't think that would be very wise," he disagreed. "One of us could very easily break a leg in the dark."

"You plan to sleep here?" she said with surprise.

"Why not? I can whip up a fire in no time and I also have a pack of survival rations for dinner—I've done this kind of thing before, you know! And you have a chaperone, so your honour is safe."

He stood up to start gathering firewood, but then stopped and listened. She heard it too, that now familiar fluttering whistle in the air. "The Pegasus helicopter once again," he said. "I wonder what the hell they're up to at this time of day?"

They both stared up into the gathering darkness and watched the navigational lights of the aircraft pass a thousand feet overhead, southwards in the direction of the monastery.

NICHOLAS BUILT a small fire in the corner of the quarry nearest the entrance, and as they sat around it he divided the pack of dry survival rations into three parts. They nibbled them, and washed down the concentrated tablets with water from his bottle.

The fire threw ghostly reflections up the side of the quarry wall and enhanced the moving shadows. When a nightjar uttered its warbling cry from a niche high up the wall, it was so eerie and evocative that Royan shivered and moved a little closer to Nicholas.

"I wonder if somewhere on the other side Taita is aware of our progress," she said. "I get the feeling that we have him a little worried by now. We have untangled the first part of the conundrum that he set for us, and I'll bet he never expected anybody to do that well."

"The next step will be to get to the bottom of his pool. What do you hope we might find down there?"

"I hesitate to put it into words," she replied. "I might talk it away, and put a jinx on us."

"I am not superstitious. Shall I say it for you?" he offered, and she laughed and nodded. He went on, "We hope to find the entrance to the tomb of Pharaoh Mamose. No more hints and riddles and red herrings. The veritable tomb."

Royan smiled, her face lighting up with anticipation. "Oh, Nicky! It is such an exciting challenge." Then her voice fell. "But is there a way? Is it possible to get in there?"

"We will find out. All I'm certain of is that it is going to take a prodigious amount of planning and hard work."

While they talked, Tamre curled up in the dust on the other side of the fire, and pulled his *shamma* over his head. Their voices became drowsier as the fire burned down, and Royan murmured, just before she fell asleep on Nicholas's shoulder, "If the tomb of Pharaoh Mamose is below the level of the river, then surely the contents will be water-damaged?"

"I can't believe that Taita would have built his dam and the tomb only to flood it deliberately. No, that would have brought all his work to nothing."

She snuggled closer, and sighed with satisfaction.

A little while later he said softly, "Good night, Royan," but she did not reply and her breathing was deep and even. He smiled and gently kissed the top of her head. Soon he too was asleep.

At the first flush of dawn in the eastern sky the little party began to stir, and after eating the remains of the survival rations for their breakfast, they set off towards the monastery. Their discussion was animated as they laid their plans. By the time they reached the lower end of the chasm it was late morning. There they met a small group of monks from the monastery coming up the trail.

Even from a distance it was obvious that something dreadful had happened: the sorrowful ululation of the monks was the universal African sound of mourning, the harbinger of death and disaster.

"What is it, Tamre?" Royan asked the boy. "Go and find out for us." Tamre ran ahead to meet his brother monks. They stopped in the middle of the path and fell into a high-pitched discussion, weeping and gesticulating. Then Tamre ran back to them.

"Your people at the camp. Something terrible has happened. Bad men came in the night. Many of the servants are dead."

They ran the last mile to the camp and arrived to find another circle of monks gathered in front of the kitchen. Nicholas elbowed his way to the front. There he stopped and stared with a sinking feeling in his gut. Under a buzzing pall of flies lay the blood-splattered corpse of the cook and three other camp servants. He went forward to identify the dead men.

"Aly is not here. Where is he?" He raised his voice and called in Arabic, "Aly, where are you?"

The tracker pushed his way forward. "I am here, effendi." His face was haggard. There was blood on the front of his shirt.

"How did this happen?" Nicholas seized his arm and steadied him.

"Men came in the night with the guns. *Shufta*. They shot into the huts where we were sleeping. They gave us no warning."

"How many of them? Who were they?"

"I don't know how many of them there were. It was dark. I was asleep. I ran away when the shooting began." He began to sob.

Royan turned away, sickened. She went to her hut and stopped in the opening. It had been ransacked. Her bags had been turned out onto the floor. The satellite photographs and the maps, the Polaroids that Nicholas had taken in Tanus's tomb—everything was gone.

Nicholas burst in and looked around quickly. "They did the same thing to me. Ransacked the place. My rifle has gone, and all my papers. But at least I had the passports and traveller's cheques in my day pack—" He broke off as he saw the empty canvas folder lying at her feet. "Have they taken the—"

"Yes!" She forestalled his question. "They have cleaned out all our research material, even the Polaroids. Thank God you had the undeveloped rolls of film with you. It's the same as happened to Duraid and me all over again. We aren't safe from them, even out here." There was the edge of hysteria in her voice. "They could return at any time, and now we're unarmed and helpless."

"All right, I agree with you that we're pretty vulnerable here. It would be wise to get out as soon as possible. There isn't any point in staying on here anyway. There's nothing more we can do."

Within the hour he was ready to start. Nicholas had decided to leave all the camping equipment and Boris's personal gear in the charge of Jali Hora, who had given them an escort of monks to accompany them to the top of the escarpment.

"Only a truly godless man would attack you while you are under the protection of the Cross," the old man explained.

Nicholas found the dried hide and head of the striped dik-dik, rolled it into a bundle and strapped it onto the load atop one of the mules, and then gave the order for the caravan to move out.

Tamre insinuated himself into the group of monks who were escorting the party. He kept close behind Royan as they set off up the trail, with the farewells of the monastic community following them.

By midafternoon they had retraced the morning's travel and once more reached the possible site of Taita's dam. Nicholas and Royan took a few minutes' breather to dip their heads in the river and sluice the salt and sweat from their faces and necks. Then they stood together above the falls, and staring down into the chasm Royan said softly, "You haven't won yet, Taita. The game is still afoot."

NEXT MORNING, while the mules were being loaded in the pre-dawn darkness, they drank a bowl of strong, bitter black Ethiopian coffee. Then they started out along the trail again.

As the rising sun lit the sheer walls of the escarpment ahead of them, Nicholas remarked to Royan, "I'll be glad to get out of here. Hell, I haven't even got my rifle. We're a flock of sitting ducks."

Aly, the muleteers and the monks seemed to be of the same opinion, for they never slackened the pace. It was midday before they called the first brief halt to brew coffee and to water the mules. While the men lit fires, Nicholas took his binoculars from the mule pack and set out on a recce. They were approaching the foot of the escarpment wall, and cliffs hung over the narrow aisle of ground that made up the river bank, sculpted by wind and weather into strange battlements.

Nicholas studied the bottom of the valley carefully through the lens. He could pick out nothing suspicious, so he raised his head and swept the cliffs. At that moment Aly's voice came up from the valley. "Hurry, effendi! The mules are ready to go on!"

Nicholas waved down to him, but then lifted the binoculars for one more sweep of the ground ahead. A wink of bright light caught his eye—a brief stab of brilliance emanating from the cliff.

It might have been a reflection from the lens of another pair of binoculars, or from the barrel of a sniper's rifle, he thought. On the other hand, a pebble of rock crystal could reflect sunlight the same way. Aly's voice floated up again. "Hurry, effendi. The mule drivers will not wait!"

Nicholas slid and scrambled down the slope. Once he reached the trail he joined Royan at the tail of the caravan.

Now that he was again part of the column, Nicholas could turn his attention to searching the skyline above them more thoroughly. As he peered upwards he saw a speck flick over the top of the cliff, twisting and falling—a dead leaf on the breeze. It was too small to be of any danger, but he followed the movement with his eye.

The brown leaf spiralled and looped, and finally he lifted his hand as a reflex and caught it. It was no leaf, he saw at once, but a torn scrap of greased paper. Suddenly all his early-warning bells jangled. He lifted it to his nose and sniffed it. The sharp, nitrous odour prickled the back of his throat. He knew the smell instantly.

Gelignite was seldom employed for military purposes in this age of plastic explosives, but was still widely used in the mining industry and in mineral exploration. Usually the sticks were wrapped in distinctive brown greased paper. Before the detonator was placed in the head of the stick, it was common practice to tear off the corner of the paper wrapper to expose the brown explosive. He had used it often enough in the old days never to forget the odour of it.

His mind was racing now. If somebody was expecting them and had mined the cliff with gelignite, then the reflection he had picked up could have been from the operator lying concealed up there, ready to press the plunger on the circuit box.

"Aly!" he bellowed down to the head of the caravan. "Stop them! Turn them back!"

He started to run forward towards the head of the caravan, but in his heart he knew it was already too late. If there was somebody up there on the cliff, he was watching every move that Nicholas made. He came up short and looked back at Royan. Her safety was his main concern. He turned and ran back to grab her arm. "Come on! We have to get off the track."

"What is it, Nicky? What are you doing?"

"I'll explain later." He dragged her back in the direction from which they had come.

They had not covered fifty yards before the cliff face blew. A vast disruption of air hit them with a force that made them stagger. Then the main force of the blast swept over them, not a single blast but a long, rolling detonation, like thunder breaking directly overhead. It stunned and battered them so that they reeled into each other and lost the direction of their flight.

Nicholas seized her in a steadying embrace and looked back. He saw a series of explosions leap from the crest of the cliff. The columns of rubble subsided upon themselves, and for a moment longer it seemed that the destruction was complete. Then the silhouette of the cliff began to alter.

Slowly at first the wall of rock started to lean outwards. He saw great cracks appear in the face. Sheets of rock collapsed and in slow motion slithered down upon themselves. The rock groaned and rumbled as the entire cliff began to fall into the river far below.

Sweeping Royan up in his arms, Nicholas guided her into the lee of the rock wall. There was a cutback here, and they crept into it. The fine dust they were breathing began to settle. The rumbling and roaring let up gradually, until the only sound was the slip and slide of settling earth and rock and the burble of the river below them.

"You're bleeding," Royan whispered, her voice husky with dust and terror.

Nicholas lifted his hand to his face and it came away covered with a paste of dust and blood. "It's just a nick," he said. "How are you?"

"I think I may have twisted my knee. I don't think it's serious. There's very little pain."

"Then we have both been ridiculously lucky," he told her. "Nobody deserved to survive that."

She made an effort to stand, but he restrained her with a hand on her shoulder.

"Wait! We don't want to give those bastards up there any idea that we have survived their little party. Much better they believe that we snuffed it, as intended."

She stared at him. "How did you know what was going to happen?"

In a few words he explained about the scrap of gelignite wrapping. "Simplest thing in the world to pick one of the narrowest sections of the trail and mine the cliff—" He broke off as there came the faint sound of an aircraft engine and the flutter of rotors.

"Quickly," he snapped. "Get in as close as you can to the overhang." He pushed her back against the sheltering boulder. "Lie flat!"

They lay and listened to the sound of the helicopter approaching. It moved up and down the valley, flying a few feet above the river.

"Looking for survivors," said Nicholas grimly. "They must have lost us in the dust of the avalanche and the breakup of the cliff face. They aren't sure where we are."

The sound of the helicopter moved off slowly along the river, and Nicholas lifted his head cautiously. One glance was sufficient to confirm all his speculations. Jake Helm sat in the front seat beside the pilot, and Colonel Nogo was in the seat behind him. They were both staring down into the river valley, but in seconds the helicopter lifted them away and the machine disappeared beyond the ridge.

Nicholas pulled Royan to her feet. "No more doubts. We know who we're dealing with now. That was Helm and Nogo in the chopper. Helm almost certainly laid the gelly, and Nogo probably led the men who hit our camp last night."

"But Nogo is an officer in the Ethiopian Army," she protested.

"Welcome to Africa." He did not smile as he said it. "Here everything is for sale, including government officials and army officers. Whoever owns Pegasus is the ugly behind all this. Helm and Nogo are merely the stooges." He looked up the slope. "Now our next job is to look for survivors."

"Tamre!" she exclaimed.

They floundered along the bank. The river was clogged with loose rock and earth that had fallen from the cliff. They found the bodies of two of the monks, both of them crushed and half buried. One of the mules lay with its body completely covered with broken rock. The pack it had carried had burst open and the contents were scattered about. The rolled skin and trophies of the dik-dik had been churned into the muck. Nicholas rescued them and strapped them onto his bum-bag.

"More to carry," Royan warned him.

"Only a pound or two, but worth it," he replied.

They made their way towards the point below the trail where they had last seen Tamre and Aly. Royan climbed as high as her injured leg enabled her, then cupped her hands around her mouth and shouted, "Tamre! Tamre! Tamre!" The echoes took her cry and flung it from wall to valley wall.

"Royan! That's enough. You're going to damage that knee even more. We cannot afford more time, if we are to get out ourselves. We will have to leave him."

She ignored him and worked her way along the rock slide, loose scree rolling under her feet. Suddenly she gave a cry of horror. Nicholas dumped his pack and went up after her. When he reached her side, he too dropped to his knees.

Tamre was pinned down in the rubble. Royan had lifted his head into her lap and was using her sleeve to wipe the filth out of his nostrils. A lump of raw rock the size of a billiard table lay across him. It weighed many tons and must certainly have crushed his spine.

"Do something, Nicky," Royan whispered. "We have to do something for him."

Nicholas looked at her and shook his head. Royan's eyes flooded with tears, and they scattered like raindrops into Tamre's upturned face. "We can't just sit here and let him die," she protested, and at the sound of her voice Tamre opened his eyes and looked into her face.

He smiled through the blood, and that smile lit his dusty face. "Ummee!" he whispered. "You are so kind. I love you, my mother."

The words were bitten off and his face contorted with agony. He gave a soft, strangled cry and then his head rolled to one side.

Royan sat for a long time holding his head and weeping softly until Nicholas touched her hand and said gently, "He is dead, Royan."

She nodded. He let her mourn a little longer, and then he told her softly, "We must go, my dear. Go down and wait for me. I will cover him the best I can."

Nicholas folded Tamre's fingers over the silver crucifix that hung around his neck. Then he piled loose rock carefully over him, covering his head so that the vultures could not reach him. He slid down to where she waited, and slung his pack over one shoulder. She wiped away the tears with her hand. "I am ready now."

They waded upstream, pushing against the current. When they reached the point on the bank above the avalanche, they climbed out of the river and picked their way up to the intact section of the pathway. There were two days' hard travel still ahead of them.

"The only consolation is that now Pegasus will believe that we're safely buried under the rock slide and they won't bother to come looking for us again," Nicholas told her.

Royan was limping heavily now, but she would not allow him to inspect the knee, and kept on stubbornly along the trail ahead of him.

They marched mostly in silence for the rest of that day and camped that night in a heavily wooded gully, below the escarpment, just before the path began the climb up the vertical wall.

Both of them were so tired that it was already half-light when they woke the next morning. As soon as Royan tried to stand she groaned and sank back. He went to her immediately, and she made no protest when he placed her bare leg across his lap.

He frowned when he saw the knee. "You shouldn't be walking on this," he told her.

"Do I have any option?" she asked, and he had no reply. He wetted his bandanna from the water bottle and bound up her leg as tightly as he dared. Then he found a phial of Brufen in his bum-bag and made her take two of these anti-inflammatories.

"It feels better already," she told him.

They shared the last bar of survival rations from his pack, then toiled upwards all that morning. The trail seemed to rise more steeply with every pace they took. She never complained, but she was ashen pale and sweating with the pain. As the day wore on, her pace was down to an exhausted plod, and she supported herself on his shoulder as they struggled over the more arduous patches.

Finally they reeled around another corner of the track and saw before them the waterfall, spilling down like a white lacy curtain across the trail. Royan staggered into the cavern behind the sheet of falling water and collapsed.

While she was resting, Nicholas gathered some wood from the monks' stockpile and managed to get a small fire going. Then he selected a round fist-sized stone from the floor of the cavern and with his first throw brought down a brace of the rock pigeons that were roosting on the ledges in the cavern roof. He pounced on the downed birds and with a practised flick of the wrist wrung their necks.

"How do you fancy a juicy slice of roast pigeon?" he asked her.

She lay propped on one elbow, and he sat crosslegged facing her, each of them plucking the feathers from one of the pigeon carcasses. Concentrating on removing the fine bristles from the puckered breast skin of the bird, she said, "It's beyond all doubt now that the material stolen in the raid on our camp is in Pegasus hands."

"I was thinking the same thing," Nicholas nodded, "and we know from the antennas at their base camp that they have satellite communications. We can place a pretty certain bet that Jake Helm has already telefaxed it through to the big man, whoever he may be."

"So he has all the details of the stele in Tanus's tomb. We know that he already has the seventh scroll in his possession. If he isn't an expert Egyptologist himself, he must have somebody in his pay who is. Wouldn't you agree with that?"

"I would guess that he can read hieroglyphics himself. I would think he must be an avid collector. I know the type. It is an obsession with them. Men like those other two on Duraid's list, for instance."

"Peter Walsh and Gotthold von Schiller." She reeled off the names.

"Those two are homicidal collectors," he confirmed. "Both of them are billionaires, and I'm sure neither of them would hesitate to kill for the chance of having Pharaoh Mamose's treasure to themselves."

"So in whoever is behind Pegasus we are dealing with a madman?"

"Much more than that," he corrected her. "We are dealing with an enormously wealthy and powerful maniac, who will stop at nothing."

THEY PICKED at the cold carcasses of the roasted pigeons for their breakfast. Then they started out on the last but most onerous leg of the trail. To begin with Royan was on her own two feet, but before the first hour was over her knee could no longer take the strain, and she subsided onto a rock on the edge of the pathway.

"I'm being an awful nuisance, aren't I?"

"Never mind," he said cheerfully. "Skinny little thing like you. Hop on my back."

"You can't carry me up there." She was aghast.

"It's the only train leaving from this station," he told her and offered her his back. She crawled up onto it.

"Don't you think you should dump the dik-dik skin?" she asked.

"Perish the thought!" he said.

With Royan perched on Nicholas's back, they toiled upwards. On the easier pitches she dismounted and hopped along on one leg beside him, steadying herself with one hand on his shoulder. Then she would collapse, and he had to pull her up onto his back once again.

He lost all sense of the passage of time. Hours blended with hours into a single unremitting agony. When he rested, he had to lean against the cliff face. He dared not lower her to the ground. The effort of lifting her again would be too much. Suddenly the gradient altered so sharply under his feet that he almost fell. The path had levelled out, and like a drunkard he reached up for a step that wasn't there.

He staggered and then caught his balance. He stood teetering on the brink of the precipice and peered into the dusk ahead of him. There were lights in the gloom, and he thought he was hallucinating.

"Oh, dear God. You've made it. We're at the top, Nicky. There are the vehicles. You did it, Nicky. You did it!"

He tried to speak, but his throat had closed up and no words came. He reeled forward towards the lights. There were startled cries and the sounds of running men. Nicholas sank down slowly into the fine highland grass and let Royan slide off his back. Dark figures gathered around them, chattering in Amharic, and friendly hands seized them and half carried, half dragged them towards the lights.

Then a torch was shone into Nicholas's face and a very English voice said, "Hello, Nicky. Nice surprise. I came down from Addis by light plane and army Jeep to look for your corpse. Heard you were dead. Bit premature, what?"

"Hello, Geoffrey. Good of you to take the trouble."

"I dare say you could use a cup of tea. You look a bit done in," said Geoffrey Tennant, and minutes later mugs of steaming, sweetened tea were thrust into their hands.

"Don't want to be pushy, Nicky, but do you mind telling me what the hell is going on here?" Geoffrey asked.

"Why don't you tell me?" Nicholas countered. He needed time to evaluate the situation. What did Geoffrey know and who had told him? Geoffrey obliged immediately.

"First thing we heard was that white hunter chappie of yours, Brusilov, had been fished out of the river near the Sudanese border, absolutely riddled with bullet holes."

Nicholas glanced across at Royan and cautioned her with a frown.

"Last time we saw him, he went off on a scouting expedition on his own," Nicholas explained. "He probably ran into the same bunch of *shufta* who raided our camp four nights ago."

"Yes, we heard about that too. Colonel Nogo here radioed in a report to Addis."

Neither of them had recognised Nogo in the crowd of men. It was only when he stepped forward that Royan stiffened. Nicholas reached across and took her hand to restrain her from any indiscretion.

"I am very relieved to see you, Sir Quenton-Harper. We had a report from the Pegasus Exploration Company that you and Dr Al Simma had been caught up in a blasting accident."

"It was probably our own carelessness. Nevertheless, Dr Al Simma has been injured and we are both badly shaken up by the accident. More important than that, however, is the fact that a number of other people, camp staff and monks from the monastery, have been killed in the *shufta* raid and in the blasting accident."

"I do hope that you don't think any blame attaches—" Nogo started, but Nicholas cut him short.

"Of course not. You warned us about the danger of *shufta* in the gorge. You have done your duty in the most exemplary fashion."

Nogo looked relieved. "You are most gracious to say so, sir."

Nicholas studied him for a moment longer. He seemed the most amiable of young men, so eager to please. For a moment Nicholas almost believed that he had been mistaken, and that it had been somebody else he had seen in the Jet Ranger, hovering over the avalanche site like a vulture, searching for their dead bodies.

WHEN THE pilot lifted the little Cessna 260 off the grass strip at Debre Maryam, the horizon over the Abay gorge resembled a field of cosmic mushrooms, vast thunderheads reaching up into the stratosphere. The air beneath them was turbulent, and Nicholas and Royan were thrown about mercilessly in the rear seats. Up in front Geoffrey seemed to be faring no better and by the time they landed in Addis Ababa he was looking a little green around the gills. Nevertheless, he handed Royan down the aircraft steps with a flourish.

"Of course, you will stay at the residence," he told them. "The hotels in town are too dreadful to contemplate. I'll rustle up some togs for both of you. My missus is about the same size as you, Dr Al Simma, and Nicky will fit into my gear at a pinch. Thank God I have a spare dinner jacket. *He* is a bit of a stickler for form."

The British Ambassador's residence had been built during the reign of the old Emperor, Haile Selassie, before Mussolini's invasion in the 1930s. Set on the outskirts of the town, it was an example of the better colonial architecture, with a thatched roof and wide verandas.

At the front entrance Geoffrey handed them over to an Ethiopian butler who showed them to adjoining bedrooms on the second floor.

Nicholas heard the bath water running in Royan's suite next door as he lay in his own brimming bath. Then there was the murmur of the doctor's voice as he attended to Royan's knee.

Geoffrey's dinner jacket was loose around his waist and too short in the arms, added to which he was in need of a haircut, Nicholas realised, as he surveyed himself in the mirror.

No help for it, now, he decided with resignation, and went to knock on Royan's door.

"I say!" he exclaimed, as she opened it. Sylvia Tennant had lent her a lime-green cocktail dress that set off Royan's olive skin marvellously well. She had washed her hair and left it loose on her shoulders. He felt his pulse accelerate like a teenager on his first date, and laughed at himself.

"You look absolutely scrumptious," he told her.

"You look very dashing yourself," she told him, and then became serious. "Did you manage to fax your secretary in England?"

"It went through at the first attempt and she acknowledged. Sends you her salaams, and promises to have some information about Pegasus double pronto."

It was a mild evening and the British Ambassador, Sir Oliver Bradford, KCMG, was waiting to greet them on the veranda. Geoffrey hurried forward to make the introductions. There were a dozen other guests and Sir Oliver took Royan's arm and led them around the group.

"May I present General Obeid, the Commissioner of Police," Sir Oliver said. The head of the Ethiopian police force was suave and elegant in his blue mess uniform. He bowed over Royan's hand.

"I believe that we have an appointment to meet tomorrow morning at eleven. I look forward to that with the keenest pleasure."

Royan glanced at Sir Oliver uncertainly. She knew nothing of this.

"General Obeid wants to know from you and Sir Nicholas a little more about this business in the Abay gorge," Sir Oliver explained. "I took the liberty of having my secretary make the appointment."

"Just a routine interview, I assure you both."

"Of course we will do everything that we can to assist you," Nicholas told him politely.

"My driver will pick you up at ten thirty and take you down to police headquarters," Sir Oliver promised.

IT WAS AFTER midnight when Nicholas and Royan were at last able to escape. At her door she offered him her cheek, and he kissed it chastely. Back in his own room, he saw an envelope lying at the threshold. During dinner, one of the servants must have pushed it under the door. Quickly he tore open the envelope and scanned the contents. Then he went back to tap on Royan's door.

After a moment she opened it a crack and peeped out at him.

"Reply to my fax." He showed her the papers. "Are you decent?"

"One moment." She closed the door, and opened it again only seconds later.

"Come in and sit down," she said.

He smiled at her. "We know who runs Pegasus now." He took the armchair facing her. He unfolded the fax and looked up at her.

"Mrs Street has worked fast. It seems that sixty-five per cent of the shares in Pegasus are owned by Valhalla Mining Company; the remaining thirty-five per cent are owned by Anaconda Metals of Austria. Both companies are subsidiaries of HMI, Hamburg Manufacturing Industries, and all the shares in HMI are owned by Gotthold Ernst von Schiller."

"Von Schiller," she repeated softly. "Duraid had him on his list of possible sponsors."

Nicholas nodded. "It would have been easy for him to sniff around the Cairo museum and find that Duraid and you were working on something big. The rest of it we know only too well."

"But how did he move Pegasus into Ethiopia so quickly?"

"That must have been a stroke of luck on von Schiller's side. Pegasus obtained a prospecting concession five years ago. Von Schiller was already in place, even before he heard about the scrolls. All that it involved was moving the base camp down from the north where they were working and relocating it on the escarpment of the Abay gorge. We waltzed right into his arms."

Royan looked thoughtful. "It all makes sense. As soon as Helm reported our arrival to his master, von Schiller must have ordered him to set up the *shufta* raid on our camp."

"Well, at least we know now who we're dealing with."

"Not altogether," she demurred. "Von Schiller must have had a man in Cairo. Somebody on the inside there."

"What is the name of your minister?"

"No." She denied it instantly. "Not Atalan Abou Sin. I have known him all my life. He is a tower of integrity."

"It's amazing what effect a bribe of a hundred thousand dollars or so can have on the foundations of even the best-constructed tower," Nicholas observed quietly.

After breakfast they were picked up by Sir Oliver's Rolls-Royce and taken down to police headquarters. There was a police sergeant waiting to meet them and usher them into the headquarters building, through the private entrance. He introduced himself as Inspector Galla and treated them with the greatest deference as he led them to the commissioner's suite.

General Obeid rose to his feet as soon as they entered his office. He was charming and affable as he took them through to his private sitting room. Once they were seated, Inspector Galla poured the inevitable tiny bowls of bitter black coffee.

After a polite interval of small talk the general said, "I won't detain you longer than is absolutely necessary. Inspector Galla here will be recording your statements. Firstly I would like to deal with the disappearance and death of Boris Brusilov."

The interview lasted longer than they had expected. General Obeid was thorough, but unfailingly polite. Finally, after they had read and signed their statements, the general walked with them as far as the entrance where their car was waiting. "If there is anything I can do for you, anything you need, please do not hesitate to call upon me. It has been a great pleasure meeting you, Dr Al Simma. You must come back to Ethiopia soon."

"Despite our little misadventure, I have thoroughly enjoyed my visit to your beautiful country," she told him sweetly. "You may see us again sooner than you expect."

Royan's words were prophetic. There were envelopes addressed to each of them lying at their places on the dining-room table the next morning when they came down to breakfast.

Nicholas opened his as he ordered coffee from the waiter. He read aloud from the note. "'You are ordered to present yourself at police headquarters at or before noon.'" Nicholas whistled softly. "Strong language. No please or thank you."

"Mine is identical." Royan glanced at the note on an official police letterhead. "What on earth do you suppose it means?"

"We will find out soon enough," Nicholas promised her.

On this occasion, when they arrived at police headquarters, there was no reception committee. The guard at the private entrance sent them around to the general charge office, where Inspector Galla, who had treated them so deferentially the day before, looked over the partition and beckoned to them to follow him through to one of the back rooms. He addressed Nicholas coldly. "You are responsible for the loss of a firearm that was in your possession."

"That is correct. As I explained to you in my statement—"

Inspector Galla cut him off. "The loss of a firearm owing to negligence is a very serious offence," he said severely.

"There was no negligence—"

"You left the firearm unlocked and unguarded. That is negligence. Criminal negligence. How are we to know that the weapon has not fallen into the hands of elements opposed to the government?"

"You mean some unknown person may overthrow the government with my rifle?"

Inspector Galla ignored the sally and produced two documents. "It is my duty to serve these deportation orders on both you and Dr Al Simma. You have twenty-four hours to leave Ethiopia, and thereafter you will be considered to be prohibited immigrants, both of you."

"Dr Al Simma has not lost any weapons," Nicholas pointed out mildly. Again this comment was ignored.

"Please sign here to acknowledge that you have received and understood the orders."

"I would like to speak to General Obeid," said Nicholas.

"General Obeid left this morning for an inspection tour of the northern frontier district. He will not return for some weeks." Inspector Galla smiled, a thin smirk. "Please sign here, and here."

"What happened?" Royan demanded as the driver opened the door of the Rolls for her. "One moment everybody loved us, and the next we're being booted down the stairs."

"Do you want my guess?" Nicholas asked, and then went on without waiting for her reply. "Nogo is not the only one in Pegasus's back pocket. Overnight Obeid has been in contact with von Schiller, and received his orders."

"Do you realise what this means, Nicky? It means that we won't be able to return to Ethiopia. That puts the tomb of Mamose beyond our grasp." She stared at him with large dark eyes full of dismay.

"When Duraid and I visited Libya, we didn't have letters of invitation from Gaddafi, as I recall."

"You look delighted at the prospect of breaking the law," she accused.

"After all, it's only Ethiopian law," he pointed out. "Not to be taken too seriously."

"YOU CAN be certain that *he* has already registered a formal complaint with the President's office," Geoffrey told them, as he hovered around them at the Kenya Airways check-in counter.

"He's most upset at the whole business, I can tell you."

"Don't fuss yourself, old boy," Nicholas told him. "As it is, neither of us intends coming back here again. No harm done."

Geoffrey waited with them until their flight was called and waved to them after they passed through the barrier, aiming this affectionate display more at Royan than at Nicholas.

As the Kenya Airways plane started its engines and began to taxi past the airport buildings, Royan suddenly stiffened in her seat. Still gazing out of the porthole beside her, she seized Nicholas's arm.

"Look! Pegasus!" she exclaimed, and pointed to the Falcon executive jet that had just taxied in to the far end of the airport buildings, where a small reception committee waited on the tarmac. The small aircraft was painted green and on its tall tail fin the scarlet horse reared on its hind legs. While they watched, the door in the fuselage was lowered and the passengers appeared. The first of these was a small man, neatly dressed in a cream tropical suit and a white panama hat. His jaw was firm and stubborn, his nose prominent and his gaze beneath dark beetling eyebrows penetrating.

Nicholas recognised him immediately. "Von Schiller!" he exclaimed, as the German raised his panama hat and ran lightly down the steps of the Falcon. "You wouldn't think that he's almost seventy."

A tall man in blue uniform detached himself from the welcoming group and touched the brim of his cap in a respectful salute before taking von Schiller's hand.

"My oath!" Nicholas was startled. "Look who's here to greet him. General Obeid. No wonder he couldn't meet us yesterday."

"Look, Nicky," Royan gasped. Her attention was focused on the top of the steps of the Falcon jet, where another, younger, man had appeared. "Nahoot Guddabi. Duraid's assistant from the museum. The man who now has his job."

As Nahoot started down the steps of the Falcon, their own aircraft trundled on down the tarmac and blocked any further view of the gathering beside the Pegasus jet. Both of them fell back in their seats and stared at each other. Nicholas recovered his voice first.

"A witches' sabbath. A convocation of the ugly ones. We were lucky to witness it. We now know very clearly who the opposition is."

"Von Schiller is the puppetmaster," she agreed. "But Nahoot must be the one who hired the killers in Cairo. Oh God, Nicky, you should have heard him at the funeral, going on about how much he admired and respected Duraid. The murderous hypocrite!"

They were both silent until the aircraft had taken off and climbed to cruise altitude, then Royan said quietly, "Of course, you were right about Obeid. He is deep in von Schiller's pocket also."

Seeing her husband's killers in the flesh had reopened half-healed wounds. Nicholas talked to her quietly, turning her thoughts away from death and vengeance to the challenge of Taita's game. By the time they had changed planes at Nairobi and landed at Heathrow the following morning, the two of them had sketched out a plan for their return and the exploration of Taita's pool. But although now Royan appeared to be her usual cheerful self again, Nicholas knew that the pain of her loss was still beneath the surface.

A little over an hour after touchdown a taxi deposited them on the pavement outside Nicholas's town house in Knightsbridge. It was only eight thirty on the Monday morning.

While Royan showered, Nicholas went down to the corner shop to fetch some groceries. Then they shared the task of cooking breakfast, Royan making the toast while Nicholas whipped up a herb omelette. After breakfast, Nicholas told her, "Take the films of the stele to be developed. There is a one-hour service at the branch of Boots opposite Harrods. I have some phone calls to make."

As soon as she had left, Nicholas settled at his desk with a note-pad at one hand and the telephone at the other. His first call was to Quenton Park, where Mrs Street tried not to show how delighted she was to have him home.

It took him ten minutes to finish his dictation, and then Mrs Street read it back to him.

"Okay. Get on with it, will you? We'll be back this evening. Dr Al Simma will be staying indefinitely. Ask the housekeeper to prepare the second bedroom for her at the flat."

Next he rang a number in Devon. Daniel Webb was ex-Royal Engineers, expert in diving and underwater construction, retired and living in a little cottage there. Nicholas suspected that he was a little short of the ready, and bored out of his considerable mind.

"Hello?" Daniel's voice was guarded.

"Sapper, I have a job for you. Are you a starter?"

"Where are we headed, Major?" Although it had been three years, he recognised Nicholas's voice instantly.

"Sunny climes and dancing girls. Same pay as last time."

"I'm a starter. Where do we meet?"

"At the flat. Tomorrow."

"I'll be there for lunch."

Nicholas hung up, and then made two more calls: one to his Jersey bank and the other to the Cayman Islands. The funds in both his emergency accounts were running low. Let's hope you're not pulling our legs, Taita, he warned himself.

He had less success with his next call, when he had to leave a message on the answering machine of Africair Services, Malta.

"Jannie. This is Nicholas Quenton-Harper. Is that broken-down Herc of yours still airworthy? This job should be a lark. Call me at the flat in the UK. No hurry. Yesterday will do just fine."

When Royan came in the end of her nose was pink with cold, but she pulled a packet out of her pocket and brandished it. "You're a master photographer," she told him. "They've turned out perfectly. I can read every character. We're back in Taita's game again."

They spread the glossy photographs across his desktop.

"You've had duplicates made? A set for each of us. Excellent," Nicholas approved. "The negatives will go into the safe-deposit box at my bank. We won't take a chance of losing them a second time."

Using a magnifying glass, Royan picked out the clearest shot of each of the four sides of the stele. "These will be our working copies. Oh, Nicky, it's so exciting to be unravelling the mysteries again!"

"Leave it alone now," he ordered sternly. "Let's get the Range Rover packed up. It's a long, hard haul up to York."

She shuffled the prints into a neat pile. "Before we go, may I make a phone call home? To Cairo? Duraid's family—"

"Please! No need to explain. There's the phone. Help yourself. I'll be downstairs in the kitchen. We both need a cup of tea before we go."

She came down into the kitchen half an hour later looking guilty, and told him directly, "I'm afraid that I'm going to be a nuisance again. I have to go back home—just for a few days. I was speaking to Duraid's brother. I have to see to some of Duraid's affairs."

"I don't like you going back there on your own after your last experiences."

"Nahoot Guddabi is in Ethiopia now. I should be quite safe."

"Still, I don't like it," he grumbled. "When do you plan to leave?"

"There's a flight at eight this evening."

"A bit sudden. I mean, we've only just arrived." He made one last feeble protest, then capitulated. "I'll run you out to the airport."

When he dropped her off at the departures entrance at Heathrow, he told her, "Phone me tomorrow morning from Cairo to let me know you're all right, and when you're coming back. I'll be at the flat."

She offered him her cheek to kiss, then slid across the seat and slammed the door behind her.

He watched her in the rearview mirror as he pulled away, and was filled with disquiet. Yet short of physical force, there was no way he could impose his will upon her. He had to let her go.

ALTHOUGH COLONEL Tuma Nogo had never entered the *maqdas*, he had often visited the monastery of St Frumentius. He was therefore aware of the magnitude of the task ahead of him, and the likely reaction of the monks to his forced entry to their premises. But Gotthold von Schiller wanted the stele and the coffin in good condition and he was a generous man to those who served him well.

Nogo was painfully conscious of his own culpability in allowing the Englishman and the Egyptian woman to escape, and he could sense the danger in von Schiller's attitude towards him. In the short time since he had made the acquaintance of Gotthold von Schiller, Nogo had come to fear him, and he realised that this raid was an opportunity to restore his reputation with the formidable German.

It took four helicopter trips to ferry Nogo's twenty men down to the assembly point in the gorge. Nogo flew with the first flight, and took Nahoot Guddabi with him. The helicopter dropped them three miles from the monastery, in the same drop area they had used for the raid on Quenton-Harper's camp. Nogo had timed his arrival at the monastery to coincide with the hour of matins at daybreak. He led his contingent to the entrance of the underground cathedral. The interior echoed with the monotonous chanting and drumming of the ceremony. Nogo paused outside the doors and his men drew up in double ranks behind him. He looked them over for a moment, then nodded at his lieutenant.

The monks were gathered in the middle chamber. Nogo crossed the outer nave swiftly, with his detachment moving up close behind him. Then he ran up the steps to the wooden doors of the middle chamber, which stood open. As he entered, his men fanned out in two files behind him and swiftly took up their positions along the side walls, their assault rifles cocked and locked, and with bayonets fixed, covering the kneeling congregation.

The chanting died away and the dark faces turned apprehensively towards the ranks of armed men. In the silence Colonel Nogo marched down the centre of the nave. When he came up behind Jali Hora he seized him by his skinny black shoulder, threw him roughly to the ground and turned to face the rows of monks.

"I am here to search this church and the other buildings of this monastery, on suspicion that there are dissident rebels harboured here. I must warn you that any attempt to prevent my men performing their duties will be met with force."

Jali Hora slowly hoisted himself to his feet. "We are holy men in a place of God. There are no *shufta* here. In the name of God the most high, I call upon you to be gone."

Nogo drew his pistol and swung its black steel barrel into the abbot's face with a vicious backhanded blow. A low moan of horror went up from the ranks of squatting monks as Jali Hora collapsed and lay on the paving stones, groaning in his own blood and spittle.

Nogo left six of his men guarding the monks, and the others followed him to the entrance to the *maqdas*, where they pushed the massive door open and peered into the dim recesses beyond.

Now suddenly even these non-Christians were reluctant to cross that threshold into the holy place. They all hung back, even Tuma Nogo. "Nahoot!" He looked back over his shoulder at the Egyptian. "This is your job now. Herr von Schiller has ordered you to find the things we want. Get in there, oh follower of the Prophet. The Christian gods cannot harm you."

Nahoot shone his torch around the low chamber, over the shelves of votive offerings. The beam stopped on the high cedarwood altar, lighting the tall silver Coptic cross.

"Beyond the altar," Nahoot cried out with excitement. "The barred gateway! This is the place where the Polaroids you stole were taken." He ran wildly across the chamber. Gripping the bars of the gate in his clenched fists, he peered at the murals of the ancient scribe. He recognised Taita's style immediately. "Open this gate!"

Nogo ran to join him, brushing past the covered *tabot* stone. "The stele!" he rasped. "Herr von Schiller wants the stone above everything else." He seized the gold-tasselled border of the tabernacle cloth and pulled it away. The tabernacle was a simple chest carved from olivewood. Picking it up in both hands, Nogo hurled it against the cavern wall, and inscribed clay tablets spilled out of the splintered chest.

"Uncover the stone," Nahoot encouraged him. "Uncover it."

Nogo tugged at the corner of the cloth, and the old and rotten material tore. Taita's stone testament, the carved stele, was revealed. Even Nogo was impressed.

"It is the stone in the photograph," he whispered. "This is what Herr von Schiller ordered us to find. We are rich men."

Nogo turned to his lieutenant and ordered him, "Break open the gate!"

Although the gate was antique, it took the efforts of several men to rip the stanchions out of their foundations in the rock. At last, however, the heavy gate fell with a shattering crash to the slabs, raising a mist of red dust that dimmed the light of the lamps.

Nahoot was the first one into the tomb. He ran through the swirling dust and threw himself to his knees beside the ancient wooden coffin. "Bring the light," he shouted impatiently. Nogo stepped up behind him and shone the torchlight on the coffin.

The portrait was in excellent condition, of a man in the prime of life with a strong, proud face. Nahoot looked up from the portrait to the inscription on the wall of the tomb above it.

"Tanus, Lord Harrab. This follows exactly the description in the seventh scroll." His voice choked with emotion. "We have the stele and the coffin. They are great and priceless treasures. Herr von Schiller will be delighted. Take them to where the helicopter can fly them to the Pegasus camp. If you can do that, you will be a very rich man indeed."

This spur was enough for Nogo. He stood over his men as they laboured, digging in clouds of dust, levering the stone out of the position in which it had stood for nearly four thousand years.

It was a solid half-ton weight. Ten burly troopers were needed to carry it, while three men were able to handle the wooden coffin and its contents. This left seven men free to provide an escort as the heavily burdened procession moved out into the middle chamber.

As soon as the assembled monks realised what they were carrying away with them, some of them leapt to their feet, defying the commands bellowed at them to remain seated. They crowded around the armed troopers, clutching at their uniforms in a challenging display of mounting hostility.

In the midst of this uproar, suddenly Jali Hora appeared, his beard and robes stained with blood. The ranks of monks opened to let him through, and he rushed straight at Colonel Nogo.

"Get back, you old maniac!" Nogo warned him, and lifted the muzzle of his assault rifle to fend him away.

Jali Hora was far past any earthly restraint. He ran straight on. Nogo fired once, hurling Jali Hora's carcass back into the arms of the monks who were crowding close behind him.

For a moment a strained, unnatural silence fell, then it was shattered by a chorus of horror from the monks. Like a flock of white birds they flew at the band of armed men, and for a short while it seemed that the soldiers would be overwhelmed by the sheer weight of numbers, but then those troopers carrying the stele and the coffin dropped their loads and unslung their weapons.

Their first burst of automatic fire, aimed into the monks at point-blank range, scythed a window through them. Nahoot cowered behind the fallen pillar, using it as a shield. The roar of gunfire deafened him. He could not credit the carnage he was witnessing.

The monks in the front rows turned to flee and ran into those behind. They struggled together, howling with agony and terror, until the storm of bullets swept over them and they fell upon the heaps of dead and dying.

It was some minutes before the guns stuttered into silence, and then the only sound was the groans and the weeping of the wounded. The chamber was filled with blue gunsmoke and the stink of burnt powder. The floor was carpeted with bodies.

"Cease firing!" Nogo gave the belated order. "Shoulder arms! Pick up the load! Forward march!"

His voice roused the soldiers, and they slung their weapons and stooped to lift their heavy burdens. Then they staggered forward, stepping on bodies that either convulsed or lay inert.

For Nahoot it was too much. Never in his worst nightmares had he seen sights such as these. He fled from the church, along the cloisters above the gorge of the Nile, following the soldiers as they carried their burdens up the stone staircase. He was so wild with horror that he did not even hear the approach of the helicopter until it was hovering directly overhead.

IT SEEMED to Royan that she had been away from Egypt for years instead of weeks. She realised just how much she had missed the bustling streets of the city, the wondrous smells of spices and the wailing voice of the muezzin calling the faithful to prayer. That very first morning she left her flat in Cairo while it was still dark, and visited Duraid's family. She had to make amends to them for her sudden departure and unexplained absence. At first her brother-in-law was cool towards her; but when she explained that she wanted to visit the cemetery, he unbent so far as to lend her his car.

As she stood beside Duraid's grave the smell of the desert filled her nostrils and the hot breeze fidgeted with her hair. Duraid had loved the desert. She was glad for him that now he would always be close to it. She hoped also that he understood why she had come back now. This was a leave-taking. She had come to say goodbye. She had mourned him and it was time for her to move on.

When at last she left the cemetery, she walked away without looking back.

Atalan Abou Sin, the minister whom Royan had come specifically to see, was out of Cairo on an official visit. She had three days to wait for his return, and because she knew that Nahoot Guddabi was no longer in Cairo, she felt safe and able to spend much of that time at the museum seeing friends and hearing about all that had happened during the time she had been away.

When at last the hour of her appointment to see Atalan came around, he was his usual urbane and charming self. He shook hands with her warmly, and led her through to his private sitting room, where his secretary served them small cups of tar-thick coffee. After the obligatory interval of polite small talk, Royan could come obliquely to the reason for her visit.

"I have spent much of the last few days at the museum, working in the reading room. I was surprised to hear that Nahoot had withdrawn his application for the post of director."

Atalan sighed. "My nephew is headstrong at times. The job was his, but at the very last moment he came to tell me that he had been offered another in Germany. I tried to dissuade him, but—" Atalan spread his hands in an eloquent gesture.

"So who have you chosen to fill the post of director?" she asked with an innocence that did not deceive him.

"We have not yet made an appointment. Nobody automatically comes to mind. Perhaps we will be forced to advertise internationally. I for one would be very sad to see it go to a foreigner."

"Your Excellency, may I speak to you in private?" Royan asked, and glanced at the secretary. Atalan hesitated only a moment.

"Of course." He gestured to the secretary to leave the room, and it was an hour later that Royan left him. He walked with her as far as the lift outside his suite of offices.

As he shook hands his voice was low and mellifluous. "We will meet again soon, inshallah."

WHEN THE Egyptair flight landed at Heathrow and Royan left the arrivals hall to stand in the taxi queue, it seemed that the temperature difference from Cairo was at least fifteen degrees.

Her train arrived at York in the damp misty cold of late afternoon. As Nicholas came striding towards her, she was surprised at how pleased she was to see him.

"How's the knee?" he greeted her.

"Almost better now." She felt a sudden urge to throw her arms around his neck, but at the last moment she prevented herself from making a display and merely offered him a cold cheek to kiss.

In the Range Rover he delayed starting the engine and studied her face in the glow of the streetlight that streamed in through the side window. "You look mighty pleased with yourself, madam," he said.

"Just pleased to see old friends," she smiled, "but I must admit Cairo is always a tonic. And now I want to see my mother. I want to know how her leg is mending."

"Popped in to see her day before yesterday. She's doing fine. I suggest we have a bite to eat, and then pick up a bottle of whisky and go and see her."

It was after midnight when they left Georgina's cottage. She had dispensed rough frontier justice with the malt that Nicholas had brought and now she waved them off, standing in the kitchen doorway and teetering slightly on her plaster-cast leg.

"You are a bad influence on my mother," Royan told him.

"Who's a bad influence on whom?" he protested. "Some of those jokes of hers turned the Stilton a richer shade of blue."

The Quenton Park housekeeper had prepared her a bedroom in the flat behind York Minster. As Nicholas carried her bags up the stairs ripsaw snoring came from behind the door of the bedroom on the second landing, and she looked at Nicholas inquiringly.

"Sapper Webb," he told her. "Latest addition to the team. Our own engineer. You'll meet him tomorrow, and I think you'll like him. I'll be in the small bedroom on the top floor. Call if you need me."

When she was alone she looked around the tiny chintzy room with the double bed that took up most of the floor area. She remembered his remark about calling if she needed him, and she looked up at the ceiling just as she heard him drop one of his shoes on the floor.

"Don't tempt me," she whispered. The smell of him lingered in her nostrils and she remembered the feel of his lean hard body, pressed against hers as he had carried her up out of the Abay gorge. Enough of that, my girl, she chided herself, and went to run a bath.

Nicholas pounded on her door the next morning on his way downstairs. "Come along, Royan. Life is real. Life is urgent." It was still pitch-dark outside, and she groaned softly and asked, "What time is it?" But he was gone, and faintly she could hear him whistling "The Big Rock Candy Mountain" somewhere downstairs.

She checked her watch and groaned again. Whistling at six thirty, after what he and Mummy did to the Laphroaig last night.

I don't believe it, she thought. The man is truly a monster.

Twenty minutes later she found him in a dark blue fisherman's sweater and jeans and a butcher's apron, working in the kitchen.

"Slice toast for three, there's a love." He gestured towards the loaf that lay beside the electric toaster. "Omelettes in five minutes."

She looked at the other man in the room. He was middle-aged, with wide shoulders and sleeves rolled up high around muscular biceps, and the top of his bald head was freckled.

"Hello," she said, "I'm Royan Al Simma."

"Sorry." Nicholas waved the egg whisk. "This is Daniel Webb, known as Sapper to his friends."

Danny stood up. "Pleased to meet you, Dr Al Simma. May I pour you a cup of coffee?"

"Please call me Royan," she said, "and yes, I'd love a cup."

As soon as breakfast was over, Nicholas stood up with the coffee-pot in one hand. "Bring your mugs and follow me."

He led them to the front sitting room. "I have a surprise for you. My people up at the museum worked around the clock to get it ready."

He threw open the door of the sitting room. On the table in the centre stood the striped dik-dik, crowned with the pricked horns and clad in the skin that Nicholas had smuggled back from Africa.

"Oh, Nicky. It's beautiful. The artist has captured it exactly."

The model brought back to her vividly the heat and smell of the bush, and she felt a twinge of sadness for the delicate creature.

"I think it's splendid. Glad you agree with me." Carefully he placed it safely in a corner of the room.

"Okay, take a seat. Now we must talk about how we're going to get into the chasm on the Dandera River. Sapper and I have talked about nothing else the whole time that you've been away. Show her your drawings, Sapper."

Sapper Webb went to the board that stood against the facing wall, pulled away the cover and proudly displayed the illustrations that were pegged to it.

She recognised immediately the enlargements of the photographs that Nicholas had taken at the putative site of Taita's dam on the Dandera River, and others he had taken in the ancient quarry that Tamre had shown them.

"The major has provided me with estimates of the dimensions of the riverbed at this point, and he has also calculated the height that we will have to raise the wall to induce a flow down the former course. As

I understand it, we will not have the benefit of concrete and heavy earth-moving equipment."

"Remember Taita," Nicholas said. "He did it without bulldozers."

"On the other hand, the Egyptians probably had unlimited numbers of slaves at their disposal."

"Slaves I can promise you. Or the modern equivalent."

"The more labour you can provide, the sooner I can divert the river. This will have to be done before the onset of the rainy season."

"We have two months at the most," Nicholas said. "As regards the provision of labour, I will be relying on enlisting the aid of the monastic community at St Frumentius. I'm still working out a reason that might convince them to take part in the building of the dam."

"You find me the labour, and I will build your dam," Sapper grunted. "There are a number of different methods of dam construction, but what this fellow Taita probably did was to weave huge bamboo baskets, which he placed in the river and filled with rock and stone. These we call gabions." He indicated the plans. "Then he would have used rough-cut timber to build walls between the gabions—the cofferdams. These he would also have filled with stone and earth."

"I get the general idea," Royan said.

Sapper went on, "I've studied the photographs taken in the quarry and I've picked out over a hundred and fifty granite blocks lying there completed or almost completed. I reckon that if we use these in combination with the steel mesh gabions and the timber coffer walls, this would give us a firm foundation for the main dam wall."

"Those blocks must weigh many tons each," Royan pointed out. "How will you move them?"

"It's possible," Sapper assured her.

"Taita did it," Nicholas said. "We will be doing it all his way. That should please you."

"You know, in a strange sort of way it does give me pleasure." She smiled at him. "When does all this happen?"

"It's happening already," Nicholas told her. "Sapper and I have already ordered all the stores and equipment. Even the mesh for the gabions has been precut to size by a small engineering firm near here. Half the shipment is already on its way to our nearest commercial airport, ready for the plane coming from Valletta."

"Valletta?" Royan looked mystified. "As in Malta?"

"Malta is where Jannie Badenhorst has his Africair base."

"Jannie who? Now you've really lost me."

"Africair is an air transport company that owns one old ex-RAF

Hercules, flown by Jannie and his son Fred. They use Malta as their base. Jannie's main employment is smuggling booze into the Islamic countries, where of course it's prohibited, but he does take on other work. Jannie will be taking us down to the Abay."

"Nicky, I don't want to be a killjoy, but you and I are now undesirable immigrants to Ethiopia. Had you overlooked that little fact? How do you propose to get back in there?"

"Through the back door," Nicholas grinned, "and my old pal Mek Nimmur is the gatekeeper."

"You've been in contact with Mek?"

"With Tessay. It seems that she is now his go-between. She has all the right connections, and she can slip in and out of Khartoum or Addis or places where it might be dangerous for him to be seen."

"One more question. Does Mek know about Taita?"

"Not in detail." Nicholas shook his head. "But he has some suspicions, and anyway I know I can rely on him." He hesitated, and then went on, "Tessay was very cagey when I spoke to her on the phone, but it seems that there's been an attack on the St Frumentius monastery. Jali Hora and many of his monks were massacred, and most of the sacred relics have been stolen."

"Oh, dear God, no! Who would do a thing like that?"

"The same people who murdered Duraid and made three attempts to wipe you out. Pegasus."

"Then we are directly responsible," Royan whispered. "We led them to the monastery. The Polaroids they took from us when they raided our camp would have shown them the stele and Tanus's tomb. Perhaps when we go back we'll be able to compensate the monks for their losses with what we find in the bottom of Taita's pool."

"I hope so," he agreed fervently. "I do hope so."

THE GIANT Hercules C-Mk1 aircraft was painted a nondescript brown, and the lettering on the fuselage was faded and indistinct.

"Does that thing still fly?" Royan asked, as she looked at it standing forlornly in a back corner of the airfield.

"Jannie keeps Big Dolly looking that way deliberately," Nicholas said. "The places that he flies to, it's best not to draw envious eyes."

"Big Dolly?"

"Dolly Parton. Jannie is an avid fan."

The taxi dropped them and their meagre luggage outside the side door of the hangar, and Nicholas paid the driver.

"There's Jannie now." He pointed to the bulky figure in brown overalls who jumped off the loading ramp of the Hercules and came shambling across the tarmac. Nicholas introduced Royan, and Jannie led them through a wicket in the main hangar door and into a small office cubicle. There he went over his flight plan with Nicholas.

"It's a little complicated," he apologised in his rich South African accent. "As you can imagine, we'll have to do a bit of ducking and diving." He pointed out their flight path on the maps spread over a desk. "Bit of a problem over the Sudan. They're having a little civil war there." He winked at Nicholas. "However, the northern government are not equipped with the most up-to-date radar in the world."

"What's our flying time?" Nicholas wanted to know.

Jannie pulled a face. "Big Dolly is no sprinter. Fifteen hours."

"Has Big Dolly got that sort of endurance?"

"Extra fuel tanks. Even with the load you've given us we can get there and back without refuelling." He was interrupted by the huge hangar doors rolling open and a heavy truck being driven through. "That will be Fred and Sapper now."

The truck parked at the far end of the hangar, where an array of equipment and stores was neatly stacked. When Fred climbed down from the cab, Jannie introduced him to Royan. He was a younger version of the father, already spreading around the waist.

"That's the last truckload." Sapper came around the front of the truck and shook Nicholas's hand. "All set to begin loading."

The cargo had been prepacked on steel pallets, secured with heavy nylon strapping, and the canvas packs containing the parachutes formed an integral part of each load. Royan called out the contents of each pallet from the typed manifest, while Nicholas checked it against the actual load. Only when he was certain that each pallet was complete in every detail did he signal to Fred, who was operating the forklift, to load it onto the Hercules.

The last part of the cargo to go aboard was the small front-end-loading tractor. Sapper had found this in a secondhand yard in York, and after testing it exhaustively declared it to be a "steal." Now he drove the tractor up the ramp and lovingly strapped it down.

It was after midnight before the aircraft was loaded. They lay down in their clothes to get a few hours' sleep on the bunks bolted to the bulkhead behind the flight deck, but it seemed to Royan that she was woken only a few minutes later by the quiet voices of the two pilots completing their pre-takeoff checks. As Jannie spoke on the radio to the control tower, and Fred taxied out to the holding point, the passengers climbed out of their bunks and strapped themselves into the folding seats down the side of the main cabin. Big Dolly climbed into the night sky and Royan turned her head to smile at Nicholas in the dim overhead lights of the cabin.

BIG DOLLY droned on steadily, and there was very little to relieve the boredom of the flight. For the first few hours Nicholas and Royan huddled on her bunk with the chessboard between them, until hunger overtook them and they moved to the makeshift galley, where Royan created a range of sandwiches. They shared the food with Jannie and Fred, perched up behind the pilots' seats in the cockpit.

"Are we still over Egyptian territory?" Royan asked.

With his mouth full, Jannie pointed out over the port wing tip of Big Dolly. "It's a hell of a big piece of country."

Nobody spoke for a while. Nicholas glanced across at Royan. She was staring out of the window at her homeland, and there was something so passionate in her gaze that Nicholas was startled.

She seemed unaware of his scrutiny. She turned to Jannie, leaning over his shoulder to ask, "When will we cross the Nile?"

"On the other side of the border. The Sudanese government concentrate all their attentions on the rebels in the far south. Stretches of the river here in the north are completely deserted. Pretty soon now we'll be going down right on the deck, to get under the radar around Khartoum. We'll slip through one of the gaps."

A little more than two hours later, when Nicholas and Royan were back at the chessboard, Jannie called them on the PA. "Another three hours' flying time to the rendezvous. We should land forty minutes before sunset. Couldn't be better."

The Ethiopian mountains came up so subtly on the eastern horizon that Royan was not aware of them until Nicholas pointed out to her the faint blue outline.

"Almost there." He glanced at his wristwatch. "Let's go up to the flight deck."

Looking forward through the windshield there was no landmark ahead of them—just the vast brown savannah.

"Ten minutes to go," Jannie intoned. "Anyone see anything?" There was no reply and they all stared ahead.

"Over there!" Nicholas pointed over his shoulder. "That's the smokestack of the derelict sugar mill on the river bank. Mek Nimmur says that the airstrip is about three miles from the mill."

"Well, if it is, it's not shown on the chart." Jannie broke off as a red flare shot up from the earth directly ahead.

"Right on the nose." Nicholas patted Jannie's shoulder in congratulations. "Couldn't have done better myself."

Fred climbed a few hundred feet and came around in a one-eighty turn. Now there were two signal fires burning out there on the plain—one with black smoke, the other sending a column of white straight up into the sky. It was only when they were a kilometre out that they were able to make out the faint outline of the overgrown landing strip Mek Nimmur had chosen for the rendezvous.

As Big Dolly finished her roll-out and the end of the pitted runway came up ahead, a man in camouflage fatigues signalled them to taxi into the space between two of the tallest thorn trees.

Jannie cut the engines and grinned at them over his shoulder. "Well, boys and girls, looks like we pulled off another lucky one!"

Even from the height of Big Dolly's cockpit there was no mistaking the commanding figure of Mek Nimmur as he emerged from the cover of a clump of acacia trees. As soon as the loading ramp was lowered, he came striding up it.

"Nicholas!" They embraced. "So I was right! You are up to your old tricks. Not simply a dik-dik shoot, was it?"

"How can I lie to an old friend?" Nicholas shrugged.

"It always came easy to you," Mek laughed, "but I am glad we are going to have some fun together."

A slim, graceful figure followed Mek up the ramp. In the olive-green fatigues Nicholas hardly recognised Tessay until she spoke.

"Nicholas! Royan! Welcome back!" The two women embraced as enthusiastically as the men had done.

"Come on, you lot!" Jannie protested. "I want to take off before dark."

Mek took charge of the off-loading. His men swarmed aboard and with so many hands to help it went swiftly. Big Dolly's hold was emptied just as the sun settled wearily onto the horizon and the short African twilight bled all colour from the landscape.

Jannie and Nicholas had one last hurried discussion in the cockpit while Fred completed his flight checks.

"Four days from today," Jannie agreed, as they shook hands.

"Let the man go, Nicholas," Mek bellowed from below. "We must get across the border before dawn."

They watched Big Dolly taxi down to the end of the strip and come tearing back in a long rolling shroud of dust to lift off over their heads. Without navigation lights, the great aircraft blended into the darkening sky and disappeared almost immediately.

"I'm leaving a full combat platoon to guard your stores here," Mek explained to Nicholas. "We will travel in a very small party as far as the border. I don't expect any trouble. The rest of my men are waiting in the entrance to the Abay gorge. We should rendezvous with them before dawn tomorrow."

"And from there to the monastery?"

"Another two days' march," Mek replied. "We will be there just in time to receive the drop from your fat friend in the fat plane." He turned away and gave his last orders to the platoon commander who would remain to guard the stores. Then he assembled the party of six men who would escort them across the border.

Thirty minutes after Big Dolly had taken off, they left the airfield and set out across the dark and silent plain, headed into the east. Mek set a hard pace, and after a while Royan lost all sense of the distance they had travelled. Only the hourly rest periods orientated her to the passage of time. Her knee was beginning to ache, and fatigue crept over her slowly, until it required an effort to lift her foot for each pace. Once she smelt the cool muddy effluvium of the river on the dry warm night air, and she knew that they must be close to the Nile.

"Crossing the border now," Nicholas breathed close to her face, and the tension was infectious. She forgot her tiredness, and this time they did not stop for the usual rest break, but continued for another hour until slowly the moon thrust above dark, far-off mountain ranges.

"All clear. We're through," Nicholas told her in his normal voice. "Welcome back to Ethiopia. How are you feeling?"

"I'm okay."

"I'm tired too." He grinned at her in the moonlight. "Pretty soon we will camp and rest. Not much further."

He was lying, of course: the march went on and on, until suddenly she heard the soft rushing flow of the Nile in the dawn. Up ahead she heard Mek talking to the men who were waiting for them, and then Nicholas made her sit while he knelt in front of her and unbandaged her knee. It was slightly swollen, and he massaged it.

She sighed softly. "Don't stop. That feels good."

"I'll give you a Brufen for the inflammation." He dug the pills out of his pack and while she swallowed one he pulled the tab on a pack of emergency rations. She fell asleep with her mouth still half filled with tasteless meat loaf and plastic cheese.

When Nicholas woke her with a mug of hot sweet tea, it was

already late afternoon. He sat beside her and sipped at his own mug.

"You'll be pleased to know that Mek now knows what we're looking for, and he's agreed to help us."

"What about men to work on the dam?"

"The monks at St Frumentius will do whatever he asks."

Mek strode up then and squatted on his haunches.

"We are very grateful for all you are doing," Royan told him.

He inclined his head gravely. "Nicholas is an old friend, and I hope that you are a new friend."

"I have been terribly distressed. Tessay told me last night that there had been trouble at the monastery. What happened, Mek?"

Mek scowled and tugged at his short beard angrily. "Nogo and his killers. This is just a sample of what we are fighting against." Speaking tersely but vividly, he described the massacre and the plunder of the monastery's treasures. "There was no doubt it was Nogo."

His anger was too fierce for him to contain, and he stood up abruptly. "The monastery means much to all the people of the Gojam. The murder of the abbot and the desecration of the church is a terrible outrage." He jammed his cap down on his head. "And now we must get on. The road ahead is steep and difficult."

NOW THAT they were clear of the border, it was safe to move in daylight. The second day's march carried them into the gorge, where the river snaked along in its depths, its entire length churned by rapids and breaking white water. At noon Mek broke the march to rest in a grove of trees beside the river.

The four of them sat a little apart from each other, while Sapper made some adjustments to his equipment. Mek and Tessay seemed strangely quiet and withdrawn, until suddenly Tessay reached and grasped Mek's hand.

"I want them to know," she blurted out. "They knew Boris. They will understand."

Mek looked away at the river for a moment before he nodded. "Why not?" he shrugged. "Do you want me to tell them?"

"Yes," she nodded, "it is best that it comes from you."

Mek was silent, gathering his words, and then he started. "The very first moment I looked upon this woman, I knew that she was the one that God had sent my way. We said our vows to each other on the night of Timkat and asked for God's forgiveness, and then I took her away. The Russian followed us. He tried to kill us."

Tessay shuddered at the memory.

"We fought," he said simply, "and when he was dead I sent his body floating away down the river."

"We knew he was dead," Royan said. "We heard at the embassy that the police found his body downstream, near the border. We didn't know how it happened."

They were all quiet for a while, and then Mek stood up and broke the silence. "We can reach the monastery before dark, if we start now."

When they reached St Frumentius, Mai Metemma, the newly elected abbot, met them on the terrace. He was only a little younger than Jali Hora had been, tall and with a dignified silver head.

After the visitors had bathed and rested, the monks led them to the welcome feast that had been prepared. When the *tej* flasks had been refilled for the third time, and the mood of the monks had mellowed, Mek Nimmur placed his arm around the old man's shoulders and whispered in his ear, and Mai Metemma listened intently.

"I HAVE OBTAINED your workers for you," Mek told Nicholas as they began the march up the valley the next morning. "Mai Metemma has promised to give us a hundred men within two days and another five hundred to follow them within the next week."

Both the women stopped in their tracks.

"What did you promise the poor old man?" Tessay demanded.

"A body to replace the one that Nogo plundered from the church. When St Frumentius came to Ethiopia he was not alone. Another Christian, St Antonia, came with him from the High Church in Byzantium. So if we do discover the tomb, then the monastery's share will be the mummy of Mamose, whom we will call St Antonia."

"That's a mean thing to do," Royan exploded. "You will cheat him into helping us."

"It is not a cheat." Mek's dark eyes flashed at the accusation. "The relic that they lost was not the veritable body of St Frumentius, and yet for hundreds of years it served the purpose of uniting the community of monks and drawing Christians from all over this land. Now that it is gone, the very existence of the monastery is threatened. They have lost their reason for continuing."

"So you are giving them a false promise!" Royan was still angry.

"The body of Mamose is every bit as authentic as the one they lost. What does it matter if it is the body of an ancient Egyptian rather than that of an ancient Christian, if it is the means by which the monastery will survive?"

"I think Mek is making sense." Nicholas gave his opinion.

"Since when have you been an expert on Christianity?" Royan flashed at him. "You're an atheist."

"You're right. What do I know about it anyway? But I do know that without the help of the monks there may never be another mummy."

She stared at him and he could see their arguments were beginning to convince her.

"You and Mek Nimmur win," she said softly. "Of course we have to accept their help, and in return they may take the mummy of Mamose or whatever mummy we discover."

They reached the head of the chasm in the middle of the afternoon, and while Mek searched out a campsite Nicholas took Sapper immediately to the narrow neck of the river just above where it plunged over the waterfall so that the engineer could take the readings with the theodolite.

It was almost dark before Sapper had made all the shots he wanted.

"You weren't too far out in your estimates," he congratulated Nicholas. "The river is forty-one yards wide at the critical point above the falls, where I want to site the structure."

"All I want to know is if you'll be able to throw a dam across it."

Sapper grinned. "You get me my ruddy front-end-loader tractor, and I'll dam the bleeding Nile itself."

WHILE IT WAS still dark the next morning, the first levy of priests that Mai Metemma had promised came filing up the valley. Nicholas went to find Tessay and told her, "You are hereby appointed official translator. Sapper speaks not a word of either Arabic or Amharic. Stick close to him."

As soon as it was fully light, Mek and Nicholas left camp to reconnoitre a drop site that was as close to the dam site as possible, for every mile that the stores had to be manhandled would add immeasurably to the time and effort needed for the work.

"Time is the major factor," Nicholas told Mek as they stood in the chosen drop zone. "Every day counts from now until the rains break."

Mek looked up at the sky. "Pray God for late rains."

They marked out their drop site a mile down from the river, where the valley was widest and there was a clear approach through a gap in the hills.

Once all the flares were in place, Mek ordered the area to be cleared. Then, lugging the radio, they climbed up to join Sapper on the high ground at the head of the valley.

"Big Dolly. Come in, Big Dolly!" Nicholas invited, but the static hummed and whined. "They must be running late." He tried not to let his disquiet show. "Jannie is a pro. He will be here soon." Nicholas held the microphone to his lips. "Big Dolly. Do you read? Over."

Every ten minutes he called out into the empty echoing silences, and at last a thin, scratchy voice floated into his headset. "Pharaoh. This is Big Dolly. ETA forty-five minutes. Standing by." Jannie's transmission was terse. He was too much of an old hand at the smuggling game to give a hostile listener time to fix his position.

"Big Dolly. Understand four-five. Pharaoh standing by." Nicholas grinned at Mek. "Looks like we're in business after all."

Mek heard it first. His ear was battle-tuned. Five minutes later Nicholas spotted the speck above the escarpment wall.

Sapper ran out to his flares and fussed over them. When he backed away they bloomed into clouds of dense marigold-yellow smoke that drifted out sluggishly on the light breeze.

Nicholas lifted his binoculars and gazed towards the other end of the narrow valley. He saw that Royan and Tessay were busy with their flares. Suddenly crimson smoke billowed from them, and the women ran clear and stood staring up at the sky.

Nicholas called softly into the microphone. "Big Dolly. Smoke is up. Do you have it visual?"

"Affirmative. You are visual. For what you are about to receive may you be truly thankful."

They watched the aircraft grow in size until the ramp below its belly drooped open and it came around, banking steeply as Jannie lined up on the smoke flares, dropping lower and still lower down the centre of the valley. The first pallet dropped out and plunged earthwards, until at the last moment its parachutes burst open. The fall of the heavy container was arrested abruptly. It dangled and swung, and seconds later struck the floor of the valley in a cloud of yellow dust. Then two more loads dropped.

Big Dolly's engines howled under full throttle and her nose lifted as she climbed out over the end wall of the valley. She came around in another wide turn and lined up for the second run.

Six times Jannie repeated the dangerous manoeuvre, and each time he dropped three more heavy rectangular loads. They lay strewn down the length of the valley, shrouded by the tumbled white silk of their own parachutes.

Then Big Dolly lined up for her final pass down the valley, and after the last pallet dropped she lifted her belly ramp and climbed away under full power. Nicholas called Jannie on the radio.

"Many thanks, Big Dolly. Safe flight home."

"Inshallah! If God wills!" Jannie called back.

"Well, now." Nicholas slapped Sapper's back. "Let's go down and see if you still have a front-ender in one of those pallets."

The battered yellow machine lay on its side with oil pouring out of her, like blood from a heart-shot dinosaur.

"You can push off. Just leave me a dozen men to help me," Sapper told them as sorrowfully as if he was standing at the graveside of his beloved.

Sapper did not return to camp for dinner, so Tessay sent a bowl of food down to him while he worked. Nicholas considered going down to offer his help with repairing the damaged tractor, but thought better of it. From bitter experience he knew that at certain times Sapper wanted to be left alone, and this was one of those times.

In the small dark hours of the morning the camp was lit up by the blaze of headlights and the hills reverberated to the roar of a diesel engine. Hollow-eyed but triumphant, Sapper drove the yellow tractor into the camp and shouted at them from the driver's seat, "Let's go build a dam."

IT TOOK THEM two full days to gather in all the pallets that lay strewn down the valley and to carry the stores into the ancient quarry. In the meantime Sapper was at work on the dam site, laying out his foundations and taking his final measurements. During this preliminary work Nicholas was watching the monks, and getting to know them individually. Of those who spoke Arabic or a little English, the most promising was a monk named Hansith Sherif, whom Nicholas made his personal assistant and interpreter.

Once they were settled into the camp, and had worked out a relationship with the monks, Mek Nimmur took Nicholas aside.

"From now on, my work will be the security of the site. Nogo and his thugs are still out there. It won't take long for him to hear that you are back in the gorge. When he comes, I will be waiting for him."

Mek took his men into the bush and deployed them in defensive positions along the trail and around the camp. When Nicholas looked up from his own work he could often make out the reassuring figure of one of Mek's sentries on the high ground above the camp.

On the fifth day the second draft of three hundred labourers that

Mai Metemma had conscripted for them arrived. These men were not monks, for St Frumentius had already given its all, but villagers who lived up on the highlands of the escarpment. Mai Metemma had coerced them with threats of hellfire.

Nicholas divided this work force into gangs of thirty men each. With Tessay interpreting for him, he harangued them heartily and then told them that they would be paid in silver Maria Theresa dollars. He set their wages at three times the going rate.

Up to this stage the men had listened to him with a sullen air of resignation, but now a remarkable transformation came over them. In Ethiopia for the past two hundred years the Maria Theresa dollar had been regarded as the only true coinage. For this reason they were still minted with the original date of 1780 and the portrait of the old Empress. One of these coins was more prized than a sackful of the worthless paper birr issued by the regime in Addis, and Nicholas had included a chest of them in the load that Jannie had dropped.

From then onwards the work began as soon as it was light enough to see, and stopped only when it was too dark to continue. The men came back to their temporary compound each night by the light of grass torches, too weary to sing. However, Nicholas had contracted with the headmen from the highland villages to supply huge pots of *tej* and a slaughter beast every day, and over the days that followed there were no deserters from Nicholas's army of workers.

MOUNTED ON THE high seat of the front-ender, Sapper lifted the first filled mesh gabion in the hydraulic arms. The mesh-bound parcel of boulders weighed several tons, and all work on the site came to a halt as the men crowded the banks of the Dandera River to watch. Sapper eased the tractor down the steep bank and drove the vehicle into the water. He locked the brakes, and then lowered the gabion into the flood before reversing back up the bank. The men cheered him, even though the first gabion was instantly submerged and only a whirlpool on the river's surface marked its position.

Nicholas shouted at the foremen to get their gangs back to work. The long lines of men came up the valley, naked except for their brief white loincloths. Sweating heavily in the heat of the gorge, each of them carried on his head a basket of stone which he dumped into the mouth of the waiting gabion. Then he returned with his empty basket to the quarry. As each gabion was filled, another team fitted the mesh lid and laced it closed with heavy-gauge wire.

At first there was little evident progress, but as a solid reef was built up beneath the surface, the voice of the water changed from a low rustle to a dull roar as it tore at Sapper's wall.

Soon the top of the wall of gabions thrust its head above the surface, and the river was constricted to half its former width. It poured through the gap in a solid torrent, and crept up the banks as it was forced to back up behind the barrier. In the meantime, two hundred metres upstream of the dam site, two teams were building a raft of tree trunks that they had hacked from the forest. The timbers were lashed together to form a grating. Over this was laid heavy PVC sheeting to make it waterproof; then a second grating of tree trunks went over this to form a gigantic sandwich. It was all lashed together with heavy baling wire. Finally, one end of the grating was ballasted with boulders, so that it would float almost vertically in the water. And while the work on the raft and the wall continued, three other work teams laboured at the head of the valley, digging out a deep canal into which the river could be diverted.

Arrangements for getting out still had to be made. One morning, therefore, Nicholas unpacked the inflatable Avon rafts from one of the pallets. These craft had been specifically designed for river-running in turbulent water, and each was capable of carrying sixteen crew and a ton of cargo.

Nicholas directed his team to strap the heavy packs onto the carrying poles that they had cut for that purpose. Five men on each end of the long poles, with the packaged boat slung in the centre, made light of the load. They set off at a cracking pace down the trail, and as soon as one team tired the next was ready to take over.

Nicholas and Royan trotted along behind the caravan, joining in the chorus of the work chant that the porters sang.

Mai Metemma was waiting on the terrace outside the church of St Frumentius to welcome them. He led them down the staircase hewn out of the rock to the water's edge. Fifty feet above the ledge, out of reach of the Nile's highest water level, was a small cavern, in which Mai Metemma gave them his sanction to store the rafts. When the porters had left, Nicholas showed Royan how to inflate them.

Royan shivered as she watched the river racing by. "You do intend coming along on this joy ride?" she asked anxiously. "You aren't planning on sending me down on my own?"

"It's best that you know how it all works," he told her. "If things start to get a little hairy when the time comes to leave here, I may need your help in launching the rafts."

When they climbed back up the staircase into the sunlight, Royan's uncertain mood changed. "It's not yet noon. Let's go back to Taita's pool again," she suggested, and he shrugged indulgently.

The porters accompanied them as far as the branch in the trail, then headed back towards the dam and shouted their farewells after Nicholas and Royan.

Even in the short time since their last visit, the path through the undergrowth had become overgrown. It was midafternoon when they eventually stood once again on the cliff above Taita's pool.

"It looks as though we were the last ones here." Nicholas's tone was relieved. "No signs of any other visitors since us."

"Were you expecting any?"

"You never know. Von Schiller is a formidable character, and he has some charming lads working for him. Jake Helm, for instance."

He cast around for any sign of intruders, then sat down beside her on the lip of the abyss.

"Once Sapper stops the river upstream, this is going to be our main area of operations, isn't it?" she asked.

"Yes, but even before Sapper closes the dam I want to move all the equipment from the quarry and open a camp here."

"How are we going to get down into Taita's pool once the riverbed's dry? Build a scaffold down the cliff, just the way Taita did?"

"What's good enough for Taita is good enough for me," he acknowledged. "One of our teams is already cutting bamboo poles higher up the gorge. We can't waste a day. Once the dam is closed, we have to get into the dry pool as soon as possible."

As if to add weight to his words there came a far-off mutter of thunder. Nicholas glanced at the storm clouds settling on the distant mountains and stood up. "Time to start back if we're to get into camp before dark."

He gave her his hand and lifted her to her feet. She dusted off her clothes and then stepped right to the very lip of the canyon.

"Wake up, Taita. We are hot on your tracks," she called down into the shadows.

THE GRATING of massive tree trunks lay on the river verge, already half in the water. Sapper slitted his eyes as he studied the layout, and then looked downstream to the partially completed dam. Two walls of gabions stretched out, one from either bank, and the river roared through the twenty-foot gap in the middle.

"The one thing we don't want is to let the plug run away from us and knock a big chunk out of the ruddy wall," he warned Nicholas. "I want to cuddle her in there, nice and softly, and let her sit snug in the gap. Any questions? You all know the signals?"

Sapper took one last drag on his cigarette and flicked the stub into the river. "Okay, gents. The last one in the water is a sissy."

He climbed up onto the yellow tractor, and with a cloud of diesel smoke the engine burst into life. He raised one hand above his head with the fist clenched, and Nicholas relayed the order to his team: "Take the strain." Sapper had rigged up a cunning series of pulley blocks through cables that he had strung across the river. One team was under the direction of Nicholas; the other under Mek Nimmur on the opposite bank.

The men leaned back against their cables, Sapper threw the tractor into extra low, eased her forward, and the timber grating slid ponderously down the bank into the river. The weighted end of the grating sank immediately and bumped along the bottom, while the lighter end floated high. Slowly they hauled it out into midstream, where the current seized it and began to bear it away, straight at the wall of gabions. It picked up speed alarmingly. The tractor blew out clouds of black smoke as Sapper threw her into reverse and backed up on the cables. The teams of men heaved and chanted.

The grating steadied across the current, and they let it fall away at a more sedate pace, down towards the open gap in the wall.

"Close the hole," bellowed Sapper, and now the full current was too powerful to resist. It dragged both teams into the river until some of them were in over their heads. However, those men who still had their footing managed to slow the rush of the grating just enough to prevent it smashing into the dam. It settled firmly across the gap, like a mammoth plug in the outlet of a giant's bathtub, and instantly the current was cut off.

While the men in the water struggled ashore, Sapper threw off the cables from his tow hitch and roared along the bank with the front-ender in its highest gear. "Got to shore up now, before the grating bursts," he yelled.

The dam was holding, but only just. Numerous jets of water spurted through every gap between the grating and the gabions. The pressure of water against the sheets of PVC in the grating was enormous. It was taking the full thrust of the river.

Sapper picked up one of the gabions that were standing ready on the bank and drove down into the riverbed below the dam. The flow of the water had shrivelled to a mere knee-deep trickle. Slowly he built up a retaining wall behind the grating, placing the gabions in sloping ranks until this revetment was as strong as the side piers.

By now Nicholas had run back upstream to the canal that the teams had dug at the head of the valley. Most of the workers had gathered along the banks of this cutting, Royan and Tessay in the front row of the excited crowd.

Nicholas pushed his way through to Royan's side and she grabbed his hand. "It's working, Nicky. The dam wall is holding."

Even as they watched, they could see the level of the trapped waters rising up the wall of the dam. While the men urged it on, the river lapped at the entrance of the canal and a thin snake of river water found its way into the canal itself. The trickle increased to a freshet, and then to a torrent. With its new strength it gouged out the canal and burst through with the full flow of the river behind it. For the time being the dam was secure.

"Do you think it will hold?" Royan eyed the structure suspiciously.

"Until the rains come, we hope." Nicholas drew her away. "We don't want to waste any more time here. Time to go on downstream to begin work at Taita's pool."

NICHOLAS WAS the first one down into the gorge. This time he had a bosun's chair to sit in and a properly rigged block and tackle to lower him over the cliff. As he swung down, the abyss opened under him, sombre and repellent. His eye was drawn irresistibly to the bottom of the gorge, and he saw at once that the waterfall above the pool had been reduced to a trickle.

The level of the great pool under him had fallen drastically. He could make out the high-water level by the wet markings on the rock cliff. Another eight pairs of chiselled niches were visible in the face. Where once he had been forced to swim down to them, they were now high and dry. However, the pool was not completely drained. It was dished below the level of the downstream outlet, so that it was unable to empty itself by gravitational flow. There was still black water trapped in the centre, with a narrow ledge surrounding it. Nicholas landed on this ledge and stepped out of the bosun's chair. It was like being in the bottom of a mineshaft. He edged his way along the slippery rock ledge towards the cliff face where the rows of dark niches stood out clearly against the lighter stone.

Now he could make out the shape of the opening in the wall that had so nearly sucked him down. It was almost completely submerged in a deeper corner where the pool flowed back against the cliff. All that was visible above the surface was the top arch of an irregular entrance at the foot of the descending rows of niches. The rest of it was still submerged.

The ledge narrowed as he worked his way along the foot of the cliff until he had his back to the rock and was moving sideways with his toes in the water. Eventually he could go no further. He squatted down and reached out towards the opening. The lip of the hole was smooth, and once again it seemed to him that it was too square and straight to be anything other than man-made.

THE BAMBOO scaffolding that Sapper and Nicholas built down the cliff was anchored in the niches that had been cut into the rock nearly four thousand years before.

The very first piece of equipment to reach the floor of the cavern was the portable Honda EM500 generator. Sapper connected it up to lights that he had rigged along the foot of the cliff. They lit the deep rock bowl like a stage.

Immediately the mood changed. Everybody became more cheerful and there was excited chatter from the men on the scaffolding.

"Now that we know they're working, switch off those lights," Nicholas ordered. "We only have two hundred litres of fuel in reserve, and we don't know how long we're going to need it in the tunnel."

When Sapper cut the generator the cavern was plunged once more into gloom. Nicholas stood back and watched the preparations to build a small cofferdam around the underwater opening and bale it out with buckets. Half a dozen empty mesh gabions were carried down the scaffolding and placed at the edge of the pool. Here they were partially filled with boulders that the men gathered up from the riverbed. There was just sufficient of the yellow PVC sheeting left over to wrap around each gabion and render it waterproof.

The depth of the water that covered the entrance to the shaft was well over the height of a man's head. They were forced to roll the gabions down into it, and complete the filling once they were in position. It was difficult and taxing work, and took almost two days to complete, but at last they had built a half-moon-shaped weir around the underwater entrance, walling it off from the main body of water in the pool.

Using leather buckets the men baled out the coffer over the wall into the main pool. Nicholas and Royan watched as the level in the coffer fell and the opening in the cliff was gradually revealed; it was about three metres wide by two metres high. Eagerly Nicholas climbed down. The water was knee-deep as he crawled forward into the opening. With his bare hands he tried to shift some of the rock debris that choked it.

"It's going to take a tremendous amount of work to clear it enough to find out where it leads to," he shouted as he clambered back out of the coffer. "Well, at least we have the floodlights," he added. "We can keep the men working in shifts, night and day, until we get through."

The debris that filled the shaft had taken centuries to wedge itself in, and it required backbreaking effort to prise it apart. Nicholas changed the shifts every hour, and at each change of shift he disappeared into the mouth of the tunnel and measured the advance.

On the morning of the second day an unusually shaped fragment in the muck at his feet caught his eye. He stooped and picked it up. As he rubbed it clean between finger and thumb, he began to grin.

Sloshing back along the tunnel, he yelled, "Royan!" Triumphantly brandishing the fragment, he said, "What do you make of that?"

She was sitting on the wall of the coffer, and reached down and snatched the object from him. "Where did you find this, Nicky?"

"Lying in the mud. Right there in the adit, where it's been for the last four thousand years. Where one of Taita's workmen dropped it."

Eagerly Royan held the broken shard up to the lamplight. "You're right," she exclaimed. "It's part of a wine vessel. The black firing around the rim dates it perfectly in our period. No older than 2000 BC." Still clutching the fragment, she jumped down into the mud and slush of the coffer and flung both arms around his neck. "Further proof, Nicky. We're on Taita's tracks."

Halfway through the next shift an excited yelling echoed out of the tunnel, and Nicholas hurried with Royan back down to the face.

Hansith Sherif appeared at the mouth of the shaft, grinning. "We have broken through, effendi." Nicholas eagerly pushed his way through the workmen. They had levered a huge round boulder out of the pack, and beyond it lay the opening to the cavern.

"What has happened here? What has caused this?" Royan's voice was puzzled as Nicholas played his torch out into the void.

"I think this is a cave-in area. There was probably a fault in the rock strata running through here and here." He picked out the cracks in the roof of the cavern.

"You think the flow of the water through the shaft has scoured it out?" she asked.

"I would say so, yes." Nicholas turned the beam of light downwards. "The floor has fallen out of the shaft also." The rock had subsided in front of them, leaving a deep hole. Luckily there was a path around this obstacle. "I think that this is the natural fault that leads the water away to the other side of the hills, and comes to the surface again at the butterfly fountain. The river has carved its own path."

"If you are right, and a section of Taita's adit has collapsed, then his tunnel should continue on the far side of this." She pointed across the hole, and Nicholas lifted the beam of the torch in the direction she indicated. A dark rectangular opening yawned at them.

Nicholas was the first one across the sinkhole. He scrambled up into the mouth of the adit, with Royan close behind him.

This length of the tunnel had also been submerged, for it lay below the natural level of the river before it had been dammed. The roof and walls of the tunnel ran with moisture, and the air was dank and cold.

They waited for Sapper to string the cables for the lights and switch them on. At once they were aware that ahead of them the shaft had begun to rise at an angle of about twenty degrees.

"You can see what that old devil Taita was up to here. He has taken us down well below water level to flood the tunnel to a length and depth that nobody would be able to swim along. Now he is angling up again," Nicholas pointed out to Royan. They moved slowly up the shaft, and eventually they came to the recent low-river level. It was clearly marked as a dry line on the walls of the tunnel. The paving under their feet was also dry and free of slime. Fifty paces further on they passed the high flood level of the river, which was just as clearly etched on the rock floor and the walls. Beyond that the tunnel had never been immersed, and the walls were in the same condition as the Egyptian slave workmen had left them four thousand years earlier.

Only ten feet beyond the highest point that the river waters had ever reached, they came out upon a stone landing.

"Let's spare a minute just to think about this as a feat of engineering." Nicholas took Royan's arm and pointed back down the tunnel. "Taita has placed this landing on which we are standing precisely above the high-water mark of the river. How did he work it out so exactly? He had only the crudest measuring equipment."

"Well, he tells us repeatedly in the scrolls that he is a genius. I suppose we will have to believe him now." She pulled against his grip. "Let's go on. I must see what lies around this corner," she urged.

Side by side they turned the corner and Nicholas held the hand lamp high, with the electrical cable trailing back down the shaft behind him. Before them rose a wide stairway, the treads polished and fitted to each other so precisely that the joints between them were barely visible. The roof of the tunnel, three times as high as it had been in the lower reaches, was of beautifully dressed blue granite blocks. The whole was a masterpiece of the mason's art.

Together they mounted the stairway. It was carpeted with a fine layer of dust that rose in soft eddies around their knees as they passed on upwards. The staircase ended on another level landing, across which a sealed rectangular doorway faced them. They stepped up onto the landing and stood before the doorway. It had been plastered over with white river clay. Neither of them had words to express this supreme moment: they stood in silence.

Two embossed seals were mounted in the centre of the door. The upper one was in the shape of the royal cartouche, the rectangular knot surmounted by the scarab.

Royan read the words from the hieroglyphics. "'The Almighty. The Divine. Ruler of the Upper and Lower Kingdoms of Egypt. Familiar of the god, Horus. Beloved of Osiris and of Isis. Mamose, may he live for ever!'"

Below this magnificent royal seal was a smaller, simpler design in the shape of a hawk, and the legend: "I, Taita the slave, have obeyed your command, divine Pharaoh." Underneath the hawk a single column of hieroglyphics spelt out the stern warning: "Stranger! The gods are watching. Disturb the king's eternal rest at your peril!"

Breaking the seals on the doorway was a momentous act, and neither of them was prepared to undertake it lightly. They needed to keep permanent records of everything they discovered, and to inflict as little damage as possible while gaining access.

Nicholas photographed the approach tunnel and the sealed doorway, while Sapper moved the Honda generator up as far as the sinkhole, to reduce the voltage drop over the distance that the current had to travel down the cable. Then he set up the floodlights on the upper landing of the staircase and focused them on the plastered doorway.

When they assembled at the threshold they were all in a sober mood. Nicholas marked out the opening he intended cutting through the plaster covering. This was large enough to afford access, but it also enclosed the royal cartouche and Taita's hawk seal. He intended lifting these out in one piece and preserving them intact.

Nicholas began on the right-hand upper corner of the opening. First he used a long, needle-sharp awl as a probe, to determine exactly what lay beneath the plaster surface. Very soon he found out that the plaster had been laid over laths of finely interwoven reeds.

He kept working the point of the awl deeper until suddenly the resistance gave way and the blade ran in its full length.

"Six inches," he said, measuring the thickness of the door off the blade. "Taita never skimps, does he? It's a heavy bit of work."

Still using the awl, Nicholas drilled all four corners of the square opening he intended cutting. Then he stepped back and gestured for Hansith to bring up the heavy four-inch drill to enlarge them.

As soon as the gimlet broke through, a faint breath of ancient air washed out through the opening. The odour was dry and dead and austere, the smell of the ages long past.

Next Sapper rigged up a heavy-duty electric blower fan which would circulate the air in the shaft, while Nicholas prepared the chainsaw. When he was ready, Nicholas handed Royan a pair of goggles and a dust mask and helped her to adjust them. Then he made her fit a pair of wax ear-plugs.

Before he started the chainsaw, he sent the rest of them back down the tunnel as far as the causeway over the sinkhole. In the confined space the exhaust fumes from the chain saw and the dust, together with the noise of the petrol engine, would be overpowering.

When they were alone, Nicholas pulled the starter cord of the chainsaw motor and pressed the spinning chain blade into the gimlet hole in the plastered doorway. Carefully he ran the cutting edge down the line he had marked out. A cloud of flying white plaster dust filled the air. Finally, when he made the last cut, he killed the engine of the chainsaw and set it aside.

Royan jumped forward to help him, and together they lifted the square of plaster out of the opening and, with the seals still intact, laid it against the side wall of the landing.

Nicholas adjusted the floodlight to shine through the open hatchway, but the dust was still too dense for them to be able to see much of the interior. They climbed through the hatch and stood quietly together, waiting for the blower fan to clear the air.

Gradually a miraculous blaze of colours began to appear through the murk, and before them opened a long straight passageway, the end of which was hidden in shadow. Nicholas turned back to the opening in the sealed door behind them and reached through it to bring in a light on its cable.

As they started forward, images of the old gods hovered around them. Nicholas and Royan passed on slowly until they came to the first of eight shrines set into the walls of the long funeral gallery. This one was the shrine of Osiris, god of the Underworld. It was a circular chamber, the curved wall decorated with texts in praise of the god, and in its niche a small golden statue of Osiris in his tall feathered headdress stared at them. The next shrine set into the wall was dedicated to the goddess Isis. The golden figure sat in her niche, upon the throne that was her symbol. The infant Horus suckled at her breast. Her eyes were ivory and blue lapis lazuli.

In the next shrine was a figure of Horus, the falcon-headed, the last of the holy trinity. In his right hand he held the war bow and in his left the *ankh*, for life and death were his to dispense.

In the fourth shrine stood Seth, the god of violence and discord. His body was gold, but his head was the head of a black hyena.

In the fifth shrine stood the god of the dead and of the cemeteries, Anubis the jackal-headed. It was he who officiated at embalmings.

The sixth shrine was dedicated to the god of writing, Thoth. He had the head of a sacred ibis and his stylus was in his hand. In the seventh shrine the sacred cow Hathor stood squarely on all four hoofs, her piebald body spotted black and white, her face benignly human but with huge, trumpet-shaped ears. The eighth shrine was the largest and most splendid of all, for it belonged to Amen-Ra, father of all creation. He was the sun, an enormous golden disc from which the slanting golden rays emanated.

Nicholas paused and looked back down the long gallery. Those eight sacred statues comprised a treasure that matched anything that Howard Carter had discovered in the tomb of Tutankhamun. But he thrust the thought aside and turned once more to face the commodious chamber at the far end of the gallery.

"The burial chamber," Royan murmured with awe. "The tomb."

As they walked towards it the shadows retreated before them, like the ghost of the long-dead Pharaoh. Now they could see into the tomb. Its walls were aflame with still more magnificent murals. The royal sarcophagus stood in the centre of the chamber, a massive coffin hewn from a solid granite block. How many slaves must have laboured to bring this mass of stone here? Nicholas wondered.

Then he felt the plunge of his spirits as he realised that the massive granite lid had been lifted from its seat and lay in two pieces on the floor beside the coffin. They moved forward slowly, the bitter taste of disappointment mingling with the dust upon their tongues, until they could look down into the open sarcophagus.

"Empty!" whispered Royan. "The body of the king has gone."

OVER THE following days, while they photographed the murals and packed the statues from the funeral gallery, Royan and Nicholas discussed the disappearance of the royal mummy from its sarcophagus.

"The seals on the gate of the tomb were intact," Royan pointed out.

"Taita himself might have removed the body."

"No, it doesn't make sense," Royan argued. "He would never have flouted the religious traditions. Something about this tomb does not ring true for me—particularly the inscriptions upon the walls."

"What do you find illogical about them?" Nicholas wanted to know.

"Have you ever heard of another tomb that did not have the text of the *Book of the Dead* inscribed upon its walls, or that did not depict the dead person's journey through the seven pylons to paradise?"

Nicholas looked startled. He left her and went back down the long gallery, ostensibly to supervise the packing of the sacred statues, but in reality to give himself more time to consider what she had said.

Before leaving England Nicholas had seen to it that all of the more vulnerable equipment that they had air-freighted into the gorge had been packed in sturdy metal ammunition crates. All these crates had waterproof rubber seals and strong lever fastenings. When they left Ethiopia the original contents would be abandoned, but the crates, together with the packing material, had been carefully preserved for transporting the treasures that they might find in the tomb.

Nicholas watched as Hansith packed Seth's ferocious head of ebony and black resin. After a while he went back to where Royan was working on the inscriptions above the empty sarcophagus.

"Very well. I agree. You are right about the lack of inscriptions from the *Book of the Dead*. But what can we do about it, other than accepting it as a mystery which we can never unravel?"

"Nicky, there is something more here. We are missing something. How long do I have to work over the inscriptions from the stele?"

"A week, two at the most. I have still to set up an RV with Jannie."

"How will you contact him from here?"

"Quite simple." Nicholas smiled. "There is a telephone at the post office in Debre Maryam. Tessay can move anywhere in the Gojam. She will telephone Geoffrey Tennant tomorrow at the embassy in Addis and he will relay a message on to Jannie. It's all arranged."

ROYAN WOULD have preferred to camp in the tomb itself, so as to be in the midst of the inscriptions on which she was working, but Nicholas had insisted that they sleep in the open air. "The musty air in the tomb is unhealthy," he told her. "Cave disease is a real danger in these old enclosed places. They say that is what killed some of Howard Carter's people working in the tomb of Tutankhamun."

"The fungus spores that cause cave disease breed in bat dung," she pointed out. "There are no bats in Mamose's tomb. Taita sealed it up too tightly."

"Humour me," he begged. "You cannot work in there for days on end. I want you at least to get out for a few hours each day."

She shrugged. "Only as a special favour to you," she agreed.

They had converted the landing at the top of the staircase, outside the entrance to the tomb, into their workshop. While Nicholas completed his photographic record of the burial chamber, Royan sat at her table and pored over her papers for hours at a time, scribbling notes in her notebooks.

At one point Nicholas found her standing in the long gallery before an empty niche. She was so preoccupied that she did not hear him come up behind her, and she started when he touched her arm.

"What are you staring at?" he asked. "What have you discovered?"

"Nothing," she denied swiftly, and then after a moment, "I don't know. It's just an idea."

"Come on! What are you up to?"

"It's easier for me to show you." She led him back to her desk.

"What I've been doing these last few days is going through the material on the stele of Tanus's tomb." She showed him pages in her neat small script. "All this is from the fourth face of the stele. It's nothing that I recognise, but seems to be only long lists of numbers and figures. Some sort of code, perhaps? I'm not sure, but I do have some ideas on it that I will come to later.

"Now this here," she showed him the next notebook, "this is all fresh material. Much of it, if not all, must be original Taita writings. If he has left any more clues for us, I believe they will be here. Look at this quotation from the third face of the stele, the side Taita has headed 'Autumn.' It's the very first one that caught my attention."

Nicholas leaned forward and read the hieroglyphics aloud: "'The great god Osiris makes the opening coup with deference to the protocol of the four bulls. At the first pylon he bears full testimony to the immutable law of the board.'" He looked up at her. "Yes, I remember that quotation. Taita is referring to bao, the game that he loved so passionately. But I'm no expert on the game. What did he mean?"

"The rules of the game have been lost. But as you know, we have found examples of the bao board among the grave goods in certain tombs, and we can only guess that it was an early form of chess." She began to sketch on one of the blank pages in her notebook.

"The wooden board was laid out like a chessboard, eight rows of indented cups wide and eight rows deep. The pieces were coloured stones. I won't go into all the details, but the protocol of the four bulls was an opening gambit."

"I'm not sure where we're going, but lead on. I'm listening."

"Come with me." Carrying the notebooks, she led him through the hatch and stood beside him at the shrine of Osiris. "This is the first shrine. How many shrines are there altogether?"

"Eight."

"And how many cups in the files of the bao board?"

"Eight across, and eight down—" He broke off. "You think—?"

She did not answer, but opened the notebook. "All these numbers and symbols—they spell no coherent words. They do not relate to each other, except that no number is greater than eight."

"I thought I had caught up with you, but I just lost you again."

"If somebody were to read the notations of a game of chess four thousand years from now, what would he make of it?" she asked. "Wouldn't it just be lists of numbers and symbols to him?"

"Oh Lordy!" His face cleared. "Taita is playing bao with us."

"And this is the first pylon, where it starts." She gestured to the shrine. "This is where Osiris makes the opening coup. This is where we counter his opening move."

They both looked around the shrine for a while, then Nicholas broke the silence.

"At the risk of seeming dense, may I ask a question? How the hell do we play a game when we don't even know the rules?"

THEY HAD spent almost two full days at the shrine of Osiris in the long gallery, taking turns to recite aloud the extracts from the stele of Tanus, repeating them until they knew each quotation by heart. While one read aloud, the other concentrated his or her full attention upon the walls, trying to discover some connecting link.

"'My love is a flask of cold water in the desert. My love is a banner unfurling in the breeze,'" Nicholas read.

Royan looked up at him from where she squatted before the shrine, and smiled. "At times Taita was really quite a romantic, wasn't he?"

"Concentrate, for heaven's sake. This isn't a poetry appreciation class. Now try this one," Nicholas ordered, and read, "'The arrow pierced my flesh but did not harm me. I have eschewed the false path that lies straight before me. I have taken the hidden stairway to the seat of the gods.' "

Royan rocked back on her heels and glanced down the long gallery. "Something there perhaps. 'The false path that lies straight before me. The hidden stairway'?" She stood up. "Oh, Nicky. It's so discouraging. We don't even know where to begin."

"Courage, lassie." He feigned a cheerfulness he did not feel. "We begin at the beginning. Let me try you with this one." He placed his hand over his heart like a Victorian actor and read, " 'The vulture rises on mighty pinions to greet the sun—' "

She laughed at his clowning, and then her eyes wandered from his face. "The vulture!" she blurted, and pointed at the wall behind him.

There was the vulture, a magnificent image of the bird, its wings spread wide, each feather outlined in jewel-like colours. It stood as tall as Nicholas, and its wingspread covered half the wall. They stared at it together, and then Royan lifted her eyes to the ceiling.

"The sun!" she whispered. The golden sun disc of Ra was painted in the highest portion of the roof.

" 'The vulture rises on mighty pinions to greet the sun,' " she repeated. "Does Taita mean it literally?"

He moved closer to the mural and examined it minutely. Beneath the paint the plastered wall was smooth. But the head was in relief, standing slightly above the level of the surrounding wall.

"Can you feel any joint in the plaster?" Royan demanded. "Try pushing the head upwards towards the sun painting."

He placed the heel of his hand under the bulge of the head and pushed upwards.

"Nothing!" he grunted.

"It's been there for almost four thousand years." She was hopping from one foot to the other with frustration. "Damn it, Nicky, if there is a moving part, it will be stiff. Harder! Push harder!"

He shifted his feet to get well under it and placed both hands under the projection of the head. Slowly he brought all his strength to bear.

"No." His voice was hoarse with the effort. "It's solid. Won't budge."

"Look on top of it, higher up the wall. There along the edge of the sunbeam. Can't you see a vertical crack in the plaster?"

He fetched one of the empty ammunition crates and placed it below the image. When he stepped up onto it he was on a level with the vulture's eye.

His expression changed. Quickly he groped in his pocket and brought out his clasp knife. He opened the blade and probed carefully. A slab of plaster the size of his hand fell off the wall.

He peered into the cavity it had left. "It looks like some kind of groove the head will travel up. I'm going to try it." He cleared the vertical cavity of plaster, then placed the heels of both hands under the head of the vulture and heaved upwards against it. The head began to move jerkily up the exposed groove in the wall. When it reached the top of the slot Nicholas jumped down from the crate. They both stared expectantly at the disembodied head, but after a long, breathless wait Royan whispered dejectedly, "Nothing! It hasn't changed anything."

"The rest of the quotation from the stele," he reminded her. "There was more to it than just the vulture and the sun."

"You're right." She looked around the rest of the wall eagerly. "'The river flows towards the earth. Beware, you violators of the sacred places, lest the wrath of all the gods descend upon you.'"

"The river?" Nicholas asked. "As Sapper might say, I don't see no perishing river."

Royan did not even smile at the cockney accent. Instead she searched the images that covered the walls around them. Then she saw it. "Hapi!" Her voice was shrill with excitement. "The god of the Nile! The river!"

High up the wall, the god of the river looked down upon them. The mouth of his hippopotamus head gaped wide to display the great curved tusks that lined his cavernous jaws.

Standing on a pile of ammunition boxes, Nicholas was able to reach the Hapi image at the full stretch of his arms. As he touched it he exulted. "This one is raised also."

"'The river flows towards the earth,'" she called up to him. "It must move downwards. Try it, Nicky."

"Give me a chance to clear the edges." He used the point of the blade to chip the outline of the god free, and then he probed beneath it and found another vertical slot running towards the floor.

"Ready to give it a go now." He settled both hands on the image of the god and began to pull steadily downwards. Gradually he brought more pressure to bear upon it until he was hanging all his weight on it. Suddenly the image of Hapi gave way under his hands, and with a sharp grating sound travelled down to the bottom end of the groove in the wall. Nicholas lost his grip, the stack of boxes toppled and he dropped back to the floor of the gallery.

"What has happened?" Royan gasped, looking around the gallery.

"Nothing," he said. "Nothing has moved."

"Perhaps there is another—" she began, but broke off at a sound from the roof above them. They both stared upwards. There was a ponderous movement from above the high plastered ceiling.

"What is that?" Royan whispered. "There is something up there. It sounds like a living thing."

A giant was moving, coming awake after slumbering for thousands of years, stretching and turning as he woke.

"Is it—?" She could not finish the question. There was a report like the shot of a cannon, and a crack appeared in the ceiling, running the length of the gallery. Then, slowly as in a nightmare, the roof began to sag down over where they stood.

"The warning!" Nicholas blurted. "Taita's warning. The wrath of the gods." He grabbed her hand. "Run! The roof is booby-trapped!"

They raced back along the gallery towards the entrance. Lumps of stone and plaster began to rain down and dust filled the passageway, half blinding them. The dull rumble overhead became a rising roar as progressively the roof collapsed. They did not dare to look back as the thunder of falling masonry swept towards them.

A jagged piece of rock struck Royan a glancing blow on the shoulder, and she would have gone down if Nicholas had not flung one arm around her and held her up, dragging her along the gallery.

"Keep going!" he yelled at her. "Almost there." As he spoke, a thick sheet of plaster came crashing down and smashed into the floodlight. Instantly the gallery was plunged into utter darkness.

Running on without a check, he dragged Royan towards the opening in the plaster wall in front of him, which was back-lit by the lamps on the landing outside.

He seized Royan around her waist, hurled her through the opening and heard her cry out as she fell heavily on the far side. A piece of rubble struck him on the back of his head and knocked him to his knees. He felt himself teetering on the brink of consciousness, but he crawled forward, groping frantically until he was able to drag himself over the sill, just as the full weight of the roof came thundering down along the entire gallery.

Royan crawled towards him, guided by the lamplight. "Are you all right?" she panted.

Without answering, he dragged himself to his feet and pulled her up beside him.

"Can't stay here," he croaked. "The whole thing might cave in."

They staggered down the steps together. Through the dust mist ahead of them loomed the broad square figure of Sapper.

"What the hell is going on?" he bellowed as he saw them.

"Give me a hand," Nicholas yelled back at him. Sapper lifted Royan in his arms and together they ran back down the tunnel.

THE POST office in the village of Debre Maryam was a small building in the dusty street behind the church. Its walls were of unplastered brick, and its galvanised-iron roof glared like a mirror in the high mountain sunlight.

Tessay strode into the small room which was filled with a motley crowd of peasants and villagers, queuing to conduct their leisurely business with the elderly postmaster. Some of the customers had spread their cloaks on the floor and settled in for a long wait.

"Jesus and all the saints bless you, Woizero Tessay." The postmaster clapped his hands in respectful greeting. "Welcome back to Debre Maryam. What is it that your ladyship desires?"

Despite two decades of African socialism, the feudal instincts of the rural population were still strong. Tessay was a noblewoman and she was entitled to this preference.

"I want to make a telephone call to the British Embassy in Addis," she told the postmaster, and there was a hum of comment among the post office's clientele. This was unusual business indeed.

"I will take you to the telephone exchange," the postmaster told her importantly, and he ushered her through to the back room of the building, where the telephone exchange occupied a cubicle.

Tessay, the postmaster and those of the other customers who could find standing room pushed their way into the tiny room. The exchange operator was almost overcome by the honour being accorded him, and he shouted into his headset, patching her call through half a dozen antiquated village exchanges to the capital. An hour later Geoffrey Tennant was awaiting her on the line.

"Mr Tennant, this is Woizero Tessay."

"I was expecting your call. How are you, my dear?"

Tessay passed Nicholas's message for Jannie to him.

"Tell Nicky it's as good as done," Geoffrey said, and hung up.

"Now," Tessay addressed the postmaster, "I want to place another call to Addis—to the Egyptian Embassy."

The second call, to the Egyptian cultural attaché, was on Royan's behalf, a message she had asked Tessay to deliver without Nicholas's knowledge.

"You are very lucky to have reached me so late," the attaché told her. "We usually close at four thirty, but there is a meeting of the Organisation of African Unity on at the moment and I am working late. Anyway, how may I help you, Woizero Tessay?"

As soon as she told him the name and rank of the person in Cairo to whom Royan's message was addressed, his condescending attitude altered. He wrote down everything she said, asking her to repeat and spell the names of people and places. Finally he read his notes back to her for confirmation. She thanked him and hung up.

It was too late to start the journey back down the escarpment, so Tessay was relieved when the headman of Debre Maryam village invited her to spend the night as a guest in his home.

The headman's house was the finest in the village, a square brick building with an iron roof. His wife and daughters had prepared a banquet in Tessay's honour, and all the village notables had been invited. It was therefore after midnight before Tessay was able to retire to the principal bedroom, which the headman and his wife had vacated for her.

She was about to pull off her jodhpurs when she heard the sound of a truck engine in the distance. She went to the window and listened.

The truck was coming fast, and she felt uneasy. It was now common knowledge that she was Mek Nimmur's woman. Mek was a wanted man. Suddenly she felt very vulnerable.

Quickly she pulled the woollen *shamma* over her head and thrust her feet into her sandals. As she crept from the room she heard the headman snoring in the room where he and his wife had moved to make space for her. She turned down the passage to the kitchen.

The truck was right outside the front of the house now. Abruptly the engine roar sank and she heard the squeal of brakes. Then there was trampling as men jumped down from the back of the stationary truck, followed by loud banging on the flimsy front door and chilling shouts of, "Open up here! Central Intelligence! Open the door! Nobody leave the house!"

Tessay ran for the back door and struggled to open it. The sound of soldiers rampaging through the house made her fingers clumsy. As she struggled with the lock she could hear other men outside running through the yard to surround the house completely. At last she got the door open. It was dark and the area was unfamiliar, so she did not know in which direction to run.

The beam of an electric torch blinded her, and a coarse voice bellowed, "There she is!" Rough hands seized her. One of the soldiers grabbed her wrist and twisted it up between her shoulder blades, laughing when she cried out at the pain.

An overweight officer came up. He was sweating heavily. "Do not hurt her, you oaf," he gasped. "She is not a criminal. She is a high-bred lady. Bring her to the truck, but treat her with respect."

With a man on each arm she was marched to the truck and shoved into the cab onto the seat beside the uniformed driver. The plump officer climbed in heavily after her, while the soldiers scrambled up into the rear of the truck.

"Where are you taking me?" Tessay asked softly, stifling her sobs.

"I have been ordered to take you to Colonel Nogo, the district commander, for questioning in connection with *shufta* activities in the Gojam," he told her, as they jolted down the track.

They were both silent for a while, and then the officer said quietly in English, "The driver speaks only Amharic. I wanted to tell you that I knew your father, Alto Zemen. He was a good man. I am sorry for what is happening here tonight, but I am only a lieutenant. I have to follow my orders."

"I understand that it is not your choice, or your blame."

"My name is Hammed. I will help you. For Alto Zemen's sake."

"Thank you, Lieutenant Hammed. I need friends now."

WITHIN AN hour of the cave-in Nicholas was ready to go back up the tunnel. When he reached the landing, he saw by the light of a lamp on the generator that the rock fall had smashed down what remained of the white plaster door that had originally sealed the entrance to the tomb. Royan had insisted on accompanying him. Her dismay, when she saw the shattered gallery, was overwhelming. "It's totally destroyed," she whispered. "All those marvellous works of art. It's going to take a lot of hard work to clear up this mess."

"What on earth are you talking about?" He turned on her in genuine alarm. "We have saved the statues, and that's all we can hope for. Now I think it's time to cut our losses and get out of here."

"Get out of here? Are you crazy? The tomb is still there. Damn it, Nicky, Taita would not have gone to those lengths if it were not. We can't give up."

"Royan, be reasonable."

"No! No! You be reasonable." She refused to listen. "You have to start clearing the gallery right away. I'm certain we'll find the entrance to the tomb behind the rubble that Taita dropped on us."

He threw up his hands in resignation. "What's the use, arguing with a crazy woman? We'll clear just enough of the scree to prove to you that there is nothing more to discover in there."

The monks accepted this new task cheerfully. They sang as they passed the chunks of broken plaster and rock down the tunnel and dumped them into the sinkhole. Even that large volume of material was simply swallowed up without trace.

Lying among the rubbish on the gallery floor, Nicholas found the remains of the mechanism which Taita had placed in the roof, and which they had brought crashing down when they had activated the device. The main part of this was an enormous stone wheel, resembling a millwheel. Moving the levers had toppled the wedges that held this in place. Once it started rolling, it tumbled all the drop stones that Taita had stacked above the ceiling of the gallery.

The crowded workings were so humid that at the change of the first shift Nicholas had to escape into the open air. Mek Nimmur was waiting for him when he climbed out over the wall of the cofferdam.

"Nicholas!" Mek's handsome face was grave. "Has Tessay returned from Debre Maryam yet? She should have been back yesterday."

"I've not seen her, Mek. I thought she was with you."

Mek shook his head. "I wanted to make certain that she had not returned without my men seeing her, before I send a patrol up the trail to search for her."

"I'm sorry, Mek. I didn't anticipate any danger in sending her up the escarpment." Nicholas felt a stab of guilt.

"If I had thought there was any danger, I would not have allowed her to go," Mek agreed. "I have sent men to search for her."

But Tessay's absence was another worry for Nicholas. It lurked at the edge of his mind during the days that followed, as the clearing of the long funeral gallery proceeded.

Royan spent as much time at the face as Nicholas did. There was no sense of time in the long gallery, and they could not tell night from day. It was always a surprise to leave the precincts of the tomb and find that the stars were shining in the narrow strip of sky that showed above Taita's pool, or to find the bright African sun burning hotly down out of the cloudless blue. They ate and slept only when their bodies demanded it, not according to the passage of the hours.

Re-entering the tomb after a few hours' sleep in their shelters beside the pool, Nicholas and Royan were crossing the causeway over the sinkhole when a wild cry reverberated down the shaft ahead of them. Immediately there was a hullabaloo of query and answer, and excited shouts from the men working in the upper levels of the tunnel.

"Hansith has found something," Royan cried. "Damn it, Nicky, I knew we had to stay." She began to run, and Nicholas hurried after her.

Hansith had cleared the gallery as far as where the shrine of Osiris had once stood. They pushed their way through the pack of workmen until they reached Hansith's tall figure.

"What is it?" Nicholas shouted. "What have you found, Hansith?"

"Here, effendi!" Hansith pointed proudly.

Nicholas went down on one knee. There was an opening in the side of the gallery. Even at first glance he realised that it was the mouth of another tunnel leading off at right angles from the long gallery. It had been concealed behind the plaster-covered image of the great god.

He felt Royan's hand on his arm. "This is it, Nicky. The entrance to the true tomb of Mamose. This gallery was a bluff."

Hansith's men set about clearing the doorway, which proved to be a dark rectangle, three feet wide by two high. When Nicholas shone his lamp into the opening he saw a flight of stone steps rising before him.

They went slowly up the steep steps. A pair of doorways led off a landing, one on either side. However, the staircase continued climbing directly ahead of them.

"Which way?" Nicholas asked.

"Keep going up," Royan urged him. "We can explore these side passages later."

Cautiously, they continued climbing. After twenty more steps they came out on an identical landing, with a doorway on each side and the stairway in front of them.

"Keep going up," Royan ordered, without waiting for him to ask.

Twenty more steps and there was another landing, with the familiar openings on either side and the stairway straight ahead. They kept going on upwards, past another landing and then yet another, each of them the exact image of those lower down.

At last they came out at the top of the staircase, with the expected doorway on each side but now a blank wall in front of them.

"How many landings are there altogether?"

"Eight," he answered.

"Eight," she agreed. "Isn't that a familiar number by now?"

He turned to stare down at her in the lamplight. "You mean—"

"I mean the eight shrines in the long gallery, these eight landings, and the eight cups of the bao board."

They stood silent and undecided on the top landing.

"Okay," he said at last. "If you're so clever, which way now?"

"Eeny-meeny-miney-mo. Let's try the right-hand doorway."

They followed the right-hand passage only a short distance before they were confronted by a T-junction.

"Take the right one again," she counselled, and they followed it. But when they came to the next junction Nicholas stopped.

"You know what's happening here, don't you?" he said. "This is another one of Taita's tricks. He has led us into a maze. Imagine being caught in here without the electric cable to follow back the way we have come. Imagine having only an oil lamp for light, and what would happen to you when the oil burnt out."

Royan shivered and gripped his arm. "Let's go back," she whispered. "We should never have rushed in here like this. I have the feeling that we are in real danger."

As they started back, picking up the electric cable as they retreated down the stone passageways, it seemed to both of them that some intelligent and malignant presence lurked behind them in the darkness, following them, watching them and biding its time.

THE ARMY truck carrying Tessay drove back through the village of Debre Maryam, and then turned off onto the track that followed the Dandera River downstream towards the Abay gorge.

"This is not the way to army headquarters," Tessay told Lieutenant Hammed. "There is only one other place in this direction. The base camp of the foreign prospecting company, Pegasus."

"Colonel Nogo is using that as a forward base in his campaign against the *shufta* in the valley," he explained.

It was almost noon when at last they reached the Pegasus camp. The truck drove through the gates and parked in front of one of the long Quonset huts.

"Please come with me." Hammed looked awkward. He led her to the door of the hut and stood aside to let her enter first.

A conference table ran almost the full length of the room, and there were filing cabinets and two desks set against the side walls. A map of the area and a few technical charts were on the walls. Two men sat at the table, and she recognised both of them immediately. Colonel Nogo looked up at her, his eyes cold behind his metal-framed spectacles. Jake Helm leaned back in his chair with his arms folded. At first glance, his short-cropped hair made him look like a boy. He chewed upon the dead butt of a cheap Dutch cheroot, and the smell of the tobacco was rank.

"Very well, Lieutenant," Nogo dismissed Hammed in Amharic. "Wait outside. I will call you when I need you."

Once Hammed had left the room, Tessay demanded, "Why have I been arrested, Colonel Nogo?"

"You have been consorting with a band of notorious terrorists," said Nogo softly. "Your actions have made you one of them, a *shufta*."

"That is not true."

They were both silent. Nogo made an entry in the notebook in front of him. Helm stood up and sauntered across to the window behind her right shoulder. The silence drew out, part of the campaign of nerves they were waging against her.

She feigned an air of confidence and crossed to the nearest chair, pulled it from the table and sat down in it easily.

Nogo frowned. He had not expected her to react this way. "You know the *shufta* bandit Mek Nimmur," he accused.

"No," she said coldly. "I know the patriot and democratic leader Mek Nimmur. He is no *shufta*."

"You are his concubine, his whore. Of course you will say this."

She looked away from him with disdain, and his voice rose. "Where is Mek Nimmur? How many men does he have with him?"

She ignored his question, turned in her chair and stared out of the window. In the long silence that followed, Jake Helm crossed the room and disappeared through the door behind Nogo. The walls of the hut were thin, and Tessay made out the murmur of voices from the room beyond. She guessed that Helm was receiving instructions from a superior, who did not want her to be able to recognise him at some later date. After a few minutes Helm re-emerged and closed the door behind him. He nodded to Nogo, who at once stood up. They both came across to stand in front of Tessay.

"It will be better for all of us if we finish this business as quickly as possible," said Helm softly. "Then I can go to my lunch."

She raised her chin and stared at him defiantly, but did not answer.

"Colonel Nogo is bound by certain niceties of his official position. Fortunately I am not. I am going to ask you the same questions that he did, but this time you will answer them."

He took a flat tin from his hip pocket, selected a fresh cheroot and lit it carefully. Then, amid a cloud of pungent tobacco smoke, he asked, "Where is Mek Nimmur?" She shrugged.

Abruptly Nogo stooped over her and seized her arms, twisting them up behind her back, and stood behind her.

"I have no more time to waste." Helm took the cheroot from his lips to inspect the glowing tip. "Let us start again. Where is Mek Nimmur?" He leaned his face closer to hers. "What are your friends doing with the dam in the Dandera River?"

She gathered saliva in her mouth and spat it into his face.

He recoiled violently. "Hold her!" he said to Nogo, and seized the front of her blouse. With one heave he ripped it open down to her waist, and with his other hand he took the burning cheroot from his lips and blew on the top until it glowed hotly.

"Where is Mek Nimmur?" he asked, and lowered the cheroot towards her skin. "What are they doing in the Dandera River?"

"WINTER," said Royan, spreading the enlargement of the fourth face of the stele from Tanus's tomb under the bright glare of the floodlight. "This is the side that contains Taita's notations, which I am postulating are those of the bao board. By a process of elimination I have determined that the first symbol denotes one of the four sides or, as he terms them, the castles of the board."

She showed him the pages of her notebook on which she had made her calculations.

"What about the verses between each set of notations?" Nicholas asked. "Such as this one here, about the north wind and the storm?"

"I am not sure about those. Probably merely smoke screens, if I know Taita. He is never one to make life too easy for us."

It was slow and painstaking work, trying to forge their way into the mind of the ancient scribe by probing the labyrinth of passages and tunnels that he had built four thousand years previously.

"Now we have to see if my theories fit into the hard stones and walls of Taita's architecture." Royan laughed—a throaty, well-satisfied sound—and looked up the staircase that led to Taita's maze.

This time they moved into the maze with more circumspection. Nicholas had filled his pockets with lumps of dried white river clay, and he used these to chalk on the stone walls at each fork of the tunnels, setting out the notations from the winter face of the stele and marking a signpost to enable them not only to find their way through the maze but to relate it to the model that Royan was drawing up.

They found that the shrine of Osiris seemed to be the north castle of the board, and they happily believed that with this as the key it would be a simple matter to follow the moves of play to their conclusion. But these hopes were soon dashed as they realised that Taita was not thinking in the simple two dimensions of the conventional board. He had added a third dimension to the equation. The stairway leading up from the shrine of Osiris was not the only link between the eight landings. Each of the passages was subtly angled either upwards or downwards.

"Three-dimensional bao, played to enigmatic rules. What chance have we got against him?" Nicholas shook his head ruefully. "What we really need is a computer. Taita really was a mathematical genius."

"You can form your fan club later," she suggested. "But right now I think we should work from the centre of the board. It may help us to visualise it."

THE ONLY sound in the room was the soft sobbing of the woman, who lay curled on the floor.

Tuma Nogo sat at the long table and lit a cigarette. He was accustomed to violence, but he was shaken by what he had just witnessed. He knew now why von Schiller placed such reliance on Helm.

Across the room Jake Helm was dabbing at the stains on his clothing with a towel. "I don't think there is anything else she can tell us," he said calmly. "I don't think she held anything back."

Nogo glanced down at the woman and saw the livid burns that spotted her chest and her cheeks. She had held out well.

Helm walked past him to the door at the end of the hut. He left the door open and Nogo could hear their voices, but they were speaking in German so he could not understand what they were saying.

Helm came back into the room and nodded at Nogo. "Very well. We are finished with her. You know what to do. Take her away. Far away. Then get somebody in here to clean up this mess."

Nogo roused himself and then went to the door of the hut.

"Lieutenant Hammed!" he called through the door.

Hammed and Nogo lifted Tessay to her feet. Hammed averted his eyes from her burns, draped the *shamma* over her shoulders and led her towards the door. When she stumbled he caught her and supported her with a hand under her elbow. He led her down the steps to the truck and sat her in the passenger seat, her burnt and swollen face in her cupped hands. The sun had set and darkness had fallen.

Nogo summoned Hammed with a jerk of his head. He spoke quietly, and Hammed's expression became stricken as he listened to his orders. "Remember!" Nogo repeated. "Well away from any of the villages. Make certain that there are no witnesses."

Hammed straightened his shoulders and saluted before he marched back to the truck and climbed up into the seat beside Tessay. He gave the driver an order and they drove back towards Debre Maryam. Tessay was so confused and in such pain that she had lost all sense of time. Eventually the truck braked abruptly, rude hands dragged her out of the cab and her wrists were bound together.

One of the soldiers yanked on her bound wrists and shoved her off the road. Two others followed, each carrying trenching tools. There was enough of a moon for her to see a grove of eucalyptus trees about a hundred metres from the side of the road, and they led her there.

While one of the soldiers aimed his rifle casually at her, the others began digging. It was only after a while that Tessay realised they were digging a grave for her. She looked around desperately for Lieutenant Hammed, but he had stayed with the truck. A feeling of weakness and resignation overwhelmed her.

When she looked up again the grave was now so deep that the two men still digging it were out of her line of sight. Her guard sauntered over to the edge of the hole. He looked down into it and then grunted.

"Good. That will do. Call the lieutenant."

The soldiers scrambled up out of the grave, gathered up their tools and headed back to the truck, leaving Tessay and her guard.

Shortly afterwards Lieutenant Hammed arrived from the truck carrying an electric torch. He flashed it down into the grave.

"Good," he said loudly. "That is deep enough."

He switched off the torch and said to the man guarding her, "No witnesses. Go back and wait at the truck. When you hear the shots come back with the others to help me fill the hole."

The guard slung his rifle over his shoulder and disappeared among the trees. Hammed waited till the man was out of earshot, then hoisted her to her feet.

"I want your *shamma*." He pulled the white woollen cloak off her shoulders, and then jumped down into the hole with it. "They must see something here. A body—"

He returned and stepped behind her. She felt the touch of cold metal on the inside of her wrists, and her bonds fell away. She gasped at the pain as the blood flowed back into her numb hands.

She looked down into the grave and saw the pale *shamma* arranged to look like a human body. "Are you going to—?"

"Please don't talk," he instructed her softly as he took her by the shoulder and led her back among the trees.

"Lie here." He pushed her down and made her lie flat, with her face to the ground.

He began piling dead leaves and fallen branches over her. "Stay here! Don't move or speak until we are gone."

Then he hurried back to the graveside, unbuckling his pistol holster as he went. Two pistol shots cracked out in the night, so loud and unexpectedly that she jumped and her heart raced wildly. Then she heard Hammed shout, "Come, you men. Let's get this thing finished."

They trooped back into the grove and she heard the sound of their spades and the thump of earth clods falling into the grave. She lay quietly, trying to stop the tremors that shook her body. At last the sound of the shovels let up.

"That will do. Now, back to the truck!"

Long after their footsteps and their voices died away, she continued to lie under the dead branches, weeping with exhaustion and pain and relief. When finally she heard the truck drive off she pushed the branches off and pulled herself up to her feet. It was only then that guilt overwhelmed her. I have betrayed Mek, she thought. I have told everything to his enemies. I must get back to him and warn him.

She blundered back through the darkness towards the road.

THE ONLY means of ascertaining if they had interpreted Taita's codes correctly was to play out the moves he had listed. They went very carefully through the tunnels of the maze, stepping out the moves and marking them on the walls in white chalk.

There were eighteen moves set out on the winter face of the stele. Using Royan's interpretation of the symbols, they were able to advance through twelve of these. Then they found themselves at a dead end, confronted by a blank wall.

"Damnation!" Nicholas kicked the wall. "We'll have to start again."

"Nicky, do you realise just how many possible combinations there are?" She was at last starting to waver. "Taita has assumed an intimate knowledge of the game. There must be another way of approaching it. Let's go over the epigrams Taita stuck between the notations again."

"All right. You read and I'll listen. Remember that even Taita had never played bao in three dimensions before. If he left a clue it would have to be at the very beginning of the stele."

"We'll try it that way." Royan ran her finger over the hieroglyphics. "'What can be given a name can be known. What is nameless can only be felt. I sail with the tide behind me and the wind in my face.'"

"Is that all?" he asked. "What can we make out of 'sailing'?"

So they riddled and wrestled with the text of the stele until they were recalled to reality by Sapper's voice echoing up the staircase. Nicholas started as he saw that Sapper's bald head was shining with moisture and his shirt was soaked.

"What happened to you?" he demanded.

Sapper wiped his face with the palm of his hand. "Didn't anybody tell you? It's pouring with rain outside." They stared at him in horror. "So soon?" Royan whispered. "It wasn't supposed to start for weeks yet."

Sapper shrugged. "Somebody forgot to tell the weatherman."

"Has the river level started to rise yet?" Nicholas asked.

"That's what I came to tell you. I am going up to the dam, taking a team with me. As soon as it gets unsafe I will send a runner down for you. When I do that, don't stop to argue. Get out of here fast. It will mean that I expect the dam to burst at any moment."

When Sapper had gone, Royan and Nicholas looked at each other anxiously. "We're running out of time fast, and Taita still has us in a tangle," Nicholas said. "One thing I must warn you. When the river starts to rise—"

She did not let him finish. "The river!" she cried. "Not the sea! I was mistaken in the translation. I read it as 'tide', but it should have been 'current.'"

They both rushed back to the desk and her notebooks.

"'The current behind me and the wind in my face,'" Nicholas quoted.

"On the Nile," Royan exulted, "the prevailing wind is always from the north, and the current always from the south. Taita was facing north. The north castle."

It was so much easier now. The intricacies of the maze had become less forbidding with familiarity. They moved swiftly through the complex twists and turns, their excitement rising sharply as they followed each notation and found the way still clear before them.

"The eighteenth move." Royan's voice trembled. "If it takes us into one of the open files that threaten the opponent's south castle, then that will be the check coup." She drew a deep breath and read it aloud. "The numbers three and five. With the lower-level symbol."

They paced it out and passed the five junctions into the lowest level of the maze. "This is it!" Nicholas told her, and they stood together and looked about them.

"There is nothing outstanding about this place," Royan said, bitterly disappointed. "It's just like any of the other turns."

"That is exactly what Taita would have wanted. He wouldn't have put up a signpost saying 'X marks the spot,' would he?"

"So what do we do?" She looked at him, for once at a loss.

"Read the last epigram from the stele."

She had her notebook in her hand. "'From the black and holy earth of this very Egypt the harvest is abundant. I follow the rhythm of the seasons and tend the earth.'"

She looked up at him. "The earth?" she asked and looked down at the slabs beneath their feet. "The promise of reward from the earth? Under our feet, perhaps?" she asked.

He stamped his foot on the slabs, but the sound was solid. "Only one way to find out." He raised his voice, and it echoed weirdly through the labyrinth. "Hansith! Come down here!"

SAPPER SAT on the high seat of his yellow front-end loader in the rain and watched the river rising sullenly, lapping the top course of gabions of his dam.

His men were packing more baskets with aggregate, using up the last of the steel mesh from the stores in the quarry. As soon as each of these was filled and wired closed, Sapper picked it up in the front bucket of the tractor and reinforced all the weak spots of the dam wall. It needed only a single breach in the wall to bring the entire structure tumbling and rolling down. He had no illusions as to just how swiftly the river could outrun any messenger he sent. His instinct was to call the others out of the chasm now—there was already less than twelve inches of freeboard at the top of the wall.

However, he knew that Nicholas would be furious if he was made to evacuate the working prematurely. "I'll give it another hour," he grunted, engaging the gears of the tractor and easing her down the bank to place another gabion in position.

NICHOLAS WORKED shoulder to shoulder with Hansith's gang as they began to lever up the paving slabs from the floor of the lowest level of the maze. His heart sank as they found nothing but the solid stratum of the country rock beneath each slab.

"It doesn't look very hopeful," he muttered to Royan as he took a short break to drink from one of the water flasks.

"I may have got the symbols for the levels wrong," she suggested unhappily. "It's just the kind of trick Taita would play, to—"

She was interrupted by a bellow from Hansith. "Effendi, come quickly!"

They ran back to where Hansith was standing, his hammer poised above a rectangular opening. Nicholas shone the lamp down into the dark shaft that was revealed.

"Another stairway," he exulted. "Surely this must be it. Even Taita must have exhausted all the false leads by now."

The workmen were crowding up behind them.

"Are we going down?" Royan asked. "I know we should be careful, but we're running out of time, Nicky."

"You're right, as always. Press on regardless!"

They descended side by side, the lamp held head-high and the shadows retreating before them.

"There is a chamber at the bottom," Royan exclaimed. "Looks like a storeroom—those objects look like wine amphorae. Probably some sort of offering to the dead."

"If this is a funeral storeroom," said Nicholas in a voice tight with excitement, "then we're getting very close to the tomb now."

They almost ran down the last few steps into the chamber lined with pottery wine jars. But as they reached the floor of the storeroom they ran into an invisible barrier that stopped them dead and sent them reeling backwards.

"God!" Nicholas clutched at his throat. "Got to get back."

They staggered up the steps and sprawled out of the mouth of the shaft at Hansith's feet, gasping and hunting for breath.

"What is it, effendi? What has happened to you and the lady?"

For a few moments, Nicholas had no breath to answer him. "I'm not sure—but whatever it was, it almost got both of us." He turned to Royan. "How are you feeling?"

"It was as though an invisible hand had me by the throat and was strangling me. I couldn't breathe."

"It must be some kind of gas filling the lower levels of the passage."

He lifted her to her feet and for a moment she swayed against him. Then she was suddenly aware of the men's eyes watching her and drew away. "What kind of gas? And how did it get there?"

"One of the gases of decay, most probably," was his opinion. "Because it is trapped in the lower part of the passage, it must be a heavier-than-air type, probably carbon dioxide."

"Did Taita do it deliberately?" The colour was returning to her cheeks and she was recovering swiftly.

"I don't know, but those jars are suspicious. I'll be able to answer that question when we've had a chance to examine their contents. Hansith, bring down the blower fan."

After half an hour with the fan speed set at "High" the gas had dispersed enough to enable Nicholas and Royan to enter the chamber again and breathe the air. They crossed the chamber, turned one of the pottery jars on its side and studied the powder that spilled out.

"Crushed limestone!" Nicholas muttered, rubbing it between his fingers. "Taita probably soaked it with some form of acid. Vinegar, perhaps. As it broke down the limestone, it formed carbon dioxide."

"So it was another deliberate trap," Royan exclaimed.

"Even so many thousands of years ago, Taita must have understood what gases those mixtures would produce."

"Furthermore, he must have known that without a draught or any movement of air, these heavy inert gases would hang here in the bottom of the chamber indefinitely," she agreed. "I bet the passage rises again—in fact I can see the first steps from here."

SAPPER HAD placed cairns of stones at the water's edge to monitor the river level. It was six hours since the last rain squall had passed, and the water level had fallen almost a foot. He forced himself not to let his optimism bubble over—after all, the final outcome was inevitable. The rains would come. The river would spate. The dam would burst. He shook his head with resignation.

He saw the men's faces turn upstream. Something was exciting their interest. He shaded his eyes. Mek Nimmur was coming down the trail from the direction of the escarpment, stocky and powerful in his camo fatigues. Mek hailed Sapper and they shook hands cordially. They had recognised in each other the qualities of strength and professionalism that they both admired.

"It is not only the weather that troubles me," Mek confided. "I have reports that government troops are moving into position to attack us. They have a battalion moving this way from Debre Maryam, and another force moving up the Abay River."

"Pincer movement, hey?" said Sapper.

Mek nodded gravely. "I am heavily outnumbered and I don't know how long I will be able to hold them when they attack. My men are guerrillas. It is not our role to fight set-piece battles. I came to warn you to be ready to pull out at short notice. If we get cut off from each other in the fighting, we will assemble at the monastery where Nicholas has cached the boats."

"Okay, Mek—" Sapper looked back up the trail, where there was a fresh disturbance among the men. "What's going on?"

"One of my patrols coming in." Mek narrowed his eyes. "There must be some new development." He stopped speaking as he recognised the small figure that was being carried on a rough litter by his men.

Tessay saw him running towards her and sat up weakly. The men lowered her to the ground and Mek went down on his knees and placed both his arms around her. They held each other in silence for a long moment. Then Mek gently cupped her face in his hands.

"Who did this to you?" he asked softly.

She mumbled through her black-scabbed lips. "They made me tell them everything. The numbers of your men. What you and Nicholas are doing here. Everything. Mek, I betrayed you."

"Who was it? Who did this to you?"

"Nogo and the American, Helm," she said, and although he embraced her as gently as a father with his infant in his arms, his eyes were terrible.

AT LAST THE lower chamber of the tunnel was cleared of gas and Nicholas led the way up the steps that rose from the far side.

They had descended forty steps down into the chamber, and the staircase they were now climbing was a mirror image of that. As their heads rose above the fortieth step, Nicholas played the beam of the lamp down the spacious arcade that opened before them, and they were dazzled by a riot of colour. Stunning paintings covered the walls and ceiling of the arcade, which was lined on each side with small chambers, like the stalls in an Oriental bazaar.

"The treasure chambers of the Pharaoh," Nicholas whispered.

The stalls were packed from floor to ceiling with wonderful and beautiful things: lions with claws of gold; a screened divan, its sides enclosed in an exquisite lacework of ebony and ivory; a chariot covered with a skin of gold leaf; the cartouche of Mamose emblazoned on the side panels; and piled beside this magnificent vehicle were war bows whose stocks were bound with wire of electrum and bronze and gold, daggers with ivory handles, helmets and breastplates made from the skin of the crocodile, and the uniforms and regalia of the famous regiments of Egypt.

They walked on down the aisle, between more paintings and murals depicting the life and the death of the king. They saw him fishing and hunting and hawking, in council with his ministers, dallying with his wives and concubines, and feasting with the priests of the temple.

Each of the persons in the panels had obviously been drawn from life. They were real breathing living men and women, every face and every expression different, captured with the keen eye, the humour and the great humanity of the artist.

"That must be Taita himself." Royan pointed out the portrait of the eunuch in one of the central panels. "I wonder if he was truly so noble and beautiful?"

They paused to admire the face of their adversary, and looked into his searching, intelligent eyes.

"It's weird to think that, although he lived so long ago, he almost succeeded in killing us," Nicholas said softly.

They went on past the treasure stalls in which were stored plates and goblets and bowls of alabaster and bronze, polished bronze mirrors and rolls of precious silk and linen that had long ago rotted.

Now they came to alcoves in which were stacked hundreds of cedarwood chests. The boxes were painted with scenes of the king at his toilet: lining his eyes with kohl, painting his face with white antimony and scarlet rouge, and being shaved by his barbers.

"Some of those chests will contain the royal cosmetics," Royan murmured, "and some of them will be Pharaoh's wardrobes, containing clothing for every occasion in his afterlife."

There were hundreds more chests stacked in the next alcoves with paintings on the lids of the king decked in all his jewellery.

"If each of those chests contains the treasures depicted on its lid—" Nicholas broke off. The possibility of such riches was daunting.

At last Nicholas and Royan came to the end of this fabulous arcade and found their way closed off by another gateway.

"That must be the entrance to the actual tomb," Royan whispered.

They hesitated at the threshold, gripped by a strange reluctance to take the final step.

NIMMUR HAD the men carry Tessay to one of the huts near the quarry, where he stripped her of her tattered clothing and treated her injuries. Then he snapped the glass phial off the needle of the disposable syringe which was preloaded with a broad-spectrum antibiotic. She winced at the sting of the needle, and he said, "I am not a very good doctor."

"I would have no other. Oh Mek! I thought I would never see you again."

Gently he helped her dress in the spare clothing from his pack, a sweatshirt and fatigues that were many sizes too large for her. His hands were those of a lover, not a soldier.

At that moment they heard gunfire, faint with distance, borne down from the north on the rain winds.

Mek stood up. "It has begun. Nogo is attacking at last."

"It's all my fault. I told him—"

"No," he told her firmly. "It is not your fault. They would have attacked us even if you had told them nothing."

He picked up his webbing belt and strapped it around his waist. "I have to go now," he told her. "These men will carry you to the monastery. Wait for me there."

"I love you. I will wait for you for ever."

"You are my woman," he told her in his deep, soft voice, and then he ducked through the doorway of the hut and was gone.

THE INNER doorway was guarded on one side by a massive statue of the great god Osiris, clutching the crook and the flail; and on the other stood his wife Isis, with the lunar crown and horns on her head. Nicholas and Royan passed between them, and found themselves at last in the veritable tomb of Mamose.

The chamber was smaller than they had anticipated; just large enough to accommodate the huge granite sarcophagus of the divine Pharaoh Mamose. It stood chest-high, its side panels engraved with scenes of Pharaoh and the other gods. The stone lid was in the shape of a full-length effigy of the king, and the clay seals which secured it were intact. The tomb had never been violated. The mummy had lain within it undisturbed through the millennia. But this was not the only thing that amazed them. Another item stood at the foot of the sarcophagus, a small human figure, one of the *ushabti* dolls. Both of them recognised the features instantly. Only minutes before, they had seen that face painted upon the walls of the arcade, outside the tomb.

Royan knelt at the foot of the coffin and picked up the *ushabti* figure. Reverently she studied the hieroglyphics carved into the base of the figure. Nicholas knelt beside her. "Read it to me," he said.

"'My name is Taita. I am a physician and a poet. I am an architect and a philosopher. I am your friend. I will answer for you.'"

"So it's all true," Nicholas whispered.

Royan replaced the *ushabti* exactly as she had found it and, still on her knees, turned her face to his.

"I have never known another moment like this," she whispered. "I want it never to end."

"It will never end, my darling," he answered her. "You and I are just beginning."

MEK NIMMUR watched them coming, skirting the bottom slope of the hill. As he evaluated them he felt a twinge of dismay. They were crack troops, seasoned during long years of war.

He glanced around at his own small force. Fourteen men among the rocks, they could only hope to hit their adversary hard while they still had the advantage of surprise, and then pull back before Nogo ranged his mortars in on the hilltop where they lay.

He looked back down the slope. The enemy was swinging around the hillside to intersect the trail along the Dandera River. Soon they must send a patrol up here to secure their flank. Yes, there they were. Ten men detaching from the main advance, and moving cautiously up the slope beneath him.

He looked across the rock-strewn slope, and saw that his RPD light machine gun was perfectly sited to enfilade their advance up the slope. Salim, his machine gunner, was an artist with that weapon.

If I time this right, we could put down more than five of them, thought Mek. He settled the pip of his foresight in the centre of the enemy machine gunner's belly, and fired a tap of three. The AKM rode up viciously and the triple detonation stung his eardrums, but Mek saw his bullets strike, stitching a row up the man's torso. All around Mek his men were firing. He wondered how many of them Salim had taken with his first burst, but there was no longer anything to see. The enemy were all down in cover. A faint haze of gunsmoke blued the air as they returned fire, and the scrub trembled and shook to the muzzle blast of their weapons.

IT REQUIRED the combined strength of Nicholas, Hansith and eight other men to lift the lid off the stone sarcophagus. Staggering under its weight, they laid it carefully against the wall of the tomb. Then they lifted the coffin out of the sarcophagus, and Nicholas carefully split the golden seals and the layer of hard dried resin that held the lid of the coffin in place. Within it they found another coffin, fitted perfectly, and when they opened that yet another was revealed.

In the end there were seven coffins, each of them progressively more ornate and richly decorated than the previous one. The seventh coffin was only slightly larger than a man, and it was made of polished gold. When at last they opened the inner coffin they found a layer of the finest linen, brown with age. Through the soft folds they saw once again the gleam of gold.

Standing on either side of the coffin, Nicholas and Royan peeled back the linen mesh. It tore like tissue paper under their fingers, but as it came away they both involuntarily gasped with wonder as the death mask of Pharaoh was revealed. It was only fractionally larger than the head of a man, but it was a perfect image in every detail. Pharaoh's features had been preserved for all eternity in this extraordinary work of art. They stared in silent wonder into the obsidian and rock-crystal eyes of Pharaoh, and Pharaoh gazed back at them sadly, almost accusingly.

It was Royan who roused herself first. "The river!" she cried. "We cannot let this be lost again when the river rises."

"Neither can we hope to save all of it. There is too much. We must pick out only the most beautiful and important pieces and pack them into the crates. Lord alone knows if we even have time for that."

So they worked in a frenzy in the short time that was left to them. They could not even think about saving the statues and the murals, the furniture and the weapons.

They removed the golden death mask, but they left the mummy in the innermost of the coffins. While Royan began selecting and packing the treasures they would take with them, Nicholas sent for Mai Metemma. The old abbot came with twenty of his monks to receive the holy relic of the ancient saint that he had been promised as his reward. Reverentially they bore the golden coffin away to its new resting place in the *maqdas* of the monastery.

Their final selection of treasures was, perforce, hurried and superficial. The death mask was without doubt the premier item in the entire tomb. It fitted neatly into one of the crates, with the wooden *ushabti* of Taita laid alongside it, packed with Styrofoam until it was firmly secured. Royan scribbled on the lid in waterproof wax crayon: *Mask & Taita Ushabti*. Fortunately, many of the cedarwood chests containing the royal jewellery fitted snugly into the metal crates, so that not only the contents but also the chests themselves could be saved. However, the larger items, the crowns and the huge jewelled gold pectoral medallions, had to be repacked.

As the ammunition crates were filled, they carried them down and stacked them on the landing, ready to be carried out. They had packed and catalogued forty-eight crates when they heard Sapper's unmistakable accents floating up the staircase.

"Major, where the hell are you? The river is in full spate, and the dam is going to burst any minute."

Sapper came bounding up the staircase, but even he stopped in wonder as he looked upon the funeral arcade of Pharaoh Mamose. It took some moments for him to recover from the shock.

"I mean it, Major! It's a matter of minutes. That ruddy dam is going to go. Apart from that, Mek is fighting in the hills at the head of the chasm. Nogo's attacked and he's trying to hold him off. You have to get out fast."

"Okay, Sapper. We're on our way. Get back to the chamber at the bottom of those stairs. You saw those ammunition crates down there?" Sapper nodded, and Nicholas went on quickly, "Have the men lug them out of here. Get them down to the monastery. We'll follow you down the trail with the rest of them."

Sapper turned and started back down the staircase.

"You know where the boats are stashed," Nicholas shouted after him. "If you get there before me, get them inflated and the crates lashed down. We'll be right behind you."

The moment Sapper was gone, Nicholas raced back down the arcade to where Royan was still at work in the treasury.

"That's it!" he shouted at her. "No more time. Let's get out."

"Nicky, we can't leave this—"

"Out!" He grabbed her arm. "The dam will go at any moment."

He ran with her down the arcade. Hansith and his men were carrying the last few packed ammunition crates up the staircase on the far side of the chamber. They balanced the crates on their heads and went up the steps with alacrity.

Caught up in the long, hurrying column, Nicholas and Royan wound their way back through the maze and down the central staircase into the long gallery. Sapper was waiting at the ruins of the sealed doorway, and grunted with relief when he saw them.

"I thought I told you to go on ahead and get the boats ready," Nicholas shouted at him.

"Couldn't trust you not to be bloody stupid." Sapper looked miserable. "Wanted to make sure you didn't hang about in there."

"I'm touched, Sapper." Nicholas punched his shoulder, and then they ran down the approach tunnel and around the sinkhole.

"Where is Mek?" Nicholas panted at Sapper's back as he jogged in front of him. "Have you seen Tessay?"

"Tessay is back. In a terrible mess. Seems like she fell into the hands of one of von Schiller's gorillas, a man called Helm, and he beat the hell out of her. Mek's men are taking her down to the monastery. I've been hearing rifle fire and mortar shells all morning. He's going to fall back too and wait for us at the boats."

They ran the last few yards down the tunnel ankle-deep in water, and at last crawled over the wall of the cofferdam onto the rocky ledge around Taita's pool. Nicholas looked up to see Hansith's porters scrambling up the bamboo scaffolding ladder towards the top of the cliff, each of them hauling up one of the ammunition crates.

At that moment he cocked his head to listen and then told Royan grimly, "Gunfire! Mek is fighting it out, but it's pretty darned close."

They swarmed up the bamboo scaffolding and when they reached the clifftop Royan was surprised to discover that, although the earth was wet underfoot from the recent rain squalls, the sun was high. She had lost all sense of time in the tomb, and now she held up her face gratefully to the sunlight while Nicholas checked the porters and made certain that they were all out of the chasm.

Sapper set off at the head of the column along the trail through the thorn forest, with the file of porters strung out behind him. Nicholas and Royan waited until all the men were on the pathway before they themselves brought up the rear of the column. The sound of the fighting was frighteningly close now, and gave a lift to the feet of the porters as they raced back through the forest to reach the main trail down to the monastery before they were cut off by Nogo's advance.

THE JET ranger was flying low, hugging the contours of the land. Helm sat in the right-hand seat, beside the pilot. Von Schiller and Nahoot Guddabi were together in the rear passenger seat, both of them craning nervously to peer out of the side windows at the heavily wooded slopes of the valley, seemingly close enough to touch, as sudden squalls of wind rocked the machine.

Gotthold von Schiller was a vegetarian, a nonsmoker and a teetotaller. Twenty years ago he had been a famous trencherman, obese, with rolls of chin sagging over his collar. Now he was as lean and fit as a racing greyhound. In the autumn of his life, his pleasures were of the mind and the emotions, more than of the physical senses. He placed a higher value on inanimate objects than on living creatures. Power and the possession of beautiful and unique objects were his passions, now that his animal appetites were losing their zest.

Every few minutes the radio crackled into life, and they could hear the terse transmissions of Nogo's men on the ground. There was a sharp firefight going on along the top of the chasm, but the *shufta* were on the run. Nogo was handling his force well.

"Call Nogo up!" von Schiller ordered Helm, leaning over the back of his seat. "Ask him if they have secured the tomb site yet."

Helm reached across and lifted the microphone off its hook below the instrument panel. "Rose Petal, this is Bismarck. Do you copy?"

There was a pause filled with static, and then Nogo's voice speaking English. "Go ahead, Bismarck."

"Have you secured the primary objective? Over."

"Affirmative, Bismarck. All secured. All opposition suppressed. I am sending men down the ladder to clear the workings."

Helm swivelled in his seat to look back at von Schiller. "Nogo has men in the chasm already. We can go in and land."

"Tell him not to let any of his men into the workings before I arrive." Von Schiller's expression was triumphant. "I must be the first in there. Make him understand that."

While Helm relayed his orders to Nogo, von Schiller tapped the pilot on the shoulder.

"How long to the objective?"

"About five minutes' flying time, sir." Suddenly the helicopter slowed, hovering while the pilot pointed down.

"What is it?" Von Schiller followed his gesture. "What do you see?"

"The dam," Helm answered. "Quenton-Harper's dam."

The wide body of trapped water gleamed grey and sullen under the rain clouds. The water diverted into the side canal boiled angrily down into the long valley.

"Deserted!" Helm commented. "Harper's men have pulled out."

"Don't waste any more time," von Schiller ordered. "Nothing more to see here. Let's get on!"

Helm tapped the pilot's shoulder and gestured downstream.

SAPPER WAS waiting for them to catch up at the junction of the trail, where the diverted river was roaring down the valley in a torrent and had washed out a long section of the original track. The porters, strung out in a long line down the valley, were picking their way along the higher ground above the water.

"Where is Hansith?" Nicholas shouted at Sapper, trying to pick out the tall monk's distinctive form.

"I thought he was with you," Sapper shouted back. "I haven't seen him since we left the chasm." Nicholas turned and stared back the way they had come, along the footpath through the thorn forest.

"Damn the man," he grunted. "We can't go back to look for him. He will have to make his own way down to the monastery."

At that moment they heard the faint, familiar flutter of rotors in the hot, humid air below the lowering cloud masses.

"The Pegasus chopper! Sounds as though von Schiller is heading directly for Taita's pool. He must have known all along exactly where we were working," said Nicholas bitterly.

Royan was also looking up at the sound, trying to pick out the shape of the aircraft. "If those swine enter our tomb it will be a dreadful desecration of a sacred place," she said angrily.

Suddenly Nicholas reached across and took her arm. His expression was stern and determined. "You're right. Go on down to the monastery. I'll follow you later." Before she could protest or question him, he strode across to Sapper.

"I am putting Royan in your care, Sapper. Look after her."

"Where are you going, Nicky?" Royan had come up behind him, and overheard his orders to Sapper. "What are you going to do?"

"One little chore. Won't take me long."

"You aren't going back there?" She was horrified.

"Don't fuss yourself, my love," he laughed, and before she realised what he intended he kissed her on the lips. While she was still flustered by this display in front of the men, he pushed her gently away. "I'll meet you at the boats."

He turned and struck out up the valley so swiftly that she had no further chance to prevent him.

"Nicky!" she screamed after him despairingly, but he pretended not to hear and kept going, back towards the dam.

THE JET ranger followed the convoluted course of the river below the dam. At moments they could look down into the narrow gap between the cliffs, into the shaded depths of the chasm, almost dry now, with only the occasional gleam of shrunken pools.

"There they are!" Helm pointed dead ahead. There was a small cluster of men on the brink of the chasm.

"Make sure they aren't *shufta*!" There was fear in von Schiller's voice.

"No!" Helm reassured him loudly. "I recognise Nogo, and that tall one beside him in the white *shamma* is the monk Hansith Sherif, our informer." He shouted above the engine beat at the pilot. "You can go in and land. There! Nogo is waving you in!"

The moment the skids of the helicopter touched the ground, Nogo ran forward, helped von Schiller down from the passenger cabin and hustled him clear of the spinning rotors. "My men have secured the area," Nogo assured him. "We have driven the *shufta* down the valley towards the river. This man is Hansith Sherif, who has been working beside Harper in the tomb. He knows every inch of the tunnels."

"Does he speak English?"

"A little bit." Hansith answered for himself.

"Good! Good!" Von Schiller beamed at him. "Show me the way. I will follow you. Come on, Guddabi, it's about time you did some work for the money I'm paying you."

Hansith led them quickly to the head of the scaffolding, where von Schiller paused and looked down nervously into the depths of the chasm. The bamboo framework seemed very flimsy. He was on the point of protesting when Nahoot Guddabi whimpered behind him.

"He does not expect us to climb down there, does he?"

Bolstered, von Schiller turned on Nahoot. "It is the only access to the tomb. Follow the man down. I will be close behind you."

Reluctantly Nahoot started down the scaffolding after the monk, and von Schiller followed him. At last they reached the ledge beside Taita's pool. There they stood in a small group, staring about them.

"Where is the tunnel?" von Schiller demanded as soon as he had regained his breath, and Hansith beckoned to him to follow him to the wall of the small cofferdam.

Here von Schiller paused and looked at Helm and Nogo. "I want you to remain on guard here. I will enter the tomb with Guddabi and this monk. I will send for you when you are needed." And with Hansith steadying him he climbed stiffly down the wall of the cofferdam into the tunnel. Nahoot Guddabi followed him closely.

"The lights? Where does the power come from?" von Schiller wanted to know, but at that moment they heard the soft burble of the generator ahead of them. None of them spoke again until they reached the landing outside the ruined gallery. By now both von Schiller and Nahoot were sweating with exertion.

"This looks more and more promising. It may very well be a royal tomb," Nahoot exulted. Von Schiller pointed to the plaster seals stacked against the side wall where Nicholas and Royan had abandoned them. Nahoot fell to his knees beside them and examined them eagerly, his voice trembling as he cried out.

"The cartouche of Mamose, and the seal of the scribe Taita!" He looked up at von Schiller with shining eyes. "There can be no doubts now. This is the tomb."

Von Schiller peered through the open doorway into the long gallery. "This has been destroyed!" he cried in horror. "The tomb has been annihilated."

"No, no!" Hansith assured him. "Come this way. There is another tunnel beyond."

As they picked their way through the rubble, Hansith explained how the roof of the gallery had collapsed, and how he, Hansith, had found the true entrance under the ruins. He led them on, and up the hidden staircase into the maze of the bao, and then through the twists and turns to the lowest level.

"Another concealed staircase!" Nahoot was amazed, and stuttered with excitement as they descended into the gas trap where the ranks of amphorae had stood undisturbed for thousands of years, and then climbed the last flight of stairs to the beginning of the funeral arcade.

Now both of them were stunned by the splendour of the murals and the majesty of the great god images that guarded the length of the arcade. They stood side by side unable to move, frozen with awe as they gazed about them.

"I never expected anything like this," von Schiller whispered. "This exceeds anything that I ever hoped for."

"The rooms on each side are filled with treasures." Hansith pointed down the arcade. "There are such things as you have never dreamed of. Harper was able to take very little with him—a few small boxes. He has left piles of goods, stacks of chests."

"Where is the coffin? Where is the body that was in the tomb?" von Schiller demanded.

"Harper has given the body, in its golden coffin, to the abbot. They have taken it away to the monastery."

"Nogo will soon fetch it back for us. You need not worry about that, Herr von Schiller," Nahoot reassured him.

They started forward together, slowly at first, and then both of them began to run. Von Schiller tottered into the nearest storeroom, like a child on Christmas morning, and gazed upon the piled treasures. "Incredible!"

He dragged down one of the cedarwood chests from the nearest stack and ripped off the lid with trembling fingers. When he saw the contents he was struck speechless. He knelt over the chest and began to weep with emotion too overwhelming to express in words.

NICHOLAS WAS banking on the fact that Nogo's men would be driving along the clifftops to reach Taita's pool, and that he would have a free run up the course of the diverted stream to the dam site. He knew that there was little time left. He could not expect the rest of the party to wait for him at the boats. The chance he took paid off, and he reached the dam site without running into any of Nogo's forces. He could see that the yellow front-loader tractor was still parked on the bank high above the wall where Sapper had left it. He could also see no sign of any Ethiopian army guards. He grunted with relief and wiped the sweat out of his eyes with his shirtsleeve.

Although the water was lapping the top of the wall and squirting through the gaps and chinks between the gabions, the wall itself still seemed to be holding well.

Well done, Sapper, he thought, grinning. You did a hell of a job.

He reached the tractor and scrambled up into the driver's seat. There was a moment of panic when he thought that Sapper might have removed the key from its hiding place under the seat. He scrabbled for it for a few seconds until his fingers closed over it. The engine fired at the first turn and Nicholas eased the tractor into her lowest gear and turned her down the bank. Below the dam wall the water that was finding its way through the gaps was less than hub-deep. The tractor bounced and ground its way through the boulder-strewn watercourse. Nicholas stopped the machine in the middle of the riverbed, downstream of the point where Sapper had shored up the raft of logs with rows of gabions.

"Sorry for all your hard work," he apologised to Sapper, as he attacked the weakest-looking gabion, thrusting at it until he could get the scoop under it and drag it free. He pulled away and dropped the heavy wire-mesh basket over the waterfall, then drove back and renewed the attack.

It was slow work. It took almost ten minutes to free the second basket and expose a corner of the log raft behind it. This was the vulnerable part of the wall. He worked the hydraulic controls and lifted the scoop to its highest travel. Then he lowered it carefully, an inch at a time, until it hooked over the end of the thickest log in the jam. He locked the hydraulics and thrust the tractor into reverse, gradually pouring on full power.

Nothing gave. The tyres spun on the boulders under them, throwing a tall shower of spray and gravel high into the air.

"Come on!" Nicholas pleaded with the machine. "You can do it."

Almost as if it had heard him, the machine lurched and hammered against the wall until, with a sound like a cannon shot, the log snapped and the top end of it flew out of the wall, leaving a long, deep hole through which the river poured triumphantly, a thick, solid column of dirty grey water.

"There she blows!" Nicholas shouted, jumping down from the seat. There was no time to drive the tractor out of the riverbed; he could move more quickly on his own feet.

The current seized his legs, trying to pull them out from under him. He glanced back over his shoulder, and at that instant he saw the central section of the dam wall burst, blowing outwards in a violent eruption of furious waters. He struggled on another few paces towards the bank before the deep and turbulent tide picked him up. He was helpless in its grip. It swept him away, down into the chasm.

"THESE ARE the royal crook and sceptre of the Pharaoh," cried von Schiller in a voice that was faint with emotion as he lifted them out of the cedarwood chest.

"And this is his ceremonial pectoral emblem." Nahoot knelt beside him on the floor of the tomb under the great statue of Osiris.

"This is the greatest archaeological discovery of all time," von Schiller whispered. He pulled his handkerchief from his pocket and dabbed at the perspiration that trickled down his cheeks.

"There is years of work here," Nahoot told him. "This collection will have to be catalogued. It will be known for ever as the von Schiller hoard. Your name will be perpetuated for all time. It is like the Egyptian dream of immortality. You will never be forgotten. You will live for ever."

A rapturous expression crossed von Schiller's features. He had not considered that possibility. Up until this moment he had not considered sharing this treasure with anybody, but Nahoot's words had awoken in him the old impossible dream of eternity. Perhaps he might make arrangements for it to be made accessible to the public—but only after his own death, naturally.

Nahoot bowed his head. "However, our main concern now must be to get all of it to safety," he continued. "Helm has warned us about the danger of the river, of the dam bursting. Nogo's men must clear out the tomb. We can ferry the treasure in the helicopter up to the Pegasus camp."

"Yes. Yes." Von Schiller scrambled to his feet. "Send the monk to call Helm. He must come at once."

"Hansith!" Nahoot shouted. "Where are you?"

The monk had been waiting at the entrance to the burial chamber, torn now between religious conviction and greed. When he heard his name called he hurried back to join von Schiller and Nahoot.

"You must go back to the pool—" Nahoot started to relay the orders, but suddenly a strange expression crossed Hansith's darkly handsome features and he held up his hand for silence.

"What is it?" Nahoot demanded angrily. "What can you hear?"

Hansith shook his head. "Be quiet! Listen! Can't you hear it?"

"There is nothing—" Nahoot began, but then broke off suddenly. There was the softest sound, gentle as the sigh of a summer zephyr, lulling and low. "Water!" he whispered. "Running water!"

"The river!" shouted Hansith. "The tunnel is flooding!" He whirled around and went bounding down the funeral arcade.

"We will be trapped in here!" screamed Nahoot, and raced after him.

"Wait for me," von Schiller yelled, and tried to follow. But he soon fell behind the two younger men. The monk, however, was far ahead of them as he took the stairs up from the gas trap two at a time.

"Hansith! Come back! I order you," Nahoot cried despairingly in his wake, but he caught only a flash of the monk's white robe as he darted into the first twist of the labyrinth.

"Guddabi, where are you?" Von Schiller's voice quavered and echoed through the stone corridors. But Nahoot did not reply as he ran on in the direction which he thought the monk had taken. He thought he heard Hansith's racing footsteps ahead of him, but by the time he had turned the third corner he knew he was lost.

He stopped with his heart racing savagely and the bitter gall of terror in the back of his throat.

"Hansith! Where are you?" he screamed.

Von Schiller's voice came back to him, ringing weirdly down the passageways: "Guddabi! Guddabi! Don't leave me here."

Panting heavily, the blood pounding in his ears, Nahoot tried to listen for the sound of Hansith's feet. But he heard only the river.

"No! Don't leave me here," he screamed, and began to run without direction, panic-stricken, ever deeper into the maze.

Hansith took each twist and turn unerringly, with the terror of death driving his feet. When he reached the doorway and eased through it onto the landing beside the generator, the low, reverberating growl of the water was much louder.

Then he heard a fresh sound, a harsher roar as the full flood of the burst dam poured down the waterfall into the pool. It found the entrance to the tunnel and came down it in a solid wave, filling the passageway to the roof.

It struck Hansith with such force that it seemed to be not mere water but the solid rock of an avalanche and he could not resist it. It plucked him away, tossing him backwards down the shaft and hurling him relentlessly towards the sinkhole beyond. He was swirled end over end by the crazed waters. The last thing he ever felt was when he was flung against the side wall of the sinkhole, and the bones of his right shoulder shattered. He opened his mouth to scream at the agony of it, but soon the pain faded into oblivion.

NICHOLAS FOLLOWED the yellow front-loader over the waterfall into the chasm. The flood that carried him cushioned his fall, so instead of being dashed against the boulders at the bottom, he bounced and tumbled in the racing torrent, surfacing fifty yards downstream. The tractor was gone, swallowed deep into the pool at the foot of the waterfall, but ahead of Nicholas was a small island in the middle of the river. With a dozen overarm strokes he swam to it and clung to a rocky spur. From there he looked up at the sheer walls of the chasm and remembered the last time he had been trapped down here. The elation he had felt at the destruction of the dam and the flooding of Pharaoh's tomb evaporated.

The volume of water coming over the falls was not as heavy as he had expected, considering the vast body of water that was being held back by the dam. He realised then that the greater part of the wall must be holding. However, he knew that the river must soon burst through, in full force. I have to get out of its way, he thought desperately.

He kicked off his boots and was about to push off from his temporary refuge when he heard the rest of the dam wall give way.

There was a rumbling roar, the crackle of logs snapping and breaking, the grating and grinding of heavy gabions being thrown around like empty rubbish cans, and then a solid wave of grey water burst over the top of the falls, carrying with it a wall of debris.

Oh Mother! Too late. Here comes the big one!

He shoved off from his rock, turning downstream, and swam with all his strength. He heard the roar of the approaching wave and glanced back over his shoulder. It was overhauling him swiftly, filling the chasm from wall to wall, fifteen foot high and curling at the top.

He felt it seize him and lift him violently, and then he was on the crest of it. He arched his back and tucked his arms behind him in the classic body surfer's position, hanging in the face of the wave, steering with his legs. After the first few terrifying seconds he realised that he was riding her high and had some control; his panic abated and he was overcome by a sense of wild exhilaration.

The increased depth of water in the chasm covered the knife-sharp rocks, enabling him to ride clear of them. It smoothed out the waterfalls and the chutes, so that he slid down them with a smooth rush, holding his position in the face of the wave with a few quick overarm strokes or a kick of the legs.

"Hell! This is fun!" He laughed aloud. "People would pay money to do this!"

Within the first mile the wave began to lose its impetus as it spread out down the canyon. Soon it would no longer have the power to hold him up in the surfing position, and he glanced around him. Floating nearby, keeping pace with him in the debris from the dam, was one of the tree trunks that had formed part of the raft with which Sapper had plugged the gap in the wall.

He steered across to this piece of timber. It was thirty foot long and floated low in the flood. Nicholas pulled himself up onto the tree trunk, lying on his belly, facing downstream, with his legs still dangling in the water. Swiftly he recovered his breath.

Although it had smoothed out and lost its wave formation, the flood was still tearing down the chasm at a tremendous pace. Looking ahead, he recognised that the stretch of the chasm he was hurtling through was the bend above Taita's pool.

The long, smooth chute of racing water opened ahead of him, and the moment before he flew down it he saw that the bamboo scaffolding had not been entirely washed away, although it was badly damaged. The lowest section was gone, but the upper part hung down the rock cliff, just touching the surface of the racing waters, and he realised that there were two men trying to claw their way up the flimsy structure.

In that fraction of a second Nicholas saw a flash of steel-rimmed spectacles under a maroon beret, and realised that the man nearest the top of the scaffolding was Tuma Nogo. Then Nogo succeeded in reaching the top of the cliff and disappeared over the lip. That one glance was all Nicholas had time for before his log was plunged into the waterchute.

For a few moments the log was stalled in the vortex below the falls, but almost at once the current grabbed it again and it gathered speed, bearing away down the length of Taita's pool.

Nicholas had a second of respite. He saw at once that the entrance tunnel to the tomb was entirely submerged and, judging by the water level up the cliff wall, it was already fifty feet or more beneath the surface. He felt a leap of triumph. The tomb was once more protected from the depredations of any other grave robber. Then he looked up at the battered remnants of the bamboo scaffolding and saw the other man still clinging to the wreckage.

At that moment the man turned his head and Nicholas recognised him. "Helm!" he exclaimed. "Jake Helm."

He had an image of Tamre, the epileptic boy, crushed beneath the rockfall, and of Tessay's burnt and battered face. His outrage and hatred surged. Instead of steering the log away from the scaffold, he swung in towards the cliff. There was a breathless interval when he thought he might miss, but at the last moment the leading end of the log swung sharply and the point of it crashed into the trailing end of the bamboo, hooking onto it. The log's weight and momentum were irresistible. The bamboo poles crackled and snapped, and the whole rickety structure tore loose from the wall and came crashing down over the log.

Helm swung out overhead, then released his grip and dropped feet first into the water close alongside the log. He went deep below the surface. While he was under, Nicholas pulled himself up to sit astride the log and grabbed a length of bamboo pole that had broken off the scaffolding and was floating alongside his perch.

A second later the Texan's head broke out, streaming water. His eyes were screwed closed, and he let out a gasp of water and air and tried to suck in a breath.

Nicholas aimed the pole at his head and swung with all his strength. Then he stretched out and grabbed the back of Helm's collar, holding him face down in the water under the log. They picked up speed rapidly down the last stretch of the canyon, but Nicholas held on doggedly, drowning any last spark of life from Helm's carcass, until at last it was torn from his grip by the current and he watched it sink away into the grey, roiling waters.

Then he gave all his concentration to balancing the log and staying aboard for the ride through the tumbling, racing current. At last he was spewed out into the bottom reach of the Dandera River. As he was swept beneath the rope suspension bridge he slid off the log and struck out for the western bank, very much aware of the terrible drop into the Nile that lay half a mile downstream. Reaching the bank, he stood up unsteadily and pushed his way through the strip of thick riverine bush which bounded the river until he struck the trail that led down to the monastery. As he hobbled down it on his bare feet he heard the sound of a helicopter taking off far behind him.

He looked back. Sounds as though Tuma Nogo made it out of there, more's the pity, he thought grimly. I wonder what happened to von Schiller and the Egyptian. At least none of them are going to get into the tomb, not unless they dam the river again. Damn me to hell, if it didn't work just the way I planned it. He began to chuckle, and started down the trail again, breaking into a trot as he reached the paved causeway that led down to the monastery.

Von Schiller still carried part of the treasure that he had been examining when Nahoot had panicked and run. He had Pharaoh's golden crook in one hand and the ceremonial flail in the other. He staggered along, his aged legs weakening with fear, turned a corner, and stopped dead as he realised that the tunnel below him was flooded, right back up to the level of the ancient high-water mark on the walls. He stared in horror at the flooded shaft.

There must be another way out of here, he decided. Perhaps Nahoot, the traitor, had already found it. He turned and stumbled back up the incline shaft, past the landing on which the generator still puttered quietly. He did not know where he was going, but followed any passageway that opened in front of him.

The steep staircase leading down into Taita's gas trap opened under his feet without him seeing it. He fell down the steps, jarring and bruising his legs and chest. Then he was on his feet again, reeling across the storeroom past the ranks of amphorae, up the far staircase and into the painted arcade that led to the tomb of Pharaoh Mamose.

Suddenly the lights dimmed for a moment, fading to a yellow glow. Then they brightened again as the generator sucked the last drops of fuel from the bottom of the tank. Von Schiller stopped in the centre of the arcade and looked up at the lights with despair. He knew what was coming. For another few minutes the bulbs burned on, bright and cheerfully, and then again they faded.

Darkness settled over him like the heavy velvet folds of a funeral pall. It was so intense that it seemed to have a physical texture. He could taste the darkness as it seemed to force its way into his body.

He struggled on, now running wildly and blindly, crashed headlong into stone and fell again, stunned. He could feel blood running down his face. He whimpered and gasped and slowly, lying on his side, he curled himself into a ball like a foetus. Thus he lay in the darkness of the tomb, surrounded by the funeral treasures of an emperor, and waited for his own slow but inexorable death.

The monastery of St Frumentius was deserted. The monks had heard the gunfire and sounds of battle and had gathered up their treasures and fled.

Nicholas ran down the long, empty cloister, pausing to catch his breath at the head of the staircase that led down to the Nile and the cave where he had stored the boats. Panting, he searched the gloom of the deep basin below him, but the clouds of silver spray from the twin waterfalls screened the depths. He had no way of telling if Sapper and Royan were down there waiting for him, or if they had run into trouble on the trail.

He started down. Then he heard her voice calling his name, and she came pelting up the stairs towards him.

"Nicholas! Oh, thank God! I thought you weren't coming." She rushed into his embrace, and he swung her off her feet as he turned her to face down the stairs again.

"Where are the others?" He hurried her down.

"They are all here," she told him. "Sapper and Mek are inflating the boats and loading."

"Tessay?"

"She's safe."

They scrambled down to the jetty. The Nile had risen ten feet since Nicholas had last stood there. He could barely make out the cliffs on the far bank through the drifting clouds of spray.

The five Avon boats were drawn up at the edge, already fully inflated. Mek and Sapper were packing ammunition crates into the boats and strapping them down.

Nicholas embraced Mek. "Thank you, old friend," he said sincerely. "Your men fought well. How many casualties?"

"Three dead, and six wounded. It could have been much worse if Nogo's men had pushed us harder."

"Still, it's too many," said Nicholas. "Where are the rest of your men?"

"On the run for the border. Kept just enough of them with me to handle the boats. Nogo has at least a full company of men guarding the river downstream. My scouts tell me that he has placed them to cover the trails on both banks."

"He doesn't know that we have boats to run the river, does he?"

"I think it is unlikely, but he knows a great deal about our movements. Perhaps he has an informer among your workmen. And he still has the helicopter. He'll spot us on the river as soon as this cloud breaks."

"The river is our only escape route. Let's pray that the weather stays socked in, like this."

Four of Mek's men carried Tessay's litter to one of the boats. Before helping her aboard Nicholas asked, "How are you feeling?"

"I will be all right now, thank you, Nicholas."

"I didn't have a chance to ask you earlier. What about Royan's message that she asked you to telephone from Debre Maryam? Did you get it through for her?"

"Yes, of course," Tessay replied guilelessly. "I told Royan that I had given her message to the cultural attaché at the Egyptian Embassy. Didn't she tell you?"

Nicholas winced as though he had taken a low punch, but he smiled and kept his tone casual. "It must have slipped her mind. Not important, anyway."

He settled her on the deck, making sure that she had one of the safety straps close at hand. After that he went back to find Mek, who was loading the precious radio onto the lead boat.

"Royan will go with me in the lead boat," he said. "You come next with Tessay, and Sapper in the one behind. Are there any of your men who know the river well enough to command the other two boats?"

"All my men know the river," Mek told him, and shouted his orders. Nicholas gave Royan a boost over the gunwale of their boat, and then helped his men launch it down the rocky bank. As they bent to their paddles, Nicholas saw at once that every man of his crew was indeed a riverman. They pulled strongly, and the light inflatable craft shot out into the main stream of the Nile.

"Bad water ahead," Nicholas told Royan grimly. "All the way to the Sudanese border." He stood at the steering sweep in the stern and looked up at the sky. The rain clouds were low and purple, seeming to sag down upon the tops of the tall cliffs.

"Luck starting to run our way," he told Royan. "Even with the helicopter they won't be able to find us in this weather. We should be able to put a few miles of river behind us before we're forced to stop for the night."

He looked back over his stern and saw the rest of the little flotilla bobbing along behind him. The Avons were reflective yellow in colour and stood out brilliantly even in the murk of the gorge. He lifted his clenched fist high in the signal to advance.

The river grabbed them and the men at the oars stopped paddling. All they could do now was to help Nicholas steer through any desperate moments, and they crouched ready along the gunwales.

Nicholas stood high and craned ahead. He had to pick his route well in advance, and once committed he had to steer her through. It all depended on his ability to read the river. They went swooping down the first run of fast green water.

"Nothing to it!" Royan laughed up at him.

"Don't say it!" Nicholas pleaded. "The bad angel is listening." And he lined up for the head of the next set of rapids.

It was only when they were halfway down that he saw the tall standing wave which marked a rock below the surface of the river. He tried to steer around it, but the river had them firmly in its grip.

Like a hunter taking a fence they shot up the front of the standing wave, and then with a sickening lurch plummeted down the far side into the deep trough. The crew were tumbled over each other and Nicholas would have been catapulted over the side if it had not been for his grip on the steering sweep. Royan flung herself flat on the deck and hung onto the safety strap with all her strength.

One of the crew had been hurled overboard and was floundering alongside, carried along at the same speed as the flying Avon, so his comrades were able to lean out and haul him back on board. The cargo of ammunition crates had tumbled and shifted, but the straps had prevented any of them from being lost over the side.

Looking back, Nicholas saw Mek's boat crash through the trough just as they had, but the following craft had enough warning to steer clear and slip through the sides of the run.

He looked ahead again, and his whole existence became the wild waters of the river as he battled to bring the racing Avon through. The onset of the African night was sped upon them by the low cloud, and in the gathering darkness another hazard leapt upon them. One instant they were running down a smooth stretch of the river, and the next the waters opened ahead of them and they were hurled out into space. It was a drop of thirty feet before they hit the bottom and found themselves floating in the pool below the falls. Here the river was stalled for a moment, revolving upon itself while it gathered its strength for the next mad charge down the gorge.

One of the Avons capsized and the crews of the other boats paddled across to drag the survivors from the water and to salvage the oars and other floating equipment. It was almost completely dark by the time they had the overturned Avon back on an even keel.

"Count the crates!" Nicholas ordered. "How many have we lost?"

He could hardly credit his good fortune when Sapper shouted back, "Eleven still on board. All present and correct." The cargo straps were holding well. But all of them, men and women, were exhausted and any attempt to go on in darkness would be suicidal.

There was a tough little tree growing out of a vertical fissure in the rock, and they used this as a bollard and made a secure mooring. Then they lashed all the Avons together in a line down the cliff and settled in for the night. There was no chance of hot food or drink, and they had to make do with some cold tinned rations.

Mek scrambled over from his own boat and squatted down beside Nicholas who asked, "How much further to go?"

"It's almost impossible to tell, but I guess we are halfway to the border. Should reach there some time tomorrow afternoon."

They were silent for a while, and then Mek said, "Your pick-up aircraft is due at the airstrip the day after tomorrow. What chances of your pilot being late?"

"Jannie is a pro. He is never late." Again a silence fell, and then Nicholas asked, "What do you want me to do with your share of the booty, Mek? Do you want to take it with you?"

"After we see you off on the plane with your fat friend, we're going to be doing some hotfooted running from Nogo. I don't want to be carrying any extra luggage. You take my share with you. Sell it for me—I need the money to keep fighting here."

"You trust me?"

"You are my friend. Sleep well, old friend," he said, and climbed across to the boat alongside, where Tessay waited for him.

Nicholas braced his back against the gunwale of the Avon and took Royan in his arms. She sat between his knees and leaned back against his chest, shivering in her sodden clothes. After a while her shivering abated, and she murmured, "You make a very good hot-water bottle."

"That's one reason for keeping me around on a permanent basis," he said, and stroked her wet hair. She did not answer him but snuggled close, and a short while afterwards her breathing slowed as she fell into an exhausted sleep.

THEY KEPT going all the following morning, and slowly the mood of the river began to ameliorate. The current was not so swift and treacherous, and the banks not so high and rugged.

"I think we are through the worst of it now," Nicholas told Royan as she sat on the deck below him. "The river is flattening out as we approach the Sudan. The border can't be too far ahead now."

Nicholas steered for the deeper water on the outside of the next wide bend, and as he came through it he saw that the stretch of river ahead seemed open and altogether free of rapids or shoals. He relaxed and smiled at Royan. "How about lunch at the Dorchester Grill next Sunday? Best roast beef trolley in London."

He was about to stoop over her and kiss her when he saw the dance of tiny white fountains on the river ahead, coming swiftly towards them, and heard the crackle of automatic fire.

His men threw down their paddles and seized their weapons. They blazed away towards the inner curve of the bank from where the attack was coming, laying down covering fire to keep the attackers' heads down and to upset their aim.

A bullet tore through the nylon skin of the Avon close to Royan's head and went on to slam into one of the metal ammunition crates. One of their crew was hit as the Avon still raced downstream on the current. It took them less than a minute to be carried past the ambush and around the next bend of the river.

Nicholas shouted across at Mek, "Are you all right?"

"One man hit here," Mek yelled back. "Not too bad."

Each of the boats reported their casualties: a total of one dead and three wounded. None of the wounded was in a serious condition, and although three of the boats had been holed, the hulls were made up of watertight compartments and were all still floating high.

Mek steered his Avon alongside Nicholas's. "I was beginning to think we had given Nogo the slip."

"We got off lightly that time," Nicholas called back. "We probably took them by surprise."

"Well, no more surprises for him now. You can bet they're on the radio to him already." He looked up at the cloud. "We can only hope the cloud stays thick and low." Within thirty minutes of the firefight, they heard the helicopter. It was flying above the clouds, and as they listened it passed overhead, but out of sight, and headed on downstream. Twenty minutes later they heard it again, coming back in the opposite direction.

"What the hell is Nogo playing at?" Mek called across to Nicholas. "Sounds as if he's patrolling the river, but can't get under the cloud."

"My guess is that he's ferrying men downstream to cut us off. Nogo isn't one to worry about international borders. He may even have realised by now where we're heading. Roseires is the nearest unmanned airstrip along the river. He could be waiting for us."

Mek steered his Avon closer and passed a line across, tying the two boats together so that they could talk in normal tones.

"I don't like it, Nicholas. We're going to walk right into them again. What do you suggest?"

Nicholas pondered for a minute. "Don't you recognise this part of the river? Don't you know precisely where we are yet?"

Mek shook his head. "I always keep well away from the river when we cross the border, but I will recognise the old deserted sugar mill when we get there. It's about three miles upstream from the airstrip."

"With this cloud cover, it will be dark in an hour," Nicholas said. "We could take a chance and keep on going. Perhaps Nogo won't expect that. We might be able to give him the slip in the dark."

"Is that the best you can do?" Mek chuckled. "As a plan it sounds to me a bit like closing your eyes and hoping for the best."

Nicholas grinned back at him. "Well, if somebody could tell me where the hell we are, and what time Jannie will arrive tomorrow, I might be able to come up with something better."

AS DAYLIGHT broke, Tuma Nogo watched the sun push its great fiery head out of the surface of the Nile ahead of them. They were flying only feet above the water to keep under the Sudanese military radar transmissions.

Nogo was a worried man. Since the debacle in the gorge everything had run against him. He had lost all his allies. Until they were gone he had not realised how heavily he had come to rely on Helm and von Schiller. Now he was on his own, and he had already made mistakes.

But despite all this he was determined to pursue the fugitives. It had gradually dawned on Nogo that Harper and Mek Nimmur were in possession of treasure of immense value, and that now that von Schiller and Helm were gone, this treasure could be his alone. There was no one to stand in his way, other than the fleeing *shufta* led by Mek Nimmur and the Englishman. And he had overwhelming force on his side.

There must be no survivors, no one to carry tales to Addis. Afterwards it would be a simple matter to spirit his booty out of the country in the helicopter. But first he had to find where the runaways had vanished to.

He had not realised that Harper and Mek Nimmur had inflatable boats hidden somewhere near the monastery. Hansith had not informed him of that fact. He and Helm had expected them to try to escape on foot, and it was quite by chance that one of his patrols had spotted the flotilla of yellow boats as they came racing downstream.

Immediately he had received the company commander's report of this contact with Mek Nimmur, Nogo had started ferrying men to the Sudanese border to cut them off. Unfortunately, the Jet Ranger could carry no more than six fully armed men at a time, and he had only succeeded in bringing sixty men into position before night had fallen.

During the night he fretted that the flotilla was slipping past him, and with the dawn they were in the air again. Fortunately the cloud had broken up during the night, and they were able to fly low along the river and search for any sign of the boats.

By now Nogo knew he had been defeated and outwitted. He brooded unhappily in the front seat of the helicopter beside the pilot, trying to fathom out what had happened to his quarry. He saw the tall smokestack of the abandoned sugar mill at Roseires and glowered down at it angrily. The factory was roofless and there was no place where anyone could hide.

"Nothing! We have lost them. Head back upstream."

The pilot lifted the machine's nose and as the aircraft banked steeply, a flash of bright yellow caught Nogo's eye. "Wait!" he shouted. "There is something there. Go back! Put us down."

As soon as the skids touched the earth, Nogo climbed out and ran to a bed of tall cane. One look was all he needed.

The yellow boats had been deflated and folded and hastily covered. The earth around them had been churned up by booted feet. The tracks led away inland.

Nogo ran back to the helicopter. "Is there an airstrip near here?" he shouted at the pilot.

"There is nothing shown on the chart."

"There must have been one. The sugar mill would have had a strip. We will find it. Mek Nimmur's tracks will lead us to it."

He left his men at the sugar mill and flew back to the border with an empty rear cabin to pick up the first load of reinforcements.

"BIG DOLLY! Come in, Big Dolly. This is Pharaoh. Do you read?" Nicholas had put out his first call an hour before sunrise. The static hummed softly, and he retuned the set carefully. He called again every fifteen minutes as they huddled around the set in the dark under the acacia trees.

Suddenly Royan started to her feet. "There he is. Listen!"

Nicholas and Mek ran out into the open and turned their faces upwards, looking into the north.

"That's not the Hercules," Nicholas exclaimed suddenly. "That's the Pegasus helicopter! They're onto us again."

As they listened, the sound of the rotors faded. Nicholas looked relieved. "They missed us. They can't have spotted the Avons."

They trooped back under the cover of the acacias and Nicholas called again on the radio, but there was no reply from Jannie.

Twenty minutes later they heard the sound of the Jet Ranger returning, and they monitored it anxiously.

"Gone again," said Nicholas after a while, but then twenty minutes later they heard it again. The helicopter moved up and down the Nile at short intervals during the next three hours.

"Nogo is up to something out there," Mek said uneasily. "He's bringing up more men. Keep calling, I'm going out to the perimeter to make certain my men are ready to hold him off if he comes."

Suddenly the radio crackled into life. "Pharaoh! This is Big Dolly. Do you read?"

Nicholas replied, "This is Pharaoh. Speak to me, Big Dolly."

"ETA your position thirty minutes," Jannie reported.

"You'll be very welcome!" Nicholas promised him fervently. But at that moment from the direction of the river came the unmistakable rattle of rapid fire, followed a few seconds later by the crump of an exploding grenade.

"Oh damn it to hell!" he groaned. "I thought it was too good to last. Nogo has arrived."

He picked up the mike again. "Big Dolly! The uglies have arrived on the scene. It's going to have to be a hot extraction."

"Hang onto your crown, Pharaoh! I'm on my way."

During the next twenty minutes the sounds of the fighting along the river intensified until the rattle of small-arms fire was almost continuous, and gradually it crept closer to the far end of the airstrip. It was clear that Mek's men, spread out thinly along the river end of the strip, were falling back before the thrust of Nogo's troops.

"What about you?" Nicholas asked Tessay. "Are you coming out with us? You're still in pretty bad shape."

Tessay laughed. "While I can still stand on my two feet, I will never leave Mek Nimmur."

"I can't understand what you see in the old rogue," Nicholas laughed with her, and sauntered back to the radio set. Royan smiled and put her arm around Tessay. "I'm going to miss you, Tessay."

"Perhaps we will meet again in happier times." Tessay turned her head and kissed her impulsively.

Royan hugged her hard. "I hope so. I hope so with all my heart."

Nicholas spoke into the microphone. "Big Dolly, this is Pharaoh. What is your position now?"

"Pharaoh, we're five minutes out, and hurrying."

From where he stood, Nicholas looked down the long strip. Mek's men were retreating, flitting like smoke through the thorn scrub and firing back in the direction of the river. Nogo was pushing them hard.

"Hurry along, Jannie," he murmured.

The rumble of Big Dolly's engines, at first barely audible, was louder than the sound of the gunfire now. Then suddenly she was in sight, coming in so low that she seemed to brush the tops of the thorn trees. Jannie touched her down short, and she blew out a long rolling cloud of dust behind her as he put the engines into reverse thrust.

Big Dolly went barrelling past the clump of acacia, spun around in her own length and came roaring back down the strip towards them, her loading ramp already beginning to drop open.

Fred was waiting in the open hatchway, and he ran down to help Sapper and Nicholas load the crates. Royan gave a hand, staggering up the ramp with one of the crates clutched to her chest.

A mortar shell exploded beyond the parked Hercules, and then half a minute later a second shell fell short.

"Ranging shots," Sapper grunted, picking up a crate under each arm and running up the ramp.

"They have us in their sights now," Fred shouted. "We have to get out of here. Leave the rest of the cargo. Let's go! Go!"

There were only four crates still lying under the acacia, and both Nicholas and Sapper ignored the order and ran back to snatch up a crate under each arm and race back. The ramp was starting to rise and Big Dolly's engines roared as she began to taxi out. They hurled the crates over the tailboard of the rising ramp and then jumped up to grab a handhold and pull themselves aboard. Nicholas was the first up and reached down to haul Sapper in.

When he looked back, Tessay was a small, lonely figure under the acacias. "Give Mek my love and thanks," he bellowed at her.

"Goodbye, Tessay." Royan's voice was lost in the blast of the great engines, and the ramp hissed closed on its hydraulic rams.

Nicholas put an arm around Royan's shoulders and hustled her down the length of the cavernous cargo hold and into one of the jump seats at the entrance to the cockpit. "Strap yourself in!" he ordered, and ran up the steps to the cockpit as Jannie and Fred pushed forward the bank of throttle levers to full power and Big Dolly built up speed.

Looking over Jannie's shoulder, Nicholas saw men in camouflage battledress firing at the huge aircraft as it raced towards them.

"Those popguns aren't going to hurt her much," Jannie grunted. "Big Dolly is a tough old lady." And he lifted her into the air.

Once Jannie had settled Big Dolly on her northerly heading, and they were sailing low over the open deserted Sudanese plains, Nicholas went back to the small, well-stocked galley behind the flight deck. He opened some canned soup and sliced hunks of fresh bread from the loaves he found in the refrigerator. While the tea water boiled, he found his small emergency pack, which contained his medicines and drugs. From one of the phials he shook five white tablets into the palm of his hand.

He crushed the tablets to powder, and when he poured tea into two of the mugs he stirred the powder in with it. Royan had enough English blood in her veins never to be able to refuse a mug of hot tea.

While Royan and Sapper sipped their tea, Nicholas went back to the flight deck and leaned over the back of Jannie's seat.

"What is our flying time to the Egyptian border?" he asked.

"Two hours twenty minutes," Jannie told him.

Back in the main hold, it was Sapper who was the first to show the effects of the doped tea. He lay back gently and closed his eyes, then a soft snore vibrated his lips. Minutes later Royan sagged drowsily against Nicholas's shoulder. When she was fast asleep, he lifted her up gently and carried her to one of the fold-down bunks. He spread a rug over her and kissed her forehead softly. "How could I ever hate you?" he asked her softly. "Whatever you did."

He went into the lavatory and locked the door. He had plenty of time. Sapper and Royan would not wake for hours yet.

When at last he had finished, Nicholas closed the toilet seat and washed his hands carefully. Then he took one last careful look around the tiny cabin and unlocked the door.

Sapper and Royan were still fast asleep. He went forward to the flight deck and leaned over Jannie's seat back. "Where are we?"

With a thick forefinger Jannie stabbed the chart. "Almost clear of Egypt," he said complacently.

Nicholas remained standing behind his seat. Suddenly, without the least warning, there was a silvery flash ahead of them as a fighter interceptor pulled up steeply across their bow. Another two warplanes rocketed up from under them, MiG 21 "Fishbeds," in Egyptian air force livery, with air-to-air missiles hanging under their wings. "ZWU 500. This is Red Leader of the Egyptian People's Air Force. You will conform to my order."

Jannie looked back at Nicholas. "Something has gone wrong here. How the hell did they tumble to us?"

"You'd better do what the man says, Dad," Fred advised. "Otherwise he's going to blow us all over the sky."

Jannie shrugged, then spoke into his microphone: "Red Leader. This is ZWU 500. We will cooperate. Please state your intentions."

"Your new heading is 053. Execute immediately!"

Jannie brought Big Dolly around into the east and then glanced at his chart. "Aswan!" he said. "They're taking us to Aswan."

Nicholas went back to Royan's bunk and shook her awake. She was groggy from the effects of the drug as she staggered to the lavatory. However, when she emerged she seemed alert and recovered from the mild draught that she had drunk in her tea.

AS THE VOICE of the military controller at the Aswan airfield gave Jannie his orders, Big Dolly lined up for the approach to the tarmac runway, sailed in over the perimeter fence and touched down. Then the controller ordered them, "Turn first taxiway right."

Jannie obeyed, and turned off the main runway to a row of camouflaged hangars in front of which a ground crew in khaki overalls signalled them with paddles into a parking stand. As soon as Jannie brought Big Dolly to a halt, a file of four armoured half-tracks raced out and surrounded the huge aircraft.

Obedient to the instructions radioed by control, Jannie shut down his engines and lowered the tail ramp of the aircraft. No one on the flight deck had spoken since they had landed. They stood crowded together, peering out of the cockpit windows.

Suddenly a white Cadillac with an escort of armed motorcyclists, followed by a three-ton transport truck, drove through the gate of the perimeter fence and came directly to the foot of the cargo ramp of the Hercules. The chauffeur jumped out and opened the door. His passenger wore a light tropical suit and white shoes, a panama hat and dark glasses. As he came up the ramp he was followed by two male secretaries.

He removed his dark glasses and tucked them into his breast pocket. As he recognised Royan he lifted his hat. "Dr Al Simma—Royan! You did it. Congratulations!" He took her hand and shook it warmly, not relinquishing his grip as he looked directly at Nicholas.

"You must be Sir Nicholas Quenton-Harper. I have been looking forward to meeting you. Won't you please introduce us, Royan?"

Royan could not meet Nicholas's accusing scrutiny as she said, "May I present His Excellency, Atalan Abou Sin, Minister of Culture and Tourism in the Egyptian government."

"What an unexpected pleasure, Minister," said Nicholas coldly.

"I would like to express the thanks of the President and the people of Egypt for returning to this country these precious relics of our ancient history." He made a gesture towards the ammunition crates.

"Please, think nothing of it," said Nicholas.

"On the contrary, we think the world of what you have done, Sir Nicholas." Abou Sin's smile was charming. "We are fully aware of the expense to which you have been put, and we would not want you to be out of pocket in this most generous gesture. Dr Al Simma tells me that the expedition to recover these treasures for us has cost you a quarter of a million sterling." He took a piece of paper from his inside pocket and proffered it to Nicholas. It was a banker's draft drawn on the Central Bank of Egypt, for the sum of £250,000.

"Very generous of you, Your Excellency." Nicholas's voice was heavy with irony as he slipped the draft into his top pocket. "I presume this was Dr Al Simma's suggestion?"

"Of course," beamed Abou Sin. "Royan holds you in high regard."

"Does she, now?" Nicholas murmured.

Then the minister stood aside and soldiers began carrying the ammunition cases down the ramp. They were loaded neatly into the three-tonner. Within ten minutes Big Dolly's hold was bare and empty. An escort of motorcyclists fell into formation around the truck, and then, with sirens wailing, the convoy roared away.

"Well, Sir Nicholas." Abou Sin held out his hand. "I am sorry to have taken you out of your way like this. I know that you will be anxious to continue on your journey, so I will not detain you further. We are planning to build a special annexe to the museum at Luxor to house these artefacts of Pharaoh Mamose. In due course you will be receiving a personal invitation from President Mubarak to attend, as an honoured guest, the opening of that museum. Dr Al Simma, who I am sure you know has been appointed the new director of the Department of Antiquities, will be in charge of the museum."

He bowed and went down the ramp. Royan began to follow him, but Nicholas called after her. She froze, then turned reluctantly to meet his eyes.

"I'm sorry, Nicky," she whispered, "but you must have known that I am not a thief. It belongs to Egypt, not to us."

She ran down the ramp to where the chauffeur was holding the back door of the limousine open for her. She slipped onto the seat beside Abou Sin without looking back, and the Cadillac pulled away.

"Let's get the hell out of here," said Jannie.

"What a splendid idea," said Nicholas bitterly.

ONCE THEY were airborne again Aswan control cleared them for a direct flight northwards to the Mediterranean.

The four of them, Jannie and Fred, Sapper and Nicholas, stayed together on the flight deck, saying little.

Nicholas waited until the Egyptian coast receded behind them and then he let out a long, soft sigh.

"Give me a hand, Sapper," he invited, and started down the staircase to the lavatory on the main deck, where he took a screwdriver from his pocket, lifted the cover of the chemical toilet and started to work on the screws holding the hidden panel in place.

Big Dolly was a smugglers' aircraft, and there were a number of these hidey-holes cunningly built into the fuselage. The location of this particular panel in the back of the toilet made it highly unlikely that any follower of Islam would want to investigate such an unclean area.

Nicholas lifted out the panel, reached into the space beyond and carefully drew out the blue war crown of ancient Egypt. He handed it to Sapper.

"Lay it on the bunk, but treat it carefully."

He reached into the compartment again. "And this is the *ushabti* of the scribe Taita."

The two relics lay on the bunk, and they stared at them reverently.

"You saved them." Sapper beamed at him. "But how the hell did you know that Royan was going to scupper us?"

"She was right when she said I must have known she was no thief. The whole lark was out of character for her. She is," he searched for the correct description, "much too upright and honest. Not at all like the present company."

"Thanks for the compliment," said Sapper drily, "but she must have given you more reason than that to make you suspicious."

"Yes, of course," Nicholas told him.

"The first real inkling I had was when we came back from Ethiopia the first time, and she immediately pushed off to Cairo. I guessed she was up to something. But I was absolutely certain only when I learned that she had passed a message, through Tessay, to the Egyptian Embassy in Addis. It was clear then that she had alerted them to our return flight."

"The perfidious little bitch," Sapper guffawed.

"Careful there!" said Nicholas stiffly. "She is a decent, honest and patriotic young woman."

NICHOLAS SAT at his desk in his study at Quenton Park. He poured whisky into a crystal glass, and while he sipped it he picked up the Taita *ushabti* from the desk in front of him and spoke to it.

"You knew the real meaning of loneliness, didn't you?" he asked softly. "You loved Queen Lostris and knew what it was like to love someone you could never have."

He set down the statuette and picked up the telephone. He dialled an international number and it rang three times before a man answered. "This is the office of the director of the Department of Antiquities," he said in Arabic. "How may I help you?"

"Is Dr Al Simma available?" Nicholas asked in the same language.

"Please hold the line. I am putting you through."

"Dr Al Simma." Her voice sent an electric thrill down his spine.

"Royan," he said, and he could sense her shock in the long silence that followed.

"You!" she whispered. "I didn't think I would hear from you again."

"I just rang to congratulate you on your appointment."

"You cheated me," she said. "You stole the contents of a crate."

"As a wise man once said, friends are the easiest to cheat—they don't expect it. You, of all people, should know the truth of that."

"You have sold them, of course. I've heard a rumour that the Texan, Peter Walsh, paid five million."

"Six million," Nicholas corrected her. "But only for the war crown. Even as I speak to you, the *ushabti* reposes before me."

"As my mother would say, 'Bully for you.'"

"The money has already gone to Mek Nimmur and Tessay."

"At least that is a good cause." Her tone tingled with hostility. "Is that all you called to tell me?"

"No. There's something else."

"Yes?"

"I would like you to marry me."

He heard her draw breath sharply, and then after a long pause she asked softly, "Why would you want anything so unlikely?"

"Because I've come to realise how much I love you."

She was silent again, and then she said, "All right."

"What do you mean, 'All right'?"

"I mean, all right, I will marry you."

"Why would you agree to anything so unlikely?" he asked.

"Because I've come to realise, despite everything, how much I love you back."

"There's a Cairo flight from Heathrow this afternoon. If I drive like fury, I may just make it. But it gets me into Cairo rather late."

"I'll be waiting at the airport, no matter how late."

"I'm on my way!" Nicholas hung up, went to the door, but suddenly turned back and picked up the Taita *ushabti* from the desk.

"Come on, you old rogue." He laughed triumphantly. "You're going home, as a wedding gift."

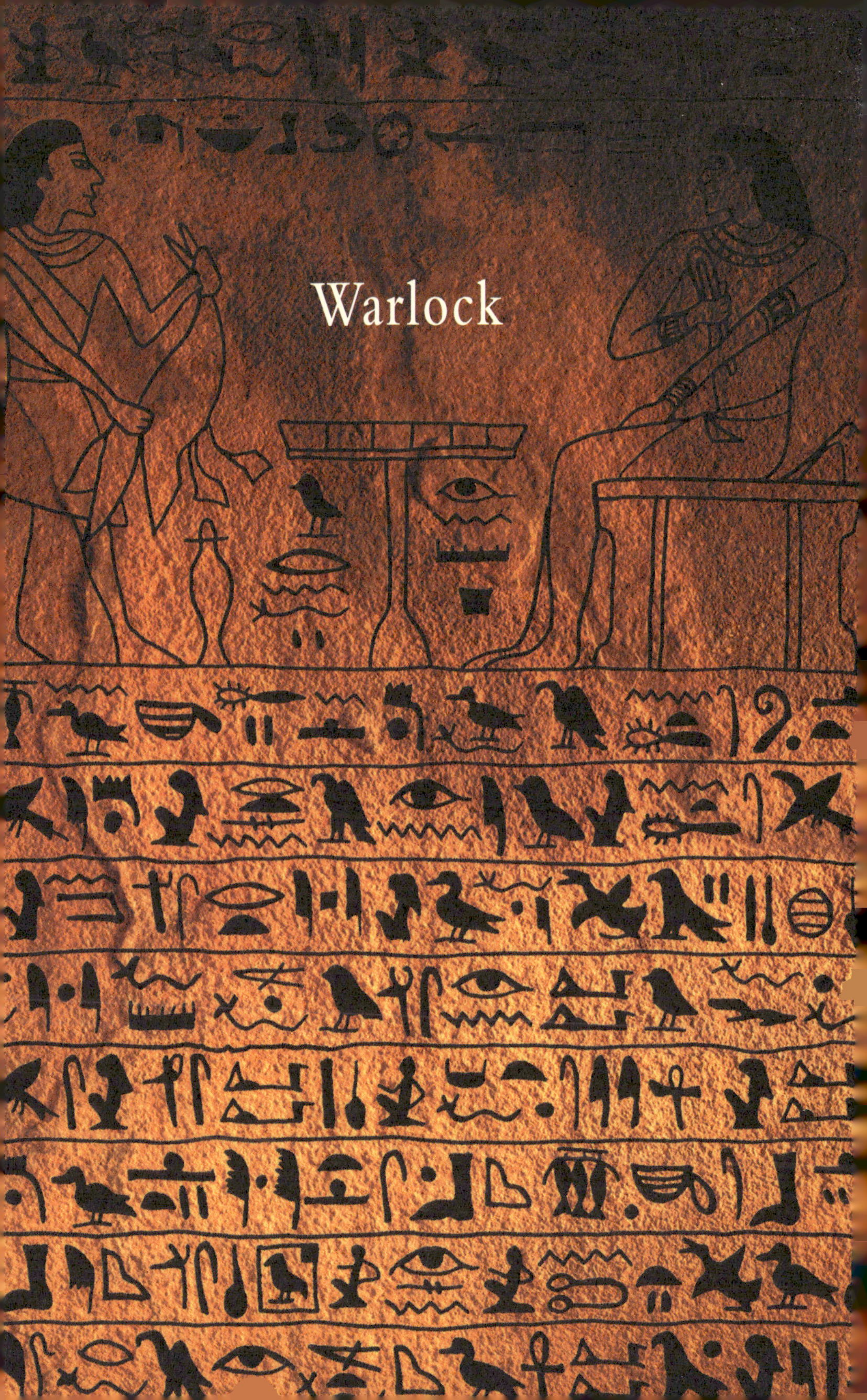
Warlock

Warlock

Wise Taita is training young Prince Nefer to bring new peace and prosperity to the ancient land of Egypt. But behind the throne a traitor lurks, as cunning and patient as a cobra. Now Taita will need all his skill to protect his country's future.

Chapter One

LIKE AN uncoiling serpent, a line of fighting chariots wound swiftly down the gut of the valley. From where he clung to the dashboard of the leading chariot, the boy looked up at the cliffs that hemmed them in. Openings to the tombs of the ancients honeycombed the rock, staring down at him like the implacable eyes of a legion of djinn. Prince Nefer Memnon shuddered and looked away, furtively making the sign to avert evil with his left hand.

Over his shoulder he glanced back down the column and saw that from the following chariot Taita was watching him through the swirling clouds of dust. The dust had coated the old man and his vehicle with a pale film, and a single shaft of sunlight that penetrated to the depths of this deep valley glittered on the mica particles so that he seemed to glow like the incarnation of one of the gods. Even at that distance his ancient eyes seemed to bore into the core of Nefer's being. Seeing all, understanding all. Nefer ducked his head guiltily, ashamed that the old man had witnessed his superstitious dread. No royal prince of the House of Tamose should show such weakness, not now when he stood at the gateway to manhood. But then, Taita knew him as no other did, for he had been Nefer's tutor since infancy, closer to him than his own parents or siblings.

Nefer turned back and drew himself up to his full height beside his father, who flipped the reins and urged the horses on with a crack of the long whip. Ahead of them the valley opened abruptly into the great amphitheatre that contained the ruins of the city of Gallala. Nefer thrilled to his first sight of this famous battlefield. As a young man Taita himself had fought on this site when Nefer's grandfather, Tanus Lord Harrab, had destroyed the dark forces that were threatening Egypt. Taita had related to Nefer every detail of the fight.

Nefer's father, the god and Pharaoh Tamose, wheeled the chariot up to the tumbled stones of the ruined gateway and reined in the horses. Behind them a hundred chariots neatly executed the same manoeuvre. Stripped naked in the heat, the charioteers swarmed down from the footplates to begin watering the horses.

"My lord!" Pharaoh hailed Lord Naja, his army commander and beloved companion. "We must be away again before the sun touches the hilltops. I wish to make a night run through the dunes to El Galsar." He glanced down at Nefer. "This is where I leave you to go on with Taita."

Nefer opened his mouth to protest. Pharaoh forestalled him. "What is the first duty of a warrior?" he demanded.

Nefer dropped his eyes. "It is obedience, Majesty."

"Never forget it." His father nodded and turned away.

Pharaoh Tamose's battle plan was bold and brilliant. If it succeeded, it would bring to a close, at one stroke, the war with the Hyksos that had already raged through two lifetimes. Nefer had been taught that battle and glory were the reasons for his existence on this earth. But even at the advanced age of fourteen, they had so far eluded him. He longed with all his soul to ride to victory and immortality at his father's side. Now he felt himself spurned and discarded. His eyes smarted and his upper lip quivered, but Taita's gaze stiffened him. He blinked to clear his tears and took a pull from the water-skin that hung on the side rail of the chariot before turning to the old Magus with a jaunty toss of his thick, dust-caked curls. "Show me the monument, Tata," he commanded.

The pair made their way through the chariots, men and horses that choked the narrow streets of the ruined city, past temples and palaces now inhabited only by the lizard and the scorpion, until they reached the deserted central square. In its centre stood the monument to Lord Tanus and his triumph over the armies of bandits who had almost choked the life out of the richest and most powerful nation on earth.

Taita watched the prince as he walked round the monument, a bizarre pyramid of human skulls cemented together and protected by a shrine made of red rock slabs.

"Tata, show me where it was that you captured the leader of the robber barons." Nefer's voice cracked with excitement and the onset of puberty. "Was it here?" He ran to the broken-down wall at the south side of the square.

"No, it was here. This side," Taita told him, and he strode on those long, stork-thin legs to the eastern wall. He looked up to the crumbling summit. "The ruffian's name was Shufti, and he was one-eyed and as ugly as the god Seth. He was trying to escape by climbing over the wall here. I brought him down with a single throw."

Even though Nefer knew, at first hand, the old man's strength, he was astonished when Taita suddenly stooped and picked up half a baked-mud brick and hurled it upwards. It sailed over the top of the high wall.

He is as old as the mountains, older than my grandmother, Nefer marvelled. Men say he has witnessed two hundred inundations of the Nile and that he built the pyramids with his own hands.

"You know the story well enough, for I have told it to you a hundred times." Taita feigned modest reluctance to extol his own deeds.

"Tell me again!" Nefer ordered.

Taita sat down on a stone block while Nefer settled at his feet in happy anticipation and listened avidly until the ram's horns of the squadron sounded the recall.

There was a great bustle and scurry outside the walls of the ruined city as the squadron made ready to go on into the dune lands. The water-skins were bulging again, and the troopers checked and tightened the harnesses of their teams before mounting up.

Pharaoh Tamose looked over the heads of his staff as Taita and Nefer came through the gateway. He summoned Taita to his side with an inclination of his head. Together they walked out of earshot of the squadron officers. Lord Naja made to join them. Taita whispered a word to Pharaoh, then Tamose turned and sent Naja back with a curt word. Flushed with mortification, Naja shot a look at Taita that was sharp as a war arrow.

"You have offended Naja. Some day I might not be at hand to protect you," Pharaoh warned.

"We dare trust no man," Taita insisted. "Treachery tightens its coils around your palace. Until you return from this campaign in the north only the two of us must know where I am taking the prince."

"But Naja!" Pharaoh laughed dismissively. Naja was like a brother.

"Even Naja." Taita said no more. His suspicions were hardening into certainty, but he had not yet gathered all the evidence he would need to convince Pharaoh.

"Does the prince know why you are taking him into the desert?" Pharaoh asked.

"He knows only that we are going to further his instruction in the mysteries, and to capture his godbird."

"Good, Taita." Pharaoh nodded. "You were ever secretive but true. There is nothing more to say, for we have said it all. Now go, and may Horus spread his wings over you and Nefer."

"Look to your own back, Majesty, for in these days enemies stand behind you as well as to your front."

Pharaoh grasped the Magus's upper arm and squeezed. Then he went back to where Nefer waited beside the wheel of the royal chariot.

"It is my command that you go with Taita into the desert to capture your godbird, to prove your royal blood and your right one day to wear the double crown."

NEFER AND THE old man stood together beside the shattered walls of Gallala and watched the column fly past. Pharaoh led it, leaning back against the pull of the horses, his chest bare, linen skirts whipping around his muscular legs, the blue war crown on his head.

Next came Lord Naja, haughty and proud, the great recurved bow slung over his shoulder. Naja was one of Egypt's mightiest warriors, and his name had been given to him as a title of honour. Naja was the sacred cobra in the royal crown.

The two were silent long after the last chariot had disappeared and the dust had settled. Then Taita turned without a word and went to where their horses were tethered. He hiked up his kilts and swung up with the limber movement of a much younger man.

Nefer, as he vaulted up onto the back of his favourite colt, cast a last, longing glance at the feather of distant dust left on the northern horizon by the squadron, then firmly turned his back upon it. "Where are we going, Tata?" he demanded. "You promised to tell me once we were on the road."

Taita was always reticent and secretive, but seldom to this degree. "We are going to Gebel Nagara," he told him.

Nefer had never heard the name before, but he repeated it softly. It had a romantic ring. Excitement and anticipation made the back of his neck prickle, and he looked ahead into the desert where jagged hills stretched away to a horizon blue with heat haze and distance.

Taita looked on this terrible place with a sense of nostalgia and homecoming. It was into this wilderness that he had retired after the death of his beloved Queen Lostris, Nefer's grandmother. He was a physician and a surgeon, a master of the known sciences, and alone in the desert he had discovered the key to doorways of the mind beyond which few men ever journey. He had gone in a man but had emerged as a familiar of the great god Horus, adept at strange and arcane mysteries.

Taita had only returned to the world of men when his Queen Lostris had visited him in a dream as he slept in his hermit's cave at Gebel Nagara. "Darling Taita," she had whispered, as she touched his cheek, "you were one of the only two men I have ever loved. My husband Tanus is with me now, but before you can come to me also there is one more charge that I lay upon you."

"I am yours to command, mistress."

"In Thebes, my city of a hundred gates, this night is born a child, the son of my son. They will name this child Nefer, which means pure and perfect. My longing is that he may carry my blood and the blood of Tanus to the throne of Upper Egypt. But great perils already gather around him. He cannot succeed without your help. Go to Nefer. Go swiftly and stay with him until your task is completed. Do not fail me, Taita."

Taita awoke, his face wet with tears, gathered up his possessions, then strode away into the western desert, back towards the city of Thebes. That had been over fourteen years ago, and now he knew that the dark powers of which she had warned were gathering around them.

"Come!" he said to the boy. "Let us go down and take your godbird."

On the third night after leaving Gallala, Pharaoh Tamose halted the squadron to water the horses and to eat a hasty meal of sun-dried meat, dates and millet cakes. Then he ordered the mount-up. There was no sounding of the ram's horn trumpet now, for they were into Hyksosian territory.

The column started forward again at the trot. As they went on, the landscape changed dramatically. Below them lay the strip of dense vegetation that marked the course of the Nile. They had completed a wide circuit and were in the rear of the main Hyksosian army on the river. Although they were a tiny force against such an enemy, they were the best charioteers in the armies of Tamose, which made them the finest in the world. Moreover, they held the element of surprise.

It was almost two centuries since Egypt had been split apart. Since then either an Egyptian usurper or a foreign invader had ruled in the northern kingdom. It was Tamose's destiny to drive out the Hyksos and unite the two lands once more. Only then could he wear the double crown with the approval of the ancient gods.

The night air blew cool in his face, and his lance-bearer crouched low behind the dashboard to shield himself. The only sound was the crunch of the chariot wheels over the coarse gravel, the lances rattling softly in their scabbards.

Suddenly a wide wadi opened ahead of him and Pharaoh Tamose reined down the team. The wadi was the smooth roadway that would lead them down to the river. Pharaoh tossed the reins to his lance-bearer and vaulted down. He stretched his stiff, aching limbs as Naja's chariot came up behind him.

"From here the danger of discovery will be greater," Naja said. "Look down there." He pointed to where the dry riverbed debouched onto the plain below. "That is the village of El Wadun, where our spies will be waiting to lead us through the Hyksosian pickets. I will go ahead to the rendezvous to make safe the way. Wait here, Majesty, and I will return directly."

"I will go with you."

"I beg you. There may be treachery. You are Egypt. You are too precious to risk."

Pharaoh turned to look into the beloved lean and handsome face, and touched Naja's shoulder with trust and affection. "Go swiftly, and return as swiftly," he acceded.

Naja ran back to his chariot. He saluted as he wheeled past

where the king stood, and whipped up his speeding horses, down towards the village of El Wadun. When he had gone, Pharaoh walked back down the waiting column, speaking quietly to the troopers, calling many by name, encouraging and cheering them. Small wonder they loved him, and followed him so gladly wherever he led them.

WHEN LATER PHARAOH Tamose saw the chariot returning, he knew by the impetuous manner in which Naja drove that something was afoot. He ordered the squadron to mount and stand with drawn weapons, ready to meet any eventuality.

The moment the chariot drew level with Pharaoh, Naja sprang down.

"What's amiss?" Tamose demanded.

"A blessing from the gods," Naja told him. "They have delivered Apepi defenceless into our power."

"How is that possible?"

"My spies have led me to where the enemy king is encamped. His tents are set up just beyond the first line of hills." He pointed back with his sword.

"What is his strength?" Tamose could barely control his own excitement.

"With his usual arrogance he has a bodyguard of fewer than fifty, and half of them are asleep. He suspects nothing. A swift charge out of the darkness and we will have him in our grasp."

"Take me to where Apepi lies," Pharaoh commanded.

Naja led them, and the soft, silvery sands of the wadi muffled the sounds of the wheels. The squadron swept around the last bend and Naja raised his clenched fist high to order the halt. Pharaoh drew up alongside him.

Naja pointed up a pathway towards the crest of the hills. "On the far side is an oasis. His tents are set among the trees."

"We will take a small patrol with us to scout the camp. Only then can we plan our attack."

Naja had anticipated the order. He selected a scouting party of five troopers. "Muffle your scabbards," he ordered. "Make not a sound." Then, with his bow in his left hand, he stepped onto the pathway. Pharaoh came close behind him. They went upwards swiftly, until Naja saw the crossed branches of a thorn tree silhouetted against the dawn sky. He stopped abruptly.

It was here, not half an hour before, that he had met secretly with his cousin Trok, a Hyksosian general. Not even Pharaoh knew that Naja's mother had been Hyksosian. In the decades of their occupation, with a dearth of their own women to choose from, many Hyksos had taken Egyptian wives, and over the generations the bloodlines had become blurred.

Naja held up his right hand for silence.

"What is it?" Pharaoh whispered close behind him.

"I thought I heard voices on the crest," Naja answered, "speaking the Hyksosian tongue. Wait here, Majesty, while I clear the path ahead." Pharaoh and the five troopers squatted beside the path, while Naja went on stealthily and disappeared from view. The minutes passed slowly and Pharaoh began to fret. As a soft whistle came down to him he sprang to his feet and hefted his fabled blue sword.

"The way is clear," Pharaoh murmured. "Come, follow me."

Pharaoh went on upwards and reached a tall rock that blocked the pathway. He stepped round it then stopped abruptly. Lord Naja faced him at a distance of twenty paces. They were alone, hidden from the men who followed. Naja's bow was at full draw, a Hyksosian arrow aimed at Pharaoh's chest. This, then, was the foul thing that Taita, with his clairvoyant powers, had smelt in the air.

"May you live for ever!" Silently Naja mouthed the words as though they were a curse, and he loosed the arrow, which took Pharaoh high in the centre of his chest, throwing him against the red rock of the boulder. For a moment he clung to the rough surface but the flint arrowhead had pierced him through, and he began to slide down, his legs buckling under him. Naja sprang forward with a wild cry, "Ambush! Beware!" and he slipped one arm around Pharaoh's chest below the protruding arrow.

Supporting the dying king he bellowed again, "On me, the guards!" and two stout troopers appeared round the rock wall, responding to his cry. They saw at a glance how Pharaoh was struck and the unmistakable bright fletching feathers on the base of the Hyksosian arrow.

"Carry Pharaoh back to his chariot while I hold off the enemy," Naja ordered, and whirled around, pulling an arrow from his quiver and loosing it up the path towards the deserted summit, bellowing a challenge, then answering himself with a muffled counter-challenge in the Hyksosian language. He snatched up the blue sword from where Tamose had dropped it, then bounded back down the path and caught up with the small party of charioteers who were carrying the king away.

"It was a trap," Naja told them urgently. "The hilltop is alive with the enemy. Hurry! The king must not fall into their hands."

The troops below had heard the wild cries in the dawn, and the regimental surgeon was waiting for them beside Pharaoh's chariot. He had been trained by Taita, and, though lacking the old man's special magic, might be capable of staunching Pharaoh's terrible wound. Lord Naja would not risk that, so he ordered the surgeon away brusquely. "The enemy is hard upon us. There is no time for your quackery now. We must get him back to the safety of our own lines before we are overrun."

Tenderly he lifted the king onto the footplate of his own chariot. He snapped off the shaft of the Hyksosian arrow that protruded from the king's chest and held it aloft so that all his men could see it clearly. "This bloody instrument has struck down our Pharaoh. Our god and our king. He wrapped the arrow in a linen cloth, and placed it in the chariot. He would need to deliver it to the council in Thebes to substantiate his report on Pharaoh's death.

"A good man here to hold Pharaoh," Naja ordered.

While the king's own lance-bearer came forward, Naja unbuckled the sword-belt from around Pharaoh's waist and carefully stowed it in his own weapons bin.

The lance-bearer jumped onto the footplate and cradled Tamose's head, as the chariot wheeled in a circle then sped back up the wadi with the rest of the squadron. Facing forward so that none could see his expression, Naja laughed softly, the sound covered by the grinding wheels. Leaving the wadi, they raced on towards the dunes.

IT WAS MIDMORNING, and the blinding white sun was halfway up the sky before Naja allowed the column to halt and the surgeon to come forward again to examine the king. It did not need his special skills to tell that Pharaoh's spirit had long before left his body and started its journey to the underworld.

"Pharaoh is dead," the surgeon said quietly. A terrible cry of mourning ran through the column.

"The state is without a head," Naja told his captains. "Egypt is in dire peril. Ten of the fastest chariots must take Pharaoh's body back to Thebes with all haste. I shall lead them, for the council may wish me to take up the duties of regent to Prince Nefer, who must be found and informed of his own succession."

He unrolled a papyrus scroll, a map of the territory from Thebes down to Memphis. "You must split up into your troops and scour the countryside for the prince. I believe that Pharaoh sent him into the desert with the ancient eunuch to undertake the rituals of manhood, so we will concentrate our search there, around Gallala, where we last saw him."

Naja held them with a final command: "When you find Prince Nefer, bring him to me. Give him into no other hand but mine."

He ran back to his chariot and seized the reins, "Onwards!" he cried with a clenched fist. "Onwards to Thebes!"

FOLLOWING NAJA'S secret orders, a full legion of the Phat Guards, his own special regiment that was oath-bound to him, were waiting for him at the oasis of Boss, only two leagues from Thebes.

The guards' pickets saw the dust of the approaching chariots and stood to arms. The colonel, Asmor, and his officers turned out in full armour to meet Lord Naja.

"Lord Asmor!" Naja hailed him from the chariot. "I have dreadful news to take to Thebes. Pharaoh is killed by a Hyksosian arrow. Egypt is without a father." He raised his voice so that it carried clearly to the rear ranks. "Prince Nefer is a child still and not ready to rule. Egypt stands in desperate need of a regent to lead her." He paused and stared meaningfully at Colonel Asmor. Asmor lifted his chin in acknowledgment of the trust that Naja had placed in him.

Naja raised his voice to bellow: "If Pharaoh falls in battle, the army has the right by acclamation to appoint a regent in the field."

Asmor took a pace forward and turned to face the ranks of heavily armed guards. He removed his helmet. His face was dark and hard. He pointed his drawn sword to the sky and shouted, "Lord Naja! Hail to Lord Naja!"

There was a stunned silence before the legion erupted in a roar, "Hail to Lord Naja, Regent of Egypt!"

THE JOURNEY from Gallala took three days of hard riding. Naja was exhausted, yet he allowed himself only an hour to rest, bathe away the dust of the journey and change his apparel. He now wore a white linen skirt, with a pectoral plate of gold and semiprecious stones covering his bare, muscled chest. On his hip he carried the fabulous blue sword that he had taken from Pharaoh's dead body.

His bodyguard formed up around him, and with five thousand men at his back the new Regent of Egypt began his march on Thebes. Colonel Asmor rode as Naja's lance-bearer. He was young for the command of a full legion, but he had proved himself in battle and he was Naja's close companion. He, too, had Hyksosian blood in his veins, and there was nothing he would not do to hasten his patron Lord Naja's ascension to the throne of Egypt.

"What stands before us now, my old comrade?" Lord Naja asked him as they rode.

"The Yellow Flowers have cleared all but one of the princes of the House of Tamose from your path," Asmor answered, pointing with his lance to the hills across the grey, silt-laden Nile. "They lie in their tombs in the Valley of the Nobles."

Three years previously a plague had swept through the two kingdoms. The disease was named for the dreadful yellow lesions that covered the bodies of the stricken. Eight princesses and six princes of the House of Tamose had died. Of all Pharaoh's children, only one girl and Prince Nefer Memnon had survived. There were those who believed that they would have died also, had not the ancient Magus Taita cut their left upper arms and placed in their blood his magical charm against the Yellow Flowers.

Naja frowned. Even in this moment of his triumph he could still give thought to the strange powers possessed by the Magus. He had already lived so long that no one knew his age; some said a hundred years and others two hundred. Yet he still walked and ran and drove a chariot like a man in his prime. Surely the gods loved him, and had bestowed upon him the secret of life eternal.

Once he was Pharaoh, that secret would be the only thing that Naja lacked. Could he wring it out of Taita the Warlock? First, he must be captured and brought in along with Prince Nefer. The chariots Naja had sent to scout the eastern deserts would bring them back.

The gates of Thebes were thrown open as soon as the sentries recognised the blue standard, and the citizens ran out to meet them. But the welcoming cries soon gave way to wild ululations of mourning when they heard the shouts of the leading charioteers: "Pharaoh is dead! He has been slain by the Hyksos."

The wailing crowds followed the chariot that carried the royal corpse to the funerary temple. The rest of the usually swarming city was almost deserted, and Naja galloped his chariot team swiftly through the narrow, crooked streets to the river palace. He knew that every member of the council would hurry to the assembly chamber as soon as they heard the dreadful news. At the entrance to the palace gardens, Asmor and fifty men of the bodyguard formed up around Naja. They marched in close order through the inner courtyard, past the ponds of the water garden filled with hyacinth.

The arrival of the armed men took the council unawares. The doors to the chamber were unguarded, and only a few members were assembled. Naja paused in the doorway and looked them over. Menset and Talla were old and past their once formidable powers; Cinka had always been weak and vacillating.

"Noble lords!" Naja greeted them as he strode into the chamber. "Pharaoh is dead. He was cut down by a Hyksosian arrow while storming the enemy stronghold above El Wadun."

The council members gawked at him in silence. Instantly Naja realised his opportunity. "I am the regent of the royal Prince Nefer." he thundered. "I was acclaimed by my legions in the field. My noble lords, is there any man among you who would question this?" He looked at each in turn and they dropped their eyes: there was no man to give them direction and the Phat Guards stood shoulder to shoulder around the wall of the chamber.

"My lord Menset"—Naja singled out the president of the council—"does the council ratify the appointment of Lord Naja as the Regent of Egypt?"

Menset raised his eyes and looked around at his fellow members, but not one would catch his eye. "The president and all the councillors of this assembly acknowledge the new Regent of Egypt," he whispered at last.

"I accept the duty and heavy responsibility you have placed upon me." Naja mounted the dais to the throne. "As my first official pronouncement in my capacity of Regent in Council I wish to describe to you the gallant death of the divine Pharaoh Tamose." He paused significantly, then for the next hour he related in detail his version of the fatal campaign. "His last words to me as I carried him down the hill were, 'Care for my only remaining son. Guard my son Nefer until he is man enough to wear the double crown.

Take my small daughter under your wings, and see that no harm befalls her.'"

It took Lord Naja some moments to bring his grief under control. Then he went on firmly, "I will not fail the god who was my friend and my pharaoh. Already I have sent my chariots into the wilderness to search for Prince Nefer and bring him back to Thebes. As soon as he arrives we will set him on the throne, and place the scourge and the sceptre in his hands."

There was the first murmur of approval among the councillors, and Naja continued, "Now, send for the princess."

When she came hesitantly through the main doors, Heseret smiled shyly around this formidable gathering. She had inherited in full measure the celebrated beauty of her grandmother, Queen Lostris. Her skin was milky, her limbs were smooth and shapely, and there were intriguing lights in her huge dark green eyes.

"Come forward, my pretty darling." Naja rose from the throne, and went down to meet her. His voice and his expression were tragic. "You must be brave now, and remember that you are a princess of the royal house, because I have bitter news for you. Pharaoh, your father, is dead." For a minute Heseret did not seem to understand, then she let out the high keening wail of mourning.

Naja put his arms around her and led her to sit at the foot of the throne. "The distress of the royal princess is plain for all to see," he told the assembly. "The trust and the duty that Pharaoh placed upon me is equally plain. As I have taken Prince Nefer Memnon into my care, now I take Princess Heseret under my protection."

Chapter Two

NEFER SAT in the shadow of the cliff that towered above Gebel Nagara. He had not moved since the sun had first shown its upper rim above the mountains across the valley. At first the effort of remaining still had made his skin itch as though insects were crawling upon it. But he knew Taita was watching him, so he had forced his wayward body into a state of exalted awareness, his every sense tuned to the wilderness about him. He could smell the water that rose from its secret spring in the cleft in the cliff. It came up a slow drop at a time and dripped into a basin in the rock. Much life was supported by this trickle of water: butterfly and beetle, serpent and lizard, the speckled pigeons that nested on high ledges, all drank here. It was because of this precious pool that Taita had brought him here to wait for his godbird.

They had begun to make a net on the day of their arrival at Gebel Nagara. Taita had bought the silk in Thebes. It was stronger than thongs of leather but almost invisible to the eye.

When the net was ready Taita had insisted that the boy catch the decoys himself. So, in the baking daylight out on the valley floor, Nefer and Taita had studied the route up the cliff to the ledge where the pigeons roosted. When darkness fell Taita had sat beside a small fire by the entrance to a cave at the base of the cliff, and Nefer had started the precarious climb. He seized two birds while they were still disorientated by the darkness, and brought them down in the leather saddlebag slung on his back.

They selected a spot close to the base of the cliff, but exposed enough to make the birds clearly visible from the sky, and tethered the pigeons by the leg with horsehair thread and a wooden peg driven into the hard earth. Then they spread the gossamer net above them, supported on stalks of dried elephant grass, which would snap under the stoop of the godbird.

When all was set up to Taita's satisfaction, they began the long wait. Soon the pigeons became accustomed to captivity, and pecked greedily at the millet that Nefer scattered for them. Then they sunned and dusted themselves contentedly under the silken net. One hot, sun-riven day succeeded the next, and still they waited.

In the cool of the evening they brought the pigeons into the cave, and then they hunted for food. They grilled gazelle steaks over the fire. The cave had been Taita's retreat during all the years after the death of Queen Lostris when he had lived here as a hermit. It was his place of power.

They had been at Gebel Nagara for many days before Nefer began to understand that they had not come here to find the godbird alone. Taita was teaching him control over his body and being, teaching him to look inward, to listen to the silence and hear whispers to which others were deaf. Even the long hours of waiting beside the decoys were a lesson.

On the twentieth morning of their stay, Nefer took up his position over the decoys. As always, he was deeply aware of the presence of Taita, whose eyes were closed and who seemed to be dozing in the sunlight. His skin was crisscrossed with innumerable fine wrinkles and dappled with age spots. It looked as delicate as the finest papyrus parchment. His face was hairless, no trace of beard or eyebrows; only fine lashes, colourless as glass, surrounded his eyes. Nefer reached out to touch the old man's arm as he slept. Nefer had heard his father say that it was because Taita was a eunuch, gelded after puberty, that his face was beardless and little marked by the passage of time, but he was certain that there were more reasons for the persistence of his strength and life force.

Suddenly Taita's eyes opened, focused and aware. Nefer knew that he had not been asleep at all, but that all his powers had been concentrated on bringing in the godbird to the decoys.

Chastened, he composed himself, and brought his mind and body under control again as Taita had taught him. It was like passing through a secret doorway. Suddenly Nefer was blessed with a marvellous sense that he, too, hung above the world and saw everything happening below him. He saw Taita and himself sitting beside the well of Gebel Nagara, and the desert stretching away around them. He saw cities and kingdoms, the machinations of evil men, and the striving of the just and good. In that moment he was aware of his destiny with an intensity that almost overwhelmed his courage.

In that same moment he knew that his godbird would come on this day, for he was ready to receive it, aware with every fibre of his being.

The royal falcon was such a rare creature that few men had ever seen it in the wild. Possession of the bird was proof that Pharaoh had the divine approval of the god Horus to reign in Egypt.

And now the bird was here. He heard its cry, a faint lament, almost lost in the immensity of sky and desert. Seconds later the falcon called again, directly overhead, its voice shriller and more savage.

Now the pigeons were wild with terror, leaping against the threads that secured them to the pegs, while high overhead Nefer heard the falcon begin its stoop on them, the wind singing over its wings in a rising note. He looked up and saw the bird drop against the aching blue of the desert sky. It was a thing of divine beauty. Its wings were folded back, and its head was thrust forward. The strength and power of the creature made Nefer gasp aloud. He wanted to possess it with a longing he had never imagined possible.

He braced himself for the moment of impact. Beside him he felt Taita do the same. The falcon dropped like a thrown javelin, and tore into the pigeons with both sets of talons.

Then Nefer heard an explosive hiss of air. Something huge and glittering black whipped out from behind the net and slammed into the falcon. He saw the thick, glittering coils of a gigantic black cobra. The snake's head was raised, its hood marked with a bold pattern of black and white. Its fathomless black eyes held Nefer in a mesmeric stare. He tried to scream, but no sound came from his throat. Each scale was polished like a jewel, each coil, wrapped around the falcon, was as thick as Nefer's arm, and slowly they revolved upon themselves.

Without thought, Nefer hurled his leather bag away from him. The cobra's fangs hooked into the leather and the bag and the snake fell away together, the sinuous body still coiling and whipping furiously. It bounced away over the rocks until Nefer lost sight of it among the grey boulders.

"Oh, Taita. It was horrible. It killed my godbird."

"Gently, lad. Drink." He offered the water-skin. "Thanks be to the great god who protected you," Taita murmured. "With this cobra apparition, Horus has sent you a portent of terrible dangers. That was no natural serpent." He turned and walked back to the entrance of the cave. Nefer followed him slowly, his heart leaden with disappointment. In the gloom of the cave Taita seated himself on the stone ledge below the back wall, and leaned forward to build up the smoky fire of thorn branches until it burst into flames. Then he sighed, and said softly, almost sadly, "I must work the Mazes of Ammon Ra."

Nefer watched in awe as Taita went through the ritual of preparing the Mazes. First he crushed herbs and poured boiling water over them. The steam that rose was so pungent it made Nefer's eyes water.

While the mixture cooled, Taita brought the tanned leather bag that contained the Mazes from its hiding place at the back of the cave. The Mazes comprised ten ivory discs, each carved with one of the ten symbols of power. Taita rubbed the discs gently between his fingers as he began to chant the incantation to Ammon Ra, and between each verse he blew on them to endow them with his life force. When they had taken on the warmth of his own body he passed them to Nefer.

"Hold them and breathe upon them," he urged, and while Nefer obeyed these instructions, Taita began to sway as he retreated into the secret places in his mind. He was already in the trance when Nefer stacked the Mazes in front of him, then offered up the infusion to him. Taita drank it to the last drop, and in the firelight his face turned white as chalk. He subsided onto the floor of the cave, and started to twitch and groan, and the sweat streamed down his face. His eyes opened and rolled back in their sockets until only the whites glared blindly into the dark shadows of the cave.

Nefer knew there was nothing he could do for the old man now. Taita had journeyed far into the shadowy places where Nefer could not reach him. Hardly able to bear the terrible suffering that the Mazes inflicted upon the Magus, Nefer lay down beside him, and after a while he fell into a sleep that was haunted by nightmares.

When he awoke, dawn was glimmering at the entrance to the cave. Taita was sitting at the fire, still looking pale and sick. "What did you see, Tata," the boy asked.

"It was obscured," Taita told him, and Nefer knew that the omen had been unpropitious.

"Explain it to me, Tata," Nefer insisted.

There was deep anguish in his voice, so Taita softened his answer. "There are mysteries here. I saw their shadows in my vision. This is a thing beyond the natural order."

Taita paused and looked to the sky, as if in deep thought. "First we must fly from the great dangers that beset us. The cobra has returned from the shadows from which it sprang."

Nefer shivered with superstitious awe, then scrambled up onto the back of his colt.

Taita led the way. By the time the sun was above the horizon they had left Gebel Nagara far behind them.

Nefer knew well that when Taita was in this mood it was wasted effort to speak to him, but he urged his horse alongside and pointed out respectfully, "Tata, this is not the way to Thebes."

"We are not going back there."

Nefer was puzzled. "Why not?"

Taita turned his head and looked at the boy with such pity that he was silenced. "I will explain when we are in a safe place."

Avoiding the crests of hills, where they might be silhouetted on the skyline, Taita wove a path through the gorges and valleys. Always he headed east, away from Egypt and the Nile, towards the sea.

The sun was setting before he reined in his mare and spoke. "The main caravan road lies just beyond the next line of hills. We must cross it, but enemies may be watching for us there."

They left the horses tethered in a hidden wadi, then climbed cautiously to the crest of the hills and found a vantage point behind a bank of purple shale from which they could look down onto the caravan road below.

"We will lie here until dark," Taita explained. He swept another look along the road below them, and immediately ducked his head. "Someone coming!" he warned.

Nefer flattened himself behind the shale bank and they watched the column of dust coming swiftly down the caravan road from the west. By this time the valley was in deep shadow and the sky was filled with all the glorious shades of the sunset.

"They are moving fast. Those are not merchants, they are fighting chariots," Nefer said. "Yes, I can see them now." His bright young eyes picked out the shape of the leading chariot. "They are not Hyksos," he went on. "They are ours. A cohort of the Phat Guards! We are safe, Tata!"

Taita reached up a bony hand and hauled him down violently. "Those are the minions of the cobra. Hurry! They must not catch us." He dragged the boy off the ridge and started down the slope, jumping from rock to rock. He reached the horses first, and was on the mare's back in a single leap.

"What is happening, Tata?" Nefer panted.

"Mount! No time to talk."

As they galloped out of the wadi, Nefer shot a longing look back over his shoulder, and saw the leading charioteer. "That is Hilto, Tata. I know his face so well. He is a good man."

Hilto was a famous warrior, who wore the Gold of Valour, but Taita told Nefer sternly, "Don't be deceived. Trust nobody."

Obediently Nefer rode on into the wilderness of broken rock. The faint sounds behind them dwindled and were snuffed out by the eternal silence of the desert. Before they had gone much further darkness forced them to dismount and walk through the difficult places where the twisting path narrowed.

At last they had to stop to water and rest the horses. They sat close together and, with his dagger, Taita sliced a loaf of millet bread, and they munched it as they talked softly.

"Tell me of your vision, Tata. What did you truly see when you worked the Mazes of Ammon Ra?"

"I told you. They were obscured."

"I know that is not true." Nefer shook his head. "You said that to protect me." He shivered from the chill of the night and a sense of dread. "You saw something of terrible portent. That is why we are fleeing now. You must tell me all your vision. I must understand what is happening to us."

"Yes, you are right," Taita agreed at last. "It is time for you to know."

He put out one thin arm and drew Nefer close under his shawl. He seemed to be collecting his thoughts, and then at last he spoke.

"In my vision I saw a great tree growing on the banks of Mother Nile. It was a mighty tree and its blooms were blue as hyacinth and over it hung the double crown of the Upper and Lower Kingdoms. In its shade were all the multitudes of Egypt. The tree gave them all protection, and they prospered mightily and were content."

"That was a good vision." Eagerly Nefer translated it. "The tree must have been Pharaoh, my father. The colour of the House of Tamose is blue, and my father wears the double crown. But then what did you see, Tata?"

"I saw a serpent in the muddy waters of the river, swimming towards where the tree stood. It was a great cobra. And it crawled from the waters of the Nile and climbed into the tree, twisting itself around the tree, supporting it and giving it strength."

"That I do not understand," Nefer whispered.

"Then the cobra reared up above the uppermost branches of the tree, struck down and buried its fangs in the trunk."

"Sweet Horus." Nefer shuddered. "What did you see then, Tata?"

"I saw the tree wither. I saw the cobra still reared triumphantly on high, but now it wore on its evil brow the double crown. The tree began to throw out green shoots. As they appeared the serpent struck at them, and they, too, were poisoned. But one grew in secret beneath the surface of the earth, until it was strong. Then it burst out like a mighty vine and locked itself in conflict with the cobra. Although the cobra attacked it with all its strength and venom, still it survived."

"What was the end of the conflict, Tata? Which of them triumphed? Which one wore the double crown at the end?"

"I did not see the conflict's end. It was obscured in the dust of war."

Nefer was silent. Then he began to shake and Taita realised he was weeping. At last Nefer spoke, with a dreadful certainty. "Pharaoh is dead. My father is dead. The poisoned tree was Pharaoh. It was the same message at the cave. The dead falcon was Pharaoh. My father is dead, killed by the cobra."

Taita could not answer. All he could do was tighten his grip around Nefer's shoulders, and try to comfort him.

"And I am the green shoot of the tree," Nefer went on. "You saw this. You know that the cobra is waiting to destroy me as he did my father. That is why you would not let the soldiers take me back to Thebes. You know that the cobra waits for me there."

"You are right, Nefer. We cannot return to Thebes until you are strong enough to defend yourself. We must fly from Egypt. There are lands and mighty kings to the east. It is my purpose to go to them."

"But who is the cobra? Did you not see his face in the vision?"

"We know that he stands close to your father's throne, for in the vision he was entwined with the tree and gave it support." He paused, and then went on, "Naja is the name of the cobra."

Nefer stared at him. "Naja!" he whispered. "Naja! Now I understand why we cannot return to Thebes."

Despite his grief for his father, Nefer slept at last, but Taita roused him in the darkness before dawn. They mounted again and rode eastwards until the ground fell away behind them and Nefer smelt the salt of the sea on the wind.

"At the port of Seged we will find a ship to take us across to the land of the Hurrians," Taita told him. "King Sargon of Babylon is bound in treaty to your father against the Hyksos."

Ahead of them the sun came up in a furnace glow, and when they topped the next rise they saw the sea below them. Taita turned to look back and stiffened as he made out not one but four separate plumes of yellow dust rising on the plain behind them.

"Hilto, again," he exclaimed. "Now he has thrown out a ring of chariots in an extended line to sweep for our tracks. He did not need a necromancer to tell him we would be heading east for the coast."

Swiftly he looked in every direction for cover. Across the open plain he picked out an insignificant fold of ground that might offer concealment. "Dismount!" he ordered Nefer. "We must keep as low as possible and raise no dust."

When they reached the hidden ground, Taita coaxed the horses to lie flat on their sides. Then he and Nefer lay beside them and watched the encircling columns of dust sweep across the plain.

"They won't be able to pick out our tracks on the stony ground, will they?" Nefer asked.

Taita grunted. He was watching the approach of the nearest chariot. In the dancing mirage it seemed insubstantial, wavering and distorted as an image seen through water. But it came on until they could make out the men on the footplate more clearly. Suddenly Taita muttered unhappily. "They have a Nubian scout with them." It was said that these scouts could follow the track left by a swallow flying through the air.

The tall black man was made even taller by the headdress of herons' feathers he wore. Five hundred cubits from where they lay concealed, the Nubian brought the chariot to a peremptory halt and jumped down. He had lost the tracks where they turned onto stony ground. Bent almost double, he circled out over the bare earth. After a few moments, the Nubian straightened with a fresh air of purpose, and gazed straight in their direction.

"He has found the twist in our tracks," Nefer said, and they watched the chariot pull in behind the Nubian as he started towards them over the rocky ground.

The boy watched in trepidation as the chariot and its outrider came on steadily. The charioteer was standing high on the footplate and Nefer recognised him as Hilto.

When he finally saw Taita and Nefer, Hilto leapt out of the chariot and went down on one knee.

"Prince Nefer! We have searched for you these thirty days. Thank great Horus and Osiris, we have found you at last." He cried out, in a voice pitched to giving commands on the battlefield, "Pharaoh Tamose is dead! Hail, Pharaoh Nefer Seti. May you live for ever."

Seti was the prince's divine name, given to him at birth but not used until this moment.

"Pharaoh! We have come to bear you to the Holy City."

"What if I should choose not to go with you, Colonel Hilto?" Nefer asked.

Hilto looked distressed. "Pharaoh, it is the strictest order of the Regent of Egypt that you be brought to Thebes. I must obey that order, even at the risk of your displeasure."

Nefer glanced sideways at Taita. "What must I do?"

"We must go with them."

THEY BEGAN the return to Thebes with an escort of fifty fighting chariots led by Hilto. Under strict orders the column rode first to the oasis of Boss. Fast horsemen had been sent ahead to Thebes and Lord Naja, the Regent of Egypt, had come out from the city to the oasis to meet the young Pharaoh Nefer Seti.

On the fifth day the squadron of chariots, dusty and battered from months in the wilderness, trotted into the oasis. Nefer stood between Hilto and Taita on the footplate of the leading chariot. His clothing was ragged and his thick locks were matted.

Hilto drove the chariot down the long alley formed by a full regiment of Phat Guards, who cheered Nefer spontaneously. They had loved his father, and now they loved him.

In the centre of the oasis there was an assembly of multicoloured tents. In front of the royal tent Lord Naja, surrounded by courtiers, nobles and priests, waited to receive the king. He was mighty in the power and grace of regency, glistening and beautiful in gold and precious stones, redolent of sweet unguents and fragrant lotions.

On his left hand stood Heseret, the princess of the royal House of Tamose. Her face was pearly white with make-up, eyes huge and dark with kohl, and her skirts were so heavy with pearls and gold thread that she stood as stiffly as a carved doll.

As Hilto brought the chariot to a halt in front of him, Lord Naja stepped forward and led Nefer by the hand to the dais of the council, carved from precious black woods and inlaid with mother-of-pearl. He placed him upon it, then went down on his knees and kissed Nefer's feet. "As your regent I salute you, Pharaoh."

He stood up and lifted Nefer to his feet, stripped away the torn kilt to reveal the pharaonic cartouche on the smooth skin of his inner thigh. Taita had tattooed the design, and it was a miniature masterpiece that would forever endorse Nefer's claim to the double crown. Naja turned the boy slowly so that everyone in the audience could see it clearly.

"Hail, Pharaoh Seti, god and son of the gods. Behold thy sign.

Look upon this mark, all the nations of the earth, and tremble. Bow down before the might of Pharaoh."

A great shout went up from the soldiers and courtiers packed around the dais. "Hail, Pharaoh! May he live for ever."

Naja led the princess forward, and she knelt before her brother to take her oath of allegiance. Then, one by one, the mighty lords of Egypt came forward to take the loyal oath. The ceremony ended when Lord Naja clapped his hands. "Pharaoh has come on a long journey. He must rest before leading the procession into the city."

He took Nefer's hand and led him into the spacious royal tent where the master of the wardrobe, the perfumers and hairdressers, the keeper of the royal jewels, the valets, manicurists, masseurs and the maids of the bath were waiting to receive him.

Taita had determined to stay at the boy's side where he could protect him. He tried unobtrusively to include himself among this entourage, but almost immediately a sergeant-at-arms confronted him. "Greetings, Lord Taita. The Regent of Egypt has sent for you."

Lord Naja's tent was even larger and more luxuriously appointed than Pharaoh's. He sat on a throne decorated in gold and silver and the sandy floor was covered with woollen rugs, woven in wonderful colours. Incense burned in silver pots suspended on chains from the ridgepole of the tent, and there were open glass vases filled with perfume on the low table in front of the throne.

At the entrance to the tent, Taita knelt to make obeisance. There was a hum of speculation as he rose to his feet. The foreign ambassadors stared at him curiously, and the warriors and priests nodded and leaned close together as they told each other, "It is the Magus, the holy Taita, adept of the Mazes."

Lord Naja looked up from the papyrus he was scanning and smiled. He was truly a handsome man, with sculpted features and sensitive lips. His nose was straight and narrow, and his eyes were the colour of golden agate, lively and intelligent.

Swiftly Taita surveyed the ranks of men who now sat closest to the throne. Many familiar faces were missing, and many others had emerged from obscurity into the sunshine of the regent's goodwill. Not least of these was Asmor of the Phat Guards.

"Come forward, Lord Taita." Naja's voice was pleasant and low. Taita moved towards the throne and the ranks of courtiers opened to let him pass. The regent smiled down at him. "Know you that you stand high in our favour. You have given Prince Nefer invaluable instruction and training. Now that the prince has become Pharaoh Seti, he will stand in even greater need of your guiding hand."

"May he live for ever," Taita responded.

Lord Naja gestured. "Take your seat here, in the shadow of my throne. Even I will have much need of your experience and wisdom when it comes to ordering the affairs of Pharaoh."

"The royal regent does me more honour than I deserve." Taita turned a gentle face to Lord Naja. It was prudent never to let your hidden enemy recognise your animosity. He took the seat that was offered him and listened as the business of the regency proceeded.

"We move on now to an important royal matter," Lord Naja said. "I come to the consideration of the well-being and status of Princess Heseret. I have consulted with the members of the council. All are agreed that, for her own good, I should take Princess Heseret in marriage. As my wife, she will come under my protection. The ceremony will take place on the day of the next full moon after the burial of Pharaoh Tamose, and the coronation of his heir, Prince Nefer Seti."

Taita remained unmoving, his face blank, but he felt chilled to his bones. He knew that Lord Naja was intent on making himself a member of the royal House of Tamose, and thus the next in line of succession. There remained only twelve days of the required seventy for the royal embalming of the dead pharaoh. Immediately after the interment of Tamose, the coronation of his successor and the wedding of his surviving daughter would take place. Then the cobra would strike again. Taita felt the certainty of it. He was roused from his preoccupation when the regent declared the levee closed, and retired through the tent flap behind the throne. Taita rose with the others to leave the tent.

Colonel Asmor stepped forward to stop him with a smile and a courteous bow. "Lord Naja asks you not to leave. He invites you to a private audience."

There was no point refusing the summons, and so Taita allowed Asmor to lead him to the back of the tent and through to a smaller, single-roomed tent, a place of secret council. At a command from Asmor, the guards posted at the entrance stood aside and the colonel ushered Taita into the shaded interior.

Naja looked up from the bronze bowl in which he was washing

his hands. "You are welcome, Magus." He waved to the pile of cushions in the centre of the rug-covered floor. While Taita seated himself, Naja nodded to Asmor, who went to take up position at the tent opening, his sickle sword drawn. There were only the three of them in the tent, and their conversation would not be overheard.

Naja had discarded his jewellery and insignia of office. He was affable and friendly, and indicated the tray of sweetmeats that stood between them. "Please refresh yourself."

Taita's instinct was to decline, but he knew that to refuse would advertise his hostility, and alert Naja to his deadly opposition. Instead, he inclined his head in thanks.

"You are a person of inestimable value," Naja told him. "You have faithfully served three pharaohs and all have relied on your advice without question."

"You overestimate my worth, my lord Regent. I am an old man and feeble."

Naja smiled. "Old? Yes, you are old. I have heard it said that you are more than two hundred years old." Taita inclined his head, neither confirming nor denying it. "But feeble, no! All men know that your wisdom is boundless. Even the secrets of eternal life are yours."

The flattery was blatant and Taita searched behind it for the hidden reason, tuned his mind to catch the other man's thoughts. They were fleeting but he captured one entire, and suddenly understood what Naja wanted from him. The secret of eternal life. The knowledge gave him power, and the way ahead opened before him like the gates of a captured city.

"My lord, two hundred years is not life eternal." Taita spread his hands deprecatingly, and dropped his eyes.

"We will speak of these deep matters another time." There was a triumphant light in Naja's yellow eyes. "But now there is something else I would ask of you. It would be a way for you to prove that my good opinion of you is fully justified. Taita, beloved of kings and gods, I wish you to work the Mazes of Ammon Ra for me."

He twists and turns like an eel, Taita thought. And I once believed him to be a dull clod of a soldier. He has been able to hide his ambition from all of us. Not only the double crown of Egypt and eternal life! He wishes also to have the future revealed to him, Taita marvelled. He nodded humbly and replied, "My lord Naja, I have never worked the Mazes for anyone who was not a queen or a pharaoh, or one who was not destined to sit upon the throne of Egypt."

"It may well be that one such person asks you now," said Lord Naja, with deep significance in his tone.

Great Horus has delivered him to me. I have him in my hands, Taita thought, and said, "I bow to the wishes of Pharaoh's regent."

"Will you work the Mazes for me this very day?"

"No man should enter the Mazes lightly," Taita demurred. "It will take time to prepare for the journey into the future."

"How long?" Naja's disappointment was evident.

Taita clasped his forehead in a pantomime of deep thought. Let him sniff the bait for a while, he thought. It will make him more eager to swallow the hook. At last he looked up. "On the first day of the festival of the Bull of Apis."

THE NEXT MORNING, when he emerged from the great tent for his ceremonial journey to Thebes, Pharaoh Seti was transformed. His dark curls had been shampooed and combed until they shone with russet highlights. On top of them he wore a circlet of gold depicting Nekhbet, the vulture goddess, and Naja, the cobra. On his chin was the false beard of kingship. His false fingernails were of beaten gold, and there were gold sandals on his feet. On his chest was one of the most precious of the crown jewels of Egypt: the pectoral medallion of Tamose, a jewelled portrait of the god Horus the falcon. He walked with a stately tread for one so young, carrying the scourge and the sceptre crossed over his heart, and Lord Naja walked a pace behind him, splendid with jewels and awesome with authority.

Next came the princess, with the golden feathers of the goddess Isis on her head, and from throat to ankles she was encased in a long dress, the linen so fine and transparent that the sunlight struck through it. Heseret's body was moulded into voluptuous curves, her breasts rosy-tipped through the diaphanous folds.

Pharaoh mounted the processional carriage and took his seat on the elevated throne. Lord Naja stood at his right hand, and the princess sat at his feet.

Companies of priests from the fifty temples of Thebes fell in ahead, strumming the lyre, beating the drum, sounding the horn, chanting praises and supplications to the gods.

Asmor's bodyguard took up their positions in the procession, and after them came Hilto's squadron of chariots, all freshly burnished and decked with pennants and flowers. The horses were curried until their hides glowed, and ribbons were plaited into their manes. The bullocks that followed in the traces of the royal carriage were all of unblemished white. Their widespread horns and even their hoofs were covered with gold leaf.

A thousand warriors of the Phat Guards fell in behind them and burst into the anthem of praise. The populace of Thebes had opened the main gates of the city in welcome and were lining the tops of the walls. From a mile outside it they had covered the dusty surface of the road with palm fronds, straw and flowers.

The procession passed through the gates, with the crowds dancing with joy, filling the narrow streets so that the pace of the royal carriage was that of a giant tortoise. It was late afternoon before they reached the docks at the riverside where the royal barge waited to ferry Pharaoh's party across to the Palace of Memnon. Once they had gone on board, two hundred rowers in massed ranks plied their paddles. When they reached the west bank another royal carriage bore Nefer through the crowds to the funerary temple of his father, Pharaoh Tamose. He rode up the causeway, lit on both sides by bonfires, and the uproar was deafening as Pharaoh dismounted and climbed the stairway into the Hall of Sorrow, that holy place where Tamose's mummy lay on its embalming slab of black diorite.

Lord Naja took up his position on the far side of the diorite slab, facing Nefer, and the high priest stood at the head of the dead king. When all was in readiness two priests drew aside the linen sheet that covered the corpse, and Nefer recoiled involuntarily as he looked down on his father.

For all the weeks after his death, while Nefer and Taita had been in the desert, the embalmers had been at work on the king's body. Now as desiccated as firewood, it had been bound up. The linen bandages were laid on it in an intricate design, as incantations to the gods were chanted by choirs of priests. Under them were placed precious talismans and amulets, and each layer was painted with resins that dried to a metallic hardness. Only the head was left uncovered, upon which four of the most skilful artists of the guild of embalmers, using wax and cosmetics, had restored the king's features to lifelike beauty.

They had replaced the eyes with perfect replicas of rock crystal and obsidian that seemed endowed with life and intelligence, so that now Nefer gazed into them with awe, expecting to see his father's pupils widen in recognition. The lips were shaped and rouged so that at any moment they might smile, and his painted skin looked silken and warm, as though bright blood still ran beneath it. His hair had been washed and set in the familiar dark ringlets that Nefer remembered so well.

The high priest came to Nefer's side and placed a golden spoon in his hand. Nefer had been coached in the ritual, but his hand trembled as he placed the spoon on his father's lips and recited, "I open thy lips that thou might have the power of speech once more." He touched his father's nose with the spoon. "I open thy nostrils that thou might breathe once more." He touched each eye. "I open thine eyes that thou might behold the glory of the world to come."

When at last it was done, the embalmers wrapped the head and painted it with aromatic resins. Then they laid a golden mask over the blind face, and once more it glowed with splendid life.

For the rest of that night Nefer stayed beside the golden sarcophagus, praying and burning incense, entreating the gods to take his father and seat him in the midst of the pantheon.

THAT NIGHT TAITA went out and prayed to Horus for guidance. At dawn he returned to the palace, and had barely time to bathe and change his raiment before he hurried to the royal bedchamber. At the door his way was barred by the two guards, who crossed their spears across the entrance.

Taita was astonished. This had never happened before. He glared at the sergeant of the guard, who dropped his eyes. "I mean no offence, mighty Magus. It is on the specific orders of the commander of the bodyguard, Colonel Asmor. No person not approved by the regent is allowed in the royal presence."

Taita strode down the terrace to where Naja was at breakfast with his particular favourites and toadies. "My lord Naja, you are fully aware that I was appointed by Pharaoh's own father as his tutor and mentor. I was given the right of access at any time."

"That was many years ago, good Magus," Naja replied smoothly, as he accepted a peeled grape from a slave. "Pharaoh Seti is a child no more. In future he looks to me, his regent, for guidance." Naja stood up from the breakfast board. His bodyguard closed in around him so that Taita was forced to fall back.

The old man watched as Naja's entourage set off towards the council chamber, then turned aside and sat down on the coping of one of the fish pools to ponder this development.

Naja had isolated Nefer. He was a prisoner in his own palace. Once again Taita considered the idea of flight from Egypt, to spirit Nefer away across the desert to the protection of a foreign power until he had grown strong enough to return to claim his birthright. However, he was certain that Naja not only barred the door to the royal quarters but that every escape route from Thebes and Egypt would have already been closed.

There seemed no easy solution, and, after an hour of deep thought, Taita rose to his feet. The guards at the door to the council chamber stood aside for him, and Taita went down the aisle and took his accustomed seat on the front bench.

Wearing the light crown of Upper Egypt, Nefer was seated on the dais beside his regent. The council was considering the latest reports from the northern front, where the Hyksosian King Apepi had recaptured Abnub after a siege that had lasted the previous three years. Taita found the council was bitterly divided in every consideration of the crisis, and he felt more strongly than ever that this war was a running abscess in Egypt's body. Exasperated, he rose quietly and left the council chamber. There was nothing further he could accomplish here, for they were still wrangling over who should be given command of the northern armies to replace the dead Pharaoh.

Next he went to the women's quarters of the palace. Because he was a eunuch he could pass through the gates, which were barred to other men. It was three days since the princess had learned that she was so soon to become a bride, and Taita knew he should have visited her before. She would be confused, sorely in need of his comfort and advice.

When he entered the courtyard, Heseret, who had been strumming her lyre, looked up at him with a sad little smile. "Darling Taita, I am so glad you have come."

"I am sorry to have kept you waiting, moon of all my nights." She smiled faintly at the pet name. "What service do you wish of me?"

"You must go to Lord Naja, and present him with my sincere apologies, but I cannot marry him."

She was so much like her grandmother had been at the same age. Lostris, too, had saddled him with an impossible task. Heseret now turned her enormous green eyes on him. "You see, I have already promised Meren that I will be his wife."

Meren was a boon companion of Prince Nefer. Taita had noticed him looking at Heseret with calf's eyes, but had never suspected that she returned his feelings.

"Heseret, I have explained to you many times that you are not like other girls. You are a princess royal. Your marriage cannot be undertaken in the light fancy of youth. It is something of dire political consequence."

"You don't understand, Taita," Heseret said softly. "I love Meren, I have loved him since I was little. I want to marry *him*, not Lord Naja."

"I cannot overrule the decree of the Regent of Egypt," he tried to explain, but she shook her head and smiled at him.

"You are so wise, Taita. You will think of something. You always do," she told him, and he felt as though his heart would break.

"LORD TAITA, I refuse to discuss your access to Pharaoh or my impending marriage to the royal princess. In both these matters my mind is set." To emphasise that he had closed the subject, Naja returned his full attention to the scroll spread on the writing table in front of him. Enough time passed for a flock of wild geese to rise from the swampland on the east bank and pass over the palace gardens where they sat. At last Taita brought his eyes down from the sky, and rose to leave. As he bowed to the regent and began to back away, Naja looked up at him. "I have not given you leave to go."

"My lord, I thought you had no further need of me."

"On the contrary, I have the most urgent need." He glared at Taita and gestured for him to sit again. "You are testing my good temper and favour. I know that you were wont to work the Mazes for Pharaoh Tamose whenever he called upon you to do so. Why do you procrastinate with me? As regent I will brook no further delay. I command you to work the Mazes of Ammon Ra on my behalf."

Taita bowed his head. For weeks past he had been prepared for this ultimatum, and had delayed only because he was convinced that Lord Naja would make no move against Nefer until he had been given the sanction of the Mazes.

"The full of the moon is the most propitious period for the Mazes," Taita said. "I have already made preparations with the priests at the temple of Osiris at Busiris. I will conduct the mystery in the inner sanctum of the temple. This holy place will magnify the force of our deliberations." Taita's voice was heavy with arcane meaning. "Only you and I will be present in the sanctuary. No other mortal must overhear what the gods have to tell you."

Naja was an Osiris man, and Taita had known that he would be impressed by the place he had chosen.

"So let it be," Naja agreed.

THE JOURNEY to Busiris in the royal barge took two days. They landed on the yellow beach under the walls of the temple, and the priests were waiting to welcome the regent with psalms and offerings of gum arabic and myrrh. Afterwards, at Taita's suggestion, they withdrew and left him to make his preparations for the evening. He would put on an impressive show for Lord Naja, but had no intention of subjecting himself to the harrowing ordeal of the authentic ritual.

After sunset the high priest entertained the regent at a banquet and Lord Naja consumed a flagon of rich and heady wine. Then, to the beat of gong and drum, the priests chanted an epic poem of the struggle between good and evil. Finally, as the silver beam of the full moon moved across the flags of the nave towards the closed door of the sanctuary, the high priest gave a signal and the other priests rose and moved out in procession, leaving Lord Naja and Taita alone.

When the chanting of the departing priests had dwindled into a heavy silence, Taita took the regent by the hand and led him down the nave to the sanctuary, which was lit by four braziers, one in each corner. There was a low stool in the centre of the tiled floor. Taita gestured for him to be seated, and placed a hand on his shoulder. "No matter what you see and what you hear, do not move. Do not speak. As you value your life, do nothing. Say nothing."

Taita left him sitting and, with stately tread, approached the gigantic statue of the god. He raised a golden chalice high and called on Osiris to bless the contents, then brought it back to Naja and urged him to drink. The honey-viscous liquid tasted of crushed almonds, rose petals and mushrooms. Taita made a mystical pass before Naja's face, and in the blink of an eye the Mazes of Ammon Ra filled his cupped hands. He invited Naja to cover them with his own hands, while he recited an invocation. "Greatness in light and fire, furious in divine majesty, approach and harken to our pleas."

Naja squirmed on his stool as the Mazes grew hot to the touch, and it was with relief that he passed them back to Taita. The old man carried them across the sanctuary and placed them at the feet of the statue of Osiris. The Magus knelt there, bowed over them. For a while there was no sound within the chamber. Then, abruptly, a terrible shriek rang out. Naja moaned and covered his head with his shawl. Suddenly the flames of the braziers flared as high as the roof, and turned from yellow to fierce shades of green and violet. Clouds of smoke boiled from them and filled the chamber. Naja choked and coughed. He felt as though he were suffocating, and his senses reeled.

Taita turned slowly to face him, and Naja shuddered in horror, for the Magus was transformed. His face glowed with green light and his eyes were blind orbs that flashed silver rays in the light of the braziers. He glided towards where Naja sat, and from his gaping mouth issued a terrible chorus of screams and moans, hisses and grunts, retching and insane laughter.

Lord Naja tried to rise, but the sounds and the smoke seemed to fill his skull, and blackness overwhelmed him. His legs gave way and he slumped forward off the stool onto the tiles in a dead faint.

WHEN THE REGENT of Egypt regained consciousness, the sun was high, sparkling on the waters of the river. He found himself lying on a silken mattress on the deck of the royal barge under its yellow awning. He looked around him blearily, and saw the sails of the escort galleys. The sunlight was dazzling, and he closed his eyes again. He had a consuming thirst, and there was a pounding in his skull as though all the demons of his vision were trapped within it.

Taita came to his side, raised his head and gave him a cool draught of some miraculous brew that soon eased the pounding in his head. When he had recovered enough to speak again, he whispered, "Tell it all to me, Taita. I remember nothing. What did the Mazes reveal?" Clearly the effects of the essence of the magical mushroom, which Taita had administered to him the night before, had not yet worn off.

Before he would reply Taita sent all the crew and slaves out of earshot. Then he knelt beside the mattress. "We have almost reached Sebennytos, my lord. We will be back at Thebes before nightfall."

"What happened, Taita?" He shook Taita's arm. "Tell it to me! Tell it all to me!"

"Do you not remember how the roof of the temple opened like the petals of the lotus, and we were borne upwards on the backs of two winged lions?"

Naja shook his head, and then nodded uncertainly. "Yes, I remember the lions, but after that it is all shadowy and vague."

"These mysteries numb the mind and dim eyes unaccustomed to them. Even I, an adept of the seventh and final degree, was amazed by what we endured," Taita explained kindly. "But do not despair, for the gods have commanded me to explain them to you."

"Speak, good Magus, and spare no detail."

"On the backs of the flying lions we crossed high above the dark ocean and over all the kingdoms of earth and heaven. We came at last to the citadel in which the gods dwell, and there it was that great Osiris rose up in all his terrible glory, lifted you off the winged lion and placed you beside him on the throne of fire and gold."

"Was he not deifying me, Taita? Surely there can be no other meaning?"

"If there had been any doubt it was immediately dispelled, for Osiris took up the double crown of Upper and Lower Egypt, placed it upon your head and spoke 'Hail, Brother Divine! Hail, Pharaoh who shall be.'" Naja stared at Taita with glittering eyes as the old man went on, "With the crown upon your brow, your holiness was manifest. I knelt before you and worshipped you."

Naja made no effort to hide his emotions. He was in transport. Taita seized the moment. "Then Osiris spoke again: 'In these wondrous things, your guide shall be the Magus Taita, for he is the Master of the Mazes. Follow his instruction faithfully.'"

He watched Naja's reaction, but the regent seemed to accept this without resistance.

"What else, Taita? What more did the great god have to say to me?"

"Nothing more to you, my lord, but now he spoke directly to me. These are his exact words, each one branded in fire upon my heart. 'Taita, Master of the Mazes, henceforth you have no other love, loyalty or duty. You are the servant of my divine brother, Naja. Your only concern is to help him fulfil his destiny. You will not cease until you see the double crown of Upper and Lower Egypt placed upon his head.'"

"'No other loyalty or love,'" Naja repeated softly. "And did you then accept the charge that great Osiris placed upon you, Magus? Say fair and true, are you my man now, or would you deny the word of the great father?"

"How could I deny the great god?" Taita asked simply. He lowered his head and pressed his forehead to the planking of the deck. "I accept the charge that the gods have placed upon me. I am your man, Divine Majesty. I belong to you."

Naja raised him up and stared into his eyes, searching for any trace of deceit or guile. Taita looked back at him serenely. The wish is father to the deed, Taita thought. He will allow himself to believe, because he longs for it to be so.

He watched the doubts clear in those yellow eyes and Naja embraced him. "I believe you. When I wear the double crown you will have rewards beyond your imagination."

Chapter Three

OVER THE DAYS that followed, Naja kept Taita close to his side, and the old man used this new position of trust to change some of the regent's intentions. He slaughtered a sheep and examined its entrails. From these he determined that the god would sanction no marriage of Naja to the princess until at least the next inundation of the Nile waters or the flooding would certainly fail. The life of Egypt depended upon the inundations of the great river, so with this prophecy Taita delayed the danger to Nefer, and the agony of the princess.

Naja protested, but he found it impossible to resist Taita's predictions. He was made more amenable by the news from the northern war front. On Naja's orders, and against Taita's counsel, the Egyptians had launched a desperate counterattack to try to retake Abnub. They had failed, losing three hundred chariots and almost a regiment of foot in the fighting around the city. Now Apepi seemed poised to come storming on to Thebes. It was no time for a wedding.

"The only way in which you can stave off an annihilating defeat at the hands of Apepi is to negotiate a truce," Taita advised the regent.

"This I believe also, Magus," Naja agreed eagerly, excited by this unexpected support. He had tried without success to convince the individual members of the council to agree to a truce with the Hyksos, but none had supported him. Even the loyal Asmor had risked his wrath by vowing to fall on his own sword rather than surrender to Apepi.

Peace with the Hyksos was the cornerstone of Naja's vision of the two kingdoms reunited and a single pharaoh ruling both. Only a pharaoh who was part Egyptian and part Hyksosian could hope to achieve that, and he knew that this was what the gods had promised him through the Mazes.

He went on earnestly, "I should have known that you, Taita, were the one person who would not let yourself be blinded by prejudice. After sixty years in the Nile valley, the Hyksos are becoming more Egyptian than Asian. Their savage blood has been softened and sweetened by ours. I know there are many among them who agree with these sentiments. It would take little for them to join us. Then we can bring peace and unity to the two kingdoms."

The regent's response to his tentative suggestion was so enthusiastic that Taita was taken aback. Then the veils began to part, and he was reminded of a suspicion he had once heard expressed but had rejected. "Who are these Hyksos sympathisers?" he asked. "Are they highly placed? Close to Apepi?"

"Noblemen, indeed. One sits on Apepi's war council."

It was enough for Taita. That faint rumour of Hyksosian connections in Naja's background must have had substance, and if it was true the rest fell neatly into place. "Would it be possible to meet these noblemen and speak to them?" Taita asked carefully.

"Yes," Naja confirmed. "We could reach them within days."

For Taita the implications of that simple statement were enormous. The Regent of Egypt had covert allies in the ranks of the traditional enemy. This was the loving friend who was at Pharaoh's side when he was struck down, the only witness to Pharaoh's death. This creature of boundless ambition and cruel purpose admitted to being an intimate of Hyksosian noblemen, and it was a Hyksosian arrow that killed Pharaoh. How deep did the plot run?

He let nothing of this show on his face, but nodded thoughtfully. "First we must determine if this treaty is feasible. Apepi might believe his military position is unassailable and might decide to prosecute this war to the bitter end."

"I do not think that will happen. One of our allies on the other side is a man called Trok, paramount chief of the Clan of the Leopards. You must go to him secretly, Taita. I will give you a talisman that will prove you come from me."

Taita sat a while longer in thought. He tried to see if he could wring any further advantage to Nefer and the princess from the situation, but at this stage he could find none. Whatever happened, Nefer would still be in mortal danger.

"It is my duty, a duty placed upon me by the gods, to help you in every way. I will undertake this mission," Taita said. "What is the safest way for me to pass through the Hyksosian lines?"

Naja had foreseen this query. "You must use the old chariot road through the dunes and down the wadi at El Wadun. My friends on the other side keep the road under surveillance. I will send my own lance-bearer and a squadron of the Blues to take you through," he promised. "But the road is long and hard. You must leave at once. Every day, every hour might make the difference."

TAITA HAD DRIVEN the chariot all the way from the ruined city of Gallala with only four halts. The troopers in the nine vehicles that followed him were in awe of the Magus's reputation. They knew him as the first Egyptian ever to build a chariot and harness a team to it. The old man's stamina was amazing, and his concentration never wavered. His gentle but firm hands on the reins never tired, as hour after hour he coaxed the horses into giving their best. He had impressed every man in the squadron, not least the one riding beside him in the cockpit.

Gil was Naja's lance-bearer. He had a rugged, sun-darkened face and was lightly built, which was desirable for a charioteer, but he possessed also a wiry strength and cheerful disposition.

With the moon waxing and the weather at its hottest they had driven through the cool of the night. Now, in the dawn, they halted to rest. When he had watered the horses, Gil came to where Taita sat on a boulder overlooking Hyksosian territory and handed him a ceramic water jug. Taita took a long swig. It was the first drink he had taken since their last stop at midnight.

The old devil-rouser is tough as a Bedouin raider, Gil thought, and squatted at a respectful distance to await any order.

"Where is the place at which Pharaoh was struck down?" Taita asked at last.

The two men had spoken briefly once or twice since leaving Thebes, but until now there had not been the opportunity for any long conversation.

Gil shaded his eyes against the glare of the rising sun and pointed down the wadi. "There, my lord, near that distant line of hills."

"Are any other men here who were with you on that day?"

"Only Samos, but he was waiting with the chariots in the wadi when we were attacked," Gil replied.

"I want you to take me over the battleground," Taita told him.

Gil shrugged. "It was no battle, just a skirmish. First Pharaoh dismounted and we went forward with Lord Naja to scout the camp of Apepi. Then I and the rest of the men were ordered to wait, while Lord Naja went forward beyond an outcrop of boulders."

"Where was Pharaoh? Did he go forward with Naja?"

"No. Not at first. The king waited with us. Lord Naja heard something up ahead, went to scout and disappeared from our view."

"I do not understand. At what point were you attacked?"

"We waited. I could see that Pharaoh was becoming impatient. After a while Lord Naja whistled from beyond the rocks. Pharaoh sprang up. 'Come on, lads!' he told us, and went up the path."

"Did you see what happened next?"

"Pharaoh disappeared behind the boulders. Then there was shouting and the sound of fighting. I ran forward but Lord Naja was shouting that Pharaoh had been struck down, and they dragged the king back to where I was standing. I think he was dead even then."

"How close were the Hyksos? How many? Were they cavalry or infantry? Did you recognise their regiments?" Taita demanded.

For the first time Gil looked uncertain "My lord, I did not actually set eyes on the enemy. You see, they were behind the rocks."

Taita frowned at him. "Did any of the others, apart from Naja, see the enemy?"

"I do not know, honourable Magus. You see, Lord Naja ordered us back down to the chariots. We could see that the king was mortally wounded, probably already dead. We had all lost heart."

"You must have discussed it later with your companions. Did any of them tell you he had engaged an enemy? That he had hit one of the Hyksos with arrow or lance?"

Gil shook his head. "I don't remember. No, I don't think so."

"Apart from the king, were any others wounded?"

"None."

"Why did you not tell this to the council? Why did you not tell them that you had not seen an enemy?" Taita was angry now.

"Lord Naja told us to answer the questions simply and not to waste the council's time with idle boasting." Gil hunched his shoulders with embarrassment. "I suppose none of us wanted to admit that we ran without a fight."

"Do not feel ashamed, Gil. You carried out your orders," Taita told him, in a kinder tone. Gil's evidence had been coherent and credible, and he had spoken out like the honest, simple soldier he was. When the Hyksosian arrow taken from the Pharaoh's body by the surgeons was shown to him, he had recognised it as the one that had struck down Pharaoh Tamose. The shaft had been snapped in two. Lord Naja had broken it off to ease the pain of the wound.

Taita, too, had examined the broken, blood-caked arrow, fletched in green and red, that had killed Pharaoh, and had peered closely at the signet etched into the painted shaft. It was a stylised head of a leopard, holding the hieratic letter T in its jaws. Now Taita was on his way to see one of Naja's Hyksos allies, a man named Trok.

THEY WAITED HIDDEN in the wadi until after nightfall. Then, the wheel hubs freshly greased with mutton fat to stop them squealing, the horses' hoofs covered with leather boots, they went on deep into Hyksosian territory, with Gil guiding them.

By now they were down on the alluvial plain of the Nile. Twice they had to turn off the road and wait while parties of armed men, anonymous in the darkness, rode past their hiding place. After midnight they came to an abandoned temple of some forgotten god that had been hollowed out of the side of a low clay hill. The cave was large enough to shelter the entire squadron, vehicles, horses and men. It was immediately apparent that it had been used before for this purpose. Lamps and an oil amphora were hidden behind the ruined altar, and bales of horse fodder were stacked in the sanctum.

As soon as they had removed the horses' harnesses and fed them, the troopers ate their own meal and then settled down on mattresses of dried straw. In the meantime Gil had changed his uniform for the nondescript attire of a peasant. "I cannot use a horse," he explained to Taita. "It would attract too much interest. On foot it will take me half a day to reach the camp at Bubasti. Do not expect me back before tomorrow evening." He slipped out of the cave and disappeared into the night.

Honest Gil is not such a simple, bluff soldier as he seems, Taita thought, as he settled down to wait for Lord Naja's allies to answer the message that Gil was taking to them.

They came in the short summer dusk, twenty armed men riding hard, Gil leading them on a borrowed steed. They swept up to the entrance of the temple, where they dismounted with a clatter of weapons. The leader was a tall man, wide across the shoulders with a heavy beetling brow and a fleshy hooked nose.

"You are the warlock. Yes?" he said, in a thick accent.

Taita did not think it opportune to let them know he spoke Hyksos, so he replied modestly in Egyptian. "My name is Taita, a servant of the great god Horus. I call his blessing down upon you. I see you are a man of might, but I do not know your name."

"My name is Trok, commander of the north in the army of King Apepi. You have a token for me, Warlock?"

Taita showed him a broken shard of blue glazed porcelain, the upper half of a tiny votive statue of the god Seueth.

Trok examined it briefly, then took another fragment of porcelain from the pouch on his sword-belt and fitted the two pieces together. The broken edges matched perfectly, and he grunted with satisfaction. "Come with me, Warlock."

Trok strode out into the gathering night with Taita beside him. They climbed the hill and squatted down facing each other. Trok kept his scabbard between his knees and his hand on the hilt of his heavy sickle sword. From habit more than distrust, Taita thought.

"You bring me news of the south," Trok said.

"My lord, you have heard of the death of Pharaoh Tamose?"

"We know of the death of the Theban pretender." Trok was careful not to acknowledge the authority of the Egyptian Pharaoh. To the Hyksos, the only ruler of the two kingdoms was Apepi. "We heard also that a child now pretends to the throne of Upper Egypt."

"Pharaoh Nefer Seti is only fourteen years of age," Taita confirmed, equally careful to insist on the title of Pharaoh when he spoke of him. "Until he attains his majority, Lord Naja acts as his regent."

Trok leaned forward. "So, then, you come to us with the authority of the Regent of the South. What message do you bring from Naja?"

"Lord Naja wants me to carry his proposal directly to Apepi."

Trok took immediate umbrage at this. "Naja is my cousin," he said coldly. "He would wish me to hear every word he has sent."

Taita showed no surprise, although it was a grave indiscretion on Trok's part. His suspicions as to the regent's connections were confirmed. "Yes, my lord, this much I know. However, I can tell you nothing more."

"As you wish, Warlock." Trok stood up angrily. "King Apepi is at Bubasti. We will go there immediately."

In silence they returned to the subterranean temple, where Taita called Gil and the sergeant of the bodyguard to him. "You have done your work well," he told them, "but now you must return to Thebes as secretly as you have come. I will remain here. When you report to the regent tell him that I am on my way to meet Apepi."

By the dim light of the oil lamps the horses were harnessed to the chariots, and within a short time they were ready to leave. Gil saluted respectfully. "It has been a great honour to ride with you, my lord."

Taita embraced him. "Go well, young Gil. I cast your horoscope last night. You will have a long life, and attain much distinction."

By this time Lord Trok's troop was also mounted and ready to leave. They gave Taita the horse on which Gil had returned to the temple, then clattered out of the cave and turned west, in the opposite direction to that taken by Gil's column of chariots.

With Taita in the centre of the party, they rode on through the night, heading west towards the main enemy base. As they came closer to the river, Taita saw the fires of the Hyksosian troops encamped around Bubasti. It was a field of flickering light that stretched many miles in both directions along the river bank, a huge agglomeration of men and animals.

There was nothing on earth like the smell of an army encamped. It was a mixture of odours: manure and smoke, leather and mouldy grain, unwashed men, cooking food and fermenting beer, unburied rubbish, and the ammoniacal reek of the latrine pits.

Underlying this stifling blend Taita picked out another sickly taint. He thought he recognised it, but it was only when one of the sufferers staggered in front of his horse, forcing him to rein in sharply, that he saw the rose-coloured blotches on the pale face and he was certain. He knew now why Apepi had failed so far to follow up his victory at Abnub, why he had not yet sent his chariots tearing southwards towards Thebes where the Egyptian army was at his mercy. The plague had struck his troops.

They passed the first of the burial carts, laden with corpses, and the men around Taita used their cloaks to cover their mouths and noses against the stink and the evil humours.

Closer to Bubasti the encampments became more numerous, tents, huts and hovels crowding right up to the walls that surrounded the garrison town. The more fortunate among the plague victims lay under tattered roofs of palm fronds, scant protection from the hot morning sunlight. Others lay out in the trampled mud of the fields, abandoned to thirst and the elements, the dead mixed with the dying.

Although his instincts were those of a healer, Taita would do nothing to succour them. They were condemned by their own multitudes, for what could one man do to help so many?

They entered the fortress and found that conditions were not much better within its walls. Plague victims lay where they had been struck down, and rats and pariah dogs gnawed at their corpses.

Apepi's headquarters was the principal building in Bubasti, a massive mud-brick and thatch palace in the centre of the town. Grooms took their horses at the gates, and Lord Trok led Taita through courtyards and dark shuttered halls to Apepi's private quarters. The walls were hung with magnificent carpets and the furniture was of precious wood, ivory and mother-of-pearl, much of it plundered from the palaces and temples of Egypt.

Trok ushered Taita into a luxuriously furnished antechamber, and left him there. It was a long wait. A sunbeam through the single high window moved sedately along the wall. At intervals Taita heard the distant sound of weeping. Finally there came the tramp of heavy footsteps down the passage outside, and the curtains over the doorway were thrown open. A burly man stood in the doorway. He wore a crimson linen kilt belted with a gold chain, there were heavy sandals on his feet and greaves of polished leather covered his shins. His beard and hair were in disarray. His dark eyes were wild and distracted.

"You are Taita, the physician," he said.

Taita knew him well: to him Apepi was the invader, the bloody barbarian, mortal enemy of his country. It took all his self-control to keep his voice calm as he replied, "I am Taita."

"I have heard of your skills," said Apepi. "I have need of them now. Come with me."

Taita slung his saddlebag over his shoulder and followed him out into the cloister. Ahead the sound of weeping became louder, until Apepi threw aside the heavy curtains that covered another doorway and took Taita's arm to push him through.

Dominating the crowded chamber was a large contingent of priests from the temple of Isis in Avaris, chanting over the brazier in one corner and shaking sistrums—percussion instruments of rods that rattled in metal frames. Twenty others, most of them women, were kneeling on the floor, wailing and keening. Only one was making any attempt to nurse the boy who lay on the couch. She seemed not much older than her patient, probably thirteen or fourteen, a striking-looking girl with a determined, intelligent face, and she was sponging him down with perfumed water from a copper bowl.

Taita switched his attention to the boy. His naked body was also well formed, but wasted by disease. His skin was blotched with the plague and dewed with perspiration. On his chest were the wounds where he had been bled by the priests of Isis. Taita saw that he was in an advanced stage of the disease.

"This is Khyan, my youngest son," Apepi said. "The plague will take him, unless you can save him, Magus."

Khyan groaned and rolled onto his side. At once the healers renewed their chants, and the high priest took up a knife and came towards the bed.

Taita stepped forward, barring the man's way. "Get out!" he said softly. "You and your butchers have done enough damage here."

"I must bleed the fever out of his body," the man protested.

"Out!" Taita repeated grimly, then to the others who crossed the chamber, "Out, all of you."

Eventually the chamber was deserted except for Apepi and the girl at the sickbed. "Who are you?" he demanded.

"I am Mintaka. This is my brother." She laid her hand protectively on the boy's sweat-damp curls. "I will not leave him."

"Good," said Taita briskly, "Then you can be of use to me. When did the boy last drink?"

"Not since this morning."

"Can't those quacks see that he is dying of thirst as much as of the disease? He has sweated and voided most of the water from his body." Taita picked up a copper jug from beside the bed. "Go to the kitchens and fetch water. Make sure it is clean. Fill it from the well, not with river water. Hurry, girl."

She fled, and returned almost immediately with a brimming jug of clean water. Taita opened his bag, prepared a potion of herbs, and heated it on the brazier. When it had brewed, he showed her how to position her brother's head and to stroke his throat as he dribbled the water into his mouth. Soon Khyan was swallowing freely.

"What can I do to help you?" the king asked.

"My lord, there is nothing for you here. You are better at destroying than at healing." Taita dismissed him without looking up from his patient. There was a long silence, then the tramp of Apepi's bronze-studded sandals as he left the chamber.

Mintaka was quick and willing. She forced her brother to drink while Taita brewed up another cup of medicine on the brazier. Between them they were able to get this down his throat without losing a drop. She helped smear a soothing ointment on his chest. Then they wrapped Khyan in linen sheets and soaked them with well water to cool his burning body. By next morning the fever had broken and Khyan was resting more comfortably.

"Look, my lord," Mintaka exclaimed, stroking her brother's cheek, "the blotches are fading, and his skin feels cooler."

"You have the healing touch of a nymph of paradise," Taita told her, "but do not forget the water jug. It is empty."

She raced away to the kitchens, and came back with a brimming jug. While she gave it to him, Taita studied her face. In the Hyksosian way, it was a little too broad, and her cheekbones too prominent. Her mouth was large, her lips full, her nose strongly bridged. Not one of these features was perfect in itself, but each was finely balanced with, and matched to, all the others. Hers was a different kind of beauty, he thought, but beauty nonetheless.

By that evening Khyan was able to sit up with a little help from his sister, and to drink from the soup bowl she held to his lips. Two days later his rash had disappeared.

Three or four times a day Apepi visited the chamber. On the fifth day Khyan tottered from the couch and tried to prostrate himself before the king, but Apepi stopped him and lifted him back onto the pillows. Even though his feelings for the boy were clear, the king had little to say and left again almost immediately, but in the doorway he looked back at Taita and ordered him to follow with a curt inclination of his head.

THEY STOOD ALONE on the summit of the highest tower of the palace. From here they had a view upriver over the captured citadel of Abnub, which lay ten miles upstream. Thebes was less than a hundred miles beyond that.

Apepi had ordered the sentries to go down and leave them alone in this lofty place, so that they would not be spied upon or overheard. He stood staring out over the great grey river towards the south.

"At least something they say of you is true, Magus." Apepi broke the long silence. "You are a physician of great skill." He looked down over the encampments of his army.

"My lord," Taita said softly, "Pharaoh will have reinforced and regrouped his forces before the plague burns itself out and your men are ready to fight again."

Apepi shook himself with annoyance, like a lion shaking off flies. "Nefer Seti is a child. I have defeated him once, I will do it again."

"What is more crucial to you, there is no plague in his army. Your spies will have told you that Pharaoh has five more legions at Aswan, and another two at Asyut. They are already on the river coming north with the current. They will be here before the new moon."

Apepi growled softly, but made no response.

Taita went on relentlessly. "Sixty years of war have bled both kingdoms white. Would you pass on the legacy of bloodshed? Is that what your sons will inherit from you?"

Apepi rounded on him, scowling, "Do not press me too hard, old man." After an interval long enough to express his disapproval, Apepi spoke again. "How long will it take you to arrange a parley with this so-called Regent of the Upper Kingdom, this Naja?"

"If you give me safe conduct through your lines, and a fast galley to carry me, I can be in Thebes in three days. The return with the current will be even swifter."

"I will send Trok with you to see you safely through. Tell Naja I will meet him at the temple of Hathor on the west bank at Perra beyond Abnub. But tell him not to expect many concessions. I am the victor, and he the vanquished. Go now."

Taita stood his ground. "Pharaoh Nefer Seti is almost of an age with your daughter, Mintaka," he said stubbornly. "You might wish to bring her with you to Perra."

"To what purpose?" Apepi stared at him suspiciously.

"An alliance between your dynasty and that of the Tamosian pharaohs might seal a lasting peace in the two kingdoms."

Apepi stroked his beard to hide his smile. "You intrigue as cunningly as you mix a potion, Warlock. Now, get you gone before you irk me past forbearance."

THE TEMPLE of Hathor had been excavated out of the rocky hillside above the river hundreds of years previously. The priestesses were a rich, influential sisterhood who had survived and even prospered during the long civil wars between the kingdoms.

Dressed in their yellow robes they were gathered in the courtyard of the temple, between the two massive statues of the goddess. They chanted and rattled the sistrum as the suite of Pharaoh Nefer Seti filed into the courtyard from the eastern wing, while King Apepi's courtiers entered through the western colonnade. Both parties had agreed to eschew the double crown. Apepi wore the red crown of Lower Egypt, while Nefer Seti confined himself to the white crown of Upper Egypt.

The entourages of both rulers packed the spacious courtyard, their ranks facing each other, unsmiling and grim. Only a few paces separated them physically, but the bitterness of sixty years' strife formed a mighty barrier between them.

The hostile silence was shattered by a rolling fanfare of rams' horns and the thunder of bronze gongs. This was the signal for the royal parties to emerge from the two wings of the temple.

Lord Naja and Pharaoh Nefer Seti paced out solemnly and took their places on the high-backed thrones, while the Hyksosian royal family emerged from the opposing wing of the temple. Apepi led them, an impressive, warlike figure in full battle armour. He glared across the courtyard at the boy pharaoh. His nine sons and his daughter followed him.

None of the Egyptians had laid eyes on Mintaka before, and there was a subdued rustle and murmur through their ranks. They had been unprepared for her beauty. The myth was that Hyksosian women were as ugly as their menfolk.

Pharaoh Nefer Seti leaned forward slightly, and Taita was so familiar with the boy, so attuned to his mind, that he could read his thoughts with ease. He sensed that Nefer was in a ferment of elation and excitement, and he felt smug at what he had achieved with so little effort. It would have complicated all his plans if Nefer had taken a dislike to the Hyksosian girl.

Lord Naja, the Regent of Upper Egypt, greeted Apepi in measured tones, diplomatically referring to him as King of the Hyksos but avoiding any reference to his claims to Egyptian territory. Mintaka stared at him with fascination. He was such a splendid sight, so different from her father. He shone with gold and precious stones, and his linen was dazzling in its purity. She could smell his perfume across the distance that separated them. His face was a mask of make-up, his skin almost luminous and his eyes outlined and enhanced with kohl. Yet she thought that his was the beauty of a snake or a poisonous insect. She shivered and turned to the figure on the throne beside the regent.

Pharaoh Nefer Seti was staring at her with such intensity that she caught her breath. His eyes were so green—that was the first thing that struck her. She wanted to look away but could not. Instead she started to blush. Then, suddenly, Pharaoh gave her a warm and conspiratorial smile. Instantly, his face was boyish and appealing, and unaccountably her breath came faster. She dropped her eyes and looked at her hands in her lap, twisting her fingers together until she realised that she was fidgeting and stopped herself.

In the ranks opposite, Taita missed not a single nuance of the surreptitious exchanges between Nefer and Mintaka. He saw more than that. Lord Trok, Naja's cousin, was standing close behind Apepi's throne, his arms folded over his chest. Over one shoulder was slung a heavy bow, over the other an arrow quiver covered with gold leaf. Trok was watching the Hyksosian princess with a dark, brooding gaze. Taita could sense his anger and jealousy. He had not foreseen this. *Is Trok's interest in Mintaka romantic or political?* he wondered. *Does he lust for her, or see her merely as a staircase to power? In either case it is dangerous.*

The speeches of greeting were coming to an end and nothing of significance had been said; negotiation of the truce would begin in secret session the next day. Both sides were rising from their thrones and exchanging salutations, and the gongs began to beat and the rams' horns to sound again as they withdrew.

Lord Trok was the last of the Hyksosians to march out between the granite pillars of the gateway. As he did so, the arrows in his quiver rattled softly, and their coloured fletchings caught Taita's eye. The feathers were red and green, and, as he gazed after Trok, something evil stirred in Taita's memory.

Taita returned to the stone cell in the temple annexe that had been allocated to him for the duration of the peace conference. His pleasure at what had transpired between Mintaka and Nefer was forgotten as he considered Trok's relationship to the Hyksosian princess, and the complications that might ensue.

Even during their long ride together, Trok had kept his war quiver firmly stoppered and it had not been possible for Taita to compare one of the arrows it contained to the one found in Pharaoh's body. How many other Hyksosian officers had red and green fletchings he could only guess, but it was probably a great number, though each would have its owner's unique signet. The only way to connect Trok to the death of Pharaoh Tamose, and through him to implicate his cousin Naja, was to study one of his arrows. But how to do this without arousing Trok's suspicions?

His train of thought was interrupted. There were voices in the passage outside the door of his cell. One was young and clear, and he recognised it at once. The others were gruff.

"Lord Asmor has given specific orders—"

"Am I not Pharaoh? Are you not bound to obey me? I wish to visit the Magus. Stand aside." Nefer's voice was strong and commanding. The uncertain timbre of puberty was gone.

The young falcon is spreading his wings, Taita thought.

Nefer jerked aside the curtain that covered the doorway, and stepped through. Two armed bodyguards followed him helplessly. Nefer ignored them and faced Taita with his hands on his hips.

"Taita, I am much displeased with you," Nefer said. "You have been avoiding me. Whenever I send for you they tell me that you are gone on a secret mission to the Hyksos. Then suddenly you pop up from nowhere, but still you ignore me. You did not even look in my direction during the ceremony. Where have you been?"

"Majesty, there are long ears about." Taita glanced at the guards.

Immediately Nefer turned upon them wrathfully. "I have ordered you more than once to be gone. Go this instant."

They withdrew unhappily. Nefer soon forgot his anger and was grinning delightedly.

"Where have you been, Tata? I have missed you so."

"I will tell you everything," Taita assured him, and rapidly, in simple outline, he told Nefer what had happened to him since their last meeting. He explained the relationship between Naja and Trok, and described what he had learned from the lance-bearer, Gil. "Now you can appreciate the danger you are in," Taita told Nefer. "I am certain that Naja had much to do with Pharaoh's murder, and the closer we come to the proof of it, the greater that danger becomes."

"One day I will avenge my father." Nefer vowed.

"And I will help you do it," Taita promised, "but now we must protect you from Naja's malice."

"How do you plan to do that, Tata? Can we escape from Egypt as we planned before?"

"No." Taita shook his head. "Naja has us too securely imprisoned here. If we tried to run for the frontier again we would have a thousand chariots hot behind us."

"What can we do, then? You are in danger also."

"No. I have convinced Naja that he cannot succeed without my help." He described the false divination ceremony and how Naja believed that Taita could share with him the secret of eternal life.

Nefer grinned at the Magus's cunning. "So what do you plan?"

"Naja sent me to Apepi to arrange this peace conference."

"Yes, they told me that when I demanded to see you."

"Well, once Apepi had agreed to the meeting with Naja, I was able to convince him that they should seal the treaty by a marriage between you and Apepi's daughter. Once you are under the protection of the Hyksosian king, Naja's knife will be blunted."

"Apepi is going to give me his daughter as a wife?" Nefer stared at him in wonder. "The one I saw at the ceremony this morning?"

"Yes." Taita agreed. "Mintaka is her name."

"I know her name," Nefer assured him vehemently. "She is the most beautiful . . ." Seeing the expression on Taita's face, he subsided. "I mean, she is quite pleasing." He grinned ruefully. "When may I speak to her? She does speak Egyptian, doesn't she?"

"She speaks it as well as you do," Taita assured him.

"Then when can I meet her? You can arrange it for me."

Taita had anticipated this request. "You could invite the princess and her suite to a hunt here in the swamps tomorrow at dawn, and perhaps a picnic afterwards."

"I will send Asmor to invite her this very afternoon," Nefer decided, but Taita shook his head.

"He would go to the regent first, and Naja would immediately see the danger. Once he was alerted he would do everything in his power to prevent you coming together."

"What shall we do, then?" Nefer looked agitated.

"I will go to her myself," Taita promised, and he did, that same day.

THE DAWN SKY the next morning was the glowing shade of a sword blade fresh from the coals of the forge. In this time before the sunrise there was no breath of air, no sound to break the stillness.

Two hunting skiffs were moored in a small lagoon, hard against the reeds that surrounded the open water. Less than fifty cubits separated them. The royal huntsmen had bent tall papyrus stems to form a screening roof over the hunters.

The surface of the lagoon was still and unruffled. It was just light enough for Nefer to make out the graceful form of Mintaka in the other boat. She had her bow across her lap, and sat as motionless as a statue. Any other girl he could think of, particularly his own sister Heseret, would have been hopping around like a canary on a perch.

Out in the swamp a heron boomed. As though this was a signal, the air was filled suddenly with the sound of wings. Nefer tore his eyes off the dainty figure in the boat across the water, and reached for his throwing sticks, determined to impress Mintaka with his hunting skills.

The first flight of glossy black and white ducks came sweeping in low out of the dawn. They turned in a wide circle then started to drop and line up on the open water. They set their wings and streamed in, losing height swiftly, passing directly over Nefer's skiff. Pharaoh judged his moment neatly, with the stick cocked and ready to throw. He waited for the lead bird to flare out and then let fly. The duck saw the missile coming and dropped a wing to avoid it.

Lost bird, Nefer thought bitterly, and before he could throw the second stick, the flight of ducks had angled across the lagoon, directly towards Mintaka's boat. They were still keeping low, going very fast, their blade-shaped wings whistling through the air.

Nefer had almost discounted the hunter in the other boat—at that height and speed the targets were too difficult for all but the most expert archer—but in quick succession two arrows rose to meet the straggle of birds. The sound of the double impact carried clearly across the lagoon. Then two ducks were falling, killed cleanly in the air at the same time. They plopped onto the water and floated there, motionless. The slave-boy retrievers picked them up easily and swam back to Mintaka's skiff, carrying the carcasses gripped in their teeth.

"Two lucky arrows," Nefer said.

In the bows of the skiff, Taita added, "Two unlucky ducks."

Now the sky was filled with birds, which rose in dark clouds as the first rays of the sun struck the waters. They squawked and honked and quacked and bleated and wailed. Mintaka's light bow was well suited to the task. It was quick to align and draw without taxing her strength unduly. She was firing sharp metal heads especially forged for her by Grippa, the famous armourer. The needle-points drove through the dense plumage and went straight to the bone. She had realised, without a word being exchanged, that Nefer intended to make a contest of the hunt, and she was proving that her competitive instincts were every bit as fierce as his.

Nefer had been badly rattled by his first failure and by Mintaka's unexpected skill. Many of the birds he brought down were only stunned, and eluded his slave boys by diving under the surface and swimming into the thick papyrus beds. The number of dead birds piled on the floorboards of the skiff grew pitifully slowly. In desperation Nefer discarded his sticks and snatched up his heavy bow, but it was too late. His right arm was exhausted by his efforts with the sticks, and his draw was laboured.

Taita watched Nefer flounder ever deeper into the trap he had set for himself. A little humiliation will do him no real harm, he told himself. For once his sympathy was not with the boy, and he smiled secretly as he watched Nefer miss again and Mintaka take down two birds from the same flight as they passed over her head.

However, he felt pity for his king when one of Mintaka's slaves swam across the lagoon, and hung onto the side of Nefer's skiff. "Her Royal Highness Princess Mintaka's boat begins to sink under the weight of her bag. Now she is hungry for her breakfast."

An untimely sally! Taita thought, as Nefer scowled furiously at this impertinence. It was time for him to intervene. "Pharaoh apologises for his thoughtlessness, but he was enjoying the sport so much that he forgot the passage of time. Please tell your mistress that we shall all go in to breakfast immediately."

Nefer glowered at him, but put up his bow and made no effort to revoke Taita's decision. The two boats paddled back towards the island in close formation. Not a word was said by the crew of either skiff, but everyone was conscious of the results of the morning's hunt.

"Your majesty," Mintaka called across to Nefer, "I must thank you for a truly diverting morning. I cannot remember when last I enjoyed myself so much."

"You are too kind." Nefer made a regal gesture of dismissal, turned half away from her, and stared broodingly at the horizon. First love is such unmitigated joy, Taita thought with sympathetic irony.

They came in to the landing on the island. The boatmen jumped over the side into the knee-deep ooze and held the first skiff steady while the slaves handed the princess and her maids across the gap onto the firm, dry ground at the top of the bank.

As soon as they were safely ashore the royal skiff came in and the slaves handed Nefer across to join Mintaka on the high bank. He led her to a giant kigelia tree under whose spreading branches a breakfast feast was laid out in the shade. At first Nefer was restrained and cool, but soon his natural high spirits reasserted themselves, and he joined in the banter and the chatter.

Mintaka loved to riddle and she challenged him to an exchange. She made it more difficult for Nefer by couching her clues in the Hyksosian language. "I have one eye and a sharp nose. I run my victim through and through, but I draw no blood. What am I?"

"That's easy!" Nefer laughed triumphantly. "You are a sewing needle." And Mintaka threw up her hands in surrender.

Of course Nefer had brought his bao board and stones. Taita had taught him to love the game, and he had become expert. When he tired of the riddles he inveigled Mintaka into a game. Bao was an Egyptian game, and this time he expected confidently to outmatch her.

Taita smiled because he and Mintaka had whiled away a few hours at bao in the palace of Bubasti when they were nursing her little brother. Within eighteen moves her red stones dominated the west castle and were menacing Nefer's centre.

"Have I done the right thing?" she asked sweetly.

Nefer was saved by a hail from the river and looked up to see a galley flying the regent's pennant coming swiftly down the channel. "What a pity. Just when the game was getting interesting."

He had been expecting this visitation all morning. Sooner or later the regent must hear about this outing and send Asmor to bring in his errant charge.

The galley nosed into the bank below, where they sat, and Asmor sprang ashore. He strode up to the picnic party. "The regent is much displeased by your absence. He bids you return at once to the temple, where matters of state await your attention."

"And I, Lord Asmor, am much displeased by your ill manners," Nefer told him. "I am not a house servant to be addressed in that manner, and neither have you shown respect for the Princess Mintaka." But there was no escaping that he was being treated like a truant from the classroom.

Still, he put a good face on it and invited Mintaka to sail back with him in the skiff while her maids followed in the second vessel. Taita kept tactfully to the bows as this was their first opportunity to hold a private conversation.

The journey was far too short for Nefer's liking, and as they came into the landing he took her hand. "I should like to see you again."

"I should like that well enough," she replied.

"Soon," he insisted.

"Soon enough." She smiled and gently took back her hand. He felt strangely bereft as he watched her walk away towards the temple.

"MY LORD, you were present at the divination of the Mazes. You know of the charge placed upon me by the gods. You know that I am committed to your interest. I had good reason to assist the boy in what was only, after all, a harmless escapade."

Naja was not so easily placated. He was furious that Nefer had given Asmor the slip and managed to spend the morning out in the swamps with the Hyksosian princess. But Taita diplomatically turned aside each of the regent's accusations, until he was no longer ranting but merely grumbling bitterly. "However, it must not happen again. Of course I trust your loyalty, Magus."

"My lord, how goes the negotiation with King Apepi? Is there aught that I can do to help you ensure a successful outcome in this matter?" Adroitly Taita set the hounds on a different scent, and Naja followed them.

"I have that old rogue Apepi at the brink," he gloated. "This morning he is about to make more concessions than he realises." He started towards the door, then looked back over his shoulder. "Come with me," he ordered. "I might have use of your powers before I am done with Apepi."

Binding Apepi to the treaty was not the easy task that Naja had suggested it would be. The Hyksosian leader was still ranting, shouting and banging his fist on the table long after the watchman on the temple walls had called the midnight hour. At last Naja adjourned the conference and staggered off to bed.

The next day, when they met again at noon, Apepi was no more amenable to reason. Taita used his influences to calm him, but Apepi allowed himself to be wooed only very slowly. So it was only on the fifth day that the scribes began to write down the terms of the treaty.

Up to this time Naja had excluded Pharaoh Nefer Seti from the conclave. But by the morning of the sixth day, when the scribes had completed their work and the fifty tablets of the treaty were ready to be ratified, Naja sent for Pharaoh to take part in the proceedings. Likewise, all Apepi's offspring, including Mintaka, were to be present at the ceremony.

Once again the courtyard of the temple was filled with a glittering congregation as, in stentorian tones, the herald royal began to read out the text of the treaty. Immediately Nefer was absorbed by what it contained, certain that he detected Taita's shadowy influence in many areas of the long document.

At last it was time to affix the seals. To a series of blasts on the rams' horns Nefer pressed his cartouche to the damp clay and Apepi did the same. Then, while Naja watched with an enigmatic expression, the new co-rulers of the two kingdoms embraced. Apepi folded Nefer in his bearlike embrace and men rattled their weapons against their shields, or hammered the butts of their lances on the stone flags. Finally Apepi turned to face the crowded courtyard.

"Citizens of this mighty land, which is once again united, I pledge you my duty and my love. In token of these, I offer the hand of my daughter, Princess Mintaka, in marriage to the Pharaoh

Nefer Seti, who shares with me the double crown of the Upper and Lower Kingdoms, and who shall be my son."

There was a long moment of utter stillness in the courtyard. Then the assembly burst out in enthusiastic cries of approval while the drumming of weapons became deafening.

Pharaoh Nefer Seti had an expression on his face that in any lesser mortal would have been described as an idiotic grin. He was gazing across the courtyard at Mintaka. She was frozen, with one hand covering her mouth, and her eyes were wide with astonishment as she gazed at her father. Slowly a dark blush suffused her face and she turned her eyes to meet Nefer's. The two gazed at each other as if no other person was in the crowded courtyard.

Taita watched from the foot of Pharaoh's throne. He realised that Apepi's timing of the announcement had been masterly. Now there was no possible way in which anybody—Naja, Trok or any other—could stand in the way of the marriage.

Standing close to Naja's throne, Taita was keenly aware of the regent's deep consternation. Naja must have sensed Taita's eyes on him, for he glanced in his direction. For a moment only, Taita looked into his soul, and saw the cobra of his vision, the cobra for which the regent was named. Then Naja veiled his fierce yellow eyes, smiled coolly and nodded in approval, but Taita knew that he was thinking furiously.

The Magus turned his head and sought out the burly figure of Lord Trok in the Hyksosian ranks opposite. Unlike the regent, Trok was making no attempt to disguise his feelings. He was in a black rage. He opened his mouth as if to protest, then closed it. With a huge effort he regained control of himself, smoothed down his beard, then turned abruptly and pushed his way out of the courtyard.

As Trok disappeared between the tall granite pillars, Naja rose and stepped in front of Apepi. "On this auspicious and joyous day, we rejoice not only in the joining of the two kingdoms, but also in the betrothal of Pharaoh Nefer Seti and the beautiful Princess Mintaka. Therefore, be it known that the marriage will take place in this temple on the day that Pharaoh Nefer Seti celebrates his majority, or fulfils one of the conditions to ratify his claim to the crown and rules in his own right without a regent to protect and advise him."

Apepi frowned and Nefer made a small gesture of dismay, but it was too late. It had been announced in full session so, as regent, Naja spoke with the authority of both crowned heads. Unless Nefer captured his own godbird, thereby ratifying his claim to the throne, Naja had prevented the marriage taking place for a number of years.

That was a masterly stroke, Taita thought bitterly. Naja had averted disaster for himself by his quick thinking. Now, he went even further. "On an equally happy note, I invite Pharaoh Apepi and Pharaoh Nefer Seti to celebrate my own marriage to Princess Heseret. This joyous ceremony will take place ten days from now, at the temple of Isis in the city of Thebes."

So, Taita thought grimly, in ten days' time Lord Naja will be a member of the Tamosian royal family, and will stand next in succession to Pharaoh Nefer Seti.

By the terms of the Treaty of Hathor, Apepi's capital would remain at Avaris and Nefer Seti's at Thebes. Each would govern his former kingdom, but in the name of the duumvirate. Twice every year, at the beginning and the end of the inundation of the Nile, the two kings would hold a combined royal assize at Memphis, where all matters concerning the two kingdoms would be dealt with.

However, before the two pharaohs parted, Apepi and his train would sail upriver in company with Nefer Seti's fleet to Thebes. There they would attend Lord Naja's wedding.

The embarkation of both trains from the wharf below the temple was a chaotic affair that took up most of the morning. Taita mingled with the throng of boatmen and dockers, slaves and important passengers. Occasionally a man would look up from what he was doing, recognise him and ask for his blessing, or a woman would bring him a sick child to tend. However, he was able to work his way gradually along the beach, casually looking out for the chariots and equipment of Lord Trok's regiment. He recognised them by their green and red pennants, and as he approached he made out the unmistakable figure of Trok among his men. Taita edged closer and watched him pause to talk to his lance-bearer, then take the path up to the temple.

As soon as Trok had disappeared, Taita approached the lance-bearer. The trooper was stripped to breech-clout and sandals, and as he stooped over one of the chests of Trok's equipment Taita saw the distinctive circular rash of the ringworm on his naked back.

"Come here, soldier," Taita called him across. "How long have you had the itch on your back?"

Instinctively the fellow twisted up one arm between his shoulder blades, and scratched himself vigorously. "Cursed thing has been bothering me ever since we captured Abnub. I think it's a gift from one of those dirty Egyptian whores—" He broke off guiltily. "Forgive me, Warlock, we are allies and fellow countrymen now."

"That is why I will attend to your affliction, soldier. Go up to the temple, ask at the kitchens for a jar of lard and bring it to me. I will mix an ointment for you." Taita sat down on the pile of Trok's luggage, and the lance-bearer hurried away down the beach.

Taita's seat was a stack of wooden chests. The top one bore the seal of Grippa, the Avaris fletcher who made arrows for all the high-ranking Hyksosian officers. Taita untied the cord that secured the lid. A layer of dry straw protected the arrows. He picked one out and turned it in his fingers.

The carved signet leapt out at him, the stylised head of the leopard with the hieratic letter T held in its snarling jaws. The arrow was identical to the one found in Pharaoh's body. It was the last thread in the fabric of treason. Naja and Trok were linked in the bloody plot.

Taita slipped the incriminating arrow under the folds of his kilt and closed the lid of the chest. Deftly he retied the cord, and waited for the lance-bearer to return.

The old soldier was grateful for Taita's ministrations, then pleaded for a further favour: "A friend of mine has the pox, Magus. What should he do?" It always amused Taita that no man ever contracted the pox himself but always had a friend suffering from it.

THE FEAST to celebrate the marriage of Lord Naja to Princess Heseret was the most lavish ever recorded. To the common citizens of Thebes, Lord Naja gave five hundred head of prime oxen, and to each of the four thousand invited guests a commemorative carved jewel with the guest's own name engraved upon it between the names of the regent and his bride.

The bride came to meet her groom on one of the state carriages drawn by sacred white oxen. The road was strewn with palm fronds and flowers, and a chariot drove ahead of the wedding coach throwing rings of silver and copper to the crowds that lined the way.

When she reached the temple she was met by her brother. Heseret was as lovely as a nymph of paradise in her snowy robes and glittering jewellery. Months ago she had come to terms with the fate the gods had apportioned her and her girlish interest in Meren had begun to fade. She came to realise that he was an impecunious boy, a common soldier without favour or prospects. Lord Naja's social rank almost matched hers, and his fortune far exceeded her own. He was also a magnificent-looking man.

Now she kept a chaste demeanour as Nefer led her down the temple to the sanctuary where Lord Naja was waiting. He wore a plumed headdress of ostrich feathers and his perfume was a blend of essences from a land beyond the Indus. The aroma stirred her, and she took the hand that Naja offered her without hesitation.

Watching from the roof of the western enclosure, Taita shuddered with a sense of foreboding. Now Naja is of the blood royal, I am the only shield Nefer has, and I am one man and old. Will my powers be enough to turn away the cobra?

LORD NAJA and his new wife rode back in splendour to the palace gates. There they dismounted and went in procession through the gardens to the banquet hall. Most of the guests had arrived ahead of them, and the commotion as the wedding party entered was deafening. The pair moved through the throng and inspected the gifts stacked in the centre of the banquet hall. Apepi had sent a chariot covered in gold leaf, so brilliant that even in the dimly lit hall it was difficult to look at directly. From Babylon King Sargon had sent a hundred sandalwood chests, filled with jewellery, precious stones or golden vessels. Pharaoh Nefer Seti, at the suggestion of Lord Naja, had deeded to his new brother-in-law three lakhs of pure gold. The regent had become almost as rich as his pharaoh.

When the connubial pair took their seats at the head of the wedding board, the palace cooks laid a feast before them, and to entertain them there were musicians and jugglers, acrobats and huge brown bears.

By nightfall most of the guests were so drunk that few could stand when Lord Naja and his bride retired. Naja led Heseret by the hand to his sumptuous bedroom, which overlooked the river. There Heseret's handmaidens took her behind a screen of bamboo to remove her wedding dress and jewellery.

Lord Naja went out onto the terrace and inhaled deeply the cool river air. A slave brought him a bowl of spiced wine, and he sipped appreciatively. It was the first wine he had allowed himself all evening. He returned to the chamber as two more slaves staggered in, bearing between them a cauldron of hot water, in which floated lotus petals. Naja set aside the wine bowl and went to bathe. One of the slaves dried and braided his hair, while the other brought him a clean white robe. He dismissed them and lay upon the marriage bed, stretching out his long, elegant limbs.

From the far end of the chamber came the rustle of clothing and feminine whispers. He propped himself up on one elbow and looked across at the bamboo screen. The gaps in it were just large enough to afford him tantalising glimpses of pale, smooth skin. Power and political aspiration were the main reasons for this marriage, but Naja had a voluptuous nature. For years he had watched Heseret surreptitiously, and his interest had increased at each stage in her journey towards womanhood. Now, at last, two of the handmaidens led her out from behind the screen, then slipped away quietly, leaving her standing alone in the middle of the floor.

Her silken night-robe fell to her ankles. It was creamy in colour and so fine that it seemed to float around her like river mist, stirring with every breath she took. There was an oil lamp on a tripod in the corner behind her, and the soft yellow light shone through the silk, highlighting the curves of her hips and shoulders. Her skin was flawless and her green eyes hinted at a sly, lascivious streak in her.

"You are beautiful." His voice caught.

Now a hint of a smile lifted the corners of her lips. "I am glad that my lord regent finds me so."

He rose from the bed and went to her. Slowly he lifted her face.

"You also are beautiful," she whispered, and it was true. In this moment she realised that he was the most beautiful creature she had ever known.

He kissed her and his mouth startled her. His tongue was as flickeringly quick as a snake's, but it did not revolt her. She closed her eyes and touched it with her own. She was so lost in his kiss that when his hand closed over her breast she was unprepared. Her eyes flew open and she gasped. She tried to pull away but he held her, and now he caressed her with a skilful touch that stilled her fears.

With a single movement he swept off her silken robe and let it fall to the floor. She had not the slightest inclination to resist.

Twice during that enchanted night she cried out in a frenzy of pleasure, and when the dawn suffused the chamber with its rose and silver light she lay still in his arms. She felt as though the life force had been drawn out of her, and there was a soft ache deep in her belly that she savoured.

When she opened her eyes he was watching her, and he smiled gently. "What a splendid queen you would make," he said softly. This he meant sincerely, sensing that he had found in her someone whose desires and instincts were in perfect harmony with his own.

"And what a splendid pharaoh you would make." She smiled back, reached up and touched his cheek. "But that could never happen." She stopped smiling abruptly and asked softly, seriously, "Could it?"

Chapter Four

King Apepi's entourage remained in Thebes for almost a month after the wedding. They were the guests of Pharaoh Nefer Seti and of his regent, entertained in royal fashion. Taita encouraged this delay. He felt certain Naja would take no action against Nefer while Apepi and his daughter were in Thebes.

The royal visitors spent their days hunting, and during these days Mintaka was often at Nefer's side. She rode in his chariot and handed him the lance when they drove up alongside a galloping oryx. She carried her own falcon on her arm as they quartered the reed beds for heron. At the hunting picnics in the desert, she sat beside him and prepared little treats for him.

Every evening there were banquets in the palace and there also she sat at his side. She made him laugh with her wry wit and she was a marvellous mimic: she imitated Heseret to perfection, simpering and rolling her eyes, and speaking of "My husband, the Regent of Egypt" in the portentous tones Heseret now employed.

As Nefer's chariot sped through the streets of Thebes with Mintaka on the footplate as his lance-bearer, men paused from their labours to shout greetings and good wishes. Their love was so apparent that it cast a glow upon all those around them. Even Naja smiled benignly upon them, although he fiercely resented the attention of the populace being diverted from his own nuptials, and he saw to it that Nefer and Mintaka could never be completely alone.

Their chance came, however, when a royal huntsman came in from the hills above the village of Dabba one day to report that a lion had raided the cattle pens during the night. It had killed eight of the terrified beasts. In the dawn a horde of villagers, brandishing torches, beating drums and screaming wildly, had driven it off.

"When did this happen?" asked Naja.

"Three nights ago, Your Grace." The man was prostrate before the throne. "I came upriver as soon as I could, but the current runs strongly and the winds were fluky."

"What has happened to the beast?" King Apepi interrupted eagerly.

"It has gone back into the hills, but I have sent two of my best Nubian trackers to follow it."

"I will have the chariots loaded onto the boats at once," Apepi decided. "With the state of the river we can be at Dabba early tomorrow morning."

Naja hesitated. He was not so addicted to the hunt that he wished to neglect the numerous affairs of state that awaited his attention. He had looked forward to the departure of Apepi, whose boisterous, uncouth presence in Thebes had long since palled. And he had other plans afoot. "Majesty, you are expected to sail back to Avaris tomorrow."

"You are right, Regent. However, most of our baggage is already loaded and the fleet lies ready to depart. Moreover, Dabba lies on my way homewards. I can afford a day or two in the hunt."

"Your Majesty," Nefer intervened, "we will join in the hunt with the greatest of pleasure." He saw an opportunity for magnificent sport, and before Naja could prevent him he turned to the huntsman, who still lay with his forehead pressed to the floor. "Well done, my good fellow. The chamberlain will give you a gold ring for your trouble. Return to Dabba at once in the fastest felucca in our fleet. Make ready for our arrival."

Nefer's only cause for regret was that Taita would not be with him during his first lion hunt. The old man had disappeared into the wilderness on another of his periodic and mysterious forays.

IN THE EARLY morning of the next day the hunting party disembarked on the river bank below the village of Dabba. All the horses and chariots were off-loaded and the lance-bearers sharpened the spear blades, restrung the hunting bows and checked the arrows. While the horses were watered, the hunters ate a hearty breakfast that the villagers had provided. The mood was ebullient.

"Sound the mount up," Nefer ordered, and the rams' horns blared as the hunters scattered to the waiting chariots. Mintaka walked at Nefer's side. In these informal circumstances all royal dignity was forgotten, and they were simply boy and girl on an exciting outing.

Led by the royal huntsman, who rode bareback astride a tough little pony, the column climbed into the bare, stony hills. They went at the trot, saving the horses, letting them blow after every steep gradient. Within the hour they found one of the Nubian trackers waiting for them on a hilltop, and the huntsman trotted back to report to the royal party, "The Nubians have cast the hills but without finding the spoor again. From where we last saw him, he may have gone to the small oasis at the head of the valley, but there are Bedouin encamped there. They might have scared off the beast. There is also a water seep below those hills." He pointed at a low line of purple peaks on the horizon.

"You have not the least idea where he is, have you?" Lord Naja complained. "We should call off the hunt."

"No!" Nefer cut in. "How can we give up?"

"We must go on," Apepi agreed, "but there is much ground to cover." He paused, then reached a decision. "We must split up and search each area separately." He looked at Naja. "My Lord Regent, take your squadron to the Bedouin encampment. I will ride to the seep below the hills." He turned to Trok. "Take three chariots down the valley." Then he looked at Nefer. "Pharaoh, you cast in the opposite direction, north towards Achmim."

Nefer realised he was being given the least promising ground to cover, but he had no complaint. This new plan meant that for the first time he and Mintaka would be away from the direct surveillance of his guardians. He waited for someone to point this out, but they were all so wrapped up in the hunt that no one seemed to realise the significance of this move. Except Naja.

He looked hard at Nefer, weighing the advisability of countermanding Apepi's orders, but in the end he concluded that Nefer was guarded by the desert as effectively as he would have been by Asmor: there was no place to run to. If he took Mintaka on some wild adventure he would soon have the armies of both kingdoms upon him.

Apepi went on to nominate an assembly point, and to give his final orders. At last the rams' horns sounded the advance, and the columns drove out of the valley. On the level ground they split into their separate squadrons and headed out in diverging directions.

There were two other chariots in Nefer's squadron, commanded by Colonel Hilto, the old soldier who had discovered him and Taita when they had tried to escape from Egypt. He had served under Nefer's father and Nefer knew he could trust him.

Nefer led them fast, and within an hour the vast green vista of the river plain opened beneath them. He reined in to admire it. "Colonel Hilto, if the lion is here it will probably be lying up somewhere on the slope of the hills down below us." He indicated the area with a sweep of his arm. "I want to extend in line abreast. The left flank must be on the edge of the plain and our right up here on the crest of the hills. We will sweep northwards." He made a wide gesture, but Hilto looked dubious.

"That is a broad front, Your Majesty. It's almost half a league to the valley bottom. At times we will be out of sight of each other."

Nefer cut in with a sharp tone and cold expression: "Do you presume to argue with your pharaoh?"

"Never, Majesty!" Hilto was shocked at the accusation.

"Then do your duty, fellow."

Hilto saluted and hurried back to his own chariot, shouting orders to his men. As the squadron wheeled out down the slope, Mintaka nudged Nefer and smiled. "Do your duty, fellow!" She mimicked his haughty tone then laughed. "Please never look at me like that or use that tone to me, Your Majesty. I am sure I would die of fright."

She lifted her face to him and her lips were parted slightly. He could smell her sweet breath, and the temptation to reach down for those lips was almost irresistible. "We have only a little time," he replied instead. "We must make the most of it, and find a place where we can be alone."

He swung the chariot down towards a small grove of thorn trees, almost hidden by a fold in the ground, where a narrow ravine had been cut into the hillside by wind and weather. There must have been subterranean water, for the thorn trees were robust. Their thick foliage provided shade and privacy in this hot midday. Nefer drove down the bank and into the shade. He jumped down and went to fill the bucket from the water-skin to water the horses. Mintaka, aware of a fullness in her bladder, picked her way deeper into the grove of thorn trees.

THE LION WATCHED her with yellow eyes, flattening its ears against its skull and pressing its body closer to the stony earth. The previous night it had missed an oryx, and hunger was a dull, insistent pain in its gut. It lifted its head, and slashed its tail back and forth, the prelude to the charge.

As Mintaka stood and started back towards Nefer, she heard the rhythmic swish and thud of the tail, stopped and looked up, puzzled. She looked straight into the yellow gaze of the beast. She screamed, a high-pitched sound that struck Nefer to the heart. He whirled round and in an instant took in the situation: the girl, the crouching beast facing her, and his bow and quiver ten paces away, in the rack on the chariot's dashboard.

At that moment the lion growled. It was a terrible sound that seemed to vibrate in Mintaka's bones and make the ground tremble.

Then its mane rose like a dark aura around its head and it launched itself into its charge, coming straight at her.

"Come! Here I am! Come to me!" Nefer yelled wildly, and it swung its huge head towards him. His arm was shaking as he reached down and drew his dagger from the sheath on his belt.

It was a flimsy weapon against this furious beast. The thin bronze blade was not long enough to stab through to the heart, but he had heard the royal huntsman tell tales of miraculous escapes from just such a deadly predicament. The lion hurled itself towards him and, as it launched into the death spring, Nefer fell backwards, not even attempting to resist the beast's weight and impetus. He lay between its forepaws, and the lion opened its jaws to full stretch and thrust its head down to crush Nefer's skull with its terrible fangs. He steeled himself and thrust his hand, holding the dagger with the blade aligned upright, deep into the open jaws. The lion bit down instinctively, driving the bronze point up through the roof of its mouth. Nefer snatched away his hand before the fangs could crush the bones of his wrist, but the lion's jaws were fixed open by the dagger held between them, and it could not bite down. It ripped at him with both its forepaws, claws fully extended. He writhed beneath the heavy body, evading some of the claw strokes, but felt the bony hooks tearing into his flesh.

Mintaka's own fear was now forgotten. She raced towards the chariot, the screams and roars behind her goading her on. Ahead of her the terrified horses reared and threw their heads. They would have bolted long ago had not Nefer secured the locking brake on one wheel so they could only turn in a tight right-handed circle. Mintaka ran in under their flying hoofs, jumped up onto the footplate and brought them under control. She knocked off the brake and drove them straight at the lion and its victim. She then snatched the long lance from its rack and, guiding the horses with the reins in her left hand, leaned far out over the side panel and raised the lance high. As they ran past the crouched lion, the back of its neck was exposed. The exact juncture of spine and skull was covered by the dense black bush of its mane, but she guessed at the spot and thrust down with all the strength of her fear and her love for Nefer.

Her lance hand had the impetus of the flying chariot behind it. To her amazement the blade slid in readily, full length through the taut hide, deep into the back of the animal's neck to sever the spinal column. As the chariot raced past, the lance was plucked from her grip. But the lion collapsed in a loose, inert heap on top of Nefer. It did not twitch again, killed on the instant.

She wheeled the crazed horses back to where Nefer lay beneath the huge carcass, and jumped down from the footplate. It was obvious how badly Nefer was hurt. She could see that the enormous weight of the dead beast was crushing the wind from his lungs. Seizing the long tufted tail she heaved with all her strength. Slowly the hindquarters began to swing, then the whole carcass flopped over and he was free.

Mintaka knelt beside him and helped him into a sitting position, but he swayed drunkenly and reached out to her for support.

"You are desperately wounded," she cried. "There is so much blood."

"Not all of it is mine," he blurted, but from his right thigh rose a crimson fountain where the claws had ripped open a blood vessel. Taita had instructed him long and earnestly in the treatment of wounds, and he thrust his thumb down into the torn flesh and pressed until the jet of blood shrivelled.

"Get the water-skin," he said, and Mintaka did so and held it for him while he drank thirstily. Then she washed the blood and filth from his face, relieved to find it unmarked. However, when she inspected his other injuries she saw how grievous they were.

"My bedroll is in the chariot." His voice was weaker. When she brought it to him he asked her to undo the bundle, where she found a needle and silk thread. He showed her how to tie off the spurting blood vessel. Her hands were bloody to the wrists, as with nimble fingers she pulled a thread round the open artery then closed the deeper rents in his flesh. She used strips torn from his tattered kilt to bind up the wounds. It was rough, rudimentary surgery, but sufficient to stem the worst of the bleeding.

"That is all we can do now. I must help you into the chariot and get you to where a surgeon can do the rest. Oh, if only Taita were here."

Nefer was staring longingly at the carcass of the lion. "My first lion," he whispered ruefully. "Unless we skin it, the trophy will spoil. The hair will slip and slough off."

In the heat of her terrible concern for him, she lost her temper. "That is the most stupid piece of man's nonsense I have ever heard. Would you risk your life for a stinking bit of fur?" Angrily she helped him to his feet. He leaned on her with all his weight as he hobbled to the chariot and collapsed weakly onto the footplate. Mintaka used the sheepskin from the bedroll to make him as comfortable as she could, then climbed up and stood over him with the reins in her hands.

"Which way?" she asked.

"The rest of the squadron will be far up the valley by now," he told her. "The other hunters are scattered across the desert. We could search for them all day without finding them."

"We must return to where the fleet is lying at Dabba. There is a surgeon with the ships." She had reached the only feasible conclusion, and he nodded. She urged the horses into a walk, and they left the grove and climbed to the high ground, heading south.

Even though Mintaka kept the horses down to a trot, the collision with every stone or hump was transmitted through the rigid chassis into Nefer's torn body. He winced and sweated, trying to hide his pain from her, but as the hours wore on it became unbearable. He groaned aloud at a particularly nasty impact, and she reined the pair to a halt.

"You are going to be all right, my darling," she told him, with a confidence she did not feel. She sponged his face, kissed the top of his dusty, blood-caked head, and took up the reins again.

An hour later she gave the last of the water to Nefer and the horses, not drinking herself. Then she stood as high as she could on the dashboard of the chariot and looked about her. At her feet Nefer stirred and moaned, and she looked down with a brave face and smiled. "Not much further now, my heart. We should see the river over the next crest."

She rearranged the sheepskin under his head, then stood up and gathered the reins. Suddenly she realised how exhausted she was: every muscle in her body ached and her eyes were sore from the sun's glare and the dust. She forced herself and the team onwards.

Soon the horses were showing signs of distress. They had stopped sweating and the salt rime had dried white across their backs. She tried to urge them into a trot but they could not respond, and at last despair overtook her. She sank down, helpless and lost, and whispered to Nefer as he lay, now unconscious, "I am sorry, my darling. I have failed you." She stroked the matted hair from his face. Then she looked up at the low hilltop to the east and blinked. She shook her head to clear her vision, then looked again, but still she could not be sure that what she was seeing was illusion or reality.

On the crest of the hills above them, a gaunt figure stood on the skyline, leaning on his long staff. His silver hair shone like a cloud and the hot, light breeze of the desert flapped his skirts against his heron-thin legs. He was staring down at them.

Beside her, Nefer opened his eyes. "Taita is near," he murmured. "I feel him close."

"Yes. Taita is here." Her voice was faint. "But how did he know where to find us?"

"He knows. Taita knows," Nefer replied, closed his eyes and slumped back into unconsciousness.

TAITA DROVE DOWN the escarpment towards the river. The horses responded to his touch, moving with an easy motion that cosseted the wounded boy on the footplate. Taita seemed to have known with some deep instinct just what medicines and dressings Nefer would need, and he had carried these with him. After he had re-dressed the wounds, he led the horses to a hidden water seep nearby to revive them. Then he took Mintaka up on the footplate and turned the horses' heads unerringly in the direction of Dabba.

A red and angry sunset was fading over the Nile like a dying bush fire as they approached the spot where the fleet was still anchored in the stream. Apepi and Naja rode out to meet them. Lord Naja was agitated, and Apepi bellowed at his daughter as soon as they were in range, "Where have you been, you stupid child? Half the army is out looking for you."

Lord Naja's agitation abated when he saw Nefer bandaged and unconscious in the chariot cockpit. Barely conscious, the boy was carried gently aboard one of the galleys.

"I want Pharaoh taken up to Thebes with all possible speed," Taita told Naja, "even if it means a night journey."

"You can order the galley to sail at once," Naja said, in front of the company, but then took Taita's arm and led him a short way along the river bank to where they could not be overheard. "Bear in mind, Magus, the charge laid on you by the gods. If Pharaoh were to die from his wounds no person in either kingdom would take it as unnatural." He said no more but gazed into Taita's face.

"The will of the gods will prevail against all else," Taita agreed.

Naja read in his reply what he wanted to hear. "We are in accord, Taita. I place my trust in you. Go in peace. I will follow you to Thebes after Apepi has been taken care of." This last remark struck Taita as odd, but he was too distracted to ponder it.

When he hurried back on board the galley, Taita found Mintaka kneeling beside the litter in tears.

She looked up at him piteously. "My father is taking me back to Avaris in the morning, but I should be with Nefer. I am his betrothed. He needs me." She seized his hand. "Oh, Magus! Will you not go to my father and ask him to let me go back to Thebes to help you to take care of Nefer? My father will listen to you."

But when Taita attempted to persuade Apepi to let her go back to Thebes with Nefer, the king snorted with laughter, "Place my lamb in Naja's pen?" He shook his head with amusement. "I trust Naja as I would a scorpion. Who knows what tricks he would try if I gave him that coin to bargain with? No, Warlock, Mintaka comes back under my wing to Avaris until her wedding day."

Sadly Mintaka went to take her leave of Nefer. He was on the edge of consciousness, weak from loss of blood, but when she kissed him he opened his eyes. She took the golden locket that hung at her throat. "This contains a lock of my hair. It is my soul, and I give it to you." She placed it in his hand and he folded his fingers tightly round it.

So Mintaka stood alone on the bank of the Nile, watching forlornly as the galley bearing Nefer and Taita breasted the current, heading upstream towards Thebes.

THE NEXT MORNING there was a final meeting between Apepi and the regent, Lord Naja, on board the Hyksosian royal barge. All Apepi's nine sons were present, and Mintaka was seated beside her father. Then, with protestations of mutual trust and devotion to the peace, the two fleets diverged, one to return to Thebes, the other to Avaris, and garlands and wreaths of palm fronds were tossed from one vessel towards the other, bestrewing the surface of the wide river.

That evening King Apepi's fleet anchored at Balasfura, opposite the temple of Hapi, where Trok and the officers under his command arranged a banquet and entertainment. On the river bank pavilions were hung with vivid red, yellow and green curtains to receive the royal family. Whole oxen were grilled over pits of glowing ash, and amphorae of the choicest wines cooled in the river waters. Slaves staggered up the bank under the weight of them as one after the other they were drained and Apepi bellowed for fresh jars to be brought.

The king's mood lightened with each bowl he lowered, and soon he encouraged his sons to join him in singing the ribald marching songs of his army. Some were so scurrilous that Mintaka pleaded exhaustion and retired with her maids to the barge.

Mintaka lay on her mattress and listened to the sounds of revelry. She tried to compose herself to sleep, but Nefer was in the forefront of her mind. The sense of loss that she had held at bay all day, and her concern for Nefer's injuries, flooded back, and though she tried to prevent them, her tears welled up.

At last she sank into a black, dreamless sleep, from which she woke with difficulty, roused by drunken laughter and heavy footfalls from the deck over her head. It seemed that her father and her brothers were being carried on board. She had sipped only a little of the wine, but she felt herself drugged and her head ached. Almost immediately she succumbed to sleep again.

The next time she woke she believed that she was in a nightmare, for she could hear screams and she was choking on clouds of thick smoke. Before she was fully conscious she found herself bundled out of her bed, swaddled in a blanket and carried on deck. She struggled, but she was as helpless as an infant in a powerful grip.

On deck the moonless night was lit by leaping flames. They were roaring out of the forward hatch of the royal barge, climbing the masts and rigging in a hellish torrent. She had never seen a wooden hull burn before and the ferocity of the flames appalled her.

She could not stare at them for long, for she found herself carried swiftly across the deck and down the side into a waiting felucca. As it pushed off into the stream she fought to free herself, but the arms that pinioned her were remorseless. She managed to twist her head and see the face of the man who held her.

"Trok!" She was angered by his presumption, at the way he was ignoring her cries. "Let me go! I command you!"

He did not respond. He held her easily but he was watching the burning galley with a calm, detached expression.

"Go back!" she shrieked. "My family! Go back and fetch them!"

His only response was to snap an order to the oarsmen. "Hold the stroke!" They shipped their paddles and the felucca rocked on the current. The crew watched the burning hulk with fascination. There were agonising screams from those trapped below the decks.

Suddenly the main hatch on the burning deck was thrown open, and a figure emerged. Lord Trok's arms tightened around Mintaka. "It cannot be!" he grated.

Through the smoke and flames, Apepi staggered towards the side of the barge. He carried his youngest son, Khyan, in his arms, and his mouth was wide open, gasping for air.

"The monster is hard to kill." Trok's anger was tinged with fear.

Even in her own distress Mintaka read the meaning of his words. "You, Trok!" she whispered. "You have done this to them!"

Trok ignored the accusation.

Apepi was no longer moving forward, but he stood with legs astraddle and lifted Khyan high above his head. Perhaps he was attempting to throw the boy over the ship's side into the river to escape the flames, but suddenly the deck under Apepi's feet burst open. He and his son dropped through, and in a tall fountain of flame, sparks and smoke were gone.

"It's over." Trok's voice was dispassionate. He released Mintaka so suddenly that she fell into the bilges of the felucca. He looked at his horrified crew. "Row to my galley," he ordered.

"You did this to my family," Mintaka repeated, as she lay at his feet. "You will pay for it. I swear to you. I will make you pay."

But she felt numbed. Her father was gone, that monumental figure in her life whom she had hated a little and loved a great deal. Her family was gone, all of her brothers, even Khyan. She had watched him burn and she knew that the horror of it would stay with her all her days.

The felucca drew alongside Lord Trok's galley and she made no protest as he carried her on board, then down to the main cabin. "Your slave girls are safe. I will send them to you," he said, and went out. She heard the locking bar placed across the door, then the sound of him climbing the companion ladder.

She hid her face in pillows that smelt of Trok's stale sweat and wept until her tears were exhausted. Then she slept.

THE BURNING HULL of Apepi's royal barge drifted up onto the river bank opposite the temple of Hapi. In the dawn the smoke rose high into the still air, tainted by the stench of burnt flesh. When Mintaka awoke the smell had penetrated into the cabin and sickened her. The smoke seemed to act like a beacon, for the sun had hardly risen above the eastern hills before the fleet of Lord Naja came sweeping round the bend of the river.

The slave girls brought the news to Mintaka. "Lord Naja has come in full array," they told her excitedly. "Yesterday he left us to return to Thebes. Is it not strange that he could reach here so soon when he should be twenty leagues upriver?"

"Surpassing strange," Mintaka agreed grimly.

Her baggage had all gone up in flames in the royal barge, but her maids borrowed clothing from the other noble ladies in the fleet, and they dressed her in a simple linen shift, gold girdle and sandals.

Before noon an armed escort came aboard the galley, and she followed them on deck. Her eyes went to the blackened timbers of the royal barge that lay on the far bank, burnt down to the water line. No effort had been made to recover any bodies from the wreck. It was her family's funeral pyre. With an effort she held back further tears, went down into the waiting felucca, and was taken to the bank where Lord Naja was waiting with all his company assembled.

She remained aloof and pale when he embraced her. "This is a bitter time for all of us, Princess," he said. "Your father was a mighty warrior and statesman. In view of the recent treaty between the two kingdoms, he leaves a dangerous gap. For the good of all, this must be filled immediately."

He took her hand and led her to the pavilion that had last evening been the scene of feasting and festivity, but where now were assembled in solemn conclave most of the nobility of both kingdoms.

She saw Trok in the forefront of this throng, and behind him in packed ranks all his officers, grim, cold-eyed and menacing. They stared at her, unsmiling, and she was bitterly aware that she was the last of the Apepi line, abandoned and unprotected.

She wondered to whom she could appeal, and whose loyalty she still commanded. She searched for friendly, familiar faces in the multitude. They were all there, her father's councillors and advisers, his generals and comrades of the battlefield. But their eyes slid away from her face. None smiled at her. She had never felt so alone.

Naja led her to a cushioned stool at one side of the pavilion. When she sat down, Naja and his staff formed a screen round her, hiding her from view. She was certain that this had been deliberately arranged.

Lord Naja opened the conclave with a lamentation for the death of King Apepi and his sons. Then he continued, "In the tragic circumstances of his death, King Apepi leaves no male heir to the Crown." Smoothly he passed over any mention of Mintaka. "As a matter of urgency I have consulted the senior councillors of both kingdoms. Their choice for the new pharaoh has been unanimous. With one voice they have asked Lord Trok of Memphis to pick up the reins of power, to take the double crown upon himself and steer the nation forward."

In the uproar that followed, strong hands took Mintaka and spirited her away through the cheering press. She struggled ineffectually, her voice unheard in the storm of cheering. On the river bank she twisted in the arms of her captors and glanced back. Over the heads of the crowd she glimpsed Lord Naja raising the double crown over the head of the new Pharaoh.

Then she was hustled down the bank to the waiting felucca, and back to her locked and guarded cabin on board Lord Trok's galley.

DURING THE VOYAGE downriver from Balasfura, Mintaka had the freedom of the deck while they were under way, but at anchor or at moorings she was locked in her cabin.

One morning Trok insisted that she join him for a lavish breakfast on the foredeck. There were twenty other guests, and Trok seated himself next to Mintaka. She pointedly ignored him and directed all her charm and wit to the officers of his army.

At the end of the meal Trok clapped his hands for attention, and was rewarded with an obsequious silence. "Your Royal Highness," he addressed her gravely, "your divine father of illustrious memory must have had some premonition of the fate that awaited him. Before his tragic death he spoke to me. He placed you under my protection. I accepted this as a sacred charge. You need never appeal to any other for protection." He placed his right hand upon her bowed head, and in the other hand he raised a scroll of parchment.

"This is my royal proclamation setting aside the betrothal of the Princess Mintaka of the House of Apepi to Pharaoh Nefer Seti of the House of Tamose. Furthermore, it contains a proclamation of the marriage of the Princess Mintaka to Pharaoh Trok Uruk. The proclamation has been ratified by the cartouche of Lord Naja, accepting and confirming it in the name of Pharaoh Nefer Seti." He handed the scroll to his chamberlain with a terse instruction. "Have one hundred copies made of this proclamation and cause them to be publicly displayed in every city in Egypt."

Then, with both hands, he lifted Mintaka to her feet. "You and I will be husband and wife before the rise of the Moon of Osiris."

THREE DAYS LATER Pharaoh Trok Uruk arrived at Avaris, his military capital in the Lower Kingdom. The populace was delirious with joy at the news of the Treaty of Hathor, and at the promise of peace and prosperity in the years ahead. However, there was some dismay when one of the first acts of the new pharaoh was to put in hand another massive draft of men for the army. It soon became clear that he was intent on doubling the size of his infantry regiments and building two thousand more fighting chariots.

The question was asked, but not to Trok's face, where he expected to find an enemy now that Egypt was united and at peace. The loss of working men from fields and pastures to the army resulted in a shortage of food, and the expenditure on chariots and equipment necessitated an increase in taxation. There were mutters now that Apepi had not been as bad a ruler as they had believed him to be.

The muttering grew louder when Trok ordered work to commence on the extensive enlargements and refurbishment of the palace in Avaris into which he intended to move with his bride. The architects estimated these works would cost over two lakhs of gold.

A revolt started in the delta, where a regiment of foot, unpaid for over a year, murdered their officers and marched on Avaris. Trok met them with three hundred chariots near the village of Manashi and cut them to pieces with his first charge. He then impaled five hundred mutineers on stakes. Like a macabre forest, they decorated both sides of the road for half a league beyond the village.

A few hundred mutineers escaped the massacre and disappeared into the desert. Trok did not bother to pursue them, for this petty matter had delayed his wedding. He hurried back to Avaris, using up three pairs of horses in his furious impatience.

There his wedding with Princess Mintaka Apepi was carried out in the ancient Hyksosian tradition. First the high priest bound Mintaka to him with a halter rope, and then, at the culmination of the ceremony, Trok cut the throat of his favourite warhorse, a beautiful chestnut stallion, as a sign that he placed a higher value on his bride than on this other precious possession. As the animal fell, the company shouted their acclamation and lifted the couple into the flower-bedecked chariot.

Trok drove back to the palace with one arm firmly round his bride. The army lined the way, showering gifts of amulets and good-luck charms into the cockpit. Others held up bowls of wine to Trok as he drove past, and he gulped them down.

By the time they reached the palace, Trok was sweating and dusty from the ride, reckless with wine, and wild-eyed with lust.

He carried Mintaka through the crowd into their new apartments, and the guards at the door turned back the wedding guests with drawn swords. However, they did not disperse but surrounded the palace, chanting encouragement to the bridegroom and ribald advice to the bride.

In the bedchamber Trok threw Mintaka onto the white sheepskin that covered the mattress, and used both hands to struggle with his sword-belt, trying to loosen the clasp. Mintaka leapt up and raced to the terrace door but locking bars on the outside had been put in place. Desperately she tried to beat open the panels, but the doors were thick and did not even tremble to her onslaught.

Behind her, Trok had at last rid himself of the sword-belt and came lumbering unsteadily after her. "Fight as much as you wish," he slurred. "It sets me on fire when you kick and scream."

He placed one arm round her waist, and threw her down again, this time pinning her with one huge muscular arm across her chest. His face was inches from hers. His beard prickled her cheeks, and his breath smelt of sour wine. She twisted her face away. He laughed and hooked one finger in the neck of her shift and ripped the silk to below her waist.

He straddled her, sitting across her lower body with all his weight so that she could not struggle, and tore off his tunic. Under it he was naked, and although her vision was distorted by terror, she had an impression of wide shoulders and bulging muscle, limbs thick and thewy as the branches of a cedar of Lebanon.

Still pinning her under him, he twisted round until his belly pressed against hers. He tried to force a knee between her thighs, but she kept them locked together, hooking one of her legs over the other. She fought not only for her modesty, but as if for her very life. Every muscle in her lower body was frozen in a rigor of fear and revulsion, hard and as impenetrable as a granite statue.

Suddenly he swung a heavy blow, flat-handed, across her face. It jarred her clenched jaws, crushing her lips. She felt blood flood into her mouth and darkness fill her head and knew she could not last out much longer.

"Hathor, help me!" She closed her eyes and prayed. "Sweet goddess, do not let it happen!"

She heard him groan above her, and her eyes flew open. She saw him arch his back and he moaned as though in pain. Mintaka did not understand what was happening. For a moment she thought the goddess must have heard her plea and struck him through the heart with a divine dart. Then she felt hot liquid spray onto her stomach. She tried to twist away to avoid it, but he was too heavy and strong.

At last, he groaned and collapsed on top of her. Then he roused himself and looked down at her. "You have shamed me, you little slut. You have made me spill my seed in vain."

Before she knew what he was about, he had grabbed her by the back of her neck and forced her face into the white sheepskin.

"Never fear, I shall use the blood from your nose if I can't have it from your honeypot." He rolled her aside and inspected the crimson stain from her bleeding face on the pure white wool with grim satisfaction. Then he jumped to his feet, strode to the shutters and kicked them open with a crash. He disappeared out into the bright daylight.

His sword-belt lay where he had dropped it. Quietly Mintaka slipped from the bed and drew the burnished bronze blade from its scabbard. She crept to the door that led onto the terrace and flattened herself against the jamb.

Out on the balcony, Trok was acknowledging the applause of the crowd and flapping the stained sheepskin for all to see. Mintaka tightened her grip on the haft of the sword and gathered herself.

"Farewell, my friends," Trok shouted. "I am going back for another bite at that sweet fig."

She heard his bare feet swish on the tiles as he returned and then his shadow fell across the entrance. She drew back the heavy sword with both hands, and held the point at belly height.

As he stepped into the chamber she braced herself and then with all her strength thrust at him. But Trok possessed a feral instinct for danger and twisted away from the sharp bronze point. It flew the width of a finger past his hairy stomach, without drawing a drop of blood. Then he clamped both her wrists in one of his huge paws and squeezed until she had to let the weapon drop.

He was laughing as he dragged her across the room, but it was an ugly sound. He threw her face down onto the rumpled, sweat-sour bed, and picked up the sword scabbard from where it lay. "This lesson in obedience is for your own good. A little pain now will save us both a great deal of unhappiness later."

The scabbard was of polished leather, bound with gold and studded with metal rosettes. He swung it down across the back of her naked legs. It left a welt with the pattern of rosettes in brighter scarlet.

He lifted the scabbard again. She tried to roll away from him but the next blow caught her across her raised right arm, and the next across her shoulder. Then he knocked her off the bed and when she rolled herself into a ball he lashed her across her back. He spoke to her while he kept the blows falling. "You will never lift a hand to me again! Next time I come to you, you will behave as a loving wife, or I will have four of my men hold you down while I mount you!"

She clenched her jaws as the blows rained down upon her until mercifully he stepped away, breathing heavily, and pulled on his dust-streaked tunic. He stalked to the door of the chamber. There he paused and looked back at her.

"Remember one thing, wife. Either I break my mares," he said, "or, by Seueth, they die under me." He turned and was gone.

IT WAS LONG after the waning of the Moon of Isis before Mintaka's bruises faded to greenish-yellow stains on her smooth, creamy skin.

Since their calamitous wedding day Trok had left her alone. Most of that time he was campaigning in the south. Even when he returned for brief periods to Avaris he avoided her. Perhaps he was repelled by her unsightly injuries or shamed by his failure to consummate their marriage. Mintaka did not ponder the reason too deeply, but she rejoiced in being free of his brutish attentions.

There had been further serious rebellion in the south of the kingdom, and Mintaka knew that Trok had returned triumphantly to Avaris three days ago, but she had still not seen him. She thanked the goddess for that, but it was premature. The summons came from him on the fourth day. Mintaka was to attend an extraordinary session of the state council. His message warned her that should she choose to ignore his summons he would send his bodyguards to drag her to the conclave. She had no option.

This was the first occasion on which Mintaka had appeared in public since her wedding. With her make-up carefully applied she was as lovely as ever as she took her seat on the queen's throne, below that of Pharaoh, in the lavishly redecorated assembly hall of the palace.

Trok acknowledged the herald, then called upon him to rise and state his news to the council. When he rose to his feet Mintaka saw that he was in the grip of deep emotion. "Sacred Majesty, I bring tragic tidings from Thebes." He paused and spread his arms in a gesture of despair. "Last month, on the eve of the festival of Hapi, the young Pharaoh Nefer Seti, whom we all loved, and in whom we placed so much trust and hope, died of the grievous wounds that he received while hunting." There was a concerted sigh of despair.

The herald spoke again: "The Regent of the Upper Kingdom, Lord Naja, who is next in succession, has been raised to the throne in the place of the departed Pharaoh. He purifies the land in his name, he endures unto eternity in his name of Naja, the fear of him through all the world is great in his name of Pharaoh Naja Kiafan."

The cries of mourning for the dead Pharaoh and the clamour of acclamation for his successor filled the hall.

In the uproar, Mintaka stared at the herald. Trok was watching her and she knew he was revelling in her pain. She listened to the rest of the proceedings, but her thoughts were with Nefer. In her mind a picture of him appeared as though he still lived. She wondered what point he had reached on his dread journey through the netherworld, and she prayed for his safety. She prayed for him to reach the green hills of paradise, and that she should soon be reunited with him there. I shall follow you soon, my heart, she promised him.

TAITA HAD BROUGHT Nefer back to Thebes from Dabba still in a deep sleep. As soon as the galley carrying them moored at the stone jetty below the palace, Taita had him carried ashore on a curtained litter. It would have been unwise to allow Pharaoh's critical condition to become widely known.

Once Nefer was safe in his royal quarters at the palace, Taita was able to work on him in seclusion. His first concern was to examine again the boy's terrible lacerations and assess if there had been any morbid changes.

He unwrapped the bandages, probed the openings gently, and was greatly relieved to find no taint of contamination. He syringed the deepest wounds with a mixture of vinegar and oriental spices. Then he stitched them closed with catgut and bandaged them.

He was rewarded when at last Nefer recovered consciousness and smiled at him. "Taita, I knew you were with me."

The following day he sat up and ate a meal of millet bread and chickpea soup. Then he looked around him. "Where is Mintaka?"

When Taita explained her absence, Nefer's disappointment was almost palpable. Taita tried to console him by telling him that he would soon be well enough to visit Avaris.

The next day the terrible news of the tragedy at Balasfura reached Thebes from the Lower Kingdom. Nefer tried to convince Taita that he was strong enough to make the long journey to be with Mintaka in her bereavement. Gently Taita dissuaded him, but promised that as soon as Nefer was strong enough he would use all his influence to convince Lord Naja to allow him to go. With this goal to strive towards, Nefer rallied strongly. Taita could see him subduing the evil humours in his blood by sheer strength of will.

Lord Naja returned from the north, and within hours Heseret came to visit Nefer for the first time since his mauling by the lion. She brought him gifts of sweetmeats and a pot of wild honey in the comb, excusing herself for having neglected him.

"My dear husband, the Regent of the Upper Kingdom, has been away all these weeks," she explained, "and I have pined so much for his return that I was afraid that my unhappiness might affect you badly, my poor darling." She stayed an hour, sang to him, and related some of the scandalous doings of the court. At last she excused herself: "My husband does not like me to leave his side for long. We are so much in love, Nefer. He is a wonderful man. You must learn to trust him completely, as I do." She rose to her feet and then, as though in an afterthought, she remarked lightly, "You must have been relieved to hear that Pharaoh Trok Uruk and my dear husband, the Regent of Upper Egypt, have agreed to cancel your betrothal to that little Hyksosian barbarian, Mintaka. I was so sorry for you when I heard that such a disgraceful marriage had been thrust upon you. My husband was against it from the beginning, as I was."

After she had gone Nefer sank back weakly on the pillow and closed his eyes. When Taita came to him a little later he was puzzled by the way in which he had relapsed. He stayed with him through that night, exerting all his powers to ward off the shadows of evil that surrounded the young Pharaoh.

At dawn he was startled to hear Lord Naja's commanding voice ordering the guards at the door to stand aside. The regent strode into the chamber and, without greeting Taita, stooped over Nefer's still form and peered into his face. After a long moment he straightened up and signed to Taita to follow him onto the terrace.

"You wished to speak to me, my lord?" Taita asked.

Naja turned to him. His expression was grim. "You have disappointed me, old man," he said, and Taita bowed his head but made no reply. "I had hoped that my way forwards would be cleared by now of impediment." He stared hard at Taita. "Yet it seems that, far from allowing this, you have done all in your power to prevent it."

"This has been pretence. I have merely made a show of caring for my patient. As you can see for yourself, Pharaoh hangs over the great abyss." Taita made a gesture towards the sick chamber where Nefer lay. "Surely you can sense the shades drawing in around him. My lord, we have almost obtained our object. Within days the way ahead will be cleared for you."

Naja was not convinced. "I am reaching the limit of my patience," he warned, and strode from the terrace. He passed through the chamber without another glance at the still form upon the bed.

During that day Nefer's condition fluctuated. Taita sat for a while collecting his thoughts, reviewing the plans he had laid so carefully over the past weeks. He could not do it alone, and would have to rely on others, but he had chosen the best. They were ready to act, and they had been waiting for his word. He could delay no longer.

AT HIS BIDDING the slaves brought kettles of hot water and Taita washed Nefer from head to foot. When he had finished, he warned the guards not to let anybody pass, and barred all the entrances to the chamber. He prayed for a while and then threw incense on the brazier, and in the blue and aromatic smoke made an ancient, potent incantation to Anubis, the god of death and cemeteries.

Only then did he prepare the elixir of Anubis in a new and unused vessel. He warmed the mixture on the brazier until it was the temperature of blood, and took it to the bed where Nefer was sleeping quietly. Gently he turned his head to one side and poured the elixir into the eardrum a drop at a time. Carefully he wiped away the excess, taking care that it should not touch his own skin. Then he plugged Nefer's ear with a small ball of wool, pushed deeply into the passage.

He watched Nefer's chest rise and fall to his breathing. Each breath was slower and the intervals between them longer. At last they ceased altogether. He placed two fingers on Nefer's throat beneath his ear, and felt the slow deliberate pulsing of the life force within him. Gradually that also faded away until it was only an occasional flutter that took all his skill and experience to detect. Gently he closed the boy's eyes and placed an amulet upon the lids in the traditional preparation of the corpse. Next he bound a strip of linen over them, and another under his jaw to keep his mouth from gaping open. At last he went to the door and removed the locking bar.

"Send word to the Regent of the Upper Kingdom. He should come immediately to hear terrible tidings of Pharaoh."

Lord Naja arrived with surprising alacrity. Princess Heseret was with him, and they were followed by the Assyrian doctor, Noom, and most of the members of the council.

Heseret was weeping ostentatiously and covering her eyes with an embroidered linen shawl. Naja glanced at the bandaged body laid out on the couch, then glanced at Taita with a question in his eyes. In reply Taita nodded slightly. Naja masked the gleam of triumph in his eyes, then clapped his hands.

"Let the good doctor Noom come forward," Naja ordered. "Let him confirm the Magus's pronouncement of Pharaoh's death."

The Assyrian's long locks had been curled with hot tongs and dangled to his shoulders. His beard had also been curled in the fashion of Babylon. His robe swept the floor and was decorated with embroidered magical symbols. He knelt beside the deathbed and began an examination of the corpse. He sniffed at Nefer's lips, then placed his ear against Nefer's chest and listened. Taita had placed much store in the Assyrian's ineptitude.

Then Noom took a long silver pin from the hem of his robe and opened Nefer's limp hand. He pricked the point deeply up under the fingernail and watched for a muscular reaction. At last he stood up slowly, and shook his head.

"Pharaoh is dead," he announced.

Lord Naja threw back his head and gave the first cry of lamentation, and Heseret, standing behind him, took up the wailing cry.

Taita waited for the mourners to file past the couch, and one by one to leave the chamber. When only Naja and Heseret remained, Taita stepped forward. "Lord Naja, I beg your indulgence. You are aware that I have been Pharaoh Nefer Seti's tutor and servant since his birth. I owe him respect and duty, even now in death. I beg you to allow me to be the one to convey his corpse to the Hall of Sorrow, and there to make the incision to remove his heart and viscera. I would take that as the greatest honour you could bestow on me."

Lord Naja thought for a while, then nodded. "You have earned that honour. I charge you with the duty of conveying Pharaoh's sacred body to the funeral temple for embalming."

THE OLD WARRIOR, Hilto, came swiftly to Taita's summons. He had been waiting in the guardroom at the palace gates. With him he brought four of his most trusted men. One of these was Meren, the friend and companion of Nefer's childhood. He was now a handsome ensign of the guards, and Taita had asked for him particularly.

Between them they carried the long woven basket that the embalmers used to transport their cadavers to the funerary temple. It was heavier than one might have expected.

Taita let them into the death chamber and whispered to Hilto, "Swiftly now! Every second is precious."

He had already wrapped Nefer in a long white winding sheet, with a loose fold of linen covering his face. The pallbearers laid the basket beside the couch and lifted Nefer into it. Taita closed the lid, and nodded.

"To the temple," he said. "All is in readiness."

Taita trusted his leather instrument bag to Meren, and they moved quickly through the passages and courtyards of the palace. The sounds of mourning and lamentation followed them. The guards lowered the points of their weapons and knelt as the dead Pharaoh passed. The women covered their faces and wailed.

In the entrance courtyard a squadron of Hilto's chariots was drawn up with the horses in the traces. The bearers laid the basket on the footplate of the leading chariot and secured it with leather straps. Taita mounted and took the reins. The rams' horns of the regiment sounded a dirge, and the column moved out through the gates at a walk.

The news of Pharaoh's death had spread throughout the city. Crowds lined the route along the river. Women ran forward and threw sacred lotus blossoms onto the basket.

Taita pushed the horses into a trot, then into a canter, desperate to get the basket into the sanctuary of the funerary temple.

The tall, rose-coloured granite walls and portico of the temple were set upon a low prominence overlooking the river. The priests, hastily assembled, were waiting to greet the column. Their heads were freshly shaven and anointed with oil. Taita drove up the wide causeway and halted the chariot at the foot of the staircase that mounted to the Hall of Sorrow.

Hilto and his warriors lifted the basket and climbed the staircase with it balanced on their shoulders. The priests fell in behind them, singing mournfully. Before the open wooden doors of the

Hall of Sorrow the pallbearers paused, and Taita looked back at the priests.

"By the grace and authority of the Regent of Egypt, I, Taita, have been charged with lifting Pharaoh's viscera." He fixed the high priest with a mesmeric gaze. "All others will wait without while I perform this sacred charge."

Taita led the bearers through the doorway and they solemnly laid the basket on the floor beside the black diorite slab in the centre of the Hall of Sorrow. Hilto closed the doors with great dignity in the faces of the assembled priests, then hurried back to Taita's side. Between them they opened the basket and lifted Nefer's body. They laid it on the black slab.

Taita folded back the cloth that covered Nefer's face, gently turned his head to one side and nodded at Meren, who placed the leather instrument bag close to his right hand and opened it. Taita selected the ivory forceps, slipped the points into Nefer's ear and drew out the woollen plug. Through a gold tube he carefully sluiced the dregs of the elixir of Anubis from Nefer's eardrum. He had the antidote ready in another phial. When he opened the stopper it released a sharp odour of camphor and sulphur. Hilto helped them to lift Nefer into a sitting position and Taita administered the entire contents of the phial.

Suddenly Nefer coughed harshly. Taita massaged Nefer's bare back and he coughed again, vomiting yellow bile. While Taita kept working steadily at reviving him, Hilto ordered his men to their knees and made them swear a dreadful oath of secrecy as to all that they were witnessing.

Satisfied at last, Taita rewrapped Nefer in the linen sheet, turned back to the basket, and lifted out the false bottom to reveal another corpse laid in the compartment beneath, also wrapped in a white linen winding sheet.

Under Taita's sharp eye they changed the two bodies. They laid Nefer in the hidden compartment in the bottom of the basket, and Meren squatted beside it to watch him and check his condition. The others laid the strange corpse on the diorite slab.

Taita swept away the winding sheet and revealed the body of a youth of about the same age and bodily shape of Nefer. He had the same thick dark hair. The young thief had been put to death by strangulation that very morning and his body was not yet cold.

The Canopic jars were arranged in the small shrine at the end of the hall. Taita ordered Meren to fetch them and open the stoppers ready for filling. While he was doing this, Taita rolled the corpse over and made a sweeping incision down his left side. There was little time for surgical finesse. He thrust his hand into the opening and drew forth the viscera. Then he cut through the diaphragm to gain access to the chest cavity, reaching deep until he could sever the windpipe above its juncture with the lungs. When all the contents of the interior of the chest and abdomen were unanchored, he brought them out onto the diorite slab in a single mass. Meren blanched, fled to the stone basin in the corner and puked noisily into it.

Bloodied to the elbows, Taita flushed out the contents of the stomach and entrails and packed them into their jars. He filled every jar with the pickling natron salts, and sealed the stoppers. Then he washed his hands and arms in the bronze basins filled with water expressly for that purpose.

Working with controlled haste, Taita stitched the abdominal incision closed. Then he bandaged the head until its features were hidden. When that was done, he and Hilto carried the corpse to the large natron bath and lowered it into the harsh alkali mixture, which would leach the fats out of the body and peel the skin away. It would remain in the bath, with the head covered, for the next sixty days. At the end of that time the priests would remove the bandage and discover the substitution. By then, however, Taita and Nefer would be far away.

It took only a little longer to sluice down the slab and pack Taita's instruments before they were ready to leave. Taita knelt beside the basket in which Nefer lay, and laid a hand on his chest to feel its warmth and check his breathing. It was slow and even. Satisfied, he stood up and gestured for Hilto to cover the hidden compartment. When this was done the bearers lifted the basket and Taita led them to the doors. As they approached, Hilto threw them open, and the assembly of priests craned forward. They gave the empty basket only a cursory glance as it was carried out, then rushed into the Hall of Sorrow with almost indecent haste.

Ignored by the crowds that had gathered outside the temple, Taita's men loaded the basket onto the leading chariot and drove it to the guard's barracks near the east gate. There the basket was carried through the back entrance of Hilto's private quarters. Here, everything was in readiness. They lifted Nefer out and Taita went to work to revive him fully. Within hours he was well enough to eat a little millet bread and drink a bowl of warm milk and honey.

At last Taita judged it safe to leave him for a while, and drove through the narrow streets. Ahead of him he heard the sudden din of wild cheering. At the palace he found himself enveloped in a dense crowd of citizens celebrating the ascension of the new pharaoh. "Eternal life to His Sacred Majesty Pharaoh Naja Kiafan!" they cried with loyal fervour, and passed the wine jugs from hand to hand.

The palace guards recognised Taita, and used the butts of their spears to clear the way for him to pass. Once he was in the grounds he hurried to the great hall, and there he found another press of obsequious humanity, waiting to swear fealty.

Pharaoh Naja Kiafan and his queen were in the private cabinet beyond the doors at the end of the hall, but Taita had to wait only a short while before he was granted access to the royal presence.

Naja was already wearing the double crown, and holding the flail and the crook crossed over his chest. Beside him Queen Heseret was as lovely as Taita had ever known her. When Taita entered, Naja dismissed those around him and soon the three were alone. Then Naja laid aside the scourge and the sceptre and came to embrace Taita.

"Magus, I should never have doubted you," he said. "You have earned my gratitude." He took from his right hand a magnificent ring of gold and ruby, and placed it on Taita's right index finger. "This is but a small token of my favour."

Heseret came forward and kissed him. "Dearest Taita, you have always been faithful to my family. You shall have gold, land and influence beyond anything you have ever coveted."

After all these years she knew so little of him. "Your generosity is exceeded only by your beauty," he said. Then he turned back to Naja. "I have done what the gods required of me, Your Grace, but it has cost me dear. You know that I loved Nefer. Now I owe you that same love. But I must mourn Nefer, and make my peace with his shade."

"It would be strange indeed if you did not feel for the dead Pharaoh," Naja agreed. "What do you wish of me, Magus? You have only to speak."

"Your Grace, I ask to go into the desert to be alone for a time."

"How long?" Naja asked, and Taita could see he was alarmed by the thought of losing the key to eternal life, which he truly believed Taita held in his hands.

"Not too long, Majesty," Taita assured him.

Naja thought about it for a while. He was never a man for hasty decisions. At last he sighed. "You may absent yourself until the next inundation of the Nile begins, but then you must return to me." Swiftly he wrote out a safe pass and sealed it with his cartouche. "This will allow you to travel at large and avail yourself of whatever food and equipment you may need from my royal storehouses."

Taita prostrated himself in gratitude, but Naja lifted him to his feet in another act of condescension. "Go, Magus! But return to us on the appointed day to receive the rewards you so richly deserve."

Clutching the roll of papyrus Taita backed towards the door making the signs of blessing and benediction.

THEY LEFT THEBES in the early hours of the next morning while most of the city still slept and the guards at the east gate were yawning and heavy-eyed.

Nefer was laid in the back of the wagon, which was drawn by a team of four horses and loaded with essential supplies and the equipment they might need once they had left the river valley. Hilto was dressed as a wealthy farmer and Meren as his son.

Nefer was laid on a straw mattress in the bed of the wagon, under a screen of tanned leather. He was now fully conscious and able to understand all that Taita had to tell him. When the sergeant of the guard climbed into the wagon to inspect the contents, Nefer peered out at him with his gaunt features spotted with the unmistakable stigmata of the plague that Taita had applied. The sergeant swore with horror and leapt down.

"Get you gone!" he shouted. "Take that poxy wretch out of the city."

It took them several days to cross the littoral plain of the river and reach the hills that marked the frontiers of the desert, following the old trade route eastwards towards the Red Sea. Now Nefer was able to climb down from the wagon, and for short periods limp along beside it. Soon he was walking more easily and for longer periods.

They rested for three days at the ancient ruined city of Gallala. They refilled the water-skins at the well and let the horses recover from the rigours of the hard, stony road. When they were fit to resume the journey, they turned away from the known way, travelled in the cool of the night, and took the path known only to Taita that led to Gebel Nagara. Hilto swept their back-trail and covered all signs of their passage.

They arrived in the cave in the middle of a night lit by bright stars. There was not enough water in the tiny seep to supply so many men and horses, so once the wagon was unloaded Hilto started back, leaving Meren to serve Taita and Nefer. Hilto had resigned from his regiment on the pretext of ill health, so he was free to return with every full moon to bring supplies, medicine and news from Thebes.

The first month at Gebel Nagara passed swiftly. In the clean, dry desert air Nefer's wounds healed fully, and soon he was limping out into the desert to hunt with Meren.

At the end of that month Hilto returned from Thebes with the news that Taita's subterfuge had not yet been discovered. He also brought news of insurrections in the Lower Kingdom, and unrest in the Upper Kingdom also, where Naja, like Trok, had increased taxation and ordered an enlistment of men into the army.

"What other news have you from the Lower Kingdom?" Nefer asked eagerly. "What news is there of Princess Mintaka?"

Hilto looked puzzled. "None that I know of. I should think she is in Avaris, but I cannot be certain."

The following evening, Hilto left Gebel Nagara at the setting of the sun, and struck out into the wilderness.

THE NEXT MOON passed more swiftly than the last, as Nefer grew stronger and more restless. Each day his limp became less noticeable. On his latest visit, Hilto had brought with him a full-weight war-bow. Under Taita's instruction Nefer now practised with it every day, building up the muscles in his back and shoulders. Hilto had also brought them a rack of heavy sickle swords, and Taita would bring them out and lead Nefer and Meren through the entire repertoire of cuts, thrusts and parries.

On other evenings Nefer and Meren stripped naked, oiled their bodies and wrestled, while Taita umpired their bouts and called advice and instruction. Then, late into the night, Taita and Nefer sat by the fire and debated every subject from medicine and politics to war and religion. Often Taita placed hidden traps and illogicalities in these lessons, and more often now, and with greater alacrity, Nefer would uncover and question them.

The month passed so swiftly that it was with a small shock of surprise that Nefer, while running through the desert in pursuit of a gazelle, suddenly noticed on the horizon the distant shape of the wagon returning from the river valley. On the instant, he forgot the gazelle he was chasing and raced to meet Hilto.

"Hilto!" Nefer yelled, still at a distance. "What news? What news?"

Hilto pretended to misunderstand the question, and as Nefer walked at his side he began a long-winded recital of political events in the kingdoms. "There has been another rebellion in the north. This time Trok found it harder to put down. He lost four hundred men and half the rebels escaped his wrath."

Later, around the campfire in the cave, it was agony for Nefer to have to listen to Hilto making a long, detailed report to Taita, the most important part of which was that the substitution of bodies had been discovered when the priests of Anubis had unwrapped the head of the corpse in the Hall of Sorrow. Pharaoh Naja Kiafan had done his best to prevent the news becoming public knowledge, for the foundations of his throne would be undermined if the populace suspected that Nefer was still alive. However, it was impossible to keep such an extraordinary event secret, and rumours were rife in Thebes and the outlying towns and villages.

Added to this, trouble was brewing in the east. The Egyptian pharaohs had sent word to King Sargon of Babylon, that mighty kingdom between the Tigris and Euphrates, demanding that Sargon's annual tribute be increased to twenty lakhs of gold. It was a crippling amount to which Sargon could never agree.

"So, this accounts for the build-up of the armies in both kingdoms," Taita said, as Hilto paused in his report. "It is clear at last that the two pharaohs are greedy for the riches of Babylon. They are intent on conquest. They know too that war is a uniting factor. If they march on Mesopotamia the populace will rally behind them in a patriotic frenzy. It is a marvellous way to take the minds of the people off their grievances."

"Yes." Hilto nodded. "You are right."

"Of course, this is to our advantage," Taita mused. "I have been seeking a haven for us. If he is at war with Trok and Naja, then Sargon will welcome us to his side."

"We are leaving Egypt?" Hilto interjected.

Taita explained, "Now that Naja and Trok know that Nefer still lives, they will come after us. The road to the east is the only one open to us. It will not be for long, just until we have built up our strength and support throughout the two kingdoms and have made ourselves powerful allies. Then we will return to reclaim Pharaoh Nefer's birthright."

They stared at him. It was Nefer who broke the silence. "We can't do that," he said. "I cannot leave Egypt. I took an oath on my life and eternal spirit that I would not desert Mintaka." He turned to Hilto. "You have been evading my questions, Hilto. What news do you have of the princess?"

Hilto opened and closed his mouth, trying to find the courage to tell him the dire news.

"Speak!" Nefer ordered. "Have you forgotten your duty?"

"Gracious Majesty, the news will not please you. Six weeks ago the Princess Mintaka was married in Avaris to Pharaoh Trok Uruk."

Nefer stood as still as if he had been turned into a granite statue. For a long time the only sound in the cave was the crackle of the acacia logs in the fire. Then without another word, Nefer stood up and walked out into the desert night.

When he returned the dawn was a faint red promise in the eastern sky. Hilto and Meren were wrapped in their sheepskins at the back of the cave, but Taita sat in exactly the same position as Nefer had left him. For a moment he thought that the old man was asleep also. Then Taita raised his head and looked at him.

"I need you now, more than ever, old friend," said Nefer. "You will not desert me?"

"You need not ask," Taita said softly.

"I cannot leave her with Trok," Nefer said.

"No."

Nefer came back to his seat opposite Taita. He picked up a charred stump of firewood and pushed it deeper into the flames. Then he looked up at Taita again. "You have tried to teach me to overlook at a distance," he said. "I have never acquired the gift. Not until this night. Out there in the darkness, I tried to overlook Mintaka. This time I saw something, Taita, but only dimly."

"Your love for her has made you sensitive to her aura," Taita explained. "What did you see?"

"I saw only shadows, but sensed sorrow and grief and despair so insupportable that it made me wish for death. I knew that these were Mintaka's emotions and not my own."

Taita stared expressionlessly into the fire, and Nefer went on, "You must overlook her for me. There is something terribly wrong. Only you can help her now, Taita."

"Do you have anything of Mintaka's?" the old man asked. "Any gift or token that she gave you?"

Nefer's hand went to the necklace at his throat. He touched the tiny golden locket that hung in its centre. "It is my most precious possession. It contains a lock of her hair."

"Then it is highly potent. It contains her essence. Give it to me, if you wish me to help her."

Nefer opened the clasp and passed him the amulet.

"Wait here," Taita said, and stood up.

He went out into the dawn and climbed to the crest of the dunes, then squatted in the sand, facing the rising sun. He pressed Mintaka's amulet to his forehead and closed his eyes. It seemed to take on some strange life of its own, pulsing softly in rhythm with his own heartbeats. Taita opened his mind and let the currents of existence enter freely, swirling round him like a great river. His own spirit broke free of his body and he soared aloft. In his mind he called for her, Mintaka! And felt the amulet grow warm then burning hot in his hand.

Slowly the images cleared away, and he heard her sweet voice reply, "I am here. Who is it that calls?"

"Mintaka, it is Taita," he replied, but he was aware that something evil had intervened and broken the stream between them. He focused all his powers upon it, trying to disperse the dark clouds. They seemed to coalesce, and took the shape of a rearing cobra. Suddenly he knew this was a direct and mortal threat against Mintaka. He redoubled his efforts to reach her, but so much pain and grief interposed between them that it was an impenetrable barrier.

Then he saw a hand, slim and graceful, reach out towards the sinister scaly head. It was Mintaka's hand and Taita understood. Mintaka, overwhelmed with grief, was about to take the way of the goddess and find peace in her bosom.

He held the serpent in check with all his life force, and prevented it from striking Mintaka's hand as she stroked the back of its hood. "Mintaka!" He exerted himself to reach her, and was rewarded.

"Taita?" she whispered, and because Mintaka was at last aware of him, Taita's view expanded so that he could see it all clearly.

Mintaka was in a stone-walled bedchamber. She was kneeling in front of a large basket woven from palm fronds. Out of it reared the deadly snake.

"You must not take this road," Taita ordered her. "It is not for you. The gods have prepared a different destiny for you. Do you hear me?"

"Yes!" Mintaka turned her head, as though she could see his face.

"Nefer is alive. Nefer lives. Do you hear me?"

"Yes! Oh, yes."

"Be strong, Mintaka. Nefer and I will come for you."

So fierce was his concentration that he dug his fingernails deeply into the palms of his hands until the blood welled, but he could hold her no longer. She began to slip away from him, but before she was gone he saw her smile, full of love and renewed hope.

"Be strong!" he urged her. "Be strong, Mintaka!" The echo of his voice came back to him as though from a great distance.

NEFER WAS WAITING for him at the foot of the dunes. When Taita was only halfway down the boy realised that something momentous had taken place. "You saw her!" he shouted, and ran forward. "What has happened to her?"

"She needs us," Taita said, and laid a hand on Nefer's shoulder. He could never tell him of the despair in which he had found Mintaka, nor of the fate she had prepared for herself. It might drive him to some wild endeavour. "You were right," Taita went on. "All my plans to leave this land and find sanctuary in the east must be set aside. We have to go to Mintaka. I have promised her that."

"Yes!" Nefer agreed. "When can we leave for Avaris?"

Taita replied, "There is great urgency. We will leave at once."

IT TOOK THEM fifteen days of hard travel to reach the tiny garrison station of Thane, a day's travel south of Avaris. En route, they discussed their plans endlessly, knowing that they were pitted against the might of Pharaoh Trok Uruk. The officers they spoke to at the garrisons and camps they passed estimated that Trok now had twenty-seven fully trained and equipped regiments at his disposal and almost three thousand chariots. To oppose this multitude they had a wagon showing the effects of long, hard service, with a back wheel that had a propensity to fall off at the most inappropriate times. There were only the four of them: Nefer and Meren, Hilto and Taita.

Hilto knew the captain in charge of the encampment at Thane, a grizzled old warrior named Socco. Long ago they had fought, roistered and whored together. After they had reminisced for an hour and shared a pot of sour beer, Hilto handed him the requisition scroll that Naja had given to Taita. Socco held it upside down at arm's length and looked wise.

"See the cartouche of Pharaoh." Hilto touched the seal.

"If I know you at all, Hilto, you probably drew that pretty picture yourself." Socco handed back the scroll. "What do you need, you old rogue?"

They selected fresh horses, then Taita went over the ranks of parked chariots in the garrison pool that had just been sent out from the makers in Avaris. He chose three vehicles, and they harnessed the fresh horses.

When they left Thane, Taita was driving the old wagon, while Meren, Hilto and Nefer each drove a chariot. They did not head directly for Avaris but made a detour to a small oasis on the edge of the desert to the east of the city.

While the others unloaded the wagon, Taita went to barter with the Assyrian master of a caravan that was encamped nearby. He bought an armful of tattered clothing and twenty woollen rugs for an extortionate price. "That Assyrian ape is a robber," he muttered, as they loaded the carpets onto the wagon.

That night Taita dyed his silver hair with an extract of mimosa bark, which altered his appearance dramatically. In the darkness of early morning they left Meren in charge of the horses and chariots, got into the dilapidated wagon and, sitting on the pile of carpets, headed west towards Avaris. They were dressed in the castoffs that Taita had procured. Taita wore a long robe and sash, the lower half of his face veiled in the fashion of a citizen of Ur of the Chaldeans. With his dyed dark hair he was unrecognisable as the Magus.

When they reached the royal city of the north, Hilto went to tour the taverns of the old quarter where he hoped to gather news from former comrades-in-arms. Taita and Nefer made their way to the palace gates, and spent the morning listening to the chatter of those around them, and gossiping with other idlers.

At last Taita struck up a conversation with a merchant from Babylon, dressed in similar style to himself, who introduced himself as Nintura. The two shared a pot of coffee and Taita exerted all his wiles to charm Nintura, who had been loitering outside the palace for the last ten days, waiting for his turn to display his wares to Trok's new bride.

"They say that Trok has been cruelly treated by his young wife. She will not allow him into her bed." Nintura chuckled. "He is wild for her, and is trying to win her favours with expensive gifts. They say he will refuse her nothing."

"Where is Trok now?" Taita asked

"He is campaigning in the south," Nintura replied. "He is stamping out the flames of rebellion, but no sooner does he turn his back than they flare up again behind him."

"Whom should I approach to enter the presence of his queen?"

"The palace vizier. Soleth is his name, the fat, gelded freak." Nintura had not realised Taita's own condition.

Taita knew Soleth only by reputation and that he was one of the secret brotherhood of eunuchs. "Where can I find him?" Taita asked.

"It will cost you a gold ring just to enter his presence," Nintura warned him.

Soleth was sitting beside the lotus pond in his own walled garden when Taita was brought to him. Taita made a dignified salutation as he introduced himself under an assumed name. He followed that with the recognition sign of the brotherhood. Soleth waved to Taita to seat himself on the cushions opposite him, and they swiftly established Taita's credentials and common acquaintances within the brotherhood. Without seeming to do so, Soleth was studying Taita's features, looking beyond the veil and the died hair. Slowly recognition bloomed in his eyes and at last he asked softly, "In your travels you might have met the famous Magus, known through both kingdoms as Taita?"

"I know Taita well," Taita agreed.

"Perhaps as well as you know yourself?" Soleth asked.

"At least as well as I know myself," Taita affirmed.

Soleth's chubby face creased in a smile. "Say no more. What service can I perform for you? You need only ask."

THAT EVENING NEFER and Hilto were on the carpet load when Taita drove the creaking wagon up to one of the side gates of the palace.

Soleth had sent one of his underlings, an old black slave, to act as a guide. He hobbled ahead of them, ushering them past the guards and guiding them through narrow passages to an elaborately carved sandalwood door guarded by two huge eunuchs. There was a whispered exchange then the sentries stood aside and the slave went through into a large airy room.

"Your Majesty," he quavered, "There is a merchant with fine silk carpets from Samarkand to wait upon Your Grace."

"I have seen enough rubbish for one day," a woman replied, and Nefer thrilled to her familiar, well-beloved tones. "Send them away."

The guide looked back at Taita and spread his hands helplessly. Nefer dropped the rolled carpet off his shoulder on to the stone floor tiles with a weighty thump, and strode onto the terrace. Mintaka was sitting on the parapet wall with two of her slave girls at her feet.

"Forgive me, Majesty," he murmured softly. "I am but a poor fool from Dabba."

Mintaka screamed, then covered her mouth with both hands. The black slave drew his dagger, but Mintaka recovered herself at once. "No, leave him." She raised her right hand to reinforce the command. "Leave us. I will speak with the stupid fellow."

Confused, the slave sheathed his blade and backed away. The curtains over the entrance fell back into place as he withdrew. Mintaka was still staring at Nefer. Her girls knew that something strange was afoot. Then suddenly she flew to Nefer and he ran to meet her, enfolding her in his embrace. They clung to each other, both talking at the same time. The slave girls recovered from their astonishment and clapped their hands with joy. Taita silenced them with a few prods of his staff, then turned back to Hilto. At his direction the man spread the largest carpet out on the tile.

"Mintaka, listen to me! There will be time for that later. We are going to hide you in the carpet to get you out of the palace. Hurry!"

"Do I have time to fetch my—"

"No," Taita said. "You have time for nothing other than to obey me."

She kissed Nefer once more, then threw herself full length on the carpet. She looked up at her girls, who stood amazed in the doorway. "Do whatever Taita tells you."

Nefer helped Hilto roll Mintaka in the patterned red carpet, while Taita instructed the slave girls: "Stay here in the vestibule. You must not open the door to any demands. Tell anyone who asks that your mistress is laid low by her moon sickness and can see no one. Delay them as long as you are able, but when you are discovered, tell them what they want to know. Do not try to hold out under torture. Now, bar the door behind us when we leave."

The old slave was waiting in the passage when they carried out the rolled carpet on their shoulders.

"I am sorry. I did my best for you," he told them, "but since her marriage Queen Mintaka has become curiously sad and angry." He beckoned them to follow and led them back through the warren until at last they reached the small side gate.

The wagon stood where they had left it. Gently they loaded the carpet and Nefer scrambled up behind Taita on the wagon box as he urged the horses forward.

Taita whipped up the horses. "The city gates will soon be closed for the night. When Mintaka's escape is discovered the first thing they will do is seal off the city."

They galloped down the wide avenue leading to the eastern gate but the way was blocked by other wagons and their progress was tantalisingly slow. The sun had already sunk behind the walls and the light was fading, but there were still two vehicles ahead of them when the captain of the guard yelled at his men, "That is enough! The sun has set. Close the gates!"

There were yells of protest from all the travellers still trying to pass out. One of the wagons drove forward and tried to block the efforts of the guards to force the gates shut. A small riot broke out, with shouting guards swinging clubs, outraged citizens screaming back at them and frightened horses rearing and whinnying.

"Help me!" Nefer shouted to his companions. Lifting the rolled carpet off the wagon and carrying it between them, they squeezed through the narrow gap between the closing gates, then ran into the encampment below the city walls. There, among the leather tents and shacks, they lowered their burden to the ground and unrolled it. Dishevelled and hot, Mintaka sat up and smiled to see Nefer kneeling in front of her. They reached for each other and embraced.

Taita brought them back to reality. He pulled Mintaka to her feet. "We have lost the wagon. Ahead of us we have a long journey on foot. Unless we set out now it will be after daylight tomorrow before we reach the oasis where we left Meren with the chariots."

Mintaka sobered immediately. "I am ready," she said.

TROK DROVE THROUGH the palace gates and reined in his dusty, lathered horses in the courtyard before his own magnificent quarters. Two colonels of his cavalry, both members of the leopard clan and his particular cronies, stumped after him into the banquet hall with weapons and bucklers clattering. The house slaves had laid out a feast to welcome Pharaoh home, but Trok was aware that the manner in which his new wife treated him was weakening his reputation, and he was determined to change that this very night.

"There is more food than even you two oxen can eat," he told his companions, waving at the groaning board. "Do your worst, but don't expect me to join you before morning. I have a field to plough and an incorrigible filly to break to my will."

He strode from the hall and two slaves with burning torches ran ahead of him to light his way. In front of the doors to Mintaka's quarters the eunuch sentries had heard him coming. They crossed their weapons over their fat chests in salute.

"Open up!" Trok ordered.

"Your Majesty." One of the sentries saluted again nervously. "The doors are barred by order of Her Majesty Queen Mintaka."

"By Seueth, I'll have none of that!" Trok kicked open the door and marched into the room beyond. The slave girls were against the far wall in a terrified huddle. "Where is your mistress?"

"She cannot see you. Her moon has come," they gabbled.

Trok laughed. "She has used that excuse too often." He hammered on the door. "Open up, you little witch!"

At his next blow the door flew open, torn off its leather hinges, and Trok swaggered through. "Have you missed me, my little lily?" he called. "Where are you?" He rampaged through the room and kicked in the doors of her closet. It took him only a minute to make sure that Mintaka was not hiding. He strode to the door and seized one of the slave girls. "Where is she?"

"She has gone," cried the girl. "Men came and took her away in a carpet."

Trok gave her a brutal kick and shouted at the sentries, "Find Soleth. Bring the fat slug here immediately."

Soleth came cringing and wringing his plump hands. "Divine Pharaoh! Greatest of the gods!" He threw himself at Trok's feet.

Trok kicked him with a full swing of his armoured sandal. "Who were these men you allowed to enter the *zenana*?"

"On your own orders, gracious Pharaoh, I allowed any vendor of fine merchandise to display it before the Queen."

"Who was the carpet seller, the last one to enter these quarters?" Trok kicked him again. "What was his name?"

"I remember now. The carpet merchant from Ur. I forget his name."

"I will help your memory." Trok picked up his discarded sword-belt and drew the weapon. "Now, tell me. Who was the carpet merchant?"

"It was Taita!" Soleth screamed, "Taita took her away."

"Taita!" Trok exclaimed with astonishment. "Taita, the Magus." There was superstitious dread in his tone. "Where has he taken her?"

"He did not tell me."

Trok touched the point of the sword to the eunuch's breast.

Soleth whimpered, "He did not tell me, but we spoke of the land between the two rivers, the Tigris and the Euphrates. Maybe that is where he intends taking the Queen."

Trok thought about it. By now Taita would know of the strained relationships between Egypt and the eastern kingdoms. He would know that he might find protection there, if he could run that far. But what was his reason for abducting Mintaka? Had she appealed to him to help her escape from Avaris and her marriage? Certainly, she must have gone with him willingly. The manner in which her slave girls had tried to cover her escape proved that, and certainly she had made no outcry, for if she had the sentries would have heard it.

He put aside those considerations for the moment. The main concern now was to get the pursuit in hand and recapture her and the warlock before they crossed into territories loyal to Sargon of Babylon. He smiled at Soleth. "I will deal with you when I return. There are hungry hyenas and vultures to be fed."

The two colonels, Tolma and Zander, were still in the banquet hall, hogging the food and wine.

"How many chariots can we have manned and running eastward before midnight?" Trok demanded.

Colonel Tolma spat out the wine he was about to swallow and leapt to his feet. "I can have fifty on the road within two hours," he blurted.

"I want that to be a hundred," Trok demanded. "And another hundred running east before dawn."

TAITA LED THEM through the night, the tip of his staff clicking on the stony path, and his shadow flitted ahead of him like a monstrous black bat. The others had to stretch their legs to keep him in sight.

After midnight Mintaka began to fail. Nefer shortened his stride to stay with her.

"It is not far now," he told her, and took her hand to lead her faster. "Meren will have the horses ready for us. We will ride the rest of the way to Babylon in royal style."

She laughed but it was a strained, painful sound.

"What is it that ails you?" he demanded.

"Nothing," she said.

He forced her to sit on a rock beside the path, and unlaced the straps of her sandals. He pulled one off and slabs of skin and flesh came with it, the blood shining in the moonlight. He gently eased off the other sandal. "You should have warned me of this earlier." He turned his back to her and braced himself to receive her weight. "Put your arms around my neck and jump up!" Then he set off after the others who, by this time, were merely a dark shadow on the moonlit desert ahead.

Before long, however, Taita and Hilto came back to search for them. Taita bound up Mintaka's feet and they took turns at carrying her. They went on faster, but the stars were fading and the dawn light was growing stronger when they finally reached the oasis where Meren waited for them with the horses.

All of them were exhausted, but Taita would not allow them to rest. They watered the horses for the last time and refilled the water-skins. While they were doing this Taita half filled a bucket with water from the well and washed the dye from his hair.

"Why does he wash his hair at a time like this?" Meren wondered.

"Perhaps it restores some of his force that he lost when he dyed it," Mintaka suggested, and no one questioned this.

When they were ready to leave, Taita took Meren in the leading chariot as his lance-bearer. Nefer followed with Mintaka clinging to the dashboard to take the weight off her feet. Hilto brought up the rearguard in the last chariot.

The Assyrian merchant who had sold them the carpets turned to watch them as they passed, and he called a farewell to Taita. But his interest quickened as he saw the girl in the second chariot. Not even her dusty clothing and dishevelled hair could hide her striking looks. He was still staring after them as they topped the last rise and disappeared into the wilderness, heading east.

THE SUN WAS HOT and halfway up the sky when Trok topped the hills above the oasis at the threshold of the wilderness. Following him were two hundred chariots, and five miles behind came Colonel Zander with another two hundred. Each vehicle carried two armed troopers, and was loaded with water-skins and sheaths of spare arrows.

Below them they saw an Assyrian trader coming up the slope from the well at the head of his caravan. Trok rode forward and reined in his chariot in front of him. When he turned from the trader a few short minutes later, Trok began issuing orders to Colonel Tolma, who followed him closely in the second chariot of the column. "They are only hours ahead of us," he exulted. "Top up the water-skins at the well, and let the horses drink their fill. But swiftly, Tolma. Be ready to leave again before noon. In the meantime send your wizards to me."

Trok found a patch of shade under a gnarled tamarind near the well. The wizards came in response to his summons and squatted around him, two priests of Seueth in their black robes, and a sorcerer from the east known as Ishtar the Mede. Ishtar had one wall eye and his face was tattooed with whorls and circles.

"The man we are pursuing is an adept of the occult arts," Trok warned them. "He will exert all his powers to frustrate us. His name is Taita."

"I know Taita only by reputation," said Ishtar, "but I have long looked for an opportunity to match him."

"Weave your magic," Trok ordered them.

The priests of Seueth went aside a short distance, laid out their accoutrements and began to chant softly. Ishtar built a small fire near the well and squatted over it, muttering incantations to Marduk, the most powerful of all the gods of Mesopotamia.

Watching him at work, Trok grunted sceptically, but secretly he was impressed. He walked a short way along the road and glared at the line of eastern hills. He was hot for the pursuit. On the other hand he was enough of a general to realise the need to rest and water the horses after the long night ride.

TAITA SIGNALLED the two vehicles that followed him to halt. They stopped in the purple shade thrown across the sands by a tall slip-faced dune shaped like the elegant curve of a gigantic seashell. The horses were already showing signs of distress. They hung their heads and their chests heaved as they breathed. Carefully he measured out a water ration from the water-skins into the leather buckets and the horses drank eagerly.

When he had finished he led Hilto out of earshot of the others.

"We are being overlooked," he said flatly. "There is a baleful influence slowly enveloping us. Do you know who Trok has with him who can work such a potent spell?"

"He has sorcerers with all his regiments, but the most powerful of them is Ishtar the Mede."

"I know of him." Taita nodded. "He works in fire and blood. I shall try to turn his influence back on him."

They went back to where the chariots waited. Before they mounted again Taita spoke to the others. "We are entering the most dangerous area of the dune-lands. I know you are all tired and thirsty, drained by the rigours of the journey, but it could be fatal for any of you to become careless. Watch the horses and the ground ahead. Do not allow yourselves to be distracted by any strange sound or sight."

They went forward again, following the valleys between the high dunes, and the heat seemed to increase with every turn of the chariot wheels. The quality of light changed: distances were rendered confusing and distorted. Nefer slitted his eyes against the shimmering glare of the brazen sky. It seemed close enough to touch with the end of his whip.

As they went on Taita looked to the sky more frequently. His expression was sober.

"I have never seen a sky like this," Hilto said, when they stopped to water the horses. "The gods are angry."

It was Hilto, with his warrior's eyes, who picked out the dust cloud behind them. "Magus!" he shouted. "Those are chariots behind us, and many of them."

Trok was there. Even at distance they could make out his bear-like form at the head of his moving column.

"One last fight!" Hilto loosened his blade in its scabbard.

Taita looked up at the bile-coloured sky as another sultry gust rippled his hair. He did not raise his voice but it carried to all of them, "This way. Mark well my wheel tracks and follow them faithfully."

To their astonishment Taita turned his horses off into the sand, heading at a right angle from the track. He went on at a steady trot and they followed him closely.

Looking back, Nefer could see there was not the least chance that, when Trok reached it, he would not find the place where the three chariots had left the track. Unless, of course, Taita could weave a spell of concealment.

They kept on for almost another league until abruptly the land ahead changed character. From the soft sand waves rose a dark island of rock, its peak as sharp as the fang of some fabulous monster.

When Nefer and Mintaka saw the rock pile looming ahead they were astonished.

"Did Taita know it was here?" Mintaka asked.

"How could he have known?" Nefer replied.

"You told me once that he knows everything."

Nefer was silenced. He looked back and saw the dust of the pursuit close behind. "It matters not at all. We might be able to defend those rocks for a while, but there are hundreds of Trok's men."

"We must trust Taita," Mintaka said.

He laughed bitterly. "It seems the gods have deserted us. Who else is there to trust but Taita."

They went forward. Behind them they heard the faint cries of the captains urging their troopers, the jingle of loose equipment and the groan and whine of dry wheel hubs.

At last they came up under the hill of black and ochre-coloured rock. The accumulated heat radiated from it like a bonfire.

"Drive the chariots close in against the cliff," Taita ordered, and they obeyed. "Now free the horses and bring them this way." Taita led his own team round the angle of the rock face. Here there was a deep fissure cutting into the rock pile.

"This way." He led them as far as they could go along the sandy floor of the deep, vertical crack. "Now make the horses lie down."

At the urging of their handlers, the horses, trained to perform this trick, lowered themselves to their knees and then, grunting and blowing, they went flat on their sides on the floor of the fissure.

Taita had brought a bedding roll from the chariot. With strips torn from it he blindfolded the horses to keep them quiet and submissive. Then he drove a javelin deep into the loose earth and used it as an anchor to tie down the horses' swathed heads and prevent them from rising again. The others followed his example.

Almost as if he knew of its existence, Taita led them to a shallow overhang in the cliff. The headroom under it was so low that anyone trying to enter would have to go down on hands and knees.

"Use the loose scree from the cliff to wall this in."

Nefer looked puzzled. "We cannot defend this place. Once we are inside we could not even stand, let alone swing a sword."

"There is no time to argue." Taita glared at him. "Do as I tell you."

Nefer glared back at Taita. The others watched with interest: the young bull challenging the older one. Abruptly Nefer capitulated. Only one person could save them now. He stooped and picked up a large rock from the scree pile and staggered with it to the shallow cave. The others joined in the work.

Meanwhile Taita climbed until he reached the peak of the hillock. He stood there gazing back in the direction from which Trok would come, and when their work was finished the little party in the gully at the foot of the hillock watched him, outlined against that dreadful sulphur sky. Nobody spoke, nobody moved, until they heard the faint squeal of chariot wheels.

Slowly Taita raised both arms and pointed them to the sky.

"What is he doing now?" Hilto asked, in an awed tone.

Taita stood as still as if he had been chiselled out of the living rock. His head was thrown back, his hair fluffed out silver on his shoulders. The heavens swirled. The light was transient, fading as the sun was covered more heavily, flaring as the clouds thinned.

Still Taita did not move, his staff aimed at the heavens. The sound of the approaching column became clearer still, and suddenly there was a distant blare of a ram's horn trumpet.

"That is Trok's battle call," Mintaka said quietly.

TROK SHOUTED at his trumpeter, "Sound the advance!"

"Wait!" said Ishtar the Mede. He was watching Taita's tiny figure on the peak of the rock hill. "Wait!"

"What is it!" Trok demanded.

"As yet I cannot fathom it," Ishtar said, without taking his gaze off the warlock, "but it is pervasive and powerful."

The column remained halted, every man in it staring at the figure on the peak with awe. Only the sky moved. It formed a whirlpool over the head of the Magus, a great turning wheel of smouldering cloud. Then slowly the centre of the whirlpool opened like the single eye of an awakening monster. From the heavenly eye a shaft of dazzling sunlight burst forth.

"The eye of Horus!" Ishtar breathed. "He has called up the god." He made a sign of protection, and at his side Trok was silent and rigid with superstitious dread.

The brilliant shaft of light struck the peak, and lit the figure of the warlock. Around his head it spun a nimbus of silver radiance.

He made a slow circular pass with his long staff, and the Hyksosian charioteers cringed like curs under the whip. The clouds opened wider, and the sky was clear. The sunlight danced on the dunes, and they lifted their hands to protect their eyes.

On the peak, Taita described another circle with his staff, and there was a sound, soft at first, like a lover's sigh, then becoming a soughing, a gentle whistling. It came from the east, and slowly all their heads turned towards it.

Out of that strange, cloudless brilliance, they saw it coming: a solid dun wall of sand that reached from the surface of the earth to the highest heavens.

"Khamsin!" Trok whispered the dread word.

The wall of sand undulated and pulsed like a demon, and its voice became a rising howl.

"Khamsin!" The word was yelled from chariot to chariot. They were no longer warriors hot for war, but terrified creatures in the face of this destroyer of men, cities and civilisations, this eater of worlds.

The column of chariots lost its formation and broke up into fragments as the drivers wheeled their teams and tried to run from it. Instinctively the horses sensed the menace and reared and screamed, trying to escape by kicking themselves free of the traces.

The khamsin bore down upon them inexorably. They looked back and saw the great storm rolling and roiling upon itself, twisting curtains of sand, brazen where the sunlight struck them, dun and sombre where their own mountainous heights shaded them.

Taita lowered his staff and, without haste, started down the hillock to where Nefer and Mintaka were standing. They welcomed him with bemused expressions. Mintaka's tone was subdued as she asked, "You called up the storm?"

"It has long been brewing," Taita said. "You have all remarked the heat and the yellow mists."

"No," said Nefer. "It was not in nature. It was you."

"Go into the shelter now," said Taita. "It is almost upon us."

Mintaka led the way, crawling into the low narrow cave through the opening in the rude wall. The others followed her, crowding into the tiny space. Before he entered, Hilto handed in the waterskins. Then, as the storm hurled down on them in all its terrible majesty, Taita stooped through the opening and sat with his back to the inner wall.

"Close it up," he said, and Meren and Hilto blocked the entrance with the rocks they had placed at hand.

"Cover your heads," said Taita, and wound his headcloth over his face. "Keep your eyes closed, or you will lose your sight. Breathe carefully or you will drown in sand."

THE STORM WAS overwhelming. Trok and Ishtar were gone with magical swiftness, they and all their men, chariots and horses, gone in the rolling billows of the khamsin. The first front picked up Trok's chariot and rolled it over with the horses screaming.

Trok was thrown free. He fought his way to his feet, but the storm struck him down again. He managed to pull himself up. When he tried to open his eyes he was blinded by sand.

As the khamsin ripped at his face, Trok screamed, "Save me, Ishtar!"

It seemed impossible that anyone could have heard his cry. Then he felt Ishtar seize his hand and together they stumbled on. It seemed endless, their tormented journey to nowhere. Then abruptly Trok felt the force of the wind diminish. For a minute he thought that the storm had already passed them by, but then a sudden gust almost lifted him off his feet and he crashed into a wall of rock.

He clung to the rock like a child to its mother. How Ishtar had brought them to it he neither knew nor cared. All that mattered was that the cliff above them was breaking the full force of the storm.

For two days and three nights the wind never relented. During this time Nefer managed to keep back the sand just enough to move his head and his arms, but his lower body was encased solidly. At times he felt Mintaka sobbing quietly beside him and tried to comfort her. She laid her head on his shoulder and they clung to each other. They were entombed in the roaring darkness, dumb and blinded, half suffocated. Each hot breath they drew had to be strained through cloth and taken only a sip at a time to prevent a rush of talcum-fine sand passing between their lips.

They drank the water that remained in their water-skin. Then the thirst came. Even though they were unable to move their bodies to use up moisture, the hot dry sand and air sucked it out of them. Nefer felt his tongue slowly cleave to the roof of his mouth.

He felt himself drifting into haunted dreams of water. He forced himself up from the darkness, and listened. He heard nothing. There was no sound. The roaring clamour of the khamsin had given way to a profound silence. The silence of a sealed tomb, he thought.

He began to struggle, to try to work his way out of the sand, but the effort soon exhausted him and his throat ached with thirst. He closed his eyes wearily, giving up. Then, even through the folds of his headcloth, he was aware of fresh air and a glimmer of light. He pulled the cloth from his face. When his vision had adjusted he saw that there was a hole to the outside.

It was the middle of the morning. Nefer did not know what morning or for how many days they had been buried. There was still a haze of fine sand like gold dust in the air.

He shook his head in wonder, and looked at Taita. He could see that he also was dried out and suffering the same agonies as they were.

"Water," Nefer whispered, touching his swollen mouth.

"Come," said Taita.

Nefer took Mintaka's hand and slowly they followed the Magus out into the sands. Thirst and exposure had taken their toll on Taita, and he seemed to be wandering aimlessly with Hilto and Meren through the new valleys of fine sand. Once or twice he lowered himself to his knees and touched the earth with his forehead.

"What is he doing?" Mintaka whispered. "Is he praying?"

Nefer shook his head as once again Taita knelt and placed his face close to the earth. This time Nefer watched him with more attention, and saw that he was sniffing the air close to the surface of the sand. Then he knew what Taita was doing. "He is searching for the buried chariots of Trok's division," he whispered to Mintaka. "He is sniffing for the scent of putrescence below the sand."

Taita stood up painfully and nodded at Hilto. "Dig here," he ordered.

They all crowded forward and began to scrape away the sand with cupped hands. An arm's span deep they struck something hard. Soon they exposed the wheel rim of a chariot that was lying on its side.

Suddenly Nefer reached deeper into the hole and they all heard the gurgle and slosh of water. He swept away more of the loose sand and between them they lifted out a bulging water-skin. The water was the temperature of blood, but when Taita held the skin to Mintaka's lips she closed her eyes and drank in a quiet ecstasy.

"Not too much at first," Taita warned her, and passed it to Nefer. They drank in turn, then Mintaka drank again.

The next time they dug they were lucky: not only was the chariot under less sand, but there were three water-skins.

"Our horses now," Taita told them, and they looked at each other guiltily. In their desperate preoccupation they had forgotten them. Carrying the water-skins they trudged back through the sand to the base of the cliff.

The narrow gully in which they had pegged down the horses was well aligned to avoid the full force of the khamsin. They found the first horse almost at once. The beast was alive, but barely. The men lifted it between them. It stood weak and shivering, but drank greedily from the bucket Mintaka held and seemed at once to improve.

In the meantime the men were digging for the other horses. They found three dead of thirst or suffocation, but another two still alive. They also responded immediately they were given water.

The men left Mintaka to care for the three pathetic beasts and went back to search for fodder and more water-skins under the sand.

Suddenly they heard Mintaka screaming.

Nefer raced back to her, a sword in his hand, the others following. Mintaka had been hiding behind a ledge in the cliff.

"What is it?" Nefer demanded, as she slid down the cliff into his arms.

"Trok!" she sobbed. "Trok is alive. Look!"

Taita stayed with Mintaka while the other three men followed a set of footprints in the sand as if they were tracking a wounded lion. They moved along the base of the cliff until they reached a second rocky fissure. Nefer examined the disturbed sand within it and interpreted the signs.

"Two of them," he said. "They were buried by the storm, as we were. They dug themselves out. One waited here." He picked up a thread of wool that had adhered to the rock, and held it to the light. "Black." It was a colour seldom worn by Egyptians. "Almost certainly the Mede."

Hilto nodded agreement. "Ishtar would have the witchcraft to survive the storm. It is certain he saved Trok, just as Taita saved us."

"Here." Nefer stood up and pointed out the sign. "They went this way."

They followed the footprints a short way out into the desert. "They have gone west. Back towards Avaris and the Nile. Will they ever reach it?"

"Not if I catch up with him," Nefer said grimly, and hefted the javelin he was carrying.

"Majesty." Hilto was respectful but firm. "They have a long start. They will be well away from here by now. You dare not follow without water."

Nefer hesitated. Though he saw the sense in what Hilto said, it galled him sorely to let Trok escape. In the end he turned aside and ran to the top of the nearest dune. Shading his eyes he looked westward, along the string of footsteps on the pristine, windswept sands, until in the distance he made out two tiny figures moving steadily towards the west. They disappeared in the wavering heat mirage.

"There will be another time," Nefer whispered. "I will come for you. I swear it."

THEY FOUND and uncovered another sixteen of the buried chariots. With such an abundant supply of water and food, horses and men recovered swiftly, and by nightfall on the tenth day they were ready to move. The khamsin had altered the landscape so greatly that Taita had to navigate by the stars. They kept going steadily through the whole of that night, and the one that followed. Before dawn on the second day they reached an old caravan road.

Here, Nefer had a difficult decision to make. "If we are to make the long journey to the east, we will need supplies and gold. When we go to King Sargon we must arrive in some state to show him the support we still command in Egypt."

Taita nodded.

"Hilto and Meren must go back to Thebes," Nefer went on. "I would go myself but all the world will be searching for Mintaka and me." He removed one of his rings and handed it to Hilto. "This will be your token of recognition. Show it to our friends. You must return bringing us men and gold, chariots and horses. Also you must gather news. We must be informed of every action of the false pharaohs."

"I will do as you command, Majesty," Hilto agreed.

"We will wait for you at Gallala," were Nefer's last words to Hilto. Then they watched him and Meren take the high road and disappear.

Twelve days later, with only a few drops remaining in the waterskins, Taita, Mintaka and Nefer reached the deserted ruins.

Chapter Five

THE WEEKS became months, and still they waited at Gallala. Mintaka set up quarters for them among the ruins. As a Hyksosian princess, she had never been called upon to cook a meal, so her efforts were disastrous. As he chewed a charred mouthful Taita remarked, "If we want to destroy Trok's army the most effective way would be to send you to them as a cook."

"If you are so skilled, then perhaps you might honour us with your great culinary skills."

"It is either that or starve," Taita agreed, and took her place at the hearth.

Nefer resumed his old role of hunter, and after his first day out in the desert returned with a plump young gazelle and four marvellously patterned giant bustard eggs that were only slightly addled.

Mintaka sniffed her share of Taita's omelette and pushed it away. "Is this the same man who complained of my cooking?" She looked across at Nefer. "You are as guilty as he is. Next time I will go with you to make sure that what you bring back is edible."

Several more hunting trips followed. Then, one evening when they came into the room in the ancient building that they had restored and made habitable, Mintaka shyly stood in the open doorway with the last light of the day behind her. "I am sorry we are late back, Taita," she said. "We followed the gazelle out into the desert." Taita was at the hearth stirring the contents of the pot upon the coals. He looked up at her. She had never apologised for their late return before, and Nefer was hovering over her with a soft, dazed expression. The emanation of their love was so strong that it seemed to form a shimmering aura around them.

So what was inevitable has happened at last, he mused. The only wonder is that it took so long. He grunted. "It is evident that you did not catch up with them. Did they run too fast or were you distracted?" They stood awkwardly, knowing that to him they were transparent.

Taita turned back to the cooking pot. "At least there is one provider among us. I have been able to snare a brace of wild pigeon. We need not go hungry to bed."

The days that followed passed for the two of them in a golden haze. The lovers spent their time in talking, making love and forming plans for the future, deciding how they might marry and how many sons and daughters she would bear him.

They were so lost in each other that they forgot the world that lay beyond the lonely desert spaces, until one morning when they left the ruined city before dawn and sat down to watch the magnificent spectacle of the dawn breaking over the blue, secret hills.

"Look!" cried Mintaka suddenly, pointing back towards the west along the old trade route. A strange caravan was coming towards them. There were five ramshackle vehicles leading, followed by a straggling column of humanity.

"There must be a hundred men, at least," Mintaka exclaimed. "Who can they be?"

"I don't know," Nefer admitted grimly, "but I want you to run back and warn Taita of their approach while I go and spy on them."

She did not argue, but set off immediately for Gallala, racing down the back slope of the hills, while Nefer restrung his bow and checked the arrows in his quiver.

Suddenly he stood up from behind the rock that had hidden him, and shouted with excitement. "Meren!" He had at last recognised the tall figure who held the reins of the first chariot. Meren pulled up the horses, then he, too, shouted and waved as he saw Nefer on the skyline. Nefer ran down the slope, and he and Meren embraced, laughing and both speaking at once.

"Where have you been?"

"Where are Mintaka and Taita?"

Then Hilto was hurrying to Nefer, and making loyal salutations. Behind him crowded a host of exhausted and wounded men. Even the men in the wagons and on the litters, who were too far gone to stand, lifted themselves to stare in awe at Nefer.

After Hilto had greeted Nefer he turned back to them, and shouted, "It is even as I promised you! Here before you stands your true pharaoh, Nefer Seti. Pharaoh is not dead! Pharaoh lives!"

They were silent. They stared at him uncertainly. Most had never laid eyes on their king before. Even the few who had seen him in formal palace processions had done so from a distance. They could not reconcile that remote figure with this strapping young man, his face tanned by the sun and his expression alive and alert.

While they still stared without comprehension, or exchanged dubious glances, another figure seemed to materialise beside Nefer. This one they knew well, both by repute and by sight.

"It is Taita the Warlock," they breathed with awe.

"I know what you have suffered," Taita told them, in a voice that carried clearly to every ear. "I know what price you have paid to resist the tyranny of the assassins and usurpers. I know that you have come here to find if your true king still lives."

Suddenly Nefer knew who they were: survivors from the rebellion against Naja and Trok. Where Hilto had found them was a mystery, but these had once been fighting troopers and elite charioteers.

"This is where it begins," Taita said softly at his side. "Hilto has brought you the seed of your future legions. Speak to them."

Nefer picked out a man in the ranks who was older than the others. His expression was intelligent and he had an air of authority. "Who are you, soldier? What is your rank and your regiment?"

The man lifted his head and squared his gaunt shoulders, "I am Shabako, Commander of the Mut Regiment."

A lion of a man! Nefer thought, but said only, "I greet you, Shabako." He lifted his kilt and exposed the cartouche tattooed upon his thigh. "I, Nefer Seti, the true Pharaoh of Upper and Lower Egypt, greet you."

A sigh went through the scarecrow ranks. As one man they threw themselves to the earth in obeisance.

Mintaka had come with Taita and now Nefer reached out and took her hand. "I give you the Princess Royal, Mintaka of the House of Apepi. Mintaka, who will be my queen and your sovereign lady."

They greeted her with a shout of acclamation.

"Hilto and Shabako will command you," Nefer decreed. "For the time being Gallala will be our base, until we return victoriously to Thebes."

They rose to their feet and cheered him, their voices thin in the silence of the desert, but the sound filled Nefer with pride. He climbed up into the leading chariot, took the reins from Meren and led his raggle-taggle army down into his ruined capital city.

LATE INTO THAT first night, and for many nights that followed, Nefer sat with Shabako and the other officers and listened to their accounts of the rebellion, their defeat by the combined forces of the two pharaohs, and the terrible retribution that they had visited on those rebels who had fallen into their clutches. They also detailed the order of battle of the new Egyptian army, and the total of men, chariots and horses that Naja and Trok had at their disposal.

In the meantime Taita, with Mintaka assisting him, set up an infirmary where they worked during all the daylight hours, setting broken bones, drawing out barbed arrowheads, stitching sword cuts and in one case even trepanning a skull that had received a blow from a hardwood war club.

When the light faded and he could no longer work with the sick, Taita joined Nefer and his commanders as they pored over maps drawn on tanned lambskins, planning and scheming by the light of the oil lamps. Although Nefer was nominally their supreme commander, in reality he was a student of the art of war and these experienced old soldiers were his instructors.

In total there were fewer than a hundred and fifty souls and fifty horses in Gallala, but within the first few days it became evident that the wells of the city could not support even these meagre numbers. Each day they emptied them and each night it took longer for them to refill, and the water became more bitter and brackish.

At last, after they were forced to ration the water, Taita took Nefer and Mintaka and a party of fifty-six men, all carrying shovels and metal-tipped digging staves, up the valley to the foot of the hill.

For two days they dug into the rock, prising out each lump, digging out the earth that lay behind it. When they struck a solid stratum of blue, crystalline rock, they stacked firewood against it, let it burn until the rock glowed, and quenched it with water from the failing wells. In clouds of hissing steam, the rock crackled and burst. They let it cool, prised out great blackened chunks of it, then repeated the arduous process until they had driven a shaft of twenty cubits into the hillside.

On the third morning, the teams of weary, disgruntled men assembled round the mouth of the tunnel to await the Magus. With his usual sense of the dramatic, Taita came up the slope with the first rays of the rising sun behind him, suffusing his silver hair with light. He stood in the entrance to the excavation and began to chant the invocation to Horus. Then he strode down the shaft until he stood before the blue-grey wall of newly exposed rock at the end. Tiny crystals of feldspar were embedded in it and sparkled in the sun.

"Kydash!" Taita cried, and struck the wall with his staff. *"Mensaar!"* He struck again *"Ncube!"* He struck for the third and last time, then stepped back.

Nothing happened, and Taita stood unmoving as the sun climbed higher. Then the men stirred and whispered as a dark, damp spot appeared in the centre of the rock face. It spread gradually and a single drop of moisture oozed out and trickled slowly down the wall.

Taita turned and walked out of the shaft. Behind him there was a sharp sound, and a fine crack split the rock from top to bottom. Water dripped to the floor. Then with a roar the entire rock face collapsed, there was a rush of mud and a gushing fountain of crystal-bright water. Knee-deep, it swept the length of the shaft, burst from the mouth and spilled down the hillside, rippling over the rocks.

There were shouts of amazement, praise and disbelief from the dusty ranks. Men threw off their clothing and rushed naked into the stream, splashing sheets of spray, throwing handfuls of mud, and ducking each other. Nefer could not long resist the temptation before he, too, shed all dignity and jumped in.

Taita stood on the bank of the stream and looked down on the mayhem with a benign expression. Then he turned to Mintaka. "Put the thought out of your mind," he said. "It would be an outrage to have a princess of Egypt cavorting with a rabble of rough, naked soldiers." He took her hand and led her away down the hill, but she looked back wistfully at the revels.

"How did you do it, Taita?" she asked. "How did you make the fountain appear? What kind of magic was it?"

"The magic of common sense and observation. The water has been there for centuries, just waiting for us to dig down to it."

"But what about the prayers and words of power? Were those of no effect?"

Taita smiled and touched the side of his nose. "Sometimes a little magic is a tonic for flagging spirits."

FOR MONTHS THEREAFTER every man was employed in the digging of a channel to lead the sweet flood of water down the hillside into the old wells. When they brimmed over, Taita surveyed the old fields at the lower end of the valley that were now a stony desolation. The outlines of ancient irrigation ditches were still visible, however, and it took small effort to clean out the contour lines and divert the overflowing waters into them, so that within months they had reaped their first millet harvest.

Almost every day more fugitives drifted into the city, having braved the desert crossing to escape the tyranny of the false pharaohs. They came singly or in small parties, weary and almost dying of thirst. The guards posted along the hills intercepted them, and sent them in to Hilto. He made them swear the oath of fealty to Pharaoh Nefer Seti, then issued them with rations and sent them to the training regiments or put them to work in the fields or restoring the city. These waifs were not the only recruits, however. A cohort of deserters from the armies of the false pharaohs marched in smartly with their javelins, shouting the praises of Nefer Seti as soon as they were in sight of the walls. Then a squadron of twenty chariots brought plundered treasure and the momentous news that Naja and Trok were at last marching against King Sargon of Babylon.

The two pharaohs had crossed the desert that linked Egypt with the eastern lands in the full of the moon, using its light and the cool nights to sweep past Ismailiya and on up to Beersheba, gathering the forces of their vassal satraps as they went.

Nefer and Taita had been preparing the defences of Gallala against an imminent attack by the false pharaohs. Their presence in the ancient city should by now have been common knowledge throughout the two kingdoms, and they had expected Naja and Trok to move against them first, before starting on the Mesopotamian adventure. They were amazed to have this reprieve.

"Can we be certain that this is not a diversion?" Nefer asked thoughtfully. "Is the eastern expedition a pretence? Perhaps their true offensive will be directed against us after they have lulled us into a false sense of security."

"There is always that possibility. Trok is a bull, but Naja is cunning and devious. It is the type of bluff he might try."

"We must keep the expeditionary army under observation," Nefer decided.

The following day Shabako and his most trusted men were sent as scouts and spies to the towns and villages of the Nile valley. They drank in the taverns and questioned the travellers they met on the road. They scouted each fort and garrison, and counted the troops they saw entering, leaving and drilling. When they returned weeks later, the intelligence they brought back was detailed and accurate.

They reported that the false pharaohs had left at least half of their army to counter any threat to their rear. All the border forts were fully manned, and the garrisons seemed alert and vigilant.

"What of the remount divisions?" Nefer asked, when Shabako had come to the end of his long report.

"Trok has taken most of his chariots with him to Mesopotamia. He has left less than two regiments in reserve in Egypt. However, all the army workshops are hard at work building more chariots."

"Horses?" Nefer demanded.

"They have commandeered every animal in both kingdoms that they could lay their thieving hands on. They have even sent army dealers to Libya to buy what they could find. It seems that the remount depots at Thane and Manashi are at full strength. However, most of these animals appear young and untrained. The battle-hardened animals have been taken with the main army to the east."

"Thane," Nefer decided. "It's much closer to the edge of the desert than Manashi." He recalled that Thane was where Hilto had used his requisition order to obtain fresh horses and chariots from Socco, his old comrade-in-arms, while they were on their way to rescue Mintaka from Avaris. "Tell me all you can about Thane. Is Socco still in command there?"

"We drank beer in the local brothel with a sergeant of the garrison. He told me that Socco has done such a good job there that Trok has promoted him to the rank of Best of Ten Thousand."

TEN DAYS LATER, Nefer and Taita sat in the thick green grass and pretended to watch over the herd of goats that grazed around them. Although the land around the garrison of Thane was rich in grazing, it was also flat and featureless. There were no hills from which they could overlook the camp.

The two of them were disguised in the ragged dusty black robes of the Bedouin and were able to blend into the landscape. At intervals they herded the goats a little closer to the garrison, then squatted down again in the characteristic attitude of the Bedouin herdsman.

Not far from where they sat, the herds of remounts were grazing.

"I would think there are upward of two thousand animals here," Nefer guessed.

"Perhaps not as many as that." Taita shook his head. "Closer to fifteen hundred, but still more than we can handle."

They watched and waited through the long, lazy afternoon. In the stockades alongside the cavalry lines the handlers were breaking the young animals to the chariot harness. Their shouted commands and the crack of the whips carried faintly to where Nefer and Taita sat.

In the late afternoon the herds of horses were driven in from the fields and stockades to the long horse lines beyond the fort. From a distance they watched them tethered and bedded down for the night.

As the sun was setting Nefer and Taita rounded up their goats and drove them slowly back towards the desert. In the dusk a small detachment of four chariots came bowling down the road from Avaris. At the reins of the leading vehicle stood a burly officer wearing the silver pectoral plate of the Best of Ten Thousand. As he came closer they both recognised him.

"The curse of Seth on it," Nefer murmured. "It is Socco, Hilto's old comrade-in-arms. Will he recognise us?"

They bowed their heads, slumped their shoulders, and shuffled along after the goats. Socco swerved off the road and drove directly at them. "You stinking scum!" he shouted. "How often must I warn you to keep your filthy, disease-ridden beasts off my grass and away from my horses?" He leaned out and struck Nefer across the shoulders.

The whiplash hummed and cracked against his flesh, and red rage blinded Nefer. Before he could drag Socco out of the chariot, though, Taita made a restraining gesture that riveted him where he stood. It seemed to affect Socco, too, for suddenly the bellicose light in his eyes faded. He stammered wordlessly. He was gawking at the cartouche on Nefer's thigh.

"Majesty," he gasped. "Forgive me! Strike! Take my worthless life as forfeit for those stupid words of mine. I heard the rumours that you still lived, but I had wept at your funeral and could not believe in such a miracle."

Nefer smiled with relief. He had not wanted to kill him—he was an attractive old rogue, and Hilto said that he was one of the finest horse-handlers in all the armies of Egypt. Hilto should know. "Will you swear the loyal oath to me as Pharaoh?" he demanded sternly.

"Gladly, for all the earth fears you in your name of Nefer Seti, beloved of all the gods, and light of this very Egypt. My heart beats only for you and my soul will sing my duty to you until the hour of my death."

"Then, Socco, I promote you to Master of a Thousand Chariots, for you turn a pretty phrase."

"Let me kiss your foot, Pharaoh," Socco pleaded.

"Give me your hand, rather," Nefer said, seizing his horny fist.

Three days later, when they rode into Gallala, they were driving nigh on four hundred horses, and Socco rode proudly at the right hand of his new pharaoh.

AS QUARTERMASTER general of the armies of the false pharaohs, Socco had been able to bring with him much of the depot's treasure store. He was also able to give Nefer and his council the exact tally of all the enemy fighting chariots and transport wagons, and where they were deployed. From memory he drew up a list of the numbers of horses and bullocks in depots of the delta, and the latest inventory of weapons stored in the armouries.

"Trok and Naja have taken almost the last serviceable fighting chariot with them on the expedition to the east. There are fewer than fifty left in Egypt, in either the Upper or Lower Kingdom. The military workshops at Avaris, Thebes and Aswan are working day and night, but every chariot they turn out is sent immediately along the road to Beersheba and Mesopotamia."

"Horses we now have, thanks to you, even though most are young and unbroken, but we cannot fight a campaign without chariots," said Hilto gloomily. "Soon Trok must hear of our successes. He will realise that we have become a real threat. As soon as he has captured Babylon, he will divert part of his army to attack us here. If he sent only a hundred chariots, we could not stand against them in our present state."

When all the others had had their say, Nefer stood to address the council. He did not speak long. "Socco, you train the horses for me," he said. "Taita and I will find the chariots."

FAR OUT IN the desert, Taita stood on a black rock outcrop. Around him the sand dunes stretched away to the limit of the eye. From the base of the rock a hundred men watched him, puzzled but intrigued. All of them were warriors who had come to Gallala of their own accord, forsaking the false pharaohs to offer their allegiance to Nefer Seti. That allegiance would wear a little thin if they found themselves without chariots, for daily there were fresh rumours that Trok was on the march to seek vengeance for their desertion.

Pharaoh Nefer Seti stood beside the warlock. They were in deep discussion. Occasionally one or the other would point towards the west, where there was nothing to see but sand. They talked through the heat of the day and came down from the pinnacle and walked out into the dunes. Without any apparent purpose the warlock wandered along one of the dune faces. He stopped at intervals and made strange, esoteric gestures with his long staff, then went on again.

At last, in the gathering dusk, the Magus planted his staff in the soft sand and spoke quietly to Pharaoh Nefer Seti. Now, suddenly, orders were shouted and twenty men ran forward carrying the digging tools with which they had been issued. Under the direction of Hilto and Meren, and under the daunting eyes of their king and the Magus, they began to dig. When the hole was shoulder deep the loose sand ran back into it almost as fast as they shovelled it out, and they were forced to redouble their efforts. Finally there came an excited shout from the bottom of the excavation. Nefer strode forward and stood on the lip.

"There is something here, Divine Majesty." A man was kneeling in the bottom of the hole.

"Let me see." Nefer jumped down and pushed the man out of the way. A patch of hide was exposed, still covered with hair.

Nefer looked up at Taita. "It is the body of a horse!" he called.

"What colour?" Taita asked. "Is it black?"

"How did you know?" Nefer was not really surprised.

Taita answered his question with another. "Does the halter carry the golden cartouche of Pharaoh Trok Uruk?"

"Dig it open!" Nefer ordered the sweating men around him. "But gently now. Do no damage."

They worked with great care, using their bare hands to sweep away the sand. Gradually they exposed the complete head of a black horse that wore on its forehead the cartouche of Trok, embossed on a gold disc, just as Taita had foreseen.

Then they went on to uncover the rest of the carcass, wonderfully preserved by the hot dry sand. Beside it lay its harness mate. Nefer had last seen these magnificent animals as they drew Trok's chariot forward under the dust clouds of the khamsin.

By this time night had fallen and the workmen lit the oil lamps and went on with the work through the night. The dead horses were unbuckled from the traces and lifted out, and the harness was recovered in a perfect state of preservation. Nefer set his grooms to work oiling the leather and polishing the gold and bronze parts.

Now they worked on the chariot itself, and a gasp went up from the diggers as the dashboard was cleared of sand: it was covered with gold leaf, and gleamed in the lamplight. The javelins and lances were still in their bins on either side of the cockpit, ready to the hand of the charioteer. Trok's great war-bow, too, was still in its rack, and only the bowstring needed to be replaced.

When the entire chariot had been uncovered they passed ropes under the chassis and lifted it out of the excavation.

Now it was morning, and the sun was climbing above the horizon. Nefer and Taita circled the chariot as it gleamed in the light. It was so sleek and graceful that it seemed already in motion.

Nefer stroked the lovely gold work. "It seems to be a living creature," he breathed. "Surely there was never a more magnificent weapon of war ever conceived. Now I need only the blue sword that Naja stole from my father to complete my armoury."

Over the weeks that followed Taita pinpointed the other buried vehicles and their accoutrements. Teams of workmen dug them out and sent them to the chariot-makers and armourers, who sharpened swords and lances, rebound the shafts and checked each vehicle, balancing and lubricating the wheels to run true and sweetly. Then they sent them on to Gallala, to equip the army that Hilto, Shabako and Socco were training.

Many of the vehicles were so deeply buried under the burning yellow dunes that they were lost for ever, or until the next great storm uncovered them, but in the end they salvaged a hundred and five. Enough to equip five squadrons.

By this time a thriving smuggling route existed between Gallala and Egypt, and other caravans came in regularly from the port of Safaga on the eastern sea. Nowadays there were few luxuries that could not be obtained in the city's souks, so Mintaka was able to procure a wagonload of the finest red wine for the welcome banquet she had arranged for the evening that the charioteers returned.

At her orders, the butchers spitted and roasted ten oxen, and fast relays of the new chariots brought up fresh fish and baskets of lobsters from the coast. The banquet was a joyous celebration, and the wine had flowed to great effect when Nefer rose to welcome the guests.

"With the weapons and chariots we now have, we are well able to defend ourselves against Trok and Naja. As you are aware, every day sees fresh recruits to the blue banner. Soon it will be a case not merely of defending ourselves but of avenging the terrible deeds that those two monsters have perpetrated. They are the murderers of King Apepi, who was the father of the noble lady at my side, and they slew my own father, Pharaoh Tamose."

The guests were silent now and puzzled.

Then Hilto rose to his feet. Nefer had primed him, and placed the question on his lips. "Divine Majesty, forgive my ignorance but I do not understand. King Apepi died in an accident when his barge caught fire while anchored at Balasfura. Now you lay the guilt for his death on the pretenders. How can that be?"

"There is one among us who was a witness to the true events of that tragic night." Nefer reached down and drew Mintaka to her feet. The company listened to her with all their attention as she related the story of the murder of her father and brothers. She used simple words and spoke to them as friends and comrades, yet she was able to share with them her own horror and grief.

Now Shabako rose and asked his prepared question: "But, Divine Pharaoh, you spoke also of the death of your own father, King Tamose of blessed memory. How was he murdered—and by whom?"

"For the answer to this question I must call upon the Magus, Lord Taita, from whom no secret, however grisly, can be hidden."

Taita faced them and spoke in a whisper that riveted their attention. His every word carried to the ears of even those on the outskirts of the gathering. At the end he held up a broken arrow with crimson and green feathers. "This is the instrument of Pharaoh Tamose's death. The arrow that bears the signet of Trok and which was loosed by Naja, the man whom Pharaoh trusted as a brother."

They howled their outrage and their craving for justice to the starlit skies above Gallala. Taita hurled the arrow onto the nearest fire over which one of the oxen was roasting. It would not have borne closer inspection, for it was not the arrow that had killed Pharaoh but one of those he had taken from the buried chariot. He sat down and closed his eyes, as if composing himself to sleep.

Chapter Six

BETWEEN THE TWO great rivers the city lay before him like a lotus flower, ready for plucking. Its walls were of burned brick. They were twenty-seven cubits thick and taller than the tallest palm trees of this fertile and well-watered land.

"How far is it to ride around this city?" Trok asked Ishtar the Mede. He knew that Ishtar had lived in Babylon for fifteen years, and had learned much of his magic here in the temple of Marduk.

"Ten leagues, Majesty," Ishtar told him. "Half a day's ride."

Trok stood on the footplate of his chariot and cast a general's eye along the wall. There were watchtowers at every two hundred paces, and at regular intervals the massive walls were heavily buttressed.

Ishtar knew what he was thinking. "There is a road along the top of the wall, wide enough for two chariots to ride abreast. Within an hour Sargon can move five thousand men along it to any point threatened by a besieging army."

Trok grunted. "Any wall can be undermined and sapped. We need only one breach."

"There is an inner wall, Divine Pharaoh," Ishtar murmured in a silky tone. "It is almost as impregnable as the first."

"If we cannot go through, we will find a way round." Trok shrugged. "Are those the gardens of Sargon's palace?" He indicated the terraces that rose in tiers into the sky. They were so skilfully raised upon each other that they seemed to float, free of the bounds of the earth.

Ishtar pointed with one sinewy, blue-tattooed arm. "There are six terraces built round a vast courtyard. The *zenana* alone has five thousand rooms, one for each of Sargon's wives. His treasure is buried deep below the palace, Majesty, and I tell you straight that in all your army you do not have sufficient wagons to carry away such a treasure."

"And I tell you straight, Ishtar, that I can always build new wagons." Trok threw back his head and laughed with animal high spirits.

Once Ishtar had dissuaded him from leading an army into the eastern desert to attack Nefer Seti and to capture Mintaka, his runaway woman, the march to Babylon had been one long triumph, an unbroken string of victories.

They had met Ran, Sargon's eldest son, on the banks of the Bahr al Milh: between the chariots of Trok and Naja they had ground his army to fragments, and had sent Ran's severed head to his father, skewered on a spear. Maddened with grief, Sargon had charged into the trap they had prepared for him. While Naja retreated before him to lure him on, Trok had circled out to the south then come at him from the rear with a thousand chariots. When Sargon turned back to defend his baggage train, they had him in a glittering ring of bronze.

Sargon had managed to break out with fifty chariots, but in his headlong retreat he had left two thousand chariots and eleven thousand men behind him. Now Babylon lay before Trok, little more than a year since he and Naja had marched from Avaris.

"You know the defences, Ishtar. You helped design some of them. How long before the city falls?" Trok demanded impatiently.

"A year," Ishtar murmured thoughtfully. "Or two, maybe three." But there was a sly look on his tattooed face, and his eyes were shifty.

Trok laughed and pushed him away so hard that he almost fell from the footplate of the chariot. "A year, you say? Two? Three? I have not that amount of time to sit here. I am in a hurry, Ishtar the Mede, and you know what that means, don't you?"

"I know, god without peer. And I am but a man, fallible and poor."

"Poor?" Trok shouted in his face. "By Seueth, you slimy charlatan, you have milked me of a lakh of gold already, and what do I have to show for it?"

"You have a city and an empire. After Egypt itself, the richest in the world. I have laid it at your feet."

"I need the key to that city." Trok watched his face, happy with what he saw there. He knew Ishtar well. "Give me the city, Ishtar. Give it to me within three full moons and you shall have two more lakhs of gold from the treasure of Sargon," he promised.

"If I give it to you before the next full moon?" Ishtar rubbed his hands together like a carpet trader.

Trok's grin left his face at the prospect. He said seriously, "Then you shall have three lakhs, and a convoy of wagons to carry them away."

THE ARMY OF the two pharaohs went into camp before the legendary Blue Gate, and Trok sent an emissary to Sargon to demand the surrender of the city. Sargon, defiant behind his walls, sent the messenger's decapitated head back to Trok. The preliminaries having been dealt with, Trok and Naja made a circuit of the walls to allow the Babylonians to view their full might and splendour.

They drove golden chariots, Trok's drawn by six black stallions, Naja's by six white. Heseret rode beside Naja, glittering with jewels. They were preceded by a vanguard of five hundred chariots and followed by a rearguard of another five hundred. The slow, stately circuit of the city took all that day, and at sunset Heseret retired to her tent with all her slave girls, leaving her husband and Trok to pore over a map of the city by lamplight with Ishtar. The map was a work of art, drawn in coloured detail on finely tanned sheepskin.

"How came this map into your possession?" Naja demanded.

"Twelve years ago, by the command of King Sargon, I surveyed the city and drew this map with my own hands," Ishtar replied. "No other could have achieved such accuracy and beauty."

"If he commissioned it, why did you not deliver it to Sargon?"

"I did." Ishtar nodded. "I delivered the inferior draft to him, while secretly I kept the fair copy you see before you. I knew that one day someone would pay me more handsomely than Sargon ever did."

For another hour they studied the map, silent and absorbed. As fighting generals with a professional eye for the salient features of a battlefield, they were able to admire the depth and strength of the walls, the towers and redoubts.

At last Trok stood back from the table. "There is no weakness that I can divine, magician. You were right the first time. It will take three years of hard work to break through those walls. You will have to do better than this to earn your three lakhs."

"The water," whispered Ishtar. "Look to the water."

"I have looked to the water." Naja smiled at him, thin-lipped. "There are canals supplying every quarter of the city, enough water to grow Sargon's six terraces of gardens for a hundred years."

"Pharaoh is all-seeing, all-wise." Ishtar bowed to him. "But where does the water come from?"

"From two mighty rivers that have not failed in this millennium."

"But where does the water enter the city? How does it pass through, under or over those walls?" Ishtar insisted, and Naja and Trok exchanged looks of dawning comprehension.

HALF A MILE north of Babylon, outside the city walls, on the east bank of the Euphrates, at a point where the river broadened and ran sluggishly, stood the temple of Ninurta, the lion-headed winged god of the Euphrates. It was built on stone piers that extended out into the river, with multiple images of the god engraved on a frieze on the outer walls.

Trok, with twenty troopers at his back, strode through into the temple courtyard where the purple-robed priests of Ninurta were gathered. He killed the high priest with a single thrust through the old man's throat. Wailing at such sacrilege, the other priests prostrated themselves before him.

Trok sheathed his sword and nodded to the captain, who commanded the guard. "Kill them all. Make certain no one escapes."

Then he turned to watch Ishtar, who had entered the courtyard to work a charm to counteract the baleful influence of Ninurta. At four corners he burned bundles of herbs, which emitted thick, greasy smoke. Once Ishtar had completed the purification, he took a bunch of heavy keys from the body of the high priest, then led Trok and his troopers into the holy places of the temple.

Their cleated sandals rang hollowly in the high cavernous hall, and even Trok felt a religious chill as they approached the image of the god on his plinth. The lion's head snarled silently and the wings of stone were spread wide. Ishtar led Trok into the narrow space between the rear wall and the idol's back. Built into the body of Nintura was a grilled gate. Trok tried two of the keys in the lock, and the second turned the ancient mechanism. The gate swung open on creaking hinges.

Trok peered down a descending spiral staircase into darkness, and he heard the sound of running water far below.

"Bring torches!" he ordered, and the captain sent four of his troopers to take down the burning torches from their brackets. With a torch held above his head, Trok started down the narrow steps. He went gingerly, for the stone treads were slippery. The sound of running water grew louder as he went down.

Ishtar followed him closely. "This temple and the tunnels beneath it were built almost five hundred years ago," he told Trok.

Now there was the gleam of water below them, and the sound of the torrent running swiftly in the darkness. At last Trok reached the bottom, and by the wavering torchlight he saw that they stood in a wide tunnel with a curved roof, an aqueduct of impressive dimensions. The roof and walls were lined with ceramic tiles, laid in geometric patterns. Both ends of the tunnel shaded off into deep darkness.

"This footpath on which we stand runs the full length of the aqueduct," Ishtar explained. "The priests who repair and maintain the tunnel use it to gain access."

"Where does it start and where does it end?" Trok demanded.

"The far end of the aqueduct emerges in the other temple of Ninurta within the walls of Babylon. Only the priests know of the existence of this tunnel. All others believe that the water is a benevolent gift from the god. After it gushes from the fountain in the temple precinct, the water is lifted by water wheels to the gardens of the palace, or sent by canals to every quarter of the city."

"I do believe, Ishtar the Mede, that you are close to earning your three lakhs." Trok laughed with delight. "It remains only for you to lead us down this rabbit hole, and into the city."

TROK CHOSE two hundred of his best and most reliable men, all members of his own leopard tribe. He divided them into two groups. Once they had fought their way through the aqueduct into the city, the first group was to secure the Blue Gate and keep it open until Pharaoh Naja Kiafan could lead the main force through it. The second, smaller group was to make its way into the palace and seize Sargon's treasury.

The chosen two hundred were dressed in the uniforms of Sargon's army, taken from the prisoners and the dead men left on the battlefield. They wore only a red sash to distinguish them from the foe. Rough copies of the city map were hastily drawn by army scribes and issued to the captains of both divisions so that they knew the layout of streets and buildings. By evening every man knew exactly what was expected of him once he entered the city.

As soon as it was dark, Naja quietly moved his assault force up into position outside the Blue Gate, ready to dash through into the city as soon as Trok's men threw it open.

In the courtyard of the river temple of Ninurta, Trok mustered his division. While it was still daylight, he and Ishtar led them in single file down the spiral staircase. They marched in silence, every tenth man carrying a torch, giving just sufficient light for the men who followed to make out their footing on the slimy stones. At their left hand the never-ending flow of water rustled darkly by.

Abruptly Ishtar stopped and pointed ahead. The faint glimmer of light was reflected off the shiny ceramic walls. Trok signalled the men following him to halt, then went forward with Ishtar. Over their own garments they wore headdresses and purple robes taken from the bodies of the slaughtered priests.

As they went towards the source of the light, they saw another gate across the tunnel, and the distorted shadows of men thrown on the walls by the light of a torch set in a bracket. On the other side of the grille two robed priests were seated on stools, with a bao board between them, absorbed in their game. They looked up when Ishtar called softly to them.

The fat one stood up. "Are you from Sinna?" he called.

"Yes!" Ishtar assured him.

"You are late. We have been waiting since nightfall. You should have been here hours ago."

"I am sorry," Ishtar sounded contrite, "but you know Sinna."

The fat priest chuckled, "Yes, I know Sinna. He taught me my responses thirty years ago."

His key jangled in the lock of the gate, and then he swung it open. "You must hurry," he said. Trok trotted forward with the hood over his face, holding his sword in the fold of his robe. The priest stood back against the wall to let him pass. Trok stopped in front of him, whispered, "Ninurta will reward you, brother," and killed him.

With a shout of alarm, the priest's companion leapt to his feet, knocking over the bao board and scattering the stones across the pier. With two long strides Trok reached him and chopped his head half off. Without another sound, the priest fell backwards.

Trok gave a soft whistle and his men moved up into the torchlight with drawn swords. Ishtar led them forward until they reached the foot of another steep stone stairway. They went up it quickly until they came to a heavy curtain blocking their way. Ishtar peeped around its edge and nodded. "The temple is empty."

Trok stepped through and looked about him. Below them the image of the god crouched over the mouth of the aqueduct from which the water spurted into a deep pond, then spilled over into the canal that carried it to the city. Although the smell of incense was thick in the air, the great hall of the temple was deserted.

Trok signalled his men to come forward. Ishtar led the smaller band through a side door of the hall into a corridor that connected with the palace of Sargon. Trok led his men out into the narrow lane behind the temple and, working only from his memory of the map, turned at the second lane into the wide avenue that he knew led to the Blue Gate. It was still dark in the sleeping city.

They met a number of cloaked figures on the way, one or two staggering drunk, but the others scurried out of their way and let the column of dark armed warriors pass. They reached the end of the avenue without being challenged, but as the gateway loomed ahead a voice sang out at them from the door of the guardhouse.

"Stand ho!" The centurion of the gate, with five men at his back, stepped out into the torchlight. But they were ill-prepared, without helmets and body armour, their faces still crumpled with sleep.

Trok gave the hand signal for his troops to charge. "Open the gate and stand aside!" he ran straight at the centurion.

For a moment longer the man stood uncertainly. Then Trok was on him, and dropped him with a single blow. His men swarmed over the other guards before they could defend themselves, but the noise had alerted the sentinels on the parapets above the gate. They sounded the alarm with braying rams' horns, and hurled their javelins down into the attackers.

"Winkle them out of there!" Trok ordered, and half of his men rushed up the ramps on either side of the gateway to reach the parapet. They were at once locked in close and desperate fighting with the guards on the wall. Trok kept half of his men with him.

Ishtar had described the gate room that housed the heavy winches and pulleys that operated the massive gates. After only a few minutes of furious fighting Trok's men had killed or wounded most of the defenders within. The survivors fled out of the postern gate, and Trok led his men to the massive winches. With two men on each spoke of the capstans they began to open the gates.

Outside the walls Naja's men had swarmed forward with crowbars and levers. They forced the heavy gates wider and wider, until at last a squadron of chariots could pass through. Then they stood aside, and Naja led a phalanx of fighting chariots in a brutal charge through the gateway, and swept the avenue from side to side. The army of Egypt poured through behind them. Trok took command of them and led them rampaging through the city towards the palace.

The sack of Babylon had begun.

THE DEFENCE of the palace was stubborn, led by Sargon himself. However, by that evening Trok had opened a breach in the outer walls of the first terrace. He led a strong contingent through and the defence collapsed. When they burst into Sargon's bedchamber he was kneeling before the image of Marduk, the devouring god of Mesopotamia, with a bloody sword through his breast. Beside him lay the body of his favourite wife, a grey-haired woman who had been with him for thirty years. Before falling on his sword he had given her a merciful death, compared to what she might have expected from Trok's men.

The women from the zenana were herded out of the palace. Trok selected twenty, the youngest and prettiest, for his personal entertainment, and the rest were given to his senior officers.

It took another two days to break into the treasury buried deep in the earth below the palace, for many ingenious constructions and devices guarded it. Without the expertise and first-hand knowledge of Ishtar the Mede, it might have taken even longer to penetrate to the chamber.

When the way was clear, Trok and Naja, Heseret following them, descended the stairway and entered the chamber. Ishtar had lit the interior with a hundred oil lamps, and even the two pharaohs were stunned into silence by the splendour of the treasure. Heseret had to shade her eyes against the dazzle of the masses of precious metal. Naja walked forward slowly between the stacks, which were higher than his head, stopping every few paces to stroke the ingots.

Trok picked up a heavy bar in each hand and laughed with delight. "How much?" he demanded of Ishtar.

"Splendid and Divine Majesty, the scrolls of Sargon's scribes record the total weight of silver at fifty-five lakhs, the gold at thirty-three." He spread his tattooed hands deprecatingly. "But who would trust the count of a Babylonian?"

"Sargon is a greater robber than I gave him credit for." Trok made it sound like a compliment.

"At least there is enough here to pay me the pittance you promised?" Ishtar suggested smoothly.

"I think we should discuss that further." Trok smiled at him genially. "I am a kindly and generous man, Ishtar, as you know full well. However, over-generosity is a form of stupidity. Stupid I am not."

There was much else to see and marvel at within the city. Trok and Naja toured the palace, climbing to the top terrace with its fountains and gardens. From this height they could look down on both the great rivers and the vista of fields, marshes and papyrus beds outside the city walls.

Next they visited all the temples, for these magnificent buildings were also stuffed with bullion, beautiful furniture, statuary, mosaics and other works of art. The greatest of these temples was that of Marduk the Devourer. Trok found this to be not only a mine of precious metal and jewellery but a place of endless fascination.

He knelt on a pile of leopardskins spread on the stone floor in the inner sanctum of the temple before the altar. The golden image of the god was of a comely youth, three or four times life-sized.

"You told me that Marduk was a terrible god, crueller than any other in the pantheon, more ferocious even than Seueth," Trok challenged Ishtar, "yet this is a pretty boy."

"Divine Pharaoh, be not deceived!" Ishtar warned him. "This is the face that Marduk shows the world. His true aspect is so hideous that any man who looks upon it is instantly rendered blind and mad."

Sobered by that thought, Trok remained silent while the priests brought in two kids and offered them to the god. Ishtar slit their throats so skilfully that they made hardly a sound as they bled into the golden divination bowl that he held beneath them and then placed before the altar into the incense braziers. Chanting and mumbling, he threw handfuls of herbs on the flames until the vault filled with fragrant blue smoke. After a while Trok found it difficult to think clearly and his vision became distorted. He closed his eyes and pressed his fingers into the lids. When he opened them again he saw that the sweet smile on the face of the god had become a leer. He tried to look away but found he could not.

"The great god Marduk is pleased," Ishtar announced, reading the auguries reflected in the surface of the blood-filled bowl. After a long silence he began to rock gently back and forth with the bowl in his lap. He looked up at last. "Behold Marduk, the great god of Babylon! Speak to us, dreadful one, we entreat you!"

He opened his arms to the golden statue, and the god spoke in the voice of a child, lisping and mellifluous.

"I greet you, my brother Trok," said this strange voice. "You wish to know about the fledgling falcon that spreads its wings and sharpens its talons in the desert places."

Trok was startled not only by the disembodied voice but also by the accuracy of this statement. Indeed, he had intended asking for counsel on his plans to attack and destroy Nefer Seti. He recalled bitterly how Ishtar had dissuaded him from leading another army into the eastern desert to attack Nefer Seti, with predictions of dire consequences, with warnings of disaster and death. Now he spoke as much to himself as to the golden god. "I must have Nefer Seti. The double crown will sit uneasily on my head until I kill him and throw his body on the flames so that he will never know resurrection."

In his anger and hatred he sprang to his feet. "I demand that you deliver the person and the soul of Nefer Seti to me, in justice and retribution. I will not accept another refusal from you and your minion here." In his fury Trok aimed a kick at Ishtar. His sandal caught the divining bowl and the blood of the kids splattered down the altar.

A hush had fallen over the sanctum. Then there was the sound of breathing, like that of a sleeping child to begin with but then growing harsher and stronger. Now it was the breathing of a wild beast, then of some monster that echoed through the temple.

Then a terrible voice spoke, harsh and unearthly. "Hear me! Trok Uruk, you mortal man who claims to be Pharaoh, part of the godhead!" The thunder rolled around the dark recess of the sanctum. "Hear me, blasphemer! If you march against Gallala in defiance of me and my prophet, Ishtar the Mede, I shall destroy you and your army just as I buried your other army in the sands of the desert. This time you shall not escape my wrath."

Even though he was fearful of the rage of Marduk, Trok still sensed some false note in the force of his fury.

He tried to identify exactly what had given him pause. He realised that the thunderous voice issued from the belly of the statue. He stared and saw that the navel of the god was a dark slit. He took a step towards it and Ishtar cried, "Beware, Pharaoh! Do not approach him."

Trok ignored him and took another step forward, seeing a faint gleam in the depths of the aperture, a shadowy movement. Often in battle he had sensed the exact moment when the fates had swung in his favour and he felt it now. He steeled himself and shouted, above the awful sound of the god's breathing, "I defy you, Marduk the Devourer! Strike me down if you are able."

Suspicion became certainty as that glimmer showed again in the slit in the god's belly. Trok drew his sword and, with the flat of the blade, knocked Ishtar out of his way. Then he ran forward, ducked down, and peered into the slit. A human eye looked back at him. The pupil widened with astonishment, and Trok gave a mighty shout: "Come out of there you slime!" He placed his shoulder against the idol and heaved with all his strength. The statue wobbled on its stone base, and Trok heaved again. Slowly the image went down with a crash onto the stone flags.

Ishtar screamed and leapt out of the way. In the silence after the shattering impact there was a scrabbling sound from the interior of the fallen idol. A trap door at the back of the idol flew open and a girl crawled out. Trok seized her by a thick head of curls. "Mercy, great King Trok," the girl pleaded, in a honey-sweet voice. "I was doing the bidding of others." She was such a lovely child that, for a moment, Trok felt his rage subside. Then he snatched her up by the ankles and dangled her upside-down in one fist, writhing in his grip.

"Who ordered you to this?" Trok demanded.

"Ishtar the Mede," she wept.

Trok dashed the child against a temple column then let her corpse drop. He turned back to the golden idol and thrust his sword into the opening, rummaging around in the belly of the god. There was another squeal and a grotesque creature shot out, a hunch-backed dwarf, the ugliest man Trok had ever laid eyes upon.

"Forgive me that I tried to deceive you, mighty god and King of Egypt!" Trok slashed at him with the sword, but the creature ducked and dodged roaring with terror. Trok found himself laughing at his antics. The dwarf shot behind the curtains at the back of the chamber and disappeared through a secret doorway.

Trok let him go and turned back to Ishtar, just in time to seize a handful of his hair as he tried to flee from the chamber. He flung him full length on the stone floor.

"You have lied to me." Trok was no longer laughing. "You have deliberately misled me and diverted me from my purpose."

"Please, master," Ishtar wailed. "It was for your good alone. How could we go against a warlock who commands the storm to his will?"

"You are afraid of Taita." Trok stood back to regain his breath. "The warlock?" he demanded incredulously.

"He overlooks us. He can turn my own spells back upon me! I cannot prevail against him. I sought only to save you from him, great Pharaoh."

"You sought only to save your own blue-tattooed skin," Trok snarled, and rushed in to slam kicks into Ishtar's doubled-up body.

"I beg of you, first of all the gods," Ishtar cried, covering his head with both arms, "give me my reward and let me go. Taita has dissipated my powers. I cannot confront him again. I can be of no further use to you."

Trok stood with one foot drawn back, frozen in the act of delivering another kick. "Your reward?" he demanded in astonishment. "Surely you do not believe that I will reward your disloyalty? If you wish to live another day then you will lead me to Gallala, and take your chances in a trial of magical strength with the warlock."

IT SEEMED THAT all Egypt had heard that Nefer Seti had an army in Gallala. Each day visitors from all over the country arrived. Some were colonels of the regiments that Trok and Naja had left to guard Egypt in their absence. Others were emissaries from the great cities along the Nile—Avaris and Memphis, Thebes and Aswan—and the high priests from the temples in those cities. Sickened by the excesses of Naja and Trok, and emboldened by their absence in Babylon so far to the east, all had come to swear allegiance to Nefer Seti.

"Egypt is ready to welcome you," the emissaries told him.

"Our regiments will declare for you as soon as they see your face, and know that the rumours of your survival are true," the colonels assured him.

Nefer and Taita questioned them keenly. It soon became apparent that Trok and Naja had skimmed the cream of the regiments for their Mesopotamian adventure, and left only the reserve battalions, made up mostly of new recruits, the very young and untried, or the elderly nearing the end of their military lives.

"What of the chariots and horses?" Nefer asked the crucial question. They shook their grey heads and looked grave. "Trok and Naja stripped the regiments bare. Almost every vehicle went with them. They left hardly enough to patrol the eastern borders to discourage the Bedouin raiders from the desert."

Taita assessed this information. "The false pharaohs are fully aware of the threat we pose to their rear. They want to ensure that if the regiments they have left in Egypt rebel against them and declare for the true Pharaoh, Nefer Seti, they will lack cavalry and chariots to be an effective force."

"You must return to your regiments," Nefer ordered the officers. "We are too many in Gallala already, and we are near the limits of our food and water. Do not allow any more vehicles or horses to leave Egypt. Keep your men in training, and equip them with new chariots as they become available. I will come to you very soon, to lead you against the tyrants."

They left, with renewed assurances of their loyalty, and the little army of Gallala redoubled its efforts to build itself into a force to challenge the might of the false pharaohs. They were inspired by their young commander, for Nefer worked harder than any of them. He rode out with the first squadrons long before dawn, and gradually forged his divisions into a cohesive body. When he rode back into the city, weary and dusty in the evening, he would go to the workshops where he cajoled and argued with the armourers and chariot builders. Then, after he had eaten, he would sit up in the lamplight with Taita, going over the battle plans and the dispositions of their forces. Usually it was after midnight when he stumbled to his bedchamber, where Mintaka took his head onto her bosom and held him until he woke to dawn's first promise.

NEFER LOOKED BACK along the column of chariots. They were at full gallop, four abreast. The platoon commanders were watching for his signal. He looked ahead and saw the line of enemy foot soldiers out in the plain, distorted by the heat mirage so that they seemed to be swimming in a lake of shimmering water where there was no water. He steered for their centre.

As they raced in he saw the enemy formation change. Like a giant hedgehog, it rolled itself into a ball, a tight circle two ranks deep, facing outwards, the outer rank with their long lances levelled, and the second rank with their lances thrust through the gaps, so that they offered a glittering wall of bronze spearheads. Nefer raced straight at the centre of the double row of lances, and then, when they were only two hundred paces away, he gave a hand signal and the formation of chariots opened, wheeling alternately right and left, spreading like wings to envelope the crouching infantrymen. The chariots whirled around them and the arrows from the short recurved cavalry bows flew into them.

Nefer gave the signal to break off the attack and withdraw. As he swept past the infantry circle, he raised his right fist in a salute, and shouted, "Well done! That was much better."

He slowed the horses and turned them, trotting back to halt his squadron in front of the ranks of infantry. Taita stepped out of the defensive circle to greet him.

"Any injuries?" Nefer asked. The tips of the arrows they shot into the hedgehog were padded, but they could still inflict damage.

"A few bruises." Taita shrugged.

"They have done well," Nefer said, then shouted to the centurion commanding the infantry, "Let your lads fall out. I want to speak to them. Then we will practise the false retreat."

There was an outcrop of rock that formed a natural podium, and Nefer climbed to the top of it while all the men—infantry and charioteers—gathered below him.

Taita squatted at the base of the rock and watched and listened. Nefer reminded him strongly of Pharaoh Tamose, his father, at the same age. He had the easy manner, and spoke simply, in language that his men understood.

Nefer reviewed the morning's exercises, giving them the credit they deserved, but ruthlessly picking out every deficiency. "I think you are almost ready to give Trok and Naja the surprise of their lives," he ended. "Now, get something to eat. We have not finished for the day." They began to disperse.

Nefer jumped down from the rock, and as he did so Taita sprang to his feet and said quietly but urgently, "Stop, Nefer! Do not move!"

The cobra must have had its nest in the rock pile, but the noise and the trampling of feet and hoofs had disturbed it. It came slithering out of the crack in the dark rock just as Nefer jumped down and landed almost on top of it. Its hood was flared open, and its feathery black tongue flickered between the thin, grinning lips. Its eyes were beads of polished onyx, with sparks of light in the black centres, and they were fastened on Nefer's long bare legs, which were within easy striking distance.

The nearest men had heard Taita's warning. They turned back but none dared move. They stared in horror at the mortal predicament of their pharaoh.

The cobra gaped wide, the preliminary to the attack, and the bony fangs came erect in the pale roof of its mouth. Drops of venom sparkled on the needle points.

Suddenly there was a shrill cry from the sky above. They had all been so intent on the cobra that no one had seen the falcon hovering high in the blue above them. Now it stooped towards the earth, and in full flight sank its talons into the flared hood, an inch behind the head. Then it rose on heavily flogging wings, carrying the cobra dangling and twisting below it.

Taita watched the bird as it bore away the snake. It dwindled in size in the distance and at last disappeared into the blue-grey heat-haze that shrouded the horizon. Taita stood a long time staring after it. When he turned his expression was grave.

"It was an omen," Nefer said, and glanced at him. He saw by Taita's face that this was so.

"Yes," said Taita. "It was a warning and a promise."

"What does it mean?"

"The cobra threatened you. That means great danger. The royal bird flew towards the east with the snake in its talons. It means great danger in the east. But in the end the falcon triumphed."

They both looked towards the east. "We will take out a scouting expedition tomorrow at the first light of dawn," Nefer decided.

IN THE CHILL darkness before the dawn Nefer and Taita waited on the mountaintop. The rest of the scouting party were encamped on the back slope. All told they were twenty men.

Hilto, Shabako and Meren had taken other scouting parties to cover the terrain to the south; between them they could sweep all the eastern approaches to Gallala.

Nefer had brought his party down along the western shores of the Red Sea, looking in on every port and fishing village along the way. Apart from a few trading caravans and wandering bands of Bedouin they had found nothing, no sign of the danger foreshadowed by the omen. Now they were camped above the port of Safaga.

Taita and Nefer had woken in the darkness and left the camp to climb to the lookout peak. They sat close together in companionable silence. Taita looked to the eastern sky, where the morning star hung low on the horizon. He stood up suddenly and leaned on his staff. Nefer never failed to be amazed by the acuity of those pale old eyes. He knew Taita had seen something.

"What is it, Old Father?"

"The omen was not false," Taita said simply. "The danger is here."

The sea was grey, but as the light strengthened, the surface was speckled with white. Like a vast flock of egrets returning to the roost, a fleet of dhows was heading into the port of Safaga.

"If this is the army of Trok and Naja, why would they come by sea?" Nefer asked quietly.

"It is the shortest route from Mesopotamia. The crossing will save the horses and men for the road through the desert. Without the warning of the snake and the falcon, we would not have expected danger from this direction." Taita nodded approval. "It is a cunning move."

They scrambled back down the mountain to the camp below. Nefer called in the sentries and gave them their orders. Two would ride back with all speed to Gallala, carrying his orders to Socco, whom he had left in command. Most of the other men he split into pairs and sent south to find the scouting parties and bring them in.

Nefer and Taita watched the men Nefer had dispatched ride away, then they mounted and rode down through the hills to an abandoned watchtower overlooking Safaga.

"The first boats are entering the bay." Nefer pointed out the largest of them all. At the peak of her stubby mast she flew the snarling leopard-head gonfalon of the House of Trok Uruk. "There he is." He pointed to the unmistakable figure in the bows.

"And that is Ishtar beside Trok: the dog and its master." Taita had a fierce gleam in his eyes as watched the strange pair wade ashore.

"Do you see Naja's standard on any of the ships?" Nefer asked.

Taita shook his head. "Trok alone leads the expedition. He must have left Naja to hold Babylon and Mesopotamia. He has come to take care of personal business."

"How do you know that?" Nefer demanded.

"There is an aura around him. It is like a dark red cloud. I can sense it even from here," Taita said softly. "All that hatred is focused on one person alone. He comes for Mintaka."

THE MORNING AFTER his landing at Safaga, Trok captured two Bedouin leading a string of donkeys down the road to Safaga. His reputation had penetrated even into these desert fastnesses, so the Bedouin were desperate to please. They told Trok of the lush pastures that surrounded Gallala. They also gave him an estimate of the numbers of chariots that Nefer Seti commanded, and Trok realised that he outnumbered his enemies five to one. Most important of all, they told him the route from Safaga to the ancient city and assured him he could reach Gallala in two days and a night of hard riding.

It took him two more days to disembark all his squadrons. On the second evening he was ready to begin the forced march on Gallala. Each of the chariots had two spare teams behind it on lead reins. They would not stop during the night to rest the horses, but would change them as they tired. Any exhausted animals would be turned loose and left behind for the remount herds to bring up.

Trok led the vanguard, and set a killing pace. Once the waterskins were empty there would be no turning back. By midmorning the following day the heat had become fierce, and they had used up most of the spare horses. The Bedouin guides kept assuring Trok that Gallala was not far ahead, but each time they topped a rise the same daunting vista of rock and baked earth shimmered in the heat mirage ahead. Fifty or sixty chariots burned out their last horses, and Trok left them scattered back along the road.

The sun came up on the second day, warm as a kiss, but soon it stung and dazzled their bloodshot eyes. For the first time Trok faced the possibility of dying here on this dreadful road to nowhere.

"One more hill," he called to his last team of horses, and tried to whip them into a trot, but they stumbled up the easy incline with their heads hanging, and the sweat long ago dried to white salt on their flanks. Just below the crest Trok looked back down the straggling column of his army. Even without counting them he saw that he had lost half of his chariots. Hundreds of dismounted troopers were staggering along behind the column, and there were vultures in the sky following them, dark specks turning in high circles against the blue.

"There is only one way," he told Ishtar, "and that is forward." He cracked the whip over the backs of his team. They went on painfully.

They reached the top of the hill, and Trok gawked in astonishment at the scene in the valley below him. The ruins of the ancient city of Gallala lay before him, ghostly but eternal. As he had been promised, the city was surrounded by fields of cool green, and a network of canals. His horses smelt the water and strained against the reins with renewed strength.

Even in his desperate haste, Trok took time to assess the tactical situation. He saw at once that the city was helpless and undefended. The gates stood wide open and from them poured the panic-stricken populace. Carrying their children and bundles of possessions they streamed away up the narrow valley to the west. There was no sign of cavalry or of fighting chariots. They were a flock of sheep before the wolf pack, but the wolves were parched and weak with thirst.

"Seueth has delivered them into our hands," Trok shouted with triumph. "Before the sun sets this day you will have more women and gold than you can use!"

The cry was taken up by the men who had followed him over the ridge, and they rode down to the first irrigation ditch and spread out along the length of it, the horses sucking up the blessed liquid.

The men threw themselves full length along the bank, plunging their faces under, or filling their helmets and pouring it over their heads and down their throats.

"YOU SHOULD HAVE let me poison the canals," Nefer said flatly, as they watched from the other side of the valley.

"You know better than that." Taita shook his head. "That would have been an offence against nature that the gods would never forgive."

He and Nefer gave their full attention to the unfolding scene in the valley below. Trok's men and horses had drunk until their bellies bulged and now they were mounting. Even though he had lost many chariots on the approach march, Trok still outnumbered Nefer's forces at least three to one.

"We dare not meet him on open ground," Nefer mused, and looked down upon the mass of refugees escaping up the valley below them. Mintaka, together with all the women and children, the sick and wounded, had been evacuated from Gallala two days before. Nefer had sent them all to Gebel Nagara, where Trok would never find them.

Now Gallala was stripped of everything of value. Nefer gazed down on the refugees with satisfaction. Even from this close it was difficult to tell that they were not women and civilians but disguised foot soldiers, stumbling in their long skirts and shawls. The bundles they carried were not swaddled infants, but their bows and swords. Their lances had been cached among the rocks higher up the valley where the main force was concealed.

The enemy's chariots were coming on across the pastures in tight formations. The water had revived them, and before them lay the promise of plunder. They were close enough now for Nefer to be able to pick out Trok's chariot at the front of the mass of vehicles, as it wheeled into a position across the mouth of the valley.

"Come, Trok Uruk!" Nefer whispered. "Order the charge! Ride into history!"

ISHTAR THE MEDE crouched beside Trok in the leading chariot. He was so agitated that he reached up to tug at Trok's beard.

"The smell of the warlock hangs in the air." His voice was shrill, and saliva frothed on his lips. "He waits for you, I can feel his presence. Look up, mighty Pharaoh!"

Trok was distracted enough to glance up at the sky. The vultures had dropped lower.

"Yes! Yes!" Ishtar pressed the small advantage. "They are Taita's chickens. They wait for him to feed them with your flesh."

Trok looked back at the prize that lay before him, but the shadows of the vultures flitted over the earth between them and he turned his head to look down at the skinny figure of Ishtar beside him.

The Mede tugged at his armour. "It is a snare laid for you by the warlock. If you never trust me again, you must trust me now. There is death in the air."

Trok scratched his beard, and glanced over his shoulder at the ranks of chariots parked wheel to wheel and his troopers leaning forward in cruel anticipation of his order.

"Turn aside, mighty Trok. Seize the city and the water. Nefer Seti and the warlock will perish out there in the desert. That way is certain. The other way is madness."

ON THE HILLSIDE Nefer narrowed his eyes as he watched his disguised troopers scurrying away up the valley, and he knew that the moment was passing. "What is holding Trok? Will he not commit to the charge?"

"Look to the head of the valley." Taita had not opened his eyes.

Nefer glanced up the valley, and stiffened with alarm. His fist tightened on the hilt of his sword.

"It is not possible!" he growled.

Near the top end of the valley, but fully visible from where Trok's chariots were drawn up, was a square slab of rock. It stood out like a man-made monument beside the road. On top of this, above the stream of fleeing refugees, had appeared a woman, young and slim, with long, dark hair that hung to her waist.

"Mintaka!" Nefer breathed. "I ordered her to go to Gebel Nagara."

"We know that she would never have disobeyed you." Taita smiled ironically. "Therefore, it seems that she must have misheard you."

"This is your doing," Nefer said bitterly. "You are using her as bait for Trok. You have placed her in mortal danger."

"Perhaps I can control the khamsin," Taita said, "but not even I can control Mintaka. What she does, she does of her own free will."

Below them, Trok had turned round and was staring up the long rising valley. He saw the tiny figure standing high on the rock platform, and recognised in an instant the object of all his hatred.

"Mintaka Apepi," he snarled, "I have come for you, you adulterous little bitch. I will make you plead for death."

"It is an illusion, Pharaoh," Ishtar howled. "Don't let the warlock deceive you. There is death all around us."

He tried to leap down from the footplate and run, but Trok seized him and hauled him back. He raised his clenched fist high above his head and shouted, "Forward! March!"

The chariots on either hand rolled forward together, and the ranks behind followed Trok into the valley. The tail of the fleeing refugees was three hundred paces ahead when Trok gave his next order.

"Forward at the gallop! Charge!"

The horses leapt away, and in a rising thunder of hoofs and wheels they swept up the narrow valley.

"Trok has committed," Nefer said softly. "But at what cost? If he takes Mintaka . . ." He could not bring himself to go on.

As the phalanx of chariots swept by below where Nefer stood on the side of the valley, he stepped out from behind the rock that had concealed him. The complete attention of Trok and his troopers was fixed on the victims ahead of their racing chariots, but all Nefer's men could see him clearly. They were hidden among the boulders down both slopes of the valley. Nefer raised his sword above his head, and as the last chariot sped past he brought it down sharply.

The wagons were poised on the steep gradient, screened from view with dried grass and so heavily laden with rocks that the axles sagged. At Nefer's signal his wagoners pulled out the wooden chocks that held them, and from both sides of the valley the wagons rolled forward, gathering speed, bounding down to the massed chariots below.

When Ishtar screamed at his side, Trok tore his eyes from Mintaka's figure at the far end of the valley, and he saw the huge vehicles tearing down upon his squadrons. "Back!" he shouted. "Break away!" But there was no space to manoeuvre.

The first wagons crashed into the head of the charge. There was the rending of wood, the screams of crushed men and horses, the thunder of wagons overturning and shedding their loads of rock. In an instant the magnificent charge was transformed into a shambles of shattered vehicles and crippled horses.

The wagons had sealed off the valley at both ends. Even the chariots that had not been smashed and capsized were now bottled up in a struggling mass, held by walls of stone, and Nefer's archers were on the slopes above them. The first volleys decimated the unprotected charioteers. Within minutes the valley was transformed into a slaughterhouse.

Trok looked around him wildly, seeking a way out of the trap, but behind him the other vehicles were so crowded that there was no room for him to turn or back up. Arrows and javelins were singing around him, clattering against the sides of the chariot, clanging off his helmet and breastplate.

Before Trok could restrain him, Ishtar took advantage of the confusion to spring down from the footplate and scuttle away between the plunging horses. Then Trok looked ahead again, and saw Mintaka still standing on the rock pile just ahead of him, a cold look of revulsion on her lovely face.

He drew his sword, sprang down to the ground and ran forward under the hoofs of his rearing horses. Two of Nefer's men jumped out from behind the rocks to oppose him but he hacked them down, his eyes fastened hungrily on the girl.

Nefer saw Trok break out of the trap, and he ran down the slope and sprang out onto the level ground in front of him.

Trok went on guard as Nefer confronted him and his face twisted into a ferocious grin. "Come, puppy," he said. "Let us test your claim to the double crown."

Nefer's men had seen him charge down the hillside. They followed his example, left the cover of the rocks and within seconds the valley was choked with struggling, hacking, thrusting men.

Nefer feinted at Trok's hip, aiming at the joint of his armour. When Trok covered, he swung backhanded at his face. Trok was surprised by the change of direction and by the speed of the stroke. Though he jerked his head back the point of Nefer's blade split his cheek open. The wound galvanised him, and Trok rushed at Nefer, his sword seeming to form an impenetrable wall of shining bronze around him. Nefer fell back before the attack until he felt the stone slab on which Mintaka stood pressing into his back.

He could no longer retreat or manoeuvre, and he was forced to pit himself against all Trok's strength, and trade him blow for blow.

In a contest of this nature, there were few men who could stand against Trok, who never seemed to flag. As much as the years of battle training had hardened Nefer they had not prepared him for this. He felt his right arm tiring. He knew that his only chance of surviving was to break away.

He caught the next cut high on his blade and deflected it just sufficiently to make an opening through which he could escape, but as he leapt into it he exposed his left flank. Trok recovered and drove in a low thrust that laid open his thigh. The blood ran down into his sandal and squelched at every pace he took. The last of Nefer's strength was ebbing away, and Trok swept up his blade and locked it with his own, forcing his guard higher. Nefer knew that if he attempted to break away he would expose his chest for the killing thrust.

Gradually Trok forced aside his blade and towered over him, so they came chest to chest, then suddenly he shifted his weight to the left, towards Nefer's wounded leg. Nefer tried to counter, but his leg gave way under him. Trok hooked his foot behind Nefer's heel and threw him over backwards.

The sword flew from Nefer's grip, and as he sprawled on the sun-baked earth, Trok lifted his blade above his head with both hands for the killing stroke. Suddenly his expression changed. He opened his mouth to say something, but a double stream of bright blood trickled from the corners of his mouth and he turned slowly away from Nefer. Trok stared up at Mintaka, who stood on the rock above him. With a detached feeling of disbelief, Nefer saw the shaft of her javelin sticking out of the back of Trok's neck.

Trok toppled forward on his face, and Nefer turned to Mintaka. She flew to him, and clung to him with all her strength. Now that the danger was past, she had lost all her icy control and was sobbing, barely coherent. "I thought he was going to kill you, my love."

"He almost did, but for you," Nefer gasped. "I owe you my life."

He became aware that the sounds of battle from further down the valley had changed. With his arm still around her, he turned to look back. Trok's men had seen him cut down, and the fight had gone out of them. They were throwing down their weapons.

With the realisation of victory, Nefer felt the last strength flow out of his body. He had just enough left to raise his voice, and shout, "Give them quarter. They are our brother Egyptians. Give them quarter!"

As Nefer slumped down, Taita materialised at his side and helped Mintaka lower him to the ground. While the two of them staunched the bleeding from the deep cut in his thigh, his officers came to report to Nefer. And with joy, he saw that his trusted captains, Hilto and Meren, Shabako and Socco, were among the men who crowded around him, exulting in the victory.

They made a litter of lances and carried him back down the valley to Gallala. Three times before they reached the gates of the city, Nefer signalled for his litter to be lowered and allowed captured centurions and captains to come forward. "I spare you from the traitor's death you so richly deserve," he told them sternly, "but you must prove once more your loyalty to the House of Tamose."

They praised him for his mercy, and his own men joined their voices to those of the defeated.

Nefer issued his orders with a frowning mien. "The corpse of Trok Uruk, the false claimant to the double crown of Egypt, shall be burned without ceremony, here upon the battlefield, so that his soul shall wander through all eternity. The name of Trok Uruk shall be erased from every monument and building in the land."

They shouted their approbation at this decree, and Nefer went on. "All the possessions of Trok Uruk, all his treasure and estates and slaves, shall be forfeited to the state. Send water wagons back along the road to Safaga, and bring in all the horses, chariots and men that Trok Uruk left along the way during his march on Gallala. If they repudiate the false pharaohs and swear allegiance to the House of Tamose, the prisoners shall be pardoned and recruited into our armies."

By the time Nefer had issued his last decree for that day, his voice was hoarse, he was pale and almost exhausted. As they carried him through the city gates he asked Mintaka quietly, "Where is Taita? Has anybody seen the Magus?" But Taita had disappeared.

ON THE HILLSIDE above the battlefield, Taita had picked up the tracks that Ishtar had left as he escaped out of the valley. He followed them until they were impossible to discern in the earth on the top of the hills, which was baked hard by the sun. Then he stopped and crouched down. He opened his mind and reached out to detect the Mede's aura, the trace he had left as he passed.

The aura was dark and tainted. Taita stood up and went on again after it, striding out on his long legs. Every so often he saw physical confirmation that he was on the right track, a smudged footprint in softer earth or a recently dislodged pebble.

Ishtar had circled round to the south then come back towards Gallala. Taita was alarmed and lengthened his stride. If Ishtar was trying to get close to Nefer again to work some mischief, Taita must intercept him. However, the pursuit led him to one of the chariots Trok had abandoned on his march up from the coast. From the wreck Ishtar had salvaged a water-skin, and had then gone back to the ridge above the city, where he had crept down to the bank of the closest irrigation canal. The imprint of his knees was clear in the wet clay where he had knelt to drink and then to fill the skin he carried. Taita drank himself. Then he rose and followed the traces Ishtar had left as he started back eastwards along the road towards Safaga and the coast.

Night fell and Taita kept on. Sometimes the aura of the Mede faded away completely, but Taita followed the road. At other times it grew stronger, until Taita smelt it, a faint, musty, unpleasant odour. When it was this strong he could fathom the essence of the Mede. He could detect his vengeful nature. He divined that Ishtar was demoralised by the turn that the fates had taken against him, but his powers were still formidable. He constituted a great and real danger. Taita himself was not immune to his baleful spirit.

A LEAGUE AHEAD Ishtar the Mede was hurrying along the track. He was by now fully aware of the pursuit. I must turn aside and conceal my path, he decided. He ran on along the road and found the place where it crossed an intrusion of grey schist, so hard that even the passing of Trok's legions had left no mark upon it.

With his left forefinger he traced out lightly the sacred symbol of Marduk on the rock, spat on it and uttered the three hidden names of the god that would summon him.

"Hide me from my enemies, mighty Marduk. Bring me back safely to your temple in Babylon." Then he turned sharply off the road and set out at right angles to it, heading into the northern wilderness. He went swiftly, trying to open the distance between him and the man who pursued him.

TAITA REACHED the point where the ridge of grey schist crossed the road and stopped abruptly. The aura that had been so strong only moments before had disappeared like mist in the warmth of the rising sun. Quickly he retraced his steps until he reached the point where he had lost the trail.

He looked up at the sky, from the starry firmament picked out the single red star low on the horizon, the star of the goddess Lostris, and began to chant the Praise to the Goddess. He had barely completed the first stanza when he felt an angry, alien presence. Another god had been invoked on this spot, and knowing Ishtar he could guess well enough who that was. He started on the second stanza of praise and on the bare rock ahead of him appeared a glow, like that of a furnace.

Marduk is affronted, and shows his anger, he thought. He intoned, "You are far from your own land, Marduk of the furnace. Few worship you in Egypt. Your powers are dissipated. I invoke the name of the goddess Lostris, and you cannot stand against it."

He lifted his kilt. "I quench your fire, Marduk," he said, and urinated on the rock. It sizzled like a bar of metal from the forge, drenched in the trough. "In the name of the goddess Lostris, Marduk the Devourer, stand aside and let me pass."

The rock cooled quickly, and as the steam dispersed the veil that Ishtar had laid was pierced and torn. Taita stepped through it and set off again after him.

The horizon paled and the light increased to a golden radiance. Taita knew that he was gaining steadily, and he strained his eyes ahead for the first glimpse of his quarry. Instead he came to an abrupt halt. At his feet gaped a terrible abyss, whose sheer sides dropped into darkness far below.

Taita looked across at the far side. It was a thousand paces across, and there were vultures soaring over the bottomless gulf. Taita shook his head with admiration. "Wonderful, Ishtar!" he murmured. "Even the vultures. That was a masterful touch. I could not have improved upon it. But such an effort called for a great expenditure of strength. It must have cost you dearly."

Taita stepped out over the edge of the cliff. Instead of airy space there was firm ground under his feet. The vista of cliffs and vultures wavered and broke up as a mirage does when you walk towards it.

The abyss was gone and in its place was a gentle plain of stony ground. In the middle of this plain, not five hundred paces away, stood Ishtar the Mede. Seeing Taita striding towards him he turned and broke into a shambling run, his black robes swirling around his legs. Taita followed him with his long, indefatigable strides, and

Ishtar was only a few hundred paces ahead when he reached the low hills and disappeared into one of the gullies.

When Taita reached the mouth of the gully he saw Ishtar's footprints strung along the sandy floor ahead of him, but they disappeared round the corner where the gully turned sharply to the right. Taita followed him, but as he reached the corner of pale limestone pillars, he heard the thunderous roaring of a wild beast. Standing foursquare in the way, its tail lashing from side to side, was a huge male lion. Its eyes were golden, the pupils implacable black slits.

Taita didn't break his stride. As he walked straight at the slavering animal, the roaring became muted, the outline of its head turned transparent and then, like river mist, the lion faded and was gone.

Taita walked through the space where it had stood and rounded the corner. Ahead of him the gully became narrower and the sides were steeper. It ended abruptly against a wall of rock.

Ishtar stood with his back against the rock, staring at Taita with mad eyes. He raised his right hand and pointed a long bony finger at Taita. "Back, Warlock!" he screamed. "I warn you!"

Taita walked towards him and he screamed again, this time in a guttural language. Then he turned and bolted into a narrow opening in the rock wall behind him, which had been screened from Taita by his body. Taita paused before the entrance, and tapped the stony portals with his staff. The rock rang true. This was no illusion, but the rear entrance to a cavern in the limestone cliff.

Taita stepped through after him, and could hear the echoes of Ishtar's footsteps distorted in the tunnel ahead. Taita counted his paces as he went forward into darkness. After a hundred and twenty the tunnel took a sharp bend, and as he stepped round it Taita found himself in a large, high-roofed cavern. From the floor rose sharp-pointed stalagmites, the crystals glimmering. From the high roof hung down matching stalactites, some shaped like spearheads and other like the shining wings of the gods. In the centre of the roof was an aperture through which a beam of bright sunlight fell to the floor.

Across the cavern Ishtar crouched against the far wall. There was no escape that way. When he saw Taita appear in the mouth of the tunnel he began to blubber, "Mercy, mighty Magus! There is a bond between us. We are brothers. Spare me."

So abject were his entreaties that, despite himself, Taita felt his resolve waver. It was just the mere flicker of doubt in his mind, but Ishtar picked up the tiny chink in his armour, and exploited it instantly. He flung out one hand with the thumb and forefinger forming a circle, the sign of Marduk, and shouted something in that strange guttural tongue.

From behind him Taita felt an insupportable physical weight bear down upon his body, trapping his arms to his sides, wrapping around his throat in a strangler's grip. He smelt scorching human flesh, the aura of the Devourer, suffocating him. He could not move.

On the far side of the cavern Ishtar danced and capered, his tattooed face contorted in a grotesque mask. "Your goddess cannot protect you here deep in the earth, Taita. You can no longer prevail against Marduk the Devourer and Ishtar, his minion," he shrieked, "Our contest is over. I have defeated you and all your wiles, Warlock! Now you will die."

Taita turned his eyes up towards the high, dim roof of the cavern and fixed all his attention on one of the long, gleaming stalactites that hung down from it like a great shimmering dagger. He gathered all his reserves, lifted the staff in his right hand and pointed it upwards. With the last breath in his lungs he shouted, *"Kydash!"* the word of power.

There was a crack like the ice shattering in the depths of a glacier, the stalactite broke from the roof and plunged downwards. Driven by its own immense weight, the point struck Ishtar on the top of his shoulder, transfixed him through chest and belly and pegged him down on the cavern floor.

As Ishtar twitched convulsively in his death throes, Taita felt the weight lifted from his shoulders and the pressure on his throat relax. Marduk retreated and the smell of burnt flesh was gone.

He picked up his staff, turned and walked back along the tunnel into the open air. At the entrance he turned back and with his staff struck the limestone portals of the tunnel, once, twice, three times.

Deep in the earth there was a rumble of collapsing rock, and a gust of air blew from the tunnel mouth as the cavern roof caved in.

"With the stone spike driven through your heart, not even your foul god can free you from your tomb. Lie in it through all eternity, Ishtar the Mede," Taita said, and he turned and struck out along the road back to Gallala.

WHEN THE MESSENGERS reached Babylon, Pharaoh Naja Kiafan gave them audience on the uppermost terrace garden of the palace of Babylon. Queen Heseret sat beside his throne, wearing the most magnificent jewels that the treasury of King Sargon had yielded.

The messengers were all high officers from the army that Pharaoh Trok had taken westward four months before. They threw themselves at the foot of the throne on which Naja sat in glory and splendour. "All hail to you, Pharaoh Naja, mightiest of the gods of Egypt," they greeted him. "We are bearers of terrible tidings."

"Speak!" Naja commanded sternly.

"In the desert that surrounds the ancient city of Gallala there took place a mighty battle between the armies of Pharaoh Trok Uruk and those of the usurper Nefer Seti," said one of the officers. "By the means of cowardly deceit the army of Pharaoh Trok Uruk was lured to destruction. He is slain. Those of his men who survived have gone over to the enemy, and have rallied to the standard of the false pharaoh Nefer Seti."

Naja sank back on his throne and stared at him in astonishment. At his side Heseret touched Naja's arm with a bejewelled finger, and when he leaned towards her she whispered in his ear, "Praise to the gods, and all hail to the one and only Pharaoh of the Upper and Lower Kingdoms, the mighty Naja Kiafan!"

Naja tried to remain expressionless but a tiny smile played for an instant over his features. It took him a moment to suppress it then he rose. His voice was soft but menacing. "Pharaoh Trok Uruk is dead. We commend his soul to the gods. I declare before you all that there is now only one ruler over both kingdoms, and over all the territories and all the conquered lands and possessions of Egypt. I declare further that ruler to be myself, Pharaoh Naja Kiafan."

The courtiers and captains who stood around his throne drew their swords and beat them on their shields. "Exalted be the king-god Naja Kiafan!"

"Send word to all my commanders and the generals of all my armies. We will meet in war council at the noon hour this same day to prepare all our forces for the campaign against Nefer Seti."

He looked at Heseret. "Do you feel no pity for your brother?"

"None!" She shook her head "You are my pharaoh and my husband. Whosoever rises against you deserves death."

"Death he shall have, and the treacherous warlock will share his funeral pyre," Naja promised her grimly.

THEY SMELLED the river from afar, the perfume of the sweet cool waters on the desert air. The horses lifted their heads and whickered. The infantry quickened their step and gazed ahead, eager for the first glimpse of the Nile's waters.

Nefer and Mintaka rode together in his chariot at the head of the long cavalcade that wound down the caravan road from Gallala. Meren rode at his right hand in the second chariot of the column.

The leading chariots topped the escarpment, and below them stretched the green valley of the Nile. Coming to meet them was the army Trok Uruk had left in Avaris, armed charioteers, generals and captains leading their regiments, legions of foot soldiers following. Behind them came the elders, the priests and the governors of every nome, all dressed in their robes, chains and decorations of office, and after them the dense masses of citizenry, laughing and dancing.

The two cavalcades came together and mingled, and elders and generals prostrated themselves before Pharaoh's chariot. Then Nefer led the vast concourse back along the river bank towards the city of Avaris. For a league outside the city the road was lined with the welcoming crowds.

When they reached the city the gates stood wide open and the populace lined the walls. They sang anthems of loyalty, praise and welcome as Nefer, with Mintaka beside him, drove under the arch of the gateway.

Beautiful as a young god and goddess, they drove first to the magnificent temple on the river bank to give thanks to the god and to sacrifice a pair of perfect black bulls before the stone altar. After the religious service Nefer declared a week of holiday, festivity and feasting.

"You are a sly one," Mintaka told him. "They loved you before; now they will adore you."

For how long? Nefer wondered. As soon as the news of our arrival reaches Naja in Babylon, he will be on the march, if he is not already. The common people will love me until he knocks upon the gates.

PHARAOH NAJA Kiafan left five hundred chariots, two thousand archers and infantry to hold and secure Babylon. Then, with the bulk of his army, he began the march on Egypt. As he went, vassal kings flocked to his standard, so that by the time he stood on the heights of the Khatmia Pass his army had almost trebled in size.

Ahead of him lay a great expanse of desert, with no spring or oasis to sustain his army until he reached Ismailiya. Once again he was reduced to laying down water points along the route ahead, and for months had been at work building up dumps in the desert, burying the filled pots in the sand, then leaving detachments of infantry to guard them while they returned for the next load.

It would take his army ten days and nights to make the crossing. During that time they would be strictly rationed, allowed just enough water to sustain the long night marches, and to eke out the burning days when they lay up to rest, enduring the heat in any scrap of shade afforded by tents or shelters made from branches and grass.

"I will ride with you in the vanguard." Heseret spoke at his elbow, breaking into his train of thought.

He glanced at her. "We have discussed this before." He frowned. "You will come up with the other women in the baggage train, under the wing of Prenn, the centurion of the rearguard."

Heseret pouted. Once, that had been appealing but now it was merely irritating.

"You become tiresome, wife." Naja lifted his upper lip in a smile that was more a snarl.

She gave him a furious glare, then she called for her litter to take her back down the column, to where Prenn was bringing up the rearguard.

ON TAITA'S ADVICE, Nefer had established a screen of scouts along the edge of the Great Sand Desert. Taita was certain that Naja's main invasion force must come this way. Naja knew the route well, and his army was too large to bring across the Red Sea in boats as Trok had done with his much smaller force.

Very soon it became apparent that Taita had assessed the situation correctly, and Naja was indeed intent on a frontal assault through the Great Sand Desert. A squadron of scouts commanded by Meren watched Naja's water carts carrying their loads of clay jars forward and building up dumps in the arid land. Meren asked to be allowed to attack them but Nefer sent orders to merely to keep them under observation and note carefully where they placed the water stores.

Then Nefer ordered the last reserves that he had been holding on the river to be brought up. When these were encamped around

Ismailiya, he called a war council of all their commanders. Mintaka sat on the council. Her contributions were invaluable: she was Hyksos born, and knew well those officers on Naja's staff who had once been on her own father's staff. As a child she had listened to her father's assessment of each of them, and she had a formidable memory.

"Now, there is one, Centurion Prenn, who commands Naja's rear-guard, who is related to me, for he was one of my father's cousins. I know him well. He taught me to ride. I used to call him Uncle Bear." She smiled at the memory. "My father said of him that he was loyal as a hound, and once he had sunk his teeth into the throat of an enemy he would hang on to the death."

All that night they sat in council while Nefer laid out his battle plan. They were to let Naja advance unopposed for the first five days. Then, once he was deeply committed, they would raid and destroy his water stores, both in front and to the rear of his advance. This would trap him in the midst of the sands.

"Taita and I have devised a plan to lead his vehicles into a trap in which we can exploit the small advantage that we have. In front of the town we will throw up a series of low stone walls behind which our archers and infantry can conceal themselves. These works will be just high enough to block the advance of a chariot." With a charcoal stick Nefer sketched out a design on the sheet of papyrus spread in front of him. "The walls will be laid out in the design of a fish trap." He drew an inverted funnel with the apex aimed back towards the fort of Ismailiya.

"How will you lead him into the funnel?" Shabako asked.

"With a charge of our own chariots and the mock retreat you have practised so often," Nefer explained. "Our archers and slingers will remain concealed behind the walls until Naja follows us into the funnel. The deeper they penetrate, the more tightly his squadrons will be compressed between the walls. I intend to shut them up in a stockade like cattle, just as we did with Trok."

They discussed the plan with enthusiasm, offering suggestions and refinements. In the end Nefer put Shabako in charge of building the walls, work that must begin as soon as it was light the next day.

The council broke up at last, the officers hurried away, and only three remained in the room: Nefer, Taita and Mintaka.

Mintaka spoke up again. "We have already discussed Centurion

Prenn," she said. "If I could meet him, I am sure I could convince him to throw in his lot with us."

"What do you mean?" Nefer's voice was harsh. "Meet him?"

"Dressed as a boy, with a small detachment of good men and fast horses, I could circle around Naja's main army and get through to Prenn in the rear. There would be little risk."

Nefer's face blanched with anger. "Madness!" he said quietly. "Stark raving madness of the kind you exhibited at Gallala when you showed yourself as bait to Trok. I will not hear of it. Can you imagine what Naja would do to you if you fell into his hands?"

"Can you imagine what Naja would do if, in the critical moment of the battle, Prenn and his legions fell upon him from his own rear?" she flashed back at Nefer.

"We will not speak of it again." Nefer came to his feet and slammed his fists down on the tabletop.

Taita looked on, expressionless. He waited with interest to see how this would be resolved.

"You deliberately disobeyed my orders at Gallala. I cannot trust you not to do the same now. You leave me no alternative." Nefer shouted to the sentry outside the door to send for Zugga, the head eunuch of the royal harem. Then he turned back to Mintaka. "I am sending you back to the zenana in the Avaris palace. You are to remain there in the care of Zugga." And Zugga led Mintaka away. At the door she looked back over her shoulder at Nefer, and Taita smiled as he read her expression. Nefer had taken on a more stubborn adversary than both the false pharaohs combined.

TAITA AND NEFER rode out and inspected the stone walls that Shabako had hastily thrown up along the eastern approaches to the oasis of Ismailiya.

"Shabako's efforts will not rank among the great architectural achievements of the age," Taita gave his opinion, "but that is all to the good. From the direction in which Naja will come, they appear to be natural features and will excite no suspicion until he enters the funnel and finds his front progressively narrowed."

Nefer nodded. "Your plan has the towering virtue of allowing us to choose our own battleground. With the help of Horus, we will turn it into a slaughter-ground." Then he laid his hand upon Taita's skinny arm. "Once again I find myself deeply in your debt, Old Father. This is all your work."

"No." Taita shook his head. "It was a gentle nudge I gave to you. The rest of it is yours. You have inherited the military instincts of your father, Pharaoh Tamose. You will achieve the greatness that might have been his, had he not died so cruelly."

"It is time for me to avenge that death," Nefer said. "Let us ensure that we do not let the cobra slither away again."

MINTAKA SPENT much of the journey back to Avaris huddled in the screened litter. Her first endeavour was to make herself agreeable to Zugga, her guardian and jailer, and impress him with her submissive resignation to his authority. By the time they reached the palace in Avaris four days later, she had him completely gulled. There, in the most convincing manner, she appealed to him to allow her to visit the temple of Hathor to pray for Nefer and his victory in the looming battle. With some misgivings Zugga acquiesced, and she was able to spend almost an hour alone with the high priestess in the sanctuary of the temple. Great was Zugga's relief when she re-emerged.

A few days later when she asked to be allowed to pray again in the temple, and to make sacrifice to the goddess, Zugga was amenable to the request. Once again the high priestess led Mintaka into the sanctum and without misgivings Zugga settled down to await her return.

Two hours later a priestess came to him with a message: "The princess has pleaded for sanctuary within the temple. The holy mother has granted her plea, and taken her under her protection."

Zugga was thrown into turmoil. The sanctuary of the temple was inviolate. He could not demand the return of his charge. The only course open to him was to return to Ismailiya and confess his failure, but that was risky. The young pharaoh had not yet revealed his true nature, and his rage might well be fatal.

THE MOMENT the temple doors closed behind her, Mintaka dropped her pretence of resigned innocence. "Have you made the arrangements, Holy Mother?" she demanded eagerly.

"Have no fear, daughter. All is in readiness." The priestess's old eyes sparkled with amusement. Clearly she was enjoying this escapade, a break from the tranquil routine of temple life. She led the way to a cell where the items Mintaka had requested were laid out. Mintaka dressed hastily in rough peasant garments and covered her head with a woollen shawl. Then she followed the high priestess out through a low doorway into the sunshine and onto the jetty where a large dhow was moored. "The captain has been paid," the priestess told her.

"You know what to tell Zugga," Mintaka said.

The old woman smiled again. "I am sure that Hathor will forgive me such an insignificant falsehood. It is in such a good cause."

As Mintaka jumped down onto the deck of the dhow, the captain steered out into the mid-flow of the current and turned the bows downstream, heading for the delta. In the late afternoon the dhow moored briefly against the east bank and two armed men came aboard. Immediately the dhow captain hoisted sail again and they pressed on with all speed downriver. The two men came to the cabin and prostrated themselves before Mintaka.

"May all the gods love you, Majesty," said the bigger of the two, a bearded Hyksos with large nose and strong features. "We are your servants. We came as soon as we received your summons."

"Lok!" Mintaka smiled to see his well-remembered face. She turned to the other man. "And surely this is your son, Lokka." He seemed as doughty as his father. "You are both well met. You, Lok, served my father well. Will you and your son do the same for me?"

"With our lives, mistress!" they told her.

"I will have hard employment for you once we go ashore, but until then rest and prepare your weapons."

The dhow captain selected one of the many mouths of the delta where the current meandered through swamps and lagoons, and steered his craft unerringly until at last the miasma of the swamps was blown away on the clean salt airs of the Mediterranean.

During the rest of that day and the following night they sailed eastwards along the coast. Next morning the dhow edged in towards the beach at El Arish, and as soon as the water was waist-deep the two bodyguards, Lok and Lokka, carried Mintaka ashore then waded back to the boat to fetch the baggage. The small party stood and watched the crew of the dhow set the sail and head back out to sea for the return to Egypt.

It was not quite as easy to find transport as Mintaka had imagined. The quartermasters of Naja's army had been ahead of them seizing wagons and horses, and in the end they had to settle for a string of five decrepit donkeys. On the third day after landing they reached the tail of the army of Pharaoh Naja, this great host filling the main east-to-west road in both directions as far as the eye could see, and fell in with the baggage train.

In her dusty, bedraggled clothing Mintaka excited little notice. Lok and Lokka chaperoned her closely, and discouraged the attentions of any other travellers. The rate of march was of the slowest, so even on the poor donkeys they were moving a little faster than the rest of the cavalcade and drifted forward towards the head.

That evening they kept on travelling after the main army had encamped, and after sunset they came upon a large zareba of poles and thorn bushes just off the road. This had been set up in an easily defended defile of low hills. The entrance was heavily guarded, and there was much marching and countermarching of the sentries around it. Above the gate of the stockade flew a gonfalon that Mintaka recognised at once: the head of a wild boar.

"This is the man we are looking for," Mintaka whispered to Lok.

"But how do you get in to see him?" he asked doubtfully, eyeing the sentries.

They made their open camp a little further down the road, but within sight of the gates of the regimental headquarters of General Prenn, the commander of the rearguard of the pharaonic army.

From one of the leather saddlebags Mintaka brought out the precious oil lamp that had survived the journey, and by its light she wrote a short message on a scrap of papyrus parchment. It was addressed to "Uncle Bear" and signed "from your little cricket".

She washed her face, dressed her hair, and shook out her tunic. Then she approached the gate of the stockade.

"You look like a kind and good man," Mintaka told the sergeant of the guard. "Will you deliver a message for me to Centurion Prenn?" She proffered the rolled parchment.

The sergeant took it, and gawked at her. She spoke the Hyksos language in the cultured tones of the aristocracy. Despite her clothes she was clearly a young woman of high rank.

"Forgive me, my lady," he mumbled. "I am sorry but I will have to ask you to wait here until I have an instruction from him."

He came hurrying back within a very short time. "My lady! I am desolated to have kept you waiting. Please follow me."

He led her to a pavilion of coloured linen in the centre of the stockade, and there was another short delay as he whispered to the junior officer in charge of the entrance. Then she was led through into the tent, its floor covered by animal skins, oryx, zebra and leopard. On these a man was sitting cross-legged with maps and scrolls spread about him. His face was gaunt, his cheeks sunken, and a leather patch covered one eye.

"Uncle Bear!" Mintaka stepped into the lamplight and threw back her head shawl. The man came to his feet slowly, then suddenly he grinned. "I did not think it possible!" He embraced her and lifted her off her feet. "I heard you had deserted us and gone over to the enemy."

When he put her down again she gasped, "That's what I have come to speak to you about."

He heard her out silently, but his expression changed as she described to him in detail the events of that terrible night when her father and all her brothers had died in the burning galley on the river at Balasfura.

When she finished speaking Prenn said simply, "I loved your father, almost as much as I love you, little cricket, but what you are proposing is treason." He sighed. "All this I will have to think on. But in the meantime, you can't return whence you came. It is much too risky. You must stay under my care until this affair is resolved."

When she protested, he overrode her brusquely. "It is not a request. It is an order."

"Can I at least send a message to Nefer Seti?" Mintaka pleaded.

"That also is too great a risk. Have patience. It will not be for long. Naja is poised on the heights of the Khatmia. Within days he will begin the march on Ismailiya." His voice dropped to a growl. "And I will be forced to a decision."

Chapter Seven

FROM A DISTANCE Meren watched the great host of Pharaoh Naja come down the escarpment from the Khatmia Pass into the arid lands. He shadowed the stately progress of the enemy legions across the desert, and when Naja's full army was committed to the crossing, and the leading elements had passed the halfway mark between Khatmia and Ismailiya, Meren circled out in front of the heavily encumbered, slowly moving host, back to where he had left the bulk of his force concealed. They were fifty chariots manned by crack troops and drawn by some of the finest horses in all Nefer's army. He paused only to water, and to change the pennants his chariots flew from the blue to the red of Naja's army. He consoled himself that this was a legitimate ruse of war. Then he drove furiously ahead of Naja's intended line of march.

The men who had been left to guard the water dumps saw the approaching chariots coming from where they expected their comrades to arrive. When they recognised the colours flying above them they were lulled. Meren gave them no time for second thoughts, but raced in upon them, and cut down any who tried to resist. The survivors were given a choice: death or defection. Most came over to Nefer Seti. A single mallet blow was sufficient for each of the disinterred clay jars, and the precious fluid poured out into the sand. Meren's squadron mounted again and went on to the next dump.

PHARAOH NAJA reined in his chariot and gazed out over the remains of his water dump. Although the scouts had warned him, he was still appalled by the extent of the destruction.

"Will you give the order to turn back?" asked one of his captains.

Naja turned on him coldly. "The next coward who suggests such a thing I will have tied behind my chariot and I will drag him into battle." He wiped the sweat from his forehead and gave new orders. "Collect all the water-skins from the entire army. From now on the water supply is under my direct control. There is no turning back, no retreat. All the fighting chariots will move to the front of the column. I will take the cavalry ahead and seize the wells at Ismailiya . . ."

HESERET THRUST her head out of the opening of her tent, and called to the captain of her bodyguard, "What is the trouble, fellow? This is a royal and sacred enclosure, so what are those rogues doing in my stockade?" She pointed at the men who were taking the water-skins from one of her personal baggage carts parked alongside her tent. "What do they think they are up to? How dare they remove our water! I have not yet bathed."

"It is your divine husband Pharaoh's order, Majesty," the captain explained. "All the water is needed for the forward squadrons."

"Such orders cannot apply to the Queen of Egypt," Heseret

screamed. "I shall go at once to Prenn. I shall have new orders for you when I return." Then she turned to the officer of her bodyguard. "Ready my chariot and an escort of ten men."

Across the flat and open plain, Prenn's headquarters camp was in clear view of Heseret's tent. It took only minutes for her chariot to carry her there, but the guard at the gate of the stockade barred her way.

"Your Divine Majesty, General Prenn is not here," he told her. "He left an hour ago with all his cavalry. He had orders from Pharaoh to join the vanguard."

"I do not believe that. I know he would not have left without informing me. Stand aside!" He jumped hurriedly out of her way, and she went straight to the yellow and green striped command tent, stooped through the doorway, and stopped dead in the threshold.

A young woman was sitting on the piles of animal skins in the centre of the floor. She looked up at her startled.

"Who are you?" Heseret demanded. "Where is the general?" Suddenly Heseret's eyes narrowed. "You!" she screamed. "You treacherous, poisonous bitch!" She pointed a quivering finger at the girl. "Guards!" Heseret shrieked at the top of her voice. "Guards, here, at once!"

Mintaka came to her senses. She darted across the tent and out through the rear opening.

"Guards!" Heseret yelled again. "This way!" Her bodyguard burst in through the doorway behind her.

"Stop her!" Heseret shouted. "Don't let her escape. She is a spy and a traitor."

Her bodyguard charged after Mintaka, shouting to the guards at the gate, and the sentries drew their swords and ran to cut her off. She fought desperately, kicking, scratching and biting, but the soldiers overwhelmed her at last and dragged her back to the command tent to face Heseret.

The Queen was smiling vindictively. "Bind her securely. I am sure that my husband, the sole ruler of Egypt, will devise a suitable punishment for her crimes when he returns. Until then she is to be caged and kept at the door of my tent where I can keep her under my eye."

One of the carts of Heseret's baggage train carried her stock of livestock in cages, chickens, pigs and young goats for her kitchen.

The cage that had contained the suckling pigs was now empty—they had been slaughtered and eaten—and the guards shoved Mintaka in through the narrow door.

"There will be guards standing over you day and night," Heseret warned her. "Should you try to escape I will have one of your feet cut off, to discourage further attempts."

FROM THE WATCHTOWER above the fort at Ismailiya the sentry shouted the warning, "Pharaoh! The pickets are coming in!"

Nefer sprang up from the table under the awning in the courtyard where he and Taita were eating the midday meal. He climbed swiftly up the ladder to the platform and shaded his eyes. Through the yellow glare he made out the chariots of his forward pickets. As they drove down the bank of the wadi, the guards threw open the gates and allowed them to enter the fort.

"The enemy comes on apace!" the sergeant of the pickets shouted up.

"Well done, sergeant," Nefer called back to him, and then to the trumpeter on the wall above the gate, "Sound the call to arms!"

The ram's horn blared out across the plain, and the entire army encamped down the length of the broad wadi began to stir. Soon lines of marching men and columns of chariots were moving forward to their prepared positions.

Taita clambered up onto the high platform, and Nefer smiled at him. "So, even deprived of his water, Naja has not turned back."

"We never thought he would," Taita said softly.

In the east the horizon started to darken, as the dust cloud of the advancing enemy army boiled like a brewing thunderstorm.

"Will you ride out to meet him with me, Old Father?" Nefer asked, as he strapped on the sword-belt that his orderly handed to him.

"No, I will overlook the battle from here. Perhaps in my own feeble way I might be of more help to you than if I wielded a javelin or drew a bow."

Nefer smiled. "Your weapons are sharper and fly more truly than any I have ever held in my hand. Horus love and protect you, Old Father."

They watched as the battalions of archers and slingers marched out of the wadi to take up their positions behind the breastworks. Every man among them knew what was expected of him, and had rehearsed this manoeuvre many times. As the last of them disappeared into the ambuscade, the field seemed deserted.

The dust cloud of Naja's advance was less than a league off when at last Nefer embraced Taita and climbed down the ladder. Meren handed him the reins as he leapt up onto his chariot's footplate. Nefer lifted his right fist high and gave the command: "March! Forward!"

The ram's horn sounded the advance and he led the van out, rank upon rank, down between the low breastworks from behind which not a single archer showed himself, out onto the open plain. On the markers he had laid out weeks before, Nefer halted his leading squadron, and let the horses rest while he studied the enemy advance.

Meren murmured, "Sweet Horus be praised. It seems he has committed all his vehicles. He holds no depth of chariots in reserve."

"They must be desperate for water," Nefer answered. "His only chance of survival is to break our ranks with a frontal charge and win through to the wells."

Closer and closer came the enemy, until two hundred paces away the mighty host rolled to a halt. A vast silence settled over the brooding landscape, broken only by the fretting susurration of the wind.

From the enemy centre a single chariot pulled forward. Even though dust coated the coachwork the gold leaf gleamed through, and the royal pennant flew above the driver's head. Naja halted less than a hundred paces to the front, so that Nefer recognised the cold, handsome face under the blue war crown.

"Hail, Nefer Seti, puppy of the dog I slew with my own hand!" Naja called and Nefer stiffened to hear him confess so openly to regicide. "Upon my head I wear the crown I took from Tamose as he was dying. Will you claim it from me, puppy?"

With a huge effort Nefer kept his face expressionless, but his voice rang like metal on stone. "Make ready!"

Naja laughed, wheeled his own chariot and drove back to his place in the centre of the opposing line.

"March! Forward!" Naja raised the blue sword. His front ranks gathered momentum, rolling towards Nefer's line. "At the gallop! Charge!" They surged forward in a solid mass.

Nefer stood his ground and let them come on. Then he lifted his sword again and described three flashing arcs with the blade above his head. His legions responded instantly, turning as though possessed of a single controlling mind, and racing away over the plain, back the way they had come, drawing together from extended order into a column of four.

Naja tore after them, but within three hundred paces his flanks came upon a low stone breastwork that slanted across their front. They could not stop now, so they veered left and right towards their own centre. Like the current of a wide river forced suddenly into the mouth of a narrow rocky gorge, they were squeezed together. Wheel snagged wheel, and horse teams were forced to give way to each other. The charge wavered and slowed as chariots and horses jammed into a solid mass.

At that fatal moment, the rams' horns brayed across the field, and the heads and shoulders of the archers and slingers rose from behind the breastworks on either hand. The slingers whirled their weapons on high, and the archers held their aim a moment, choosing their targets with care. The first volley was always the most telling.

The slingers loosed their missiles and the archers their arrows in a single concerted volley. They had been ordered to aim for the horses, and to pick out the enemy captains. The first rank of Naja's charge was shot down, and as the horses fell the chariots piled up over their carcasses, swerving out of control into the stone walls on either hand, or capsizing and rolling.

The vehicles that followed were unable to stop the charge, and crashed into the wreckage of those in front. Wheels shattered and were torn from their axles. Men were hurled from their cockpits and trampled under the frantic hoofs of the rearing, milling horses.

At the head of his squadron, Nefer gave the signal that the men following him were expecting, and foot soldiers leapt out of hiding and dragged away the thorn bushes that concealed the openings that had been left in the walls on either hand. In quick succession Nefer's chariots swerved through them and into the open ground beyond the walls. No longer constricted, they doubled back, circling in behind Naja's trapped squadrons, and falling on their rear echelons.

Now both armies were locked together. Not all of Naja's vehicles had been lured into the trap between the walls. These chariots now came rushing forward to engage Nefer, and a traditional chariot battle swiftly developed. The squadrons broke up into smaller units, and across the plain single vehicles viciously engaged each other, wheel to wheel, and man to man.

Despite the frightful losses he had inflicted on the enemy in the opening phase, Nefer was still heavily outnumbered. As the advantage swung back and forth, Nefer was forced to call in more and more of the reserves he had been holding concealed in the wadi behind the fort. Now he signalled in the last of them. He was fully committed. But they were not enough. Slowly his horses and his men were being ground down by the sheer numbers of his enemy.

In the dust and clamour and turmoil, Nefer knew that his army would soon be in rout, and he shouted encouragement to the charioteers close enough to hear him, to rally them. Then beside him Meren shouted, "Look, Pharaoh!" and he pointed to the east out into the desert. With the back of his hand Nefer wiped his sweat and splashes of enemy blood from his face, and stared out into the glare.

He knew then beyond all doubt that it was over, and that they had lost the battle. A fresh mass of enemy chariots was tearing in towards them. He had thought that Naja had committed all his vehicles. That did not matter now, for the battle was lost.

"How many?" Nefer wondered, black desolation filling his soul.

"Two hundred," Meren guessed. "Maybe more." His voice was resigned. "It is all over, Pharaoh. We will die fighting." As the enemy closed he saw that the leading enemy chariot flew the pennant of a general, a centurion. "By Horus, I know him," Meren cried. "It's Prenn—and he flies the blue!" Prenn's pennant was streaming back, directly away from them, which was why Nefer had not noticed it until this moment, but Meren was right: Prenn was flying the blue of the House of Tamose, and all his chariots with him.

Now Prenn slowed, held his right arm across his chest in salute to Nefer, and shouted in a great voice, "What are your orders, Pharaoh?"

"What strange business is this, General Prenn? Why do you call on me for orders?" Nefer called back.

"The Princess Mintaka delivered to me your message, and I have come to place myself under your command."

"Mintaka?" Nefer was confused, for surely she was still in

Avaris. But his warrior instincts took over and he thrust aside those thoughts. "Well met, General Prenn. You arrive none too soon. Lay your chariot alongside mine and we will sweep this field from end to end."

They charged side by side, and Nefer's broken and scattered legions saw the blue pennant coming and took new heart. The red squadrons of Naja Kiafan were in hardly better case and could offer only scant resistance as Prenn's fresh troops charged into them. They fought on for a while, but the heart was torn out of them.

Nefer quartered across the field with Meren, searching for Naja. He reached the stone breastworks and looked over the low wall into the narrow defile where he had trapped the forward legions of Naja's army. Around each smashed chariot lay the dead and the wounded. Some were still moving and weeping, calling to the gods and to their mothers. Others sat dazed with the agony of their wounds. Nefer looked for Naja's body among the dead, but all was confusion. Then he picked out a flash of gold leaf, and the royal standard of Naja Kiafan lying in the dust.

"I must find him," Nefer told Meren. "I must know he is dead." He jumped down from the chariot.

"I will help you search." Meren tethered the horses to the walls.

Nefer vaulted over the breastworks and scrambled over the other wreckage until he reached the golden chariot. It lay on its side, but the cockpit was empty. Suddenly Meren shouted and stooped to pick up something from among the debris. He lifted his trophy high, and Nefer saw that he had found Naja's blue war crown.

"His body must be close," Nefer called to him. "He would not have discarded that. It means too much to him."

At that moment Nefer caught a flash of movement from the corner of his eye. He ducked and whirled about. Naja had risen from where he had been crouching behind the dashboard of the chariot. He still carried the blue sword of Tamose and he launched a double-handed blow at Nefer's head, but Nefer ducked under the hissing blade and drew his own sword.

Naja stepped back and looked about him. He saw Meren coming to Nefer's aid and he saw the empty chariot hitched to the wall. He drove Nefer back with another thrust of the blue blade, then whirled and sprinted away. As he jumped over the wall he cut the horses free and leapt up onto the footplate. Startled, the pair lunged forward together and within half a dozen strides were both at full gallop.

Behind them Nefer jumped to the top of the wall and saw Naja being carried away across the plain. He drew a long breath and whistled, the high piercing blast his horses knew so well. He saw their heads go up, their ears prick and swivel towards him. Then they changed gait and swung into a tight turn, and came pounding back towards where Nefer stood poised on the wall. As they swept by below him, Nefer leapt lightly onto one horse's back, and with his knees steered it onto the open plain. He glanced back and saw Naja climbing out of the cockpit, then edging along the shaft to get at Nefer.

Nefer leaned down and sliced the leather rope that hitched the horses to the shaft. Running free, the chariot veered off to one side. The shaft dug into the soft earth, flicking the vehicle over, and Naja was thrown clear. He struck the ground with his shoulder and even above the sound of hoofs Nefer heard the bone break.

Nefer charged at him. Naja had climbed painfully to his feet and stood swaying, clutching his damaged right arm across his chest. In his fall he had lost his grip on the hilt of the blue sword. It had spun out of his hand, and ten paces away from where he stood the point had pegged into the earth. The blade still quivered from the impact. The wondrous blue metal threw slivers of blue light, and the jewelled hilt whipped from side to side.

Naja staggered towards the weapon, but then he saw Nefer bearing down on him, and an expression of utter terror turned his face the colour of cold ashes. When Nefer leaned down and plucked the sword from the sand, Naja knew then that he could not escape his terrible vengeance. He fell to his knees and lifted both hands in supplication, as Nefer jumped down and stood over him.

"Mercy!" Naja sobbed. "I yield to you the double crown and all the kingdom." He crawled pitifully to Nefer's feet.

"I already have that. I lack only one thing. Vengeance!"

"Mercy, Nefer Seti, in the name of the gods and for the sake of your sister, the goddess Heseret, and the infant in her womb." Suddenly there was a dagger in his right hand, and he stabbed up viciously at Nefer's groin. Nefer twisted away just in time, and struck the weapon out of Naja's grasp with a flick of his blade.

"I admire your consistency. To the very end you are true to your base nature." Nefer smiled down on him coldly. "You I grant the same mercy that you showed my father, Pharaoh Tamose." He drove the point of the blue sword into the centre of Naja's chest, and it came out between his shoulder blades.

Naja toppled face first into the dust, and drew one more ragged breath, but the air from his lungs bubbled out of the wound between his shoulder blades and he shuddered and died.

Nefer hitched Naja's body by its heels to the traces that dangled from the horse's harness, then mounted and dragged it back across the field. Cheering followed him as he rode up to the gates of the fort. He cut the rope and left Naja's bloody corpse lying in the dust.

Then he looked up to the figure who stood high upon the watch-tower of the fort, and raised the blue blade to him in salute. Taita lifted his hand in acknowledgment.

He was on the tower through the whole day. What part did the Magus play in the battle? Nefer asked himself. There was no answer, and he put the thought aside. He mounted the ladder to the top of the tower and stood beside Taita. From there he spoke to his men. He thanked them for their duty and their bravery. He promised them their rewards, a share of the plunder to all, and the honours of valour to the captains and centurions.

By the time he had named them all the sun was sinking through a low bank of purple thunderclouds towards the horizon. He ended his speech with a call to prayer: "I dedicate this victory to the golden Horus, the falcon of the gods," he cried, and as he prayed there was a wild cry from above. Every head lifted and every eye turned towards the sky. A great murmur went up from the multitude. A royal falcon hovered in the air above the head of Pharaoh, and as they stared in wonder it uttered that strange, haunting sound again, then circled three times, and at last shot away in a straight line on rapid, incisive wingbeats into the eastern sky.

"A blessing from the god," the soldiers chanted. "Hail, Pharaoh! The gods salute you."

But beside him Taita spoke softly. "The falcon brought a warning, not a blessing."

"What is the warning?" Nefer demanded.

"When the bird called, I heard Mintaka cry out," Taita whispered.

"Mintaka!" Nefer had forgotten her in the exigencies of the battle. "What did Prenn tell me about her?" He turned to the ladder and shouted down to the guards. "Prenn! Where is the centurion Prenn?"

Prenn came at once, and knelt before Pharaoh. "You have earned our deepest gratitude," Nefer told him. "Without you we could not have prevailed."

"Pharaoh is gracious,"

"At the start of the battle, you spoke of the Princess Mintaka. I thought that she was safe in Avaris."

"Pharaoh, you are mistaken. Princess Mintaka is not in the temple. She came to me with your message. I could not bring her into battle with me, so I left her two days ago in my camp in the desert."

A foreboding seized Nefer. "Who else is in the encampment?"

"Some of the royal women. Her Majesty Queen Heseret—"

"Heseret!" Nefer wrung his hands. "If Mintaka is in her power, what will she do to her when she hears that I have slain her husband? We must ride at once."

HESERET AWOKE in the darkness and chill of that dread time before the dawn when the human spirit is at its lowest ebb. At first she was uncertain of what had interrupted her sleep, but then she became aware of the sound of many voices, faint but growing stronger. She sat up and tried to make sense of the distant hubbub. She was able to make out words now: "defeated" and "slain" and "flee at once". She called for her maids and two stumbled in.

"What is going on?" Heseret demanded.

The eldest maid was breathless. "They say there has been a great battle at a place called Ismailiya, Majesty."

Heseret felt a great surge of joy. Naja had triumphed: in her heart she was certain of it. "What was the outcome of the battle?"

"We don't know, mistress. We did not ask."

Heseret seized the girl nearest to her by the hair, and shook her violently. "Have you not a speck of brain in your thick skull?" She slapped her across the face, and left her lying on the floor of the tent. She grabbed a lamp and hurried to the door.

The guards were gone, and she felt the first pangs of fear. She ran to the cage outside and held up the lamp, peering into the pig cage. Part of her anxiety was allayed as she saw that Mintaka was still pinioned and tied to the struts at the back of the cage.

Heseret left her and ran to the gate of the stockade. In the starlight she made out a dark cavalcade streaming past. She saw the loom of carts and wagons being drawn by teams of oxen. Some were piled high with bales and boxes, others were crowded with women clutching their children. Hundreds of soldiers hurried past on foot and Heseret saw that most had thrown away their weapons.

She picked out a soldier in the passing throng, who wore the collar of a sergeant. "What news of the battle? Tell me. Oh, please tell me," she begged.

He peered into her face. "The most dire news, Majesty." His voice was gruff. "There has been a terrible battle and our army has been defeated. The enemy will be upon us soon. You must flee at once."

"What of Pharaoh? What has happened to my husband?"

"Pharaoh Naja Kiafan is slain, cut down in single combat by Nefer Seti himself."

Heseret let out a keening wail. She gathered up a double handful of dust and poured it over her head. Still wailing she clawed her face with her fingernails.

Her handmaidens came out of the stockade to fetch her in, but she screamed incoherent obscenities at them. She ran to the pig cage on the cart, and screeched at Mintaka through the bars: "My husband is dead. Slain by my own monstrous brother."

"Praise be to Hathor and all the gods," Mintaka cried.

"You blaspheme!" Heseret raved. "Naja Kiafan was a god." She turned to the captain of her guards. "Drag the sow from her cage."

The captain hesitated. Nefer and his captains would be here soon.

Heseret grabbed a spear out of the hand of the nearest soldier and struck him across the back. "I order you, Captain, to obey me."

The man backed away. "You are mad. What punishment would Nefer Seti heap upon my head?" He turned suddenly and bolted from the stockade to join the flood of fleeing refugees in the roadway. His men hesitated only a moment longer, then rushed to the gate hard after him.

Heseret ran after them. "Come back! I order you!" But they mingled with the crowds and were gone. Dazed as a sleepwalker she went to her tent. She picked a robe at random from the pile in the corner, and pulled sandals onto her feet.

"I am going to find Naja," she said. Then with new determination she headed for the door.

As she stepped out into the early sunlight, Mintaka called to her from the cage. "Please release me, Heseret. In all charity, let me go."

"You don't understand." Heseret shook her head wildly. "I have to go to my husband, the Pharaoh of all Egypt. He needs me."

She did not glance at Mintaka again but hurried out of the stockade, shaking her head and muttering incoherently to herself. She turned towards the west, in the opposite direction from the flood of terrified humanity, and started to run back towards Egypt.

MINTAKA STRUGGLED against her bonds, bracing her bare feet against the struts of the cage to give herself better purchase. She felt the skin smearing from her wrists, and blood dripping down her hands, but the leather thongs were tight and strong and she could neither stretch nor snap them.

Once Mintaka heard a stealthy scuffle at the entrance to the tent and saw Heseret's two maids creeping out, each carrying a large bag crammed with valuables they had looted. Mintaka called to them, but they glanced at her with startled, guilty expressions and scurried from the stockade.

Then she heard something else, hoofbeats and the sound of men's voices growing stronger, and stronger still, until she could recognise one. "Nefer!" She tried to scream his name, but her voice was a draughty whisper. "Nefer!"

She twisted her head and saw Nefer storm through the gateway, Meren and Taita close behind him.

Nefer ran to the cage. He tore the gate off its hinges with his bare hand and pulled his dagger from its sheath to slash loose the leather thongs from her wrists. Gently he drew her out of the stinking cage and held her to his chest. Mintaka shut her eyes and slumped into unconsciousness. Nefer was weeping as he carried her into the tent.

MINTAKA CAME awake slowly as though she were rising up from the depths of a pit. When she opened her eyes she saw with immense relief the two most beloved faces in her world. Taita sat at one side of her couch and Nefer at the other.

"How long?" she asked. "How long was I gone?"

"A day and a night," Nefer answered her.

"You are not angry with me for disobeying you?"

"You have given me a crown and a land." He shook his head and one of his tears fell upon her face. "Above that you have given me your love. How could I ever be angry with you?"

Taita rose softly and left the tent, and they stayed together all the rest of that day, speaking softly together.

In the evening Nefer sent for two priestesses from the temple of Hathor. "You have come to see justice done," he told them, then turned to the guards at the door.

"Bring in the woman named Heseret," he ordered.

Mintaka started and tried to sit up, but he pushed her gently back upon the bolster.

"Where? How did you find her?"

"Our pickets found her wandering in the desert on the road back to Ismailiya," Nefer explained. "At first they did not recognise her or believe her claims to be a queen. They thought her a mad-woman."

Heseret came into the tent. Nefer had allowed her to bathe and provided her with fresh raiment, and Taita had treated the grazes on her face and body. Now she shrugged off the hands of her guards and looked around her. "Prostrate yourselves before me," she ordered. "I am a queen."

No one moved, and Nefer said, "You are a queen no longer." He stared at her so coldly that Heseret started to weep.

"I am your own sister. You would not harm me."

"You are right, Heseret. I will not harm you."

He sighed and turned to the two priestesses. "I give into your keeping the body and the life of Heseret Tamose, who was a princess of the royal House of Egypt."

Heseret began to scream but no one took notice of her cries as gently they dragged her blubbering and wailing from the tent.

They sat in silence, and through the linen walls listened as Heseret's wailing, entreaties and blandishments faded into the distance. Then Mintaka covered her face with both hands and Nefer made the sign against evil with his right hand.

WHEN MINTAKA had recovered sufficiently to begin the long journey back to Avaris, Nefer insisted that she be carried in a litter to ease the jolting over the rough road that lay ahead. They travelled slowly, and it was fifteen days later that they reached the escarpment and looked down upon the wide green valley of the Nile.

Nefer helped Mintaka from the litter, and together they walked a short way from the road, so that they could be alone and savour this joyous moment of homecoming. They had not been there long when Nefer stood up and shaded his eyes.

"What is it, my heart?" Mintaka asked.

"We have a visitor," he said, but when she exclaimed with annoyance at the intrusion he went on, "This visitor is always welcome."

She smiled then as she recognised the figure approaching them. "Taita. But what strange attire is this?"

He was dressed in a simple robe and sandals, and slung on his back he carried the leather satchel of a holy man on a pilgrimage.

"I have come to take my leave of you," Taita explained.

"You will not leave me now." Nefer was dismayed. "Will you not attend my coronation?"

"You were crowned on the field of Ismailiya," Taita told him gently.

"Our wedding!" Mintaka cried. "You must stay for our wedding."

"You were married long since," Taita smiled, "perhaps on the day of your birth, for the gods intended you for each other."

Nefer knew that there was nothing further to say, that more words would degrade this moment. He did not even ask where Taita was going. Perhaps he did not know.

He embraced Taita, then he and Mintaka stood and watched him walk away, and his distant shape slowly dwindle in the shimmering wastes of the desert wilderness, and they shared the same deep ache of regret and bereavement.

"He has not really gone," Mintaka whispered, when at last he had disappeared from view.

"No," Nefer agreed. "He will always be with us."

WITH THE HIGH priestess and fifty acolytes from the temple of Hathor preceding her, the Princess Mintaka Apepi came for her marriage to Pharaoh Nefer Seti.

They stood together on the terrace of the palace of Thebes that overlooked the broad brown floor of the Nile in flood, in the season most propitious to all living things in the land of this very Egypt.

It seemed that all of Egypt had come to bear witness to the nuptials. The crowds stretched back along both banks of the river as far as the eye could see. The couple embraced and broke the jars of

Nile water, and then Nefer Seti led his new queen out by the hand and showed her beauty to the populace, who fell to their knees and wept and cried out their loyalty and their love.

Suddenly a silence fell over this vast congregation. Slowly every eye turned upwards to the tiny speck in the vaulted sky above the palace.

In the silence there was the wild, lonely cry of a royal falcon, and the bird began its stoop out of the high blue. Just as it seemed it must come into violent collision, the falcon flared its wings wide and hovered over the tall figure of Pharaoh. Nefer lifted his right arm and held it out, and softly as a feather the magnificent bird alighted upon his fist.

A sound like the sea on a stormy day rose from ten thousand throats as they greeted the miracle. But Nefer's eyes fell on the loop of gold that was fastened about the bird's right foot. Engraved into the precious metal was a symbol that made Nefer's heart race.

"The royal cartouche!" he whispered. "This was never a wild bird. This is Nefertem, my father's falcon. That is why it came to me so often in times of greatest danger, to warn and guide me. It was my father's spirit."

"And now Nefertem has come to affirm before all the world that you are king indeed." Mintaka stood closer to him and gazed into his face with eyes that glowed with pride and love.

About the author

WILBUR SMITH was born in 1933 in Northern Rhodesia, now Zambia. The wildlife of Africa and the vast open spaces fascinated him as a child, and early travels with his father took him to Ethiopia and the Upper Nile. Before long he was reading avidly about Egypt in the time of the Pharaohs, building up such a fund of knowledge that years later he was able to create his stories of ancient Egypt with little extra research.

He also loved reading a wide range of novels, a passion he shared with his mother. He was especially fond of adventure stories, which seemed in tune with the extraordinary environment where he was growing up—physically majestic, but also riven with political tensions. Keen to write himself, he planned to become a journalist, but his father said, "Don't be a bloody fool. You'll starve to death. Get a real job."

Wilbur Smith's years as a tax accountant, "probably the lowest point of my entire life", prompted him to write fiction as an escape. His first novel, *When The Lion Feeds*, was an instant success when it was published in 1964—then Reader's Digest produced a select edition, film rights were sold, and Wilbur Smith found himself contemplating a career as a novelist.

Now, after a lifetime of best-sellers, Africa is still his inspiration. He says, "Events that took place on this continent centuries ago are still determining the lives of those who live here." He knows Egypt well, and *River God* grew quickly from an idea about the life of an Egyptian slave that had been "buzzing around" in his mind for some time. He started with the few known facts about the period of the Hyksos invasions, and built the story of Taita around them. "My books are always such a mixture of fact and imagination that not even I know where one begins and the other ends." *The Seventh Scroll* grew out of his interest in archaeology, and frequent journeys along the Nile. "That part of Africa is very much a part of my life's experience." *Warlock* shows the Taita at the height of his powers and brings to a climax the long war between the Hyksos and the Pharaohs. As Wilbur Smith points out, the recorded history of that time is very confused and obscure, so he can counter any Egyptologist who might challenge him on his accuracy by saying, "You don't know for certain either!"

The author's life these days is based on a work-hard, play-hard cycle, with one year to complete a novel and the next year at leisure. He enjoys diving and fishing in the Seychelles, safaris in Botswana and Zimbabwe, skiing in Switzerland and sea fishing around Australia and New Zealand. He has a deep concern for the peoples and wildlife of his native continent, and spends much of his time on his 60,000-acre ranch in South Africa, which he has turned into a wildlife reserve.

Acknowledgments

River God: Original full-length version published by Macmillan, London © 1993 by Wilbur Smith.
The Seventh Scroll: Original full-length version published by Macmillan, London © 1995 by Wilbur Smith.
Warlock: Original full-length version published by Macmillan, London © 2001 by Wilbur Smith.

Design for this edition by Mark Thacker – Big Cat Design.
Map by Alex Stafford.